J

C000081871

Flashbacks

Ottery Books

Flashbacks

Published in Great Britain by Ottery Books
7 Riverside View
Ottery St Mary
EX11 1YA

First published 2016

ISBN 978 0 9955035 0 2 (hb)
ISBN 978 0 9955035 1 9 (pbk)

Typeset in Helvetica

Cover picture by istock, cover design by Short Run Press

This novel is a work of fiction. The names, characters, incidents and
locations are the product of the author's imagination and any resemblance
to actual persons, places or events is entirely coincidental

website: jehallauthor.com

A full CIP record for this book is available from the British Library

Printed and bound by Short Run Press, Exeter

To

Rosie with all my love, who knows writing is not my first love, Ben whose own cycling exploits fired the imagination, Tom whose insights into crime and the criminal world informed my thinking, Sam who lent his literary wife Irene to critique the writing; and, to the countless other people of many cultures, faiths and backgrounds whom I have had the privilege to meet and whose lives have so enriched my own.

I owe a special debt of gratitude to the members of the Ottery St Mary Writers' Group and The Seasons Tea Room where we meet. Local writers have been a great source of advice and encouragement. I am most grateful to the kind friends who read and offered advice on early drafts of the novel, including Jeni Braund and Sheila Walker who provided much needed editing skills The use of the correcting red pen has still got a valued place amongst us!

There is a wider circle of writers and academics who have, over the years, stimulated my imagination and a love of literature. The freedom to enjoy literary self-expression is something I do not take for granted. It is a precious social gift to be treasured, a necessary, even essential medium, for exploring, knowing and loving the world around us.

To those other friends and family who fed back their wisdom, I owe much thanks.

"Flashbacks & nightmares

You find yourself re-living the event, again and again. This can happen both as a 'flashback' in the day and as nightmares when you are asleep... You see it in your mind, but may also feel the emotions and physical sensations of what happened - fear, sweating, smells, sounds, pain.

Ordinary things can trigger off flashbacks."

Royal College of Psychiatrists

1

They said it was a British fighter bomber. It came in low and fast from nowhere with the unexpected roar of an Arabian lion lusting for a kill. Then it had gone, but not before releasing its deadly cargo. The flashes came, the shock waves and booms, the sounds of falling masonry and pitter-pattering dirt, followed by swirls of hot red dust and silence.

As the noise dissipated and the grey smoke began to rise, a middle-aged man ran out across the Mosul street to try to seek cover with his teenage son on the opposite side. They were apart when it happened, which was fitting, for neither could really say they had ever truly been together. But for once in his life he wanted to be there for his son.

He was flushed out, exposed, in the middle of an empty road, caught under a clear blue sky and white hot sun with nowhere to hide. His white robes clung to his legs as he ran, slowing his movement, his sandals flapping and clapping against the soles of his feet, his thin arms flailing in a circular movement as if to try to generate extra speed.

He looked so ungainly, his sprint so unlikely and he slowed as he got half way across.

That was when the uniformed Iraqi soldier, waiting in the cover of a bombed out building at the end of the street, saw him. A turkey shoot presented itself. So easy there was no need to be cautious. He had time to stand, raise his gun slowly, wait for the man to turn and realise his fate, his staring, disbelieving eyes looking his killer straight in the face.

At his leisure, on the count of three, he squeezed the trigger, held it, watched the man dance, his arms once again swinging outstretched, circling the empty air as he flew back and up and down. Twitching, his empty face looked upward, his dark eyes closing out the clear blue sky for the last time; and, then he had gone, his life blood pulsing into the sandy earth.

Across the street, frozen in the shadows, waiting for his father to join him and watching everything was Ali Muhammed. There had been many times when Ali had wished his father dead, but this was real, played out before his wide, still disbelieving eyes.

Crouching next to Ali, Salim Ismat saw the gunman and fired, watched him fall, then firmly grabbed Ali by the shoulder and dragged him over to look at his father's killer. Taking the AK47 the man was cradling in his arms, tearing it from his dying grasp, he handed it to Ali.

'This is yours, now execute your vengeance my brother,' he said.

Ali, traumatised, looked straight ahead, his gaze a frozen mask, the matching image of his now dead father's face.

Salim saw the look on Ali's face and understood the boy's hate and loneliness. He could be useful to IS, he thought, as he put his arm around the lad's shoulder to lead him away.

2

It was late evening. The yard at the back of the red brick Edwardian terraced house was quiet but for a solitary person. A lean, tall figure was fastening things to his bike in readiness for a long ride. Adam Taylor was an ordinary sort of guy, or at least he thought so. Life was full of good things to do. School and college in Muswell Hill, north London, had been the centre of his world. He'd got by and a couple of part-time jobs since the start of his Gap Year last summer had given him some cash in his pocket. Life was pretty good, is how he'd describe it.

Now it was time to get away, spread his wings, occupy his space and see what the world had to offer. With two splayed hands he pushed back his dark hair from across his forehead and behind his ears. It was the middle of May, the days were beginning to stretch out, summer was coming at long last. In the light from the kitchen window he gazed fondly at his Marin bike. It was ancient but sturdy, with a triple butted steel frame the like of which was hard to get today. It was his bike, every part of which he knew; and, it had all the accessories he'd saved for, swapped things for and then added to over the years.

He had packed the panniers, front and rear, clothes fit for a long ride, just enough to stay fresh, not too many to slow him up. Swiss army knife, multi-tool kit, GPS, maps, all the kit he'd acquired and got familiar with after years in the local scouts. It was done. Hands on hips he stood back to admire his world - everything he'd need. He felt fit and ready.

A quick feel of the brakes, a lift up to test for weight, one hand on the handlebars, the other hand gripping the traditional but comfortable Brookes leather saddle. Manageable, he thought. A new Shimano gear set would propel him up any incline, even fully loaded. Living at home had had its benefits, giving him money to spend on bike parts, many bought through successful on-line bids. Sometimes he

3

missed out, but often he'd strike gold. But living at home also had its downside: parents. Inside, he knew his pending ride was screwing them up and in turn they always seemed to get to him with their worries. Soon, very soon, he'd be free.

He double-checked his cycle repair kit, that tools and selected spare parts were stowed away. The excitement and anticipation caused a rush of adrenalin. He knew there would be adventure, perhaps risk, even danger in it. He even had a small first aid tin. On his bike he felt king, tall and with the wind in his face. London's traffic had not defeated him, he'd always emerged from scrapes unscathed, he'd get through, he always did. He was the one in control and all the confidence of youth surged through his veins. He'd cycled every day for months, he was fit. Nothing was left to chance. How could anything go wrong?

Stepping back, he once again admired the bike's black sturdy frame, the neat packing of all his gear, his machine that would carry him across Europe to the Middle East. In the morning he was off, the first part of his Gap Year adventure. So long in coming, so eagerly awaited, ready at last. Ever since his great uncle had first told him about his war time exploits in 'Persia', modern Iran, he'd been captivated by the country and desperate to get there and see the place for himself.

Leaning the bike against the wall of the house there was a final glance as he stepped out of the quiet evening and inside into the warmly lit kitchen where his mother was leaning over the sink clearing up the crocks.

'Night Mum', he said, hoping to make a quick exit up to his room and avoid emotional last minute conversations, but he was not quick enough to make his exit. Her call of, 'Adam,' caught him midway across the tiny kitchen and he stopped at the kitchen table.

'A drink? A Coke, a beer maybe?' she enquired, but he knew this was just a preamble. He nodded a 'No', but she followed up, 'You will keep Dad and I posted each day where you are, what direction you will be taking.'

It was more an anxious statement than an enquiry. She made him aware he was to sit down and he steeled himself for he knew a parental conversation was coming. He submitted, thought it best to hear it out, the clock was ticking. Besides, she meant well, he reasoned.

'You know Dad and I care and we're worried that you haven't planned things sufficiently. You're taking a huge risk not booking up in advance where to stay,' she said.

'I'll be fine, got my one-man tent for emergencies and there are lots of places to put me up.' He didn't think he sounded convincing enough, and anyway he knew there was no convincing to be done in this conversation.

'But you can't simply pitch up at the side of the road, you might get arrested for vagrancy. It's not like England. They can be very strict on that kind of thing abroad,' his Mum added.

'I'll be fine. If I get arrested they'll look after me, but it won't happen. I'll be absolutely fine,' said Adam.

'How will you charge your phone? Have you got a medical kit?'

'Everything's sorted, all packed ready to go. I just checked my first aid tin and spares. Everything's sorted. My friends are going away for a year, I'm only going for two months - it's no time at all.'

'If you get in a fix and need some extra money, or anything...', she added a little too desperately, her voice petering out. Adam's chair scraped on the tiled floor as he stood up to make his exit.

'I need an early night Mum, need to be fresh for an early start. Got to reach Gravesend tomorrow and then it's Dover. Good night Mum,' and he was out the door, in the hall-way and a few strides upstairs into the sanctuary of his room. Relief. He could hear her downstairs busying herself again with the last few pans, trying to keep her worries at bay.

It was approaching midnight. Just a few final checks to make. His last remaining things to take with him were laid out on his bed. His red cycling jersey with several really useful zipped pockets, his black and yellow Gortex cycling jacket with extra pockets inside, his new cycling shorts with cushioning protection - he'll need that he thought. His cleated cycling shoes that gave him that extra power on the pedals, his shiny new red British passport, his wallet, his mobile which he intended to keep switched 'off' except to listen to music and Facebook his friends, his new soft notebook which he'd use as a travelogue diary. He placed them all neatly on the floor.

He'd left nothing to chance. An organised and self-disciplined guy, he had long relished this challenge, the freedom of the road, the adventure ahead. He had a nagging doubt that being an only child made him a little too cock-sure of himself, a little less well attuned to other people; maybe he had a chink in his armour, but he quickly pushed the thought to the back of his mind as his eyes rested on something unexpected.

There was an extra item by his things, a brown envelope. He picked it up, turned it over in his hand, then opened it. Mum and Dad had put 250 Euros inside for him. It was good, it would be that extra cushion. He might hide it somewhere just in case, maybe in his Brookes saddle seat post. Never can be too careful. OK, he thought, I might be one of life's best-organised people, but I'm lucky too.

A final glance, nothing missing, no more to be done. Yet one last look at his kit before diving into bed. Then twenty minutes after flicking through Cycling Weekly, he was sound asleep.

3

Hot sand. White searing light. Dry air that caught the back of your throat. No-one about, everyone hunkered down out of the light. The family's beat up old Toyota Hilux truck looked grimy yellow in the courtyard. Once shiny white, it was now dirty and scarred. It hardly needed the camouflage colours it had been painted, the desert was claiming it. He wondered how the car's Japanese makers felt knowing that IS had endorsed the vehicle, so unwisely sent by the Americans to the Al Nusra Front in Syria, before becoming the must-have all-terrain technical vehicle of choice in Iraq.

He shrugged as he looked at the vehicle's battered state. In the end the desert took everything. My, the stories that motor could tell, he thought. The removable rear-mounted gun poked awkwardly out from under grey plastic sheeting, the grenade launcher half tucked away. It was all looking old and worn, but mechanically it was still in good order and totally reliable.

The Toyota had seen a lot of action in recent years. He depended on it and it reflected his own status - as a significant and loyal revolutionary. Anyway, that was how they saw him. To them he was the best of the mujaheddin, the holy warriors; and like the best of the shahadah, the martyrs, he had always taken care to be seen in the front line of battle.

It was too hot to stay outside. Ramadan changed everything. No food, no drink, no patience. Sawm, the season's compulsory fast, made everyone short-tempered. Ali kicked the ground in frustration, sending up a small cloud of hot red dust before stepping back inside the cool dark interior of their Mosul home.

Frustration, he mused, had come to characterise his life, a feeling he did his best to conceal. He could hear the high pitched murmur of the women and children's voices from across the yard. His sister Fatima and his brother Mo's wife, Maryam, would no doubt be organising something simple for the two younger children to eat. Not for them the strictures of Ramadan; the innocence and blessing of childhood, he thought.

Less than a week in, still in the long days of the month of May, the fasting practices of the season with the day and night prayer times were yet too new to have bedded into bodily adjustment. The routine, once established, would make it all easier to bear. But then it was all worth it, he told himself, God would count it as merit. Hunger gnawed and thirst dried the lips and mouth. God was hard, he thought, putting Ramadan in the height of summer when the days were long and the sand was hot, but who am I to question God? He shrugged his shoulders involuntarily as in private, he realised, he often did question God.

The house felt safe as well as cool, the mud brick walls shaped into an enclosed courtyard of several family buildings served their purpose well. Indeed, for as long as anyone could remember his family had lived here. Once sited on the edge of the city, sprawling new builds now threatened to surround them. Everywhere vertical concrete seemed to be replacing the buildings of the past, but in recent times all building work had stopped. Inside, his brother Mo was sitting at the single table trying to get an internet signal and hissing through his teeth as each time when he hit the 'search' key the little blue tracer line hardly marched a tenth of the way across the screen - nothing doing.

'How are we supposed to know what is going on?' he muttered under his breath as he pushed the laptop away and turned to Ali who was now leaning over his shoulder. It had been a few years since IS had taken their town in northern Iraq, and they were feeling more and more embattled. It was important to know what was going on. Mosul had settled into a pattern of life which was at one and the same time perfectly relaxed and orderly, but always fearful of terrors from without and, if lines were crossed, terrors from within.

The combination of clear rules to live by and strict discipline to enforce things wasn't so bad. In fact it had improved life in many ways, but you needed to know who was

8

saying what, and know what to say to whom; and, when the internet was down, you felt more insecure. Ali fought back his sense of frustration. Information was safety, and it was a help to know what local leaders were up to and what they were reporting about the war. Just now in Ramadan it was vital not to miss what the spiritual leaders were saying each day. Success in life was not just about who you knew, but often about proving how well you were following what people were teaching. With a final shrug Mo gave up, pushing the laptop away from him in frustration.

Ali flopped into a nearby chair. He glanced around at the familiar room, bare walls, a rug on the floor, an oil lamp next to the door. This was the time of year when nothing happened, everything shut down. Ramadan's call to discipline the faithful was hard, austere, unforgiving. The super-spiritual seem to welcome it, but for Ali, each time it came around, it was an ordeal.

The hours were punctuated by the regular calls to worship and prayer by the Adhan; and, the five times a day electronic broadcast voices of the Muezzins penetrated everywhere - no escape for the would-be heretics, the thought amusing him. All would have to hear, all would hear the Takbir and Shahada proclaimed - God is great, there is no God but Allah, and Muhammed is his messenger. One day, it was said, everyone would share this common vision for the world, but for the present, Ali knew jihad must continue and only in struggle would he find his way to glory.

'Let's head over to the mosque for midday prayers', he heard himself say. Mo responded with a nod and picked up a magazine. Ali wondered what it was. There was so little permitted, it was easy to be looking at the wrong thing. He knew how to make out in these times and the excitement of being part of something new, an Islamic State which had even left the great Satan, the United States of America wondering what it could do, was a marvel of the age. IS had survived, it had grown, and he was part of its success. It was an exciting adventure, an experiment, an ideal here to stay, so he was always being told and sometimes he almost believed it.

9

It had been nearly five years since Ali had given up his engineering course at Mosul University. At that time he knew he was needed elsewhere to serve the revolution; and besides, too many students were rebellious. Ali had always been a pragmatist. It was safer to leave his studies, for loyalty to IS had to be demonstrated. Anyway it wasn't long before only IS run schools were allowed and pretty well everything else had to close. There was no room for lukewarm ambivalence in a time of jihad. They found they could use his engineering and language skills and it helped that they welcomed him.

It had all worked out well in the end, he mused, the Toyota had been an early gain and he could get fuel for it on request. The steady income also helped and his family never went hungry. In fact, like most god-fearing people, life had gone on much as before but with fewer uncertainties and far fewer corrupt officials and politicians to negotiate. The imposition of strict Shari'ah had given a much needed order to the community and anyone stepping out of line paid the price. Truth to tell the only future was in serving IS, and it wasn't so bad. He'd learned to handle it, even if he didn't like it.

But the trouble was, as the years passed, Ali was increasingly bored as well as frustrated. He was so bored it was becoming dangerous. When he had nothing much to do he suffered from flashbacks, it made him restless. He would yearn so deeply for something colourful, something different, he would take risks.

'Come on Mo,' he called across the room to his brother, 'get that laptop connected, I want a quick look before we go to prayers.'

He hoped Mo would just pass him it and then leave him in peace so he could surf the net for things to lift his spirits. He wanted real news of the world outside, not religiously sifted, heavily censored news that didn't tell you what you really wanted to know. One last attempt and Mo gave up trying to get anywhere and passed him the ancient grey laptop before disappearing to lie down for a few minutes - the heat sapping all energy. That suited Ali just fine.

10

He had better luck than Mo and connected almost immediately. Emails came pinging in. First, he'd better check whether he was required for duty by his unit commander. Young men like him had to be ready to serve at all times. No, nothing. Next, he started searching. He fancied looking at what was happening in London. He got the BBC, but hurriedly checked to see the sound was switched right down so that he'd remain undetected.

There was a strike on the London Underground and people were struggling to get to work. Wouldn't happen here, he smiled. Strike leaders would be called in, told to stop or taken out and beheaded. An agitated black woman, her face bare and clothes bright, seemed to be telling a reporter how difficult it was for her that morning, her young child pulling at her arm as she spoke. No, we wouldn't let that happen. He flipped to another story, concern at how wet the summer was and the impact this would have on the south coast resort towns. There were pictures of deserted beaches and miserable looking hoteliers. No bikini clad women on these beaches today, he noted.

He flipped again, this time it was about preparations for the autumn, when London would commemorate all those who had died in war. Armistice Day was apparently getting to be a bigger event year on year. Pictures of the first World War, red poppies, lines of military aligned white headstones of the fallen, filled half a screen page. The Prime Minister, had apparently appointed a minister to take charge of events for the coming November and the PM had promised resources to give London an occasion to remember. There would be military parades, fireworks and street parties, even a special one in Downing Street.

He's after popular sympathy, Ali thought, it's just the same with leaders here. The Prime Minister desperately wants to present himself as a man of the people, introduce some informality to his latest term in office. Hmm, a bit over the top, a few shots in the air was about as celebratory it got here. Mind you when Eid al Fitr arrives after Ramadan, we'll feast and party in our own way. As all this was some weeks away

11

the thought didn't particularly lift his spirits. Then his laptop flashed up a new message. It was his commander. He immediately clicked on it.

He'd been called in for special training starting tomorrow. He was to report to the nearby souk, his community cell, at 6am next morning, his community cell. Well, he thought, as he typed his acknowledgement, at least something is happening; and, that he'd got on to it straight away, that was fortuitous. He logged off, throwing the laptop on to the chair seat as he made his way into the courtyard of the family home. Washing was drying on the line. His Mother, sister and sister-in-law had been busy. Lines of grey and black cloth waved in the breeze, the bright sun never brightening the clothes. Why does God want it all so dull? he pondered.

He went over to a small store in the compound, secured by a wooden door with a high bolt to keep the youngsters out. His younger brother, sisters and the children would be in there going through his things given half the chance. He reached inside and pulled out an oily sack from the back. He took out his prized AK47 and decided it was time to clean it up and get ready for whatever the morning might bring. He always found it immensely comforting to hold his automatic in his hands. The engineering was perfect. Such a debt of gratitude was owed to its Soviet designer Mikhael Kalashnikov. Ali's had a standard 30 round magazine feed system, less cumbersome than the 100 round drum version.

Cradling it, he felt so powerful, even invincible. It had served him well and he looked after it lovingly, cleaning and oiling it most days. It had been taken from the dead Iraqi soldier who had shot his father at the time of one of the many failed attempts by the corrupt politicians of Baghdad to retake IS lands. He'd never forgotten how the soldier, even in death, seemed to clutch his gun with such affection. He understood that, now it was his. The memory of the street scene, his father's dead grimace, unsettled him and he turned his attention back to the task ahead.

He set about stripping the weapon down on the laid-out cloth, using the smaller cloth to clean and polish each part in turn. It took him the best part of an hour. Then the job was done and he placed it carefully back in its wrapper ready to take with him in the morning. The mosque muezzin was calling the men for prayer, it was time to go. He called his brother who dragged himself up, and they were out of the gate moving with others in one direction mosque-ward.

The sun seemed to stay overhead for ever in Ramadan. Though the calendar dates varied year on year, he felt it always fell on the hottest time of summer when the days were longest. Twenty-two years old and he was bored. He was desperate to do something that would make a difference. IS seemed to have stopped still since the incredible successes of the early years in 2013-14. There had been no recent territorial gains after the early successes, only stalemate and setback. The dream was beginning to tarnish.

Increasingly life felt under pressure now. As they headed across the street toward the mosque, he glanced skyward, he routinely did. Drones were a real threat. The coward foreign forces relied on them more and more. A leader would be taken out, a weapon store blown up, a vehicle hit, a useful building demolished. Intermittent electric supplies and a subterfuge half-life in the shadows were part of the price that had to be paid, but Ali thought, their own leaders were cunning tacticians. They knew drones could never win and had now so dispersed communications and command into the lives of the whole community, things were certainly no worse and possibly even better than they were.

What was so encouraging or delusional, thought Ali, was that our commanders were still thinking ahead, dreaming big dreams; and, their resolve in God and their belief in ultimate victory as unshakeable as ever. He passed the now empty neighbour'ing house marked with a large 'N' for Nasrani. They, like all the Christians he knew, had fled - very wise he thought, they're not like us. They must convert or die. There's no place for them here.

'Mo' he murmured, 'I've got a call from the CO. I'm needed first thing tomorrow. Now what do you think that will be about?'

13

'No idea', he replied. 'You'll find out soon enough.'

But Ali knew different, to call me just before prayers in Ramadan, he thought, something's up. He felt an extra spurt to his step as he moved from the white sun into the shade of the mosque, kicked off his sandals and stepped into the cooler interior of the wudu area. He began washing - hands, forearms, face and feet. Was this a preparation for something more than prayers? They joined the men and boys crowding into the mosque's worship space. He was always impressed as silently everyone stood shoulder to shoulder, side by side, numbers building line after line. Maybe we are truly invincible, he thought.

When they were inside, his ritual preparations began, so well-known and ingrained in his life he was barely conscious he was performing them. Then the IS appointed imam began the Dhur, the second round of the day's five prayer times.

Ali went with the familiar flow, but his mind was elsewhere. He felt his boredom, his frustration, his need for escape and dreamed - maybe, just maybe, he hoped, something better might be coming his way; and, the hungry eagerness to know what his CO had in mind gnawed away at his insides, adding to the biting hunger of the Ramadan fast.

4

The Christian Ministry Channel 128 studio had an afternoon guest preacher. North London's Bishop Sam Kone, originally from Jamaica, had huge amounts of energy and a larger than life personality to match. If he was asked what made him happiest, he wouldn't have said, but he'd have thought to himself, why being on TV as a successful preacher giving my all for the good Lord, that's paradise. He craved being the centre of attention and he loved leading and telling. Today was good, very good. He imagined the many thousands, even millions watching on God TV, tuned in to him, or planning to listen to him later on-line. It made his very soul almost burst with satisfaction.

The shiny black London taxi had collected him from his home in Edmonton at 8.30am and his neighbours had seen it. He kept the taxi waiting outside with its door open as he made a point of making his loving goodbyes to Shazee, his wife and Kaylah his teenage daughter. His lad Clive was nowhere to be seen - but then he wasn't an easy son.

As he took the ten steps from door to taxi, rushing parents were taking children to school, casting glances in his direction. Others were off to work or college - the perfect time to get noticed, he thought. Just over 30 minutes later he arrived at the foyer of the Beta TV studios in Tower Hamlets ready for action. About half an hour more of pre-broadcast checking and make up and he was pumped up and all set to go. Just a few minutes more to wait, the adrenaline began to build and he thought it time to offer a quick silent, final, arrow prayer to the Almighty. The familiar words, 'anoint' and 'bless,' came to mind.

Sam's north London black pentecostal congregation had grown over the eight years he had been pastor. He'd been called by the Edmonton elders whilst serving at a mission chapel in Islington. It was there he had cut his teeth. Today he was leading a congregation drawing worshippers from all over London and the church now had a fine building in Edmonton Green, a former suite of council offices which the London Borough of Enfield had found to be yet another building too many to finance in an era, now decade of, austerity and public spending cuts.

After interminable discussions with council minions, a compromise had finally been achieved when, rather than see the building lie empty and fall into dereliction, Bishop Kone had persuaded them to make it over to him to meet the community needs of north London's marginal Black and Minority Ethnic community. The fact that the building appeared in the local Enfield Gazette newspaper as a future venue for the care of the homeless and recovering drug users, an article that Sam had had tactfully placed there, led to a rapid signing of documents, anxious councillors relieved and Sam triumphant. Councillors were glad on two counts - having no longer to face the complaints of local residents on the one hand nor having the deal cast as socially irresponsible on the other hand.

Only months later, with the building safely signed over to him in a 99 year lease and with his carefully chosen management committee in place, did Bishop Kone start shifting away from the community use focus the council had wanted to see, to one of out and out religious zeal and evangelical fervour. All this didn't trouble him, his life was a mission! Currently he was on a roll and saw his precious reputation scaling new heights through TV exposure.

Today he had chosen to preach on faithfulness in a diverse and sinful world. He was waved at by a heavily made-up, plump, white-uniformed blobby, filling an office chair who signalled him forward, it was time. In through the opaque glass door he strode in his purple episcopal shirt and pinstriped suit and into the regulated atmosphere, dimmed lights and absorbed sound of the clean studio. He noted with satisfaction the purple backlighting behind his seat and the halo-shaped tinge of white light that would be directly above his head. This can only go one way, he thought.

He pulled out his well-thumbed, black, Authorised Bible from its leather case which he discarded by the door and made his way to his Mastermind style seat, balancing the good book open in his ample lap. The green light came on, 'Kool Kone Komments' flashed up behind him. He was live.

Sam made a serious face, leant into the nearest camera and began addressing his audience with a question.

'Do you really know your neighbour, the person next door to you? The person who travels next to you on the bus or in the tube? How can you know your neighbour? There's only one way to really know your neighbour, be they a Muslim, Hindu or Jewish neighbour. Only, and only through love, God's love. God's all-embracing lo-ve.' He leant back confident his viewers were now with him.

'And make no mistake, God loves everyone.' Lifting his Bible confidently, he continued, 'John 3.16, "For God so loved the world," (giving 'the world' a bit of added emphasis), "he gave his only begotten Son, that whosoever believeth in him should not perish, but have everlasting life."'

He paused for a moment. He was building his baseline, he was gathering momentum like an express train, he was on his way and soon as it always did, the sweat would start to break on his brow and his body would grow in agitation as the Spirit of God took hold of him. He failed to notice the expanding line of dark sweat now staining the purple shirt. All Sam could think was, this was going to be good.

Twenty minutes later and his emotionally charged final appeal delivered, his voice dipped to a calm and reassuring tone and he signed off with his catch phrase, 'Am-en my friends, A-A-Amennnnn.' He stepped down from his chair and wiped his brow, feeling and feeding on the deep self-satisfaction welling up inside him.

Back in Edmonton, watching TV in their front room were his wife Shazee and daughter Kaylah. Shazee as ever thought Sam's performance top drawer.

'He just gets better and better,' she said.

Shazee liked her husband to have success, a commodity so hard to find. Kaylah didn't want to upset her

17

Mum who never seemed to have a view of her own on anything, so she bottled her thoughts and feelings and smiled sweetly. It was easier that way.

To her eyes, life was not black and white as her parents saw it, but all manner of shades of grey. Simple prescriptive answers to life on the street in Edmonton were not to be found by quoting a Bible verse here and there or in the Sunday School stories about Shepherds and Fishermen. So, she had to dissemble a bit to get by. If she didn't do so, she'd be shown the door and that didn't suit her. After all, where would she go?

Show over, Kaylah fled to the sanctuary of her own room and picked up her new mobile, glancing at the stream of messages and Facebook pictures and comments, but there was nothing from her older brother Clive. Clive being a boy had always had it easier, she thought. As far back as she could remember he had a freedom to do and say what he pleased. Maybe that had been her parents' mistake, spoiling him so, but she'd always loved him for the likeable rogue he was. Life for girls was never fair. Mum gave him the money he asked for without the questions she always got. The injustice of it bothered her, but never enough to make her argue out loud.

The trouble was, Clive worried her sick. His smiles and confidence, so winsome and charming as a younger boy, no longer reassured Kaylah. For much as she privately distanced herself from her parent's fundamentalist over-zealous religion, Clive's life was rapidly heading in the opposite direction as she saw it - bad friends, bad lifestyle. Clive was a walking disaster waiting to happen - and their parents hadn't a clue.

'Come on Clive, why don't you text me?' He hadn't been home in nearly 24 hours. Last time she saw him, his mate Winston had called to pick him up in his blue BMW yesterday morning. They were up to something, her instincts told her. Winston was a nice enough, ever cheerful guy, but bad news. Where could he get the money for that car other than by serious crime? Her friends were more relaxed about him, Monique loved being taken for a ride, living the life, glamourising his car. She's behaving like a gangster's Moll, she thought, becoming ever more alarmed at the direction her thoughts were taking her.

People said Winston had done time inside, but he always said not. Clive was generally pretty good at judging characters, so why would he spend time with Winston? She sent another text to Clive and threw her phone on the bed in frustration.

It was nearly time to head to college. She'd get the bus up to Southgate, but first she needed to go through her business studies notes. She aimed to do well, to succeed and that meant getting rich, but more than that, she wanted to be able to stand on her own two feet and walk away from here. Some of the people in this terraced house were just cramping her space, she thought. She needed to breathe, have more fun.

Her papers finally sorted, neatly in order, she slid them into her bag. Then she scooped up her pink short jacket and slipped out of the front door. She should just make the bus.

5

If only Clive had known Winston's BMW was taking him along the same stretch of road as his Dad. They passed each other at speed in Tottenham High Road, the black taxi and the BMW going in opposite directions, rather like their lives. Sam Kone was staring straight ahead, onward and upward.

Clive was glancing out of the window, a pretty girl here, a shop window there. They'd spent most of the past 24 hours at Winston's flat listening to music, picking up a pizza, chilling out. Then, this morning, Winston had taken a mobile call; on his instruction they'd hastily grabbed their things, jumped in his car and without a word of explanation headed off. Moments later they passed Tottenham Police Station, for decades a focus for black resentment. Too many brothers and sisters had died at the hands of white policemen - Roger Sylvester, Cynthia Jarrett, Mark Duggan... .

'No justice, no peace,' Clive said out loud as they passed.

Winston Sinclair, was too far away listening to music on his oversize headphones to hear him. Soon they were in Stamford Hill, then Hackney. Winston slowed the car to a crawl.

'What are you looking for?' shouted Clive.

'There's a package I'm taking delivery of. Wind your window down, get ready to grab it,' said Winston. The electric window slid down quietly and effortlessly as everything seemed to do in Winston's car.

'See that kid, grey hoodie, by the post box,' said Winston as he slowed still further, much to the annoyance of the queuing motorists behind. The lanky lad, no more than 14 or 15 years old, saw them approaching and lifted a sports bag from by his feet, up to waist height. Even at a crawl they were closing fast.

'Grab it for fuck's sake', said Winston.

Clive did what he was told, bag safely drawn inside the car on his lap, the BMW quickly accelerating away. Through the nearside wing mirror Clive could see the kid disappearing down the side street back into the Manor Estate. Clive reckoned he wouldn't have grabbed the bag if the kid hadn't looked like he wanted to hand it over, so he felt OK if still puzzled, by what he'd done.

'OK, what have I got here then?' Clive asked. He felt the weight of the bag again - not heavy really. 'Did you forget your kit for the gym today or something?'

He had pushed his headphones down to his designer shirt collar and was now on high alert looking around him quickly and anxiously.

'Hang on. We might have a problem', said Winston.

Clive could see him looking in the rear view mirror. He turned his own head to better see what it was. A police car, four or five cars back, had put on its blues and twos and was trying to get by. Winston quickly left the traffic by turning left, clearly wanting to avoid it. He took a left again, and then a right. They were heading back north again. The police car could just be made out still tied up in London's as ever frustratingly congested traffic.

'What's going on?' Clive quizzed, making another start at unzipping the bag, but Winston's large left hand shot across and held the top of the bag firmly shut.

'Nothing, just business. Throw it on the back seat will you. Thanks for your help, it meant we didn't have to stop. When we get back to Bruce Grove we'll grab a bit of nourishment, you hungry?' asked Winston.

Clive knew better than to argue with Winston, he did what he was asked and they drove in silence the remaining fifteen minutes it took to get to Cliff's Coffee House at the back of Broadwater Farm.

Winston pulled the car off the main road. Clive knew this was not normal behaviour either, for Winston always parked outside wherever he was going, double yellow lines or not. Then, just to seal the matter and leave Clive in no doubt something serious was up, Winston threw the sports bag in the boot and did something he'd never seen done before: check he'd locked it! Clive knew for certain whatever was in that bag was precious!

His phone went, another text from Kaylah. He flicked the phone off. It could wait. He loved his sister, but she so mothered him and now was not a good time for a conversation. Inside he was wrestling with what had just happened. Same excitement as a movie, but this time it was different for he had the feeling he was with the bad guys. They hurried into Cliff's.

A crowd was there. He followed Winston deeper inside, turning over again what had happened. Winston wasn't what he'd call a bad guy, now was he? If nothing else, a bag grab, a chasing police car and a mysterious holdall brightened up a dull day; nothing had gone wrong now, had it? Yet somewhere, deep inside, a little voice was telling him something bad was going to happen.

Then he thought of his Dad. That was what he was always telling Clive. He had kind of got so used to being told something bad would happen because of the company he kept, it was a slippery slope and he now found himself thinking it too. Part of him was worried. These days he felt like he was always letting his Dad down, never meeting his expectations. He was always the bad thing that happened. 'But what's done is done,' he concluded. 'Best just go with the flow and let things be what they will be.'

6

Adam had got away later than he'd hoped. Last minute, he'd popped into Tottenham to pick up a second spare inner tube, cycled there of course, but on his old mountain bike. He rode more cautiously than usual and thought to himself that he mustn't do anything at this stage to jeopardise his chances of getting away - last thing he wanted was to be inadvertently knocked off his bike before he'd even left home.

Fred Striker's cycle shop in the High Road had always been good for bike parts and servicing advice; and, besides he wanted to say goodbye to Fred, to tell him he was finally off. The shop was an Aladdin's cave of bikes and bike parts and had that garage smell of metal, rubber and oil that pleasured the senses.

The two had talked many times about cycling adventures. Fred himself, as a young man, had cycled the length of Britain and it pleased him hugely to see the spirit of adventure alive and well in young Adam.

Adam selected and paid for his spare tyre and as he turned to leave, Fred, with a shrug, thrust in his hand a couple of energy bars as a present to send him on his way. Adam had done well out of Fred, getting second hand quality parts for his bike, all provided by a genuine bike enthusiast secretly wishing he was sharing Adam's forthcoming adventure.

Leaving the shop, Adam was nearly knocked off his mountain bike by a blue BMW, the driver and passenger clearly miles away. Just as well he was careful. He watched them disappear up the road and then swing left into Bruce Grove. He was heading that way and then along Lordship Lane and back to Muswell Hill. He half-heartedly thought of hurling some abuse at them if he caught up, but quickly told himself that around here that was dumb, plain stupid and in any case it could undo his play it safe strategy until he left.

He soon forgot the incident and saved his energies for the uphill ride home.

Back home, he wheeled his mountain bike through the house and put it back in the shed, wondering when he'd next climb into its saddle again; and, with a bit of a struggle, gathered his things, pulled his bedroom door firmly shut and pulled his loaded Marin tourer out and through to the front of the house, leaning it on the wall by the front porch. He looked at his home, a pretty ordinary Edwardian terraced house in red London brick, but more spacious on the inside than it looked from the outside. It would be some time before he saw it again.

He could hear voices inside, the moment had come for saying goodbyes. Best get them over with quickly, he thought. His parents had taken time off and were hanging around to see him leave. Last hugs and well wishes and from Mum tearful words urging him to take care. His Dad didn't say much, but he kind of understood what Adam was about, which was good to know. He pushed his bike to the metal front gate and it swung and clanged shut behind him for the last time, his parents following, leaning on it for a lingering, farewell. There was a last silent look and a wave as he cycled off, that image of them together fixed in his mind.

He quickly forgot about home as his mind tuned to the turn of the wheels, the gradient of the road, the click of the gears, the weight of his machine loaded with panniers and the direction of travel. A red London Routemaster bus broke the breeze in front of him and helped him gain ground, but only so far as the end of Muswell Hill Road. From Muswell Hill it was downhill practically which ever way you went and certainly all the way toward central London. Not quite believing it, he was on his way at last, the wind in his face, the freedom of weeks, the call and excitement of the unknown journey.

London's traffic flowed past him, around him, either on the inside or the outside, which was something to constantly watch for. To them he was just another cyclist heading for the city, but he knew he was bound for Iran and it made him feel special. Initially, his plan was to take himself south and west before heading east, toward the city of London. He'd chosen the route carefully, determined to look at the sights one final time.

His route was sentimentally circuitous to begin with. He headed for the green lungs of the city - taking himself past the oak trees and glades of Highgate Wood, then around the wider panoramas of Hampstead Heath, down through Primrose Hill, into Regents Park with its many memories of zoo trips with his parents in past years. A rhythm soon set in as he clocked up the first few miles on his Garmin Edge Cycle Computer and odometer.

Then he was heading towards the seat of government - Hyde Park, Green Park and St James's. He circled round a bit to look into Whitehall and Downing Street and then backtracked and zigzagged to find a way down to the River Thames and the Embankment. The tide was in and river boats were busy criss-crossing the blue water.

The day was glorious, non-stop sunshine and cool fresh air with a gentle westerly breeze. People everywhere seemed to be enjoying the city as he was. Every Thames Embankment bench was taken and lots of people were sitting out on the grass or walking to see the sights, enjoying the early summer sunshine. He paused briefly by the river to take stock and have a drink from his water bottle.

Moments later he was off again, making his way past the Houses of Parliament, the giant blue, white and red union flag billowing majestically above, catching the afternoon sunlight. He spotted the big Ferris wheel, the London Eye, with queues of tourists waiting the chance to have their turn. Now he was heading east through the City of London's monuments to finance, big business and commerce, the shiny high rise temples to capitalism.

He nodded a respectful glance at St Paul's Cathedral, winding his way through narrow city streets with ancient names like Cheapside (how ironic was that, he thought) and Poultry (where the only poultry today was to be found in expensive sandwiches and wraps).

Then down towards the Thames again and past the white ramparts of the Tower of London, that turreted symbol of royalty since the time of William the Conqueror. He could see yellow-jacketed workmen behind crowd barriers trying to get the grounds of the Tower ready to install another exhibition to mark Armistice Day later in the year. He didn't think anything they could possibly do could eclipse the sea of red ceramic poppies that had commemorated the hundredth anniversary of the outbreak of the First World War.

Adam had decided to follow the straight Roman Road line of Watling Street to escape London. Today it was called by the functional name of the A207. It was just fine, but for the maddening sea of potholes, not nearly as bad as those in north London, but irritating with a laden bike all the same. He also found it impossible to miss all the annoying traffic-calming humps. Despite endless traffic lights with a penchant for the colour red and over-long changes just to madden and slow him, he made good progress riding steadily east.

So far as conditions would allow he kept his legs turning rhythmically and smoothly. It was a different thing cycling fully loaded. With a heavy bike he had to turn the pedals efficiently, to conserve energy and do things smoothly, always thinking, anticipating, that bit further ahead. It felt so good to hear the well-oiled, clean clicking, of the gear change and chain set sounding crisp to his ears; and, the cable tensions feeling just perfect to the touch for his gear changes. He knew full well that things didn't stay that way, but it was certainly good while it lasted and his increasing tiredness was more than compensated for by the sense of satisfaction he had at the progress he had made on his first day.

The afternoon was wearing on, the sun now low on his back, and he was glad to be on to the A226 heading through Dartford and taking the bridge over London's orbital motorway, the M25, with its eight lanes of continuous motor noise. It was only at this point, he believed, he was really leaving London. He was now in Kent, the garden county of England and he applied a little more energy to the pedals to wind in the remaining ten miles.

The first night's stop would be in Gravesend. Head down he pressed on, relentlessly turning those pedals, putting the past behind and heading for, well, he wasn't quite sure. He wondered what the journey would do for him, but couldn't come up with any ideas.

Maybe it would be simply a useful conversation starter to have up his sleeve when he went to Uni. in the autumn. Well, all that was an age away. In the back of his mind he had a persistent nagging thought, that this would be a real adventure, combining excitement and risk. What kind of risk, he couldn't guess, but instinctively. Well, he would find out soon enough.

7

At last the cool of evening had come and it was time to break the day's fast. First a few dates, a little water, then something more. Ali wanted to eat more quickly but knew that it wasn't going to be possible. He had to proceed at the pace the family produced the food and he had to be patient. Besides, he reminded himself, eating slowly aided the digestion after the rigour of the day's fast. Those first juicy sweet dates very quickly lifted his blood sugar.

He felt energy coming back. Looking again at the message he'd received at the end of midday prayers telling him to report to his CO after evening meal, he felt both excited and impatient. That time of meeting was soon.

Some Kibbeh had been cooked by Fatima, the minced lamb or goat inside coated with cracked wheat and cooked in the frier, a family favourite. There was flat bread with it and fruit juice. Some Palestinian-sourced Cola drink was also available and he wondered just how that had made its way to the table. Often meals were hit and miss affairs, always a surprise, no-one quite knowing what if anything was to be had. At times it felt like the family were endlessly living on short rations, but then at other times, like now, food seemed plentiful and the hungry days were forgotten.

He was done and pushed his plate to the side as he stood up. Excusing himself to his uncle, the senior male in the house since his father had been shot, he stood up. His uncle knew better than to ask him his business, for he knew that it was dangerous to know too much in these times and he was all the more cautious knowing Ali had aligned himself closely with the town authorities. On balance his uncle viewed the arrangement as beneficial, for Ali was the one who made sure the whole family got the fringe benefits of keeping in with the Caliphate leadership.

Ali slipped out of the front door, patting his niece and nephew affectionately on their heads as he left, everyone else either too engrossed in the important matter of eating to notice he had gone or just being sensibly discreet.

Ali walked purposefully, striding through the virtually empty streets. Most families, like his own were focussing on the evening meal. Two, three streets later he stepped into the foyer of an apartment block. It had some minor pockmark mortar damage to the third floor outside walls, but the lower two floors were as yet unscathed and he knew Salim Ismat as regional IS CO had acquired the place because it was pretty well attack-proof, either from overhead bombers or low flying drones. It was surrounded by family homes and had a school to one side and a hospital opposite.

For such a nice place, Salim had made it a model of unpretentious austerity. Just inside the front door, he'd placed the opening words of the Qur'an, the Al Fatihah. There was no other internal wall decoration. Clever, Ali thought, to put words about opening hearts next to an opening door.

Salim needed to be fed regular communication like a vampire needed blood. Salim didn't lock his front door, he argued he had nothing to hide, but out of respect Ali called out a greeting and paused rather than walk right in.

'Salaam Alekum', he shouted, which was followed almost immediately by a quietly spoken call from somewhere inside to come in.

They entered a small first floor side room with a window to the dark street outside. It was simply furnished, with a desk and two chairs. Ali was invited to sit and refreshment was sent for. After the usual and expected exchange of polite pleasantries, Salim took a sheet of paper from under his robes and laid it on the table. The business was about to begin.

'We are keen to take the IS cause beyond our borders and into the heart of Kuffar lands. We are convinced that our Muslim brothers and sisters are gradually being won over to our cause here in the Middle East. Yes, I admit it is taking a little longer than we thought, but enshalla,' he grinned.

'The tide is turning and the misguided ones among us are losing ground. The fight is not in them any more and we have right on our side. In their hearts they know that. Our illustrious leadership are now thinking much further ahead strategically and we have decided that we have reached a point when our hard-pressed brothers and sisters in the West who have had to give up so much to survive in the face of rampant Islamophobia and oppression, need, let's say, a helping hand. The kind of helping hand that encourages our brothers and sisters here too,' he said, rising to his theme.

'Sounds interesting,' Ali interjected, adding keenly, 'and how can I help?'

Maybe he was a bit too impetuous. Interrupting the CO wasn't wise, especially as he was clearly warming to the sound of his own voice. The CO ignored the interruption as if it hadn't occurred and pressed on.

'Our contacts in London are aware of certain opportunities now open to us. Through our foreign fighter returnees we know there is some support waiting to rise up at the right time. For them life is very tough: they are monitored day and night, their homes are watched, they are denied electronic communication and some have to wear tagging bracelets. Others are under house arrest and are even denied access to a mosque as well as to spiritually pure leaders. Sadly some of our best and strongest warriors are to be found in the prisons. That said, there's still much opportunity to do something glorious.'

There was a pause as Salim stopped speaking and motioned silence putting a finger to his lips. There was a noise outside in the corridor. A knock, the door was pushed open and a shrouded person, completely hidden behind veil and black cloth, carried in a tray of soft drinks with two clean glasses. Some small, sweet, honeyed biscuits were on a side plate. Salim served in silence as the woman made her exit. When Salim was quite sure she was out of range he began talking again, this time in a lower conspiratorial tone.

'I have been most impressed by your loyalty and faithful service to the Caliphate, and your jihad has not gone unnoticed at the highest level. You are the kind of person who will run straight at the enemy, neither turning to the left or the right, a soldier ready to fly to the highest paradise chambers of Jannah. For this reason we wish to bestow even greater honour and blessing upon you and your family. Your background in engineering and your ability to speak English mean that very soon we are expecting to enable you to travel to the United Kingdom, to London.' He paused to make sure Ali had registered what he was saying.

'Your journey there is still some weeks away. In the meantime I want you to begin a programme of training to prepare you for what lies ahead. You will attend daily English classes with your former secondary school English teacher, straight after morning prayers. He has been told to expect you, but he has no idea why he has to give you this English refresher course. If he must know or suspects anything, you are to simply say you need it for commercial purposes, nothing more,' Salim instructed. Ali nodded.

'You will also go to our communications centre for more training, here in Mosul. It is in the basement of the hospital if you hadn't guessed already. A very safe place,' he smiled, 'and no enemies would dare to attack it. There, on Sundays from 10am you will be briefed on how to send electronic messages and codes. When we get nearer the time when you leave, they will also issue you with some equipment you will take with you. It is really important you know all these things - you must learn well, very well. Lives will depend on it, not least your own.'

'But how will I get into the Communications Centre?' asked Ali.

'Good point.' Salim knew Ali would ask and had already been reaching inside his robes again, this time to take out and place a small plastic oval object on the table between them.

'Take this key fob when you go to the hospital. Say at reception you are visiting the classes for disabled fighters.'

'I didn't know there were any,' said Ali.

'Exactly, there isn't any such thing. You will be sent to the staircase. Unhook the plastic "no entry" red and white chain, pass through, and hang it back as it was. When you get to the bottom of the stairs there will be a guard at a desk in front of a locked door who will want to see your IS identity card. He will take things from there. You will need your fob to gain entry. Just show it to the electronic door reader.' Salim pulled out his mobile phone and tapped on it. He was reminding himself of something before continuing.

'Oh yes, there is a third element to your preparation as well as improving your English and technical skills. You are to get fit, very fit. For this reason, each day, you are to report to the military gymnasium after midday prayers. It is also in a basement. We provide everything nearby just for you,' he laughed.

'It is in the school basement opposite to the hospital! Your fob will also allow you into the school and the same chain arrangement applies when you get to the stairs. This time you are to say you are there for Jihad Warrior training. You will be told what to do. Hmmm, the good thing is, you are given special dispensation to stop fasting immediately. In fact you are to drink and eat as instructed by your sports trainer.'

'But what am I going to do?' Ali enquired.

'Wait and see. The less you know until you need to know, the better it is for all of us and the more likely you will be to succeed. Be assured what we have lined up for you could change the whole course of world history and your name will be known and celebrated for ever. In the meantime, you are excused all other services to the Caliphate. In fact we would rather you lie low and drop out of popular circulation. You are also excused regular mosque attendance. We want you to prepare to disappear for sometime. There will be some further instruction nearer the time.'

'But what will I say to my family?' asked Ali.

'Your Uncle will be told to manage his household discreetly as the Caliphate have need for your services. He will know he is not to make enquiries or raise eyebrows. He will know if either he or you betray us, then the penalties will be very severe. Everything you ask of him he will do and he will supply you with whatever you require. Any problem, you come straight to me. When you wake up tomorrow morning your life will be different,' said Salim.

'You are on special duties and total, I mean absolute secrecy is required. You speak about this, you lose your tongue. You write about it, you lose a hand before you lose your head! Understood?' Ali nodded to indicate assent to what was now a quite normal method of getting things done, but the terror of its impact still made him shudder inside every time. He knew full well such punishments were all too frequently used.

His CO sat there, now leaning back in his chair. Ali knew today's conversation was over. He couldn't quite believe what he'd heard. Shown the door, he was out in the dark silent street before he realised it. No this wasn't a dream, in his hand he was clutching a fob on a silver chain. He put it around his neck and tucked it down inside the front of his vest. Furtively, he scurried in the shadows, glancing just to make sure no-one was watching. This was like life was going to be. He was alone, he had to learn to start living in secret.

Moments later he was approaching his own home. His uncle was standing at the door and Ali knew from the serious look on his face he had already been briefed. His uncle didn't say a word, but Ali could tell he was feeling very uncomfortable and vulnerable. That was the way it was and nothing either of them might say or do would make it any different. At least an opportunity beckoned, a break in the humdrum routines. Quite what to make of it as yet he wasn't at all sure.

Every now and then in the coming hours Ali had to push down his rising sense of dread and fear, telling himself that even if so many things here ended very badly, maybe whatever this jihad was, it just might prove otherwise. It could well be the breakthrough that was needed, but the fear in not knowing what exactly was expected of him in London filled him with apprehension.

8

Cliff's Coffee House was a good location to chill out and meet up. The car park to the rear of the probation and fire service buildings was a handy place to pull into and it was situated discreetly just off the main Tottenham High Road. Getting to or leaving Cliff's offered three different routes, north up through to Edmonton, south towards the city or west toward Wood Green and Muswell Hill. It was an excellent location.

Cliff himself was a no nonsense, mind your own business kind of guy. He was built like a brick house they said, but most of his six foot two was pure fat, the body-building muscle of past years having degenerated into fat through self-neglect and a fondness for rum. Though Cliff might have his name on the board outside it was really his partner Tracy who ran the place and it was Tracy who saw the familiar faces of Winston and Clive making their way inside.

'Hi you guys, what will it be, the usual?' she said with a smile.

The two both agreed, asking for jam donuts to be added; and, after exchanging pleasantries sat down some way back from the door, but facing it so they could see who was coming. This was a habit Winston had taught Clive. 'Always watch your back' was a favourite saying of his. Tracy disappeared behind the counter and the coffee machine started making its wondrous hissing sounds as their order took shape - a double Expresso for Clive and an Americano with hot milk for Winston. The jam donuts were brought over, fresh smelling and warm to the touch. The whole while Clive couldn't get Winston's black sports bag they'd collected out of his mind. It was time to ask for some explanation.

'I think you'd better tell me what I've got myself into,' he found himself saying. Winston gave Tracy a tenner and she left them to themselves. Clive waited for Winston to speak.

Winston thought for a moment. He debated with himself. He hadn't intended to pull Clive into his world and he weighed up the risks. Clive had no form, his family were "good Christian stock" and who knows which way Clive might turn once the chips were down. Could he be trusted? Yet, Clive was in it now. Hadn't he collected the stuff, collaborated in its collection, got involved? He couldn't deny that and besides Clive could be useful for some of the things he had in mind for the coming weeks. So, yeah, he decided to tell him all.

'Yes, buddy, I need to explain things. It's only fair and I owe you. You were great today and I needed your help to pick up the stuff,' he said.

'What is it?' asked Clive.

'It's a package I said I'd deliver to someone in Muswell Hill. It's come a long way, Afghanistan originally, but via Iraq and somehow across Europe by lorry. I don't know all the details, best I don't really. All I know is that when I do these deliveries I get paid well and no questions asked. It's easy money and I need the cash.' He saw the look of shock on Clive's face.

'Yeah, I know it's probably drugs, but I don't use and the trade will go on whether I help out or not. I'm not a pusher, a dealer, a user - just a set of wheels, a postman if you like. Besides, you know how the dice are loaded against black guys getting by - how long you been looking for work then? A year? More? It's a racist world out there and a guy's got to live. I'm not doing anyone any harm. It gives me bit of a buzz to be honest, it paid for your coffee too! There you go, living off immoral earnings!' and he rolled around in the chair amused at the situation. That was the thing about Winston, he was so upbeat and cheerful much of the time. The two friends went way back.

Clive was telling himself this hadn't happened. This was not what he had planned for himself, but hindsight was a marvellous thing, and he could see no other way forward other than to accept the realities of his new situation. He certainly had no intention of running to the police to tell them his best friend had just taken delivery of some drugs. Drugs were everywhere and Winston had a point.

'The incident's over so far as I'm concerned. Just do me a favour will you and when we get out to the car, give the handles on that bag a good wipe. I don't want any trace of my fingerprints on it,' said Clive thoughtful of the situation.

'OK, if it'll humour you. I think that's really funny - your prints wouldn't be on any index anyway, but I'll clean up, and hey presto, nothing to do with you. I'm impressed. Lots of guys don't think, they're not careful,' said Winston.

'Now the thing is, we don't want to hang on to this any longer than we must. So after coffee, I need your help to pass it out through the car window to a guy in Muswell Hill Broadway - just like you collected it, you now dispose of it. When it's gone, it's gone and over with. OK with that?' asked Winston waiting for an answer.

'Suppose so. Then that will be the end of it,' said Clive.

'Sure pal, sure,' said Winston, knowing they both knew that not to be true.

Sometimes Winston said things people wanted to hear him say and he was doing it again now with his best friend, maybe his only friend. The world's a stinking mess, he thought to himself, and I've dragged Clive down in the shit but he still doesn't seem to know it. It somehow made him feel bad about himself, but only briefly, his irrepressible smile winning out and lifting their mood.

After Winston had sent a brief text message and checked the time, he said, 'time to make the drop' and nodding farewell to Cliff and Tracy who noticed everyone's coming and goings but knew better than to comment on what they saw, Clive and Winston strode purposefully round to the back car park and climbed once more into the blue car, still warm from the earlier run. Winston took the sports bag from the boot, made a point of wiping the bag's handles and Clive found himself once more its unwilling minder, using his sweater sleeve to grip it by. He looked at it as if it were some kind of infection, a contamination.

Moments later they were on their way and in fifteen minutes cruising slowly in heavy traffic along Muswell Hill Broadway, the spire of St James's church ahead and the sweet smell of roasting coffee beans wafting in the open car window from a deli. They went along the full length once and saw no-one, turned round at the roundabout and headed back the way they'd come. And there he was, this time a smart guy, in blue jeans and a designer T shirt. He was already carrying a sports bag which he seemed to be offering them. His hand reached out into the road and Winston yelled.

'Be ready with the bag and do a swap - just do a swap. He knows the drill, just swap the fucking bags,' ordered Winston, Clive now on the front edge of his seat.

'Just don't drive so fast then,' shouted a panicking Clive; and Winston, who realised he really was driving far too fast for a bag swap, slowed right down. The change was fluid and done. They waved goodbye trying to make it all look normal and drove off slowly so as not to attract undue attention. Very soon they were heading back down Muswell Hill and toward Tottenham Lane.

'Open the bag' said Winston. At first glance it looked empty and it felt light. Clive wondered if it was empty.

'Nothing in it,' said Clive sweeping his hand round the inside almost turning it inside out in the process.

'Check again'. Clive's hand smoothed the bottom of the small sports bag and then slid under the firm board base which gave the bag its shape. There was a plastic bag. He pulled it out.

'Count it,' said Winston glancing at Clive rather more than the road.

Keeping the wad of notes low in his lap, Clive did as he was told.

'Two hundred,' he said, after double checking.

'Take forty and put it in your pocket,' said Winston.

Clive hesitated.

'OK,' he said finally.

He knew he needed some cash.

'Thanks,' he said meekly, feeling inside that he had sunk even lower into something deeply unpleasant.

'No worries, you earned it,' said Winston.

Winston was smiling again and both sensed a moving on from the earlier tension. The bags with their money and drugs were already history. Life was already progressing forwards, leaving the tawdry world of drug dealing as history, or so Clive thought.

Back near the North Middlesex Hospital, Winston pulled off the North Circular Road and let Clive out of the car for the short walk home. Clive preferred it that way, and often asked to be dropped off away from his front door, allowing for some separation between his world and that of his family. Time to go home, no doubt to face more hard to handle parental nagging and sisterly over-concern, he thought.

This time as he walked home he felt strangely more vulnerable, but the feeling soon passed and he smiled as his hands felt the crisp notes in his pocket.

9

What a grey day for summer. Inside the house, colours seemed to be in shadow and Ruth thought how wonderful it would be when the family got away to France in a few weeks' time. Such welcome bliss, a holiday - she was desperately in need of it. Rev. Ruth Churchill found it tough being a Church of England minister in London, even though part of her thrived on meeting the challenge and the reward in being constantly needed. Being a white woman, middle class and visibly Christian in the urban multi-ethnic faith mix of Edmonton made stepping outside her door in Windmill Road an expedition into the unknown every time, that too made life infinitely varied and stimulating.

Edmonton was such a highly contested and contradictory Christian community for her to find her place. There were so many varieties of Christian, so many elements in the mix, so many who just didn't get on. In her own Enfield Deanery there were Church of England clergy who were more Roman Catholic than Roman Catholics and others who were either raving charismatic or determinedly fundamentalist evangelical church planters. Every now and then she felt her own parish to be the target of someone else's mission - which felt more like an attack than a blessing. Add to the mix an absence of financial support for such a tough parish, it made serving here feel like a constant battle. In truth it ground one down, and it was high time for that holiday, she thought.

She and her husband Phil, who worked in the city as an accountant, had two young children, a girl Olivia and boy Paul. Juggling, husband, children, work and keeping on top of looking after the biggest house in the area had become so stretching she'd taken on some extra help. Aneni Chigowe from Zimbabwe helped out a couple of times a week in their six-bedroomed Edwardian house and Joseph Museve kept the garden presentable.

In the past she would have found the idea of employing help in this way so counter-cultural and impossible to justify in ordinary circumstances but now, she told herself, this bit of self-help entrepreneurism was actually a constructive means of being supportive of the Asylum Seeker and Refugee project she ran in the church hall next door. Today being Wednesday, Aneni was helping out in the house, and she could hear the rhythmic rise and fall of the noise as the vacuum cleaner was being pushed back and forth along the long landing carpet upstairs.

'Aneni, Aneni,' she yelled as loud as she could.

You couldn't become a preacher without knowing how to project your voice, she thought. But it made no difference; Aneni was energetically manoeuvring the vacuum into the bedroom doorways, engrossed in her job and Ruth had to go virtually all the way to the midpoint on the landing to tap her on the shoulder to get her attention before the machine was finally switched off and she could ask her question.

'Coffee?' she said, knowing that Aneni would of course say yes and they could have a break together at the kitchen table downstairs.

In truth, that break was more welcome to Ruth than Aneni. Ruth liked to talk, to find out more, to be a friend. Aneni instinctively knew this was the score, but without any good reason she could call to mind not to stop, the machine stayed off. Yes, she was wary, but Ruth was a good person without guile and so conversation time was reasonably relaxed and certainly Aneni didn't want to jeopardise the cleaning arrangement she had. She suppressed, as best she could, those deep voices which told her she was nothing but a servant in the home for Ruth, a legacy of a colonial past that still hadn't quite disappeared and she should really be steering well clear of it. But Aneni was nothing if not pragmatic, she needed the money and formal employment wasn't an option.

So at Ruth's bidding Aneni left the Dyson where it was, ready to resume later where she had left off. She followed Ruth downstairs, past the front door, across the hallway and

40

into the spacious kitchen. The big square kitchen table had been reclaimed from a second hand shop and semi-restored. It looked well used, but then it was and the kitchen everyone knew was the real hub, the warm centre, of the house. Aneni took a couple of blue and white striped mugs from a cupboard, grabbed the Fairtrade coffee jar from a shelf and a spoon from the drawer and put them on the table and sat down whilst Ruth put the kettle on, but she got up again remembering to fetch the milk from the fridge. It was time to start a conversation, and as ever Aneni let Ruth lead the way.

'Any more news yet?' asked Ruth.

'No, from what other people say it is too early. The Home Office will call me to Croydon for an interview when they are ready. They seem to think that because we're from Zimbabwe there's no problem there and they can send us back. Joseph's heard nothing either. I don't like to think about it. I don't want to talk about it. I like to help out here in the house. I like to be busy, but please Miss Ruth don't tell them I work for you as they will surely send me to Detention,' she pleaded.

Aneni immediately regretted having said so much, but she knew it was her nature to wear her heart on her sleeve.

She needed Ruth's reassurance and really needed the extra cash in hand Ruth gave her, but she felt so vulnerable and insecure. It meant she couldn't plan ahead, even thinking about that very evening felt like a bridge too far. Life was lived moment by moment. That was the only way to survive.

'Not to worry. It'll all sort itself out in the end,' Ruth told her, as she had numerous times before.

Ruth liked her kitchen, not only was it the warmest room in the house, but it also commanded a view of the street outside and everyone who walked by. People she knew would slow and wave a greeting if they saw her in the kitchen's triple sash window; and, she would wave back, each wave a little victory in her battle to win local acceptance.

Aneni, however, had chosen the chair at the end of the table, the one that meant she couldn't be seen by passers by. By contrast she wanted to live in the shadows. Her victories

41

came with staying hidden. She wondered whether Ruth had noticed and whether she really had any idea what it was like to live like she did. But, whether she did or not, what Ruth had done in opening up the church hall to people seeking asylum like herself was something for which she would be forever grateful. It was a veritable water hole in the jungle, for she knew of no other project to help people like herself.

The thought made her feel more kindly toward Ruth, who after all was a well-intentioned person and much as she hated being dependent on someone else, she needed her support. The kettle boiled, vibrating the metal pan next to it, and then the coffee mugs were steaming, filling the air with their burnt caramel aroma. Today Ruth found shortbread biscuits. It was a vicarage whose life was built around innumerable hot drinks and mountains of biscuits.

Coming to England several months earlier on a false passport, travelling via Lagos, Nigeria, Aneni had immediately claimed asylum on arrival at Heathrow and after only a short while had been allocated a place to stay in Edmonton. She remembered the high, the sheer elation she felt then, when she was able to say those words, 'I want to claim asylum here.'

That seemed ages ago and she now felt she had only lived a half life since, in which her emotions were battered down and the future looked, well - bleak, so much so she could no longer think about it. With each passing day, life's continuing uncertainty was grinding her down: too, in different ways and for different reasons she and Ruth were embattled conjoined sisters. A silence descended as they sipped coffee together, each retreating into their own thoughts.

Aneni recalled how, on the grapevine, she had soon heard that there was free food and a warm place to meet at Ruth's 'Holy Trinity' Drop In Centre. In a vast, hostile, vast or at best indifferent city this was a rare place of sanctuary. She'd expected life to be much much better here than this. England was after all the mother country, the leader of the Commonwealth, the place as a young girl in a village school she'd been taught to look up to, even if its colonial past and exploitation of her country had somewhat sullied its reputation.

Since those early days before she was born and UDI under Mugabe had increasingly tyrannised and robbed free Zimbabweans, driving political opponents into prison or killing them, and ruling the country as his personal fiefdom. Her father had been bold enough to oppose Mugabe, joining forces with Morgan Tsvangirai's Movement for Democratic Change party and had paid the price with his life in the violence of the 2008 elections. The family home and land were taken by Mugabe's cronies days later. She'd had no choice but to flee Zimbabwe. Why would no one believe her?

An uncle in Bulawayo had fixed things to get her some exit papers and passport. He'd spent his own money and taken a huge risk to do it. She couldn't even say thank you or send him a message for fear of placing him in danger. Indeed where else to go but England? She could speak the language, she respected the Queen, it was just and fair and the rule of law was applied, ever since Magna Carta. But this England wasn't home and it didn't sit right with what she felt England ought to be.

On arrival in London she discovered she'd been totally naive to think the family of someone who opposed Mugabe would be supported, even praised. She'd been quite wrong about that and the surprises were many. Reality dawned slowly from that first ride locked in the back of a police van from Heathrow Airport. She was like some unwelcome piece of lost luggage that had to be processed and sent on. The resentment was not spoken, but she felt it and saw it in their eyes. She felt she was no longer Aneni, no longer a person. People always mispronounced her name or misspelled it.

She soon realised that her ebony black skin became a new identity marker for oppression and her accent an insuperable barrier of separation though she spoke good English, didn't she? It had been nearly a year now and truth to tell she had new unwelcome feelings of fear and despondency. Not being officially allowed to work was a real blow. It knocked her professional pride as a teacher. All her

43

training and her teaching qualifications were worthless here and she had not a piece of paper or certificate in her hand to prove anything.

It made her dependent on charity and handouts and undermined her sense of pride in herself as a person. She was increasingly feeling hopeless and helpless, and these black moods were becoming all the more frequent. She began to wonder where things would end and the conclusions she drew were more and more depressing with each passing month. Sipping the last of the comforting warm coffee, she placed her mug back on the kitchen table.

Ruth had instinctively warmed to Aneni. A teacher herself before going into the church, it was nice to have her around and she was great with her two kids - and she really did need someone to help fill the gaps and mind the kids with all the demands on her time. Aneni had been good like that, in fact she was more of a Mum to them than Ruth herself sometimes and would invent all kinds of activities to keep them happily occupied - it was so good to get them away from their computer games and TV screen.

Aneni's up and down mood swings were nothing to be concerned about, Ruth told herself, understandable in her situation and nothing too serious; and seemed to mirror her own, though Ruth did her best to manage and hide how she felt. Ruth needed to stay in control and always felt better about herself when she did. She genuinely wanted to make things work for Aneni and had written letters to the Home Office and her own MP on her behalf to try and push her case. She couldn't understand why Aneni still held back from her after all she had done. She wanted them to be co-conspirators, fighting sisters, but it was as if unspoken past agendas kept getting in the way.

Attempts to make email contact back to Zimbabwe and get useful letters and documents from friends there had so far drawn a blank and no replies had come. Aneni was insistent that her own identity and that of her family were kept out of this, to protect them. In the meantime, useful occupation, coffee and conversation helped pass the hours and days.

Ruth found it reassuring that Aneni had some background in a lively African Christian tradition and Ruth felt a pastoral responsibility to help her find solace in her faith and reassurance in belonging to the branch of the Christian family in which she now found herself.

A comfortable arrangement or compromise had been found to enable Ruth to pass money over to Aneni through this cleaning job which she told herself was a legitimate form of direct action wholly justified on the grounds of the demands of true justice. If the government wouldn't treat Aneni as an equal human being, she would do her best to remedy that. In fact Aneni was now spending three days a week helping out and in return Ruth only had to give her some cash in hand, every Friday morning. Ruth pushed to the back of her mind the difficult conversation she ought to be having with Aneni about a more generous arrangement, it could wait until another day. It would be embarrassing for them both, she reasoned.

The conversation about Aneni's situation was not going anywhere and Ruth began to talk about a safe subject, the Drop In Project. It was where they had first met. The Project had been Ruth's idea when she had first come to the parish and now it was the biggest thing in her life and the life of the church. It had been noticed too and the Archdeacon of Hampstead, under whose loose jurisdiction she fell, had asked to visit it, with the press in tow, on no less than three occasions.

She'd found success, in the form of attention and media coverage, comes at a price in the church and there was some resentment amongst her congregation that her time and their precious resources were being expended at such a rate on the project. The opposition took many forms and when Aneni dropped into the conversation, that Sid, the elderly Churchwarden had been to the Drop In the previous day, she wanted to know more.

'Why was Sid there?' she enquired. 'He doesn't normally come down during the week unless he has a reason.'

'Well, he wanted to see what state the hall was in. Some people had said that the toilets were dirty and paint work needed seeing to. But while he was down he ended up in an argument. I thought he might have a heart attack or something. He went so red in the face,' said Aneni.

'Why's that then?' asked Ruth.

'Seems like he didn't like what a Muslim guy was doing. It was lunch-time-ish and the Muslim guy, Abu Tariq was calling out to the other Muslims there that it was time for prayers and the brothers should be faithful brothers and should pray. Abu didn't speak to the sisters, only the brothers. He wouldn't take no for an answer; and, within five minutes he had eight or nine of them in the toilets doing their washing thing, water everywhere. Then they took themselves off to the far end of the hall and started prostrating themselves and chanting and so on. That's when Sid got all uppity. He went over and told them to stop it, saying this was a Christian place.' Aneni paused to draw breath.

'That's when it got really heated. I thought at first they were going to pick him up and carry him outside, but Ishmael stepped forward and ensured they just ignored him. Ishmael's some kind of leader. I'm not sure I trust either Abu or him. There's such a dark side to them both and no fun, none at all. But not getting anywhere in spite of his protests, that just made Sid more and more mad,' said Aneni, Ruth listening carefully to her every word.

'Thankfully, in the end Sid realised he was being stone-walled and took himself off and waited at the other end of the hall until they had finished. Then he had another go. He was calmer by then, not much mind - "You can't do that here," he told them, wagging a finger. This is holy ground, it's a Christian church. You've done a terrible thing, it'll need cleansing and prayers. I've heard that you Muslims claim possession of places where you pray. This project will have to close if this kind of thing is going on." You should have heard him! "The vicar will get to hear about this," he said. Oh yes, he also complained that the building's getting to be such a mess and because of the Drop In we don't have space in the

46

diary for the local community to hire our facilities. It was terrible,' reported Aneni.

'How did it all end?' asked Ruth, glad to have been given Aneni's story.

'Ishmael more or less took him to one side. I could hear what they were saying, but not every word mind, as I was helping tidy up the tables ready for lunches. Ishmael told Sid he shouldn't worry. Prayer to God was a duty and God would be pleased that prayers had been offered.'

'And how did Sid take it?' inquired Ruth.

'Sid wasn't having it, Mohammed this and Allah that, no way was he happy. Ishmael took issue with what Sid said about it being holy ground. He said, he understood the church was a sacred space for Christians to worship, but was the hall sacred space? Would Sid call the car park outside sacred space too? And where did sacred space begin and end? Surely in England there was freedom of religion and Muslims were allowed to say their prayers at the appointed times. Wasn't it people like Sid who had prevented them finding somewhere to pray in a building of their own? By now Sid was getting hot under the collar again. In the end Ishmael, who had kept his cool throughout walked away with Abu who told him to leave it. Sid then told Carol there were too many Muslims coming to the Drop In now, and he was going to speak to the vicar about it. I'm really surprised Sid hasn't been in touch with you already,' said Aneni.

'That's really interesting', Ruth reflected quietly. 'We've had many more Muslim asylum seekers coming to our hall recently haven't we? It's like the pressures really on them and quite a few have horrendous stories to tell of living under so-called Islamic State.'

Aneni shuffled in her seat, took a second biscuit, before volunteering the comment she had only half a mind to share.

'But they are so rigid and I don't feel comfortable with so many of them around in the Drop In. To think some have escaped Islamic State, you'd think they'd be a bit more grateful to the country giving them asylum, wouldn't you?' she said.

47

Ruth glanced up and saw Sid moving across the window. She knew from the look on his face he was headed straight for her front door.

'That's Sid now, coffee break over,' said Ruth, moving toward the door.

Aneni was already half way up the stairs retrieving the vacuum. In that split second, in what later Ruth would say was an answer to prayer, a strategy came to mind to counter Sid's concerns. If I could get at least one of the other local churches on board to shoulder some of the load, that would take the pressure off. What about the Pentecostals? There's Bishop Sam Kone for a start, she thought. Now there was a man, if ever there was, looking for some way to boost his local community profile still further; and, from what Ruth had heard, he had a pool of younger people to draw on who might like to be volunteers.

As she strode to answer the repeated ring at her front door, she felt her confidence surging back. In the background, Ruth heard Aneni start up the vacuum again somewhere upstairs. She was trying to carry on as if things were normal.

Ruth was determined her project would continue to help Aneni and all those like her. It was not going to be thwarted by the likes of Sid. Little did she know Sid's visit would later be remembered as but a minor skirmish.

10

Kaylah had no idea Ruth was on her way to their front door and when the chimes rang she found she was the one nearest to open it. She looked twice at this woman in a ridiculous cycling helmet and pale pink clerical shirt and collar.

'You must be Ruth Churchill,' she said as Ruth firmly chained her bike to the metal gate post.

'Hope it'll still be there later,' Kaylah said, as Ruth walked straight past her into the front room of the Victorian terraced house.

Kaylah wondered why she'd bothered to cycle round to Cheddington Road, you could almost throw a stone at the vicarage from the corner of the road. Maybe it was to make an eco-point, something her own father never did. A door straight ahead led into the back room where she knew her father was making one of his interminable mobile calls to one of his flock.

'Dad', she called loudly, 'someone to see you'.

Much to her annoyance, though he had clearly heard her call, he didn't appear and Kaylah knew she would have to make some polite conversation with Ruth until he appeared. 'Not for the first time Dad,' she muttered under breath as she turned to give her attention to their visitor.

'You must be Kaylah,' said a well-informed Ruth, 'I've heard about you.'

'What you heard?' replied Kaylah nervously.

'You're one of the business students at Southgate Community College. One of the Brown sisters in Huxley Road told me,' explained Ruth.

'That's right,' said Kaylah.

Then for the next ten minutes Kaylah ended up telling this woman far more than she had ever intended. Perhaps it was because, unlike her own over-busy parents, this person actually gave her time and listened. Maybe it was also because Kaylah knew that in a man's world and a man's church, here was someone she had a sneaking respect for.

'Isn't it tough being a woman in the church?' she found herself asking.

That opened the flood gates and she began hearing Ruth's story, how her ministry election panel had been all old school males, right up to the opposition she'd had in setting up an asylum seeker Drop In project. Kaylah, thinking business studies now, was impressed at what it had taken to get such an initiative off the ground - organisation, finance, commitment, local leadership - you name it Ruth had had to find it all.

Moments later, she'd agreed to visit the Drop In Centre the following day. Yes, tomorrow, she'd actually committed herself to meet Ruth there; and then, immediately regretted having done so. At this point her father's bulky presence rather belatedly appeared, the extended mobile conversation being wound up as he entered the room. At this point Kaylah quietly absented herself and made her way upstairs to the sanctuary of her own room, still feeling rather foolish and thinking to herself, she'd just got to get out of this. How the hell had she got herself talked into meeting this vicar woman again tomorrow?

Kaylah could overhear Ruth and her Dad's conversation downstairs. She was trying to persuade her father to lend her the support of Bethel church. He was wiser than she and Kaylah knew her Dad wouldn't be pinned down to something he'd later regret as she had. A few minutes later, no doubt leaving with a few platitudes rather than promises from her Dad, Ruth could be heard outside unchaining her bike, her Dad once again back on his mobile phone. Ruth had gone and the coast was clear.

A rustle of movement and she knew her younger brother Clive was in his room. She hadn't seen so much of him recently. Now might be a good time to touch base.

'Hi Clipper!' she called out. She called him by the familiar name she'd always used.

'You got five min?' she said.

50

No negative was a positive and she pushed open his bedroom door. He had his earphones on and she could make out the tinny regular rapping as he was listening to something on his phone. He switched it off and casually pushed the earphones down like an outsize necklace, setting off his designer sweatshirt. Image was all to Clive. He was altogether a cool dresser - skinny jeans and designer trainers, immaculately clean and with the laces undone. The white Ikea sofa bed he was lounging on made him look so very relaxed. He had done so much more than she to cultivate a good street cred which was why he was the one always out with friends, being picked up in fancy cars and living the high life.

'How's it been?' she enquired, 'got anything going I should know about, any parties this weekend?'

Clive liked his sister's attention to a point. So often they were allies in the face of parental moral onslaughts. Like her, he didn't feel much connectivity with Mum and Dad and had created a sanctuary in his room walled in by his music. He had kind of separated out two modes of living, the one for time with his parents and the other for himself, but it was hard keeping his life together on track and, as he saw it, somehow Kaylah always seemed to manage life better.

'How's it been?' she asked again.

For once Clive didn't know what to say to her question. Memories of recent events with Winston and bag swaps came flooding back; so, he hesitated, long enough in fact for her to know he was discomforted by her question. He wanted to deflect what would surely follow, a more searching personal enquiry, so he tried to convince her he was really debating with himself between two options open to him that evening, either time with Winston down in Tottenham or listening to music with Raff and Jaydee at their house in Fore Street. Raff did some DJ work and what his brother Jaydee didn't know about music whether Soul, Reggae, Blues, Folk, Rap was nobody's business.

'Mmm' he mused, 'maybe cruising with Winston and who knows where we'll end up, or doing music with Raff. Then 'tis possible I'll stay in tonight. No parties I know of Sis - you'll have to wait for the weekend. Anyway, what's up with Southgate, they got nothin' happening? You surely not tellin' me it's all quiet in your world now?'

Clive was a little envious of Kaylah's ordered world, her business ambition, her college place, her homework to do, her regular rhythm of life which meant getting up in a morning and being out the house with good reason. Her world looked like a safe world, no stop and searches, no gangs, no drugs, no brothers to please or upset. But then, it was her choice. It was easier for a girl to make out. Racism hits harder if you're a young man. Just what were the options he really had, he thought. Winston's right. Good choices didn't come their way.

Kaylah really wanted to do something with her brother. It had been ages since they'd been into London or had a day out, so she asked if she could join him that evening.

'I'll change into something a bit more fun,' she added.

He couldn't say no.

'OK, I'll give Winston a buzz. He's calling by later, he'll be happy to have you along. Better watch him with you though,' he teased.

'Let's say, leave here about 8,' she said, ignoring his playful gibe.

It was agreed. Kaylah, left his room, noting the earphones being raised again to his head as she went out of the door. That's good, she thought. Clive needed her, she knew it: and, 'no way is that Winston my type, he just makes me uneasy,' she said out loud; but, in her head, not quite being able to forget what a cheerful, happy-go-lucky guy Winston always seemed to be, she could see why Clive and he were such close friends. A night out would be fun.

11

There's a rhythm to get into and then it's OK, said Adam to himself. Life on a long bike ride required the regular, steady circular rise and fall of the pedals; and a degree of order, and it was only some hours after he had left Calais that he began to find it. The ferry from Dover to Calais had provided him with his first real sense of departure, the English Channel something defining in its separation of home from what was foreign. He'd watched the white cliffs of Dover disappear over the horizon, then the French coast and sandy beaches slowly appear as the ferry cautiously slipped into port.

Language and currency changed and he knew he didn't belong any more. Only now he truly felt he was on his own, but he didn't mind, nor did he feel any less self-confident. He'd prepared for this and so far so good. At school he'd been pretty good at languages, had once been on an exchange with a lad called Etienne from Boulogne. He could get by in French and soon he'd begin using it again, a greeting at customs, a few sentences to buy supplies at a supermarket.

Once off the ferry and through the slow procedures of customs and port roads which took him with all the rows of cars and lorries in giant loops of endless concrete, he finally broke away from most of the port traffic as he sought out the local D119 to take him north to Dunkerque and the Belgian border.

Thank goodness it was a pleasant day with a westerly wind on his back and mainly sunny skies ahead. Rhythm was found, the miles or should he now say, kilometres, passed effortlessly by. There was not a hill worth mentioning, all pretty straight and level with occasional final glimpses of the sea to his left. He knew this easy cycling would change, but while it lasted he cruised on.

He cycled through nondescript Gravelines, then took a detour left along the port and industrial roads around

Dunkerque avoiding the busy N1. The road became the D60 once outside Dunkerque and before he knew it he had crossed the Belgian border. He realised it was now getting late in the afternoon and he would need to find somewhere for a night stop soon.

He turned and headed east and it was not far from Veurne, a pleasant enough Flemish market town, where he found a public camp site he knew would serve his purpose. There was a shop nearby and by the time he had pitched his one man tent, collected water, erected his little Gaz stove and put pasta on to boil it was dark.

After eating and cleaning up, there was enough public street light to enable him to check his bike over and play with the gear and brake cable adjustors to fine tune them. A small roll mat and sleeping bag took hardly any space in his Dutch waterproof pannier and he marvelled at how simply one could actually live travelling alone; and, he thought, to be wonderfully free of having to consider anyone else.

He was organised and, parents and friends in mind, he took out his mobile to switch on, check and send messages. He had a signal and whilst water boiled to make a hot drink, he sent a one-liner home to say where he was and that everything was fine. Rather more time was spent chatting with friends on Facebook, most of them greatly impressed by his ride, albeit only just begun! By 10pm he was in his sleeping bag, the wind now ruffling and tugging at the tent, the soft sound of nearby cars whooshing anonymously by. Feeling relaxed and tired he was soon fast asleep.

Dawn marked the start of new day. By the time grey light gave way to sunrise he was on his way again. It was quieter first thing, though a bit of a nuisance sometimes squinting into the sun straight ahead. He'd stop somewhere for coffee and breakfast, but was determined to get a couple of hours riding done first. The mornings always passed quickly. The days, too, soon fell into a pattern.

He'd noticed that it was a more solitary life than he had anticipated and he had consciously begun a new practice, talking to strangers as he went and this had grown on him.

Yes, there had been the occasional 'oddo', but then every community, even Muswell Hill had its eccentric characters who wandered up and down the Broadway. Jimmy, who smelled of vagrancy and the distinctive aroma of the unwashed, wore an old duffel coat tied round the middle with a piece of blue nylon rope; and he recalled the 'bag lady' everyone called Lil, who pushed a battered supermarket trolley along with everything she possessed inside it.

Strangely, for the first time he felt himself to be a kind of kindred spirit with Jimmy and Lil, like them occupying the public space, having for now no place to call home; and, he supposed no certainty as to what the day would bring either. In all he'd sum up the experience of Europe so far as being one where people generally got on with their own business and left him to his. All his conversations he felt were initiated by him. He'd been to more friendly places, he thought. By now he'd crossed Belgium.

Germany was similar, smart cars passed at speed. He was finding the good thing about cycling on the continent was that, unlike in London, motorists seemed to respect cyclists and allowed him room on the road. Perhaps it was the national obsession with the annual Tour de France, that mad dash round France every July, culminating in the sprint circuits in Paris, that made every continental driver hold a sneaking respect for any cyclist on the road. Whatever the cause, the respect was definitely there and it felt good. Whether he was right to allow himself to feel so safe might be mistaken, but in these early days Adam felt good, really good.

Since crossing the Channel he'd tried to average around seventy miles a day, but soon found his heavily laden bike, coupled with the arrival of the first significant hills to climb, his own level of fatigue and his unintended detours often taken to avoid busy roads, pushed down his daily mileage, despite his good intentions, to below sixty miles. He was not overly concerned. This was no race and he'd allowed himself a couple of weeks leeway in Iran before his pre-booked return flight home from Tehran. All was well.

Each night camp sites had been found, apart from one night when he'd had to simply pitch up at the side of the road. That had almost resulted in a hefty fine for vagrancy, something he hadn't counted on, but the policewoman on hearing his story had been sympathetic, back-tracked and allowed him to make a hurried re-pack and continuation instead of imposing an on the spot penalty. Just a few miles further on, he'd found a lorry park with a grass verge and friendly night-stop cafe, just the thing. He'd be more discreet before pitching up at the road side in future, thinking he'd choose somewhere less obvious, where he wouldn't attract attention.

It was a Friday evening and two weeks into his ride east, whilst in Bavaria, heading south from Bamberg and into the outskirts of Nurnberg, that he decided he'd have a day off from cycling and explore this historic city. Why not? He'd committed himself to navigate by the Main-Danube canal and river; he'd be doing this for the coming days, so it was time for a weekend break. He would give himself a little luxury and book the weekend in a Rough Guide suggested hostel. It was his chance to clean both himself and his clothes properly and maybe eat out once or twice.

The hostel had a secure area for his bike and after washing clothes and hanging them out in the laundry area, he walked off into town. A cafe boasted free Wi-Fi and he used it to catch up on emails, chat with friends in north London, update his Facebook page and send an extended report home to Mum and Dad.

Around him on the other tables there was a motley group of mainly young people and after a few minutes he found himself chatting away in English to a guy from Eastern Europe. He learned that in fact he was from Sofia in Bulgaria, having formerly lived in Kosovo. Sofia lay on Adam's route and the conversation was well lubricated by the German lager that his new-found Kosovan friend, Gezim, was now buying. Gezim wanted to hear all about where he was from and Adam's story of his adventurous journey to date. He was clearly impressed and Adam for his part enjoyed having the chance to relive his travels with a ready listener. Gezim, in return, told him how he, as a small boy, together with his family, had fled Kosovo in the troubles of 1999 when Milosovic's army's 'Operation Horseshoe' had driven out the Kosovar Albanians.

This was such a different early life to Adam's. Gezim's family had escaped north and he'd since made a life for himself in Sofia. Now he was a postgraduate student, currently taking a year out to learn German, before returning to Sofia at the end of the week when term finished. Things went so well, Gezim and Adam exchanged mobile numbers by the end of the evening and Gezim promised to put him up and show him round Sofia when he turned up.

'See you in Sofia,' he called out as he finally disappeared up the road walking back to his flat. Adam watch him go and observed Gezim busy on his mobile before he turned the corner of the street.

Next morning, feeling slightly the worse for wear after the lagers of the night before, Adam took himself off to see some of the sights. One "must see" his Rough Guide said, was the Nurnberg court, where the Nazi post-World War 2 trials had taken place.

As he was leaving the hostel on foot to make his way there he spotted his drinking partner of the previous evening, Gezim, standing still on the pavement facing him apparently taking a photo in his direction on his mobile. He waved back in a friendly fashion before walking off briskly away down the street opposite. Adam soon forgot about him, his attention moving to something he'd heard about at school, the Nuremburg Trials; and, he very soon arrived at the court buildings where he found the Nurnburg Trials court room had been preserved just as it was.

This was where it happened then, Adam said to himself. He tagged on to a tourist group which fortunately had an English-speaking guide and he heard how the US Chief Prosecuting lawyer, Judge Robert Jackson had framed the Nuremburg Charter which allowed a proper prosecution for breaches of human rights, and laid a foundation for the subsequent development of human rights charters in the UN and Europe. Long since dead, Jackson's legacy lived on in his ideals which had since found themselves enshrined in various charters now taken for granted at the UN and in the European Union.

Adam felt buoyed up by the thought that bad leaders couldn't get away with it and that there was such a civilised way to bring them to justice and deal with them. Maybe, that's what I'll be one day, a human rights activist he thought, someone needs to defend these ideals when politicians seem so determined to undo them. Open to any promising vocational ideas, he recalled that he was still feeling quite unsure what direction to follow when he got back. The group he'd joined were now moving away, to look at the rest of the building, but that didn't interest Adam. He'd seen what he wanted and made his way back to the centre of the town and its old market.

There was lots going on in the characteristic European way of doing these things. There was a motley gathering of white vans with shady awnings side by side with civic erected, purpose made, market stalls with striped canvas roofs and the sweet meaty smell of boiling wurst. Why not? he thought, and bought himself one to remember, all of a foot long. He also bought bits and pieces to take with him to eat later and made his way off the side of the street market and along the waterside to find a quiet spot to eat, concluding Nurnberg wasn't such a bad place to rest up in.

Sitting on a public bench he looked back at the bridge he'd just crossed and there to his surprise, he spotted Gezim once again, this time with a couple of middle-eastern looking friends. He was pretty sure Gezim was looking in his direction, but whether deliberately or not Gezim turned to his friends to direct their attention away from where Adam was sitting and then they had gone.

Adam felt just slightly uneasy. In London he'd been quite good at keeping his wits about him and was generally good at reading what was going on around him on the street. Once again his instincts were telling him something wasn't

58

quite right here. It was surely more than coincidence he'd spotted Gezim eyeing him, and though he couldn't put his finger on it, the guy had unsettled him. In such a situation the sensible thing was to get back into the crowd and lose himself, which is what he decided to do.

A little later he was making his way back to the hostel for a restful end to his Nurnberg stay. He thought he might give his bike a bit of a service, check the tyre pressure, lubricate and clean the chain set, and re-pack everything very tidily ready for leaving early next day. As he prepared himself to move on, he was ready to put Nurnberg behind him.

The city itself was delightful and fascinating, but the strange sightings of Gezim and his middle-eastern friends had disturbed him. He'd be relieved to be on his way once again in the morning. Then, he thought, his troubles would all be behind him.

12

This was no sports trainer, this was one sadistic bastard. It was 9am on a Sunday morning and Ali felt he'd done enough scrunches, pull ups, press ups and sprinting with and without heavy weights, that he could lay off a bit and sit out on the side benches that lined the underground gymnasium. He made the mistake of betraying his feelings in his face and the result was he was singled out, shouted at, prodded hard with a baseball bat and told to do another five circuits. The heat made him sweat profusely. He gritted his teeth and pushed his tired body on as instructed.

This arduous get fit programme had been going on for over three weeks and much as Ali wanted to ease up, even give up, he knew that wasn't an option. No-one in IS was allowed to say they'd had enough. In Mosul everyone had to do what the CO said; and equally, whilst in the gym, what the sports trainer said, was law. He knew, because he'd been told time and time again that nothing less than unquestioning obedience was permitted and it was only this that meant survival and reward, and in the promises of IS sometimes reward and not survival.

He had to admit that since the CO spoke to him all of three weeks ago, life had generally been better. He liked having something to do, a reason to get up for, some goal to aim at, though he still didn't know exactly what it would be. It helped that despite the on-going strain of a long-term war, extra supplies of fresh, top quality food had been delivered to the family home in Mosul and he'd been personally sent special extra nutritious meals with plenty of lamb and chicken, fresh pomegranates and oranges - all intended to build him up for what lay ahead. And as to what exactly lay ahead, day after day had passed and nothing further had been said. All the focus had been on getting him into shape, his English polished up and his communication and technical skills up to the mark.

Though the gym workouts were very tough, the toughest thing he'd ever done, he knew that he was getting into better physical shape than he'd ever been in. The night runs had built his stamina and he'd entirely lost the roll of fat that had begun to press on his belt. People in the West would pay a lot of money to have a personal sports trainer like Hakim! He laughed out loud at the thought, picturing Hakim yelling and prodding westerners to make them workout ever harder. Hakim noticed the laughter and Ali wondered how he would cope with yet another five circuits as punishment for what he'd see as this latest subordination, but surprisingly Hakim yelled at Ali to stop.

'Come here,' he ordered and then motioned to the bench indicating he was to sit down.

'You are to have a rest day tomorrow and I mean rest. Be idle, let your body repair and get stronger. Come back the following day and we will begin the final phase of your programme.' This was news to Ali.

'The final phase', Ali echoed back.

'Yes, just a few weeks more, no more than four, we think, until you begin the task we have in mind for you.' Ali felt a buzz of excitement mixed with apprehension.

'You had better head off for your communications skills training soon. Just get a shower first,' he said.

'OK, thanks,' said Ali.

He swept up his kit bag and towel and headed for the changing room. The showers were always really cold and the water supply was a bit hit and miss. Today, though, it was fine and he had all of five minutes before the pressure started to fall. When the water finally failed, he called it a day, quickly dressed and walked over the way to the hospital where his weekly espionage skill training took place. This was always very exacting and exciting. He had to remember exactly what he was told and repeat the programmes and practical exercises perfectly. The good thing was he got to spend time with Sarina. He'd not expected a female trainer, men and women were so rigorously segregated by the regime, but he told himself she was the best and he had found the weekly lessons something he really looked forward to.

Ali drew out his fob as he approached the hospital basement where everyone was led to believe there was a disabled soldiers rehabilitation programme running, but no-one actually believed it as they never saw any disabled soldiers and everyone was too sensible to ask what was really going on there, with the result everyone went along with the charade, not daring to do otherwise. Ali followed the now familiar routine to get himself into the communications suite. He unclipped the flimsy red and white plastic chain that symbolically closed off the downstairs, carefully clipping it back in place before he made his descent down the white concrete stairwell.

At the bottom there was an elderly soldier whose task was to check all arrivals and departures. His authority was marked by his clip board and of course the ubiquitous AK47 leaning against his chair. His gun looked badly neglected and Ali wondered whether it would actually work. Personally, he was obsessive about cleaning his own weapon and he realised that he had made a habit of regularly looking at other people's AKs to see how they looked compared with his own. He recalled his CO first handing him the weapon that had killed his father and as he always did, involuntarily shuddered at the memory.

The nameless elderly gatekeeper did not rise from his chair, though he knew full well who Ali was. The man was a complete and total jobs-worthy who went through the full ID check, made Ali sign in with date and time, explaining each time how the fob entry door worked and finally, before letting Ali through, undertook a meticulous bag and body search. Maybe it was understandable; failure in Islamic State was ruthlessly punished, the guy was probably doing all this out of self-preservation. A moment's reflection and Ali knew he was probably much the same, falling in line like the rest. It was, he realised, the norm in order to survive. Then, he was in.

Sarina was sitting at the work station which was laden with computers, mobiles in various states of completeness and boxes of electronic kit. She was bent over a small device with a long thin screwdriver in her hand. She greeted him warmly.

'Salaam Alekum,' she said and beckoned him to come and sit beside her.

He noted that her required male relative minder was sitting uncomfortably, looking in their direction from the other end of the room, bored, clearly out of place; and, stealing the occasional glance at Sarina as she began to explain to Ali how to construct mobile-linked trigger devices for improvised explosive devices or IEDs.

Her male relative had been told that on the one hand he was required to see no impropriety occurred and on the other hand he must not overhear any conversation or know what was going on. He shuffled where he sat knowing he was neither near enough to keep a proper eye nor far enough away not to have heard something. He'd be glad when the session was over and he could get Sarina back home.

Ali had already been told how to use a command wire to detonate bombs in an earlier class and briefed on hand grenade use in the previous session. Today he was told that for where he was going he needed to forget the wire option. It was not realistic. Sabrina said it was time to concentrate on what he really did need to know and he was shown an array of different grenades.

Sarina sat very close, and though veiled, so that he could see only glimpses of her eyes, to Ali she looked to be a young, intelligent and attractive woman. Clearly she was well educated and her family had money, he could tell that from her clothing, education and speech, indeed from the very way she walked. He also, just occasionally caught the scent of her perfume, flowery, unknown to him, but stirring in him some deep feelings inside.

The CO would not have allocated Sarina to teach him had she not been excellent in her craft, probably someone educated at a foreign university at some point, he surmised, though he knew better than to ask questions.

Ali very quickly learned that she was truly expert and not only knowledgeable of her subject but a natural teacher, able to convey complex procedures and tasks in a readily accessible way. In just a few weeks, through a mixture of desk top practicals, blackboard diagrams and laptop demonstration clips he was beginning to feel confident in his own ability to assemble explosives from raw materials and handle the delicate chemical and electronic elements to ensure a reliable outcome every time. His own fingers became more dextrous in making wiring connections as he mirrored her own.

She called her brother across the room and told him to turn out the lights. He shrugged and did as he was told. In the pitch black he felt her hands on his as she led the way in training him in how to dismantle and reassemble the mobile detonation send and receive components in the dark. He felt clumsy and stupid, but patiently time and time again, he had to go through the same routine, until he found her hands were no longer guiding his, and he was able to master the process for himself.

'Yes', he cried out.

Next, she placed what he knew was a grenade in his hand.

'Find the firing pin to pull, but don't pull it or we both die. This is the type of fragmentation grenade you will be issued with, remember the feel of it,' she said.

He did as he was told, very gingerly, finding the pin; then lights went on again and with much relief he passed the heavy grenade back. He knew IS only trained with genuine weapons not dummies.

At the end of the lesson, Sarina gave him a USB stick to take away with him. It was password protected and contained his week's homework.

'It covers all the training you've done with me so far, the communication routes we use, the codes, what electronic addresses you use and when to switch, something about SIM cards, and today's fact sheet and Youtube clips on how to disassemble and assemble bomb detonating equipment. The most important document covers the effective use of fragmentation grenades in urban settings,' she said.

This time she gave him a plastic bag of mobile phone parts and some tools and tapes to take home.

'You'll need these, and you will keep these. The smaller black bag contains what you will actually be carrying with you to London. You will especially need to know how to disable these if need be so they can never incriminate you or us. They are issued to you and must not be lost. They are for your mission. These things are to be so well known to you, so familiar, you can see them in your imagination, you can take them apart and rebuild them in the dark. It is time for you to go,' she said, hesitating before adding a surprise to his routine.

'But Ali, I am told you are not to go home from here today but to go back to the gymnasium where you were earlier. Go there now. I'll see you next week,' said Sarina leaving Ali puzzled at this change.

'Bye, and thanks,' he added, his mind now elsewhere, wondering what the CO had lined up for him as an extra. 'See you next week, and yes, I'll do my homework.'

At the other end of the room Sarina's male minder was clearly relieved to see him go.

Ali quickly headed for the exit, Sarina's minder moving just as swiftly to talk to his charge. She didn't seem to like his pushy way with her, rushing her to gather her things and make her way back home with him. Ali turned back. He thought he could get away with a bit of insubordination.

'Just like to say how much I appreciate my sister's help in the cause. Now, let's show a little respect here. I've given her a hard time. I'm a very demanding student. May I help you with your things Sarina?'

She turned, for a moment flustered.

'No, time for you to get to your next appointment. But thank you anyway. We will be fine,' she said, turning away from him.

The relative just glowered, but Ali could tell he was not the powerful one in the situation. Ali knew he was important to the Caliphate and woe betide anything or anybody which interrupted his mission. Having made his point, he swung round and briskly exited through the door, nodding to the sleepy white-haired guard and headed up the stairs two at a time and out into the bright sunshine which cut into him like a searing blade and made him screw his eyes almost shut after the cool semi-darkness of the basement he had just left.

Moments later he was over the way and back in the gym. He sensed things were different and walked in cautiously. A curtain had been slung across the one end, to hide whatever it was that was there. To the left there was a table and on it, to his surprise, he saw his own AK47 - he'd know it anywhere. His uncle had probably been told to produce it. A new trainer in the familiar black military fatigues, a middle aged man with a face of stone, a man he'd not seen before was sitting behind the desk.

'Ali Muhammed,' he called out, 'come here my friend.'

It was more an order than invitation, delivered coldly, like steel. There was no chair so he had to stand. Behind the curtain he heard a shuffling sound.

'What's going on?' Ali asked.

'Training', was the one word reply.

'Pick up your weapon,' he said.

Ali did as instructed.

'Follow me,' he ordered as the man got up from where he had been sitting.

Again Ali followed, as the guy who'd still not introduced himself and showed no intention of doing so, marched briskly down the gym toward the curtained off area. He's seen action, thought Ali and won't be taking any nonsense. With a guy like this he told himself he'd need to be ready to up his game here. As Ali approached the screen he saw numbers from one to ten had been etched on the curtain with a broad tipped marker pen of some sort.

'When I call a number, holding the point of your gun, swing the butt end to strike the number I call to connect with the number on the curtain. I will call the numbers and you are to move as swiftly as you can and strike fiercely hitting the number I call. Clear?' he said.

Sounds easy enough thought Ali as he nodded and prepared himself. He stood in a get set position.

'Two.'

He struck Two.

'Eight.'

He moved quickly and struck again. Then he received a deafening blow to the side of his head.

'Not quick enough, not hard enough', said his instructor.

The number sequence continued and Ali upped his game. Thankfully no further blows followed.

'At ease,' the guy ordered.

'That's a relief,' Ali found himself saying.

Attempting to be friendly cut no ice, and almost immediately the number sequence calls began again. Moments later he took another blow to the head.

'Not hard enough,' were the words given as justification.

By now Ali was building up a sweat and feeling angry. On the shout of 'Five', this time his AK connected hard with something or rather someone the other side of the curtain almost forcing the weapon out of his grasp. It was not a thing, it was definitely a person, he'd hit a person, he'd hurt someone. No comment and no let up.

'Six', and he took a hit again on the head for pausing too long.

This was painful, he dreaded five coming up again, but when 'Nine' was called he experienced the same thud of gun butt on flesh, this time guessing he'd hit someone hard in the torso, and a groan came from the other side. Ali was quick and did not slow. No choice here but to follow orders and continue striking quickly and hard for what seemed like an eternity. Many times after he'd convinced himself the rest breaks were going to be the end of the session, the session did finally come to an end.

There was the sound of someone being dragged away on the other side of the curtain and a far door out of Ali's sight, opened and shut. He wondered what he'd done, but this

67

was war and he was a soldier. He'd counted seven times when the number called had led to him striking some unseen person hard. Inflicting pain was something you did. He was beginning to feel faint and sick, but he dare not betray how he felt. This was training and as a trainee he must not fail.

Finally, he was told to get himself a drink, go home and rest. That was one order he had no trouble following and as he moved out into the sun he felt something fundamental had happened inside him.

He was beginning to forget what innocence and goodness were, he was being sucked deeper into some evil vortex he could not fight. Ali knew that obedience was his only option if he and his family were to survive. He'd just been given a hard lesson in the realities of jihad, a necessary foretaste of the toughness the Caliphate needed their most promising warrior to display.

Unknown to Ali, the message went back to his CO that the recruit's training was progressing nicely.

13

It had been a difficult journey getting into the Metropolitan Police, numbers admitted by direct entry as a PC had been subject to successive government spending cutbacks. There was only one route in still open to her. As it was, the number of would-be recruits had so swamped the application process that she'd been rejected three times before she was finally able to join as a PCSO or Police Community Support Officer as they were more formally called. She was lucky; soon, she knew, even that route in would be closed.

April Cooper's Dad had also been in the Met, made a lifetime career of it and on retirement ended up a security consultant for a large delivery company on the nearby Brimsdown Industrial Estate. He'd enjoyed life in the police, though the anti-social hours had placed a huge strain on life at home. However, enough of his enthusiasm for the police life had rubbed off on his daughter April who was determined to make it, in what many still saw as a man's world.

Her Mum had been none too pleased when she'd made her plans clear, but she had at least giving her blessing and supported April all the way since her mind was made up. As a PCSO she was still able to do what she thought was real policing, working at grassroots with the community. In fact, she told herself, this is real community work. She believed most people appreciated what she did and if you asked them, they wanted to see the police right where she actually worked, on the streets, walking the beat, calling in their shops, listening to their woes.

Three months into the role, her uniform no longer quite so brand spanking squeaky clean and sharp as it was, she was thoroughly enjoying herself. Her Mum and Dad were pleased, she was happy and fulfilled, the future looked great; soon enough, she told herself, the door would open to allow her to become a proper police constable.

Today in the north London YE division, she was walking a new beat with an experienced constable, Bob Steer. Bob knew Edmonton like the back of his hand.

'Walk more slowly,' he had told her, 'walking fast means you don't notice things.'

It was good advice, the wisdom of an experienced copper. She began to notice things, look inside parked cars, spot the doorways which suggested trouble behind them, take in the atmosphere in the Silver Street pubs as she passed by. She became aware of where people were on the street, even those behind her. Most of all she observed people, infinitely interesting, never two the same, ever changing, all to be weighed carefully as either criminal or law abiding.

'April,' Bob said, 'things are changing round here and the atmosphere isn't what it was.'

'What do you mean?' she replied, curious to know the facts behind such a statement.

'The people are changing. Once upon a time, this used to be a respectable, white working-class neighbourhood. It was full of decent hard-working moral people. They didn't have a lot of money, but they were decent people. Now, no-one knows their neighbour, still less whether they are good or not. Now, we see crimes here we never saw back then. In the past, people left their front and back doors unlocked, even open. People chatted to one another, in the street, over the garden wall. But, so many new people have come into the area, everything's changed for the worse,' said Bob, stopping to peer into a litter bin before walking on.

'Some people living next door to each other you just know will never get on, from areas of the world where they hate each other's guts and we house them without a thought as to where all that hate is going to go to; and, then it's us, the police who get asked to sort it. It's demoralising. It's impossible. We're on a downhill slope and we're given fewer resources to cope.' He paused, until the gloomy expression suddenly lifted. Something brighter had clearly crossed his mind.

'Mind you, there's a project with good intent round the corner, here in Windmill Road, and we need to pop in on it. You need to know about this, the Holy Trinity Drop In Centre,' he said.

He pointed past the large Victorian Ashford Community College, to the church behind metal railings between it and the street. Then his attention switched back to the college opposite.

'That college is now home to over one hundred and twenty different first languages and where there is an ever-worsening immigrant problem. Look at a school and you see what the future holds that's what I say, and what I see scares me,' said Bob.

April followed the line of his gaze, her eyes then returning to the church, a building without tower or spire, squat and undecided whether it was made from brick or stone. Next door was the Centre, looking like some old Victorian brick school room. They were almost there.

'The local vicar is a bit of a good thing, Rev Churchill, or Ruth to her friends. That's her house there, between the Church and Centre.' He pointed it out.

'She asked me to keep an eye on it for her whilst she was away in France. She'll be back now. Bit of a target that house, biggest around here and burgled twice to my knowledge. It would kill two birds with one stone us popping into her hall. I could tell her we kept an eye on her place and she could tell us about her Drop In project. That part will be about us gathering local intelligence, but we don't tell her that. Right?' He winked in April's direction and she noticed he'd quickened his pace.

'That Drop In club she's got running is one of the few positive things I see going on. Don't know how she does it. Doesn't get much local support as far as I can see. Even some of her own flock think she's got it wrong. Step to it, we might even get a cup of coffee. In we go,' he said, letting her lead the way.

They swung right through the dark green doors of the Victorian church hall. Police boots always made such a noisy entrance, she thought. It smelled warm and of people. The inner swing doors revealed a quite unexpected scene, one that in the next few minutes became more subdued as people realised they had visitors. This was an all too familiar response April had begun to see when she walked into places in her uniform - embarrassed cafe owners, market traders at Edmonton Green, or even at football matches.

Police work always felt like you had one arm tied behind your back because so many Joe and Josie public were not on your side, that was until they got to know you as a person, she thought. Recent scandals hadn't helped. Un-investigated grooming of kids who were supposed to be in the care of their local authority, the failure to recruit more police from ethnic minorities and the softly softly approach adopted when there was real trouble on the streets. The public just didn't understand and were merciless.

Even police officers themselves wondered whether it was worth arresting people half the time, for the CPS, the Crown Prosecution Service or the courts themselves seemed to either throw the case out or let people off. April reckoned it was deliberate. Politicians wanted to pay less for a prison service, they wanted fewer police and they were frightened of a backlash if they gave the police the go-ahead to be firmer on crime. April just wondered if anyone outside the police had any idea how many difficulties policing faced even before an officer left the station.

Her thoughts were interrupted as they were offered a cup of coffee by a young Afro-Caribbean girl whose job seemed to be to welcome everyone as they came in. This is amazing, she thought, there's maybe seventy or more people here. After coffee had been handed over, the girl wasn't sure what to do with these visitors and looked around anxiously. Moments later someone was bringing, or rather steering Rev Ruth Churchill across the hall in their direction and visible relief spread over the girl's face.

Bob was gazing around. April knew he'd be assimilating all he could through his finely honed powers of crowd observation. Bob could sense when something wasn't right, he had the policeman's nose. There weren't many like him and she was glad to be training with him. Old school yes, bit misogynist, yes, but loyal and knowledgeable. He was not bothered about what the top brass thought, as all thoughts of promotion had long passed him by. She noticed that he was watching the far corner of the room intently, even as Ruth Churchill greeted them both with a warm welcome.

'I'm glad you've been offered coffee. Welcome to Holy Trinity Drop In,' she said with a genuine smile on her face.

'This is PCSO April Cooper, new to us, and with me for now. I trust you had a good holiday?' Bob added.

'Yes, but Paris seemed a stressed kind of place this time. People were worried that discontent in the suburbs might flare up again, everyone looking over their shoulders the whole time. Fear of extremists is all people talked about. Such a polarised place, thankfully we all get along better here. The English way seems so much more easy going, even relaxed and laid back by comparison,' she said, as she took a cup of coffee for herself.

Ruth was invited by Bob to tell April how the project had started and what they were hoping to achieve. April only half took in what Ruth began to tell her. She was half watching Bob and she could tell that he was once again more interested in watching the robed young men at the far end of the hall, about half a dozen of them.

They were a very definite little group, and she too had that feeling they were up to something. It was the half glances they kept casting in their direction. Well, maybe if not exactly up to something, she thought, a group with something to hide. She didn't feel comfortable. As the minutes passed and Ruth kept talking, she read their occasional gaze in her direction as more than dismissive. She decided it was contempt. It was Bob who interrupted Ruth's story.

'You've got some new takers then,' Bob said, glancing up the hall as if to read April's mind.

'Oh yes,' she said, 'Middle East and out of North Africa. Some are the lucky ones that didn't drown in the Med. We never know who is coming next under the European Asylum

Dispersal Agreement. These Muslim guys have made themselves quite at home here, but having said that, they do very much keep themselves to themselves. Where they come from the idea of a woman religious leader is total anathema. I'm hoping they won't just come and use the amenities we provide like the advice service, food, laundry and free Wi-Fi, but I hope they will let me get a bit closer to their world and share with me their hopes for their future,' said Ruth with a note of concern in her voice.

Bob, April thought, is not convinced by this idealistic vicar, he thinks these newcomers are trouble. When he bluntly asked Ruth, 'where are they staying?' April knew for certain she was reading the situation accurately. Bob's policeman's nose was twitching!

'Most of them are in the flats on the Red Brick Estate, Silver Street. I haven't yet visited. They are just into observing Ramadan, and in a few days' time when things are more relaxed I plan to make calling on them a priority,' said Ruth.

April turned round again and to her surprise she could see none of the young men. They'd quietly slipped out the door. Bob was already trying to politely extricate himself from his conversation with Ruth, to thank her for the coffee and make his own way to the door. They were not quick enough. The men had already turned the corner of the street, half way to the no-go world of the Red Brick Estate.

'I thought you said we need to walk slowly to notice things,' April chided, as Bob began to slow his pace. He turned, he slowing more.

'You're right,' he said without smiling.

'We both know something's not right, something's brewing,' she said.

'It is not just Paris that needs to worry about extremism. But then again they might be into some other racket. Maybe drugs? Who knows?' he said with a shrug.

'You need to tell me how we move on this, when all we've got to go on is our gut reaction,' said April.

'Not easy, let me talk to a few people,' said Bob, leaving April unclear as to how much of what they'd noticed would be followed up. She had no idea who Bob intended to talk to.

Just then a call came through for them to attend a vehicle accident on the Great Cambridge Roundabout just yards away. They dashed across to where they could see the traffic was already building. For now the mysterious robed young men from North Africa and whatever it was they were up to was not a priority.

14

Ruth left the Drop In soon after April and Bob. She knew she had a church council meeting to prepare for that evening and it weighed heavily on her mind. Feeling anxious, she wondered how to organise the agenda; the wearisome weight of the looming meeting depressed her; her shoulders sagged as if gravity itself had been turned up several notches. Questions kept attacking her and eroding her self-confidence - How do I keep everyone together? How on earth do I get sufficient support to keep this Drop In going?

The previous meeting, only four weeks earlier, had been a disaster. Alex Sutton, the treasurer, had made it clear that the budget for the current year was already sliding into a serious and unsustainable deficit and only significant new fund-raising initiatives and, or, new regular giving through the stewardship programme would keep the church afloat.

It was then that Sheila Parker, the Church Hall Secretary, had piped up and said that the hall could be made to positively contribute to church funds if only the Drop In were not such a huge drain. She suggested other local churches help share the burden, even by offering to host the Drop In itself. Sheila made her argument all the more persuasive by saying that a new Mums and Toddlers group had asked if they might use the hall and pay a weekly rent, but she had had to tell them, 'no' because the vicar said the Drop In had first call on the use of the hall.

'It wouldn't be so bad saying 'no' to the Mums and Toddlers, if I were able to say the Drop In paid something to rent the space - but they don't, they don't pay a single penny, do they?' said Sheila.

Sheila had been in full flow that night and begun exactly where Ruth felt most vulnerable.

'You know as well as I do the local authority give no money but make lots of fine noises about how good the Drop In is. Now what is it they say again, oh yes, "it's a superlative

76

example of a community-led sustainable networking initiative." Fine praise indeed, but that doesn't provide us with a single penny toward our bills. In my view it has got to come to an end. We have to close it, and close it now before it bankrupts us!' Sheila had said.

Ruth hadn't been able deny it, Sheila had stunned and shut her up; council support for Ruth had melted; and now, to her dread, all this was to be re-run again tonight.

It hurt Ruth to recall all those nodding heads at that point. She had felt so alone and isolated and, only managed to persuade them to hold fire on stopping the Drop In by promising to have a conversation with other local churches to get their help, but she knew that tonight she would have to report back the fruitlessness of her efforts and face the music. Even her most likely source of support, the lively free church under Bishop Sam Kone had not yet produced anything concrete in the way of help. Tonight looked grim.

She tried to rally herself. When things get tough, she said to herself, the tough get going; with an air of resignation, mixed with a little new found self-determination, she grabbed her bag, her pile of papers for the evening's Parochial Church Council, its PCC, and headed for her study tucked away in the labyrinthine vicarage. She hoped she might be spared, today of all days, that bane of her life at such times, the unexpected crisis call to go to the hospital or see a parishioner in crisis. Even her family needed to know that for the next couple of hours she must not be disturbed. The very future of the Drop In depended on her coming up with something, however futile such a hope now seemed.

It turned out that that this afternoon she was lucky, more than lucky. There were no interruptions, except at about 4.30pm when her husband Phil, home early from an accountancy and tax conference, popped his head round her study door with a pot of tea on a tray. There were two mugs. She half stretched as she leant back from her paper-strewn desk. He flopped into the easy chair she had set up for visitors. He could read the struggle and stress in her face.

'Time for a cuppa,' he said kindly, which was more a gentle command than a question.

'That's nice,' she replied, 'I'm ready for one.'

Five minutes to regroup she told herself. By the time she was half way through the mug of Earl Grey tea, she'd told Phil what lay before her.

'I'll be a lamb led to the slaughter. I can't think of any way I can give the project a future,' she said in desperation. 'When it goes, there'll be nothing left like it for needy asylum seekers north of the Thames.'

Phil just listened to her; it was all of ten minutes before he was able to comment.

'What they need,' he said slowly, 'is some reassurance that a panicky situation is under control. More fundamental than that, they need to believe in the work the church is doing.'

'The only way they'll believe things are under control is if I can find the funds to cover the budgetary shortfall, and I simply can't see it. Have a look at these,' said Ruth. She pushed a spreadsheet of income and expenditure, assets and liabilities across for him to see.

'Alex the treasurer sent these latest figures across earlier for tonight's meeting,' she explained.

Phil stared at them. It only took him half a minute. This was just his thing. Some said he was boring, safe to the point of utter predictability, but like a good labrador he was a faithful and homely, unquestioningly loving companion.

'I can't see any problem here,' was his surprising remark.

'What! Just look at the bottom line, the income coming in is already over £1,000 in arrear for the first half of this calendar year. That figure in red is all the PCC will see. Don't you see, that's enough to close the Drop In, especially as the Mums and Toddlers are offering to pay us a rent that will pay off that arrear and put us in the black by the end of the year. It's a disaster!' she said, head in hands.

'But hang on, there's nothing to show that Alex has been doing his job collecting Gift Aid back from the

78

Government. Pass me last years accounts, they're behind the annual meeting papers,' Phil said, pointing to the top drawer of the open filing cabinet.

She pulled them out and handed them over. He ruffled through them until he found what he was looking for.

'Just as I thought, he didn't do them last year either. As far as I can see, the accounts don't indicate this money as debtor income. I'll bet he's totally forgotten to claim it, must be all of several thousand pounds given the number of signed up people you've got. Look, give me the accounts file and I'll give you a more accurate figure as to what you can claim back from the government. You're not in debt, you're in surplus! I don't do guess work, but the figures are definitely in the black!' said Phil, throwing his hand down firmly on the papers to emphasise the point he was making.

Ruth was stunned. A light switch flicked on in her head. Phil was right, she knew it. Gift Aid returns had been overlooked. This could take the financial pressure off for now, but the question Phil had also raised about the PCC believing in what they were doing was going to need work too. She left Phil to re-work the financial sums and began to reflect on what direction the church was moving in, and slowly, very slowly she began to see a way forward.

Two hours later Ruth gathered up her papers again and made her way back to the Church Hall where this evening's PCC would be held. She always made certain she was there well ahead of everyone else. A seven thirty start meant she was in the hall by seven.

She began to take down the stacked blue plastic Gopac chairs and arrange them in a semicircle. It was more unifying to lay them out this way, less hierarchical and gave everyone a chance to engage. The circle was broken by the table she erected, bending and locking with some difficulty the table's metal legs. She would need to sit behind this to chair the meeting.

Beside her would be Julie Brown, the PCC secretary, who would be taking notes of the meeting. Julie always insisted on having something firm to write on. The table served to hold the meeting papers and the jug, water and plastic mugs. In just a few minutes the room was ready and Ruth sat herself down behind the table for a moment of quiet prayer and contemplative preparation.

When she next looked up no-one was missing. All twelve PCC members had arrived; and, by seven thirty-five were busily chatting with each other until she called the meeting to order. Stephanie was always so loud and had a habit of standing far too close when speaking to someone. Ruth particularly disliked that as particles of spit inevitably parted company from her lips and open mouth to fly in her direction. It felt rude to be brushing them off whilst she was still talking. Ruth told herself that Stephanie wasn't aware of this habit and she herself shouldn't be the first to throw stones.

Lionel and Ollie were talking conspiratorially, about what she couldn't imagine. Jill, Arun and the Churchwardens were listening to Alex, who in his one hand held an open copy of the latest accounts and with a pointy index finger was prodding them meaningfully, as he explained them to his attentive coterie.

Ruth called them to order; the hubbub died and everyone sat down. The Council became attentive remarkably quickly. Not only was everyone present, but also everyone appeared engaged. This was promising, but what direction would they be going in, were they with her or against her? Would her resignation letter be in the post by the end of the evening? She wouldn't have long to wait to find out.

Church Council meetings always began with a Bible reading and a prayer before the main agenda. The task of reading was passed round on a rota and tonight it was Lionel's turn; after Ruth had given him an affirming nod, he cleared his throat and announced the reading formally - it was the Anglican way.

'The reading is taken from the Gospel according to Matthew, chapter fifteen and beginning at the twenty-first verse,' he intoned.

The thing about stories is the way they draw you in and, though the story wasn't long, it seemed to have everyone hooked. It wasn't an unfamiliar story. Being pretty clued up on their Bibles, this PCC knew this story well; but there was something in the way Lionel read it that grabbed them.

He told them about Jesus, when he was a long way from home in the borderlands of Israel, and was verbally cornered by a loud-mouthed foreign woman. Even those friends Jesus normally counted on, his closest followers, his disciples, wanted to shut this nuisance of a woman up and send her on her way. But this woman was upset, she was crying out for help because her little girl was seriously ill. She wanted Jesus' help. 'Send her away,' the disciples pleaded of Jesus, 'she's a nuisance.' Jesus at first seemed to agree with them. He told the woman he wasn't there to help people like her, foreigners, but only 'the lost sheep of Israel' - his own people.

But this woman was feisty and having none of it. She kept screaming at Jesus; and, you know what, he gave in to her banging on. He told her, that her daughter would be well again and then he rounded on his own disciples to tell them what great faith this foreign woman had shown. The result was, that when Lionel had finished and closed the book, there was an attentive silence and this allowed for a moment's reflection before Ollie spoke up to offer a brief prayer.

Ruth reassumed the chair, thanking Lionel and Ollie, who in turn smiled politely back. The Council quickly signed off the previous meeting's minutes, matters arising and a piece of meaningless correspondence about General Synod, the Church's highest governing body.

'Now to the main item on this evening's agenda, "The Future of the Drop In Project." Let me begin by reminding everyone where the last meeting left things. If you recall, the future of the Drop In was called into question because of concern that the church was not paying its way and we were headed in an unsustainable financial direction. I agreed. I offered to talk to some of our neighbouring churches to see if they would share the burden, share the financial load, and then report back to our next meeting - which is tonight. I have to say that my conversations with the other churches in the neighbourhood were helpful and supportive, there were even offers of voluntary help; but disappointingly, as of now none of the other churches have sent us any money or pledged any,' said Ruth.

At this point Sheila interrupted her.

'I'd like to say something,' Sheila said, piping up rather too shrilly.

Perhaps she's anxious, Ruth thought. Sheila wasn't to be stopped.

'Tracey, at Mums and Toddlers, has told me she has enough people on her waiting list to book the church hall every morning of the week, and she'll pay enough rent to more than cover our shortfall. It's the answer to our prayers,' said Sheila.

Amanda beside her voiced her support.

'If we expand our Mums and Tots work then we can grow new Christians, it'll help the mission of the church. At All Saints, Edmonton, they have a Mums and Tots and the numbers of children being baptised has shot up and their church is growing. This is a real opportunity. I think we should support Sheila's suggestion. We've done our bit for the foreigners. If we don't look after our own, the church won't flourish. I support Sheila's proposal to close the Drop In and let Mums and Tots pay to use the hall,' said Amanda.

A lively debate immediately followed and at one level Ruth was pleased that they were so energised and enthusiastic - and pretty well everyone had something to say on the subject. After half an hour the conversation was only going one way and Ruth felt things were slipping rather too quickly away from her. People felt insecure about the Drop In, and some unsavoury remarks had started to slip into the debate about undesirable migrants, people who didn't contribute to society.

'We didn't fight the last war for this and those who gave up so much for this country and this church in the past would turn in their graves if they saw the way things were today,' someone muttered.

And then things took a surprising turn. Lionel who had been unusually quiet, spoke up.

'Haven't we all heard the reading tonight? Call ourselves followers of Jesus do we? Then we need to set an example. The other churches might not give their support, but here's the chance for us to lead the way in caring for the most needy members of our community. How many of you have been to the Drop In and talked to the people coming to us, people who are hungry, traumatised, homeless and hopeless? I have. I called in for the first time last week. Our hall was full of needy people, all races, all faiths, women as well as men. There are needy Muslims, like Abu and his family, living in limbo, they've been waiting years for a decision as to whether they can stay or must be deported. Have we really any idea what Abu's life must be like? Our vicar is doing an amazing job on our behalf. It strikes me if we can answer two questions, then we must allow this work of pity to continue. These people are our own Canaanite women, the foreigners Jesus commended,' said Lionel.

'What are the two questions Lionel,' Ruth asked.

'First, we need to ask ourselves, is there no other way we can find somewhere for Tracey's Mums and Toddlers to meet? And second, what can we do to balance our books?'

There was a pause as everyone took this in. Ruth remembered Phil had handed her a piece of paper as she left the vicarage for the meeting with his calculations of the value of outstanding Gift Aid and now seemed the right moment to produce this to the meeting.

'On your second question, the finance one, I think our accounts fail to show the Gift Aid contributions we can claim back from the government for all the regular stewardship giving. Is that correct Alex?' asked Ruth.

She saw Alex blink, blink again, and then he spoke.

'Oh no! Sorry, it completely slipped my mind. Judy used to do it in the past, to help me; and when she left, it must have got overlooked,' said Alex apologetically.

'I thought that might be so,' said Ruth, 'and my husband Phil, who is an accountant, did a quick back of the envelope calculation as to how much money we might collect in outstanding Gift Aid. Alex, it looks like three tax years unclaimed, and we're talking about several thousand pounds due to the Church.' There was a gasp among the members.

'I think we have the answer to our immediate budget concerns, but how can we help Tracey?' asked Lionel.

The PCC spent a further twenty minutes going through various options. The longer conversation went in this direction, the more certain Ruth was that she had saved the day. The Drop In, the finest, indeed the only one of its kind in north London would continue.

Eventually, the PCC agreed to meet with Tracey to see if the old choir vestry, which was a very large space, might be suitably adapted for her new group. Everyone seemed happy to be offered a solution and Ruth asked finally if there was Any Other Business. She looked around to see Stephanie had her hand half raised. Items of Any Other Business, or AOBs were always so unpredictable, thought Ruth, and even with tonight's victory won, she was apprehensive as to what was to come.

'I have something to ask. I'm glad the Drop In will continue. I went in there myself. But does everyone know that Muslim men are using the hall? And Vicar, is it right they treat it as their sacred space and offer their prayers to their God? I came away feeling our hall had been spiritually defiled. Someone told me that Muslims claim our Christian space when they pray in it. Can you have a word with them, Vicar and ask they do it elsewhere.' She was spitting out her words now. 'And what about the Gospel, Vicar. If this were a Salvation Army Hall we would ensure every visitor heard the Gospel. What are you doing about preaching the Gospel to these Muslims? It's a heaven sent opportunity, a mission opportunity on our doorstep. Can you tell us how the Gospel is being preached to these Muslims, what we are doing to convert them?' spluttered Stephanie.

Ruth's mind was going back to the group in the hall earlier that day and Sid's conversation with her. She felt that as a woman, she would be at a disadvantage trying to talk

84

with them to start with and her heart sank at trying to tell them what Stephanie had in mind. The days of megaphone evangelism were hopefully over, but there surely was a need for some positive dialogue, inter-faith conversation, not least so they could get to know the new Muslims in the neighbourhood, but could she do it? Ruth felt very tired all of a sudden.

'Thank you for your important question Stephanie,' she found herself saying, 'there are a lot of issues wrapped up in what you say. I will certainly speak with them. The time is late, and I don't normally like to cut things short, but if the Council would be happy to leave me to follow this one up and report back next time, that is what I propose.'

Thankfully, there were nods of agreement all round as people wanted to get off home. The meeting swiftly concluded and people disappeared making their separate ways, mostly on foot, in ones and twos into the night.

Ruth for her part swept up her papers under her arm, grabbed her handbag and made her way next door to the vicarage where she would forgo the usual bed time cuppa and see if Phil would join her in a celebratory G and T.

The Drop In had been saved and that was a victory to celebrate, even if she had to think further about how better to engage with the Muslim men coming in ever-increasing numbers.

15

Ali was at home, lying on his bed in the heat of the day, reflecting in the quiet moment the direction his life was now taking. He knew the brutal training he had been put through was designed to equip him for what lay ahead and told himself he had absolutely no choice but to attack the man behind the curtain screen, do it or die was no choice at all. That didn't make it any easier to come to terms with inside.

He had found his sleep pattern, normally so deep, had been broken since and he had woken in the night with sweats and panic attacks. He wondered whether he had actually called out as he woke, but no-one in the house said they'd heard him, so Ali told himself to keep calm, others had been through far worse and it was all a matter of time before he could move on. The dead face of his Father had started reappearing in the night, and sleep for now was proving elusive. He tried to tell himself sleep would return and the nightmares and panic attacks would ease eventually.

Soon, he knew, he would complete his preparation and he had begun to look forward to when he would be released from the constant rigour and discipline of training in weapons, bomb-making, communications and English language revision, to which had recently been added what was euphemistically called the 'London Visitor' briefing module.

In sum, all the various components of his personal programme, with their attendant 'homework', were beginning to make his head spin - too much pressure, on-going training, broken nights and mission uncertainty. Being allowed food and drink during Ramadan was certainly a welcome dispensation, but all in all he was beginning to hope that sooner rather than later things would move on. Inside he felt he'd had enough, he just wanted to get on with it.

Life in Mosul was, for the citizens living in the 'perfect' Islamic State, also presenting increasing numbers of challenges, though again this was not something anyone dare voice out loud. In fact it was wise not to even think about it in case an unguarded look or comment slipped out. He knew people had lost their lives through unwise talk even for what they had said within their own homes. It was dangerous to think, he thought; and deadly to speak. His training had brought it home to him that the way things worked here was through fear and terror. It was a very simple transactional way of doing things and remarkably effective in its own way.

There was a clear leadership structure, it was a given and things got done. He had to admit, sometimes decisions were rough and ready, but it worked. The state didn't yet have the luxury of being able to afford fully-functioning courts with legally-trained Sharia-compliant advocates and judges. Even so, crime was something that just didn't happen because people knew 'justice' was done, handed out once and for all. That was it. His CO reminded him time and again of the importance of commitment, loyalty to his faith, his people, his family. Such commitment to Islam, he said, sometimes required sacrifice of the bravest ones, only in that way can the commitment to the faith and to the community be shown.

The rest of the world had so demonised IS and all who lived within its world. Life within the state had to function simply, or simply function, so as not to distract from the ongoing jihad against the infidel, the evil corrupt empire of America and all its allies. Life was raw at the edges, he admitted, but that's temporary and generally things weren't so very bad - taxes were paid and everyone felt they belonged.

The powerful ideal they had begun within, creating both the vision for and the reality of an Islamic Caliphate, had united people together, provided a rallying call bringing brothers and sisters from all over the world to give their support. Look at the stirring film clips, he told himself, consider the successes so proudly reported.

Though territorial gains had been slow in coming and the hunkered-down feeling of constant attrition from allied air attacks had ground people down, there was still a really strong grass-roots camaraderie and that's what would win out in the end. There was no crime, no corruption or immorality that he could see. Life here had a certain simple purity. The dream was worth fighting for.

Nevertheless, what had really surprised Ali was how divided the Muslims outside were on Islamic State. He'd thought it was a no-brainer. Surely everyone in the umma would fall in behind the black and white flag. Not so, though many faithful men and women had come from Europe and North Africa rallying to the noble jihad.

A thousand people had come from Britain in the first three years, now the number must be double or even treble that, he calculated. But support was hard won where he thought it most naturally ought to come from. Even Saudi Arabia - home to Sunni Wahabism, or Jordan - home to so many conservative revolutionaries; or Turkey - which had so wonderfully opened its huge long 500 mile adjoining frontier to make it porous, allowing as many who wanted to find their way here to IS - even these places you would assume were natural 100% allies, these places had not signed up.

What a difference it would make if they all did, he mused; but it continued to trouble him that not all his Muslim brothers thought the same way, and nagging doubts about the IS course sometimes tugged at his inner being.

Rallying behind a single Muslim cause wasn't reality, it was still a dream. Muslim on Muslim conflict seemed to be increasing everywhere Ali looked. Indeed the future battle for Muslim minds, as well as the military battle, seemed ceaseless. In the end our sacrifice and our commitment would decide it, he told himself, repeating the mantra he had been taught. However, the more he pondered the more he doubted, for since March 2013 when Raqqa in Eastern Syria had been won, the years were going by and it was getting harder and harder to see what had been achieved or where the next victories were going to come.

The battle had ebbed and flowed, sometimes IS taking more territory, sometimes the Iraqis with their infidel Shia militias and US planes in the ascendant. However, with al-Qaeda affiliates now stretching the fingers of their operations into the heartlands of the enemy and brothers and sisters across the globe now linking up operations there was some hope. 'Take the battle to the Kuffar', was the new rallying cry giving rise to new optimism and he knew that was why he had been chosen. It would be him, Ali Muhammed, spearheading a targeted campaign right at the heart of the enemy and they would surely want to give up after that.

Year after year of constant revolution is hard to sustain, thought Ali; he wondered how, in a more normal world, the engineering training he'd had in pre-war Mosul University might have set him up in business, allowed him to have a family, to prosper, to enjoy holidays and leisure. Occasionally he reflected on what other forms his life might have taken had the world been different. He knew he was thinking dangerous treasonable thoughts but he couldn't help himself.

Ali had noticed how IS had increasingly had to put in place some local government to handle tax collection, military service, security, water and electric supplies. More than this, creative businesses had had to flourish so that vehicles could be fixed. Even his own Toyota Hilux needed a service and attention from time to time. People demanded bread and medical care and in troubled times considerable local organisation had had to be put into making sure people had the basics to survive.

Some of these things were only now being put in place and he knew this was a huge distraction from the revolutionary jihad. Some understanding and agreement as to what the mosque controlled and what the military controlled had also had to be ironed out using new legal structures. This was leading to internal argument and people being allocated work away from the war effort. Local bureaucracies were now springing up everywhere and what was a revolutionary country on a continuing war footing seemed to Ali to rather resemble some third world developing country.

Revolution was becoming tired and normal. Jihad was in danger of losing its momentum without something to get things moving in the right direction again. Ali knew that the weapons available to IS were never going to win a conventional war. IS hadn't a single plane to his knowledge and their enemies were using ever more advanced technological weapons to target all that really mattered. Drones and Reaper bombs would never win a war either but, like mosquitoes, enough of them wore the people down, wore him down, sapped morale and seemed to eliminate key individuals all too regularly with scarily forensic precision.

It had been a long day and Ali was deeply self-absorbed, lost in his own thoughts for what felt like hours. It was then he heard a knock at the front door. He raised himself to a sitting position on his bed and listened. Mo had gone to the door to open it. From the overheard murmurs, he knew a message had been delivered for him. He never saw the messenger and his brother Mo didn't say more than to tell him he was to see his CO straightaway.

Ali leapt to his feet, put on his sandals and outer robe and slipped out of the door. Moments later he was outside his CO's apartment. He called out in greeting and opened the door once he'd been acknowledged. Taking off his sandals as custom required Ali entered. Salim was sitting, concentrating on his laptop. He waved Ali in without looking up. This time Ali was to sit on the rug. Mint tea was brought in and Salim lifted his gaze and focussed his sharp eyes on Ali. Beside his laptop, Salim had a well-thumbed booklet open in front of him.

'You've done well my brother,' he said smiling.

'All the training reports tell me you have learned well from your teachers and that is excellent news for I truly believe that in the service of the Prophet, Peace be Upon Him, your name will be great. In just a few days you will embark on a journey that will change the course of history. Our esteemed leader Abu Bakr al-Baghdadi, now in the eighth year of his rule, has given us the green light. The time has come for us to shake the infidels to their rotten and corrupted core. We will strike the Great Satan at its head and its heart when they all gather in London on November 11th. You, you Ali, are going to London to deliver the mightiest jihadi victory since 9.11,' Salim announced.

Ali felt himself tremble. This was it. He was indeed going to London, his earlier suspicions now confirmed. How

90

was this to happen? he wondered, and what plan had they come up with to get him there? He was hungry to know more.

'Let me read for you the wise words of Sheik Ibn Taymiah, in the Al Quaeda Training Manual,' said Salim.

His finger fell on the booklet in front of him searching for his place. His finger stilled.

'"The interests of all Adam's children would not be realised in the present life, nor in the next, except through assembly, cooperation and mutual assistance,"' he read, then lifted his face to look Ali in the eyes.

'And you, my brother, are about to undertake the mightiest possible gift of mutual assistance you can possibly afford for the sake of your people. What a great honour you have.' He flipped the Manual shut.

'Our sources tell us that the greatest collection of western leaders, political, military and religious, will gather in London to mark Armistice Day. This is so ironic. They think they are celebrating peace, but you my brother are going to shake their ridiculous delusion and remind them they have created a world at war. You my brother are going to London, first to lie low as a wolf in its lair, until we tell you exactly what to do. You will then deliver the greatest military victory the world has ever seen. You will shake their foundations of government so they fall and you will give them something to remember for ever. It will be the beginning of the end for them. They will melt before us and the ultimate victory will be ours. Others who have wavered will see that it is right to come over to us and we will have not only an Islamic State right here, but also we will rule right across the globe.'

'What am I to do?' asked Ali.

'A young man from London is cycling into our web. He has been identified as a suitable target. He is heading our way. Very soon he will be taken hostage and brought here. His passport will become your passport, your identity, and your safe ticket to London. Our contact says he is, even as we speak, approaching the Turkish border. The fact he is cycling alone and is not being closely monitored in his travels is ideal for our purposes. He is an innocent abroad, a fly who

91

has absolutely no idea he is already the spider's prey. He's in a web with no escape,' said Salim rubbing his hands together.

He paused to draw breath, whistling through his teeth as he did so.

'We believe he sends an occasional email to his parents in London, updates his Facebook page for his friends from time to time, but that's it. We'd rather he spoke less often than he does to them, but no matter, the intervals are long enough to suit our purposes. Just to help you have the maximum head start in your mission and for there to be absolutely no risk you will begin your journey to the West assuming the identity of this young man, though you will not have to cycle all the way like him. No, we have arranged for you to be helped on your way,' he said.

Salim grinned. There were those teeth with gaps again. The continuing smiles made this particular feature of his CO's appearance very noticeable today and Ali found himself thinking the treasonable thought that he didn't like his CO very much.

'When Adam Taylor gets into Eastern Turkey and as soon as we are sure he has just sent his last message home, we intend to speed his journey up to get him here. He'll be picked up by our friends from Istanbul. No-one will know he's gone for weeks. We will bring him here, to Mosul, together with his bike, with all his neat panniers full of his things and with his mobile phone and passport. We will make sure his stay with us is comfortable, but let's say without the usual communication channels he might have hoped for. A healthy young hostage from London is always such a useful commodity in support of our cause,' he said, enjoying the telling of his tale.

'We will give you the perfect chance to make your way to London unnoticed. We have already notified a friendly van driver to take you on the first leg of your journey to the West. You will carry Adam Taylor's identity as your identity as long as possible on your journey, but obviously you will cease to be him the minute you arrive in England,' Salim explained as Ali was giving what he said his full attention.

'Maps are even now being prepared for you, together with an electronic briefing folder on a mobile - everything will be encrypted and password protected - it'll have everything in it you need to know and I will reach you on it. We had wondered about either you or he continuing to send messages to his parents to keep the enemy off your trail, but if we send them, or you send them, or we get our hostage to send them, the risks are greater. Better to have a silence. We want the authorities to conclude he made his own way back and then disappeared. He simply chose not to go back home. Young people do this all the time in the West. They have no family loyalties like we do. Either way, no-one will have any idea that someone from here has got in behind their security. They simply won't have any idea you are there, and that is just perfect. Perrrrfect!'

Salim seemed pleased, smiled and began to chuckle. He looked odd when he laughed thought Ali, it made his face look distorted. Ali kept his thoughts to himself and his emotions locked down. Salim could read people so well and now was not the time to put any doubts in his mind. Ali's mind was racing and he could feel the adrenaline rush as he began to contemplate the turn his life was about to take. Goodbye boredom, hello excitement, he thought.

'It will suit our purposes for his bike to reappear in London which is why you will need to take it all the way there. When you get to London, you will need to dump it, but to do so in such a way as to complete the illusion, that people will think its owner is truly back there, back home again. Our thought at the moment is that once we've ascertained his home address, you will leave the bike there, where it will be found. We want them to think he has come back, not you. You will be an undetected lone wolf and as a lone wolf you will live in the shadows. No-one will know your real name or your real purpose. But don't worry, that's easy in London - so many illegal immigrants and many of them are on our side. You'd be amazed how many people come over here from London and then we send them back to be sleepers. Whatever happens you must not be picked up with the bike. No CCTV must spot you on it. You will need to be smart, very smart. Attention to detail will be everything. Learn from me,' he laughed.

'Over the next few days, your preparation will change. You are to come here and you will go through the mission, time and again, so that you are fully aware of every detail of your journey, your communication arrangements with me, your minder, and your life in London. The prisoner, this Adam is from north London, which suits us well. We have a supporter there, Abu Tariq, a dear friend. He's an older man, been there a few years with his family. Sends us money, helps us out, fixes things. Now he's the one guy in London whose loyalty you can count on and we know that once you've got yourself to north London you'll be taken care of. There will be ways for you to hide,' he said.

For the first time Ali realised everything was leading up to an event in London, but nothing was said, nothing was included about what happened then, what happened after that. Did he come back? Did he become a prisoner in England? Did he die a glorious martyr? These things he didn't feel he could ask Salim. The man was definitely leading the conversation and telling him only what he needed to know. Oh well, thought Ali, things will become clear, one step at a time. There's more than enough for me to get my head round from what I've been told already. Best to show some enthusiasm, even though I feel a dark reality dawning.

'OK, that sounds pretty clear. Now I know a bit more and you say that I begin my journey west in just a few days - do you know how soon?' asked Ali.

'Just a few days. Maybe a week.' Salim shrugged his shoulders before adding, 'some things are out of even my control.'

'What will I do for clothes and money?' asked Ali.

'You will be given what you need over the next few days. The trickiest part will be getting from France to England, but we've thought of that and you won't simply be taking your chances with the thousands of Calais migrants waiting to jump on an unsuspecting lorry to get across the Channel and then usually getting found out at immigration control. No, we have a better route planned for you. Yes, you'll need money, that's no problem. Clothes, that's being seen to as we speak. Also equipment for your mission in London - we're arranging for that to be prepared separately and Abu will help us with arrangements for when you get there. It is better for you and for us if the weapons and explosives go by our commercial courier, though I have to say it is getting harder to get things through the searches. You will need to adapt to whatever we can get to you. We will give you further instructions on arrival in London. Understood? Got that?' he asked, before continuing to speak without waiting for Ali's reply.

'Don't be surprised if days or even weeks go by before you hear from us. We are very, very, careful. There are loyal brothers who will look after you in London, but they do not and must not know your mission. You must keep yourself apart from them. Understand?'

Ali nodded.

'You are a lone wolf operative and to stand the best chance of success nothing must compromise your control of the mission. Even with Abu, keep a safe distance. Is that quite clear?' Salim asked.

'Total secrecy, no-one in London to know why I am there - absolutely fine,' Ali replied.

'Your sole contact for this mission will be with me, no-one else. We are to communicate exactly as I arrange. It is too dangerous to do otherwise. I don't need to remind you that the future for your family and mine depends on your as well as my attention to detail and on the project's success. Failure is not an option,' Salim told him, in a serious tone of voice.

Ali felt a sudden weight of unwelcome responsibility at this. He was doing what he did for his wider Muslim family as well as his own kith and kin. He realised now that the future lives of others like Salim and his family depended on how well he did his job for the Caliphate. He realised how much weighty power Salim had over him and how in the years since his father's death his CO had personally guided him into the

95

path now open before him. Involuntarily he shuddered once again as the unbidden image of his dying father flashed before his eyes, making him tremble inside.

'Our leaders have great faith in us. That's all for now, you are dismissed,' concluded his CO.

With that Salim waved Ali away. That was it. He did as instructed and slipped back into the dusty, empty, street and moments later he was back inside the family home.

He looked at the family busying themselves with their daily tasks. His Mother washing some big red tomatoes, his brother Mo trying to connect his laptop with the internet - usual stuff - little did they know that their future rested on the success of his jihad to London. He began to feel overwhelmed by it all and took himself straight back to his room, where, in the dark, he lay down and stared at the ceiling. What have I got myself into, he asked himself and more importantly, is there any way out? Once again, he did not expect to sleep that night.

16

Clive had sent a long text to Winston explaining how his sister Kaylah wanted to come into London with them, perhaps go to a club, something relaxing. That first evening didn't work out, Winston had cried off, saying his Mom was not well. The following week, once again nothing had transpired even though Kaylah had asked twice and he'd passed on the messages to Winston. He supposed he could have just organised something without Winston, but he felt more comfortable about the three of them going out clubbing. So he waited.

About three weeks went by until one evening Winston had surprised him by instantly replying to his message text suggesting a night out, with the reply, 'Gr8. C U both 9pm outside your door.' Clive knew Kaylah would be pleased and simply forwarded Winston's message on to her. She in turn replied, 'will start getting ready as soon as I'm back from college.'

Clive didn't have much to do, so crashed out in his room, put his headphones on and lost himself in some music he'd had since school days. For longer than he cared to think about, he seemed to have little focus to his life, felt himself drifting, lethargic and certainly wanting to keep out of the way of his Dad. Dad was becoming more and more of an embarrassment. He didn't like the way he and Kaylah were seen by many of Mum and Dad's people as some kind of holy family, which Clive for his part utterly resented.

This can't go on, he said to himself. He was stuck between a raving charismatic churchman father and a best friend on the edge of, if not actually practising evil. What was Winston up to? What was he dragging him into? Where would it all end? What could he do with his life? With all the questions and the absence of any answers, Clive stepped up the volume and shut himself down in his make-believe music world. The empty hours would soon pass until Kaylah was back.

As good as his word, Winston in his blue Beamer drifted up Cheddington Road and pulled to a smooth halt at the front door. He didn't move, didn't toot a horn or anything. He knew they'd be watching and waiting for him. He thought he'd make an effort too and had pulled his best shiny black leather jacket and matching narrow-cut leather jeans out of the wardrobe for the occasion. An immaculate white Nike baseball cap was perched jauntily atop his head.

Sure enough they emerged from the house a second later. Winston greeted them with an ear to ear smile as they gazed in wonder at his outfit. Winston even got out of the car to open Kaylah's rear door. He could tell she liked that and Clive felt all the brotherly protection hackles begin to rise before they'd even left the street. He recognised that he really did care about his Sis.

The car's music went on, strangely some Motown to start with, but by the time they'd turned down the Great Cambridge Road, Winston had gone back to his favourite rap artist JME, his Grime Group bringing joy to his heart, his humour bringing laughter. They sped round the Roundway, overtaking a red double-decker London bus on a blind bend, much to the bus driver's annoyance; then swung left into Lordship Lane, and headed down Bruce Grove. They passed by Cliff's Cafe and then turning right were into Tottenham High Road heading south toward the city. Winston then made a surprise left turn and pulled up outside an apartment block.

'Give us five minutes,' he said, more a command than request, 'got a call I must make.'

He disappeared inside after using the door call system. It was nearer ten minutes before he reappeared and he was not alone.

'This is Dillon,' he said, as Dillon climbed in the back next to Kaylah.

Kaylah eyed the surprise new arrival with suspicion. This was not her area, and she didn't know this guy. Her instinct was he was bad news. He smelled of weed and he didn't look after himself, his teeth were brown round the gums and his eyes were watery. She began to get bad vibes about her plan for an evening out with Clive. Things were taking off in directions outside her control and this guy, Dillon, was well..., she already knew he was no good. Clive seemed unaware of the fact and leant over from the front seat to chat.

'Hi, I'm Clive. How are you doing? This is a surprise. Fancy a night clubbing then?' he asked.

Dillon responded in a friendly enough manner, but didn't mention the clubbing. Perhaps he's not coming with us, just having a lift, Kaylah wondered, her spirits lifting.

Soon they had passed through Stamford Hill, then Hackney, before heading for Islington. Finally they pulled up near Highbury and Islington tube station. Dillon showed no sign of leaving. Winston announced that there was a bit of a party going on at Sonia's flat and that 'we're all invited.' It was something of a relief to both Clive and Kaylah that there was something tangible happening and going to this stranger's party, one of Winston's many friends, no doubt, seemed a reasonable way to spend the evening.

'Perhaps we'll go clubbing later,' Winston half whispered into Kaylah's ear as she stepped out of the car.

Clive scowled at him for making such an obvious pass. They all got out, leaving the car on a double yellow and dived into a large three storey house in Petherton Road. There had been something like 20 doorbells at the entrance, but Winston had got them in straight away. They could hear the music upstairs and the three of them followed Winston's enthusiastic strides upstairs. Their feet echoed on the wooden boards and Kaylah's assessment was the whole place could have done with a lick of paint and probably a total refurbishment.

The top floor had three doors on the landing and the left-hand orange one was open invitingly. They strode in, the music now really quite loud. At least it was something you could dance to, Kaylah thought. There were three girls in tight skirts and clingy tops in the hallway, clutching drinks and giggling. The bright block colours of their outfits would look OK, thought Kaylah, if only they weren't standing next to each other. She nodded to them as she and the lads passed. It was good to make contact with the other girls. She couldn't think she would know anybody here and some effort at communication on her part was required. Security was in who you knew and being on your own patch and here she felt, well a little vulnerable, slightly uncomfortable, and not completely at ease.

A table had been stacked high with bottles and Winston yelled to them to help themselves, which they did. They now saw where the music was coming from. A young overweight guy with a purple mullet was perched on a three-legged stool playing the part of DJ, clutching a fist full of cables and with an open laptop displaying his playlist. He was so into his music, Kaylah couldn't think he'd even noticed they'd come into the room.

Moments later Kaylah had seen all there was to see and she couldn't think the evening was going to go well. The flat was tiny, there was no space to turn round in, let alone dance and of the half dozen or so people leaning on walls some chatting to one another, there hadn't been the slightest glimmer of connection. Kaylah began to think that maybe the night out idea was not such a good one. Then she thought of Clive and made an effort to strike up a conversation above the music.

'Been here before?' she asked.

'Nah,' said Clive.

'Has Winston talked about this place?' she followed up.

'Nah,' Clive said dismissively.

This conversation was not going anywhere and even the little there was, was brought to an abrupt halt when Winston grabbed Clive by the arm and led him toward the kitchen. When Kaylah tried to follow, Dillon stood between them and she had to watch helplessly as the kitchen door shut. Some private conversation to which she was not invited was no doubt about to take place. Her indignation rose, the more so at Dillon's behaviour. How dare he treat her like this? However, before she could remonstrate verbally, Dillon as cool as you like spoke to her.

100

'Winston said you like to dance. Let's dance, you and me,' he said, getting much too close.

Against her better judgement and telling herself she really had no choice, she unenthusiastically moved toward the centre of the floor and the two began to gyrate in time to a piece of blues. She didn't like the way Dillon kept looking at her. Was she meat? How could she escape this repulsive man, she asked herself. The one dance ran into two, then three and each time she felt Dillon moving nearer, closing in on her. She could smell his fetid breath and feel the hot warmth from his body. He seemed high on something, more so than when they'd picked him up. She desperately needed a way out of here. Where was Clive all this time? she asked herself.

Clive was surprised to be taken away from Kaylah, but when he saw Dillon moving in as he was smoothly ushered into the kitchen he interpreted that positively, thinking he would look after her whilst Winston and he were gone. My, how things work out, he thought. There was he, worrying Winston would move in on his Sis, and Dillon's the guy to watch. In that moment he forgot about Kaylah and turned his attention to the group round the kitchen table.

There were two empty chairs and they sat down. The flat felt more like a squat than someone's home, not the best venue for a party he'd ever been to, he told himself. Clive knew the moment he saw the fellas this was a serious set of hard-nosed people. Time to focus. He knew he had to simply do what he was told. Even Winston seemed unusually deferential.

The guy opposite introduced himself as Will Williams and said, 'me and the brothers have heard you two guys are cool. You drive a good set of wheels,' he said, nodding at Winston, 'you don't mess up and you, yes you brother,' he then looked straight at Clive, 'you have a clean record, you're a squeaky-clean virgin, whom the good Lord has blessed with goodness since the day he was born.'

Will growled a chuckle. Clive felt really uncomfortable, this menacing guy seemed to have been spying on him. He shot Winston a glance wondering whether Winston had been spilling the beans. He must have.

'You two guys are just who we've been looking for and after the help you've given us in north London with the delivery runs, you've proved yourselves ready to graduate and do a decent day's work for a decent day's pay,' said Will.

He paused to look round at his friends, his bald head with some kind of shine to it reflecting the white light of the long-life bulb immediately above his head. Winston made as if to object.

'Only came over 'cus I heard there was a party, just the driver for my mate Clive and his Sis,' Winston said meekly.

'No such thing as a free meal Win-ston, stay sat down whilst I tell you what's what,' Will ordered putting a restraining hand on Winston's shoulder.

Winston knew better than to argue. He had better be compliant or else, thought Clive, quickly wising up to the situation.

'I've a sister who works in the South Tottenham Post Office in Seven Sisters Road and she says that Mondays are a big day for her. The Group 4 truck delivers all the pension and benefit money on Mondays. She says they are a tad careless. She says they wouldn't miss a bag of money if someone were to help themselves. She says she'll help us. Now Dillon tells me,' he threw his thumb in the direction of the other room, 'Dillon tells me, when he came to see me this afternoon, you two guys are good at picking up and dropping off the odd bag of stuff,' said Will.

The pressure was on and Clive felt it. He felt trapped and looking at Winston he could see he was feeling the pressure too.

Clive suddenly recognised the guy sitting silently next to him was the hoodie man who made the black sports bag exchange. This was 'Woody the Hoodie' as Winston called him. Now what was he getting himself into here? he thought. Will continued to speak.

'My Sis says she is ever so willing to help us because the window to the street next to her Post Office desk opens wide enough for her to hand out a bag to anyone standing outside. Now, knowing how you Winston like to drive by and you, Clive, like to do the exchange, me and my friends here, are setting up the perfect little lifting and picking job for you two to maximise your talents. Like I say, you are about to graduate in Will's school of life,' he said, now placing his other hand on Clive's shoulder. He had both Winston and Clive under his thumb.

'Dosh deliveries are every Monday, but on the first Monday of the month there is an extra large delivery and one bag is filled with £100,000, all in bank notes. Naturally, my Sis says the first Monday of the month is the day when she would prefer to hand a bag out the window to her friends. In fact I've been so good to her, providing her with what she needs, she says she wants to be able to repay me. So listen here. You like your smart black and white clothes and your blue car, Winston; and you, Clive, you like your goody-two-shoes family and your let's go to a party sister. If you want a future, then on the first Monday in September you'll listen to what Wise Will says and collect another bag for him. The job is easy, you won't fail; and you will find that where there's a Will there's a way!' he said, rocking both of them toward each other, the puppet master in control of his own.

He leaned back and smiled at them a slimy, threatening, you do what I say, kind of smile. Will went on to tell them where exactly the Post Office was and which window the drop would be made from. Although the times of cash delivery were varied for security, Post Office staff didn't start early and so deliveries always happened between 8.30 and 9am as the cash had to be prepared quickly, ready for the first customers coming in once the Post Office opened to the public.

So much for security thought Clive. Winston was going to have to find a suitable place to loiter with his engine ticking over and then make his advance once he saw the window open. The box would be dropped to the pavement five feet below precisely 30 seconds later. Their job, Clive's job, was to scoop up the money bag and deliver it to an address they would be given. Clive noted Will had carefully ensured he himself wasn't personally directly linked to the proposed crime. He was masterminding this whole thing at a distance. Clive couldn't yet see an escape from all this. Then Will began to explain why all this was necessary.

'Once business in north London was straightforward, but now with so many gangsters from abroad muscling in, it's hard for the original hard-working Londoners to make a living. The immigration policy in this country is all wrong. I never thought I'd say it, but these days even Will is thinking of supporting the English Defence League! Once we were able to buy and sell our stuff without troubling anyone, but now even in your neighbourhood, Edmonton, we have Arab guys with Middle East contacts dealing with drugs and guns and making life difficult for us, right here in our own back yard. They need to go back to where they came from. Bottom line is, we need a bit more equity, a bit more cash to keep ourselves at the head of the game, to buy a couple of shooters to even things up a bit; and, you two guys are going to be helping your north London black brothers to a happier future and for this we will be truly grateful,' continued Will, very much in charge.

'One final thing. I don't do failure,' he added, and taking a long knife from his trouser pocket, he spun the weapon on the formica table top with practised ease just so it stopped spinning with the point in Clive's direction. 'Off you go boys, enjoy yourselves, the party's on me!' he suddenly said smiling again, terminating the meeting as abruptly as it had begun.

With that Winston and Clive were ushered out of the kitchen, only to be confronted by loud banging and shouts from outside the flat.

'Police, Police, come out one by one with your hands on your heads,' voice shouted.

It was a raid. Eight blue clad, perspex-helmeted officers brandishing truncheons and spray canisters burst into the already crowded tiny flat. Out of the corner of his eye, Clive spotted Will back in the kitchen placing his shiny metal blade on to the outside window sill, sliding shut the window once he had done so. This guy was sharp.

Kaylah was pleased there had been a police raid. It had halted Dillon's unwelcome advances in their tracks. The raid was exciting, something she'd heard about but never experienced before. This was something she could tell her friends at college about later. They'd been present at such things and now she could hold up her head as they compared notes. She had nothing to fear, she was innocent and, as she soon found out, none of the police officers was rough with her. They weren't interested in her, they were after bigger fish.

It was all over very quickly. Once all had given their names and the officers had checked everyone for illicit substances, disappointingly for them only finding sufficient for personal use, they suggested everyone go home, adding, 'the music's disturbing the neighbours.' One girl, wearing a leopard skin top insisted on staying, claiming the flat was hers.

Once in the fresh air of the street, Winston reached his car to find a ticket on his windscreen. He screwed it up and dropped it in the gutter.

'Let's go,' he said, as Kaylah, Clive and Dillon climbed back inside the Beamer.

Thankfully, so far as Kaylah was concerned, Dillon was dropped off in Hackney. 'Have some business to see to,' were his parting words, 'see you around Kaylah. Get Winston to drop you at my place in Muswell Hill. Let Dillon give you a good time,' he offered from the pavement. Kaylah grabbed the car door handle to pull it firmly shut.

'Suppose we go to Cliff's Cafe,' Winston said, 'we've got some thinking to do.'

Strangely, Winston never put on his music this time and the short journey to Bruce Grove and Cliff's passed in almost total silence. Clive was wearing a far-away expression which Kaylah just couldn't read, but it deeply concerned her. It was a weird night, only just after eleven, the night was still young. The long midsummer evenings meant there was still a hint of light in the sky as they swung the car off the road into the lights of Cliff's Cafe. They had a lot to chew over.

17

Adam had been cycling for a month. He felt supremely fit. His self-confidence at his own mastery of the cycle ride had grown with the miles, despite the few navigational failings which had never been too bad to count as a disaster. Turkey felt very different to the countries further west, it was Muslim, Eastern, the relic of a once great Ottoman Empire. It oozed a very different history in its pores beneath a superficial western air. Negotiating his way in Istanbul was a challenge, but its people proved helpful and places to stay the night were easy to find and really, really cheap. He'd not yet had to touch the Euros his parents had given him, having in mind to save them to buy something special at the end of the ride, perhaps to get a memento of some sort, though at this point he had no idea what. He thought he might get Mum and Dad something too.

Thinking about home and his parents unsettled him. He found himself feeling uncharacteristically emotional. Admitting to himself he missed them, he realised he missed his friends too. He'd never been so far, so long, from those around him; and in the moment, he realised for the first time he was incredibly lonely. The journey he had set himself was not just one of miles, but about finding independence and that journey, just now, was inwardly proving its most challenging. Only by going over how far he had come, reflecting on what he had achieved, could he begin to reassure himself and find some composure, some calm, some personal sense of security once again.

He passed a Starbucks Metropole and a Pizza Hut which felt slightly odd, out of place and yet reassuring at the same time. He didn't want to go inside somewhere so western and cycled on, all the time getting nearer the Bosphorous. He spotted a corner cafe with Wi-Fi. It had an unpronounceable Turkish name, but instinctively it appealed, there were people inside and he pulled off the road.

Locking up his bike outside the window where he could keep an eye on it, he pushed open the glass door. Lucky so far, he'd not once lost anything and the bike itself had stood up to the journey well, that is regular punctures aside, but then he'd expected those. He'd got to be quite adept at getting punctures quickly repaired at the roadside.

Much to his surprise, the cafe looked pretty international inside. There were lots of younger people of different nationalities, but there were still spare places to be had and the cool air conditioning was a delight after the furnace outside. He ordered a Turkish coffee, a honey cake, and some cold water to go with it. When the coffee arrived it was sweet and very strong and the water thick with ice and topped with lemon. He enjoyed having a polite conversation with the waitress, a friendly albeit superficial conversation with another person. Thinking he was another tourist she tried to tell him the places he must see whilst he was in Istanbul.

As he sipped the hot liquid, he plugged in his phone, checked Facebook and laughed at his friends holiday frolics on a Majorcan beach. Just looking at what they were up to made him feel better. After posting a quick selfie from the cafe, he tapped into his email account and composed what he thought would be a quick email home, his latest travel bulletin of reassuring detail that he knew his parents would be glad to receive. He'd sent them a message almost every day in the early days of his cycle, but he realised as soon as he logged in that he hadn't written home for almost two weeks.

Oh well, they'll be glad to get this one, he thought. He'd managed to take another reasonable selfie, one taken earlier outside the Blue Mosque which he thought would appeal more to them and added that to a paragraph of text. Looking at the picture again, he was pleased to have got the bike in the shot. He realised as he looked at the photo that he now looked sun tanned and perhaps thinner than when he had set out. His face too had the rough stubble of a new beard and his black hair, longer than before, was sticking out from beneath his cycle helmet. I'll get it cut when I get back, he thought.

107

All this took quite a while and the email wouldn't send for some time, so he ended up using almost an hour of his time anchored to a metal chair, the coffee long since finished. From time to time he cast occasional sideways glances to see his bike was still secure. The email finally sent, he spent his remaining minutes taking the opportunity the Wi-Fi afforded to enable him to catch up on the news both at home and in Turkey.

There was some BBC News report about traffic jams on the motorways at the start of school holidays; and IS continuing to pose a threat in some countries, but he couldn't see Turkey in the list of Foreign Office places not to visit. In fact the rest of the news seemed pretty much what he'd expect to see, Wimbledon tennis championships over for another year, a Cricket Test Match about to start; in France the Tour de France well under way. Hmm, he thought, they'll be going a lot faster than me, but they won't have covered nearly the distance. It must be great cycling as part of a pelaton, a back-up crew ready to help with every puncture and meal.

The time connecting with back home and events elsewhere reminded him of the loneliness he was currently feeling in being on the road. This was the first time he had done something just by himself. It had been something he had long wanted to try, but today, he knew he much preferred the company of others, though right up until now he realised he hadn't found being alone too bad. He smiled at the thought that he had succeeded in putting up with just his own company these past weeks. He told himself it wouldn't be long until he'd be back with everyone, it wasn't so bad. Switching his mobile off, he unplugged it, went over and paid for his coffee, cake and water and returned to his bike. The heat hit him as if he'd opened a fan oven door.

He remembered there was something else he needed to do before leaving Istanbul. It had proved impossible to pick up maps of eastern Turkey in London. It was as if this next stage of his ride east were that bit too far off the tourist trail and no-one back home sold enough maps this far east to make it worthwhile to stock them, but here in Istanbul surely he should be able to find what he needed.

Adam asked a couple of passers by and was eventually given directions to a promising shop a couple of streets away, an old place, he was told, in a row of shops, the second one along, a book and map shop. He unlocked his bike and rather than ride, wheeled it along the pavement. It was heavy and unwieldy this way, the panniers front and back making it difficult to balance, so much easier to handle when being ridden.

Minutes later he guessed he was outside the right shop with its peeling green paint and dusty canvas awning. He fastened his bike to the railings running either side of the door, thankfully in the shade; and disappeared into the shop's dark interior.

A short young man, sporting a thinly-sprouting moustache and attired in a suit despite the heat, immediately found what he was looking for. Adam had got used to people knowing he was English, though occasionally they thought he was German.

As the assistant unfolded the map to show him the area it covered, Adam realised that getting the right map had proved easier to obtain than envisaged, the assistant speaking English surprisingly well. However, even though the conversation flowed, he felt he was being eyed suspiciously and after some hesitation, the shop assistant began to ask why he wanted the map. This wasn't just curiosity, it was as if the map would allow Adam to intrude on some private agenda, the part of Turkey that Tourists weren't supposed to go to.

Adam tried to explain in as relaxed a way as he could, how he had cycled from London, across Europe and was about to complete the last leg of his journey before returning home and to university. The young assistant didn't seem impressed.

At this point an older man, sorting books from a cardboard box, grunted disapprovingly at the young man on the desk. He had been watching the transaction unfold. Clearly the senior person there, he nodded vigorously toward the till indicating that he was wanting the assistant to see a sale made and not missed.

The young man took the hint, asked Adam for 15 Euros and started to gift wrap the map in white tissue paper. At this, Adam explained that it wasn't necessary for it to be wrapped and taking the map from the beginning of the parcel being assembled on the wooden counter top, he thanked the assistant for his help, left the premises quickly and returned to his bike.

Before heading off he paused to open his new map again, this time in the shade of the shop's awning and marvelled at how big eastern Turkey was. Goodness, he thought, such a long journey still lay ahead. More than a few days cycling, a week at least, maybe more, lay ahead, before he would arrive at the Iranian border; and then, a straight road across the desert down to Tehran and his flight home.

It seemed strange looking at the paper delineating the final days of his ride east. All too soon the adventure would be over and for the first time he began thinking of the stories and fun he would have meeting up with friends again to chat about what they had all been doing over the summer.

Ending the ride was not a thought he was entirely ready to relish, his adventure still having days to run and he now felt impatient to get into it and leave Istanbul behind him. He began quickly folding away his map, the route for the next few miles of his journey now clear in his mind.

Happening to glance up as he slid the into his front pannier, he noticed two guys opposite watching him. He knew it to be so, for the two men looked away all too quickly when he gazed in their direction. It made him feel uncomfortable, a little vulnerable, targeted even.

He quickly finished putting his map away and firmly closed his front handlebar bag. What were they up to? he wondered. Perhaps being away from the main thoroughfare had made him a target for opportunistic thieves, it could be they wanted to steal his bike. Well, he thought, they'd have had to be quick if they wanted to catch him.

Determinedly, he unlocked his bike, pulled it away from the railings, swung his leg over the cross bar, clicked his cleats securely in place as he moved off, this time pumping the pedals hard in a low gear to swiftly build up speed.

As he moved down street after street in the busy traffic, he realised how polluted the city air had become, cars, lorries and buses poisoning every breath with their black fumes. He pressed on, breathing hard and unavoidably taking in the poisonous clouds of diesel smoke as he did so.

Within ten minutes he was reasonably certain he must have lost the two guys. He tried to tell himself it was nothing and hoped he could soon slow down. It was hot and he was sweating already in the afternoon sun.

Easing back the power to the pedals a little to regain his breath and recover from his exertions, it took him a while to get into his normal cycling rhythm. He pushed himself on, winding in the kilometres, wanting to put himself well into the outskirts of Eastern Istanbul before finding somewhere to stay by nightfall.

Though he'd looked round more than once and seen no-one, the uncomfortable sense of being spied on never entirely left him. He felt on edge. Irrational though it might be, he wanted to be absolutely certain he'd put those two Arabic looking guys well behind him, but he kept seeing them in his mind's eye. Being on one's own was fine, he told himself, but could he be getting paranoid?

Thinking again of the absence of friends whose presence for the first time he would have much appreciated, feeling a little anxious, he told himself to take control, it was time to relax, he ought to just chill out and enjoy the ride east. After all, nothing had gone wrong hitherto and all would be well.

He felt the hot breeze on his face, the comforting rhythmic turn of the pedals driving him ever forward. As each kilometre passed he tried to convince the anxious part of his mind that life didn't get much better than this. But for some reason he couldn't explain to himself, he didn't quite believe it.

18

The worst part of his cycle ride was the big cities, their endless suburbs and busy roads; and Istanbul was no different. So it was with some relief that over the coming days he found himself on quieter roads, albeit these were often hilly roads, even mountainous roads or gorges with steep sides, sometimes dried up stream beds and many, many, dusty villages.

At this time of summer the vegetation seemed to be just hanging on for a lucky thunderstorm or autumn rain. Human settlement was becoming more sparse and gathered into what felt like eternally unchanged rural communities, often strung out along his road necklace like, usually with a sort of square to mark the centre, almost always having a place to pull up and grab some water.

After the diesel fumes of Istanbul and the heat-reflecting concrete, this rural landscape made for an altogether much more enjoyable ride. Villages often had some roadside cafe for refreshment and people were so much more friendly than their urban counterparts. Indeed he began to see a level of generous hospitality toward him as a total stranger that he'd been quite unaccustomed to in Western Europe. Maybe the recent end of Ramadan with all its restrictions helped as people now seemed more cheerful and even festive. He'd noticed how there were far fewer European-looking faces east of Istanbul. It was as if he'd left the West behind him.

On more than one occasion, people who met him in a shop or at a roadside halt would invite him back to their house or village to share a meal or kebab BBQ, pressing him to have some of their food and meet their families before allowing him to travel on. Often, as he left, they would make him take with him some bread, hard cheese, grapes or figs. How could he refuse? He truly felt that the best part of his journey was right now. New friends were not old friends, but he felt accepted and genuinely welcomed.

It was hot, so hot the black Tarmac was soft under his cycle tyres and the light searingly white bright, so he measured his rides carefully, avoiding the worst heat of the day by setting out early in the morning and trying to find somewhere to stay before the sun was at its height; and he always ensured he carried plenty of water in spite of its added weight.

A room to stay in cost so little. For a Euro a night he had done well, even once being provided with a clothes wash service thrown in, a basic drying line strung out for him in his room, his refreshed cycling gear ready for him by the time he hit the road at dawn the following morning.

Yes, there were unsettling moments and, in some of the villages, some strange people who back home would be medicated or kept indoors by caring relations. There was one odd man with cuts on his arms and face, wearing a torn shalmar kameez and battered fez who had run after him waving a stick, not really posing any threat and without a hope of catching him, but not something he could ever recall seeing back in Muswell Hill. Even Jimmy in his duffel coat or Lil with her trolley were, by comparison, really quite civilised. The neighbours of the man with the fez seemed to just accept him for who he was, giving Adam a knowing shrug as if to say, 'he's our village 'oddo''. What was strange was that every village seemed to have its own version of the man or woman in the fez. Spotting the mentally ill before they eyeballed him became a new hobby as he pulled into each new habitation.

As the days passed and Istanbul was but another distant memory of yet one more city he'd visited, he began to notice the character of the area changing. There were more Turkish military vehicles and convoys on the road. He never liked to see the military who made little attempt to hide the weapons they were carrying and definitely didn't move over much for a cyclist. They were always there, passing him or waiting at the road-side, but there was never any communication with him, sometimes a dismissive or even a curious glance, but never a word. They seemed to endlessly patrol the roads he was on now. The raw edge of the state-sanctioned killing machine seemed to be only a trigger pull away and his own mood began to darken the more military he saw.

There were also increasing signs that Kurdish sympathies were strong, as graffiti on walls and houses, made clear the ongoing battle for a free Kurdistan was where local sympathies lay. Vivid aerosol scripts and base images showed the contempt in which the Turkish 'occupiers' were held. He detected and felt, with each mile he travelled, he was entering a more conflicted world in this mountainous dusty terrain, a conflict he had not fully anticipated. It made him feel increasingly on edge.

He began to ask himself if he really belonged here. Wasn't he just intruding on someone else's private grief? Maybe all this was why he'd been quizzed when buying his map in Istanbul. The feelings of loneliness he had had were now accompanied by a growing anxiety for his own safety in an area where he had no idea what the real issues surrounding local conflict were all about. He feared he might inadvertently cycle right into the middle of a fire fight. Who, he wondered, is the 'oddo' here if it isn't me?

It was past midday, and he was well east of Ankara, probably over half way to Erzurum, the next big city and looking forward to getting to the next village in the hope of finding somewhere for the night. It had been a particularly hard cycle with long uphill mountain stretches and very little respite. His legs ached and his throat was parched.

At last he spied what he was looking for up ahead and a road sign indicated he was entering the village of Zara. It was a typical village, but bigger, more a small town, with dry dusty mountains around. The road had been getting more mountainous and he knew there were some tough, long, stretches ahead before he got to the Iranian border.

On the outskirts of Zara there was a petrol station, its elliptical red neon sign advertising its presence many minutes before he would actually arrive. He aimed for it, knowing he'd be able to get chilled water before he began his now routine early afternoon search for something to eat later and somewhere to stay that evening.

He didn't normally give the occasional whoosh of a passing car a second thought, but as he slowed, he heard a car coming up behind and, rather than overtake him, the engine noise slowed as if it were reluctant to do so. Indeed, it followed him on to the garage forecourt.

Turning his head, he observed a rather old, once white, VW Golf pull up by the pumps and a lean young man in jeans and white T shirt climb out and begin to fuel up. He had long dark hair held in place, but not really controlled, by a black bandana. Adam's gaze meant they exchanged glances, almost a greeting.

Adam leaned his bike up against the small kiosk shop with the usual range of confectionary, news and magazines, as well as rows of multi-coloured chilled drinks in a cooler display. He grabbed a couple of bottles of water, checking they were properly chilled before going inside to pay.

The woman behind the counter gave him a contemptuous look as if to say he ought to have spent more. Adam returned to his bike. As he went to put one of the bottles into his pannier and drink from the other, he noticed his back tyre had gone flat. Strange, he thought, it must have happened suddenly on the forecourt. He was certain all had been well until then. Anyway, he reasoned, it wasn't such a bad place to have to make a repair.

He reached inside his pannier for his cycle repair kit, feeling for it by touch in the dark interior, thinking to himself how very hot the interior of the bag was. He'd just got the white plastic box in his hand, was opening it to grab the two metal tyre leavers, when the young guy with the Golf came outside the kiosk, having paid for his fuel. He walked across and stopped to chat, leaning casually on the free air machine, taking care to position himself in the shade as Adam had done.

'Got a problem?' he asked. Adam had found Turkish people invariably friendly and wanting to talk. Often they thought he was German, but this young guy had correctly taken him for an Englishman.

'Not really, I'll have it fixed in less than ten minutes.' His English is good, thought Adam, wondering where he'd learnt it.

'Where are you headed?'

'I'm riding east, Iran soon, then fly home from Tehran,' said Adam.

'Where's home then? Is it a long way from here?'

'London actually, and it is a long way from here on a bike!' Adam told him.

'You mean, you cycled from London? All that way. Wow! I'm full of admiration. Me, I have a bike, but me and my brother, we've never cycled further than the next village. That's amazing! I'm just full of respect for what you've achieved. Have you done it alone? All by yourself? Bet you've got some stories to tell. When did you leave England?' said the guy enthusiastically and obviously in no hurry to leave.

'Mid-June, five, no six weeks ago now, and yes, I've cycled alone. It's been fine, really, just fine,' said Adam.

'Hey, my family would love to meet you. Have you got somewhere fixed for tonight?' He paused, before adding, 'I'll take that to be a no. My family are having a bit of a party, call it an extended Eid family celebration. Everyone's welcome. You must come as my guest. Our home's here in this village, literally half a mile away. I won't take no for an answer.'

He grinned. Adam looked up from his wheel. This guy wasn't going anywhere. From his front shirt pocket he pulled out a pack of cigarettes, half-offered one to Adam, rightly knowing Adam would refuse.

'Guess not,' he said, as he put his pack back in his pocket and lit up. Cigarettes on petrol station forecourts seemed to be allowed here then, Adam thought.

By this time, Adam was pretty well done on the puncture. An odd one this, a sidewall blow out as if something had sliced into the tyre. He couldn't recall clipping a curb or a bottle, but these things happened. The job was done and taking his small but efficient pump from the bike frame, he started putting some air back into the tyre, a little at a time, watching carefully to see the inflating tyre was seating on the rim correctly. It was, and he continued pumping. An invitation to dinner tonight, he was tempted. The guy seemed OK, if a little pushy.

'Tell you what,' he said, 'You just follow me, I'll drive slowly. You'll love it, you really will. My Mum and sisters are great cooks, you must taste authentic local cuisine, our lamb kebabs in the outdoors are irresistible. It'll be really relaxed. Look, you won't be the only visitor and we'll put you up in the barn and set you off on your way first thing in the morning. That's if you can move after the kisir and goat and dates and apricots and all that goes with them,' he persisted.

This guy's a real motormouth, thought Adam, no stopping him, it'll be hard to refuse.

'You should taste the lemonade my uncle makes with his own lemons, and between you and me, we have a few beers - now you won't find that anywhere else round here will you?' he grinned.

'OK, I give in,' said Adam. 'Puncture's fixed, let me pack these away and I'll be on your tail. Just keep your speed down and give me space to brake, the bike's so heavily loaded it won't stop quickly.'

'The name's Yusuf,' he said offering his hand, 'what's yours?'

'Adam, Adam Taylor,' he replied, pleased to have company. 'Let's go then, and thank you. I'm really grateful. Do I need to pick up anything to bring?' He nodded in the direction of the garage shop.

'No, no, no - just come. I'll just call them to say we're on our way,' he said, as he pulled his mobile out of his back pocket and began walking back to his car.

He was chatting away, but turned to check Adam was set and called out a parting comment.

'Think nothing of it. Let's hit the road!' He skipped the remaining steps to his Golf, started the engine and led them both off the forecourt along what was a longer road than Adam had anticipated.

Adam could see Yusuf never stopped talking, his mobile pressed to his ear as he drove, steering and gear-changing with just the one hand. He found himself pedalling harder than he might normally have done, but they both slowed as they entered the village centre.

Every now and then Yusuf would very obviously glance in his rear view mirror and throw a reassuring wave. There was a sharp right and a left and half a mile of scattered reddish brick houses and then they swung through a gate into what looked like any one of the ubiquitous farm courtyards he'd passed many times before.

He spotted a secure looking barn with a stout door and wondered if that would be where he'd be sleeping. He made a mental note of the route back to the main road so that he could make a good start in the morning. There was a big, scruffy, black and white farmyard dog which barked nonchalantly to show he'd done his guard duty, but then settled down again almost immediately, the late afternoon heat probably sapping the dog's energy as much as his.

Yusuf pulled up next to the front door behind a yellowed and rusty van. He leapt out and waved Adam over to the barn.

'Here,' he shouted, 'drop your bike in here.'

He had to wrestle with the old sliding bolt to get the door open. Inside it was dark with the warm inviting smell of cut hay. Adam rolled his bike round to the left and leant it on the wall, putting his cycle helmet over the seat before swiftly emerging again into the bright sunshine.

'Follow me,' said Yusuf, beckoning keenly with his hands.

They crossed back over to the farmhouse and walked straight in. There was the smell of a wood fire or stove, the clatter of pans or baking tins and Adam spotted a couple of women of indeterminate years bending over what looked like a bread oven. He waved and said 'hello' but there was little response.

Yusuf muttered something in Turkish to them and got a kind of grunt by way of acknowledgment. He was surprised they didn't really lift their heads, offer a greeting, or even

118

show any curiosity at their western guest. It seemed quieter than he had been led to expect, but then it was early yet, he told himself.

'Adam, you can use this room to freshen up. The towel on the back of the door is for you, then come and join me in the courtyard. I'll get the iced lemonade. No rush my friend, take your time, we've hours before dinner,' said Yusuf, looking quite at home.

The room was pretty sparse, an old wooden table, a wash-stand with a water stand-pipe and jug. It had an old stone floor and the grey breeze block walls were crudely cemented. The towel was hanging on a rusty nail on the back of the door. There was a latrine bucket and toilet roll suspended by a piece of old fence wire. A freshen up wouldn't take long in here, Adam mused. He noticed there was no sign of electricity in this room, just a shelf to one side, maybe for an oil lamp or candle.

Minutes later he walked back through, passed the two women who barely seemed to notice him, flour dust powdering the air around them in white clouds as they hastened to knock the pitta bread into shape and get it baked. Hot work, he thought.

Three lemonades were on the veranda table. Yusuf had been joined by a larger, slightly older man, with big swarthy hands and a weatherworn face.

'Meet my cousin Stefan,' he said, 'just in from the fields. We have to get the sheep in for the night here. Look, they're over there, by the far wall.' Yusuf pointed toward a dozen or so scrawny looking leggy sheep.

Adam offered his hand to this giant of a man, who looked most unlike his cousin Yusuf.

'Me, Stefan,' was all he said, and crushed Adam's hand in his for what Adam took to be a welcome. There was no smile from Stefan. Adam was beginning to wonder if Yusuf would be the only cheerful guy at the party.

The lemonade was excellent and a cool jug, covered with condensation on coming out of a fridge somewhere, appeared to replenish supplies. So they must have electricity,

Adam thought. Then he heard the distinct sound of an electric generator somewhere over by the house. That'll be it, he concluded, as he took another sip of refreshing lemonade.

'How long have your family lived here?' he asked, trying to be sociable.

'Generations, since the time of Saladin, or so the story goes, though this isn't the original house,' said Yusuf.

He poured Adam more lemonade from the jug as he spoke.

'For my part I'm a newcomer. The extended family here only took me in when I came to college. That was four years ago when I started my English language course. My ambition is to become a tour guide. The money's not bad for tour guides and we have such a rich cultural heritage in this country. Muslims lived here under the Ottoman Caliphate for many hundreds of years, a vast empire it was, ruling over large parts of Africa, the Middle East and even Europe. Their history is all around us.'

Yusuf could well become a tour guide, he'd be able to talk for Turkey, thought Adam. He had never found history easy to concentrate on and this evening was no different. Yusuf was going on and on, and he was feeling so incredibly tired. Tired, like never before. Fight it. Fight it, he told himself, but embarrassingly, he was finding he couldn't speak, even to excuse himself. The hum of Yusuf's voice was becoming ever more distant, the light dimming.

'Sorry,' he tried to say, and that was the last thing he could do as he felt himself slipping down from the chair and on to the floor, and then he had gone, he was out of it, gone, completely gone.

The darkness was intense, the floor hard under the thin spread of hay, his head hurting so much he could hardly gather his thoughts. Where was he? Something must have disagreed with him. He remembered the lemonade, the first glass sweet and fresh, the second less so and cold, very cold, and then he'd fainted, he must have done.

Where had they put him? He must have been out cold for ages, for it was now so dark. It was then he began to feel anxious and he tried to kick-start his mind, to appraise his situation more carefully, to deal with his rising sense of foreboding and alarm. He had the unsettling sense, a feeling he couldn't yet rationalise, that things were far from quite right.

First, a quick check, to see if he was hurt. No problem there. He was beginning to feel reassured. His body was OK: but why was it so dark and why did his head hurt so, like the worst of all hangovers?

Then he remembered the barn and he thought Yusuf must have laid him down in the barn thinking he was tired and left him to sleep off whatever it was, that was it. He felt the stone wall to his side and could make out the light boundaries framing the wooden door and he pulled himself to his feet. His bike would be to his right. Groping like a blind man, he found it was; he reached across and flicked on his bike light. Yes, he was in the barn, safe and secure. He looked round for his cycle jacket. It wasn't there, maybe they'd hung it up or did he leave it on the veranda? That was funny, his watch had gone from his wrist, how annoying.

Adam reached for the circular iron hook that was the only handle, turned and pushed. He leant harder. Nothing moved. He thought it must be stiff and gave it as big a shove as he could muster. It felt like it was fastened on the other side and he remembered the iron bolts. That's when he yelled.

'Yusuf! Yusuf!' he called.

There was no response and he thought he would have a look around for another way out, maybe a window or a hay loft balcony, anything. But it was hopeless, nothing; and, despite several more calls as loud as he could make them, there was still no reply. This is stupid, he told himself. Obviously they can't hear me. I'll just have to be patient and collect myself.

Frustration began to build as fear too began to eat into him. He pressed his ear to the door to see if he could hear any sounds, and there was nothing. Had they abandoned him and gone off somewhere? It slowly began to dawn on Adam that there was a possibility he was in serious trouble, but he couldn't quite bring himself to believe it, though with every passing minute he suspected it to be true.

What may have been as long as a couple of hours passed until Adam heard the sound of a vehicle start up, which could have been the old van in the yard. Its engine noise increased and it seemed to drive over from the house to pull up by the barn. Moments later he heard footsteps approaching. At last, he thought, the promise of relief and the possibility of release. He called out just as the bolts slid back and the door was pulled open.

It was dark outside but as his eyes grew accustomed to the night he could see the yellow van had been moved across the dusty courtyard with its open rear doors now facing the barn. Yusuf was sitting in the passenger seat leaning out of the window looking toward him. Adam called his name, but at that moment Stefan suddenly grabbed him from the side in one of his burly arms, as his other arm slid a sack over Adam's head and upper body. A cord tightened around his hands and waist.

'Be quiet, little kuffar, if you know what is good for you,' Yusuf instructed from the front of the van in a tone quite different from his engaging manner of the previous evening. This change of persona brought its own terror.

It was still more night than dawn. Noise carried easily and if there was anyone about, Adam didn't see or hear anything. There was no sign of the women. The next instant Adam felt himself being thrown into the back of the van, which he was. It was impossible to protect himself against the fall and he felt winded as a wheel arch crashed into his side. Then he heard the unmistakeable sound of his bike being wheeled, the regular click of the wheel race bearings and then the clatter as it too was lifted into the back of the van beside him. He was terrified.

The doors were slammed shut and locked. He heard the handles being yanked to check; and then he heard Stefan walking away up the side of the van, moments later opening the driver's door and under his considerable weight, tilting the van as he climbed into the driver's seat beside Yusuf. He slammed his door shut after him, evidently not worried that someone might hear him. In the total darkness that smothered, suffocated and stifled him, Adam could hear words were being exchanged in the cab. They were just checking things out, he thought. Obviously all was well for them as the engine started up again and with a few bumps and lurches a journey into the unknown began.

'Where the fuck are they taking me? What will they do to me?' Adam murmured, trying to manage his overwhelming fear.

Helpless as a fly in a web, Adam could do nothing. He tried to think, he had to think, but his head still wasn't clear and it took all his concentration to keep himself from injury as the van noisily bumped along, throwing Adam from side to side as it took every corner. Even his bike had become his enemy as it kept poking and pressing into him, more sharp metallic edges than he could count.

The sack he was in was old; there were holes, useful for breathing, but also to see just a little. No matter, he was trapped. He needed to think in terms of survival, only right now there was not one single thought that came to mind that was of any help in his situation. It was all he could do to cope with the rising levels of panic that came like surges threatened to overwhelm him.

A few minutes later he told himself to count the positives. Well, he could breathe, he could move slightly, he was still alive. Next minute he was afraid, very afraid. He'd been such a naive idiot.

His mind went back to the garage forecourt. 'Idiot,' he said to himself again and again as he thought about the puncture, which was, with hindsight, nothing less than a knife taken to his tyre wall. What did they want? If to rob him, they'd done that, his jacket had gone. If to make him some sort of slave, no, not that. Or maybe as in one film, set in Morocco had shown, to sell his living donor body parts to the highest paying bidders who would pay handsomely to have good quality organs extracted. Even now they could be on

123

their way to some back room operating theatre. He felt wet with fear.

He quickly told himself he was being stupid, his imagination simply running away with him. No, he was a hostage and a price would have to be paid and everyone says kidnap situations usually end up OK. Terror grabbed him again making him sweat more as he thought of bits of his body being cut off to ensure the hostage ransom would be paid.

Dismissing his dark thoughts, he tried to start making a mental note of their direction and the distance travelled. He'd got quite good at judging these things after so long navigating his way here. Taking control, occupying his mind positively, even in such a little thing as knowing the direction and distance might help overcome, distract him from, his fears. His mind played his pannier map in front of his eyes as he knew they had now pulled back on to the main road near the garage and were definitely heading east in the direction he would have taken without all this happening.

He levered himself up so his back was on the near side of the van, if there were any roadside drains or raises for turns he'd be better placed to pick up on them. He pushed himself up further and sat on the wheel arch that had so cruelly assaulted him earlier. They must have set off not long before dawn as now he could make out strips of light around the van doors. The van kept going with no let up. Now and then there was the whoosh of a passing vehicle. There were times when the van laboured, going down through all its gears to negotiate what was an increasingly mountainous terrain.

Definitely going east, said Adam to himself. No turnings off as far as he could tell, no stops, just mile after unrelenting mile. His bound wrists were now sore, the rope cutting into his skin, sufficiently tight to restrain him, but not loose enough that he could work them free even though he tried. He was now getting hot and very thirsty and this new worry for his health and well being began to occupy and take over all his thoughts.

Then the van began to slow, by which time Adam estimated that a journey east of some one hundred and forty miles had been covered if the van had averaged 35 mph which he reckoned was not unreasonable. His calculations were interrupted as there was a change, the van lurching right, then left, then reversing up. Adam began to feel tension building. Being a prisoner was one thing, but not knowing what might come next filled him with dread and foreboding. He could feel his armpits were as damp as the palms of his hands.

The doors swung open. The daylight was so intense, that even looking through the loose weave of the sacking made him screw up his eyes. They'd reversed against a wall. Very clever, thought Adam, so I can't see or be seen. Yusuf spoke first.

'Stay there,' he ordered.

Stefan heaved himself into the back. With a swift movement he undid the rope securing Adam's hands and pulled the sack off Adam's head. Dusty bits from the sacking filled the air and got into his eyes. His legs were pulled round, none too gently, so they overhung the back of the van.

'Say nothing,' he was told.

'Now drink this,' Yusuf instructed.

A plastic bottle of water was passed to him. He took it.

'We're not inhumane, but we won't be messed around with. We're to deliver you safely. In what condition is up to you. Now drink. If you need to pizz, then pizz against the wall,' said Yusuf.

Adam did as he was told, taking the opportunity that time for a pee would give him. Though he couldn't see much, he noted the pavement, the dust colour, the slope of the ground; as he gazed up, giving the impression he was tilting his bottle up for a drink, he could see how the old stone wall joined the roof, what kind of guttering it had and even the ridged red roof tiles. He estimated the angle of the sun in the sky. It's not far off midday, he thought. Six hours at 35 mph, around 200 miles. No doubt sensing Adam's actions, Stefan anxiously ordered him back in the van.

'In. In now. Behave and maybe we no tie your hands. You trouble, we tie you up like a chicken for the market. Geddit?'

Adam knew better than to argue and swung himself back into the van. No chance for conversation, but maybe with hands now free and his bike accessible, surely he could work out something. No sack, such a relief, maybe he could leap out and run. Fat chance. The van doors slammed shut even as he thought it; after the bright sunlight, back in the pitch black he could see nothing at all for several minutes. He fell into the side of the van as they pulled away. A quick right and left and their speed picked up again. He knew they were back on the main road and still heading east.

He felt for his bike, reaching for the handlebar. 'Damn, they've taken the front light,' and as he felt in his panniers, one by one he found they were totally empty. No tool kit, no pen knife, nothing. He kicked his bike in frustration before he remembered he'd been instructed to behave. Fortunately, the movement of the van sufficiently disguised his frustration and no response from his two captors was forthcoming. The journey east continued.

He resumed his search, remembering he had no jacket now and all his documentation, his wallet, his money, his mobile, were in it. No doubt these guys had taken them too. He wondered if these things were in the cab and just what he could do without them. If only he could get out and get them back. 'Idiot,' he said to himself yet again.

Then Adam remembered the 250 euros his parents had given him. Money that he'd hidden in the seat post.

'Right, you bastards, bet you didn't get these,' he said under his breath.

He wrestled to rock the Brookes saddle back and forth to give him the access he needed. It took ages and it was very difficult to lever up, but finally he managed to get his little finger in to pull up the wedged euros inside a plastic money bag. He decided that the inside of his cycling shoe was the safest bet, and carefully rolled the few notes to make toe cushions for both shoes. Job done, he sat back again on

126

the wheel arch, his spirits lifted momentarily, to continue his geography mind map exercise.

The hours went by and he was feeling really hungry. There was a stop and fuel was being added. He heard the hum and click of the diesel pump and the sound of the nozzle being returned to its holder. It must have been Stefan who went to pay, the van lurching as he climbed in and out of the driver's door. Adam guessed it was probably his van. He'd failed to look for any vehicle registration when he'd got out, and kicked himself for being so stupid. 'Idiot', he found himself saying once more.

'Next time,' he told himself, 'next time.'

He curled up in a ball sitting near the wheel arch. He was feeling frightened now, so very, very, frightened and this time he wasn't able to quell his fears. What torments might lie ahead? Would he have the strength to survive his ordeal?

19

Jim and Sue Taylor were enjoying summer in London. They had their home to themselves for the first time for as long as they could remember. Since their son Adam had cycled off, school term had ended and both were occupying that summer space which, as teachers, they felt to be their due entitlement after the stresses of the academic year.

The end of July had not disappointed, with wall to wall sunshine and almost every evening, joyous relaxation and rest, time to sit and drink chilled New Zealand Sauvignon Blanc on their small patio. Thirty years in the same house had served them well. Bought when they fully stretched themselves on a maximum mortgage, the Edwardian terrace house, though small, was now worth a six figure sum and they had created a home that fitted them perfectly. Contentment didn't go nearly far enough to describe their feelings right now.

This evening would be nice, Sue thought, as she put down her glass and threw a pink table cloth with white polka dot spots over the patio table just outside the south-west facing back door. She plugged in the fairy lights to the exterior electric plug, ready to switch on later when dusk fell. As she was bending down near the wall she felt the late sun's warmth radiating back comfortingly from the orange-red bricks of the house.

It would be so nice sitting outside, a just perfect evening, she thought. She adjusted the positions of the four metal chairs, not that they needed it really, and dead-headed some of the many bedding plants she had potted up back in the May half-term. Glancing around, it looked nice - red geraniums, blue lobelias and white petunias, inadvertently patriotic, she mused. Now well established, the carefully chosen shrubs and small trees screened the garden from the eyes of neighbours. The smell of the white orange blossom drifted pleasantly across.

It was nearly six, time to call her sister to find out what time the two of them would be over for supper. Life in a vicarage always seemed so unpredictable, even chaotic and wouldn't suit her, she thought. At least these days Ruth had got some domestic help in that big vicarage house and, even better, the same young African woman would be babysitting Olivia and Paul tonight. There wasn't anyone else she had to make last minute checks with, only her sister. She grabbed her mobile from just inside the door and then paced the patio as she made the call.

'Hi Ruth, it's Sue. How are you doing? Kids OK? Still on for this evening?' There was a pause at the other end. 'You alright?' asked Sue, wondering what Ruth was busying herself with this time.

'Yes, sure, just putting down an armful of gifts for the Drop In as well as trying to answer my phone! Yes, Phil and I are really looking forward to coming over. Aneni is taking the kids down the road to Pymme's Park before putting them to bed. It'll help them settle if they let off a bit of steam in the playground. It's so nice to have a few hours out of the house. We're really looking forward to it. Do you want me to bring anything?' Ruth asked.

'No, just yourselves. I've got it all in hand,' said Sue.

'It'll be so nice for the five of us to catch up, it's been weeks,' said Ruth.

'Just the four of us, Ruth. You know Adam's off on his bike, touring, not back yet,' corrected Sue.

'Oh yes, er, of course. Is seven-thirty OK with you?' checked Ruth.

'Sure, just great, see you later, seven-thirty it is, bye.' With that Sue hung up, her mind going back through her menu plans for the evening.

'Jim,' she called loudly. 'We need to get started. Leave the laptop until later. They'll be here for seven-thirty.'

She heard him slide a chair in the small computer room/ study they had created upstairs, followed by the steady callump callump as he dropped quickly down the stairs and into the hallway.

129

Jim joined Sue in the kitchen and together, in a well oiled routine, they prepared the table and the three courses. Jim even found time to give the areas of the house that mattered a quick vacuum round and the downstairs cloakroom a clean visitor's towel and spare loo roll. Then it was time; and, after a waiting period when time seemed to hang in the air unwilling to move forward, the door bell went at precisely 7.40pm, as near on time as Ruth and Phil ever were, thought Jim. He rushed to the door and threw it open wide.

Hugs and kisses on both cheeks happened in the hall way. No coats - too hot and though told not to bring anything, Ruth passed over a box of M&S luxury mint chocolates with the one hand, whilst with the other, very obviously placing an appeal leaflet about the Drop In on the hall table for reading later, or so she hoped. Everyone went through, and then on again to the patio as Sue announced they would be eating outside this evening. This was a relief to Ruth and Phil after the warm journey they had just made, stop-starting along the North Circular Road and then, shuffling along Muswell Hill Broadway.

'Great idea!' said Ruth, 'Can I do anything to help?'

Sue had anticipated the offer and got Jim to move her and Phil outside. Jim, glasses in hand, left Sue to make the final check on the pears and proscuitto starter which was just finishing nicely under the grill. He passed a bottle for Phil to open, whilst he grabbed a bowl of stuffed olives to hand round.

'You hardly ever need a bottle opener these days, even the better wines are screw tops,' he added.

Sue sprinkled watercress from the fridge on four small plates as artistically as she could to form a bed for the pears and proscuitto.

'Oh dear,' she called out, 'I've made a hot starter, but not too heavy; and, it will be cool by the time I get it outside to you. Here love, be a dear and pass these through,' she told Jim.

As she scurried round the kitchen lining up things to follow, she could hear the others busy catching up, chatting on the patio. Minutes later, all were sitting relaxed and enjoying the first course.

'What a lovely way to spend an evening', she said, interrupting the conversation.

Ruth and Phil didn't make their usual obvious dig about teachers' holidays, merely saying they had noticed this summer how things had quietened down a bit for them too.

'And, isn't it nice that half of London has vacated the city to free up the roads for those who are left,' Jim added. A comment which elicited a predictable reply.

'Try driving from Edmonton to Muswell Hill like we just did,' said Phil.

'People in Edmonton can't afford to go away on holidays,' added Ruth.

The conversation ebbed and flowed, all of them relaxing, as nothing of any real substance was actually said. No-one wanted to argue or pressurise and nobody seemed to mind simply chilling out together on a balmy evening.

By the time the nicely presented Tuna Nicoise was served and a second bottle of Sauvignon had been opened, everyone seemed pretty happy, if not merry. The progress of the meal slowed.

Sue had recounted the highs and lows of her teaching year at East Finchley Academy. Jim had lamented how OFSTED failed to understand his Primary School when they made their latest surprise visit. Phil, for his part, reassured everyone that accountancy really was a boring profession though it paid well, whereas it was agreed Ruth did more than enough needy people work for all four of them put together. Ruth got away with about two minutes talking about her Drop In before the conversation was taken on; and, 'what makes for a good holiday?' became a more lively if not contentious subject of conversation. By then it was time Sue decided to go and switch on the fairy lights which glinted white and blue, adding a festive air to the evening warmth.

'Come on,' said Ruth, 'tell us how that nephew of mine, Adam, is doing on his epic cycle holiday. How's it going? I'm so full of admiration. Such confidence in taking himself off on

131

an adventure like that. These things are character-forming. It'll be the making of him. Our two are nowhere near that stage yet. Adam sets them such a fine example. Shame not everyone takes Gap Years, though not everyone can afford to,' she added quickly remembering her parish.

'Well, Adam's made a great start,' said Jim. 'He left in the middle of June, and he's already crossed France, Belgium and Germany, and in very quick time. We were surprised.'

'If it were our kids, if I'm honest, I'd be worried he was travelling on his own,' Phil offered, 'but Ruth's right, Adam's such a capable lad, so very organised. Always was. I remember last Christmas he wanted a set of the right make of cycle panniers as a present from us, nothing but the specified make would do, some waterproof Dutch ones if I remember.'

'Yes, he got them and he took them with him, though I doubt he's seen hardly a drop of rain since he left England! We've been following the forecast on the internet, best we can. He doesn't email that often, which we think is a good sign, since things are obviously going well. You really don't want to feel your parents are checking up on you at that age, do you? I have to say he was better keeping in touch in the first few weeks, but then I suppose, in Western Europe, sending regular messages was a lot easier for him than where he is now. He sent the odd picture too which is nice. Last one we got was from some cafe in Istanbul. I'll just go and get it, I printed it off,' said Jim.

Jim disappeared inside the house and was back almost instantly, the photo clearly ready to hand.

'This is it,' he said, passing it to Ruth.

'My, he looks so handsome,' said Ruth smiling, 'and well,' she added. 'What an adventure. I'd love to see the Blue Mosque. When was this taken?'

Sue thought, but couldn't bring herself to say, 'too long ago.' Ignoring the question, she began clearing away the empty main course plates and turned her mind to the strawberries and cream all ready to be brought out from the fridge. Ruth, as she had a habit of doing, seemed able to touch her raw spots every time and seemingly without trying.

The question 'when was this taken?' kept repeating itself inside her head. She began to worry and found she couldn't stop herself.

When she got to the fridge she looked at the magnetised calendar on the fridge door. Every day when Adam had emailed or messaged them, she had marked the date with a blue asterisk. As she stared, she saw a pattern. The number of contacts he had made was steadily declining. Her eyes followed the blue asterisks again, up until they stopped. The calendar stared back at her as one big blank white card.

When was he in Istanbul? she wondered, hesitating before counting the days a second time. She couldn't help herself calling out, 'just over two weeks ago, that's when it was taken.' Still feeling anxious, she wondered what Adam was doing right now, hoping against hope he might send another message, perhaps this very evening, whilst they were all here. That would be so nice.

Returning to the table, she placed plates piled high with the best-tasting English strawberries in front of each person's place and returned to jug up the double cream before returning to the table herself. There was, for the first time that evening, an awkward silence hanging in the air. Even the garden birds seemed to have stopped singing and the night air was still, heavy and warm. Yet what began as relaxation now felt strained.

'If he was my boy,' said Ruth suddenly, voicing what everyone was thinking, 'I'd like to have heard from him again by now. Where do you think he is tonight? Let's look at a map and see if we can work it out and then when he calls we can see who was right.'

Everyone liked the idea. It kind of placed Adam within their sight. Jim seemed to have a world atlas in his hand even as Ruth spoke. Sue suddenly realised he must have had it out earlier to look at himself. He opened its giant pages in a space they all helped make for it on the patio table as Sue carried out the now empty strawberry bowls to the kitchen. The fairy lights cast a magical glow and added an exotic air to the experience, evoking romantic places and images as they fingered Adam's route page by page until minutes later they had Istanbul and Turkey open before them.

'Now where was he headed, you two?' asked Phil peering over, his reading glasses perched right on the end of his nose.

'He's got an open air ticket back from Tehran, where his great uncle was stationed in the war. That's there; he was going to go straight across eastern Turkey and dive down through into Iran, like so. He didn't want to fix dates to his travel too tightly,' offered Jim.

'Wow, look at the scale,' said Phil, jabbing his pointy finger toward the horizontal grid at the bottom of the page. 'The distances are pretty big, we're talking a thousand miles across Turkey, that's weeks of cycling. You say he was here two weeks ago, Istanbul, well he's made some progress east. What a ride! I think, if he was cycling thirty miles a day on average, he'd be moving quite well and be somewhere in this sort of area.'

His finger landed on a mountainous, little inhabited area, a single main road striking through it.

'No,' said Jim, 'he was always going to be going further each day than that. He'd be much further east, in fact somewhere near, if not in Iran, already.'

'In which case it won't be long until he's back,' said Sue in a voice which was less reassuring in tone than she had intended.

'I'm sure he will,' Ruth added soothingly, only serving to put Sue further on edge. 'Well, all in all, he's nearing the end of his cycle ride and I wouldn't put it past him to just turn up on your doorstep one evening and surprise you!'

The atlas was folded closed and Jim put it away. Ruth started to help clear dishes and offered to load the dishwasher, an offer she knew from past experience was always firmly refused. Sue turned off the fairy lights and ushered everyone into the cosy front room, swishing shut her terracotta Laura Ashley curtains.

'Coffee anyone?' she asked.

Minutes later with a cafetiere of best Ethiopian Sidamo coffee earthily scenting the room, Sue remembered the M&S mints and brought them in, tearing off the cellophane with a single scrunch. Soothing sweet mint and smoky coffee aromas filled the air.

Nothing more to be said about Adam, the conversation switched to a different subject, one that always energised them, immigration and the diversity of north London's population. Somehow Adam's cycle ride was the trigger that set it off. Ruth held the advantage in always arguing from irrefutable first-hand contact with all kinds of people. She seemed to have her finger on London's diversity pulse.

But Sue and Jim, being in education, brought their own angle. They had accurate numbers for the direction things were taking. In their view, pupil diversity figures were an irrefutable future trend marker. The number of ethnically white and Christian pupils was dropping and this section of the community was even disappearing from classroom rolls as they saw it. A battle of the best stories began.

Whereas Ruth didn't see any problems arising from increasing diversity per se, she did argue that resources were needed to cater for the newest arrivals who slipped through the margins of decent British society.

'People needed a hand on the first rung of the ladder,' she added.

Sue and Jim always felt held back by subconscious guilt at their own relative wealth, though hadn't they, by hard work and yes, it had to be said, good fortune, earned every penny of it? When Ruth mentioned some of the more recent Muslim asylum seekers had arrived at the Drop In from Turkey and Iran, in fact where Adam was, she'd now hit Sue's raw nerve hard three times that evening.

Sue and Jim felt uncomfortable at being in the front line of government agendas to ease the complications a diverse society brought. Mandated just a few years ago by The Department for Education to promote British Values, they now had to go further and lead assemblies, American flag and anthem style and conduct regular assessment tests on pupils to appease the ever more frequent and unannounced OFSTED inspector visits. Sue and Jim agreed with Ruth that more government help was needed for these things.

Phil's contribution to the conversation was to support Ruth, saying just how unfair it was that the government expected the voluntary sector, even the established church, to provide and continue to give out from their own resources what, in his view, were essential services for the new arrivals. Phil had a surprisingly good awareness of how much the members of Ruth's congregation were giving to make the Edmonton programme work and his knowledge of the Diocese of London's wider contribution across the whole of the metropolitan area led him to give some eye-waveringly high numbers to the care figures required to look after all London's new arrivals.

'I wonder what Adam thinks about this as a young person? He took it in his stride being in a multi-faith, multi-this and multi-that school. His friends are all backgrounds. He's so good at mixing with anyone. In his travels he'll have been meeting people from all over, even I guess Muslims, especially in Turkey and Iran? I think young people are so much more adaptable and accepting than us older fuddy duddies,' Sue added pensively.

'We've got a new group of Muslims from the Middle East at our Drop In. He needn't have gone further than Edmonton if he wanted to meet some!' joked Ruth. 'In fact I'd rather like someone to get to know them. They don't seem to want to talk to me. There's a guy called Abu who's been coming regularly, mainly for food for his big family and yet I hardly know him. It could be because I'm a woman, but you know I don't think it's just that. Something else lies behind his reticence. Give me time and I'll find out!'

'Sure you will,' said Phil. 'She usually does get to the bottom of things eventually.'

Jim responded with, 'I'm not so certain. I think there is trouble brewing under the surface, but I wouldn't say so to anyone else. We paper over the cracks and fault lines. First it was multiculturalism, then it was British Values, but I know that even in my Primary School the kids carry different identities and, well, conflicts are just boiling up. Sometimes it gets called bullying, that's dressing it up as something it's not, but we all know its more complex than that. There's race and religion involved today, even in primary school. No-one seems to want to see it that way. Everyone wants to think we all get on. Truth is, some of the most difficult kids are only reflecting views they've heard from their parents or at the madrasas.'

On that unsettling note, the conversation drifted nowhere in particular. Some future holiday plans were discussed, a date put in the diary for a return visit to Ruth and Phil's in September, Ruth saying Adam was to come along too to 'tell us all about it' and 'put us right.' Then it was time to go and Ruth followed Phil out of the door taking the few steps to their car and the journey home.

Sue and Jim set about the late evening clearing and cleaning routine with determination, never known for leaving the dishes until the following morning. Once everything was on the side in the kitchen, they talked.

'Went OK, didn't it?' ventured Jim. Sue, quite unexpectedly, was head down, tears dropping into the sink.

'What is it dear? What on earth is it?' he asked, putting his hands on her shoulders, knowing exactly who was on both their minds.

'Oh Jim, I'm worried sick, it's Adam. We shouldn't have let him go. It's so long and we should have heard something. I'm frightened for him. My life's so empty without him,' she said, sounding more negative and pessimistic than she intended. 'This Gap Year adventure of Adam's has become a living nightmare. When will it all be over?'

20

Next morning, all thought of a pleasant evening with Sue and Jim had pretty well vanished from Ruth's mind as she searched her bag for her bunch of house, church and church hall keys, determined not to be late to greet the Drop In volunteers getting ready for a busy Saturday shift. As she pulled the vicarage door closed behind her to make the short walk next door to the hall, she found her keys awkwardly heavy. Always so many, every church the same, as heavy as the weight of responsibility she felt she carried. Shrugging her shoulders, she launched out into the day.

It was a very different morning, the warm summer sun had given way to a steady drizzle, shrouding everything in a monotone greyness. She'd left Phil to mind Olivia and Paul, something she knew she did all too often these days. It just didn't do to think about the impact of this continuing. It can't be helped, she told herself, and dismissed the thought as futile.

She then laughed to herself as she remembered she'd left Phil having to remove nail varnish from both children's hands. Aneni had amused them whilst babysitting last night by applying her Rimmel bright pink varnish to their finger and toe nails. It would take Phil a while to clean that lot off, she thought. The good thing was, the kids' evening had passed off well. Though they'd stayed up far too late and were bad-tempered this morning as a result, they'd clearly enjoyed the time of licence and freedom Aneni had permitted them.

Ruth pushed her way into the church hall. The battered green door yielded to her touch without a key being needed. She wasn't the first in and to her surprise and pleasure, there was Kaylah Kone apparently helping sort out the latest food donations with a couple of the regular helpers.

'Hi Kaylah, how nice to see you,' Ruth said bounding up to her enthusiastically, 'this is a nice Saturday surprise.'

'Not half as surprised as I am to have got my brother Clive along too! He's over there, with more time on his hands than me. To be honest our Dad felt bad he hadn't offered your project more help and asked me if I'd give a hand. I just couldn't think of an excuse quick enough to say no,' she said with a smile.

'Clive, poor guy, I've been pestering him ages for us to spend more time together and when I said today wouldn't cost him anything, and I knew he wasn't doing anything until tonight, he fell into line and here he is! Please just find him something to do, he needs something positive in his life, he really does, but don't tell him I said so,' Kaylah hastily added.'

Ruth felt she'd been let in, and her heart warmed to the girl.

'Leave him to me,' she smiled. 'OK, come on, you've got to introduce us properly.' She took Kaylah's arm and almost marched her across to the back of the hall where Clive was using a beaten up two wheel tubular metal truck to move stacks of chairs into the body of the hall.

'This is Ruth who I told you about Clive,' Kaylah said, as she parked herself in front of his chair trolley. 'Ruth's running the show here, just so you know.'

'Hi Miss Ruth. This isn't really me, but I promised my Sis here, so that's it,' he replied in a manner Kaylah knew to be Clive on his best behaviour.

'Delighted to see you. Want a coffee?' she offered.

'OK,' he said hesitantly, 'Americana, oh, it's instant, black will be fine,' Clive said in response to Ruth's friendly welcome.

Once coffee was gathered from the kitchen hatch and the remaining chairs allocated to their allotted table places, Ruth got Clive to sit behind a desk and work with one of the regular advice givers. The two sat together, Larry taking Clive under his wing and explaining the format. This all looked to Ruth to be going well. And when Kaylah, moments later, glanced over she too was likewise pleased to see Clive happily settled, the first of the Drop In clients going over to talk to them. Ruth and Kaylah exchanged a knowing smile.

Kaylah busied herself organising the food donations. She'd spent worse Saturday mornings. It amazed her that so much had come in through voluntary gifts and arrangements with local supermarkets. Why, she asked herself, in the twenty-first century was it still necessary to run something akin to a workhouse?

Looking around she was truly amazed at the work Ruth had going on, the variety of human flotsam and jetsam that had floated by and been washed in by tides and forces she could only guess at. It struck her almost immediately just how kind of desperate, hungry some of them were: not just for food, but also for warm human acceptance and a place off the street. For the most part they were wanting to move on, get things sorted but needed help.

By now a little queue had formed at Clive and Larry's table, some people holding official letters they'd received, clutching them in their hands all ready to present them, each in turn thrusting them down on the folding table under Clive's nose. Such letters, Kaylah mused as she watched them, were signposts of destiny. Momentous forces she could only guess at were shaping the lives of those around her and this raised a deep curiosity in her and pulled at her heart strings. She reflected for a moment on the history of her own people, as slaves, as objects of racism, as an underclass; and she knew that today she had come to the right place.

Ruth then busied herself with the routine organisational chores and quick phone calls that so preoccupied her, and the next hour passed in an instant. Next time she looked up from her corner table, the hall was filling up with people and it wasn't even noon.

It was then she spotted the Middle Eastern group of guys, just three of them, who'd made the far corner their own. They were talking excitedly to each other. Maybe now was a good moment to go and get to know them better; there would still be time before they did prayers, she was sure of it. Part daunted by the invisible barrier posed by being a woman, she nevertheless decided the direct no-nonsense approach was

140

her best tactic. She folded her note book, picked up her mobile and wandered down to the far end.

That's good, she thought, Clive and Kaylah are still here. Kaylah was now busy stacking a new delivery of food items into the storage area, clearly already aware how the system worked, so absorbed in what she was doing she didn't lift her eyes in Ruth's direction. 'I hope I can keep her,' voiced Ruth to herself. Clive for his part was also energised, busy talking to a young man waving his letter in his hand. The Muslim guys didn't seem to notice her approach. They were talking away to each other in an excited manner.

'Abu,' said the scruffy bearded man with the piercing eyes. 'The one we are waiting for, he's on his way now, he'll be here in north London very soon, I had a text message. Enshallah, he'll arrive safely.'

He was abruptly silenced with a quite unsubtle, winding elbow jab, by the guy Ruth knew to be Abu, the one she'd assumed to be a kind of leader to the group who invariably kept themselves on the edge of all that went on at the Drop In. Abu had seen her approaching and moved a couple of paces toward her. It seemed strange to Ruth that the guy's conversation with Abu was deliberately cut short, but it wouldn't help to mention it to start with.

Abu's hand went to his long black beard, stroking it with a polished and deliberate calmness. He had the air of a leader. Ruth spoke first.

'Sorry to interrupt you guys,' she said, sounding a conciliatory tone. 'It's nice to see you here again. Is there anything you need? Anything you'd like help with?' She tried to be jolly and inclusive, seizing the moment.

Abu seemed about to send her away as he usually did but, possibly because he didn't want to appear unsociable, and maybe also to distract her from what she might have overheard earlier, he chose now to make an effort.

'Rev Churchill, we're very grateful to receive your hospitality. This is a safe place for us. You allow us to say our prayers, to meet our friends here and the internet connection is excellent.' Abu laughed in a strange mix of formality and informality.

'I've often wondered why you come here rather than the mosque, or maybe you go to both places,' Ruth replied. She wondered whether she was being too inquisitive too soon.

'It's the internet you provide. The men can call their families back home in Iraq,' Abu said. 'Beside those Shias don't want us around.'

The comment reminded Ruth of the deep and conflicted traditions within Islam, all too resonant of the divided history of her own Christian Church with its many denominations. As some parishioners reminded her on more than one occasion it wasn't so long ago since the IRA had planted a bomb under the Silver Street railway bridge a short walk from her church.

Ruth engaged quickly, seizing the conversational opportunity, 'And is it good news from home? Have you been able to get through to your families? What's it like there now, more settled?' Abu took the role of spokesman.

'Our families chose to send us out of the country because we were not safe, I'm lucky I have my family here, but these guys' families live in a very difficult place and our contacting them is full of risk. You've no idea what it's like for us. It's your foreign policy that caused them to lose families, homes, people,' he said bitterly.

Abu started jabbing his finger in Ruth's direction. She took a step back.

'Your western ways are wrecking the world. I am surprised at you, Rev Churchill for allowing parties in this hall where alcohol is consumed. Don't you think we live in very decadent times?' he asked.

His arm was tugged by the man with the piercing eyes and immaculate cream robes, whose tilt of the head was as if to say, be careful, you are going too far, and on this prompt Abu fell silent, though Ruth knew he'd been cut short in full flow.

'Well you are very welcome here. I'm glad you have the internet and I want you to feel this is your home, whatever our foreign policy has done to your country. I do hope your

142

families stay safe. We've got a couple of new volunteers helping us today, Kaylah and Clive. You may like to introduce yourselves,' said Ruth, pointing the two out.

The third man had been glowering resentfully since she came over. He definitely had business on his mind, business he wasn't going to share with Ruth. He showed no intention of striking up a conversation and just stood sullenly by. A few minutes later, this same man pulled the other two away to the back of the hall and left Ruth standing alone.

Abu took a mobile call. It was to say his delivery had arrived, but there had been a problem: a man known to the guys on the street as Winston, driving a flash blue BMW with wide wheels and one of his Afro-Caribbean friends had stepped on their north London turf, into their territory.

'It was their territory, we took it from them. Thought they might try something like this,' replied Abu.

'Whatever. They intercepted the delivery. A lad in a hoodie knocked Riyaz to the ground outside his house, snatched the bag, and was seen handing it to a guy in the BMW with Winston. Don't know who the other guy is, just that he's young and black. It will need to be recovered and soon. We need to find a way. Abu, it's a loss we can't afford to take,' the man told Abu.

Abu said, 'leave it with me' and ended the call. He had an idea and telling his two friends to remain quietly at the back of the hall he joined the queue with some questions for Clive.

'How can I help?' said Clive, looking up to see who was next in line. His eyes tracked up the Middle Eastern robes to the beard and face of Abu. Their eyes met and Abu said nothing. Larry had gone to speak to someone and had left Clive to run the advice table alone. 'What can I do for you?' Clive said, repeating his offer of help.

'I'm trying to do some business in the area and I need to get in touch with a guy, an Afro-Caribbean guy. This is a long shot, but do you know a guy called Winston, who drives a smart blue BMW with wide wheels? Need to get in touch, can you help?' asked Abu.

It was not a question Clive had anticipated. Where was this coming from, he wondered, anyway it was a chance to make a good impression. Winston surely wouldn't mind.

'Er, yes, could be the same. Why? Winston, blue BMW, wide wheels, lives Crouch End? Is that who you mean?' asked Clive.

'Sounds like him. He's trespassing. Tell him,' said Abu, amazed at his good fortune.

'I'll give him a call later, you ought to speak to him yourself, talk to him, sort it out,' said Clive.

As soon as Abu had stepped away, Clive got out his mobile and Winston picked up.

'Hi, it's early for you to call!' said Winston.

'Just down the Drop In with Kaylah, but a guy down here called Abu is asking after you. Well, I think it might be you from his description, thought you ought to know,' said Clive.

'Fuck! You got yourself into deep shit. Be careful, he's dangerous and no, I don't want to speak to him,' and quite unusually, Clive found Winston had hung up on him.

The call had left Clive feeling perplexed. When he next looked up it was to see Abu standing right in front of him. Clive guessed, from the angry look on his face, he had pretty well overheard every word. Suddenly, Abu grabbed Clive's arm holding it down firmly on the desk.

'Get this Mr Clive, your Winston and his crew are stealing what isn't theirs and I want to get what's mine back,' said Abu menacingly.

'I don't know anything about this, and bloody well let go of my arm,' said Clive, not knowing whether to stand up, retaliate and get physical with this objectionable man.

'I want him to know I don't mess about. If you know what's good for you, you'll keep quiet.' Swinging his right arm out and holding a short metal blade to Clive's neck, Abu added, 'make sure your friend Winston gets my stuff back to me. I want you to make sure it's delivered here, to me personally. Talk and you're dead. Tell him I'm making a point.'

With that he swung the blade down away from his neck and to Clive's horror pierced the back of his hand, pinning it to the table, the blade shaking as Abu moved away.

Clive felt no pain at first. He watched the pool of red blood flowing off the top of his brown hand. He fought hard not to yell out. What to do? No-one seemed to have noticed, or didn't want to. He stood up carefully, fought the feeling of nausea, leant over and after steeling himself, with a fierce swift yank pulled the blade out of the desk and back through his hand, before clutching a tea towel from the nearby kitchen server hatch. Larry was coming back over.

'Cut my hand, Larry, take over will you, need to clean up.'

He said this trying to sound calm as he wrapped knife and hand in the now bloodied tea towel and made his way to the door.

'I'll get the Accident Book, need to make an entry, got to keep the Health and Safety brigade happy,' said Larry.

By then Clive had gone out through the door. He had an urgent call to make to Winston. What the hell had he got himself into? Shit, he said to himself. Remembering he'd left his sister in the hall, but looking again at his bloodied hand, he thought to himself, Kaylah, well she'd have to take care of herself.

21

Next morning, Anna Simonsson thought something was odd, not a lot, but odd all the same. In the great stream of thousands of lines of moving data on the screen in front of her, here was a line with a pattern. Well for her it was a pattern. Nothing much, might be nothing at all, just one of many slight changes, the things that caught her eye, a ripple on the surface of the pond, but one that registered with her unusual mind. This mobile signal trace shouldn't move across Europe for weeks at a steady slow pace and then all of a sudden in the middle of Turkey move very rapidly at another pace. She made a note of it on her long list electronic report file as the latest item in need of an explanation and then went to get a coffee.

It was Anna's job to listen and look for the odd and the irregular. Her brain worked that way; and Mossad, the Israeli intelligence service, knew how to use a brain like hers whilst she was serving her country, doing her turn as a member of the conscripted military. It was still early days as a conscript. Everyone had to do it, the Israeli Security Service Law required it. She told herself this was a lot better than being out on the Golan Heights or facing hostility at a Gaza crossing check-point.

Here, she simply sat looking at screens all day, looking for patterns, reporting things that needed a second look, easy work, second nature, what she liked doing more than she'd let on. When she was at school they'd talked about her being assessed for autism, just because she liked numbers and patterns, but she'd talked them out of it. This was serious work she was doing, made for her; she believed, her country's security relied on her skill. Always under threat, always worried where the next attack would come, Israel expected her to do a thorough job and she did, every time. Though still early days, she loved it.

She often wondered why her compatriots always felt so threatened. Her grandparents' generation, when they could speak of such things, told the story of the Shoah, the Holocaust, and how the few had had to build the nation of Israel in the face of huge hostility. Ever since its creation in 1948, Israel had been at the heart of conflict in the region - conflict from within, whether Palestinian or extreme Israelis; and conflict from without, with every surrounding Muslim land seemingly ready to fight them by fair means or foul. The big picture, why people hated each other, she just couldn't get, but she could understand the need to protect her family and friends and, for this reason too, she gave what she did here every bit of her attention and effort.

Working in Tel Aviv whilst living in Jerusalem meant commuting between the two cities. As she travelled, she was well aware of the need for her own personal security and what it was like living under what at times felt like a defending army of occupation. Her own family, with a mixed marriage on her sister's side, her younger sister having fallen for a non-Jewish man from Bethlehem, struggled with the day to day border crossing rigmarole never knowing whether work or family gatherings would actually happen. Her sister's husband just didn't fit the system and no one seemed able to offer a hopeful future. What a mess, she thought.

So life was just more of the same, hard line responses, endless surveillance for survival and for too many people, the joy in life slowly dying. Life here was just getting more unpleasant and conflictual, she thought. This is all too gloomy, she said to herself, and as she usually did at such times of despondency, decided to add a chocolate snack to her coffee to cheer herself up.

Back from the vending machine in the corner of her nondescript office on the outskirts of Tel Aviv, Anna looked at the line of electronic pulse signals once again. Yes, definitely a pattern, she concluded. She called up the data on the phone trace using the passwords and pathways only she could find her way through. Thank you UK for sharing data with us, she said to herself, as she did every time she opened these files.

There it was, an Apple iPhone 7, owner Adam James Taylor, purchased last March. She opened the message and email trails, accessed the Facebook page and began reading. Soon she had a picture of a young man with lots of friends, a young man called Adam from Muswell Hill, north London, apparently taking a Gap Year adventure and cycling east with the plan to fly home back to his parents at the end of his ride.

I knew he'd be a cyclist, she said to herself. Only a cyclist moves at around 12 miles an hour, day in day out. He's probably my age, she mused. Then she widened her search and found images and pictures to see what Adam looked like. Facebook was always so easy to get into. He's nice after all, she thought. Within half an hour she had read everything. She walked over to get another coffee and some more chocolate. If only chocolate didn't give her so many spots.

No, it's still a pattern and now it's more so, she told herself. Not only has his phone signal trace pattern changed to average around thirty-five miles an hour, he hasn't communicated; and, since his silence, his trajectory is east toward Iraq and not toward Iran where his messages say he intended travelling. It just needs looking into. He might be going over to IS, but she dismissed that idea for nothing in his profile suggested that was likely to be the case. More likely he's a hostage.

A few more searches and she'd found he'd obtained a visa to allow him into Iran, probably aiming to take the road route through the Bazargan border, it was just about the only option open to travellers these days. That's it, there's the payment, he's also got a pre-paid open return flight home from Tehran. So he's definitely not going over to IS, glad about that, he looks nice. Mustn't think too much of it at this stage, there's time yet for his route to change, but why has he headed so near Iraq? she asked herself, getting more and more drawn in.

Now where is he right now? She called up a map and then superimposed Adam's phone signal on it as a series of coloured dots. Maybe I've got it wrong, perhaps he's simply had the offer of a lift on the last leg and he's going where his driver is going. It has to be a vehicle happy to take his bike too. But he's not making calls or sending anything. She still thought it needed to be checked out, simply because it didn't rest easy with her, the pattern wasn't right.

She stood up and walked round the office to gather her thoughts; knowing she wanted, but didn't have the authority to access visual satellite surveillance. A junior like her wasn't privy to such things, but it would be nice to see what was on the road where Adam was. Spy satellites were now so good she felt sure the very vehicle he travelled in could be identified. That might settle it. Just maybe there were also drone images she could get hold of. Again, that was out of the reach of someone of her low rank.

Going back to her desk she typed a briefing report for her CO, and an hour later she pinged it over the email, job done. Time to shut down, clear the desk and make a long commute back to Jaffa Gate, Jerusalem and the family apartment they called home. At least today had been interesting. Something very promising had definitely come up, she knew it, but whether it got taken any further was now someone else's decision and they wouldn't understand the flow of numbers like she did. Keeping an eye on Adam Taylor's erratic journey was soon forgotten about as she signed out and left the building.

22

Sue Taylor wasn't one given to worrying, but at no time in her life had there been such a long space, such an empty void, when she'd neither seen nor heard from her Adam. She was walking to Sainsbury's in Muswell Hill and, as she came out, clutching her two orange recycled bags containing the day's shop, she looked across the road and stopped. She'd noticed it many times before, but this time, as she paused, the midday sun behind the spire of St James's Church cast a shadow over the west door. It felt like what she would call a spiritual moment.

She noticed a small sign by the door stating, 'This building is open and invites all who pass to come in.' In spite of her sister Ruth's frequent invitations to do so, she hadn't been inside a church for ages, probably not since her Mother's funeral eight years ago. Mum always found such comfort in her religion, she thought, as she took the zebra crossing and pushed open the heavy oak side door, the west door itself being resolutely closed, no matter how hard she pushed.

Once inside she found it was clean and warm, reassuringly spiritual and she could see the brass cross on the altar table at the east end and the coloured lights of the stained glass east window making their magic pictures shine brilliantly above. She shuffled herself sideways, her shopping and handbag, into a row of chairs just inside, the bench pews she remembered of old clearly having been long removed. Some things do change in the Church of England then, she mused.

After a few minutes enjoying the peace and feeling a sense of serenity she'd not felt for days, she stood up, leaving her bags on the chairs and went looking for somewhere to light a candle. Peering in vain into a side chapel to the left, she could see there was no votive candle stand in there or indeed anywhere else. Then moving silently on the plush red-carpeted floor, she found herself up by the main altar rail itself.

Turning back and to the right she noticed a door going through into further buildings and walked on through. Until now she'd seen no-one, but in the extension there was some sort of meeting going on. People were sitting in a circle and in earnest conversation. Hoping not to be noticed, she started to retrace her steps back into the main body of the church when a friendly female voice asked, 'Can I help?'

Then for some unknown reason; and, quite unlike her usual self, Sue burst into tears. She was sat down, tea was administered, and a kindly lady sat next to her.

'I'm Molly. Are you alright? You seem a bit upset dear,' she said.

'Sorry, this isn't like me, I don't normally get like this,' Sue replied, pulling a tissue from her pocket.

'Well, take as much time as you want and just feel at home. It's my job to look after visitors today. I'd popped into the hall, to the loos, turned around and then there you were,' Molly said.

'It's just that our son Adam, I've not heard from him for over two weeks. Sorry, there's too much to tell. I'm frightened for him. Something dreadful might have happened,' Sue said, somewhat incoherently.

She hesitated about saying anything further and was all for going to collect her bags from where she'd left them and head off home, but then there was the half drunk cup of tea still in her hand. It wasn't possible to move quickly and politely away. She certainly didn't want to appear ungrateful or rude, so she stayed put.

'How old's Adam?' asked Molly.

'Nineteen. He's having a Gap Year before going to Uni. He's a mad keen cyclist. Been saving up for this trip, doing odd jobs to pay for it. He's been working toward it all last year. But he's been gone since the beginning of May,' she said.

'And gone off on his bike somewhere, has he?'

'Yes, right across Europe.'

151

There was a pause to take a deep breath, before she added, 'across France, Belgium, Germany, Eastern Europe and he's making for Iran before flying back with his bike. But we, that's Jim, my husband and I, we haven't heard from him for two weeks now, and that's longer than he's ever left sending us an email or message. I'm worried.'

'That's an amazing journey. Has he gone with anyone?' asked Molly.

'No. He took it as a very personal challenge to ride east on his own. He's got loads of friends round here in Muswell Hill, but wanted to test himself I think. He really is a very sensible boy. He can look after himself or thinks he can and he was really well organised, planned every step of the way for months beforehand. We went along with it, and now, I'm worried for him. Perhaps we shouldn't have been so easily talked into it. We were wrong. I'm frightened something terrible has happened to him,' said Sue, beginning to feel she couldn't hold back her tears again.

'They say no news is good news. I've a son myself and it's hard letting go of them, whatever their age. Did Adam say when he would next call?' asked Molly.

'No. Last time we heard from him he was somewhere in Turkey, so nearing journey's end,' said Sue.

Sue realised Molly had put her arm over her shoulder. She didn't mind, in fact it was a comfort.

'I just wanted to light a candle for him. That's why I came in. But I couldn't find one and, I guess I feel upset because I haven't been able to do anything. I can't do anything, nothing, nothing at all,' said Sue despairingly.

'We don't have candles here. Perhaps we should, but I can promise you we will pray for Adam if you'd like that,' Molly added caringly.

'I'd like that. That'll be all, I'd better be going. Thank you for the tea, and for listening to me,' she said.

'Not a problem, but we will pray for Adam. Let us know when you hear from him, and do come in again. I'm here most afternoons. Just ask anyone for Molly.'

She was kindly and not pushy and Sue was grateful. In fact she felt she'd unburdened herself somewhat and felt more composed. Adam's situation, whatever it was, had been put into the greater scheme of things, into the hands of the Almighty.

Now what had Molly said, 'no news is good news.' That was something positive to hang on to. And though, unlike her sister Ruth, she wasn't much of a praying person, except in a crisis, she felt warmed by the thought that they'd be praying for her Adam. Perhaps she ought to suggest Ruth's church prayed for him too, the more support the better in that department, she reasoned.

'I'll just go and retrieve my Sainsbury shop from the back of church.' Sue said, as she stood up. 'Then I'll be on my way.'

Molly followed her through to the main body of the church.

'Oh no, it's gone,' Sue cried out.

Moving the orange Sainsbury bags to the side, there was no room for doubt.

'Gone, I've lost my handbag. I left it here on the seat with my shopping.'

Molly called the police, to be told the local Muswell Hill Police Station had closed long ago and presently they were too stretched to send anyone immediately. Molly kindly called Jim on his mobile. Molly heard him repeating himself, before passing her phone over to Sue.

'You're where? Where? What, Sue, are you doing there?' he said, more puzzled than anything.

A few minutes later and he'd swung the Ford Focus into St James's church car park and shepherded his distressed and by now silent wife into the front seat to get her home and begin the tedious process of cancelling bank cards and changing locks. Sue was waiting for him, standing there clutching orange shopping bags, looking totally crestfallen, all forlorn.

As the car moved slowly into the traffic to take the few streets to their home, Sue watched the red brick London

153

houses of well-to-do Muswell Hill pass by in a daze. Then in a flash of realisation she felt more composed.

'My bag, the cards, the cash, they all don't matter Jim,' she said. 'What matters is that our Adam is OK, that's all that really matters and it's only just now I realised that. In spite of what's happened I'm going to go back to the church from time to time until our Adam comes back. Until my bag went, I was finding it such a comfort,' she told him.

For his part, Jim realised that Sue was only mirroring the anxieties he had been trying so hard to keep hidden from her. In reality, they were both desperate for news from Adam. It was as if their instincts told them that something dreadful had happened.

23

Winston ran fast out of the church. It wasn't every day there were such easy rich pickings. That white lady was bloody stupid, virtually giving her stuff away. He'd been lucky, so lucky, but wasn't he always lucky? Fate always dealt him a good hand. He hadn't intended to take anything, but when it's there for you, what do you do when there's no-one around? He'd simply followed her into the church and watched her.

Sitting at the back to case the joint, he noticed things. Alert, he'd checked there was no CCTV, felt the sharpness that comes with the adrenaline build; and then, when she went through the side door, he'd snatched her handbag from beside the orange bags of groceries. Once outside, joy of joys, he found her purse and cards inside; she must have just got a load of cash out too, one hundred and fifty pounds, very nice.

Bag inside his jacket, Winston had moved quickly outside and crossed the road from the church. The handbag's too conspicuous, he thought; at the first street bin, he off-loaded it and everything in it, apart from the cash and cards, which he stuffed in his pocket. She'd as likely get the bag back later, if she got lucky, he told himself. Just redistribution from rich to poor. No-one hurt, a Robin Hood crime, he reasoned, trying to justify to himself what he had done.

Moving casually and mingling with all the pedestrians in the busy Broadway, he continued on his way to Dillon's flat. As he walked, he felt the buzz beginning to subside. It was so easy, so normal. He knew someone he could trade the cards to, but would need to be quick, before they were stopped.

He made a mobile call to Toby who dealt in these things and minutes later was one hundred pounds more better off, as he handed over the cards. Then Winston retraced his steps back along the Broadway, moving more quickly to get to Dillon's place in time.

There was to be a big meet. It wasn't usual to get called to a big meet and he was curious to know what it was about. Glancing at the fake Rolex watch he'd picked up in Edmonton Market, he thought it was high time he joined the others. Being late went down badly with the ever unpredictable Dillon whose mood depended on which drugs were flowing through his veins at the time.

Earlier, he'd sensed anxiety in Woody the Hoodie's voice when he'd called. Then he thought of Clive. How the hell had he got dragged into all this and got himself bloody well stabbed too? Need to see him later and find out more. Did he tell the others what Clive had said to him? Suppose he ought to, he reasoned. It might be all the worse for Clive if he didn't.

He'd need to keep his wits about him, didn't want things to spiral out of control. Wanted to avoid Dillon rushing in and making more trouble for Clive and himself. Seen it too often before. Easy pickings, an over-hungry desire for vengeance, get sucked in, get careless, get caught, everything ending up pear-shaped. Not him, never caught, not going to start now, but it was getting harder to stay ahead, to keep on top, to keep paying the bills.

He put his hand in his pockets and squeezed the £250 roll of notes and felt better. He'd see Clive later, after the big meet. They'd do something to chill out. Clive was a decent guy, a good guy, he always made one feel better. He was lucky to have one good friend.

Winston arrived in Prince's Avenue, eyeballed his blue BMW, checking it was still where he'd left it and hadn't been messed with. It gleamed back at him reassuringly in the sunshine, sitting low on the road. My other true and loyal friend, he thought. He walked out across the busy road prising his way through the traffic which seemed reluctant to let him cross. 'Racist bastards,' he muttered quietly, before pressing the intercom of Flat 1b at number 19.

There was no wait, no voice either, just the buzz of the door release solenoid. He pushed his way in and then through the inner door where Dillon, Will, Woody and a mean-looking bald guy he didn't know, but instinctively didn't like, were already gathered.

'Time for business, now the latecomers have deigned to join us,' said Will looking in Winston's direction, as ever in charge and making sure everyone knew it. Dillon, whose flat it was took a back seat. Will sat in the best leather chair. Winston thought discretion the better part of valour and kept his mouth shut.

'We've a problem brothers. It's getting busy in the park. Know what I mean. Good thing is, there's nothing busted that can't be fixed,' said Will.

'Need to pass on a message before we go further,' interrupted Winston. All eyes turned to him. My brother Clive's been told he's meat if he doesn't let you guys know the Arabs want you off their turf,' he said.

'Fuck 'em,' said Dillon standing up, 'it's our turf. They've been using their stuff from Afghanistan to undermine us. I just put things right by relieving them of some cash, teach them a lesson. If they don't like it, they can just push off.'

He tipped back his baseball cap and stomped his feet like some weird overgrown kid having a tantrum. Winston wondered what he'd taken today. Dillon used whatever he could get his hands on. He was none too fussy and always experimenting. Winston interrupted him anyway.

'It's not so easy, Dillon, these guys not messin' any more. You gonna have a war. They drawn blood. They hurt my bro Clive,' he said.

Will broke in and allowed Winston a few minutes to tell Clive's story. Unlike wild Dillon, Will was thinking through what to do, Winston could see it, like a clockwork winder in the dark mind lying behind those ever watchful eyes.

'OK, OK, like I was telling you before, we have to go to the Post Office first, make a withdrawal, buy ourselves two shooters, and take Edmonton back the hard way, just leave it to Wise Will to think it through and get things fixed. Now listen good everyone for an important update. My Sis says the Post Office cash is all lined up for us to collect next Tuesday.

It's not Monday any more. It's Tuesday. Get it? Big day for you Winston, pay day, and don't worry about your precious Beamer, I got a different car ready for you to drive for the Post Office job! Untraceable! Now look here,' said Will, pushing his i-pad forward on to the coffee table for all to see.

He typed into his i-pad and they all leaned in to see a Google earth picture of South Tottenham Post Office.

'Follow what I is saying very carefully. We do this right. There's easy money here and there's lots of money in it for us,' said Will.

To Winston's ears, Will was a man obsessed, he rattled on about places, meetings, times, tools, bags, where to drive, how fast to drive, what route to take. It didn't quite all hang together, like something from a poor film. At one point he even told Winston where he was to leave his Beamer for the car swap, just off Archway Road. An unnecessary piece of detail.

'And there are no cameras nowhere thereabouts,' he concluded with a lopsided smile, 'it'll work like a dream.'

Finally, it was explained that it would be a case of all meet up here at Dillon's flat after it was over, count the money and split. Winston logged in his mind that Will was deliberately keeping his own flat in Tottenham out of it, keeping himself well behind the exposed front line. Clever move that, Winston thought. The good bit was that everyone would have their payout in cash there and then, Will keeping the lion's share for 'business'. Then after it was over, on the Tuesday night, he would need Winston to drive him to Stamford Hill to collect a couple of shooters with a couple of boxes of ammo freshly arrived from Eastern Europe.

'Then, and only then,' said Will banging the coffee table with his fist, 'we go and get the Mother-fucker Arabs and take back our turf, and you Winston can tell that clean lad Clive he's coming with us on a mission. Tell him his true brothers will look after him, but first he needs to help us at the Post Office. I take it that excellent grabbing hand of his still works Winston?' asked Will, leaving Winston without the option of keeping Clive out of it.

158

Winston nodded. He had no choice, he told himself.

Will sent everyone off from Dillon's flat, not together all at once, so as to attract attention, but singly over the next ten minutes. Winston squeezed the roll of notes in his pocket for comfort. He didn't like what he was getting into one bit and didn't for one minute think Clive was going to just volunteer his services as Will was presuming he would. The others had been dismissed and Dillon had gone into the kitchen. It was just him and Will left in the room.

'What car you getting me?' Winston asked, making an effort at conversation.

'Silver Vauxhall, but with a big engine - it's being given me anonymously for the occasion. Don't worry it's totally clean, won't be traced to you,' said Will. 'I've got everything sorted.'

'You sure about all this Will? I mean we could just stay out of Tottenham and Edmonton. You is doing just fine I know. This is going to get attention, lots; and, we'll not be able to move for cops. It'll be lock down, stop and search. This is going to upset loads of people, big time,' said Winston.

'Are you chicken-shitting me? This is dog eat dog, we do it or we die - get my meaning? It's all sorted, we get the money, I get shooters, we clean up, job done and life gets back to normal. We rule our turf!'

Dillon came in from the kitchen. He tapped out white powder on the back of his hand and snorted before looking up again. Where it had come from, Winston had been too lost in his own thoughts to notice. He looked across at Dillon, so drug-soaked as to be a liability. Then he looked back at Will, so obsessed with being king of the jungle, he could kill anyone in his way. Winston didn't like it one bit and knew he needed to find a safe way out for him and Clive.

'But what you need Clive for?' he asked Will.

'I need him to help sort the Edmonton business, but first we need to get him in properly, to get him to be a good boy for the brothers. He's part of my future investment. He needs to be with us on Tuesday, right? Right?' ordered Will.

159

Winston gave a meek 'OK' as Will ushered him out of the door. The meeting was over.

Winston didn't like it. Too many unstable guys, too many risks and what had he got Clive into? First, he gets his hand stabbed and next, well what will happen next, it's like bloody dominoes, the first one falls and then everything falls, bang, bang, bang, until every last one lies down flat.

Even the roll of notes in his pocket didn't seem to offer him much comfort now.

24

Southgate Community College was a handy location for Kaylah. Easy to get there on the W6 hopper bus from Silver Street or simply a 30 minute walk up Hedge Lane and Bourne Hill. That was of course only on nice sunny days when she felt like walking, which to tell the truth was, well, hardly ever. Having the Piccadilly Line running through Southgate also made it easy to get into central London, and the Piccadilly was in her view the best Tube line of them all. Southgate was not a bad place to be at College at all.

Now it was September, the college was running some pre-Freshers Week summer school seminars; the Students' Union, recognising that so many students were local and not going anywhere over the summer, had broken with all tradition and decided to organise a programme of events. Today it was to be an afternoon debate on a contemporary issue, with a BBQ at a local park the following day.

The debate was on 'religious freedom' and, having nothing better to do, Kaylah had decided to put in an appearance. She thought she might have some knowledge of the matter, having grown up in a home where prayers were said before meals and her Dad had, as he saw it, always led his home on Christian principles. Her Dad reckoned that he was in a long succession of elders preaching and singing hymns in a foreign land. His folkish Christianity was infused with warm memories of the Caribbean, a world where the Bible had the answer and everything could be readily judged as right or wrong.

She might disagree with her Dad on many things, but she was still fond of him, a feeling she knew was reciprocated; she hoped she might please him further by her commitment to college and her studies.

Of course she knew her Dad hadn't really any significant first-hand knowledge of the Caribbean, having been sent over here from Jamaica as a five year old to his London Aunt.

Kaylah reminded herself that she didn't think like him; like her friends, she was thoroughly post-modern in thinking she could create a spiritual potpourri from the many different religions and philosophies to suit herself. No longer would the old literalism and unquestioning certainties of her Dad's world do for her. Yes, she'd have something to say about hard-won 'religious freedom' today and found herself with a definite spring in her step as she arrived at the college gate.

As she approached the College's Number 2 lecture theatre, guided by the signs the SU had put up, there were other students arriving too, she guessed for the same event. There was Keith who'd tried unsuccessfully, on more than one occasion, to recruit her to the Christian Union, even chatting her up to get her to come. He had a handful of leaflets in his hand. This was one guy who never missed an opportunity to proselytise. No way was she falling for that! Keith was just like her Dad, evangelical and forceful and wanting to see the world ruled by men.

Not far from him were a couple of Muslim guys from FOSIS, the local Federation Of Student Islamic Societies group. They and Keith should get on fine together, she mused, both tarred with the same black and white brush. FOSIS had their literature to hand too, all very organised. She wondered which one would give her the best price for her soul. Anyway, she concluded, neither are interested in women, so they can get lost.

An outspoken atheist student, called Melissa, who'd gone to the trouble of signing up with the Humanist Association was hurriedly running the gauntlet between the two groups and Kaylah quickened her pace to join her. She'd found Melissa to be a good friend and she rushed over to grab her arm.

'Hi there Melissa! How you doing?' she said in greeting.

'Kaylaaaaah. You here for the debate too?' she replied in her high-pitched voice. 'Thought you might be, your Dad being Bishop Kone and all that.'

162

'Yes, but just steer me past these scary fundamentalist guys first. Had a good holiday?' she asked.

'Mmm. Bit boring really. At home all summer, which is why I've come along,' Melissa said.

They pushed through the doors into the Number 2 lecture theatre, the stage area glowing in a soft light with everywhere else dark and atmospheric. As her eyes adjusted she could make out dozens of students already seated, others leaning against walls chatting. A member of the SU committee was hastily putting up a SU debate poster behind the podium, 'Religious Freedom - Yes or No', whilst a colleague clutching a set of wires was trying to check out the podium microphone. Moments later, the microphone obviously working, everyone was summoned to take their seats. By now the theatre was more than half full.

'Wonder who's speaking?' quizzed Kaylah.

'They got people I've never heard of, a Muslim guy from Egypt, supported, I mean seconded by, a Christian woman, from London, I think; and then, speaking against, we've got our Sue Harper and she's seconded by one of the college's new Sociology lecturers, Baz Reid. Look they're coming in now.' Kaylah's heart missed a beat. The second person in the line was Ruth Churchill.

'I know her, it's Ruth Churchill. At least she uses her religious freedom practically to help people who need it,' she whispered into Melissa's ear.

There were the usual safety, admin and social notices from the SU secretary, before the Chair introduced the debate proper and then the speakers in turn. Kaylah was busy trying to switch her mobile to silent and didn't really pay attention at this point.

She was back on message when the proposer of the motion, Ibrahim Modood, stood up to speak. He looked just like an Imam and began by talking to himself as far as Kaylah was concerned. Didn't anyone tell him it was a debate in English? Then she realised he was quoting the Qur'an and offering a prayer. Once that was over, he spoke clearly in good English.

163

'I'm a Salafist,' he began, 'and what I am going to say may be enough to get me arrested under the draconian Prevention of Terrorism legislation in this country, but thank you to this college for allowing free speech this afternoon.'

There was some polite applause.

'I tell you there is no freedom of speech, no religious freedom here in England. There are so many anti-Terrorist laws in this country you dare not open your mouth today. But "Allahu Akbar" God is Great!' he confidently stated.

'Allahu Akbar,' returned the murmuring echo somewhere in the darkness of the hall before all eyes again turned to the robed man Ibrahim.

'Omar Bakri Muhammad helped many of us - Farid Kasim, Dr Abdul Wajid and others, along with myself to find our true selves and to discover now is the time for the new Khalifa, the Caliphate, where there is true religious freedom. But here in so-called Great Britain, I can't raise funds for the cause, I can't travel to the Middle East and I have to watch what I say. My brothers are being locked away or tagged, or put under house arrest, their computers and phones taken from them - freedom, what freedom is this I ask you?' Ibrahim asked his audience.

'No freedom here,' a voice echoed from the back.

This is going to be fun, thought Kaylah.

'For decades the foreign policies of the west and their genocidal wars have oppressed religious freedom and supported Zionism at every turn. Back in 2003 the imperial armies of the Americans and their allies invaded our lands. Look what evil they did, what great civilisations they crushed and how many innocents they killed,' he said.

'And don't just look abroad, brothers. Here in the UK the moral war has already been lost. Here society is corrupt, decadent, like a stinking apple at the bottom of a barrel. I'm put on a platform with women who ought to be properly covered and feeling fulfilled managing their homes, not being let out unescorted, albeit one is arguing the same case for religious freedom as myself,' he said begrudgingly.

He turned and cynically half bowed toward Ruth. Then he was back in full stride again.

'These western ways and western laws are to oppress us, can't you see it? What I want to tell you my Muslim brothers is this, it is time to stand up and be counted. Call yourself Muslim, then act like Muslims. Whilst your brothers and sisters are suffering for religious freedom in Iraq, in Syria, in North Africa, in Afghanistan, in Palestine, you just carry on as normal giving in to western ways, forgetting their suffering; and, decadently lapping up corrupt entertainments, forgetting your true loyalty, your duty to your own people. Religious freedom is about jihad, devotion and duty. It's a non-debatable reality,' said Ibrahim now in full flow.

Kaylah saw his conviction causing discomfort amongst the Muslims in the room. This wasn't what she had expected and he only seemed to be speaking to Muslims. Ibrahim then began giving an extended history and holy book lesson. She used to feel the same way when her Dad got all fired up about the legacy of the slave trade, the slave risings and rebellions in Jamaica. It was all rather lost on her and she drifted off into her own thoughts.

Then at last, to the relief of many, Kaylah included, the red light bulb in front of Ibrahim lit up to show 'time', and he sat down. Sue was up at the podium next, her bright red hair standing up on end, all spiky as if in shock. Ibrahim didn't even register her, he didn't even deign to look in her direction. How rude, thought Kaylah, her blood beginning to boil.

'I'm a secularist, a humanist, an atheist, a liberal, a democrat, a feminist and an advocate of human rights. Personally, I don't see any grounds for a belief in God and on that basis any religious freedom should only be allowed in so far as it relates to private belief and personal prayer. That is about as far as religious freedom should go. The public realm, the life of the nation and the life of our communities belong in that common space which we all have equal rights to shape. The minute we let religion into it there's trouble. With all due respect, balls, to your Caliphate, Mr Modood! It doesn't give a shit about freedom or rights or anyone who isn't made in the same fundamentalist mould as yourself,' Sue said forcefully.. In her own mind Kaylah could hear herself thinking, 'hear! hear!'

At this point, Ibrahim turned his head toward her, half rose to his feet, just as the Chair stepped in and reminded the panel of the rules, urging respect and moderation in the use of language. Ibrahim sat down again and began shuffling his papers. Sue Harper apologised.

'No offence,' she said, at which Ibrahim waved a hand in contemptuous acknowledgement.

'Just to be even-handed, I have to say the fact that we have an established church, which is a total anachronism in today's Britain, is another example of where religious freedom ought not to be allowed. What are we doing with Bishops in the House of Lords? What are we doing having prayers before Council Meetings? What the hell are we doing with Church Schools with their proselytising school assemblies and corrupt entrance criteria? Opening a Sikh School in Leicester, Muslim Schools in Birmingham or Hindu Schools in Brent isn't the answer. Where will all this madness end? These schools are forcing us into parallel lives,' she confidently asserted.

'We need the secular state to have some muscle and hold the ring. We need reform to limit religious freedom to bedside prayers or within the walls of church, mosque or synagogue. I've no time for the Charles Taylors of this world who want a 'pragmatic secularism', it won't work. I want to see things change. Let me give you one tiny example. In the past, Christians wanted to Keep Sunday Special and as Christian culture ran the show in those days, that was what we had. It took decades of campaigning before we had the freedom to shop on Sundays. If we give more religious freedom today, it won't be just the Christians who want a day off, but Muslims will want Fridays, Jews Saturdays and all the other religious festivals will knock a chunk out of the rest of the week. It's ridiculous. Only having a secular state means fair play,' she said.

Sue went on to talk about how hard it had been to get abortions when religion ruled the roost and how sexual abuses were covered up by all religions. Kaylah felt Sue was looking straight at her when she said that the churches had long delayed any challenge to slavery or apartheid. Finally, she went political, talking about what she saw to be the religious contribution to so many of the conflicts in the world.

In a finishing flourish, she concluded, 'Ibrahim's view of the world as a radical Muslim who believes in a Caliphate, requires the rest of us who don't share his view to be killed or exiled. It is easy to reject that kind of religious freedom. To those multiculturalists among you who say, it is possible to have a relative separation of religion from the executive function of the state, I say you need to think again. You need to look at the difficulties. Multiculturalism is crap. It's all about sandwiches and samosas. It needs to grow up and get real. It doesn't address religious bigotry, racism or equality. I'm not against people being religious, but they shouldn't have the right to impose it on me! History proves there isn't any compromise to be had with religion. So I urge you to vote against the motion,' concluded Sue.

With that she sat down, and this time there was some polite applause, but not from the Muslims in the audience. Kaylah had quite liked what she had to say and found herself enthusiastically applauding. This was all shaping up into a good afternoon. It had been worth the effort, thought Kaylah.

The Chair then invited Ruth to the podium to conclude the arguments in support of religious freedom. Ruth spoke in a measured quiet tone, with a typical English lack of passion, thought Kaylah. She just wasn't going to cut it with the students there. People's attention was wandering. Ibrahim gave the impression he wasn't even listening, and was busy doing something with his mobile. Ruth looked over-tired and too old for the audience gathered. She only had a couple of minutes and one minute she seemed to be arguing with Ibrahim and the next with Sue. That's blown it thought Kaylah, there'll be no support for religious freedom here.

Sue's seconder, Baz Reid, had clearly been roped in from the institution. As a new sociology lecturer he'd been set up by the College Vice Principal for this debate but his presentation went way over the heads of everyone present. He was totally impenetrable, lost in the world of Descartes, Ricoeur and the post-modernists Barthes, Foucault and Derrida. Kaylah had never heard so many names mentioned in so few minutes. It lost her and lost everyone else. Kaylah found her lip balm and was absorbed in its application; her mind wandered until Baz had finished. He sat down pleased with himself, but there was not a murmur of interest in the room in what he'd said.

There was a hushed silence after the last speaker, giving the Chair chance to thank all the speakers in turn and throw the debate open to the floor. After some initial hesitancy several students stood up to make a lively contribution both for and against the motion.

It was then Kaylah saw more people she recognised. There were those three guys from the Drop In. What were they doing here? They weren't students so far as she knew. She hadn't spotted them earlier. They must have slipped in at last minute on the far side, but it was definitely them. Abu, the older guy, with his two friends, one either side of him. Then Abu stood up.

'Abu,' he said, by way introduction.

'Thank you to my brother Ibrahim for his excellent speech, and to sister Ruth for her support and all she does in the community. We don't need to debate religious freedom. Islamic law makes it clear the apostate takfir and the disbelieving murtad should die, for the Qur'an tells us in Surah 4.89 "they wish that you should disbelieve as they disbelieve, and then you will be equal; therefore take not to yourselves friends of them, until they emigrate in the way of God; then, if they turn their backs, take them, and slay them wherever you find them." It is a hard truth, but Muslims must be faithful and obedient to it.'

At this, there was heckling and shouting from the floor. Someone threw a shoe in the direction of Abu, who sidestepped it with ease. Then three or four guys started moving toward the front, yelling abuse about Islam being the religion of the Devil; cries of 'England for the English' could be heard. It was turning ugly.

The Chair stood up in a desperate and doomed attempt to regain control. To Kaylah's surprise Melissa was getting in on the act and heading straight for Abu. When she got near, one of Abu's two friends stepped between them and she saw Melissa fall to the floor.

The Chair was on his phone calling for security, frightened that he'd opened Pandora's box and the whole SU programme would end up being suspended because of this. A fire alarm went off deafening everyone amidst cries of, 'clear the building!'

Kaylah went across to help Melissa up, but withdrew in horror, a crimson stain of blood was pooling across the floor and Melissa wasn't moving. 'Get some help,' yelled Kaylah, but it was chaos and no-one was listening. 'Help! help! Please someone, Help!'

25

The van slowed to a crawl after taking a couple of turns off the main road. This was no tarmac surface, thought Adam. By his reckoning it was early evening as the light was fading. Maybe they had travelled some three hundred miles.

In a moment of lightheadedness it amused him to think that if he could get out of this fix and on to his bike, he'd be so far ahead of his schedule he'd be in Tehran in no time; and what a story he'd have to tell! The imagination is running away again, he told himself, and pulled himself together to concentrate on the now, the terror of his present predicament. Reality and make-believe played with his head like demon brothers.

The van stopped. The engine cut and all was quiet, apart from Yusuf and Stefan having another of their animated discussions in the cab, no doubt working out how best to deal with their passenger. Adam couldn't make it out. Then he could hear a mobile in use with its speaker on as both men talked with a third party. It was a brief conversation and then the van moved off again, but it was only a matter of minutes before it came to a final stop and both men leapt out and moved swiftly round to the back of the van. Adam felt extremely apprehensive, finding himself involuntarily backing away from the van doors, fearful of what might happen to him next.

The doors were flung open and before he could do anything his head was inside a sack again and he was pulled off the van. He was petrified. A brief pause and with one person gripping each of his arms, he was walked some dozen paces before he heard a door of another vehicle open, then shut and a third voice give instruction, the one he'd heard on the phone moments earlier. Then he was inside a building, footsteps echoing as was walked through one room, then another, outside again and then into another room. Finally, Yusuf spoke.

'Now listen carefully. We are spending the night here. You will be given food and drink. Rest. Do what we say, no questions, that's it.'

The whole while the grip on his arms hadn't lessened, then a sudden pain as something struck the side of his head. Again, then again, knocking him to the ground, his head ringing, his heart pounding. In his terror he was willing it to stop but suddenly both his captors let go of him simultaneously. ;Helpless, he collapsed on the floor, the taste of blood in his mouth. He felt the sack pulled back off his head, the men taking steps away behind him laughing, a door creaking and slamming shut. They left him alone, curled in a helpless defensive ball in the dirt.

As Adam felt his battered face, wiping blood on his shirt, he tried to pull himself together and see where he was. He was in a small store room of some kind, and a quick look round ended any idea of escape.

High above he could see the first of the evening stars through a glass skylight. In the corner were two plastic bowls, no cutlery, some kind of food in the smaller bowl and water it looked like, in the other. He was so hungry he knew that he had to attempt the food, better now before it was totally dark.

It tasted like lentil and onion. Having no cutlery of any sort made it difficult and messy to eat; a cut lip and bruised jaw made it painful too, but he wolfed it down like a man possessed. He felt better having something inside him. The water was cool and tasted fresh. This too he took in quickly, in deep gulps.

He sat back against the wall, a throbbing pain in the side of his head which he found himself holding as if that would ease it. No noise, no cars, no animals or birds, just silence as evening fell. He decided to try and use some of the water by carefully pouring it into his hand to wash, first his hands, then his face, using his wet hands to smooth back his long hair. That too felt better.

Looking up at the stars, he felt deeply aware of his own imprisonment and the freedom that lay just beyond his grasp. As the night progressed, the combined effect of his fears and

171

the pains in his head prevented any possibility of sleep. He began to talk through his scenario to himself as if it were some kind of police movie; it seemed like the best use of his time.

First, he asked himself why they hadn't simply robbed him and left him. The answer must be they had another purpose for him. He was being personally held, at greater risk to them, so there must be some other reward for them - perhaps he was being kidnapped. All this travelling, he reasoned, was to hide him until a ransom was paid. That was how it worked wasn't it? His parents weren't well off, but surely kidnappings were managed and most people were released. No, that didn't feel like the whole picture, this massive drive doesn't fit in with kidnap for ransom.

Second, maybe they must have some other use for a kidnapped westerner. They'd taken his passport and cards. People-smuggling was big business and they were going to use his identity to smuggle another asylum seeker into Britain. Then, maybe then, they'll let him go. No, that didn't feel right either. Having taken his documents, surely they didn't need to keep hold of him.

Third, what's third? He stood up and thought it would be useful to exercise in the small cell-like room. Movement might help him concentrate and distract his mind from his painful bruises. He began circulating clockwise seeing if he could do so without crashing his shoulder into the walls, a walk lit very dimly by the limited starlight from the skylight above. It was good to move his legs. Weeks of cycling had led his legs to expect to be worked hard each day. Moving around might stimulate his mind too.

After several perambulations, a third option did come to mind. It made him stop to think it through. Given his probable location now in the borderlands of eastern Turkey, he knew things were a good deal less stable here. Different groups in the vicinity had their own agendas. He could have been caught by one of these factions to serve their ends. The Kurds were determined to prise a free Kurdistan from Turkey's grasp, but Yusuf and Stefan weren't Kurds. Who then were they? Whose mind was behind this?

On reflection they didn't seem like Turks either. He was pretty sure they were Muslims, but of their ethnicity he couldn't be certain. The nearer they were to the Iran border, then... and then it hit him, the journey east could also be toward Iraq, and that would certainly manifest all the worst scenarios for a kidnap he could imagine.

A final thought crossed his mind before he sat down again with his back to the wall. What had happened in Nurnberg was no accident. Now what was the guy's name, 'Gezim!' He said his name out loud. Then there were those two guys outside the map shop in Istanbul. I know I'm in danger of getting paranoid here, he told himself, but I knew something was going on back then, I couldn't put my finger on it, but I've been tracked and followed half way across Europe.

As he tried to curl up in a comfortable ball on the hard earth floor, another thought struck him. The kind of planning that had gone into this was professional and organised by a Europe-wide group. They could have taken him anywhere, but they were deliberately taking him east. There was one other group out this way: Islamic State. The very memory of the name made him shake.

'I'm an idiot in deep shit,' he told himself, 'a prize, top of the class, idiot. How the hell am I going to get out of this?'

No way would sleep be an option tonight. A cloud passed in front of the moon and he was left in total darkness.

26

The only good thing about the night was that Adam was left alone. He'd felt his way round the walls looking for any way he might prise bricks loose or find footholds up to the skylight, but his frantic searching was entirely fruitless. These guys were careful and thorough. He used the remaining water to drink, not knowing when next he'd be offered any.

At first light, there was the sound of approaching footsteps outside, the jangle of keys and the sliding of unwilling bolts. They were coming to get him. It raised Adam's adrenaline levels. There was a pause before the door opened. Adam pressed himself against the back wall for fear he might be hit again.

As the door swung open, he caught a brief glimpse of a nondescript courtyard and a woman, arms folded with a veil and headscarf, standing by the far door of what looked liked the main house. As soon as his eyes met hers she turned and that was when the sack went over his head, dust once more getting into his eyes such that he could do nothing about until it worked its way out to the sides. The claustrophobic sacking smelled of damp earth and in his panic he drew hasty breaths to make sure he could breathe, his heart beating fast and furiously.

They yanked him out none too gently and without saying anything pulled him along quickly by the route he'd arrived and moments later he was once more in the back of the van. Once inside, Stefan held his arms viciously pinioned behind him making both his shoulders hurt. Then the sack was unexpectedly removed from his head and his arms allowed to fall. Next, Yusuf secured his hands in front of him with self-locking plastic ties, Stefan with a big arm around Adam's neck as they were fastened. The ties were OK as they didn't do them too tight, but there was no way he was going to be able to break them.

Yusuf then grabbed Adam's hair and pulled his head back, grinning as he did so. In his other hand he had a wet cloth, dripping wet. Adam feared he might try and suffocate him. Another wave of panic, but no. Yusuf roughly wiped Adam's head to clean off what crusted blood came free easily, then playfully slapped him across the face to show he had finished, pushing him away from the van doors as he closed up. In the next instant they were on the road again.

During the long night of imprisonment Adam had had the presence of mind to tear off the edge part of his plastic bowl and push it down the inside of his shoe, reasoning that any tool might prove useful. Once they were under way, he edged himself off the wheel arch and as his eyes got used to the dim light he tried several ways, none successfully, to use his plastic wedge to trip the van door lock or force the doors open, even a fraction more, so he could see something.

It was a waste of time and all he was doing was destroying the plastic and punishing his tied hands. He gave up in frustration and resignation and slipped the shard of plastic down the inside of his cycling shoe once more, hoping it would be more useful at some future time. The activity, however fruitless, meant he he had attempted to exercise some control over his desperate situation and this gave his pitifully low self-confidence a little boost. For the moment he felt better about himself.

The first stop came surprisingly soon and some flat, but fresh, Turkish bread, two figs and a bunch of red grapes were given him. He said, 'thanks,' but there was no flicker of acknowledgement and no word exchanged. Adam thought the two cousins looked preoccupied. Stefan and Yusuf seemed more nervous today. The van made more and more stops. Sometimes there were mobile calls, other times it sounded like one or other just got out to stretch their legs or look around. Adam couldn't make it out, but he sensed something was soon to happen and his feeling of deep unease crept back.

Then, round about midday, the van pulled up for a longer spell. More phone calls were taking place, he guessed about him. Another vehicle pulled up and Yusuf and Stefan got out and walked away. Presumably they were meeting someone, but he could be completely wrong. He decided to press his ear against the middle of the side of the van in the hope that he'd be able to hear more of what was going on. Yes, a conversation was taking place outside, but he couldn't understand what they were saying. It was getting very hot: he was sweating, and the uncertainty was beginning to take its toll.

He heard the other vehicle door open and slam shut, the engine start up, and the distinct sound of it moving closer. It pulled up, and he knew it must be very close. Footsteps approached and his door opened, just a fraction. A black robe of some kind and a matching head scarf were pushed in, a knife flashed, slashed his wrist ties free and disappeared as quickly as it came; and, he was told to put the new clothes on over his cycling gear and do it quickly.

This was difficult. He didn't have room to stand, he had hardly any light, he had no idea how to wear them, but he tried. After a few minutes both the rear doors then opened simultaneously. Two more men had joined Yusuf and Stefan, two to either side of him, the one holding an automatic weapon and the other opening the rear tailgate of a Toyota Hilux which now faced him. Adam realised his situation had just entered a new more perilous phase.

'Get in,' the man to his left said, using the end of his weapon as a visual aid. The sight of weapons added a new dimension to the situation.

He opened the secure box-back which had darkened windows. As he did so, Stefan moved into the back of the van, seized Adam's Marin bike, and after a look around to see they weren't being observed, re-located it in the back of the Hilux next to Adam. There was just enough room for it.

Stefan shuffled across and handed a large plastic bag over to one of the newly arrived men, the top of Adam's jacket showing it was probably all his possessions. Stefan had done all the physical stuff, though Yusuf, it was clear to Adam, was the one in charge of the two. It was Yusuf who'd talked him into this mess, who'd taken his passport from the inside pocket of Adam's jacket and now handed it over separately to the waiting young man.

'Hands,' the younger man with dark eyes, demanded of Adam.

Adam obediently put his arms forward. This guy looked fit, as if he worked out. Ties were once more put on his wrists, this time woven through with a metal chain that was anchored somewhere to the structure of the vehicle. He saw an envelope given to Yusuf and then his kidnappers turned, climbed back into their battered and dusty van, reversed, and drive off, but not before Adam, in their moment of carelessness this time, had managed to see and read its vehicle registration plate.

The blue TR strip indicated Turkey, then 06 which Adam knew was Ankara and the bit he then had to really commit to memory was ET 6898. He kept repeating it over in his head. The ET he linked with Extra Terrestrial and the Hollywood blockbuster of a generation ago - 'got it' he said to himself, and 6898, it's just 6898, and the number kept tripping off his tongue rhythmically the more times he said it.

I'm still in control he tried to remind himself. It was, he told himself like those hard moments on the cycle, when he was tired, when he wasn't sure where he was, when it was a long uphill. He knew he was having to dig very deep into his inner resources to keep control. He reminded himself that in his shoes he had some euros and a shard of plastic and in his head, a good idea of the geography where he was being taken and a van registration. Who could tell if any of these things might be useful? Yusuf and Stefan's faces were also etched indelibly in his memory. In spite of these little victories, every now and then he felt he was losing it, as fresh waves of panic threatened to take over.

Whereas the back of the van which had been his home smelled of hay and grass and farmyard, this Toyota smelled of grease and oil and metal. This vehicle, with its battered desert camouflage paintwork had immediately signalled the idea of armed militia to Adam, and he knew he had now been passed over to a much more dangerous adversary.

Bolt heads standing proud from the floor suggested some weaponry had been fastened there at one time. In this vehicle, he could both see through the box unit's darkened windows of the side and rear, and forward into the double cabin of the front. He could observe his captors as well as the direction and landscape in which they were headed. He knew his captors were confidently in control otherwise they'd have blindfolded or hooded him.

As the Toyota set off he made every effort to observe every detail. The task usefully occupied him. After a while he could tell from the position of the sun they were headed in a southerly direction. The terrain was rough and dry, dusty brown mountains could be seen. The road became more a dirt track. For the first few hours his captors appeared quite edgy, glancing up at the sky or across to the side or into their mirrors.

The hours passed and the afternoon lengthened into dusk, the men in front visibly relaxing and increasingly chatting to each other. Then they halted and waited. The still times were the worst.

An old plastic bottle of water was passed into the back together with a piece of dry flat bread. The warm water inside tasted OK and was particularly welcome; as Adam tried his best, ties permitting, to lift it to his dry lips, he could just make out the words 'St Elijah's Monastery, Mosul'. It was then he knew for certain, he was headed for Iraq. This was a seriously dangerous place for him to be and any chance of surviving his ordeal seemed to diminish with every passing moment. He slumped, tired and despondent, simply waiting for what would happen next.

When it was quite dark, but for the quarter moon and myriad stars, the Toyota started up again and began to creep forward, making only slow progress for what seemed like hours.

Then the mood of the two guys seemed to change again. There was a definite high five enthusiastically shared and soon the vehicle was accelerating on a better road; headlights were switched on, and then Adam saw it. A street sign, saying 'Mosul'. He was inside the Islamic State. Adam squeezed his hands together and closed his eyes. He'd seen what they did to western hostages.

27

Driving into Mosul wasn't easy, debris from bombed and damaged buildings spilled into the road. No-one seemed to be about. Occasionally the bright headlight beam picked up black graffiti on the houses with red circles and what looked like a letter U with a dot between the two uprights. It was how the seized houses of Christians were marked - so reminiscent of the yellow star of David used by the Nazis. A cold shiver passed through his spine.

It was hard not to be totally distracted by the passing sights, the few things caught briefly in the headlights, but he told himself to try and observe his two captors, to gain any insight or detail, however slight or apparently insignificant, anything in fact that might prove useful later.

He watched them, trying not to look obvious as they were also watching him. Both had their sun visors down, the vanity mirrors aimed in his direction. They were not like the rough and ready thugs who had been paid to kidnap him. These guys were altogether more sinister, cloaked, organised, poised and focussed.

In turn, their mirrors allowed him to see their faces, the area their black headwear left uncovered. Occasionally the vehicle would slow as if passing through some checkpoint hardly visible in the shadows. At no point were they challenged, which made Adam conclude these guys and their vehicle were both well-known locally and they had the necessary authority to move around unhindered.

The young fit-looking guy with dark eyes was driving. The other, who could be his brother, as their faces bore a resemblance, had been trusted with the automatic, and he was definitely the more nervous of the two. The driver carried authority, the other guy did what he was told and was less self-assured. This was clearly an experienced driver and he knew the vehicle and route well, taking the Toyota past obstacles and debris with consummate ease, at times barely slowing up even through gaps which looked too small to pass.

They drove down by a large river, must be the Tigris, flowing dark and wide, some larger houses still standing on its banks, then swung and moved toward the outskirts of the city. There were now more low rise rustic-looking collections of buildings amongst typical city apartments. Adam concentrated his attention now on the landscape outside, sensing they were near their destination; it would be important to get what bearings he could. He spotted the minaret of a mosque and, as it was a bit of a local landmark, committed to memory its minaret complete with metal-railed platform.

Then they were going straight toward two metal gates, which swung open by some hidden hand as they drove up. Once they were in the courtyard, the vehicle stopped, the lights were switched off, the gates clanged shut and all was dark. The two guys in front exchanged words and got out, the interior light briefly illuminating them. He saw their shadows move to the rear of the vehicle, the driver carrying Adam's bag of things slung over his shoulder, the more nervous guy told to stand several yards back from the car with the automatic pointed toward the vehicle. Finally, the rear door was opened, Adam's chain was unlocked and he was pulled, none too gently, from the vehicle so that his ties cut into his wrists making him draw a sharp intake of breath. He was led to a metal door with a metal grille set about head height. He guessed it was once an animal stall; the image of a lamb being led to the slaughter came to mind.

He felt his cycle shoes kicking dusty ground as he obediently followed the young guy to what he rightly guessed was to be his next place of detention. The door was unlocked and Adam simply walked straight inside and there he was left. He was glad of the open grille. He could see by the moon and starlight the yard outside. The two guys, then a third person, disappeared into a door opposite. It was night, dark, he was alone, so very alone.

There was no food or water that night; crushed by a great weariness, he slept fitfully, the cold earth offering no comfort. The muezzin's call to prayer broke and marked the hours. First light saw him up and looking out of the grille long before he heard sounds of other people.

The Toyota was parked against the far wall. He could just hear sounds of the city coming to life, occasional vehicles starting up and the sounds of distant voices as people got up and went out, perhaps to get bread. However, it wasn't until the sun was well up that anything happened in the courtyard and by this time he was really hungry and thirsty, his stomach persistently gnawing at his insides.

Ali Muhammed was both pleased and unsettled. This captured lad, Adam Taylor, reminded him of when he himself was a young student at Mosul University. He was a living symbol of what might have been and it now seemed to him that that was a quite different age, a separate life, a dim memory.

Since then he'd been part of the fighting militias and indeed part of the group capturing his home city of Mosul back in June 2013. His own knowledge of the city had been invaluable as Iraqi troops had been forced on the back foot. He recalled how many thousands of ordinary people had been killed in Mosul alone since then as unquestioning loyalty to the Caliphate had to be imposed.

He reckoned about 2,000 people a year were having to be summarily executed, according to the regular lists posted up by the Ministry of Forensic Medicine. Their offence was uniformly described as 'promoting ideas contrary to Islam' which was a blanket crime that he knew could cover anything they chose. It was not nice, but there could be no room for sentiment. Well, that's what their leaders kept telling everyone, in a hard place suffering hard times.

That battle for internal order had been won long since, but the sleepless nights from the blood-letting and rooftop falls for which sometimes he himself was responsible, never seemed to go away. He hated what he had become, all innocence destroyed, committing easy acts of cruelty toward others as he'd become increasingly anaesthetised to violence in a system that fed off fear and violence.

How near they had been then to taking the whole of Iraq. Again, it was mainly the American infidels who had halted the Iraqi rout and prolonged the years of suffering since. Everyone then had talked about when the Mahdi would come and liberate his people from pain and struggle. It couldn't be long now everyone said, but Ali was beginning to doubt, thoughts he kept wisely very much to himself.

But this lad, this Adam Taylor, he thought, as he held and read his open passport in his hand, was to provide his own new persona. He was to become this Adam. As he looked, he realised this Adam, dark haired and youthful in the passport photo, looked to a casual observer not so very different from himself.

The reality of taking Adam's identity, albeit a temporary expedient, had led him to think he was more like him than he cared to admit. Seeing Adam, being Adam, had touched him, it was something to do with how identity worked. No one person was a fixed thing, no matter what they told you, bits were borrowed and stuck for however long they were useful, that was how it was.

This was troubling, so he then reminded himself again that, as a faithful foot soldier of the Caliphate, all personal thoughts and sentiment had to be subsumed by duty. That was the answer. He was in the business of changing the world and nothing and no-one was going to get in the way.

He had done everything his CO had asked of him, even calling him that very morning to give him the latest briefing. There was no point in thinking of Adam as any more than a delivery parcel, a meat parcel, here today, gone tomorrow - best not to think about it.

The links in the chain had all held good, from Germany, through Turkey, and now here in Mosul. Satisfaction was to be found in obedience to the cause, seeing true purposes fulfilled. In the mobile calls he'd taken overnight from his CO, he could tell that for all his restrained leadership and controlled emotion, his CO gave enough indication of heartfelt praise to leave Ali feeling he'd done well so far. For the moment his own situation and that of his family remained safe.

His sister, Fatima had unsettled him earlier. She had put out an extra plate of food, one for Adam, and told Ali, to take it to him. That wasn't her place, she should have waited for instructions, but in providing for Adam as if he were a guest, this too had touched some raw nerve of humanity and reached deep inside him. Against all military sense he found himself walking over to the makeshift cell opposite the kitchen, the very plate of food Fatima had so carefully prepared in one hand and hot coffee in the other.

He had to put them both down in the dust to open up. Adam had been watching him approach. He could feel his eyes on him from behind the metal grille, like gluey filament strands reaching out to stick themselves to his very soul. He tried to steel himself and look tough. He couldn't afford any mistakes, no undue risks must be taken.

With the door open, Adam didn't look any kind of threat, just a tired, fearful young student, still in his ridiculous cycling gear, the black robes he'd been given to travel in now cast to one side, a victim caught in a snare not of his own making.

Ali offered the food and Adam took it meekly.

'Thank you,' he said.

Ali then did something that surprised him. Subconsciously lowering his guard for the first time, he responded to Adam in English.

'My sister, she cooks, it's not so bad. You will be here for now. Try to make yourself as comfortable as possible. I'm afraid there won't be any privileges and there will be no communication. Being here is not without risk to you or to us. Don't ask me or anyone for anything. That's it.'

With that and without waiting for Adam to say anything, he turned, stepped outside and locked the door behind him, but even as he did so, he heard the sound of his own closing the cell-like door and locking it up as being more gentle than before, more as if he were making his favourite pet safe for the night.

As he walked back across the yard, he kicked the ground deliberately, a cloud of dust rising as he did. He could have kicked himself for such a betrayal of feeling, for he knew Adam would have seen this frustrated outburst of emotion from behind his grille. Indeed Adam's watchful eyes were on him and had read exactly how Ali was feeling.

Ali knew he had to get on and finalise his packing. He was now this Adam Taylor and there was no time to waste if he was to maximise the advantage of using his stolen identity. He needed to be on his way today and head as far west as he could in as short a time as possible. A barber had been called to give him an Adam style hair cut and a shave to match his passport picture.

Once done, Ali checked he had everything he needed. He knew Adam's bike had been thoroughly examined overnight by IS's own mechanic to ensure it was in a tip-top state to carry him when necessary. The panniers had been carefully re-packed with all the authentic paraphernalia of a long-distance cyclist. It was time to get into his own cycling kit, collect his wheels, prepare himself, his kit and the bike. He was now ready and waiting outside with red cycling jersey on under his robes.

Finally, his CO called to give him the signal. After weeks of waiting and training, it was almost time to head west. But it was the way of commanding officers to keep juniors waiting and as dawn gave way to morning Ali was still being held with no call coming to release him on his mission. At long last, a text came: his transport, for him and his bike, was on its way to collect him.

Meanwhile, a few hundred miles south and west, Anna in her office in Tel Aviv was checking her latest emails. Her boss had been through her day lists and flagged interesting items to be followed up.

There was that Adam Taylor case again. Her boss had looked at it and agreed it didn't check out. It was now red-starred, the mobile trace having definitely gone over into IS territory. Latest position gave the phone's position as Mosul, Iraq, right in the devil's mouth.

The only trouble was, it was very difficult getting intelligence back from Mosul. How the hell was she to follow this one up now? She called up an on-screen picture of Adam Taylor again and looking at him she despaired that anything much could be done to save this young man from the fate that undoubtedly awaited him.

28

The small terraced house in Cheddington Road was not a place to have a family row. The walls were so thin the neighbours both sides could hear the Kone family shouting and carrying on and, for those engaged in the fracas, there was nowhere to escape. Kaylah might be the youngest but she could hold her own when it came to having it out with the family.

Today was a case of everyone for themselves. First, it was Sam calling the shots, then Shazee telling him he had no right to shout at her and he was equally responsible for the way his kids turned out. Clive for his part found his way to his usual bolt hole, his room, blocked off by his Dad. Sam Kone was standing across the bottom of the stairs using his bulk to create an impassable barricade.

This had all been brewing up for days. Bishop Kone's 'Kool Kone Komments' TV contract had not been renewed for the autumn term and this had left his status badly dented, given him unwelcome extra time on his hands and left his self-image in urgent need of a pick-me-up.

His way to rationalise this was to bring in God. He interpreted what had happened as a judgement and a punishment for sins, and the only way he could understand this was to conclude that he had failed to bring his family up in the ways of the Lord. The rebellion of the children was what lay behind this latest catastrophe, of that fact he was quite certain. He rounded on Clive again.

'You turnin' into some kind of roadman, useless wasteman these days. You either just lying in bed listenin' to music, hip hop, rap, whatever. Ain't no future for you in it. Fillin' your head so full of nonsense you turnin' out no good for nothing. Don't ask much of you, but man, when are you goin' to get out there, grab the world and do a decent day's work for a decent day's pay? What you bringin' into this family? Nuthin', nuthin' nuthin',' Sam shouted, his disappointment and frustration taking hold of him in equal measure. His finger was wagging right under Clive's nose, but he hadn't finished yet.

'That no-good criminal Winston is corruptin' you. Don't want to see him round here no more. People will think this house is some den. Dat boy don't know day from night. Mark my words you are headin' for a fall. The good Lord says in Deuteronomy 6, the commandments of the Lord should be on your heart, and Fathers must impress them on the hearts of their children. I tell you boy, I ain't ever been a failure and I ain't beginin' to start failin' my own offspring now. So tell me son, what you goin' to do? What the hell are you goin' to do?'

Sam Kone hadn't dropped a decibel in ten minutes. He didn't wait for an answer, he was like an express train at full speed.

'Your sister here, she started right, she goes to college, she learn real good. That's what I thought until today; but no, she goes up there in the holiday. I thought she go there for her learnin', but no, look at this, looook at thiiiis!' Sam said as he reached to the coffee table where he picked up the latest copy of the Hornsey Journal, jabbing at the front page story.

'Some lecture that. Girl gets stabbed; and you Kaylah, end up in the front page picture! Everyone t'inks it you what's involved. Trouble-making Muslim terrorists you went to listen to. Trouble-making knifemen and you right there and get yourself on page one. Police will be at our door next. Neighbours will think we is criminal no good wasters. Think on the shame, the shame and disgrace,' he said.

Clive was quiet, leaning on the wall, his face not betraying any emotion. A deadpan expression was a step of defiance he knew he could get away with, but Kaylah was having none of it. Stepping up to Sam, matching his fierce gaze, eyeball to eyeball, she launched herself at her father.

'You are so out of order! I went to a lecture on freedom of speech and religion along with lots of other students. None of us knew it would turn out like this. Anyway, that newspaper make a mountain out of a mole hill. I did what anyone would have done if someone gets hurt. I look after them, I get help, I

188

stop her bleeding till help comes. I'm working my socks off on this course, I passed my year exams and what's more I'm doing your work for you. These past weeks I've been helping out at the Drop In. You were asked to go, I was here when the vicar came round to ask you, and I never seen you there once, not once! What else you expect of me, eh?' said Kaylah, almost matching her father for volume.

Her Dad stepped back, taken aback, momentarily stung by guilt. He didn't know what to say. He was proud of his daughter and he knew he'd overstepped the mark. Maybe she hadn't been at the heart of the trouble herself, if it was as she described, then it could only be simply bad luck or rather good luck she was there at the time. He was confused, didn't know where to go next, so he turned to face Clive, a softer target, but Clive beat him to it.

'I've been helping with the Drop In club too, but as Kaylah says, we don't see you down there, so you wouldn't know. As it happens, me and Winston have got some work goin'. Should turn a tidy profit in a few days, so keep your hair on and give us a break. We can't all sit around all day natterin' on our mobiles and drinking tea with old folks. Make no mistake, I'm all in favour of gettin' out of this yard as soon as I can,' said Clive.

'Oh my days!' came in his Mum, fearing an empty nest. 'Now come on, we all need to cool. Dear,' she said reaching for her husband's arm, 'don't you think they're doing alright. Listen to them. Makes you proud doesn't it? They're young, the world's against them. This is still a racist country and we must stand together or else disaster will visit us. The house that doesn't stand firm together will surely fall. Isn't that right? Isn't that what you always tell us?' Shazee said softly.

'That Drop In's trouble if you ask me,' Sam said more quietly, trying to defend himself. 'It's a base for puttin' poison into our ends. Edmonton ain't seen nothing like the drugs trouble before that place opened. Can't put my finger on it, don't know who, but been happenin' since it opened. If you two goin' there, you better watch yourselves, go in with your eyes wide open! No good will come of it. Send them all back where they come from I say. Send 'em all back. Country can't afford them. They bring their gangs, their drugs here. A door to evil that's what it is,' he said, but this time not knowing where to direct his ire.

With that he turned on his heels and went to the desk in the corner of the back room, the place he euphemistically called his study. He pulled some papers from the corner toward him and began to shuffle them. The signal was sent, the row was over.

Kaylah gave Clive a nod, indicating they step outside the front door. Her Mum was heading the other way and through into the kitchen leaving the front door exit clear. Clive followed and the Yale lock snicked shut as they stood out on the street.

'Come on, let's get some fresh air,' Kaylah suggested.

They began walking down their road of tired -looking red-brick terraced houses that made up most of the Huxley Estate of uniform Victorian homes. Minutes later they were in Haselbury Road and headed for the Angel. Their local MacDonald's would do nicely, they agreed. It took thirty minutes to wander down, until they were ordering burgers and Coke.

They both knew they were living on the thin surface crust of life and could fall through any time. There were no safety nets in this part of north London. Kaylah was worried for Clive and truth to tell she was worried for herself. She wanted to hear more from Clive. Her Dad had softened him up. Could she now prise him open a bit more.

'How's the hand?' she asked, seeing the raw stab-like wound as he lifted his Coke cup to his mouth.

'Oh that, it's fine, I was lucky, no damage done to nerves or tendons. Almost healed up. It's nothing,' Clive said dismissively, hiding his scar from her sight as he spoke.

'You never actually told me the story of how it happened. It was more than a cut. It was bad, it bled for ages, I had to clean up the mess; and, look it went right through,' she said, taking and turning his hand in hers.

'You were white as a sheet when I got to you. You got stabbed in the hand, didn't you? Come on. Tell me,' she persisted.

'Not much to tell really. As you know I was helping out, Larry stepped outside a minute, I got the difficult customer and somehow spiked myself as I stood up.'

'Skeen! No way! Clive, Clive, it's Kaylah, your Sis. Tell me.'

'T'ing is, this can't go further, promise?' he said, knowing he was beaten.

'Sure, sure,' she reassured.

'Dem Muslim guys are trouble. One of dem, that Abu guy, stabbed me as a warning. "Tell Winston and his friend stay out of our area," he said. And then this. It could have been so much worse. Truth is, Winston's doin' some runnin' around for the bruvvers. There's some opportunities in this, Winston's careful, I can make some money,' explained Clive.

'So it's fightin' over ends?' to which Clive nodded and suggested she lower her voice.

'This stuff just gets worse, you ain't gettin' a knife through your hand next time Clive. You will be dead on a mortuary block. My friend Melissa got a cut belly, probably a Stanley Knife or something. That guy Abu and his friends came to my college, they did it. They're dangerous, someone is going to die soon. You can't deal with this stuff. It's not what you know. How come you got into all this?' she asked.

'Winston took me out in his car. We picked up some stuff. You know what it's like. You came to the party. You saw Dillon and the others. This is life on the street Sis, no escape. I squeal now and they stick me like a pig. They got to sort out something and then it'll all quieten down, promise, then it's back to normal,' Clive said.

'What you mean?' she said.

'Got to deal with these Muslim guys before things get out of hand. Not me personally, they'll do it. Things will be OK then, you'll see. It'll be over then,' said Clive.

'What you goin' to do with your life, Clipper, after all this is over?' she said affectionately.

191

'It's gettin' too hot around here. Come the autumn, might take myself off to do a course like you,' said Clive.

He smiled cheekily at her and tweaked her chin. Burger eaten, Coke finished, they got up to leave. They'd enjoyed being together, just chatting, hanging out, away from the claustrophobia of home. Somehow they both felt closer to each other. Clive pushed open the glass door to leave and they stepped onto the pavement. Outside, on Fore Street, they saw them: Abu and his two friends, walking in their direction.

'Hell,' said Clive panicking and pulling Kaylah to a stop. She watched as Clive quickly pulled out his mobile.

'Winston, am at Angel, MacDonald's, with my Sis, need help now. That guy Abu's outside with a couple of fellas, bring back-up. Make it quick! Please,' pleaded Clive.

Turning them both round, he pulled his sister away from the street.

'Need to get back inside Sis, it's safer inside, it'll be OK, the cavalry are coming.'

He watched Abu and his friends walk past the open glass front doors, glancing in, looking around, hesitating, but deciding against coming in. They walked on.

Kaylah knew better than to argue with Clive and agreed to wait with him. In not much more than a few minutes the familiar and welcome sight of Winston's blue BMW with two guys inside screeched to a halt, Winston, as ever, ignoring the double yellows.

They stepped out on the street, climbed in the car and were chauffeur-driven back home. For all the shouting earlier and excitement at MacDonald's, home now felt a safe place to be, but Kaylah's concern for her brother had only deepened. He was getting in way over his head.

How can I get him out of this? she asked herself. Where can I turn for help?

29

10 Downing Street had been the seat of power and home of British Prime Ministers since 1735 and people the world over knew this to be no ordinary London house. It had the very smell of government oozing through the mortar holding the bricks of history of which it was built.

The PM was glad to be back, even though it looked such an unprepossessing place from which to run a country. To look at it, one could be forgiven for thinking it was little different to the London brick terraced houses of Cheddington Road and the Huxley Estate, or for that matter any of London's ancient, terraced, urban housing stock; but in so far as it had another floor and a highly polished black front door with a posh light above, it was an improvement. The PM pondered, asking himself why people in power; liked the colour black so much, why not a blue front door? Strange this was the seat of power, No 10 didn't have even a slither of front garden to lighten the greyness, just black railings. Notwithstanding its ordinariness and shortcomings, this terraced house with its modest black front door still meant everything to him as he was welcomed home.

The summer recess had come to an end and now in early September Parliament was again coming back to life, the long holidays over. the PM was gathering his troops.

Ministers were beginning to arrive, some having the luxury of a chauffeur-driven journey to allow extra minutes to work at the their laptops or on their phones. One by one they were let in the front door by the duty policeman with a polite nod, past the security desk just inside, which only they knew was but the tip of a security network trying to protect them against any one of many possible dangers.

Even the IRA had made explosive inroads in the past, the Tory PM John Major being the target of a mortar attack in February 1991. Fortunately the shells had been poorly aimed and then failed to explode and in the fashion of stiff upper lip, ministerial business just went on in Downing Street much the same as before. The current PM tended to be in this very British tradition.

Things were, everyone told themselves, much better now. Security improvements had been made, safe areas created, escape routes built and barriers constructed at the entrance to Downing Street itself. Even the tourist icon, the ubiquitous London policeman, was now more likely than not to be armed; and, if he wasn't, then he'd have hidden colleagues no more than a call away who most certainly were.

The Prime Minister had finished breakfast in the tiny top floor kitchen. After swilling his mouth with water and adjusting his dark blue tie, he was ready to go straight down to the Cabinet room. He noticed there was still a smell of fresh paint about the place, work that had to be hastily completed over the summer, just before Tabitha, their children and himself arrived back from their brief seaside holiday in the South West. The hallway mirror showed his face had a reassuringly healthy tan. That's the face of a leader, he told himself.

Stepping onto the landing he began his descent, the wooden staircase winding down round a central void, the outside walls covered with painted portraits of his predecessors. Nearly all the more modern portraits were photographs, though Lady Thatcher had had hers done in oils. He rather thought that was how his ought to be, a thought he'd keep to himself for now, but it wouldn't be long, he told himself, before he could sign out for the last time. Today he gave this hall of witnesses barely a glance.

There was a creak on the wooden boards in two places as he descended and he made a mental note to get it fixed. He'd been PM for two long terms in office, built a solid reputation, a strong economy and was now trying to build a platform for a Tory majority and a third term in government. Having a parliamentary majority had meant that he could do pretty well as he wished. The thought of near invincibility put an added spring in his step.

Just one thing on his mind today, one agenda item, one event to host to conclude his personal time in office.

194

Something significant on the world stage; and then, perhaps, semi-retirement and a place in the Lords. He couldn't wait to share the idea he'd conceived and been quietly working on. He'd been developing it for months, taking key figures into his confidence as he explored and planned. Even whilst walking on the sandy beaches of south Devon more ideas and detail had come to him. He was bursting to get on with it, though to any observer he looked cool as ice.

Wearing his trade mark immaculate blue suit, he pushed open the Cabinet Room door and strode in, a picture of poise and statesmanship. Faces turned toward him, faces he could read like a book - allies, rivals, advisors and support team, all in their places. They might think they had achieved their positions, but the reality was, it was him who had appointed every last one of them.

The Cabinet Room was little bigger than an ordinary front room, and - like the house itself - too small. Only the wooden panelling on the walls gave it a distinguishing feature and a little character. Sliding his way behind the chairs holding seated colleagues, he sat himself down in his usual seat about half way down the table. It was time, and almost all the seats were taken. It wasn't his practice to hang around waiting for latecomers. He looked up, got everyone's attention and began to set forth the one agenda item.

'Thank you for your attendance here today. I do hope you all feel refreshed after the summer recess. Things are going well presently, except in one particular direction - polls indicate, and this time I am inclined to believe the thrust of what they are saying, that ours is not a popular government. Our policies are seen by too many people as divisive, elitist and uncaring. People are also finding the necessary police and terrorism measures we have taken as overly oppressive and intrusive.'

He kept his voice low and serious as he had been trained to do, to make his point. Then he pressed on.

'People are demonstrating, protesting even; and, some are complaining that either we let too many migrants in, or we are not doing enough to look after the ones who are here.

195

Even our international partners are wanting more from us. It seems whichever which way we try, we lose. I'm only comforted by the fact that the Opposition are even less popular, less credible and certainly less organised; but I've never been one to judge who we are and what we do by things pertaining to the Opposition. So let's move on.' He could see they liked that!

'When we came to power, the exiting party wrote to the Treasury saying, "there is no money left in the coffers." Yes they did, I have the very letter here,' said the PM.

He lifted it from the top of the pile of papers on the table in front of him, then waved it demonstrably.

'Labour's legacy was a disaster for this country. When we came to power there was no money! To turn our economy round is taking years, and yes we will succeed; but the necessary austerity cuts have undermined many people's sense of pride in our country. The pervasive negativity all around us attacks the very British Values we hold so dear. Let me tell you with all sincerity, if we continue like this, yes we will have balanced the books, but we will not win the next General Election. Given the present political climate of widespread disillusionment, most of you look set to lose your seats and will have to find other jobs,' he said.

He paused to let it sink home.

'I don't jest, this is the reality we face. Read the papers, look at the polls yourselves, talk to your constituents.' He paused reached for the carafe in front of him, pouring water into his glass before taking a sip and placing it carefully back on the table. Only when he felt that the dead weight of his last point had truly sunk home, was he ready to move on.

Raising his index finger to call them back, he continued, 'what we need is to restore British pride. Remember when we hosted the Olympic Games in London, in the glorious summer of 2012. The whole world came to London for the best games ever. We won many medals, we discovered new heroes and heroines, the nation felt good, the nation was united. Colleagues, I want to present you with a unique, once in a generation opportunity to do something even better, to rekindle that British spirit; and, if we do it right, we will be back in power on the crest of a wave of unprecedented popularity.'

There were grunts and hurrahs of approval from around the table. He knew they were with him and he pushed on.

'This coming 11 November marks a significant anniversary of the end of the First World War. At different points during these past years people have enjoyed observing and commemorating the anniversaries of the War, such as Armistice Day on the hundredth anniversary of the commencement of hostilities. You will recall how the Tower of London captured the population's attention with their field of red ceramic poppies. This coming November could become something equally memorable. It could unite us as British people and I bring before you today some ideas I have been finalising over the spring and summer, to provide us with an occasion of public spectacle that will endear everyone to us.

'First, this country will host a gathering of world leaders; political and military leaders of course, but many ordinary people will be invited to take part too. The present international state of flux guarantees us their support. It will be held here in London underlining our position as a leading world democracy and an unrivalled cultural and economic force. It is not only Moscow who can lay on big military parades, we can too! In all these years of public expenditure cuts, we said we would not allow the armed forces budget to suffer and I am counting on them to respond by laying on a military display in London the like of which this country has never seen before.

'The military Chiefs of Staff received scoping papers outlining this proposal of mine and indications are they will rise to the challenge. Incidentally, the exercise is an opportunity for us to see our own arms sales benefit to the tune of an estimated £2 billion.'

The Chancellor whom he had briefed earlier added a timely, 'Hear, Hear.'

'I have also asked the Home Secretary, the Chief Constable of the Metropolitan Police, and the Mayor of

197

London to come up with the best route for such a procession to take. After observing the necessary poppy wreath protocol, those leaders gathered will all be walking from the Cenotaph to a marquee by Parliament Square and Westminster Abbey. This will be the ideal place for them to watch a military procession pass the Houses of Parliament itself. There will be a specially constructed stage built on the grass opposite for the dignitaries. The very seat of government, Parliament, with the River Thames as a backcloth, at the heart of London and the nation, will take pride of place, as we ourselves will too,' he enthused.

'Second, the covert aim in all this is to get public participation. You will recall how the success of the 2012 Olympics was built on the work of the 70,000 Games Maker volunteers, all in their uniforms, all welcoming everyone to London. This is what British Values are all about. Modelling on their great success, I propose that we will have an army of British Values Volunteers the like of which we have never seen in this country before. They will form the vanguard for what I plan to be an ongoing initiative to build a new and integrated sense of community in this country. All this is going to be a huge logistical challenge, but I want to see not 70,000 Games Maker volunteers in November, but 888,246 volunteers. Those of you good on figures will follow my thinking.'

He nodded again at the Chancellor, who smiled in affirmation.

'You will recall that Paul Cummins and Tom Piper created 888,246 ceramic poppies, each representing one serviceman or woman from Britain or its colonies who died in World War One. What better way to mark the year's commemorations than to have that same number recalled by the presence of 888,246 living people who are our hope for the future of this great country?'

He wasn't inviting an answer, they all knew it was rhetorical and he hadn't finished with them yet.

'These ordinary people - men, women and children will be from every walk of life. They will embody our British

Values, they will all wear red and hold hands in a giant circle around this great city, together forming one huge symbolic poppy shape. They will all wave their Union Jacks in a choreographed media event the like of which no-one in this country will have ever seen before. We get this right and the mood of the country and our ratings will soar. Are you with me on this? Are you with me?' he urged, rallying his troops.

Initially, it was quiet as people reflected on what was said and took in the sheer audacity of the plan. Quiet was followed by growing murmurings of approval, and then the Chancellor motioned to speak.

'Yes, Prime Minister,' he endorsed, his response quickly followed by enthusiastic table thumping and more calls of, 'Yes! Yes!'

Once things had quietened, the PM spoke again.

'I take that to be a unanimous "yes". No need for any formal votes. A set of confidential briefing papers for each of you will be with your offices by later today. The Chancellor's office have already done some sums and can give departments a heads up on draft budgets for this. You will see that it is generous. A press briefing is being prepared by Comms even as I speak and this story will be fronting the news bulletins by the time of today's BBC One-O-Clock News. Thank you everyone, let's get to it.'

The PM rose from his seat to signal the meeting was over. He moved quickly through the corridor to a quiet room where, with his already assembled and briefed secretarial team at the ready, he could begin working through the list of calls to heads of state and foreign governments whom he would personally ring today to ensure they would be present. He was fully confident that this London event was one no-one would want or could politically afford to miss. First on his list was the Palace. From earlier soundings made, he knew they would play their part and, once they were signed up, other heads of state would fall in behind like dominoes, their own status flattered and their own egos propelled upward and onward by the royal endorsement to their personal invitations.

He was just putting through his first call, when he was tapped on the shoulder. It was Andrew Baker, long-serving Director General of MI5, the Head of UK security.

'May I have a word?' Andrew asked, his familiar insistent tone, bespectacled gaze, pudgy face and knowing voice always guaranteeing him a hearing. the PM dropped the call he was about to make and gave him his full attention.

'Our listening friends tell us this may be a difficult time to do this. Something is being planned out there. This event must be risk-assessed again, but even now I can tell you it will very likely be the target of unwelcome terrorist attention. We've had a leak somewhere. One of your early conversations went viral. We're investigating, haven't found who it is yet, but I'm afraid indications are that our most extremist friends are already on to it,' warned Andrew, speaking in the PM's ear.

'That, my friend,' he said, 'is your job to deal with. You have nothing specific, otherwise you'd have said. When you have something more definite, let me know. Life, as you and I both well know, is never without risk. What we need to do is make sure the next external threat to our security becomes useful to our purposes, something we can use, something around which I can unite the British people. Remember the war time spirit? In politics, it's the threats that forge unity! Threats, Andrew, present political opportunity. Simply cruising safely along is the road to many a government's political ruin,' said a confident, unstoppable PM.

'I don't want to be a party-pooper, but I am not sure it will be as easy as that this time Prime Minister. Indications are that IS are moving to put someone into London as we speak, and we know there are sympathetic supporters here already. Trying to stop funding from here getting there is like trying to plug a leaky bucket. IS have the resources and some are provided from people raising funds here in London,' said Andrew.

The PM could not stop himself involuntarily shuffling uncomfortably at this persistent problem he'd not yet found an effective method to deal with. Many hundreds of potential

200

terrorist plots had been foiled by Andrew's MI5 department and he was grateful; he knew he owed it to Andrew to hear him out.

'Trouble is, we don't know where they all are, who they all are or what their precise intentions are. All we know is, that with IS internationally now on the back foot, they are desperate to bring the conflict to our very door and once news of November is out, I am certain they will see it as their chance to have another go. It's rather like Adolf Hitler's last gap Ardennes Offensive; the war was lost, but he could still give a nasty surprise with a sting in its tail. Increasingly they see one-off attacks in our cities as an effective strategy, creating a spiral of fear.'

He paused, wanting to present another safer option.

'Can't you consider something small-scale for November, something we can manage? What you have in mind is going to prove a major challenge for us, one I fear may be a bridge too far.' As he was speaking his phone buzzed in his hand. Instinctively he glanced at the screen. He turned and showed it to the PM. It read, 'Israeli intelligence say they have something that may be coming our way.'

'Prime Minister,' he said seriously, 'Even as we speak the devil is making work for idle hands.'

'Thank you Andrew. The overall political plan will only work as I have outlined it. You will have all the resources you need to keep us as safe today as you have until now. I have every confidence in you and your team. This is, and I repeat is, going ahead. Keep me posted. I need to press on,' and with that Andrew was dismissed.

The PM began re-tapping his phone, simultaneously waving a signal to his waiting secretarial team to get going. Andrew Baker on the other hand was stepping out of Downing St a very worried man. We need some good intelligence, he told himself, but as of now we simply don't have it. He too was in a hurry, important calls of his own to make if a looming disaster on Armistice Day were to be averted.

30

Sunrise was often a spectacular sight over Mosul, orange and reds in the dusty sky dissipating as the rising sun scorched everything back to dryness, the blue above turning to white heat. Ali, having eaten an early breakfast was ready and waiting to depart when he received a text calling him to meet his CO before leaving. Salim Ismat, his regional IS CO, had groomed him carefully over the years since his father had been shot in front of them, overseen his military career and in recent weeks carefully supervised and prepared Ali for his mission.

Ali's training in communication skills, his English refresher classes and the rigorous fitness regime to toughen and prepare him physically had, thankfully, all gone to his satisfaction so far as Ali could gather. To Salim's mind, Ali was as ready as could be and the time to send him on his way had come, but to be absolutely certain, to give him peace of mind, he had to see Ali one last time before sending him on his mission.

Ali made his way over to his CO's apartment and as usual did not proceed through the unlocked door without respectfully announcing his presence. There was, as ever, a meticulous attention to hospitality protocol with mint tea and sweet biscuits being brought in on his arrival. Once left alone, Salim was impatient not to delay things unduly and was quick to get to the point.

'You have the Englishman, you have his passport, his cards, his bike and possessions. I trust you have memorised all the details - address in London, date of birth, place of birth, make of his bike?' checked his CO.

'Yes, yes,' said Ali.

'Then we cannot delay any longer. We must get you to London as soon as possible. Your family will be instructed to keep Mr Adam Taylor secure while you're away. It may be that your safety and return will be determined by this Adam being kept alive and useful to us. I know that rather depends on how co-operative he is, but I understand he is little more than a school boy and should pose us no problem. So, forget about him for now. I will see that your family are told what to do and are rewarded for their work for the Caliphate. You just focus on your personal jihad,' he said.

'You need to say goodbye to your family properly, tell them you will be away on military service for the coming months; they are to come to me if they have any concerns. Today you will be leaving at noon precisely. Your transport will pull up outside your house. Once on your way you will not have contact with me. It is safer that a communication silence is observed as much as possible. We cannot be too careful,' his CO continued.

'We can get you into Europe, no problem there, but then it is all up to you. Since the Schengen agreement, Europe is one land of open borders, that is until you try to get into the United Kingdom. The UK still retains a tight control over who comes in. The use of iris technology and the degree of customs and immigration surveillance at all the main access points means you will need to be intelligent how you find a way into England. I'm afraid there is no technology here to match theirs yet,' cautioned Salim.

'But that's a big problem isn't it? What should I do?' asked Ali, for the moment seeing this as one huge insurmountable obstacle in his getting to London. Looking into Salim's eyes, he could see the man was all set to demonstrate he already had a solution lined up.

'Well you can take your chances with the other groups of would-be asylum seekers and refugees who gather at favourite migrant camps up and down the coast at the French and Belgian ports, but your chances of getting through that way are, being realistic, only slight. There is more risk to the success of the mission if you are seen in these places and besides, you could be too long delayed. No, the best I can offer by way of a solution and we know it worked with one of our London contacts in the past, is to pay off a yachtsman in Calais to smuggle you across. We reward our agent in Calais well, she knows we can get to her if she fails us. You may have to wait for a few days, but she'll get you a safe passage to England. It will work again,' he said smiling as if to say he'd thought of everything.

'This is a mobile number you can use to call her when you get to Calais.' He slid a small card with hand-written blue inked numbers on it across the table. Ali slipped it into his pocket. 'She'll be there by the end of September, plenty of time and she's been told to wait for you. Her contact will take you across to a place called Blackwater, Essex - and you shouldn't have to even think about Customs. If by misfortune you do have to be checked in by Customs, it will be one man without any technological back up - they can't afford to watch everywhere. Here, take these.' He passed over some neatly folded maps in plastic cases.

'We have got these for you. They cover Western France and the South East of England. We have also found a map app on Adam's phone, which is useful back-up and could be especially helpful when you get to England. Don't use the phone until you are in England. You'll be using the SIM phone you've been issued with until then. Let me explain why,' he said. Ali listened politely, not having the courage to say this had all been explained to him already in training.

'It is vital to the success of our mission that no-one knows you are in London. They must only think Adam has returned. Doing that may just buy you more time before they discover you are in the country. People will believe Adam is back when they find his bicycle - it will be what the police call hard evidence. It just might throw them off the scent. This is where you will leave it, as near his home as you dare, though you must take every care not to be seen with the bike until then. If you must, use your mission mobile which you are familiar with from your training. It is clean and untraceable. You will use it as little as possible to communicate with me, our enemies are keen eavesdroppers of any conversation.'

'You will need to transport the bike with you, as you are Adam Taylor the cyclist from London. The driver here, the man collecting you shortly, has been instructed he is meeting

Adam. Your driver's taking carpets west, to an auction in Germany, and is happy to have a hitch-hiker on board as company. From this point on, you are Adam, to me, to everyone, especially to your driver. Keep yourself well-shaved and practise that half-smile on the passport photo. Your hair style is just fine. Any questions?' asked the CO.

Ali's mind was racing. This was his last chance to get some control over all this. He blurted out what was on his mind rather more hastily than he'd intended.

'There are a couple of things. If I make people think Adam Taylor is in London, won't they come looking for me? And Adam's got an open flight return from Tehran to London. Why haven't I flown back? And also, how do I get back after?' asked Ali.

'That's three questions. Each is important. Yes, they will come looking for you in London, but they won't find Adam. You will be Ali Muhammed once again, an anonymous asylum-seeking refugee hidden in the hoards of people without papers all currently seeking asylum in Britain. For this reason, north London is a good place to hide yourself. England is full of anonymous refugees and immigrants. You will, in common with many in that situation, present as not having any papers or passport, but if you say genuinely you are who you are, that you fled the evil IS regime, they'll assume you are like any number of similar asylum seekers who have arrived in Europe - no problem.' He opened wide his hands in a gesture of feigned innocence.

'But until then, why will they think Adam has travelled back if he's not showing himself to prove it and, he's not used a plane ticket to get back that he's paid for?' asked Ali.

'Now listen carefully. Adam has unwittingly cooperated with us on that point. Our friends in Istanbul were able to access his email, which is, so far as we can ascertain, the last one he sent home. They will today send a message to his parents to say that Adam met a girl in Turkey and rather than travel on to Iran is travelling back with her as she is starting a course in London in September. Her father is a lorry driver who regularly travels between Turkey and England and is

205

bringing them both back for the start of the autumn university term.'

'Very clever,' said Ali.

'His family will think he is coming, and when he doesn't show, they'll think he has linked up with her. When you leave the bike to be found they will feel reassured he is back in London, but no-one will be interested in one more young person who has disappeared in London. Family life there is not like it is here where we value our families and watch over our youngsters. Who would let a young person cycle on their own the way this Adam has done?' said Salim.

'You will need money. People give most generously to God's work. Our contacts in London have raised us considerable funds by trading in substances we condemn here. They both make money and watch the infidels decay through their own decadence. You will need enough money to live on and get yourself around. Here is £5,000 and €2,000. Your contact in London will provide any further things you need. His name is Abu, but don't get too close to him, it will be risky for both you and him.'

'And getting back?' said Ali, mindful of his future.

'That will all be taken care of at the right time. May God grant you success in striking a blow to the heart of the infidel nations. Do not forget the teaching of the Qur'an that, "those who believe and have left their homes and striven with their wealth and live in Allah's way are of much greater worth in Allah's sight. These are they who are triumphant," and this is your jihad, and you will be blessed in this honour, and you will be victorious. The final detail of your mission in London will be given you when you are safely there. For now it is enough for you to go and be on your way. It is time.'

Ali stood up to leave. They embraced formally and he knew then it might well be a final embrace. Jihad took no prisoners, jihad meant total service, total sacrifice. Salim reached down and took a small black scarf from his desk. On it were embroidered words he had seen on the heads of the martyrs. It was an honour being bestowed and it was placed in the palm of his hand. Then reaching down again, a folded

206

black IS flag was also placed in his hand and it was understood between them what he was to do with this when the time came.

His question about getting back had not been answered and he knew his return wasn't a planned-for eventuality. The unspoken truth was he was being sent as a martyr. And with that, Ali turned and let himself out of the door, clutching his emblems of holy office, feeling both the apprehension and the excitement which comes with stepping out to face the enemy.

Right now he should be thinking there could be no better place to be, but inside, behind the pumping adrenaline, were rebellious Jinns, supernatural beings bringing doubts and fears of every kind to distract and torture him. Amongst them was his dead father, grinning at him, goading him, making him feel bad. He felt bullied and pushed around, a creature formed to be hurt and led by others.

The world in which he lived offered no safe havens in this life. All he could do was be obedient to the cause. Surely, he thought, to fight to make the world a better place has got to compensate for this tortured life. He walked back home for the last time, and pushing open the metal gate to his family courtyard sat in the shade against a wall, waiting for the transport taking him west to arrive.

31

Within the hour a newish, white Mercedes van, had pulled up slowly outside the metal gates, the driver calling out his new name ever more loudly.

'Adam! Adam! Adam!'

It was time. As Ali wheeled Adam's shiny black bike smartly from against the wall to the gate, he was sure that Adam Taylor's eyes were boring into him from the other side of the yard. Adam would have heard his name called. That was an unnecessary slip up, thought Ali, but nothing would come of it.

Once in the street, the bike was loaded with its full panniers now containing Ali's own things. He slid the metal gate bolt closed behind him. Would he ever be back to see home again? The regular click click of the bike's bearings sounded loud in his ear as he rolled it to the van.

For now he had decided to wear customary clothing, but had Adam's red jacket in a plastic bag and Adam's washed cycling clothes on under his robe. A number of western items of clothing had been sourced, jeans, T shirts, a fleece and sufficient socks and underwear. He preferred to wear his own sandals for now, having slipped a pair of new cycling shoes together with a pair of his best Nike trainers in a second plastic bag. A sports bag had been rolled up and put in the panniers for use in London.

Fearing he might have overlooked something important, he double-checked in his head that he had everything, before finally pushing further out from the gate to meet the van driver. All was ready, or as ready as it could be, he said to himself. Farewells to his family had been brief, his sister Fatima crying, his brother Mo looking lost, his Uncle anxious, his Mother distant, his nephews and nieces playing noisily somewhere in the house out of sight. He was all too aware they knew their very future was bound up with his jihad.

'Salaam Alekum, I'm Ali, er Adam, you ready?' he called out to the driver. That was, he realised, his second mistake and he hadn't yet left.

The driver, a short guy with the belly of the self-neglected middle aged and a short beard of barely permissible length, replied anxiously, 'We'd best get going. It's a long road ahead. Van's fuelled up, I've got food and drink for the two of us. I don't need to know any more. I just drive and get paid for it. Now bring that bike of yours round the back. So far as anyone else is concerned who might search for it, it's not ours. We've no idea how it got in there, probably left by mistake by the last delivery driver. OK? We've a long road ahead of us. You ready?' He was speaking quickly and anxiously, his body jerking involuntarily. His presence was not reassuring.

'Sure,' Ali agreed.

He did as he was told, wheeling the bike round and leaning it against the rear of the van. He wondered where the driver was from. It certainly wasn't a local accent, Turkish, but which district, which part? The metal roller back door shot up into the van's roof as the driver released the catch.

'Now get up here and give me a hand,' he instructed Ali with an air of impatience.

It took several minutes to remove the top layers of rolled red and brown rugs and lean them up on the ground against the rear of the van. Adam's bike was then lifted up high by the two of them, slid over the top of the pile of rugs, then dropped unceremoniously where it slipped out of sight with a clunk somewhere behind the driver's cab. It was well and truly out of sight. No-one would find it unless they were prepared to do a lot of carpet lifting to do so. The two of them reloaded the rolled rugs and tied them down to ensure the rug pile, stacked from floor to ceiling, would not shift as they drove.

Ali then clambered into the cab and moments later they were finally on their way, dust rising from their wheels in the midday heat, a fan blowing a welcome blast of air-conditioned coolness over their now sweating limbs. To anyone looking they were just another couple of guys in a van, a familiar sight the world over, nothing deserving of a second glance.

The driver told Ali that if anyone asked, he would do the talking, but if they asked him questions directly, which wasn't likely, he was to say he was simply a day labourer hired to assist with the loading and unloading of rugs. Ali could well appreciate why two people were needed to handle them, so the story sounded entirely plausible, but he hoped they would not be asked to give explanations.

As they set off, Ali noticed his mindset had already begun to change. Whereas until today he lived with time punctuated every few hours by the regular calls to prayer from the muezzin or his mobile app announcing the same, now he was counting and living by the minutes on his or rather Adam's watch and his nerves heightened.

He realised he was living on the edge again, like he did when he was fighting as a soldier. This must be what it was like on stimulant drugs, he guessed. He seemed to notice everything and time seemed to move in a different frame. Though outwardly nothing untoward seemed to be going on, in his head everything was significant, every breath a milestone. He told himself to try and relax. There was a huge journey yet to be made, he needed to relax, that was how the best soldiers made it through.

It took the rest of the day to get to a point on the Turkish border safe enough and with a good enough road surface to cross back into Turkey. In recent years the Turks had done much to fence and guard the border, fearful of IS attacks or Kurdish ascendancy. The borderlands were, however, impossible to fully police with large numbers of migrant populations constantly on the move and the drivers of trade and commerce demanding the flow of traffic be maintained in both directions. The smoothness of passage for anyone wise to the practice was greatly eased by monetary notes passing between drivers and border police.

By this point Ali had discovered his driver was indeed Turkish, and as they talked about their intended route, he learned here was someone clearly well used to travelling back and forth between Iraq and Europe.

Suddenly, to Ali's horror there were two armed Turkish Army personnel ahead of them, the road closed by a metal pole barrier. They were waving the van to slow down and halt beside them.

'Say nothing,' said his driver calmly.

The van came smoothly to a stop. As they pulled up and the driver's window was cautiously wound down, Ali immediately sensed that driver and army officer knew each other from previous crossings. A light-hearted conversation developed, slightly forced maybe, but the two were party to a regular charade. Ali's driver offered to open the back of the van for inspection. It seemed to be the routine thing, but Ali felt numb with the dread of early discovery.

He tried to reason with himself, there was nothing to incriminate him, the bike - well that was the driver's responsibility, but if they searched his things they'd find Adam's passport and cycling gear. He felt exposed, inadequately prepared and terrified of discovery. It could all end here before he'd got anywhere. He tried to make himself as inconspicuous as possible, a normal van driver's assistant, but he felt incredibly at risk of an early arrest.

Then he heard the shutter roll up at the back and felt the van move as someone clambered into the back. They began walking about in the limited space, then moments later, a sudden movement as the same person alighted. No sounds, nothing giving anything away. His driver was then back in his cab.

As he turned the key in the van's ignition, he reached forward for a white envelope on the dashboard and handed it to the guard, who looked at Ali before opening it to check the contents. He looked across at his colleague in uniform who was giving his attention to another vehicle pulling up behind them, then back to the envelope. Hesitation, tension, blood pumping in Ali's head; and then, his driver, smiling, broke the moment saying he would be back later in the month and who knows maybe with another delivery. The soldier seemed satisfied, slipped the envelope discreetly into his trouser pocket, stepped back, lifted the red and white pole barrier and waved them through.

It was then Ali noticed his driver had beads of sweat across his forehead.

'You must be pretty important. I've never paid so much before, and that soldier knew it. I think it's alright, I know his family and he wouldn't want to risk anything happening to them. Hell, it used to be a lot simpler trading carpets in the old days!'

For the first time, Ali's driver pulled out a packet of Turkish cigarettes, put one to his lips, extracted a lighter from his jacket, lit up and took a deep drag before filling the cab with the pungent tobacco smoke. He wouldn't have dared produce them in the Caliphate.

'We will be sleeping in the van tonight. You're in the back. You'll use the rugs to make yourself comfortable. I'll sleep in here. Its a low-key roadside halt with no amenities, best that way,' he explained.

Even as the driver talked, Ali's eyes were fixed on the side mirrors trying to see what the diminishing figures behind were up to. Would they be stopped again further up the road? Would there be a reception committee? So much risk, so much uncertainty - life today was so very different to yesterday. He wondered how long he could live on his nerves before he began to fray at the edges. At this rate, not very long, he concluded.

After many hours travelling and as dusk fell, they pulled up on an extended lay-by where many other drivers were making preparations to rest up. Some of the larger lorries had flung open their trailer doors to discourage would-be theft. A small coffee and fast food kiosk constructed from an old caravan had been set up, an electric generator humming away providing it with a lit string of orange lights, a garish neon sign and the necessary heat to create a haze of kebab oil smoke. It drifted their way and made Ali feel hungry. As if reading his mind, his driver reached under his seat and pulled out a couple of plastic food containers and four drink cans of fruit-flavoured water.

'You don't go wandering off. You want coffee or anything, I get it, but you stay quiet and low. Understand?' he ordered.

Ali nodded. He was handed plastic cutlery and a container of cold lamb kebab on a skewer and then a separate bag of pitta bread. Somehow his driver magicked a salad with cucumber, tomato, shredded lettuce and a small bottle of olive oil for a dressing.

'Fit for a sheikh!' he said with a smile, Ali realised this was a man who liked his food; fruit followed, red grapes and oranges, honey cakes to finish.

As the evening wore on, conversation remained vague, impersonal, boring and most of all how his driver wanted it - safe. Ali thought he'd excuse himself by finding somewhere to use as a toilet. His driver produced a large ten litre water container and a towel before once again firmly instructing Ali.

'Don't go wandering off,' he said sternly.

Ali still needed to stretch his legs. Having spent weeks shaping up physically, his body rebelled at the forced immobilisation of travel. He told his companion, 'Don't worry,' and then stepped out of the cab into the cool of the evening.

The lay-by was quiet and he decided to walk up and down, stretching himself and filling his lungs with air. The cicadas were making a noise in the nearby verges. With the surprise police stop safely behind him, he allowed himself to think that an adventure was beginning, and at last some purpose had come into his existence. Maybe God had chosen him for special blessing and for a moment he felt he had new life pulsing through his veins.

Then his thoughts plunged in another direction - he mustn't fail. His family and the people of Mosul needed him to succeed, their lives depended on him. He must get to London, and this was but the first night of his journey there. The army checkpoint was a salutary reminder he would need to be more careful in future. It was stupid to have kept Adam's stuff on his person instead of putting it in the back of the van with his bike. Turning on his heels at the end of the lay-by he made his way slowly back to the van. Any longer and Ali would be just too anxious. Later, settling in the back of the van he felt safe and secure and sleep came easily.

One night followed another. Their travelling became more relaxed. Once they got to western Turkey he changed his clothes in the anonymity of Istanbul and became just another western young person. He put his own robes in a roadside rubbish bin and bought himself a peaked cap to pull over his eyes and keep the sun off. He purchased some English designer shades too. When he looked in the vanity mirror to shave he began to see not Ali but Adam Taylor, a cyclist who had decided to hitch back to England. Maybe he was passable as Adam and this jihad possible, he told himself.

Crossing eastern Europe was easy. He'd showed Adam's passport and simply been waved through. Country by country he ticked them off in his head - Bulgaria, Serbia, Hungary, Slovakia, then the Czech Republic. His driver became less tense with every border crossing and at the regular stops to break their drive they began using the service areas for refreshments and the public washrooms to refresh themselves.

It was reassuring that no-one gave them a second glance. He was just another traveller on the road. After three nights sleeping in the back of the van and too many miles of endless dual carriageway they were driving into Berlin, and his overweight companion started telling him to look at his maps, for soon he would be on his own.

His still nameless driver finally parked up the Mercedes van in a quiet modern industrial estate in Berlin. He was increasingly impatient to say goodbye to Ali, clearly all too relieved to be off-loading a great burden.

First, there was the awkward task of trying to retrieve Adam's bike from behind the pile of Persian rugs, but there were no curious eyes, and with panniers loaded, Ali finally straddled the cross bar, map in hand. His driver, clearly relieved to see the back of his high-risk passenger, gave a half-hearted farewell wave of his hand and simply said, 'that way,' and with a couple of turns of the pedals Ali was on his own, the van and its driver no longer visible.

It was a further week of outwardly uneventful cycling before he found himself near Calais. People he came into contact with didn't show any inclination to engage in conversation with him and he was happy for it to be that way. But it was a ride west which Ali personally found surprisingly difficult. Maybe he was out of condition after so long sitting in a van; maybe the prevailing wind was always against him,. Or was it his nerves? He didn't know. He wondered how Adam had managed it, cycling all the way to eastern Turkey. Adam, though, hadn't had to cycle carrying the burden now pressing down on his shoulders: that of responsibility and fate.

He was finding the assumption of the name of another was a peculiar experience, now that he called himself Adam and had to think like him. As Adam, he found his admiration and respect for the young lad began to grow and at one point he even imagined liking him, in different times, as a fellow student, a younger brother, or pen pal; but told himself sternly, not for the first time, there was to be no room for sentiment. Being Adam had even got him to use his English rather than try French, and he felt pleased he usually got what he wanted.

Ali had chosen a route west along quieter roads wherever he could, passing through some pleasant touristy areas. There had been the hilly Black Forest in Germany and the just as hilly Ardennes in northern France, but for many days since the landscape of northern France had been by comparison boringly flat. Ali had taken the D roads, passing through villages and towns without raising a single eyebrow. Where once or twice people had tried to engage in conversation he had deflected their polite engagement and quickly got back on his way.

After all the effort, it was with some relief and mounting excitement he began to approach the outskirts of Calais. He spotted the tower of the town hall, 'La Mairie', on the skyline marking the 'Centre Ville' and he felt some extra energy come

215

with the sense of achievement at having made it to the English Channel.

As he approached, the roads became busier with every passing mile, international traffic heading up and down the coast or linking with the ferry or Eurotunnel. Heavy articulated lorries thundered by on the smooth fast tarmac. He continued to avoid the worst of the heavy traffic. The map he had was good and he made his way through suburban streets until he reached the port canals right at the heart of the town.

Once there he leant his bicycle up against a factory wall and took a deep draught from his bottle of water. He'd made it this far, but the sea view stretching out in front of him looked to be an insurmountable obstacle. He recalled that people said that on a good day you could see England from here, but not today. The sea air was fresh and cool in his nose, England though not yet quite in sight, he told himself, was now but a breath away.

His wistful confidence soon ceased as he realised how risky this next stage of his journey was. His safety would be in the hands of an unknown contact in Calais he had yet to call and an unknown sailor prepared to smuggle him across the sea. His fate was not in his own hands, his plans could so easily collapse around him at any point; and, he saw his father laughing at him, and Ali fought back, willing him to go on his way, pleading that he leave him alone.

32

As he pondered on his situation, Ali knew this point in his journey was a particular place of risk, another step into unfamiliar and dangerous territory. At any time he could be discovered and he now had to make a call on a mobile to a stranger he had little option but to trust. Full of apprehension, he dialled up the number he'd been issued with, and the call was picked up immediately. Surprised at first to hear a female voice, he then remembered that his CO had told him it would be a woman.

'It's Ali, I'm here, in Calais.'

'Quai d'Angouleme,' she said in a squeaky voice, 'find it. Can you be there in ten minutes? Find the Chamber of Commerce building. Then you can't miss it. There's a tall pillar, a column with a round ball on the top, right outside. You'll be met by an older man on the steps beside it.'

'OK, I'll be there in ten minutes,' and she cut the call.

He decided to get there quickly as it was literally a street away. He needed to be cautious and to check the place out. The last thing he wanted was to be arrested at this point and he was somewhat alarmed at how Calais just seemed to be swarming with police and army personnel. Were they looking for him?

Everywhere there were people wandering the town's streets, people from his part of the world wanting to get to England, some Muslims he guessed. He couldn't trust them. 'Traitors', he muttered under his breath, worried he might, at any time, be recognised or compromised by someone not loyal to the cause.

He sped through an archway, then under a modern concrete building with the canal on his right and the smell of the sea in his nostrils and there, in a street of red brick offices, he spotted the Chamber of Commerce, a red-brick, concrete-panelled building with a peculiar glass and metal entrance area. Right outside was the ball on a column he'd been told about. He cycled past it, staying with the traffic and without slowing he took himself round to the left before pulling up two blocks away to watch the rendezvous point from what he thought was a safe distance.

As he waited, he couldn't see anything suspicious and there was no-one there yet to meet him. He therefore decided to swing off the road and continue watching from a distance. After five minutes an older-looking European man, carrying a small rucksack on one shoulder, wandered up to the steps. It can't be, thought Ali, but she'd said, 'you'll be met by an older man' so it must be him.

As he watched, the man put his rucksack down and sat beside it on the steps looking round. He was balding, to Ali's eyes the other side of middle-aged and slightly untidy-looking. Ali climbed back in the saddle and began moving slowly back down the length of the canal-side to pull up by the steps, casting a wary look round as he approached.

'You Adam?' the man called out, in a friendly enough manner. 'The name's Dave Tranter,' he said, offering an outstretched hand.

'Had a nice holiday? You got a good tan mate.' He didn't wait for an answer and they shook hands, Ali feeling rather awkward.

'Yep, that's me, pleased to meet you. I've been told you can get me to England,' Ali said, anxious to get on with things.

'Sure can. We ought to make our way over to the Yacht Club mooring, store everything away and take the evening high tide. We've not that much time if we're to catch the ebb tide. The 'Maid of Margate' is just a couple of minutes walk from here. I've got some food stored in the galley, some fresh bread, and supplies. She's all ready. If it is all the same with you, we'd best get going,' he said, grabbing his rucksack as he got to his feet. Ali nodded, glad to be moving.

They walked along the dockside, Ali wheeling his bicycle beside Dave. In the direction they were headed Ali could see the masts of yachts bobbing up and down. The wind blowing through them rattled and whined eerily in warning. As

218

they walked, he thought his best strategy was to stay quiet. He didn't know what this Dave knew and probably the less he knew the better all round. But he couldn't be unfriendly, and noticing that Dave seemed to be limping slightly, sought to engage him in light conversation.

'You got a problem with your leg?' asked Ali, trying to sound sympathetic.

'It's a bugger getting old, hip is giving me gip. I'm waiting to have it done, six months they tell me. Bloody Health Service, it's underfunded. But you can't keep an old sailor down, just you might have to do some of the running round for me on the boat, Adam. The weather's set fair, but you can never tell in the Channel. How's your sea legs? Last lad I took with me was sick as a dog,' said Dave laughing at the memory.

Ali had never been on a yacht before. He'd never thought about whether he'd be sick or not. He shrugged his shoulders adding, 'we'll see.'

Alarm bells started to ring in Ali's head as the path narrowed and a metal gate appeared, barring their path to the yacht club area ahead of them. As they approached they were attracting stares from other sailors. One man, looking officious, started to approach them to challenge them and Ali almost froze in his tracks. This is it, he thought, I'm for it, I've been spotted and I'm not going to get through. Then Dave came to the rescue.

'He's with me,' he said, and the man with a shrug, backed off before turning away. Ali noticed for the first time there were other people wheeling bikes around, some looking as if they were going or coming from Calais' shops. True to Dave's word, almost immediately they slowed up by a yacht that he introduced to Ali as, 'my long-time luvver.'

The crisis at the gate now in the past, Ali's next fear, on seeing such a small, ramshackle boat was, is she seaworthy? Was he, after all the risks to get here, about to die at sea? But Dave seemed to have total belief in his 'luvver' and strode confidently across the deck, sliding back a hatchway near the forward end.

'Throw your bike down there, will you and bring what stuff you need with you for the crossing into the cabin. Make the clasps secure after, or we'll fill up with sea water!' He laughed and disappeared briefly out of sight.

Ali did as he was told, sliding the hatch back in place and locking the clasps, then double -checking them just to make sure not a drop of water would get in that way. He glanced around again at the boat. It was made of timber with a battered varnish finish. He thought it was old, probably as old as Dave. That worried him. His curiosity got the better of him and he called out to Dave.

'How old's the boat?'

'Built her myself with my brother in '75. Sailing's my life since he died. I go back and forth across the Channel in the summer months. Love to eat at bar 'Le Detroit' just over there,' he gesticulated waving his hand airily in the direction of the town. 'Bloody port's a bit of a nuisance unless you know it. Too many ferry boats in Calais that don't give a damn. There's only access into this basin a couple of hours before and after high tide, so it's not everyone's cup of tea. Too much red tape as well. Bloody checks everywhere you go. Bloody migrants wanting to stowaway. All a bit much these days, and I'm not getting any younger,' said Dave, clearly a man with strong opinions. Dave continued to chatter on, doing odd jobs preparing the boat ready to set sail as he talked.

'Anyway, there's a group of us who come here regularly to Calais. Over the summer we go up and down the coast, Ostend, Boulogne, Dunkirk, sometimes further. It's the getting together over some sea food and vin blanc that makes it all worthwhile. Now come on there, put your stuff inside the forward cabin. That's where you're sleeping. Your travel agent young lady said you'd like to go back a different way to the way you came, you fancied trying some proper sailing, she said. Afraid I'm only going over to Blackwater, Essex, I told her, but she seemed happy with that, though her squeaky English was rubbish. Thing is, she paid up front for you, in cash. Suits me, carrying the odd passenger helps pay for my boat repairs. That's my winter job, repairs in the boatyard, making her seaworthy for the next season. Scrape her bottom and varnish her myself every year I do.'

Ali didn't like to hear that the boat needed so much attention and so many repairs to keep it seaworthy. It was bad enough knowing it was old and made of wood. He still wasn't convinced it was safe.

'Anything I can do,' he offered cheerily.

'Put the bloody kettle on will you. We've got another hour to kill before we set sail. Make sure you light the gas otherwise you'll blow us to high heaven!' He laughed again at the worried look on Ali's face.

Ali reached for what looked like a tap and after a few moments fiddling, water magically appeared. Tea made, milk and sugar added in the English style, he decided his best plan until they were off-shore was to take a rest in his bunk and keep out of sight. He ducked down and whether it was the motion or tiredness, or a combination of the two, he found his eyes closing and he drifted off to sleep.

It was the motion of the boat that woke him. Raising himself on one elbow he looked out of a round porthole window to see a long concrete wall some hundreds of metres away with waves breaking against it. He needed to steady himself against the motion of the sea. The movement wasn't unpleasant, and so far he wasn't feeling ill. He panicked and jumped quickly to his feet as he heard Dave's voice on what he guessed was the yacht's VHF radio. He froze, not knowing what to do.

'Calais Port,' he kept calling. 'This is Dave Tranter on the 'Maid of Margate'. Tango Romeo call. Just myself and Adam Taylor leaving for England, thank you, over and out.'

Ali had been alarmed at the official sounding call, but when he put his head round and asked what was up, Dave explained it was just routine, a lot easier than going through customs any other way.

'Don't even have to show my passport as a yachtsman,' he went on, 'in fact, come to think, I never have,' which was reassuring news.

'What did you say Tango Romeo for?' asked Ali fearful this was a police message.

'Oh that. We sailors use the Tango Romeo protocol going in and out of ports. It's a kind of understood polite convention which means they trust us yachting guys and don't worry about checking passports and all that stuff,' explained Dave.

'That's great,' said Ali, genuinely relieved.

The crossing took longer than Dave had expected with the shipping lanes proving tricky to navigate, the large vessels looking perilously close to Ali's eyes and their wash from powerful propellors alarmingly high. As darkness fell, he was surprised how much illumination came from the moon and stars. It was not unlike being in the desert at night. Despite all the creaking and groaning, Dave's 'luvver' rode the waves with ease and Ali felt this was in itself an unexpected adventure he was actually enjoying. He decided to venture out on deck and see if he could learn anything.

'Thought you was out for the night,' ventured Dave seeing him emerge on deck. 'Watch your footing there. Take the wheel for me, just hold her steady for a minute whilst I tie up and stow away that loose sail.'

Ali did as bidden and felt the shudder of the boat and the force of the sea against the rudder. A surge of exhilaration rose within him. He could like this. As he entertained slight adjustments to the wheel, he sensed the responsiveness of the boat, but by then Dave had all too quickly returned.

'The gods must be with us. Not usual to get a south easterly this time of year. With this wind we will be home late morning I guess. Wind, sea and currents are in our favour, only the bloody cross-Channel ferries to worry about. I've got to keep her straight across the sea lanes at ninety degrees otherwise we will have the Customs after us. Can you cook?' asked Dave.

'A bit,' responded Ali, wondering if his non-existent English cooking skills were about to be tested.

'Take yourself down into the galley. In the cupboard opposite the cooker there's French bread, a selection of meats and some French cheeses. Make a few sandwiches mate, and bring 'em up here. Help yourself to the lagers down below. I always ferry a few boxes across for my mates. They expect me to try them,' he laughed.

After a few minutes in the galley, Ali put together what he thought Dave wanted. He even opened a bottle of lager for him and, bracing himself, stepped back on to the deck, bread roll in one hand and lager in the other. Dave took them eagerly and pushed them into the front pocket of his sailor's waterproof trousers.

'You grab something to eat yourself,' he shouted, the waves now crashing against the front of the boat making such a rise and fall they caused Ali to hold firmly to the side rails. Dave was clearly in his element, thoroughly enjoying himself.

Back in the galley, Ali made himself a roll from the french loaf and stuffed it with cheese and meat, wondering if he was eating pork. As he was now Adam he thought he wouldn't enquire too closely and he'd better have a lager himself to play the part. It was only after eating he felt queasy, the motion of the sea making his head pound, or could it have been the lager? He didn't know. Being down in the galley definitely didn't help, so he dragged himself out on deck once again and grabbed a rail near Dave.

'You're looking green mate,' Dave ventured, 'and this ain't rough.'

'I'm OK,' he offered, but not very convincingly. He was feeling better being outside: having sight of the horizon definitely helped.

'Cycled far have you?' said Dave, happy to chat.

'Across to Eastern Europe,' Ali said hesitatingly, not wanting to give too much away, or find himself trapped in a conversation he didn't want to have. 'A Gap Year thing.'

'So, are you off to Uni when you get back?' asked Dave.

'Yes, more or less straight away,' Ali replied.

'What you study?' said Dave.

'Engineering,' Ali ventured, thinking it was a safe enough subject to offer; and, one he knew something about from his Mosul University days.

223

'No call for engineers any more. You ought to do something different, like Business Management or something. More future there from what I hear,' said Dave, who always seemed to have an opinion on everything.

'Well, it's engineering. Too late to do anything about it now,' said Ali.

'Where will you read it?' enquired Dave.

Ali hesitated, then said, 'London Brunel,' and hoped his inspired choice would end the conversation, but Dave was sociable and genuinely interested which meant the pressure to keep telling and stringing along the story didn't let up. Ali was finding it hard and was torn between keeping Dave on board and needing to get out of a conversation which could trip him up at any point.

'Are you from London then?' was Dave's next question. An easier one this time.

'Yes, Muswell Hill.' Ali then wished he hadn't gone this far and wondered how he could get himself off the hook.

'Nice place. Love it. Often go to London from Essex. Now, don't get me wrong, but your roots aren't London are they, it's your accent, your skin, and Adam's a funny name for a lad like you,' said Dave with questions too close for comfort, but put in a disarmingly friendly manner.

However, Ali suddenly felt exposed. If it was this easy to see through his cover he was in deep trouble. He wondered whether when they got to shore Dave, who was nobody's fool, would give the game away. The threat of exposure suddenly felt very real.

A moment's thought and he came up with a storyline. 'Well, you're right, my Mum is from the Middle East and my Dad's English. They met at university in the UK, which is why I thought I'd cycle across Europe this summer to, to touch base with Mum's side of the family.' He congratulated himself for thinking so quickly. He thought it sounded totally believable as the story came out his mouth.

'Sounds quite an adventure. If you want to take a nap, I'm happy to be keep watch until first light, then I'd be glad for a hand. You seemed OK with the wheel earlier, must be the engineer in you!' said Dave, making himself comfortable behind the wheel.

'OK,' Ali replied, only too glad to end the conversation. He stepped back toward the cabin, making his exit before Dave asked him any more searching questions.

As he went below he thought hard. Did he risk Dave talking to the port people in England as he had on leaving Calais, telling them he had a passenger called Adam Taylor, or did he take a look at giving Dave's VHF transmitter a breakdown?

Dave wouldn't have any choice but to sail into Blackwater and it would look when he docked as if he'd just been along the coast, no-one would be any the wiser. Ali wasn't familiar with this Tango Romeo thing, so whilst Dave couldn't see him from the wheel, he took his chance, and took a good look at the VHF transmitter sitting on the shelf.

It was one of those ICOM fixed-mount machines with a long curled wire like an old telephone hand receiver. This meant if Dave should want to, he could still speak whilst holding the yacht's wheel. It was not one with a portable handheld device. Like everything else on the boat it was quite old, with a simple dial for power and a channel selector.

The set sat between angled shelf brackets and Ali's job inspecting it was made easier by the fact he could lift the set and turn it. The back plate had just four Philips-head screws. He was going to use a knife from the drawer to undo them but he could see an easier way to put it out of action. Powered by the boat's battery, the power lead which was fastened to the side of the craft with clips, helped to secure the set in place to prevent it from falling in rough weather, one end of the cable disappearing into the darkness down the side of the wooden hull. The other end was joined to a simple electric connector on the transmitter itself which he had simply to pull slightly for the corroding wires to come entirely away from the set. Job done.

Let's hope the rest of this old craft doesn't come apart quite so easily, he thought. The now disabled unit was repositioned, so a quick outward glance would show nothing amiss. Pleased with his handiwork and certain that Dave hadn't noticed his sabotage, he decide to make the most of the chance to get some rest. Tomorrow he would be in England.

Ali woke to Dave's call. His mobile showed it was only 5.30am but Dave said he needed a break if 'Adam' didn't mind. Ali pulled himself up and staggered out into the grey dawn, wrapping a sailing jacket round him as much to keep the wind out as the steel grey cold, on a morning when it was impossible to see where sky and sea met. The wind was gentle enough to keep the boat moving slowly in the right direction. Steering shouldn't be difficult, he thought.

'Call me if you see anything and keep her lined up with the compass bearing I've set. You should be OK for a couple of hours, and anything big should mind you! For god's sake call me if need be, but it had better be an emergency,' and with that he disappeared down the hatch.

Ali took over and found he enjoyed the experience. Some dolphins, or he assumed they were, poked their black heads up playfully ahead of him, but they didn't hang around long before disappearing. There were no boats nearby to worry him. Two hours on, Dave pushed his head out again, looked at Ali and glanced around to see what was what.

'Ta, anything to report?' he said sleepily.

'No, all quiet here,' replied Ali, and asked if it was alright for him to place himself up on the bow. He thought he'd be able to keep himself to himself better, away from any further questions and Dave would just think he was doing it to enjoy the experience.

Later, after more French bread, now soft and chewy, they spied the Essex coast and the long slow process of getting nearer began. More sea birds appeared. It seemed to take for ever to get to the mouth of the Blackwater estuary and the grey in the sky never seemed to lift, even though by now it was late morning.

Dave, sure enough, tried to get his VHF set to work, but gave up without comment after tapping the hand held piece a couple of times on the bulkhead. It was almost as if he expected things to go wrong on his old boat. He carried on as normal, seemingly not giving it another thought. It certainly didn't bother him enough to want to mention it, which Ali took to be a good sign.

A line of buoys was sighted and Dave eventually dropped the sails and started up the boat's diesel engine to motor them in the last stretch, the rhythmic rumble driving them forward toward land with every minute. Unlike Calais, it all seemed pretty quiet. Dave waved to a couple of passing yachts. He was on his home territory and Ali could sense this was all very familiar to him.

As they pulled up and Ali had to help moor the boat up against a floating pontoon, linked by a ramp to the firm land beyond, he called to Dave, 'Mind if I get straight off, I've got a long ride ahead of me?'

'Sure, and all the best with Uni. Good to have you along. You can check in with Border and Customs over there if you want before setting off. Likely as not there won't be anyone there. If it were me I wouldn't bother. I couldn't get through to them earlier.'

'I enjoyed the crossing Dave; soon found my sea legs, didn't I?' Ali replied, as he released the forward hatch clasps and opened and retrieved his bike.

Lifting his bike and bags on to the quayside, though still feeling slightly wobbly, he was safely ashore. As he wheeled his bike on to solid ground, Dave's yacht soon became only visible because of its mast, with a triangular courtesy flag flying from its tip.

He was amazed by the sight of even older Thames barges moored up at Malden, which made Dave's craft look, by comparison sleek and modern. But he didn't want to hang about near the coast sight-seeing and definitely not stopping by the Customs building, which indeed looked empty. He therefore pressed on out of the harbour area, just in case there were any curious officials about.

Minutes later he was well on the road, heading for Chelmsford. He was here, he'd made it to England and he gave a cry of delight into the wind. This land might be grey, but his heart was bright, brim full of joyous elation. It took until dusk to cover the fifty miles or so and get to north-east London. He called up the contact number he'd been given by his CO.

'Abu, it's Ali, I'm here, in Walthamstow, in London.'

A dour-sounding Abu told him to make his way to Edmonton Green Railway Station. When he got there he was to ring again.

Not much of a welcome there, Ali thought. He was thinking he needed to to start looking for somewhere to spend the night. Some shelters in a local park looked promising. He saw one was already occupied, so he made for the other. No-one gave him a second look, which suited him just fine.

33

Winston's second-floor bedsit overlooked the clock tower in Crouch End. Upmarket, he called it. It was a precious plot and he kept it clean, clean of dust and clean should any prying police eyes ever want to look inside. Smart clean mind, from smart clean habits, to ensure he stayed one step ahead of the game, he told himself. His 'Hornsey Housing Association' property was perfectly located, so far as he was concerned, the only trouble was finding a nearby parking space. Sometimes it meant driving around for ages to find somewhere to leave his Beamer.

He had a sort of on-off girlfriend, Etta, who dropped in from time to time and stayed over, but not this week. She was an art student and the new term had kicked in, meaning she was up to her eyes in it, wouldn't be until next weekend he'd see her again. Winston was pretty chilled about it, as he was about most things, and his loping walk with easy strides gave a picture of self-confidence and control.

Only Winston really knew it was mainly bullshit. His actual life, like that of a summer butterfly was a precarious floating thing, easily blown about or worse. He had to settle for living in the now, the future was a banned thing and he knew his life as he saw it, living on the edge, could all too easily be snuffed out. Making out in north London as a black young man was mean, without a future, so he needed to steel himself, toughen up, be sharp, just to get by in the present, in the here and now.

This week he'd been more scared than he could remember ever being scared, like a chicken knowing its neck was about to be wrung. Monday had been get ready for the Post Office job day, Dillon as high as a kite, Will phoning his orders through like it was a military op. Then the whole thing was suddenly called off. Dillon said Will's sister at the Post Office had called to say cash delivery days had changed without warning to a Sunday, and there was nothing to collect.

'Abort it, abort it, there's nothin' for no-one,' a pissed-off Will had told Dillon. Dillon relayed the message to Winston, adding that Will was proper deflated.

'How was Will going to buy his shooters and ammo now? How was he going to get his ends back?' Winston had never heard Dillon sound so high and low at the same time.

After the call, he himself felt hugely relieved it was all off, though he knew they'd come up with something else, a Plan B. Dillon and Will were getting into more and more risky things and dragging him in. At this instant, however, with the immediate pressure off, Winston felt light as air, even carefree. Will and Dillon's problems weren't his problems right now and his mood brightened!

Nice day, he thought, as he strolled up Shepherds Hill to collect his car. Maybe the walks to his parked motor did him good. He didn't take much exercise. With nothing much doing, he decided he'd give the Beamer a ride and pop over to see Clive, a quarter of an hour away in Edmonton. Once in the car, it felt good to be behind the wheel, it always did, and before pulling away he lined up some music, this time old Reggae for a change. He pulled away, turned right into Muswell Hill Road and headed north over Alexandra Palace, with its stunning views over the flat urban wastes of north and east London.

First, he thought he'd get the car cleaned up, though to be honest it didn't look too bad. Even so, he pulled into the Palmers Green 'Wash and Shine' run by some asylum-seekers. For a fiver they did a good job and he felt sorry for them. He believed newcomers deserved a chance, his own people had come to their mother country and had doors slammed in their faces. 'Nigger' this, and 'black' that. The racism was still there, usually covert but insidious, more carefully exercised so as to seem not to give offence. He saw every institution from school to police like a fixed deck of cards all stacked against him and his 'tribe.' 'I'm better than them,' he said to himself, 'these poor bastards can have my business.'

Twenty minutes later, with a gleaming car, he slipped again into the post-rush hour traffic which actually meant it moved slowly rather than stood totally still. Unusually, he found he had barely a wait at the Great Cambridge Roundabout at its normally chocker intersection with the North Circular Road. It was then his mobile rang. He took the call as he slid to a halt in a vacant bus lay-by outside a secondary school in Silver Street.

'Fuck, it's Dillon, and I'm almost at Clive's door,' he muttered.

'Hi Dillon,' he said cheerfully, 'what's up?'

'I've been trying to get you. We need to be active. We've been neglectful and the grass is being grown in our territory.'

'What you meanin?' Dillon sounded both high and hysterical.

'There's some greedy fuckin' Arab guys selling grass in our garden. Word has come to Will that they are taking our business away in Tottenham, supplying Broadwater Farm this very morning my contact tells me. It can't carry on. It has to stop now, we're losing big money and some of our best delivery guys are switching sides, so I've got a job for us.'

'What you wantin' me for?'

'You pick up Woody and then me and drop us off so we can sort these bastards out and put things right, how they should be. Just get over here, pick us up, as fast as you can, I know what needs to be done. All you got to do is drive, so don't shit yourself. It's what Will expects,' said Dillon settling the matter.

'OK, OK, just need to turn the car around. Give me twenty minutes,' said Winston. Dillon had hung up. Winston knew his promising day had just begun to go seriously downhill.

Woody in his hooded jacket was waiting in the street and climbed in the back seat as Winston pulled up. He had his trademark black sports bag embraced in his arms. Winston thought he could smell petrol, but thought nothing of it. He accelerated away and a few minutes later they were cruising along Princes Avenue in Muswell Hill.

'Tell Dillon we're here will you,' said Winston chucking his mobile in the back. Call made, Dillon appeared moments later and sat next to Winston.

'Where do you want to go then?' asked Winston.

'Tottenham, back of the Farm, Broadwater Farm, Mount Pleasant Road will do nicely,' said Dillon, rocking his head and trying hard to stay focussed.

Winston swung the car round, then he was on the roundabout, the waiting red London buses parked up waiting their turn, as he shot passed them down the hill and toward Tottenham Lane.

'Take it easy man, don't want us pulled up by some nosey cop,' said Dillon looking anxiously behind him at Woody.

Winston eased back his speed. They passed Wood Green Crown Court with police cars and others pulling in for another day in the crime business. Winston eyed the scene nervously; before a little further on they swung right into Mount Pleasant Road next to the Farm. Dillon made them do an anticlockwise circuit twice, the one way system directing their route. Dillon ordered Winston to cruise along even more slowly. Like some movie gangster, he then peered out through big reflective shades he'd pulled out of his top pocket.

'Yep, someone's in,' he said with satisfaction, 'next time around, pull up over there about five cars away, past that green front door.'

He thrust his pointed finger into the windscreen. Winston did as instructed and pulled up. They waited. Dillon was looking up and down the street. Winston could bear it no longer.

'What we doin' here Dillon? I don't want to be part of any trouble. Don't mind driving you and Woody around, but I don't want no trouble,' he said.

'Keep cool Winston, I knows what we are about. Wait here and keep the engine running until Woody comes back. Woody, you know what to do. All we are doin' is looking after

232

our business, our ends is our ends and no-one else is muscling in on what is ours. See,' said Dillon.

'I'm just giving you a lift, want nothin' to do with this, understood?' repeated Winston, only to be met with a blank stare. There was no way out and the uncomfortable reality sunk home.

He looked at Dillon like he'd never looked at him before. The two went back, school pals, which was until Dillon had dropped out, and by the time both were fifteen, neither was at school. The street was where they gained their education. It had its own laws and rules and it involved sticking by one's friends. It was how you survived. Dillon returned a steely look through vacant eyes, and Winston thought this wasn't the friend he once knew. His one-time friend was now a starry-eyed manic addict. He knew he was trapped, he wasn't going anywhere until this was done. He shrugged his shoulders, signalling compliance. Dillon turned away and looked at Woody.

'No problem with you is there Woody? Time to get to work. You know what to do, street's clear. It's the house with the green door two doors down. Go, tell that Turkish Arab Abu to go fuck himself and make sure he understands,' said Dillon, reaching round and starting to push Woody out of the car.

Woody grabbed his bag, stood on the pavement a moment and glanced up and down the road, his movements accentuated to compensate for the effect of his hood over his head which slid across his field of vision whenever he turned. It was almost comic, an impractical adherence to dysfunctional fashion.

Woody walked slowly down the street. He looked like just another youth with his sports bag. Then he turned into the short pathway and up to the front door. There was a kind of porch so Winston could no longer get a full view through his car mirror. He wound down his driver's side window so that he could listen. He thought he heard the chime of a door bell and watched as Woody took a step back and came into view again.

A door opened and a conversation began. He couldn't hear every word and he could only see the outline of a robed guy whose outstretched arm appeared and pushed Woody away, almost toppling him back the short distance onto the pavement.

Woody stepped forward again, and then there was a simultaneous shriek as Winston saw the glint of a blade strike across toward Woody's face, Woody then turning to move away clutching his head.

'Hell,' cried Winston, 'the guy's cut Woody up.'

Winston instinctively started up the BMW's engine, by which time Woody was fumbling the car door handle, dripping blood from his face, falling into the back of the car.

'He's slashed my face, slashed me. Help me guys,' he pleaded. 'How bad is it? How bad?'

Dillon looked over his shoulder, his face strangely sober, looking grim. He grabbed a towel cloth Winston used to clean his windscreen.

'You'll be OK,' he said. 'It's bleedin' a bit and Winston's precious about his car. Press this on it until we get you seen to.'

There was more crimson blood and Dillon grabbed another cloth from the glove compartment, passing it to an ashen-faced, frightened-eyed, Woody. As Winston put the car into gear ready to move off, Dillon ordered him to wait.

'This ain't over yet. We ain't done what we came to fix and Will wouldn't want us back without doing our job. Just wait here two ticks Winston bruvver. Won't be long,' ordered Dillon.

Dillon stepped out of the car, opened Woody's door and grabbed the black sports bag. Winston didn't know which way to turn. Woody was groaning in the back, the fresh towelling also rapidly turning red from what he could see was a three inch slice across Woody's flapping left cheek. And in the mirror, there was Dillon, reaching down into Woody's bag to pull out a petrol can. Then Dillon had gone, striding down the street, making for Abu's house.

'Hell, no,' said Winston out loud, 'is he going to start a fire, Woody, is that what he's got in mind? This is getting serious. What do I do?'

But Woody gave no answer, his head hidden for the most part by crimson-stained hood and towels., Winston just waited and watched apprehensively through his mirror.

Dillon was pouring petrol into the porch. He could hear it splashing and sloshing it about. He was taking for ever and now he could smell petrol on the breeze. As he put his hand to the ignition itching to leave, there was an explosion and flash of orange flame and Dillon was picking himself up off the pavement, clutching the petrol can in one hand and the sports bag in the other. He was running crazily for the car. Once inside, he shouted right in Winston's face.

'Put your foot down and get the fuck out of the area,' he shouted gesticulating wildly.

Winston glanced back as he pulled away. Already there was smoke and flame at the front of the Victorian terraced house. He hoped people would be getting out at the back. There was no way out to the front through those flames.

The acrid smell of burning and petrol had been brought back into the car by Dillon. Winston shot him a glance.

'What the hell you done?'

Then he noticed Dillon wasn't right. His appearance had changed. Half his hair had gone, and his face, partially protected by his shades, had blistered. He'd been caught in the fireball.

'Don't tell me you're hurt too? Two fuckin' invalids. What the hell am I to do? This ain't no bloody ambulance service,' said Winston.

'Drive up to the North Middlesex Hospital A and E and drop Woody off to get his face cleaned up. And don't say nothin' about it to anyone Woody, right,' said Dillon, to Winston's mind making one sensible statement for a change.

Woody grunted an incomprehensible reply, sitting there in a kind of shocked, lock-down. 'Then we head back to my place and take things from there,' said Dillon.

'OK, can't think of anything better to do to get us out of this shit,' said Winston, deliberately cutting back to the speed limit, realising his early morning cool had totally evaporated.

Fifteen minutes later he dropped Woody off in Wilbury Way, and watched him walk slowly toward the A and E entrance at the North Middlesex Hospital, clutching his face in a crimson towel.

'He'll be fine,' said Dillon. 'Let's get back, I need some fuckin' painkillers.'

'Why did you do that Dillon? People could have been hurt,' asked Winston.

'People were hurt, look at Woody. Besides, Will says that guy Abu is cooking his own white at his yard. Must be taking a load of our business. Our runners have started going over to him and he had to be stopped. That's what we've done. Stop him. I fuckin' hope he's dead, the bastard! We've stopped a trespasser, stopped him working our manor.' There was not an iota of conscience left in Dillon, thought Winston.

'Will said we had to do something. He was angry. He'll be happy now. He'll step back in, get his ends back. All over. You done well. I need to get on my mobile to pick up Abu's runners and get them back on our books. It'll take me half a day. I got plenty of cut brown ready to sell, it's been stacking up. Good stuff, tested it myself. Need to get the message out and the runners running. Big money for you too Winston, but hell, get me some pain killers from the chemist's will you,' begged Dillon.

Winston pulled up in Green Lanes outside a chemist, a green flashing cross indicating its location well before he arrived. He dived in, ignoring double yellows as he usually did. The young Asian girl on the counter wanted to chat, but Winston was having none of it.

'Just the strongest you got, I'm in a bit of a rush,' he said.

He also bought a bottle of water and dashed back to the car. Dillon was moaning about his head and face.

'It bloody hurts,' he cried out. 'Give them here, for fuck's sake.'

236

Winston handed him the pack of Nurofen Double Plus and the water and watched him swig back four times.

'Need to get back,' he directed.

Ten minutes later they were back in Princes Avenue in Muswell Hill, just a few doors down from Dillon's flat.

'Job done, Winston, no more bother now. I'll see you're rewarded, bruvver. I'll call you,' and with that Dillon had gone.

Wondering what to do next, Winston thought he'd take himself down to Tottenham, to the cosy comfort of Cliff's Coffee House. He needed time to chill out, to consider his situation, to calm his ragged nerves. Only now he realised he was shaking. Then as he glanced in his driver's mirror he spotted Woody's bag on the back seat, partly unzipped with the red plastic petrol can sticking out.

'Fuck!' What did he do with it? He pulled off Bruce Grove and round to the rear of Cliff's Coffee House, and in the relative seclusion of the car park area moved the bag and the petrol can, which still had some petrol in and put it out of sight into the boot of his car. Woody's blood on the car seat would have to wait. He used his hands to smooth down the front of his T shirt, trying as much to smooth and calm his ruffled self as he strode into the cafe and ordered a double shot Americano. He seated himself in the quietest corner hoping that no-one would be asking him his business. Cliff had the radio on, rubbish music, background sound wallpaper, that was until there was an interruption for a news bulletin.

'Reports are coming in of a house fire in Tottenham. The police and fire service are on the scene, and it is feared that there has been a tragic loss of life. Neighbours are saying that they were unable to help a family on the first floor who were trapped by the fierceness of the blaze. It is believed an older man managed to climb out of a lower window to safety. Buses in the area have been re-routed and there is inevitably traffic congestion as road diversions have been put in place. We'll let you know more when we have it. Remember you heard it here first on LBC,' said the reporter.

The canned music resumed where it had left off, leaving Winston frozen with shock, his coffee half-spilled in his saucer.

Ten minutes later, Winston picked up his mobile. First, he called Dillon, but the line was constantly engaged and he didn't pick up. So he gave up. Then he called Woody, who was still waiting for an available medic to stitch up his face. He'd no idea how long that would take, but he sounded calmer. When Woody heard the news Winston had to give him, he simply said, 'when I'm out of here I'm lying low.'

Finally, Winston called Clive. He felt, beside Etta whom he couldn't possible tell, Clive was the only real friend he could confide in and the only decent nice guy he knew. He asked if he could come round. He felt he needed to tell someone, talk to someone he could trust and he had got it into his head that Clive, only Clive would understand and help him. Clive, sensing the urgency and need said, 'sure, come over, soon as you like.'

Leaving his Americano unfinished, Winston climbed back into his car and moved off in the direction of Edmonton for the second time that day. This was how the day had started, he recalled, he had been on his way to see Clive, a good day until all hell broke loose. Now, here he was, setting out again, the same start, the same journey. If only he could set the clock back. He felt he was in replay. What the hell had happened to him? How did he get himself into this fucking mess by just driving his car?

34

On the second ring Clive opened the door, Winston stepping into the cosy front room.

'You look awful. Want a coffee?' asked Clive. 'Must be something up for you to come round here.'

The cinema-size TV was on BBC24. Kaylah was spread out on the couch, not yet dressed, even though it was the afternoon. Her eyes were flicking between her mobile and the TV screen. Though she knew Winston was there, she never even acknowledged his presence. Winston sensed the disapproval and felt he deserved it. He liked Kaylah and it hurt. Clive disappeared out the back to make the coffee, leaving Winston stranded, standing awkwardly by the door.

Then he was seeing it on the TV, the house in Mount Pleasant Road, only he couldn't be sure, it looked different. The once green front door had gone, leaving a smoking black hole. It was live coverage and the reporter was being made to move further away behind a blue and white safety tape cordon. She was continuing to talk as she walked backwards.

'No-one's sure how many have died, but the neighbours say that they were a very nice, quiet, Muslim family. Even the girls wore headscarves, a family who kept themselves to themselves. The head of the household is a man neighbours call, "Abu". He's believed to have survived. Somehow, he climbed out of a downstairs window and is now being cared for by friends. Here is a friend who knows the family well, Imam Ibrahim Modood, from the East Tottenham Mosque. What do you know about Abu and his family, Ibrahim?' she asked, assertively pushing a microphone in front of his mouth.

'Abu is a dear friend. Only a few days ago he came to support me as I gave a talk to the students at Southgate Community College. He's a loyal and faithful Muslim man. He is a good man. I can't believe what he must be going through. His whole family taken in a tragic fire like this. We dreaded something like this might happen.'

239

Kaylah made a sudden movement to glance up at the screen.

'People are saying, it was an arson attack,' the reporter added. 'Neighbours heard arguments outside and then, the fire broke out. What do you think happened and why do you think they were targeted?'

'Islamophobia. People fear and mistrust us. Some people hate us. But our community will rally round. Everyone will turn out to show their support and pay their respects,' he replied.

'Did you know Abu's family well?' she persisted.

'As well as anybody. His four children all attended my Madrassa School, their Mother or indeed Abu himself, ensuring they attended regularly. They were amongst my most able and most promising pupils. Their oldest, I think she was eight years old, she could already recite much of the Qur'an by heart,' he said.

'Thank you Ibrahim,' said the reporter, 'and now back to the studio.'

Kaylah was still gazing at the screen.

'He spoke at my college, that man Ibrahim. Didn't like him. Upset everyone. Intolerant man. Wondered how the hell he'd been invited. He wanted to see, now what did he call it, a Caliphate, yes, here, with people like him ruling over the rest of us, though I'm not sure he'd want the rest of us around if he was ruling. Didn't trust a word he said. Hateful man. Mind you, wouldn't wish what happened to that family on anyone,' said Kaylah.

Winston hadn't said a word by the time Clive reappeared clutching two mugs of steaming coffee.

'Let's go through to the back room, quieter there,' he said, holding the door open with his foot so that Winston could follow.

As they made their way through, Kaylah was already lost in her own thoughts again, fiddling with her mobile. The back window looked out onto a small narrow lawn surrounded by brick walls on three sides. Winston dropped on to a dining chair.

240

'You look awful,' said Clive again, passing him a coffee.

Winston's phone sounded a discordantly cheerful note.

'It's Will, I'd better take it,' he said.

'Winston, you seen the TV, you heard the radio?' Will's voice was loud and excited. 'This thing's gone viral. Good thing is we won't get any more trouble from them Turkish dealers. That Abu guy's been undercutting me with Afghan brown for too long, but this is the end of him. Trouble over. With Dillon's help I've already reclaimed most of my old runners this afternoon and got them on my roll. Dillon's doing a great job getting them back. It's given us a reputation and it's helping. Even now we're hoovering up Abu's business. Profits are going up by the hour.' Will was in one of his best moods ever.

'Need you to do me a favour. Dillon's face and arm are blistering up. Says it's painful even with those Nuros you bought him. He needs something else. He phoned the health line. They say he mustn't pop the damn blisters and needs to cover them with a dressing. Boots, the chemist in the Broadway have got the stuff, just need you to collect it for him - I'm too busy here. Can you do that this afternoon? They shut by six, and get him more painkillers, will you. I can't stand his moaning. See if they have anything stronger, he's complaining like hell and getting on my nerves every time he calls,' said Will, in a less aggressive, even amenable frame of mind now he'd got what he wanted.

'OK. I'm round at Clive's place. I'll pick the stuff up. Be over later. Bye,' said Winston compliantly.

He hung up. This was one job he didn't mind doing. Clive was looking at him with a strange expression.

'What's up with you? Come on, tell me. I knew something was up when you arrived, when you were watching that TV like a man possessed. I could hear what Will was saying. You were there weren't you? You were at that house fire. It's about Will and his dealing,' said Clive, accurately interpreting the situation.

Winston didn't know what to say and that was all the confirmation Clive needed to know he was right. He simply

241

shrugged his shoulders the way he did when words failed him. He grabbed the coffee mug with two hands, whether to steady it because of his shaking hands or for comfort, he couldn't think. Clive knew, he'd guessed. Winston voiced the all-important question.

'What do I do? Thought you might know. That's why I came round. I was only driving. I had no idea. You need mates at a time like this,' he said pathetically.

Clive insisted Winston tell him the whole story. He listened to its telling in silence, only once suggesting Winston keep his voice down. When Winston had finished, their coffee mugs were empty and they sat once again in quietness looking out at the grey uninspiring brick wall outside. In his mind's eye, Winston imagined it was a prison yard. He began picturing a bleak future and his head slumped into his arms.

'Would your car have been seen?' asked Clive suddenly.

'I hadn't thought of that. Not sure. Anyway, I've got to pick some medical stuff up for Dillon. Do you want to come for the ride?' he asked.

'OK. I think you could do with the company,' said Clive, grabbing his jacket.

'Thanks mate. I just got caught up in something. All I did was drive them. I'd no idea all this was going to happen. You believe me, don't you?' he asked.

'Let's go,' said Clive, not knowing what to say to his troubled friend.

They drove down to the end of the road, taking a right and right again to head back west. Minutes later they were in Muswell Hill, Winston leaving Clive in the car whilst he dashed to the chemist's shop. Clive spotted with alarm the red and brown patches of Woody's blood, all over the back seat of Winston's car.

Winston had still not reappeared. An officious-looking parking enforcement officer was standing outside the car, looking in through the front windscreen, his face very close to the glass. Clive tried to smile, but it cut no ice. Winston always took no notice of double yellows. Then he was back.

'Emergency medical supplies,' Winston said to the attendant, holding up the blue Boots bag as evidence, which left the attendant undecided, giving Winston time to start up, reverse and pulled away.

'Close call,' he said, smiling.

That's more like the old Winston, thought Clive. Clive watched the attendant in the nearside mirror. He was still watching them. He had taken out his mobile, taken a picture, and was now lifting the phone to make a call, watching them still.

'He knows, he knows,' said Clive. 'He's making a call. This car's a liability Winston, that guy knows. The back seat's covered in blood.'

Winston swung his head round.

'Not good, not good at all,' was all he could say.

'Let's chill, take Dillon his supplies and then maybe we'll go down to Bruce Grove, Cliff's,' Clive said, trying to think of something positive.

'Grab this, take it to Dillon's front door, number 19, flat 1b. Just ring his bell. I'll wait here for you. There really is nowhere to park this time. If I'm not here it's because I've gone round the block. See you in two ticks,' said Winston.

Clive got out and Winston immediately pulled off. Dillon opened the door on the first ring. Clive saw his face. All down the right side was fiercely blistered, his one eye swollen and almost totally closed. Dillon recognised, but didn't acknowledge him.

'Got them?' was all he asked.

Clive handed the bag over. The door slammed shut. There could be no doubt Winston's story was true, now he too felt he was getting written into the script. Got to be careful, he told himself, as he stepped outside again, looking down the street for the blue BMW.

Soon enough Winston was back, just moving along very slowly, so as to pull up briefly and sweep him up. Clive jumped in. They moved off, but as they were going round the traffic island at the end of the Broadway. Winston looked agitated.

243

'The answer to your earlier question Bruv, is they know about the car. Hate to tell you this, but there is a jam sandwich so close to my backside I can smell it. Hold tight,' Winston said.

They moved slowly down Muswell Hill, then, judging his moment to perfection, Winston did a power u-turn in front of a bus and they shot down a narrow road to the right. There was no chance the police car could have made it too with heavy traffic coming up the hill. Moments later, the narrow side road ended in a T junction, the steep slope of St James' Lane going left and right. They turned left, then left again and were passing an assortment of businesses occupying the arches of the long-disused railway line to Alexandra Palace. Clive was looking out of the back.

'We lost them,' Clive said with relief.

'Won't be for long before they find us, and the helicopter will be up in no time. Get ready to get out,' said Winston looking agitated.

He pulled the car into the vegetation. They leapt out. Winston opened the boot, poured the remaining petrol from the red can inside the car on the back seat, then standing back gave his pride and joy one last look, gleaming still from its early morning clean. He struck a match, reached in, arm out-stretched and it was ablaze.

'Get up there on the nature trail, the old railway track, quick. Don't look back. Then we'll be clear,' ordered Winston, pointing the way.

They scrambled through the briars and up the muddy slope, joined a well-worn path and were back on the roundabout in Muswell Hill Broadway once again, mingling anonymously on the crowded pavement.

'Suggest we split,' said Winston. 'You take a bus home from here. I'll call you. Thanks for being with me. Will owes me a new car!'

Clive wandered up to the bus stop and joined the queue. Two police cars were cruising up and down as he waited. He didn't dare make himself conspicuous. A bus arrived, he was away. Soon he'd be home.

Winston was also lucky. A bus arrived immediately. He was home in minutes. Then he had a good idea. He picked up his phone and called the police.

'I'd like to report the theft of a motor vehicle,' he told the switchboard operator.

There was no real interest and that suited him fine. He gave the registration, make, colour, his name and address and then was asked to hold. Then a different voice came on, a more searching male voice, asking where he was calling from. He gave his address.

'We'll have someone with you in just a few minutes sir.'

Winston hadn't thought this far ahead. He had to think of a story quick. Better say he was at the Car Wash when it was taken, yes, and that when he'd got out to let them clean it inside, it had been driven off. He'd walked home, called the police when he'd got over the shock. It' would have to do. Ten minutes later there was a firm knock at the door. It would be them.

Surprisingly, the interview with the police passed off easily. The man and woman who'd come accepted his account, even venturing to say that it wasn't the first time something like that had happened at the Car Wash. A lucky break. Minutes later he was showing them out of the door, smiling and politely thanking them.

Dillon called again, 'I need you to deliver some stuff, the light and dark are are sold out now we've got Tottenham back.'

'Hold it right there. The police have clocked my car, so I've torched it. It's burned out, can't help you. You owe me a set of wheels,' said Winston.

'Good move burning all the evidence. Excellent! No worries. The way things are going I'll have you a new motor by the weekend,' said Dillon.

Winston wasn't sure if Dillon was lucid and meant it or deluded, because he was high on painkillers and whatever else he'd got hold of.

'Thanks Dillon,' was all Winston could think to reply.

245

Winston couldn't put his finger on it, but this wasn't the Dillon he once knew. This was a new Dillon increasingly getting out of control, sort of freewheeling in his mind toward chaos and being steered by Will. Winston felt he was caught up by the movement, like a surfer caught by a wave, who can't get off without going under. 'I'm a lost man, I'm on the very edge of drowning,' he muttered under his breath.

Dillon's one good eye was flashing as he chatted with Will, who'd called round on him later. Dillon's injuries and dressings made him look quite mad, like someone out of a horror movie. Was his face actually smiling or was it a grimace? Will couldn't read him, yet he relied on him. Dillon after all knew everybody on the street. But he was so high on drugs and painkillers, Will wondered if it was even worth trying to talk with him.

'Oh yes, now we got our ends back and the cash is rolling in, pressure's off; don't know whether it's the painkillers or what I took with them, but things are on the up. Feeling good, Will, feeling ace, feeling I could fly,' Dillon said.

'I've decided when we do the Post Office job,' broke in Will soberly.

'The idiots did us a big favour when they switched cash day from Tuesdays to Sundays. Heard on the news there's to be a big Sunday 'do' in London, something to do with the Armistice. Lots of foreign visitors and military. Won't be a policeman in north London for love or money that day. That's when we'll do it,' he announced.

'Spoke to my Sis earlier, she can't see any snags. She'll be there and it'll be quieter. "Put Sunday 11 November in your diary," she said, so I'm telling you and bruvver Winston, pay day is 11 November. It's when we all get to be rich! I want that lad Clive in on this too. My bald bruv is doing a few months inside until the New Year, so there's a place in the team. When you've dealt with those remaining deliveries, I need you to call up Winston and then Clive; make sure Clive understands it's all in a good cause. I still need to pay for those shooters to be sure to hold our ends now we got them back. Clive will join us, he's in and he knows it; after all he's the last one to want to see Abu bounce back, now isn't he!'

Will looked again at Dillon. He wasn't sure if he'd heard a single word he'd said.

'Are you with me Dillon?' he asked.

'Oh yes, all the way. Today we fixed Abu, one Sunday in November we fix the Post Office; and you want bruvvers Winston and Clive in. I'll tell them.' With that Will decided he'd achieved all he could. He knew Dillon was getting seriously unhinged and before long he would have to do something about replacing him. It was time to leave.

35

After Ali had gone, Adam thought no-one left behind really knew what to do with him. He'd soon learned that his minder, Ali's brother, was called Mo. Mo was learning how to mind Adam, treating him as if he were a new pet, some exotic but wild animal. At first he was very wary of Adam, as if he might be attacked. He'd only ever push food in on a tray if Adam were squatting down at the furthest corner away from the door, and then he'd back off quickly. Of course Adam obliged. Then Mo tried practising words in English, 'OK,' 'food,' 'eat,' and 'no,' and this felt better for Adam who was desperate for some kind of human connection.

On the second day after Ali left, Adam asked for water to wash with and a towel to dry himself, then a tooth brush, and a clean T shirt to wear. Each time Mo hesitated and without acknowledging the request disappeared back to the house, only to reappear, sometimes a few minutes later, sometimes half a day later with what was requested in his hand.

Adam frequently watched Mo from his window grille, the slow loping walk, the flat usually emotionless gaze in his face. Over the days he began to see Mo as much imprisoned by his life as himself. Mo was a damaged guy, dutifully following routines not of his own making, in a regime of harsh obligations. It was clear he'd much rather not be looking after Adam.

One day someone had called out several times, 'Mo Muhammed,' until Fatima hurriedly crossed to speak to whoever it was through the grille on the gate and hush their calling. Adam thought the family name Muhammed was probably like Jones or Smith back in England but more so. How confusing to know whether you'd got the right person. Gradually, over the days and weeks Adam was building a picture of the family holding him.

With each step back and forth across the yard little puffs of dust rose from Mo's sandals, which made him seem weary, a man dragging himself along. Adam thought the oppressive weight of the IS regime was almost tangible in the compound. These routines made the days pass in some ordered fashion, but did little to lessen Adam's sometimes crippling feelings of anxiety nor lessen his desperation to be free.

He'd watched carefully, observing every detail from his window. Fear heightened his attentiveness. Of the world outside beyond the compound he heard nothing apart from the calls to prayer, the low growl of a vehicle passing, distant voices and just occasionally the explosive dull reverberating crumph of an explosion, usually some way off.

From time to time the creaking metal compound gate to the courtyard opened. Usually it was Fatima accompanied by an older relative leaving to buy food, the gate opening again maybe twenty minutes later, sometimes longer, when she returned. She always looked across to where he was. He liked to think it was because she cared, as if she wanted to connect with the human person separated by his door, her veil and so much more. He'd heard her name used. She did all the fetching, carrying and sometimes she'd escort the young children through the gate. Children were the same everywhere, innocent, curious, bounding energetically along cheerfully, their high-pitched voices carrying across the yard, oblivious to the cares of the adult world.

Mo rarely left. Adam thought he'd undoubtedly been charged with being his gaoler, and that was that. Sometimes Mo left the door opposite open and he could just make out Mo's seated shape in the shadows facing him. Yes, he was the gaoler, Adam the prisoner, with a profound space, more than the several metres of red-brown dust, dividing them. They watched each other in an awkward distant silence.

Adam wasn't normally given to claustrophobia or panic or depression; but these feelings were increasingly his companions. He'd always thought of himself as was one of those eternal optimists, who saw life's glass half full and not

249

half empty. Now, he felt his very personality was changing into someone else's, with dark moments getting ever longer. This meddling inside his head, as he understood it, further added to his fears.

But not all the time was stressed; unusually for him, he sometimes began to see his cell-like existence as a religious experience, a lesson in living, a reflection on mortality, even a wilderness time from which something positive might come to make him stronger. Occasionally, he felt a connection with the faith of his Aunt Ruth whom he'd always been fond of. Unbidden, he found these new feelings not entirely unwelcome or unhelpful as he got used to the privations of his new life. Sometimes there was a sense of what he could only describe as God's presence, making him feel less lonely, feelings he found hard to define or explain to himself.

It was amazing, he thought, that a person could live like this, on almost nothing, and as the days passed he began to use his simple cell as a laboratory to test himself, utilising the choices he felt he still had. Routine days were the easiest to bear, when he felt the most normal. It was the uncertainty and unpredictability that was torture. On good days, he realised that even though his life was limited, the best thing he still retained was the freedom he had to think. His mind was not yet their prisoner.

Bizarrely, he made friends with the hard-packed red dust earth beneath his feet and saw the speckled paint work on his metal door as art and tried to count how many shapes, patterns and pictures he could decipher in this decaying fresco. When it was dusk he could imagine all manner of fantastic imaginary animals, reptiles and birds. He also liked to see the occasional ground or flying insect come and share his space. They could come and go, but for him there was no escape, the enclosing 116 grey block bricks with their vertical and horizontal mortar lines made an impenetrable solid wall.

The simplicity of his transactional relations with Mo, centring on his personal needs, he reasoned, could become the basic building blocks for an experiment. Put simply, the question he asked himself was, 'is it possible to build a relational bridge between Mo and myself?'

The idea of an experiment then broke down in his mind into a series of pilot exercises. There was the relational language between them to learn and it was to be as much about the silences in their conversation, the unspoken, the ritual forms of their communication as it was to ever be tied down into flowing words. There were the limited everyday transactions to be made the most of, these occasional exchanges to be stretched to become more dynamically personal. There was also respect to be built and a trust to be forged. Then, between times, there were the opportunities, even unexpected opportunities, to be taken full advantage of.

Adam also realised that any experiment happened in a context; and he took it upon himself to make imaginary journeys in the long hours when he was left entirely alone. Funny how childhood events came back. When he was small, just a kid, his father had told him many imaginative stories about two brothers, Gerry and Terry, taking him on such creative journeys, the present was left behind. He revived the memory of story as a place to transport him to new realities and played with ideas and stories in the long hours of captivity.

These stories began to take flesh, keeping him alive especially at night. They kept him thinking, helped him feel alive. Through story, he began to try and re-enter the worlds around him. There was the Muslim family here in the compound, the Muhammed family world - different in its bonds to Adam's western nuclear Taylor family and middle class liberality, where everyone in their freedom chased their potential, whatever that meant.

Here though, family life was constrained by unseen custom and religious rules, shrouded and buried in distinctive clothes and behind high walls, the demands of poverty further eating away their freedom. Even so, he recognised the bonds of family affection at work, the considerations, the taking care for the older man, the help with carrying parcels and shopping, the working together on household chores. Here were the beginnings of a family story he could build on.

Mo was definitely in charge with Ali away, even the older man doing his bidding. Fatima, together with unseen other female hands in the house, and the younger children, he guessed lived a second-class life. There were only rare glimpses of a domestic world of cooking and cleaning and minding the children.

Theirs was a family story different to his, but in some ways not so very different. Just maybe, he might connect his family story with their family story. Just maybe, if he told them about his Mum and Dad, they might help him; but, to make that happen meant a lot of other things had to fall into place first.

Another story Adam told himself was one he called his 'Mosul Magazine.' He created mental pictures of the city outside with which to fill the imaginary pages. He recalled from school the rich history of Iraq, its many civilisations before its recent downward descent. He wished he'd read more. He knew his parents had marched in London with a million others to stop the 2003 war, a war that deposed one savage ruler in Saddam Hussain simply to open the door for all the other waiting demons to rush in. It was a disastrous piece of western political and military intervention, and he wondered whether that piece of remembered information at some point might win him favour. Another picture he had was of the River Tigris on which Mosul sat and the images he glimpsed on his ride here in the Toyota of a once-great city largely destroyed by constant war and bombardment so that it was now a shadow of its former glory.

He tried to picture a geography of Iraq for another page. He could visualise the two great rivers, the Tigris and Euphrates running north to south, meeting near Basra, the capital of free Iraq, Baghdad to the south, and the vast empty desert spaces to the north and west. Iraq was labyrinthine in his mind. He had no idea where roads from Mosul led to. Imagining possible roads radiating out from Mosul, one of which might lead to freedom felt totally impossible, like being in a dark underground system of caves, like when his father had first taken him potholing. The geography story he was inventing was not getting him far.

But then, as he was looking outside one evening, he saw the stars high above, and he thought of his past holidays spent on scout camp and how their leader had told them where to find the Pole Star and how it was possible to find one's way by the light of the moon and navigate by the stars. No, he was not lost in a labyrinthine pothole with no map and no sense of geography, the stars and remembered patterns of the starry heavens went into his imaginary magazine. Adam looked again and again at the stars at night, eventually working out which way was north. He had a map.

The last part of his imaginary journey pulled him within the IS story and he knew he had to better fathom out its life. Whether justifiable or not, the media back home had demonised the ruling regime here as one of Islamic extremism. In his imaginings he felt he had to try and understand that world in its own terms: his survival might depend on it. He found himself transported back to his secondary school days.

At school he'd once been put in a classroom peer group with Mark John, or 'Bible John' as everyone called him. No-one at school was friends with him. Mark John held a view of the world surprisingly resonant with that of the Caliphate. His 'Brethren' Christian brotherhood religion was, as he saw it, the only way to live and it was based on the literal truth of the scriptures. He belonged to the Muswell Hill Exclusive Brethren Church who didn't just meet on Sundays, but seemed to meet every day of the week for something or other. 'Bible John' was going to work for his Dad's garage as soon as he could leave school. No-one in his family went on to further education, he said, for 'real education was serving the Lord.' What was it, he said, 'the knowledge of God was the beginning of wisdom, and a millstone round your neck if you follow other ways.' Adam thought, if Mark John had been born here, he might even fit in! Same story, different context. Bloody similar selfish stories, both wanting an untidy world sewn up in a neat cosy package where they held control over the rules, where they were guardians of the truth and to hell with everyone else. He'd never won an argument with Mark John. He imagined he might find it was the same here.

This was day-dreaming, for Islamic State was more unsettling than any Brethren Brotherhood. Adam could call to mind no memories of 'Bible John' being anything but a peaceful, polite guy. Why then was IS so violent? His Mum had always said the bullies at school were the ones whose parents were bullies. Maybe that was it? Violence was passed on down the generations here, something everyone got socialised into. That didn't convince, violence couldn't just be the result of mass personal trauma.

He began to wonder whether people got locked into patterns of violence by patterns of social, political and even religious life that left no room for manoeuvre. This made some sense. Intuitively, he felt as he gazed once more toward the house opposite, Mo's situation was one of victim more than perpetrator of the violence against him. All the generous Arab and Muslim hospitality he'd been shown on his cycle ride had been pressed down and forced to hide itself here, but like some Jack-in-the-Box could one day be released back to life again. There must be some mechanism to release it, but what was it? Or was that just the now faint voice of the optimist in him speaking again?

On day eighteen of his solitary confinement things were different. He felt himself to be in limbo, between the fragile safety of each day turning out the same and still being alive and the dangerous uncertainty that one day something terrible would happen to him. It was an impossible emotional roller coaster ride. Today, Mo brought him a better breakfast, dates, apricots, cheese, fresh bread, and a coffee. Soap and a plastic safety razor were produced afterwards, then a bundle of new clothes - a cleaned and ironed T shirt and shorts.

'Get ready, soon,' said Mo, leaving him to himself again.

This made Adam extremely anxious. He needed to use his toilet bucket. His insides knotted up. What was going to happen? He'd seen videos made of western hostages who

254

were reading statements, then sometimes they were shot or beheaded. Were his options being closed down? Was this the hangman victim's last meal? It took away his hunger at first, but then he began to think about choice again. He could eat or leave the food. It made more sense to make the most of the present time and eat it, a choice he would make, not one driven either by hunger or by fear. So despite his knotted inside, he forced himself to eat.

When Mo returned half an hour later, the morning sun already burning the sandy courtyard, Adam asked, 'You write to my Mother?' He signed a writing motion with his hand. Mo didn't respond. Had he understood? Adam repeated the request.

'Me Adam, Me write to My Mother?' he pleaded. Mo knew full well what he meant, but he was not in charge. The request registered and was brusquely ignored.

'No, give hands,' he ordered and the plastic self-locking tie restraints went on, this time behind his back.

Mo stood behind him and then began to push him out of the cell across the yard to the Toyota Hilux. Adam noticed the keys were in the ignition and thought to himself that would never happen in Muswell Hill. Then he realised the keys were always, always left in the ignition. In a country where limbs were lopped for theft, no-one worried that the Hilux could be stolen. These things didn't happen.

He was pushed into the back of the vehicle and directed painfully into a seating position, Mo then leapt into the front, picked up a hand gun on the adjacent seat and waved it at Adam.

'No trouble please,' he ordered.

Adam gave a compliant nod, glad this time not to be hooded. Being outside his cell after so long was beginning to terrify him and he fought against the sensation he needed to shit again, concentrating hard until it passed.

It was just a short ride, a few blocks. They were expected. A group of men in fatigues were lined up outside an apartment block. Any civilians had been kept well away. The Hilux glided slowly up to the door, pulled past it. Then the

255

waiting men moved to surround the back of the vehicle, opened the back and dragged Adam out.

One man pushed his head forward so that he was forced to look only at the ground in front of him. Another person helped the process by grabbing his tied wrists and lifting them. He felt the pain in his shoulders and tilted even lower to avoid it.

Once inside the building he was made to go upstairs. Thoughts of people being thrown off buildings came to mind. A door opened, he was in a room with a fan whirring somewhere. Then, with the door closed on him again, the pressure eased and he was allowed to look up, gently raising his head. There was a brown wooden desk and standing behind it a man in black robes. A calm and measured voice addressed him in English.

'Good Morning, Adam. I trust you are being well looked after?' Adam felt he had to reply and chose to do it deferentially, an approach that tended to work well at school when in front of a reprimanding teacher.

'Yes, Sir,' he said, barely audibly, then remembering the Muslim greeting, added 'Salaam Alekum.' Then quickly he added, 'Can I write to my Mum please, she'll be worried.'

He'd exercised choice and he'd taken the initiative even if this man opposite hadn't realised it and he himself didn't show it. For an instant he felt better, he looked at his inquisitor's face. The fleeting feeling passed and his request was totally ignored, was as if it had never been made.

'Let me introduce myself. I am Salim Ismat, enshallah, the Commanding Officer here. You are a guest of our Caliph. We are indebted to you for helping us Adam, maybe not intentionally, but helping us nonetheless. Your epic cycle ride from London has given us the route into that city we have been looking for, and I have to tell you, so far as anyone is concerned you are safe and well on your cycle ride and even now we're letting everyone know you are back home in London,' he said.

Adam was puzzled.

'As we speak, Ali, whom you have already met, is now in London. He is Adam! He did it! He got there all because of you!' Salim said. A self-congratulatory smile passed across his face. 'Please sit down Adam, I can see this is hard for you,' he said, his arm motioning Adam toward the empty chair.

His manner was slimy and greasy, repulsively patronising, in the manner of the playground bully, thought Adam. Salim called across to one of his men and uttered a command and Adam's ties were cut. His arms fell forward and he rubbed his wrists to restore the circulation. Then mint tea was brought in on a silver tray.

'Please have some tea Adam. Please, believe me, it isn't poisoned.' He grinned again. Adam did as he was instructed. 'I have been told we need to make a short film together, a procedural thing, all very straightforward.'

He pulled a drawer open in the desk in front of him. Some sheets of A4 paper with handwriting on were placed in front of him and revolved slowly through 180 degrees so Adam could read the words. Salim summoned another unseen man into the room with his hooked finger, this man carrying a small handheld camera.

'This may take more than one shot,' he said as he stood up and moved his chair further back and sat the camera man in it, the camera now pointing straight at Adam.

'Begin reading, and keep your voice up please,' ordered Salim.

As Adam took the papers in his hand, he exercised his second choice, to move the mint tea out of shot. Why should he be seen drinking tea with his captors? Salim didn't seem to notice, but words were said by the cameraman and moments later the tray was moved right back next to him.

Most of what he had to read was boringly routine, who he was, that he was in Islamic State and that he was being treated well. Then the text began to get more problematic. 'I am most appreciative of what is being done here,' it read, 'this is a peaceful place and these peace-loving people only want to follow in the ways of the prophet, peace be upon him.

I have decided to stay on here for a while to learn more about the way of life here.'

After reading it once, Adam was asked to make a re-run and put more feeling into it. He decided to stumble over the words deliberately on the second run and told himself he had now made three choices, small but important statements of self-identity and control. However, he knew that he had little option but to comply with their need for propaganda and when it was done to their satisfaction, he felt dirty inside, and to rub the dirt in further, Salim gave an ingratiating and quite insincere thanks.

'Thank you for your cooperation in this Adam. You will appreciate we need to keep an historic record of your stay until such time as it is useful, if ever, to release it.'

The visit was over. Adam began to feel incredibly anxious inside as to what would happen next. They didn't bother to re-tie his wrists, simply marched him head down, a hot and heavy hand on the back of his neck, returning him to the waiting Hilux. Mo, looking anxious too, was still in the driver's seat. Adam was ejected into the back and locked in, this time with an extra man for the return trip sitting in the front next to keep an eye on him.

Relieved to be back in the compound once again, he was returned to his cell; and yes, thought Adam, as he eye'd the Hilux parked in its usual place opposite his metal grille window: they really do always leave the keys in.

In his cell he argued with himself whether to play the long game, to wait and see what fate determined, but increasingly told himself he must attempt to get away. Maybe it was a fanciful thing every prisoner did, he didn't know, but he told himself he had to find a way of escape. He believed his life was useful here only so far as it served the regime and then he was finished. Today he was grateful Mo had left him in his change of clothes, had given him an ample breakfast, some of which still lay on the tray.

He began to think what further choices he had. He could try to save some food, keep one of the plastic water bottles he'd been given to wash in, to scrutinise the old locking

258

mechanism of his door, to observe and log in his mind the patterns of movement over in the house. Yes, he still had the freedom to think, a few choices, and doing nothing was not a choice, he, Adam Taylor, was going to take. Driven by fear for his survival, he looked at everything with a view to it helping him one day to make his escape.

Four days later a chance plan began to form. A sandstorm was definitely brewing and by late afternoon the sky had turned red-brown shutting out the sun. A wind got up, even stirring the dust in the courtyard. For three days Adam had scraped and sanded the saved plastic bowl edge in the instep of his shoe. He used the abrasive concrete bricks of his cell as a file until he had fashioned it to make a rectangular block he now thought given a quick and often practised movement, he might be able to introduce into the mortise mechanism of his door. It was a long shot, but it might just stop it locking fully shut. It was worth a try, he had nothing to lose.

Mo had become more relaxed about Adam since the visit to the CO, perceiving him to be little threat, a frightened lad, totally compliant and even friendly. In recent days he'd allowed Adam to come to the door as he approached on his regular visits with food and water and both yesterday and today permitted Adam to stand just outside the cell door to take his stinking sluicing pot with its circular cardboard lid and tip it into the drain himself. It hadn't taken Adam much power of persuasion to get Mo to agree to this.

It was this move that allowed Adam, in the fading light of dusk and in a building wind, to quickly insert the plastic piece he'd shaped into the mortise bolt-receiving hole. With a firm push it fitted tightly. Whether or not Mo would either spot it or whether this would work he didn't know, but he told himself he'd exercised another choice.

Back inside, Mo slammed the cell door shut and Adam heard the key grind squeakily, not once, as it usually did, but three times. Then the key rattled its exit. In a near moment of panic, Adam grabbed the back of the door with both hands pulling it toward him with as much weight as he could as, sure enough, Mo tried testing the door to see whether it had in fact locked by giving it a sharp pull. Why hadn't he anticipated he'd do that? thought Adam, his heart thumping.

Mo seemed satisfied and Adam watched him, without taking a second glance, walk hurriedly back toward the house with its orange light glinting inside. With bad weather approaching, the front door opposite was promptly shut for the night. Some time later, when all noise was drowned by the now howling wind, Adam put his hand to the door and gently, firmly and slowly pushed his shoulder against it, for the first time in three weeks hoping against hope that this was the moment to seize his freedom. He was so scared he could barely control his shaking.

36

Kaylah's mood was upbeat. Her new autumn term at college was going well and the 'frees' she had, gave her pretty well half a day to herself every day, which suited her just fine. She got up late on 'free' mornings, but not that late because she had found herself getting a real buzz from helping at Ruth's Drop In and was spending more and more time there. She felt useful, needed, purposeful, and for the first time in her life doing something for herself outside the family. Clive had stopped coming ever since his hand was stabbed. She continued to worry about him, for he was increasingly evasive with her and was spending ever more time with Winston.

The College was now saying she should do a placement as part of her Business Studies course, but the promised help they offered in finding a placement had yet to materialise. Her friends had been asking relatives in shops, or the more fortunate ones, their friends in the City of London, to give them a work shadowing experience, but for Kaylah there was, as yet, nothing on the horizon.

In the meantime she was filling her time any which way she could. If anything the Drop In was busier by the day and the logistics in keeping it going had become ever more testing, and so it was she had ended up there helping out most days of the week.

After the house fire, the Centre had rallied behind Abu Tariq brilliantly. Wider community support had come in with all the media coverage and sympathy generated. Visitors had been bringing in anything from food to envelopes of cash. A good number had also turned up for the funeral gathering. People with nothing understood these things better than people with much, thought Kaylah, and she felt herself changing her views, once so quickly judgemental, but now softening to be more understanding.

After the fire Abu had continued to come along to the Drop In, though less frequently than before. Kaylah noted he was invariably on the edge of things, never really mixing, except with two or three guys from the Middle East. They were always on their phones, collecting free food and making use of the free internet service laid on.

Kaylah could see that the demands on Ruth, juggling this surge in activity, alongside her family and church responsibility were straining her to breaking point. She was getting more abrupt, more irregular, sometimes forgetful and things were beginning to slip. Then Kaylah had an idea. She decided to approach Ruth when she next had a chance to offer her support on a different footing, to offer some business skills to the Drop In in addition to just helping out. In return, all Ruth would have to do would be to complete a placement report for her college at the end of term.

It wasn't until late Thursday afternoon she had a chance to broach the subject when Ruth suddenly appeared, swinging two large bin liners full of food items which had been mistakenly dropped off at the vicarage next door. Kaylah stepped across quickly to assist and they began emptying them together, putting them on the shelves in the store.

'Ruth, I was wondering if I might help out here as part of my college course, because we are expected to do a placement and I haven't been able to find one. No, what I mean is, it's not that I haven't been able to find one, it's that I think I could do something useful here. Well, I know I am doing something useful, but... I'm not explaining myself very well am I?' blurted out Kaylah.

'Carry on. You're doing a great job here and I'm so grateful you are around to help. What do you want to do?' asked Ruth kindly.

'My course is Business Studies, and this term we're supposed to find a business to do a placement in. Well, they're supposed to find a placement, but they never do. They leave it to the students. We've all ended up finding our own, only I haven't got one yet and the term's moving on. I was thinking this Drop In is, in its own way a business, a social

262

enterprise project. It has resources, it has staff, it's located in a premises, there is a business side to it. It has to be sustainable. If it's not managed, then it will collapse and all these people will be let down.' She drew a breath, then pressed on.

'I guess it's complicated when you think about who owns the business too. The church are kind of stakeholders, they have to raise their income and pay their bills, and this Drop In must figure significantly in the church accounts, which raises questions to my mind about where its priority lies. I ask myself how does this activity get measured against other activities of the church? It has to make its case doesn't it? My Dad, as you know, runs a church which places mission as its number one priority and resources just wouldn't be given to this kind of social caring work. We argue about it sometimes. Whatever. From what I've learned at college, a project as big as this can only flourish, be sustainable as a business if there is a business plan, a budget, a fundraising strategy, communication, good governance and so on and so forth. Can I help you with any of these please?' said Kaylah, now breathless.

'There is a God!' Ruth suddenly exclaimed, raising her hands to the sky, the expression rather shocking Kaylah.

'You've really been thinking about this haven't you? I'd be so pleased to have you help with this. You wouldn't believe how much sense what you've just said is making. It's music to my ears! I just can't do any more than I am doing. You'll need to give me some sort of CV and outline of what the college requires as soon as possible, I guess. Look, get Olive to bring us over a couple of mugs of tea or coffee, whatever. Let's park ourselves up over there and get this sorted now,' said a delighted Ruth.

Kaylah's eyes lit up, her face beamed. She moved over to the table with a new spring in her step. There was a girlie conspiratorial air which both of them felt, a unity found in a shared enjoyable purpose.

'It's a feminist issue too,' added Ruth some minutes later. 'You forgot to say that. In my church it's a feminist

263

issue, because it's about women taking responsibility for business issues, for leading things, for taking power and control and running things. You need to think about this too if you do a placement here. Women don't have an equal place here or in the nation's board rooms. Just remember that when you're here, especially when you get to talk to our treasurer Alex Sutton. Even when you speak to the women in positions of responsibility, remember to always read the feminist agenda,' said Ruth.

'I hadn't thought of that one, but you're right. We did some lectures on that last year. You've met my Dad, he's so traditional, he's so, what you'd call, patriarchal. I've seen a lot of it, it's crushing,' said Kaylah, sensing a need to be more personally empowered too.

'I was thinking, is that going to be a problem? I mean you doing your placement in a different church to your Dad's? Will that be alright with your Dad? Will it be OK for you too?' asked Ruth.

'Leave him to me. He's full of contradictions. Sometimes he wants me to be successful, other times he just wants me to find the right kind of Christian boy, get married and have kids - then be a stay at home wife like my Mum. Other times, I don't know... I think he's like a lot of people like him, stuck in the certainties of past dogmas because they give a safe framework for life. He's alright, his heart's in the right place, but the world I live in is different to his. I really want this placement. It'll be good for me to work with you and it will give me something on my CV too. I want a future rather than settle for old Edmonton,' she said with some conviction.

The tea had long been finished. Taken into her confidence, Ruth had given Kaylah her personal mobile details and they had already fixed up some diary dates to talk further. Pressed for time now, Ruth excused herself.

'Look, make sure you start logging the hours you've done this week. They all count. Got to go. Tell you what, it would really help me if you could drop round to Abu's place to take him a basket of things we've been given for him. Any chance you could do that when you've finished here today?

Since the fire, he's been moved from Mount Pleasant Road. The Wood Green Housing Association have put him round the corner from here on the Red Brick Estate. He's on the ground floor at number 52.'

'That's fine, leave it with me. I'll find it,' said Kaylah, happy to help.

Ruth passed her the correspondence she was to take with her to Abu and showed her where the basket had been stored. A new group of African asylum seekers pushed open the door and stood, not knowing which way to turn; Kaylah moved across to engage them in conversation and feed them into the system.

Things had been getting busier and busier as the EU had worked to get Britain to take a fairer share of the ever greater numbers of desperate people fleeing to Europe. For some time, the PM had stuck to the line that Britain had secure and tight island border controls as a key policy message but events had turned this into an embarrassing fiction as on the one hand business leaders had told him how helpful it would be for the growing economy to let these motivated workers in, and on the other hand to get the policy support he needed from Europe on other areas, like defence, agriculture, Gibraltar and fishing quotas, he'd been forced to open the migrant door a little wider.

'So you're from Libya,' Kaylah beamed, 'so nice to welcome you here. Come over here and let's get you registered and let's see what we can do to help.'

The half dozen, mainly women in coloured robes, seemed happy, the more so when mugs of steaming hot chocolate were brought over by Olive and her team.

Mid-afternoon, Kaylah noticed things were beginning to quieten and some new helpers were coming in. She told Olive that she was off to deliver the food parcel to Abu and would be back in the morning.

It was awkward carrying the wicker basket laden with dates, fruit and other good things to eat, but it wasn't so far down Silver Street. She crossed over the road in front of a red London Routemaster bus and into the discrete world of the Red Brick Estate.

She'd never really cared for these modern featureless blocks, built when the old hosiery factory on the site had closed down. There were always 'problems' here she'd heard. She soon found Abu's front door and pressed the bell. He answered and looked at her with a puzzled expression on his face.

'Abu, its Kaylah, from the Drop In. I've come to deliver these for you.' She lifted the basket toward him and removed the cover to reveal the contents, but rather than receive it, his hands remained resolutely at his side.

'What's this for?' he asked her stiffly.

'Well, some people heard about what had happened, the fire,' she wished she hadn't mentioned that bit and hurried on, 'and they dropped this in, saying it was for you. People rally round when something awful happens, yes they really do,' she said, trying to be friendly.

He was keeping her on the doorstep and not inviting her in, but that was OK. He started staring at her, peering right into her face.

'You're that guy's sister aren't you,' he said looking at her coldly.

'You mean Clive,' she said, recalling that Abu and Clive had clashed when Clive had come to help recently. She was getting apprehensive about where the conversation was going and what might happen next. It was Abu who was also close to her college friend Melissa when she was hurt; and it was then she remembered what had happened to Clive's hand. She was feeling more uncomfortable and unsafe with every passing minute and wished she hadn't agreed to make this call.

'That's right. Thought it was. I don't want anything from you,' he said bitterly, 'Go.'

Kaylah was taken aback, shaken, but told herself Abu had been through trauma she could only imagine and so she would simply leave the basket and make a polite exit. She bent down and put the basket by the door.

266

'I'll leave this here for you,' she said not knowing what else to say.

As she reached down, a young man in his late teens rushed up to the door on a battered blue racing bike, mobile pressed to his ear, calling Abu's name.

'Need another twenty brown, got to get them to Edmonton Green right now,' he said. He hadn't really noticed Kaylah, but Abu's face was red with rage.

'Shut up you foolish boy,' Abu shouted, cuffing him around the ear.

Kaylah backed off. She'd never liked Abu and she liked him less now. It was time to make a hasty retreat. She knew about what happened on the street, she knew a drugs 'runner' about his business when she saw one.

The Red Brick Estate had its own ways of dealing with people and it was time she got away. She could feel Abu's eyes boring into the back of her head as she smartly headed off. The placement wasn't intended to start quite like this, but it certainly wasn't boring, she thought, as she headed swiftly away and toward home.

Then as she retraced her steps her mind wandered. She imagined what it must be like to do a business placement with a drugs cartel. Now twenty wraps of your average street deal at ten quid each, that's £200, she calculated. 'Bloody hell,' she said out-loud. She laughed at the impossibility of such a placement. The College Ethics Committee would have apoplexy - but it was a fun idea and lifted her feelings after the stand-off with Abu.

Sobering up, she realised she had just seen the drugs business for real, right under her nose. It was right on her doorstep. She asked herself what no good thing Abu might be up to and pondered why he had asked about Clive like that?

The thought sent a shiver down her spine. Abu was responsible for what happened to Clive. She surmised Clive had wrangled him somehow, heard something he shouldn't have, but by then she was turning into Cheddington Road and it was time to put her feet up and listen to some music. She

267

told herself she must remember to tell Clive what had happened and warn him about Abu.

37

Ali had one problem as he cycled through Walthamstow next morning. He suddenly found his bike wobbling all over the road. Looking down over the handlebars, he saw he had a puncture in his front wheel. That in itself wasn't the problem, the issue was, he'd never before mended a bike puncture. He pulled the bike off the road and onto the pavement. Reaching into the pannier bag he retrieved Adam's repair kit with its tube of glue, abrasive strip, chalk block and rubber sticking plasters. By trial and error he released the front wheel, but only after much futile pulling did he realised he had to release the brake callipers first to get the wheel off.

Two young white lads had gathered to watch him. Couldn't have been more than ten or eleven years old. One of the boys, the older one, watched as Ali tried to peel the tyre from the rim by brute force.

'Hey mate, you use them wheel levers,' one of the boys said, pointing to the two curved metal rods with notched ends in the repair box.

'Come on then, show me,' invited Ali, seeing these street kids as the same as any the world over.

Moments later the tyre was peeled free, the inner tube revealed and the valve retaining nut unscrewed to release it. The next part of the process was to find the point of the puncture itself. Here again the lads proved useful. The older one told his younger friend to go home and bring back a bowl of water. The boy ran off into the nearby apartment block, to appear with a sloshing bowl of water, spilling some of it on the pavement as he tried to carry it quickly across to the bike. It took half an hour to get it fixed, the lads enjoying working with him.

'Where you going Mister?' the second boy asked as Ali was about to climb on the bike again.

'Edmonton, north London,' he replied.

'Spect you'll go down the Lea Valley then, nice way that, avoid the traffic,' the first boy guessed.

The lad proceeded to offer directions which proved to be reliable and a good choice. Ali had hated the increasingly heavy traffic, especially the lorries with their fumes and their complete occupation of the road space which had led him more than once to have to take evasive action.

The Lea Valley was a delight. The pathway was as pleasant as the lad had promised, the valley so green and lush and the fields so productive and the houses so well cared for and prosperous. Where was all the litter that so desecrated everywhere back home?

In Mosul this oasis wouldn't exist and the river would not be clean. He spotted fish in the water, fishermen trying to catch them, and so many different birds and ducks. The only problem was, so many people trying to use such a narrow path, though everyone he met was polite and good-humoured. All too often he had to slow up to get by. People even seemed to love their dogs here and what surprised him most, and made him laugh, they cleared up after them. He'd never do that, he told himself. Soon it was past midday and he was feeling hungry again.

He spotted a pub garden beside the waterway and, setting aside any religious scruples, excusing his behaviour as needing to blend in with the locals and doing what Adam would have done, he wheeled his bike into the garden and leant it against a trestle table. Using one of the twenty pound notes he had been given by his CO, Salim, he ordered a burger salad lunch and a red juice J2O with ice.

He carried his drink outside; the burger soon followed, served by an attractive girl in an outfit no doubt acceptable here but which would be reviled as decadent back home. The contrast between the cultures was taking some adjustment. He asked himself whether it was his own decadence in eyeing the girl's curves that was the problem, for she seemed quite comfortable in how she was dressed. Some other cyclists pulled up, but he studiously avoided them, not wanting to be drawn into conversation, particularly now he was getting so near his destination.

On the trail again he saw a sign saying Pickett's Lock and then one for Edmonton. His heart missed a beat. He pulled off the trail and began cycling on roads again. It was mid-afternoon and he wanted to get to meet Abu at the Drop In rendez-vous soon. He decided now was the right time for his second call to Abu. He pulled over by a fish and chip shop, the familiar smell of stale oil the same the world over.

'Salaam Alekum. Abu, that you... Ali here. I must be near you. This is Church St, Edmonton near a rail station bridge. Know it?'

'Ali, you've done well my brother. I know exactly where you are. Wait there. I'm going to send Chris to meet you and bring you here. He'll be on his bike. You'll spot him by his red T shirt. You're just five minutes away. We'll meet at the door of the Drop In. You can leave your things, then get rid of the bike, the sooner the better. I'm on my way there now, after that we'll let the Drop In fix you up. Just wait there, wait'! and with that he hung up.

Ali spotted the lad approaching from under the railway bridge, cautiously as if expecting a trap, but once his searching eyes were satisfied he moved in quickly to Ali and told him simply, 'follow me.'

They went up the road, swinging right into Haselbury Road and past some fancy school, smart blue blazers and mothers in cars everywhere.

'Land of the bloody middle classes,' was his companion's only comment. Then it was right and left, and then into Windmill Road. Moments later they were pulling up outside some old brick buildings. A shuffling man in a white Arab tunic was at the door.

'That's Abu,' said his companion, 'No worries, I'll watch your bike. I ain't goin' to nick it now am I? He's all yours Abu,' he said and then moved off a few yards to have a smoke and give them some space.

Abu embraced Ali as a dutiful father might a son. For Ali it was heartfelt, he took Abu at face value, believing him to be

271

a true and faithful brother and elder living as best he could in the land of the infidel. Abu saw the embrace as custom, what was expected and was the first to let go.

'Before you go in, Ali, it's important that your story is good. Tell it to me as you intend to tell them,' said Abu.

'There's nothing to it really. I have escaped as an asylum seeker from Mosul, brought here by people smugglers to escape persecution by Islamic State. I am an engineer and want to find work in the UK. But I have nowhere to live and no money... that's my story anyway. Will it do?' asked Ali.

'For now it's fine. This Drop In will get you fixed up with somewhere to stay. I'd have you stay with me, but it's better we are in separate places. Anyway it's orders from above. The lad Chris is going to take you to where you drop off your bike. He looks rough but he's trustworthy, just leave your own things here with me while you're gone.'

Ali unpacked his bike's panniers, but slid the contents of the front pannier into his jacket pocket rather leave his documents, passports and money, just in case. Ali didn't trust this lad Chris, though Abu might. Whilst this was going on, the lad Chris, leaning on the wall was drawing on another cigarette and going through something on his mobile phone as he did so. Abu went across to him. Ali decided it was time to go to Muswell Hill before it got any later and asked Chris if he was ready. Leaving Abu with the contents of his panniers, the two cyclists set off again.

Ali decided his bike needed a bit of a clean so they bought wet wipes at a corner shop in Westerham Avenue where the friendly Asian Hindu guy who sold him them asked him if there was anything else he needed. They went to a park nearby, Tatum Park, where Ali began a meticulous bike clean. He didn't want to leave any personal clues on the machine. Chris was getting through his cigarettes. He had only one comment to make, 'it's nicked, innit?' which Ali thought was spot on, but made no comment.

Once done and everything remaining dumped in a waste bin, they set off again. It began to rain. He'd forgotten how

England was so frequently grey, dull and wet more days than not. He had to accept he'd get wet.

It was a mistake, a big mistake, to follow the North Circular Road east. The traffic gave them no quarter and the spray from the passing cars and lorries soaked them both to the skin. They turned off, making their way up Colney Hatch Lane, into what he took to be a nicer part of town. He could tell by the shops, at one point enjoying the sweet smell of roasting quality coffee from a delicatessen called 'Taylors', the aroma carrying across the street. Chris wanted to wait in the Broadway and pointed Ali in the direction he was going to dump the bike. He agreed to wait until he was back.

Cautiously Ali turned into what he knew was Adam Taylor's road. For a while he parked up outside a pub called the Royal Oak, just so he could watch and get a feel for the place. From there he could actually see Adam's house. It was a weird feeling. For so long he had been Adam, and now he was in London he was Ali again. Who was he really? He felt so close to Adam's world. He felt he understood him intuitively. So this was where Adam lived. This was his home. The thought unsettled him. It was too personal.

His plan was to dump the bike where it would be found by Adam's parents. He'd been told they would maybe believe Adam wasn't missing abroad, but safely back locally. It was all part of setting a false trail, and he told himself it was a good thing to let them kind of believe their lad was fine, even though they didn't know the half of it. They wouldn't worry so much, would they? They'd tell themselves he's back, he wants his independence, and is leaving his bike at home to collect later. Perhaps they'd think he'd really got a girl friend like other western lads do and he couldn't tell them for shame. Whatever. He admitted to himself he didn't understand how these things worked here, but he had nagging doubt the IS story-line he'd been sold would ring true here.

Ali ended up waiting longer than he'd intended in the hope of seeing what Adam's parents were like, but they didn't show and Chris was fretting and getting impatient. It was just he was curious. He decided when the road was quiet to

273

quickly wheel the bike up to the gate, open it, and then lay it in the small front garden behind the hedge. That way it would be seen when someone came back to the house later and being behind the front hedge it stood a better chance of not being stolen.

It was kind of sad to part with a bike he liked. Part of him would have liked to continue cycling with its freedom and independence. He quickly moved away, confident he hadn't been observed and retraced his way up the hill and back to the shops. Chris walked him to the bus stop and gave him directions and then he had gone, but not before he had asked Ali for money for cigarettes.

Half an hour later he was back near the Drop In Centre. Abu was still there, but now sitting on the step, beside Ali's things, everything he possessed in one sports bag. Abu stood up and indicated they should go inside.

Once inside the hall, Ali was surprised how many people there were. He was a little alarmed because he thought he might be drawn into conversation with other Arabic speakers he heard here and there. Abu first took him over to where two robed friends of his were standing against what was formerly the stage area of the hall. Ali was introduced to them as if he were the Mahdi himself. Clearly these two guys were part of Abu's cell and they were very excited to know the long-awaited Ali had now arrived. Abu was keen though not to draw undue attention to Ali as part of their circle, and soon pulled him away from the others.

He took Ali across to a desk where a young black woman was sitting. Abu snorted with discomfort as they approached. Ali thought the young woman had a lovely warm engaging smile and captivating eyes. Abu brusquely introduced Ali.

'This man was outside. He needs some help,' said Abu. At that he turned and walked back to rejoin his friends.

'Please take a seat,' the young woman said. She reached across for a sheet of paper and a pen.

'Welcome to Holy Trinity Drop In. We are here to provide support for everyone who needs it. I'm Kaylah Kone and I am an Advice Worker here. What is your name please?'

'Ad... Ali, Ali Muhammed from Mosul, Iraq,' he said.

Kaylah wrote it all down, carefully checking the spelling and accuracy of her understanding as she went. Occasionally she would veer off as when she said 'your English is really very good, Ali, that will be such a help to you.'

'I studied English at School and at Mosul University,' he said.

Then the questions became more searching, 'Where will you be staying?' she asked.

'I have nowhere to stay.' Ali detected a flicker of genuine concern in Kaylah's eyes.

'Maybe we can find you somewhere,' she said. She picked up her mobile, but before making a call, waved across the hall to another helper, 'Olive, can you get Ali here something to eat and drink please.'

Whilst Olive provided some welcome tea and cake, Kaylah deftly called up two or three people before announcing, 'it's not the Ritz, but Flo and Bert offer a room to us round the corner. They're a very sweet older couple, used to come to the church here when they were younger, but they still like to help. It's basic but clean. Here's how you get there,' Kaylah instructed.

She drew a simple map, Ali captivated by her slender fingers and beautifully manicured pink brown nail polish.

'Tell you what,' she said, 'I'm just finishing for the day, I'll walk you round there and introduce you. Is that all the stuff you've got?' she asked.

'Yes, just this,' Ali said.

He discreetly waved farewell to Abu as he left. They walked for not more than five or ten minutes, turning right after the streets of terraced housing Kaylah called 'The Huxley', had given way to slightly bigger semi-detached houses with larger gardens to the front. They stopped at a well cared for house with climbing roses each side of the shiny front door, the last of their scented pink blooms flopping

275

with heavy heads. An elderly white lady with glasses opened the door on a chain. When she saw it was Kaylah, the door was immediately released and flung open wide.

'My dear, how nice to see you again! And you have a handsome young man for us,' she added, spotting Ali right behind her.

'Bert,' she called back into the house, 'come and see who we've got this time, a handsome young man!'

As Bert made his way to the door, Kaylah said, 'Flo, this is Ali Muhammed, Ali this is Flo and Bert.'

Bert was using some kind of metal aluminium frame to shuffle down the hallway. He called a friendly enough 'Hello,' adding, 'Well, it ain't that bad, don't just stand there on the doorstep, come on in, come on in,' he said to Ali.

Ali could hear a very loud TV on somewhere in the back of the house. It felt homely and he couldn't resist holding out a hand to have it shaken, asking as he did so, 'have you lived here long?'

Flo looked at him quizzically.

'This one speaks English Kaylah! Handsome and speaks English. You've done us proud Kaylah,' Flo said.

She shook Ali's hand with her thin pale fragile hand, Ali taking care to be gentle. Bert had both hands firmly holding on to his walking frame.

Kaylah told Flo to ring her if she needed to, Flo saying, 'Don't worry love, we'll see he's alright.'

As Kaylah turned to go, Ali couldn't help but turn too.

'Thank you,' he said, finding himself gazing into her dark eyes, 'thank you so much.'

He then took her hand and awkwardly shook it. Unlike Flo's hand, hers was warm and soft. Releasing his hand, she told him, she'd see him at the Drop In tomorrow if he called; and, then she could check he was properly registered with the authorities and that he got the money and vouchers to which he was entitled. All this kindness left Ali feeling confused. If this is the decadent west, maybe I'm not understanding something, he thought.

276

Moments later, the front door firmly shut, Flo was showing him the upstairs room they'd set aside, saying, 'it is for anyone who has need of it. We might not get to church much these days, but making a spare room available is something useful we can still do,' before adding, 'and we've met the most wonderful people from all over the world.'

Ali again felt uncomfortable and confused, overwhelmed by the human kindness and genuine hospitality of this elderly couple. They made him feel dirty inside.

Flo and Bert, Ali soon discovered, had made the downstairs their home, so he found he had the complete use of the upstairs floor to himself, which suited his purposes ideally. He had still further privacy too, aided by the deafness of Flo and Bert which meant they would never overhear any of his phone calls even if they could understand what he was saying. They were unbearably kind, making sure he had an evening meal, a bath if he wanted it, which he did, and then, after the best night's sleep for ages, a hearty breakfast to start the next day. They kept calling up to him to see if he was alright.

Breakfast was a bit of an ordeal. He had to sit with them and he felt obliged to eat what they had provided - a lumpy porridge cereal, tasteless slices of white toasted bread with butter and marmalade, and a brand of fair-trade instant coffee which had less flavour than desert sand only it was smoother. For all this he knew they meant well and he thanked them.

As soon as he could, he got himself ready to go out. Before leaving, though it felt entirely unnecessary, he hid Adam's passport, his phone, the Euros and nearly all the Sterling he'd been issued with. The free-standing wardrobe had old boxes of children's games on top. It amused him to see one called Risk, so he pulled it down and hid everything inside the Risk box before carefully replacing it in the middle of Flo and Bert's collection of old board games.

Before leaving the house, Flo insisted Ali should have his own front door key and come and go as he pleased. They were kind enough to lend him a London A-Z which they said he'd find really useful. Flo made him try the key in the lock

277

twice to be sure it worked before she would finally let him go. Bert watched him leave from the front window, Flo from the porch step. He felt obliged to give them a friendly farewell wave and a 'see you later.'

As he walked off he tried to tell himself he wasn't here because of people like Bert and Flo. He was here because the west was decadent and godless. Bert and Flo were god-fearers, people of the book, and they could hardly be decadent, but they were watching some sexual content on TV, something about London people, a programme called 'Eastenders' so maybe even they had been corrupted. Even so, he couldn't bring his heart to condemn them for it. He walked slowly down to the Drop In and wandered inside. There was Kaylah.

'Hello,' he called, 'it's me again, can you help me?'

She looked genuinely pleased to see him, as indeed she was. She took him over to the table where they had first met yesterday.

'How did you find staying with Flo and Bert?' she asked.

'Good. They're very kind. I think I'll be alright there. But I am worried how I will be alright in your country. I need to be an asylum seeker don't I?' he asked her.

'You do. Have you claimed asylum before?' she said.

'No,' said Ali.

'Did you come here through Europe? Did you get any help with asylum?' she said.

'No. People-smugglers helped me get here in a van,' he lied, but then it was a half truth, his journey had begun that way. 'They dropped me off on the North Circular Road,' he added, knowing this was a complete lie. He remembered the name of this busy thoroughfare where half the world's lorries had seemed to thunder past him, the biggest risk to his mission so far. She seemed satisfied, and pulled out a piece of paper. He knew he had to be careful.

Half an hour later, his signature on the form, Kaylah promised him she would get it sent off today and they should hear something back after the weekend. He would be quite safe at Flo and Bert's house in the meantime, but once his

278

claim was processed then the authorities would offer him somewhere official to stay in, for longer.

'Oh, but I like Flo and Bert's,' he said.

'I think you'll be there for a while yet, given the pressure on places,' she told him.

Ali found it really easy to talk to Kaylah. Here was someone who could be useful to him, he thought; and, as she wrote down the answers he gave her, he found himself kind of checking her over. He'd noticed her perfume when he first arrived, and was aware that his own clothes were damp and probably smelled of sweat and worse. He noticed her clean stylish shoes, her figure hugging blue jeans, and the cheerfulness of her shapely silk top. He saw how smooth the skin of her face was and how gentle and happy were her dark eyes. In fact it was her eyes that had first caught his attention yesterday.

Then he felt guilty. He tried to concentrate on why he was here and the job in hand. But then he'd be distracted again and when Olive brought her some coffee, and himself a cup too, he watched how she drank it, how she smiled, how she was so at ease with herself and the world. If only, he caught himself thinking and it was then his elbow was pushed, nearly causing him to spill what remained of his coffee. He turned to see Abu standing there and his distracted thinking came to a quick end.

'Oh Abu,' said Kaylah seeing him there. 'Would you mind looking after our new arrival Ali for a few minutes whilst I try and get this to the last post. Ali, this is Abu, he's had a terrible thing happen to him recently, had a house fire, terrible thing.' Her words trailed off, Ali sensing an atmosphere between them. Not knowing what else to say, she marched off clutching the newly filled and signed form in her hand, grabbed an envelope off the shelf and was out of the front door before Ali could say 'thank you.'

'Abu, what's this about a house fire?' asked Ali.

Abu looked up and down the hall.

'Come over here,' he said, leading Ali into a quiet corner.

279

'Life here in the land of the infidel is hard and sacrificial. It is the will of Allah. I have lost my wife and children, burned by these infidels. An innocent Muslim family burned in their own home by decadent western gangs. Just a couple of weeks ago. My home was destroyed, much of my livelihood taken away, all my loved ones gone. I have little left. But this isn't about me. There is God's work to be done my brother, no room for sentiment, only sacrifice. We are so glad you have made it safely. It is you who will have the privilege of striking a great blow to the heart of this faithless country and its evil ways. You are the chosen one,' he said stiffly.

Sitting in his still damp, western clothes, Ali didn't know what to say to Abu. This man had lost his family, yet all he could talk about was the sacrifice that had to be made. He'd heard this kind of talk in Mosul and it always filled his own heart with a kind of despair. Had all human relations come down to this - blood and sacrifice? For now he knew he must keep in with Abu, but he was glad it would be at a distance. Dutifully, he shared his commiseration by hugging Abu, which seemed appropriate, though Abu in response was cold, formal and seemed quite without sentiment.

It was then, like a ray of late afternoon sunshine, Kaylah reappeared, and Ali took this as an opportunity to turn away from Abu.

'Kaylah,' he called, 'did you make it? Did you catch the post?'

The smile she returned told him all he want to know.

38

Adam's bike had lain on the grass nearly three hours before it was discovered. Sue had arrived back from work clutching bags of marking which she knew she probably wouldn't look at until the weekend. As she struggled up to the front door her head was so full of the school term and her hands so encumbered by bags she simply didn't notice the bike there. It was only when she looked out of the front window later to see if Jim was coming, that her eyes suddenly spotted it.

Her first thought was that someone making deliveries had wheeled their bike in, but then that would be impractical, she told herself. Then she thought, maybe it was stolen and had been dumped, another bloody thing to sort out. Then she spotted the distinctive Dutch panniers, and her heart missed a beat. They had to be, Adam had insisted on the best, and she yelled out loud.

'It's Adam, he's back!'

Her heart immediately filled with sunshine, the trials of the day were forgotten and with new-found energy she raced to the front door expecting to see Adam. Unlatching and opening the door, she looked up and down the road, she couldn't see him, her eyes couldn't search him out. She ran inside and yelled upstairs, in case he'd come in earlier. No answer. Perhaps he'd dropped his bike and finding no-one in, he'd gone up the road to the shops or popped round to one of his friends. That's probably it, she thought.

She decided to retrieve the bike, wheel it into the hall, it would be safer there. Adam can put it away later, she thought. It was awkward and heavy and she was determined to avoid marking the wallpaper like Adam used to. The wall was still streaked with black marks from those same handlebars. It was inside. Adam, she repeated to herself, was back.

She went and found a tea towel to cushion the handlebars from the wall and then she stood back to look at it. Yes, Adam's familiar bike. She felt warmth and pride in the achievement of her son. She thought she'd send a text to Jim. It simply said, 'Adam's back.' Then she rang Adam's mobile.

Many times she'd tried in recent weeks. She could never really understand why he didn't answer, but she'd persuaded herself that trying to reach him abroad was problematic, but now he should pick up. She tried several quick successive calls. Each time it rang out with no reply, but she was on such a high, nothing worried her. Then she wondered what they would do to celebrate and threw a bottle of sparkling white Cava into the fridge, a bottle she'd kept by for weeks ready for this day. Leaving it to chill she had a look round for what to cook. Jim arrived moments later.

'He's back then,' he said cheerily as he eyed the bike in the hall.

'Don't know where he is exactly, haven't seen him yet. Probably out at friends, dumped his bike on the front lawn. I found it when I got back,' she told him.

They went through the usual homecoming ritual of sitting in the kitchen to enjoy a mug of Earl Grey Tea.

'Strange no sight or sound of Adam yet. You did check his room? He might have just crashed out,' said Jim.

'No, pretty certain he's not been inside. Wondered whether he'd lost his key,' said Sue.

'I'll ring his friend Seb. If anyone's seen him, Seb will have done.' Jim picked up his phone, Seb picked up.

'Hi Mr Taylor, how's Adam?'

'Don't know. His bike's here but we've not seen him and wondered whether you had,' asked Jim.

'No, not yet. Tell him to call me when you see him,' said Seb.

'Do us a favour Seb and ask around Adam's friends. Put something on Facebook. It's a bit strange for us not hearing from him at all,' asked Jim.

'Sure thing. I'll put something up, and Twitter too, right now. Bye,' and Seb was gone.

Sue and Jim didn't know what to do with themselves. An hour later Jim said he was popping out in the car for a drive round.

'Might look in the 'Baird' and the 'Royal Oak, won't be long,' he said. He found it easier than sitting waiting at home.

Half an hour later he was back and shaking his head from side to side as Sue opened the front door. Both were getting worried, but neither wanted to admit as much to the other. They decided to prepare supper, agreeing to make up a third portion they could keep by for Adam when he came in. Time passed ever more slowly and Sue's visits to the front window became ever more frequent. In the end she said, 'I'm worried Jim. Do you think we ought to report him missing?'

'No, we'd look silly when minutes later he comes waltzing in the front door. He'd tell us off for making such a fuss,' he said, not wanting to make a fool of themselves.

'OK, but at what point do we try and find out more, report him as missing or something,' she persisted.

'I think we should wait until the morning, and then if we've still not heard, we'll phone the police. Let's put the TV on and keep ourselves occupied,' said Jim.

They sat next to the TV and ate their long over-cooked supper from trays on their laps. Neither ate everything on their plate. Neither could concentrate on the romcom Sue had chosen.

'You can watch the football if you like,' she offered, being unable to sit any longer.

She got up, cleared the dishes and tidied up. Doing something was better than doing nothing. It was now dark outside. Jim called Seb again at 10pm. Still no news.

'Let's hit the deck,' he said, 'just got to wait until he turns up.'

A night of listening for the sound of the front door opening left then sore-eyed and weary by first light. They looked at each other and, after dressing and coffee, they finally agreed to call the police.

'We'd like to report our son Adam Taylor as a missing person,' said Sue, fighting hard to hold back the tears.

The elation of yesterday afternoon had turned very sour. As she fed the bureaucratic responses to the policewoman's questions, delivered in a cultivated sympathetic tone, her heart sank lower and lower. After, and with no more assurance from the police than, 'we'll make some enquiries with Border Control and get back to you,' Sue told Jim she was phoning in to East Finchley Academy to report herself sick.

'They'll manage without me. I couldn't concentrate on teaching today,' she moaned.

Jim left for work, dragging himself out of the front door.

'You'll call me soon; I'll keep my phone on today,' he yelled as he pulled the front door shut.

Sue thought she should check out Adam's bike for any clues. Besides, he'll be glad if I put his dirty washing on. Pannier bag by pannier bag, she went through them. Empty! That was unexpected. She didn't know what to make of it.

At morning break time when she knew Jim was free, she phoned him and told him what she'd discovered. By then her mind had dreamt up half a dozen conspiracy theories to explain the mystery of Adam's disappearance. She knew she was getting hysterical as she spoke on the phone, she couldn't stop herself. She heard Jim tell her what to do.

'Call the police again and tell them all his things are missing, and ask what they've found out,' he said.

She did so. This time a more serious-sounding officer promised to send someone straight round to the house. Waiting in their front room for the police to arrive, she was in tears. If only she knew where Adam was.

She heard the police car pull up outside. She could see there were two uniformed officers, a man and a woman and she panicked, thinking they only came in twos to bring bad news. She hardly heard them introduce themselves as Bob and April from Edmonton Police Station, as they strode into the hallway.

'You must be Sue Taylor. You called us yesterday evening to say you believe your son Adam to be a missing person. Perhaps you could tell us what has happened. Take it slowly madam, and start at the beginning,' said Bob.

He pulled out a notebook from his top pocket. He seemed kindly. His companion seemed new.

'Sorry, do come into the front room; would you like some tea?' asked Ruth.

'That will be nice in a minute Madam, but first tell us why you think Adam has gone missing,' said Bob.

When Sue had regained her composure, reminding herself she was a professional person and mustn't come across badly, some twenty minutes had passed. Still the questions went on.

'Has he ever disappeared before?' said Bob.

'Do you have a photograph of him?' asked April.

'Have his friends heard anything from him?' questioned Bob.

Then they asked if they could see his bike. Bob peered into the empty panniers asking what she thought should be in them and she told him about her search for washing and all the missing cycling things.

'I can see dust, maybe sand in the bottom of this one, we'll get forensics to take a look. Don't touch the bike again, Mrs Taylor. Someone will be around to collect it,' instructed Bob.

It was then a call came through on the officer's radio. He said, 'excuse me whilst I take this call,' and stepped outside the front door leaving her with April.

'You must be worried,' said April, 'so out of character. These things usually resolve themselves, don't you worry.' She tried to sound reassuring, but the look on Sue's face told a different story. Bob stepped back into the hall way.

'Mrs Taylor, that was UK Border Control. We asked them to check on Adam Taylor. The peculiar thing is that they have a record of him leaving the country in May, but as yet no record of him returning. They said they'd check again for us. The fact his own emails home trace his journey out the country as far as Turkey and you've had none since, suggest she didn't travel back. I agree the very presence of his bike

285

here implies he did in fact return, so there is some explaining to be done. You did the right thing to call us. Look, there is nothing more for us to do here right now. Just to rule it out, we will check with local hospitals, it's routine with missing person inquiries; and, Mrs Taylor, should you hear anything give us a call. Here's my card,' said Bob kindly, giving Sue his business card with his name and direct line contact details.

When they stepped outside and the car pulled away, she saw a neighbour's window blind opposite twitch, an unseen watcher looking in on other people's business.

Sue turned away. She felt she had been abandoned in a hostile wilderness, on her own, inconsolable and now the police were checking hospitals. She couldn't stop thinking of Adam, her only and precious son, as dead.

39

Tel Aviv was always hot at this time of the autumn, summer dragging its heals. Anna Simonsson darted into the cool of her air-conditioned Tel Aviv office, showed her passes and made her way into the building's secret heart. She pressed the buttons and entered her encrypted password sequence to start up her computer and then strode over to the water dispenser whilst it searched for the latest emails to dump them in her inbox.

On her return, there it was, like a red ruby jewel, highlighted on the flickering silver screen. She peered in, so excitedly she nearly made the classic mistake of spilling her drink on her keyboard.

She sat down to compose herself. Opening the file attached to the email which she'd called 'Adam Adamant', the name based on some adventurous heroic guy from a TV series in the last century, Anna was like an excited dog with a bone. Her instinct was throwing up more and more connections. It had all started, she reminded herself when a lone British cyclist heading east across Europe had changed his pattern of movement. His changed mobile trace had given him away.

Since then things had moved on. The mobile had travelled into Mosul and after barely any pause at all it had travelled at the speed of a vehicle by a most unusual route up into Turkey and eventually into Germany. Curiously, since Berlin, it had reverted to cycling speed and now, wonder of wonders, the latest report showed it back in London. But though the phone signal showed everything should be OK, Adam's bike had reappeared at his home, but her Adam had not reappeared in person; and, in Muswell Hill, a police missing person report had been filed following a call from his parents, UK Border Control reporting no indication that Adam had actually entered the country. Somehow he'd passed from

Calais to Essex, with apparently no-one knowing anything about it!

Someone always knows, she told herself. 'My story is still running,' she said out loud, as she began scanning the intelligence service reports for any unusual activity. There it was, a cryptic intelligence line from inside Mosul, hard-gained rare news from inside IS, but there it was, one report of a new western hostage from the communications surveillance of the Mosul IS CO's office. Apparently a new video headed 'Adam-Ali' had been sent on to IS HQ in Raqqa. That settled it. Without any further delay she decided to call her boss.

'I think we have an IS sleeper in London,' she said in an understated tone. He gave her his immediate attention.

'An English young man, Adam Taylor, is being held by IS and a lone wolf operative, a man called Ali, has been sent over there,' she said.

'Come on through,' her boss replied instantly, as she knew he would. They walked the few paces and closed the door on the soundproofed conferencing room.

'Right, what do we have?' her boss asked.

After she had finished speaking, he said, 'I need to think about permission from the top to share this information with the FBI and MI5 in London. First, let's get the team in and try and read what this might be all about. I want everyone in here, in fifteen minutes sharp.'

Six people in the tiny conference room was a crowd and the air con struggled, failing to compete with the combined body odour and heat of those present. After just a few minutes they were agreed that Anna had landed on a pre-prepared IS strategy, which had as its aim the abduction of a young male UK citizen with the purpose of getting one of their own extremist operatives into the UK to perform an as yet unknown act of terror.

It was the little irregularities that shot through the IS planning that gave it away. The erratic mobile trace movements Anna had spotted early on, the communication loss since Adam made his last email home in Turkey, the particular location within Mosul which put the phone and

Adam right in the centre of radical operations. Then there was the entry into the UK without passing through regular border control suggesting that the person and passport didn't hold up to the close kind of scrutiny now standard at all the main points of UK entry. Her boss, once he got going, built a momentum into the case that sounded persuasive to everyone present.

'We reckon he was probably taken by small boat from Calais to Essex, and Ali, whoever he is, once in England cycled from Essex to north London where he still is. We have various mobile movements logged around Walthamstow, and Edmonton in north London. Yesterday, Adam's bike turned up at his home without him, purely and simply as a clumsy attempt to throw us off the trail and lead us to think Adam had in fact come home and is simply choosing not to go back to his parents. His parents have unsurprisingly reported their son missing to the Metropolitan Police, which strengthens the profile we have of a fairly normal north London family where neither the parents nor indeed Adam do unpredictable things.

The fact is we have someone IS went to a lot of trouble with to have them located to London, which means we have some serious possibilities to consider. Listening analysis of IS messaging suggests they have deliberately minimised the number of their communications in order to keep this from us, but we have learned that a video file named 'Adam-Ali' has been sent by IS Mosul to IS HQ Raqqa suggesting Adam is or was held hostage in Mosul. The fact it hasn't yet been put up on social media, taken with everything else we know, suggests they have something big in mind. There are various possibilities.

'We need to know who is the most likely person to have been sent to England? Who is this Ali?' he said, looking round at everyone, as if seeking an answer. He was met by a silent row of blank faces.

'We also need to understand what has happened to Adam Taylor. My guess is, as a high value western hostage, he will be brought out later when the time is right. That time is clearly not yet right, because they think it will betray their own operative in London should they do so. They want to keep their London guy under the radar until he has undertaken whatever evil purposes he has been sent to perform. That could possibly give young Adam Taylor a little longer to live.'

'However, the reality is, his personal prospects I'm afraid look rather poor. The chances of getting a rescue team in there don't merit the risks involved, but we do need to put extra listening resources in. We need to get the occasional drone over to recce Mosul and we might get lucky doing some snooping around. But we need our friends, our allies, in on this too,' he said, waving to his international liaison officer.

There was the usual meeting summary of the briefing and a who does what allocation of duties and tasks as they wound up. As everyone left but for Anna and her boss, she knew there was still more to be said.

'Well done Anna, being meticulous about your job has paid off,' he said, 'I just hope we can spare London; but for young Adam, if he's still alive, I'm afraid there can be very little hope.'

Anna was pleased to be praised, more pleased still to have all the lights go on in her head as the entire Adam Taylor case developed in front of her, but another side of her felt she knew Adam as a person, like a school friend she once had and really liked. The thought upset her for some reason.

'I do hope you are wrong about Adam's future,' she said under her breath, but inside she feared that soon she'd be looking at another execution video from IS. They came out with alarming regularity. She shuddered at the thought.

40

Ali was getting used to things. He had all the privacy he wanted at Flo and Bert's. They accepted his offer of cleaning and vacuuming upstairs, for it meant they themselves never needed to go near his room. He thought they actually liked having him around. Yes, they got some money for looking after him, but nowhere near enough to call it worthwhile in any material sense. He'd come to know them as genuinely well-meaning good people. They knew he was a Muslim but weren't bothered, not even asking him what he thought about this or that. To them he was just another lad who needed somewhere to stay, had come from a place of horrors and needed caring for. It would have been far easier for him staying there if they were less nice.

For their part, he imagined, they were happy to support him. He was grateful they should continue to think the way they did, and even more grateful they spared him detailed questions. It would have felt more normal had he been in a house with other Muslims, but, he reasoned, had that been the case, the risk of discovery might be that much greater. All in all this was a good place to wait up. With Kaylah's help he was well hidden, under the radar so far as security services went. Here he could keep himself to himself and wait for that instruction to 'go' call he knew would come one day.

Life had entered an easier phase for him. No-one was curious about who he was or what he was here to do, but as the days went by and he was not doing anything much he once more began to feel listless and lacking in direction. Waiting reminded him of how frustrated and bored he'd felt in Mosul until the chance to do something had come along. Was it just the need for excitement that had brought him this far? Did he still really believe in the cause? Was he a victim of a conflict not of his making? Or simply doing what his CO told him like he always did? These dark thoughts increasingly nagged at him and he tried to push them to the back of his mind.

He could see no threats of discovery. Even the two police, Bob and April who called in at the Drop In just seemed to wander round and then leave as happily as when they arrived. He did not even attract a second glance. He was just another service user, another nobody as far they were concerned. He hoped he'd hear something from Mosul soon.

Kaylah had been as good as her word and got him registered with the Home Office and he was now in a long processing queue and in the meantime was provided with small amounts of cash and vouchers to get by on. Not that he really needed them as the money his CO had given him when he left Mosul was going a long way. Instinctively he moved his hand to his inside zipped pocket to check its comforting presence.

He often thought about the Mosul he'd left behind. It was such a different place. It was hard not checking to see how Mo was getting on running the house in his absence. Mo wasn't like him, he wasn't so focussed or ambitious and sooner or later he feared Mo was prone to take short cuts and make mistakes. It worried him he'd left him in charge of the home, but then he'd had no choice, had he? None of them had. They all simply had to do what they're told, he reasoned. He knew the safety of his family now rested on his shoulders. Their fate depended on his success. If only they were all here, life could be so very different, better even, he thought, but this was an impossible dream.

His mind came back to the present. He had no way of knowing whether Adam's bike had been found or that the ploy had had the desired effect. He wondered whether it was naive of his CO to really think they could fool anyone into believing Adam had come home. Anyway, any local search for him here would surely be called off very soon. What do the English say? They'll think it's like looking for a needle in a haystack, which made him laugh.

There was no way of knowing what the security services were up to, so Ali dismissed any further thinking about his adversaries as futile. He reassured himself with the knowledge that London was a vast city and thousands of young people went missing every day. What could anyone conclude - only that he may be in London. He was confident no-one would look for Adam where he was safely hiding at Flo and Bert's.

Sometimes in the night he would think of Adam, the lad whose identity and freedom he'd taken. It concerned him that a guy in many ways like himself, just a little younger, was locked up in the sheep pen. What was Adam now but another sheep for the ritual IS slaughter? He wondered how he'd be holding up, whether Mo and Fatima were feeding him, a prisoner with no future, now confined for a month. Like many other troubling thoughts, he tried to push Adam to the back of his mind, but he could never fully do so. He felt the certainty of his mission sat uncomfortably with all the less certain bits of his life. He believed himself to be a misfit, a creature of contradictions, always belonging in the shadows, destined to do so. The thought was depressing.

Autumn sunshine, if this cool English light could have any real claim to be the sun he knew, filtered in through his bedroom window announcing another day. He could hear Flo and Bert downstairs talking to one another at a volume so loud that even upstairs he could hear every word. They spoke to each other endearingly even if loudly, Flo asking if Bert was ready yet for his second cup of tea of the day.

Ali got up, washed, tidied his short beard, dressed in a new set of trousers and a T shirt and jacket Kaylah had sourced for him at the Drop In. They smelled clean. He was fresh and smart and that felt good.

He went through his small collection of possessions, laying them out on his bed cover. Taking down the Risk box where Adam's things were hidden he couldn't resist opening Adam's passport to see his picture, and realised that, at a casual glance, the two really could be one and the same person.

He picked up Adam's mobile which he kept on silent, the mobile charged up so he could keep regular checks on what incoming messages and calls were coming in. Nothing to worry about, just more calls from Mum to Adam, now some guy Seb and a girl Millie had also tried to reach him, both messages he chose not to read. They must think he's nearly home, if only they knew. Whilst such messages continued to come in, he thought he himself remained safe and hidden.

One day his CO would send him instructions but that would be to his own SIM only, untraceable pay as you go phone, his new phone which now sat next to Adam's silent Apple I-Phone 7. Taking Adam's phone, he reached up high and pushed it out of sight on top of the wardrobe. Safer there than him carrying it around, he reasoned.

He put all Adam's other things and his own few papers together in an A4 white envelope Flo had given him, folded it and squeezed it into his inside pocket.

Still on the bed were two pens, his Yale front door key on a Margate fob, his phone chargers with neatly wound cables, a small pile of clothes, his A-Z of London, his small thin paper Qur'an which he flicked through occasionally. Looking at it he realised he found it hard to be self-disciplined in religious things, it was so much easier when everyone practised the faith, then he was just carried along by it. He then swiftly scooped everything up in one sweep and placed them in the top drawer of the chest of drawers. This drawer of things and his sports bag - all he had in the world is here, he mused.

Then finally grabbing his own phone off the bed he skipped downstairs with a cheerful 'good morning' to Flo and Bert, still at their breakfast. Looking at them, he saw in their old age a mutual contentment and it nagged at him again that what he was going to do in a couple of weeks time would, when all the connections were inevitably made, trace him back to their address and turn over their quiet good lives. It troubled him more than he cared to acknowledge.

Feeling guilty, he quickly excused himself and walked to the nearby corner shops, picked up a chocolate bar and a Coke at the always friendly, Hindu-run, corner shop. Then he began walking down toward the Drop In.

Before he'd left Mosul, his CO had said that Abu was his point of contact, describing him as a loyal man who collected and regularly sent through large financial contributions from London to the Caliphate. He'd now met Abu discreetly several times and he still felt he didn't know him. Kaylah had explained the tragic fire which police were still investigating as an arson attack, but no-one had been apprehended and the word on the street was it was a drugs gang dispute that had gone wrong.

Ali couldn't work Abu out. Maybe he held collections at the mosque, but then he'd be watched by the authorities. Things were very tight in the UK as attempts to deal with any blatant support for so-called terrorism were stamped on hard. Maybe Abu had a network of people who secretly gave him money; well, it would have to be very secretly done.

Abu never mentioned his activities to Ali. Ali thought this was possibly a means of protecting him from knowing too much. He'd noticed how Abu often seemed to have two or three Muslim acquaintances with him at the Drop In and would generally lead them in the midday prayers whenever he was around at that time. Two of the regular guys, he'd go so far as to call Abu's friends, but thinking about it, friends would be too strong a word. Ali wasn't at all sure about them either. All this meant that Ali had made his own mind up, that he'd keep his links with Abu to nodding acquaintance, a little distance between them would serve to protect them both. It's what his CO would have expected anyway. It wouldn't be difficult, given that instinctively he didn't like the guy one bit.

Who saw the other first he wasn't sure, but there was Kaylah, shoulder bag, trousers, nice on the eye, and with a cheerful, 'Good morning Ali,' to lift his day. They walked side by side together the remaining few minutes to the Centre. No woman walked like this on her own in Mosul, no woman walked with a man either, and where were the smiles there? Ali imagined in those few strides they were together, and the thought cheered him, lifting his spirits.

'Do you want to give me a hand this morning?' she said. 'The food store needs to be totally emptied, cleaned and re-ordered. It'll be hard work and will take most of the day.'

'Sure, I haven't anything planned,' said Ali, glad for the opportunity.

The physical work would be good for him, get a bit of tone and condition back into his body. Kaylah locked her bag in a cupboard and came over to work with him in the small hall in the centre of the building complex which had been given over to hold the food. Donations had come in thick and fast and many were simply piled high on the floor. The place was a disorganised mess. Kaylah took charge and they began by taking all the items from the metal shelf racking and placing them in the central space.

'Why do you do it?' Ali asked, a little while later.

'You mean, help here?' she said, puzzlement in her voice.

'Yes.'

'I feel useful, I can make a difference. It fits with my college course and I get to meet people like you!' she teased.

'You don't really know me,' he said smiling.

'Well, I know you a bit. You arrived hidden in a vehicle. You escaped from Mosul where life is unbearable. You live with Flo and Bert at the end of the road and you come in here to help sort out and plan your future. How's that for starters?' she said, stopping to look him directly in the face.

'It's a start! But what about you? Do you have brothers or sisters?' he asked her.

'I live at home with my Mum and Dad. I've a younger brother Clive who doesn't really know what to do with himself and I worry about him lots. He came down here once to help, but gave up after his first visit. I suppose worrying about younger brothers, that's what older sisters do,' she said.

'Why do you worry about him?' asked Ali.

'I am not sure about the friends he has and I worry he'll get into trouble. If you are a black guy in London, it's still hard to make your way even when everyone says we're an equal society; the reality is we're not! I worry Clive's drifting downwards. My parents have given up on him. Dad just falls back on throwing his weight around and sounding off, but Clive just withdraws from him. As I said, Clive came down here a few weeks ago when I asked him. I tried to get him involved again, but he hurt his hand and he won't come back,' she told him, Ali listening attentively to her story.

After an hour of heavy work Olive put her head round the door and asked if they'd like coffee and cake. They took a break and wandered into the main hall. Kaylah excused herself saying she needed to get some booking figures so that she could appraise the Drop In's finances later. Ali spotted Abu alone. Clutching his coffee Ali felt obligated to strike up a conversation and wandered over to him.

'Salaam brother, how are you?' he asked.

'Could be better. Things are not going well for the Caliphate, pressure from all directions. We need to turn the tide, strike back. I've no news for you, just advice. Stay low, keep below the radar. Don't mix with me. I know how to reach you if I need to,' and with that he shuffled off. What a soul-less codfish of a man, thought Ali.

Ali rejoined Kaylah and they worked well together making a significant difference to the food store by the end of the morning. Ruth looked in to inspect their efforts as they were leaving.

'I'll have to get you two working together again if this is what you can get done in a morning,' she beamed.

'That's fine by me,' said Ali realising just how much he'd actually enjoyed himself, not least because he found he really liked Kaylah's company.

Kaylah told Ruth how helpful Ali had been and a little about Ali's story and how he had got to be there. Ali shuffled uncomfortably at this disclosure. It was hard never being able to be fully at ease.

It was time to be on his way. Kaylah said she was off to college for the afternoon.

Over the next couple of weeks Ali called into the Drop In most days. He wanted to keep a low profile and it was somewhere safe. Feeling less vulnerable there, off the street, he liked the social company and helping out.

Whenever Kaylah was there on placement he made a particular point of helping her with what she was doing. It was a friendship he was determined to cultivate. Gradually, he began to feel he had some call on her beyond her expected role and decided he would work still harder to take their growing friendship further. For him this was a deliberate plan to widen his network. Being totally on one's own cut the options if problems came along. Kaylah was in his strategic sights, useful and pleasurable in one package.

One late morning, when Kaylah was finishing, she said she was off to Southgate, to college. Ali seized his chance.

'Where's that?' he enquired.

'Southgate, never been there?' she said.

It was an opportunity for Ali to get even closer to her. He sensed she could be helpful to him, she seemed so naive, so very malleable, and unless he were mistaken, entirely possible to shape to his will.

'No, do you mind if I string along? I've nothing else to do,' he said.

Moments later they were heading out of the door together making for the Hopper bus stop to wait for the next bus for Southgate. Ruth watched them going. She'd been observing them over the weeks and thought she might need to take some time with Kaylah when she was next in, to explain setting appropriate placement boundaries.

Her professional eye could see dangers of which Kaylah seemed blissfully unaware.

41

Adam pushed. Nothing gave. He put his shoulder to the door, and with a metallic scrape whose white noise rose to terrify him, the door swung slowly open. He pulled it in again almost closed, holding his breath, his heart pounding, whilst he planned his next move. Freedom called more loudly than the rattling wind.

The howling black night wrapped round him comfortingly like a protective shroud and he hoped it would last. The dusty darkness meant he could barely make out the shape of the house on the opposite side of the yard which signified in turn that it would be hard for them to see him. There was a glint from the Toyota to his right. Dust blew everywhere, fine and penetrating everything, even inside his clothes and made him hold his towel close across his face just to breathe. This might be his only chance. Choices were limited and he knew this was one opportunity he had to grasp. Clutching a rescued plastic bag with what food he'd been able to hide, he moved out, immediately feeling exposed.

Once outside the door, he pressed his back against it. He'd prised free his plastic wedge in the lock's retaining slot, sliding the door shut so the lock sprung closed. No way did he want to leave the door to blow open and betray him. There was now no way back.

He moved quickly, creeping like some furtive animal against the low corners of the wall, moving so very slowly round to his right, willing himself to appear invisible. By feeling the rough wall with his hands he slid around to the gate, eyes searching, ears listening, like some hunted animal on high alert. There was a startling crash as if a shutter had blown open somewhere. It made him stop and snatch a breath. Every sound became terrors.

Opening the courtyard gate meant releasing a retaining bolt on a metal chain and sliding a noisy metal bar along a runner from left to right, before swinging the the gate inwards.

This was slow and tricky, and as he did so the wind almost took the gate from his grasp. It took all his strength to hold it and stop it from crashing into the side wall. He used the wooden prop to hold the rusty metal gate open whilst he turned his attention back to the Toyota. The shrieking wind was doing its job, there was still no sound from the house, nobody was about.

As he opened the Toyota's door the interior light came on, exposing him in its deadly pale glow and then to his immense relief he saw the keys just as he'd imagined, sitting there invitingly in the ignition. The still-lit interior light was panicking him. After much fumbling, he hit the light switch correctly plunging the interior once again into darkness. Now he couldn't see a thing. Panic built inside. With the light off he couldn't see the vehicle controls. He tried to look small, crunched up and low in the seat and hurriedly felt around with his hands. Pedals under his feet, a gear shift in his hand, he was ready.

He took a deep breath, flicked the interior light on again and quickly took in where everything was. Light off again, hand on ignition, he couldn't afford to tarry longer. He had rehearsed this in his mind many times, but the reality of driving a vehicle and not a bike was something else. The driving lessons he'd had in London had not been in a vehicle like this.

The moment of truth came. When a particularly strong gust of wind blew in, he turned the ignition key and the engine fired up. With only the gentlest press of the accelerator to keep the noise down, but not so gentle as to stall, he crept toward and then out of the gate, his sweating palms struggling to grip the steering wheel.

Once outside, his immediate aim was to make a break for the desert to the north and, if he could make it, follow the course of the Tigris. Then he would head back toward the Turkish border and hopefully get picked up by Kurdish troops without getting blown up or shot en route. It was a wild aspiration, a desperate throw of the dice. It was all he had.

Pushing his foot down to build more speed and gain immediate distance from the house, he almost hit another vehicle. It had side lights on, and Adam instantly realised he had no lights on at all. Side lights now on, he re-wrapped his dirty towel around his head. It served as a useful disguise. He moved the Toyota forward slowly, and as inconspicuously and smoothly as his limited driving skills would allow. There were no sounds, no vehicles following, no shots behind him, just the buffeting sand-filled wind clouding everything.

Twenty minutes later, under the cover of the storm, he was driving on a desert trail. In one sense the storm hid him from sight, but it also made it almost impossible for him to judge where he was driving. Normally he reckoned he had a fairly good natural sense of direction. He knew as he pulled out the gate which direction was north, and he tried to hold a path in that direction. He feared a chase, a road block, an insurmountable obstacle, but to begin with none came.

After an hour or so, the wind was dying and the visibility was starting to improve. He was more visible, but he could see around him in the inky blackness; whether the dying storm was a blessing or a curse, he couldn't yet tell. Soon he could see stars and he paused to take stock of his direction, mangling to glimpse the Pole Star.

He had time to look around in the vehicle. Fuel tank needle almost half full. In the glove compartment he touched the metal form of Mo's hand gun. He then spotted a half full water bottle lying horizontally in the passenger door. 'Half full,' he said to himself, 'my life is now more half full than half empty.' He took a swig to dampen his dry, sour-tasting mouth, before moving off again.

Pushing his foot hard to the floor, he began to rap along to Justin Bieber's 'Rucka Rucka Ali,' - 'I been in bad Korea, And fought in Vietnam, And I would be in Afghanistan, but I left my legs back in Taiwan. I see what's goin' on, and I think it's fuckin' wrong...'

It didn't matter he couldn't get all the lyrics; just repeating any words that came, like some mind-filling mantra, some driving rapping rhythm, helped keep him going, and with every minute he felt more free.

For now, this precious time, he was the one in control, yes, his situation desperate, a shot or explosion ending things quite probable at any moment.

Must keep going, pushing on, he told himself, his wild eyes constantly flicking between rear view mirror and trail ahead. He wondered how soon it would be before they discovered he'd gone. When that happened the chase would be on to find and get him.

On that thought he stopped looking in the rear mirror. He put all his concentration into the road ahead. Adrenaline rush, mind racing, he drove as if each moment were his last. In his desperation, he almost felt reckless. Dying out here had to be better than seeing his life slowly draining away back in the cell he had left.

42

MacDonald's are the same everywhere. For Ali it represented every bit a sign of rampant western imperialism, an American plan to culturally and economically take over the world, sliding in western decadence and loose morals over the counter with the burgers and fries. So it was both exciting and unnerving to be in MacDonald's, Southgate, with Kaylah at his side. She insisted on paying which also felt strange.

He had a Coke. He couldn't bring himself to have anything more. They found a table. She had a quarter-pounder meal which in spite of his initial reluctance, he later helped her eat. The fries were great. All around were other young people, all nationalities and as far as Ali could tell, all religions too. People were laughing and chatting without a care in the world and sitting together, the two of them were soon doing the same.

Was it something they put in the food, he wondered, that set the happy mood? In his mind this experience of MacDonald's briefly recalled his own Engineering days in University, a past era, when students also laughed and joked and played. It was a warm and pleasant memory, but so very long ago he couldn't quite believe that was really how it once was in his country.

Ali asked Kaylah about her course at college, what she was studying and how it was going. He told her about how he'd studied engineering at Mosul until the troubles had come, then he'd had to give it all up. He wouldn't be drawn into saying anything more about his life and she didn't push him.

For his part Ali deliberately set to work to show an interest in her world, to give her his full attention. They talked about each other's families and discovered that families were much the same the world over, squabbling over which TV programme to watch, who had control of the remote, women ending up with the domestic chores, which was one matter they argued over, but Ali took care not to let their argument reach the point where they would fall out over the issue.

Kaylah had heard about the fighting in Iraq and told Ali that she had been shocked by what she had seen on TV, the beheadings and ethnic cleansing.

'Is it really like that? Can people do such things to each other?' she asked him.

He marvelled at her innocence and couldn't bring himself to tell her the truth. He wanted her on his side, he wanted her sympathy, for her to be his friend, he didn't need her understanding.

'It's bad out there, my home city is poor and life can be brutal, but it can be good too,' but to his surprise he couldn't immediately think of one good thing to tell her.

Then he reflected on the morning light across the desert, the colourful life he'd once known when the bazaars had had plentiful produce, the calm grace of the Tigris and Euphrates rivers bringing life along its banks, the rich history of Iraq he'd heard about when he was a child. He told her about these things and Kaylah's eyes went into a distant stupor. She was enchanted by his oriental, exotic, far away world.

It changed when he mentioned his fantastic Toyota he'd had to leave behind. That brought her back to the present. 'Guys are all the same when it comes to cars,' she said provocatively.

'What about girls?' asked Kaylah, with a twinkle in her eye.

Ali was thrown, he was speechless.

'You're embarrassed,' she laughed.

He forced himself to laugh at first, but then it came naturally. He couldn't remember when he'd last laughed and their laughter joined the laughter all around and the afternoon drifted on in a haze of fries and donut fat and Kaylah never got to her lecture, and time stood still.

'Are you a Muslim?' she suddenly asked, 'I guess you are. I've never really known what that means, only Muslims get such a bad press here. Some of my friends say they should be all sent home.'

He nodded. He didn't know what say.

'You know we had a debate here at College at the end of the summer, about a month, maybe six weeks ago. It got very heated. Security had to be called. And you know what, Abu from the Drop In was there, a right stirrer he was and he was speaking up for this extremist guy from Egypt and it almost ended up a fight, well it did I think. Me, I just wanted to leg it, but my friend Melissa got hurt, her belly knifed and she was knocked to the floor. They were supposed to be talking about religious freedom, but the violent ones there put an end to that. You're a Muslim, what do you think about that?' she asked him.

Ali couldn't handle it. He had been silenced. Talk of Abu made him suddenly feel out of his comfort zone. His world had been brought to the table and she seemed to be on to it. He made some excuse about it all being too heavy for him. Having fled to England, he'd put all that behind him. Abruptly he rose, saying he needed to get back. They walked in silence to the bus stop round the corner, the conversation closed, but not forgotten by Ali.

Back in Silver Street, Kaylah gave him a hug on the corner of her road. He didn't know whether he should have held her, kissed her even, but he didn't do that, you didn't. Confusion welled up inside like a volcano. Not for the first time, he didn't know who he was or how to behave. Forces had been unleashed in him he hadn't anticipated.

As he walked on alone, he knew he liked the warm sexual awakening of it all, and the way he'd got Kaylah to be his friend and the possibilities that now promised, but as he strode off back to Flo and Bert's his mind was in a whirl. He was liking this naive girl, he needed her but increasingly he realised he didn't want to hurt her.

He couldn't allow himself to get entangled like this, but he couldn't see how he could now disentangle himself. She could be useful and he didn't like being so on his own. He felt like a drowning man. Being with Kaylah was useful, confusing, exciting and dangerous all at once.

Kaylah opened her front door. She'd loved her day, thinking it was the best time she'd had in ages. Pushing the door shut behind her she spotted a brown envelope on the mat, hand delivered and with her name written on it.

She picked it up and opened it. It was a brief note from Ruth Churchill saying Ruth would be calling to see her tomorrow morning to discuss an aspect of her placement with her. She threw it on the side and called Clive. She wanted to tell him about her brilliant day.

43

Lena Bloom was assigned to the Culture Department of the Israeli Embassy, London. The posting was a lucky break, it was a great city to find oneself in, especially as the Embassy was located in attractive South Kensington.

People often wondered what Lena actually did, and those who had worked there longest knew that when it wasn't obvious what someone was doing then you certainly didn't ask, because they were really engaged in much more serious undercover work. This was precisely the case with Lena, whose role in the promotion of Israeli Culture and Tourism proved such an easy facade to hide behind, Lena didn't really have to try.

It was now October and London was looking particularly autumnal and beautiful, the large leaves of the huge plane trees falling, plate size, to carpet the pavements and parks. It made Lena's short walk into Palace Gardens and work an absolute pleasure. Usual security checks complete, she found her way to her very private work station which was tucked away in what once was a servant's bedroom when the Embassy was a private residence.

She loved the thought that long before Israel located its diplomatic mission here, the great Victorian literary giant, William Thackeray had made this his home, designing it using red London brick. A prolific writer, second only to Charles Dickens, it amused her to think, had he been alive today, he'd have found a rich contemporary source of material for his historical fiction! The building still hadn't lost the sense of once being a home and Lena felt contentment within its walls.

As she breakfasted on an apple, her computer showed it was lunch time in Israel. Her day began as usual with the mundane administration anyone working on a computer had to face, so she was pleased when almost immediately her mobile rang. She saw it was Dan Abrahams, Head of Political Section. He asked her to come straight to his room.

Dan always wore a suit, but never a tie and today was no different. She detected the scent of his aftershave, sweet, even fragrant for a man, she thought.

'Morning Lena. This is a code red conversation,' he said, sounding unusually business-like, pushing his door closed.

She knew then something was up.

'We have a problem,' he said, his face deadly serious, hands resting on the desk between them.

'A message came through in the daily security bulletin to inform us that a high level, lone wolf IS operative has actually made it to London. Sometimes we get to take them out on the way, but not this one. We don't yet know who he is or where he is exactly. We don't yet know his precise mission. But it has got to be big, very big; they've gone to some trouble with this one. They took risks to get this particular operative to London. He's undoubtedly been prepared well, and IS tried to disguise him, to make us all think it was a young Englishman, name of Adam Taylor, who'd slipped back into the country,' he explained.

'Sounds interesting, but how sure are we about this?' ventured Lena.

'Absolutely! 100% sure. Our people in Tel Aviv are certain on this. As we speak our guys are going through Turkish and German border videos to try and spot who this lone wolf is and we're also looking at satellite and drone imagery to try and discover more. Our closest allies are currently being told and they may find out something from their own sources. We might get lucky, but all this takes time and we might not have enough of it,' he said.

He paused. A serious silence hung for a moment like a still frame between them. Then he was animated again.

'What we do know is that this guy travelled under the name of a nineteen year old north London young man, called Adam Taylor, whom we believe was captured in Turkey and is now being held secretly by IS in Mosul, Iraq. I'm afraid that young man's life is in grave danger, that is if he is still alive.'

308

'That's unfortunate, but this isn't really about him, it's about what might happen here, yes?' asked Lena.

'Spot on. In the jargon, Adam might be collateral, but we can't say it,' said Dan.

'Do we know anything about the sleeper or his plans?' asked Lena.

'I was coming to that. He passed through Turkish customs using Adam's passport and he's kept hold of Adam's mobile. But after entering Germany this guy never went through British Border Control to get here. That's a give-away, that is! Then a rather clumsy attempt was made using the bike Adam had cycled on to Turkey, laying it in his parents' front garden, trying to suggest Adam had come back to London and gone off somewhere. They thought it might have bought them more time; it gained them half a day, that's all,' he paused thoughtfully.

'Knowing what we do about Adam, and the psychological profile we have on him, intelligence suggests there's no way he ever came back. Our friends in forensics in the Met have just told us that grains of desert sand from Iraq have been found on the bike and the bike has been deliberately cleansed so that all finger prints have been wiped. There are some items being further checked for DNA but that's going to take weeks to get results on. Even the forensics we have for now definitely confirm our worst suspicions.'

He leant back, hands on hips.

'In sum, what we have is an attempt to secretly plant a top level IS operative here in London. We know IS are desperate for a high impact act as on so many fronts their military campaign is failing. They are increasingly relying on carrying out major terrorist incidents in key city locations. Who would have thought they would have held together for nearly two decades? We also think he will have people ready to assist him, sympathisers in London and we have a short list of possibles. One man in north London in particular, name of Abu Tariq, has been doing some substantial fund-raising for IS. This is where you come in.'

309

'What can I do?' asked Lena, her day having suddenly got much more interesting.

'I want you to attend a meeting of Prevent Police Officers and a few others to be held at the Metropolitan Police's Edmonton HQ in north London this afternoon. The Prevent personnel are those assigned to address extremism. The meeting's at 1400 hours. They are expecting you. Earlier, I phoned through and arranged for your attendance there. On this occasion, you are not from the Cultural Department, you are an Assistant Political Officer. They'll accept that. Pick up some new business cards from the print room before you leave.' Dan looked as if he had finished, but hadn't quite.

'Incidentally, I don't want you briefing them on everything you've just heard from me. I just want you to find out what they are hearing on the street about IS sympathies. A few names would be good and I don't want you coming back empty-handed. If you have to take one of them out for a drink after then do it. OK.' he said.

It was an instruction not a question, and she nodded. She kept a wardrobe in her office and was already thinking what might be appropriate to wear.

'Call me as soon as you have anything,' he said, before adding, 'but call me anyway.'

'Dan. What do you think this guy has in mind that's so big a target?' she asked.

'That's for me to guess and for you to find out', and with that, keeping his remaining cards close to his chest, he signalled the briefing was over.

Dan then called his contact in the Met Police's SO15 Counter Terrorism Command to get any updates, and was told that the mobile signal location provided a specific area of one street in north London and the local area was now being put under immediate surveillance. Much to Dan's frustration, his contact wouldn't say which street. So much, he thought, for allied cooperation.

Lena hurried on her way, changed into a silk blouse and black pencil skirt. Clutching her bag under her arm, she flew out through the embassy gates and dashed down to the tube station.

Within the hour she was at Edmonton Police Station, sitting in an interior room with all the window blinds drawn. The building already felt like an enclosed box with not even a passing nod to architectural style. To Lena's mind this meeting room felt as lifeless as a tomb, devoid of all character. There were just five people present, a couple of dedicated Police Prevent Community Engagement Officers, a guy from the Met, and two others who were introduced as, Bob Steer, a long-serving beat PC who knew the scene on the ground better than anyone and April Cooper, a new Police Community Support Officer, who had been accompanying Bob in Edmonton.

The meeting had its own agenda and it took forty minutes before talk turned to the real issue, so far as Lena was concerned. The guy from the Met gave a simplified version of Dan's earlier talk to her, which grabbed everyone's attention.

At this, ironed white shirts positively bristled and crackled with electric excitement. The atmosphere changed. Voices were reduced to a hushed conspiratorial tone. Everyone was reminded of house rules to keep everything discussed within the four walls. The local Prevent Community Engagement Officers didn't seem to Lena to have anything to add. One had only been transferred in from another Borough, Islington, a week ago and the other didn't seem to know as much as Bob. It was Bob who'd noticed things and was invited to report.

'April and I have been keeping a low-key eye on the asylum seeker Drop In at Holy Trinity Hall in Windmill Road. It does a good job making new people welcome. Bit of a meeting point for all migrants, no other place like it that I've found. It's a good place to have your ear to the ground, to see what's happening. There've been a few guys from the Middle East come in over the months. Abu Tariq, you'll have heard of him, he's been here a while. His house was fire-bombed a month or so ago, wife and family died in the inferno, people tend to

311

focus round him. The arson attack is still a live investigation. Don't know exactly Abu's Muslim views, but from what I've picked up, he's pretty conservative and can't stop himself having a go at the decadent west. Oh, and he won't talk to April unless he has to, so he's a bit anti-women too, bit like one or two officers here,' joked Bob.

Only an old sweat like Bob could get away with that, thought Lena.

'He's just been re-housed since the fire, now living on the Red Brick Estate, 52 Silver Street, one of those owned by Wood Green Housing Association. It's a ground floor flat, I've seen him outside it once or twice. He never wants to talk to me and he's got some strange friends - local drug-runners for a start. There's a small following of Muslim guys he has, sometimes as many as seven or eight. He acts as a bit of a religious leader, always reminding them of their prayers. They are never any bother, but within these walls, April and I don't like Abu much and to be frank, we wonder what he's really up to. If he's not into drugs, he's right on the edge of it.'

'Why does he go to the Drop In?' Lena asked.

'Like many of the others who go there, they get free food and advice; and the Wi-Fi facilities there are particularly good. Oh yes, and spare laptops are made available so that people can try and reach friends and family overseas. That's about it really,' said Bob.

'Any changes you've noticed, anyone else in particular who has recently started attending,?' asked Lena. April turned to face her and replied.

'Several guys from the Middle East arrived over the summer, then, after a lull, one new person turned up toward the end of September. Looks like he might be from the same part of the world. Seems OK, a young man, bit of a beard growing, name of Ali, I recall. He was helping reorganise the food cupboard last time I called. Haven't spoken to him yet personally. Not sure he and Abu have much in common. Word is Ali escaped from the conflict with IS, an asylum-seeker, like many others,' said April.

Lena wrote down three things on her mobile notes page, 'Abu Tariq and drugs - Ali new arrival from Caliphate - Drop In, Windmill Road.'

She decided there was nothing further to be learned here. To her mind the meeting was over. She excused herself, went outside and made a call straight to Political Secretary, Dan Abrahams. Job done and out on Fore Street, she then hailed a taxi.

'South Kensington High Street, please.' The taxi driver smiled at his lucky break, a decent fare, the first of the day.

As Lena made herself comfortable on the back seat of the black cab for the hour it would take, he wasn't the only one to think they'd done well. With what they now knew, this guy Ali's mission was as good as over, she thought, before continuing to check the tedious list of unopened inbox emails she'd never got round to at the start of the day.

44

Ruth set off on foot to call on Kaylah. It was only a five minute walk, that was had she not seen Flo walking down to do the flowers in the church and felt she had to stop and chat. Flo told her about the nice, handsome and helpful young man she had staying with her, and Ruth told her in return what a good thing she was doing in putting him up. She had to excuse herself, extricate herself from the conversation, as she couldn't afford to be late with so many scheduled appointments to keep. Flo would have easily chatted on for an hour!

Ruth was mindful she wanted to stress to Kaylah the seriousness of the placement arrangement and being punctual about appointments was her keeping her own side of the bargain. As she rang the Kone door bell she glanced at her watch. Only four minutes late was within the bounds of acceptability, though she couldn't allow herself to relax knowing what needed to be said. It was Kaylah who opened the door, mug in hand.

They moved into the front room. Ruth began by asking Kaylah how she felt her business placement at the Drop In was going.

'You certainly have put in some good work in just a few weeks, but there is a difference between helping with a project and being on a placement. It's the focus required, do you see that?' said Ruth.

'Why yes, but when something is worthwhile and you're enjoying it, I agree it's easy to let your heart rule your mind. But I know what I have to do, it's still early days,' answered Kaylah.

'Kaylah, I hope you won't mind me saying this, but I need to say it. Please don't get me wrong. Yesterday, after you had done all that brilliant reorganising of the food store with Ali in the morning, I saw you leave with Ali, going off with him and it concerned me that maybe I hadn't talked with you about boundaries. There must be a professionalism as well as an awareness of risks. I know it isn't possible to create two entirely watertight compartments between the project and your personal life, but I'd be failing you as your supervisor if I didn't talk about the need to keep the two worlds as separate as you can,' she said.

'I understand what you are saying, but there was no harm done. In fact I think Ali gained from the experience. I took him up to Southgate where he'd never been before. He hasn't been in the country long. I think he doesn't have many friends. He's fled IS; and his family were all left behind.'

'There I think you have it. He's needy and vulnerable and may become rather more dependent on you than you anticipate. You might also find yourself caught up in a relationship of friendship which is something that changes everything,' Ruth said, worried she might overstate how things really stood between the two.

'How is that a problem? I can be friends with whom I like,' said Kaylah rather defensively.

'Of course, and I believe in friendship, believe me. But it can become very complicated in the context of a placement,' Ruth added.

Without realising it, Ruth's anxiety had raised the level of her voice and this had prompted Sam Kone to put his head round the door from the back room.

'Everything alright in here? I thought it was you Ruth. Thank you for giving Kaylah a placement. She's doing well at college and I feel sure you will want to give her a good report,' he said politely, though much to Kaylah's embarrassment.

Ruth didn't rise to this, but seeing Sam Kone gave her another chance to try and get him to put some resources into the Drop In.

'I am thrilled Kaylah has joined the Drop In team for this term. We will certainly do our best to make it a good experience for her. Kaylah may have already told you this, but the needs of those who call make very great demands on just a few people's pockets and it would thrill my heart to see your own congregation more closely and more generously involved,' suggested Ruth.

'The scripture tells us that we must first seek the Kingdom of God. What if a man gains the whole world and loses his soul? That is the bigger issue. If you were to open the door to my preaching to the many idolaters, Mohammedans and unbelievers who use your Drop In, I'd be very pleased to come along. How about it? It's about Christian priorities, mission before service,' he replied, putting Ruth on the back foot.

Ruth didn't want to have an argument. She could see Sam Kone's line of argument taking shape much as it had at her own PCC church meeting some weeks ago.

'Well, if I can get you along as a guest preacher that will be a start. I'll mention it to the Committee and see what they say. In the meantime, if you could only up the number of food donations from your congregation that would really help us, given all the new asylum-seekers finding their way to north London.'

This seemed like as good a point as any for Ruth to make her exit. She was nearest person to the door and moved quickly into the street.

With a 'God bless and thank you,' she was out of Sam's reach and on her way to take Home Communion to an elderly parishioner just out of hospital. Life for her was one of being stretched in many different directions like a piece of elastic webbing. Her fear was that at one or more points something might break.

Back in the house, Sam was yelling, 'Clive, get yourself up Son. The world's waiting for you.' Then to Kaylah, 'I really worry about that boy. All the people I know who get up as late as he does are no good loafers and into trouble.'

'I'm sure Clive's not one of those, Dad,' Kaylah said, once again defending her brother.

A bleary-eyed Clive stumbled down the stairs and into the front room, shielding his eyes from the sun's glare through the window.

'What you want?' Clive asked.

316

'I want to know what you're doing with your life, Son. You're not a kid anymore. I don't see you tryin' no more, no mo-tiv-a-tion that I can see. So what's goin' on in that head of yours? Time for a man to man. The Devil makes work for idle hands,' his father railed.

'Don't push me Dad, and lay off all that old-time religion. I just get me some breakfast I think,' said Clive. He made to move toward the kitchen, but Sam stood in his way. 'C'mon Dad, a guy's got to eat.'

'You're not contributin' nothin' to this house. Our people didn't go through all the sufferin' so you could loaf around. Why don't you do a college course like your sister here? Why don't you get a job so you can hold your head up? I watch that Winston troublemaker guy come round, showin' off his latest set of wheels, but I don't see where he earns the money. He's like you, on the high road to trouble. You don't need to go lookin' for it you two, it'll come and find you. Mark my words.'

Clive looked at the floor throughout, like he was waiting for a storm to pass before moving on, but Sam was in no mood to give up, he was just warming up.

'You just think you can take no notice of me. You're wrong. Either you give me some idea what you're goin' to do with your life, or, or you'll be out the house fendin' for yourself. I've given you long enough. You're out by sunset Son, sunset today, and leave your keys on the table in the hall as you go.'

With that Sam stormed out of the front door, grabbing his large fleece-lined anorak off the hook by the door as he went, leaving Clive going into the kitchen muttering.

'Huh! What's got into him?' Clive said, not quite believing what he'd heard.

Kaylah knew her Dad wasn't a man to joke about these things. Everything was black and white and his word was a matter of pride to him. Clive would be out by sunset unless something could be worked out. She tried to talk to Clive but he just shrugged her off too. She looked at her watch; time for her to get to the Drop In. She'd agreed to meet Ali there at

317

10.30. In two minds about whether to go, she moved toward the door.

'See you at lunchtime Clive,' she called, which gained another 'Hmm' which she took to mean 'yes, if nothing else has come up.'

Closing the door behind her, clutching her bag under her arm, it troubled her that her own family looked set to fall apart. Yes, Clive hadn't yet found himself, but many of his friends and hers were in the same situation. Clive had never been one to respond well to being pushed into things and Dad had once again used his overbearing bullish force of character with disastrous consequences. She really must talk to Clive at lunchtime.

As she hurried to the church hall, she saw Ali waiting outside for her to arrive. He seemed uneasy, looking around, glancing up and down the street.

'Now what's got into you,' she said.

'Nothing, just that I thought I was being followed here. Some guy in a silver Ford. When I slowed, he slowed. No more than that. Do asylum-seekers get watched round here?' he asked her, anxiety written on his face.

'You're paranoid,' she laughed, 'who'd be watching you? Come on in, I guarantee the only person keeping an eye on you will be me.'

Was she flirting with him, he thought.

'That's alright by me,' he replied, trying to draw her in. After the row at home, Ruth's words to her about boundaries had been forgotten. Here was the friend Kaylah thought she'd been looking for.

'Let's go in, there's things to be done,' she said cheerfully.

At the end of the morning they left together. Bob and April had been in, spent longer there than usual and April had made a point of asking Kaylah what she knew about Ali.

'What, is he under surveillance or something?' she'd replied.

April all too quickly backed off, so Kaylah got her answer. Kaylah was good at reading these kinds of things. So

318

Ali could have been right earlier, about being watched. Ali was a great help in getting the clothing storage area cleared, cleaned and reordered, even whilst there was a steady stream of people coming in to try things, generally warmer clothes to wear as the autumn was progressing.

'All done,' Kaylah announced at the end of the morning, telling Ali she was going home.

'I'll walk with you, if that's OK,' Ali offered.

Going out the hall door first, Kaylah saw a smart-looking white man, not a local, parked up about fifty paces away, sitting in his silver Ford, observing, yes definitely watching the Drop In door. She stared back at him and he looked away. Ali was right. There was surveillance. She immediately turned on her heels and went back inside, bumping into Ali in the hallway behind her. He didn't seem to mind, nor did she.

'Ali, your man in the silver Ford is sitting in his car over the road. I don't know whether he's watching you, me or the Centre. Ali looked anxious, his eyes uncertain.

'Maybe old enemies want to settle scores,' he offered.

'I have an idea.' She beckoned to Ali to follow her back inside.

'There's a little-used rear exit. We can leave that way, walk across the back of the vicarage garden, round the church and into Silver Street. That way we lose him. Don't owe money to the bailiffs do you?' she asked with a conspiratorial smile.

'No, no debt to anyone, but I had to flee people persecuting my family back home. I don't like being followed around, so let's do what you suggest,' agreed Ali, realising his friendship with Kaylah was paying its first dividend.

Moments later they were walking round the block and came into Cheddington Road, arriving at Kaylah's front door from the other end of the road. Kaylah hesitated, but then said, 'come on in, I'd like you to meet Clive, my brother.'

She was still worried about Clive and thought it wouldn't do any harm to bring Ali in on this one. Ali's presence might bring a bit of harsh reality to bear after all Ali had gone through; Ali might feel comforted by being in a family home,

319

albeit a rowing one! Thankfully Clive was now dressed and sitting brooding in the front room as they walked in.

'Dad back yet?' she enquired.

'No, thank God,' Clive answered.

'This is Ali, a friend,' she said.

'Hi, pleased to meet you Ali. Not the best of days for me,' said Clive.

'Nor me,' said Ali, 'some guy's following me around. Putting the wind up me actually. Where I come from, when you're followed, a bullet usually follows not far behind,' said Ali, unintentionally shocking Clive and Kaylah.

'Police?' asked Clive.

'Could be, but I don't think so. I don't like it,' Ali said.

'Yes, I didn't tell you earlier, that police support woman, April, she asked after you this morning, reckon it could be police,' said Kaylah.

'Might be Border Control or Immigration,' ventured Ali, 'maybe they want to send me back. That would kill me.'

Kaylah then explained the little game they had played to lose the guy in the car.

'Exciting,' said Clive, his eyes lighting up for the first time that day, his spirits lifted.

'Not for me,' said Ali, 'I can't face going back to Flo and Bert's tonight, not until I'm sure to be alright. I don't feel safe.'

'You know what, Sis, I've had an idea. That pain in the arse father of mine would be off my back if he heard I was helping asylum seekers. You're doing something useful at last he'd say. So how about Ali and me swop digs for a day or two, just till things cool down for both of us. You can have my room here Ali, I'll use yours at Flo and Bert's. You can explain to Mum and Dad, Kaylah. Honestly, it'll be better like this.'

The more they talked, the more they agreed. Clive gathered some things in a sports bag. Kaylah called Flo to explain and fix it, Clive checked the number of the house he was going to and it was settled. Ali was evidently much relieved, which left Kaylah wondering what Ruth would make of the direction this developing friendship was taking.

'One thing,' she added, 'we don't tell Ruth Churchill. In fact we keep it low profile for now, OK?'

'OK,' echoed both Ali and Clive simultaneously. With bump fists it was agreed. Ali explained to Clive that all his things were in a top drawer, and if he put them into the sports bag and brought them round here that would be just great. Clive agreed, and said he'd drop Ali's things in later and leave them in his own room ready for Ali to retrieve.

When Sam Kone arrived back at 4pm to find Kaylah and Ali sitting on the settee deep in conversation in the front room, he raised an eyebrow. He didn't know what to say and thinking discretion to be the better part of valour, he skipped straight through to the kitchen. Kaylah got up and followed him, closing the door behind her on Ali.

'You what! You've done what,' Ali heard Sam Kone shout out. She explained the situation twice over.

Finally, her Dad said, 'But what's your Mum going to say?'

With that remark, Kaylah knew her Dad was won over. A few moments later when he'd calmed down, Sam smiled as he thought to himself, I'm doing more for asylum-seekers now than you are Ruth Churchill, I've even got them living in my home! He couldn't wait to tell her!

As Ali listened, he breathed a sigh of relief. He was still on mission, still one step ahead of any pursuers. His friendship with Kaylah had not only paid its first dividend, but she was now tied closer to him than she knew. He had her in the palm of his hand.

45

After driving round the block several times and waiting outside Bert and Flo's house until five o'clock, Charlie Spiller hit his dashboard with his fist and resignedly gave up, pulled his Silver Ford Mondeo away from the surveillance area and called his boss at SO15.

'I lost him,' he confessed.

'Don't know what happened, one minute I saw him go into the Drop In in Windmill Road, but he never came out. Well, I never saw him. Maybe there's a back way off site. I couldn't exactly go nosing around, I would have given myself away,' he said, feeling frustrated.

To which he got the anticipated sarcastic remark about needing further training and being assigned to watch the office kettle boil to hone his observational attention span.

'Good job we don't just rely on you. We're pretty sure the mobile signal is still coming from the house you're supposed to be watching, so grab a coffee and go and park up and keep your eyes peeled. He'll probably show up there later. You'll be relieved by Sean at 8pm,' his manager said.

Charlie did as he was told and sped off to find somewhere to get a coffee and chocolate bar fix. As he looked at the older housing of the estate and the struggling people, he thought how nice it would be to get away from all this depressing urban grime at the end of the day, back to his modern flat in green and leafy Hatfield.

It was just after five when Clive knocked on Flo and Bert's door. Charlie saw him, made a note, but decided this wasn't Ali and he once more relaxed back into his driver's seat, some Chopin playing on the radio.

Kaylah had told the couple about Clive which kind of made it easier to introduce himself, but he still felt somewhat awkward when Flo opened the door.

'I was expecting you. Clive isn't it,' she said. He was immediately at ease. You couldn't help but like her.

'So Ali thinks someone's watching him. Only to be expected after all he's probably gone through, all that nasty fighting and killing. Must have seen some terrible things. Kind of your Mum and Dad to put him up and you're the one who had to lend him a bed. Well, come in, would you like a cuppa?' offered Flo.

'No thanks Flo. If you wouldn't mind showing me the room, I'm off out for the evening shortly. Do you mind if I come in late? I've got Ali's front door key and can let myself in,' he said.

'No, don't you worry dear. Bert and I are very sound sleepers, in bed by nine-thirty. Using the downstairs room as a bedroom these days. Just do what Ali did and make yourself at home upstairs. Bert and I will just leave you to it. Call us if you need anything, and shout loud, neither of us can hear anything! Use the front room upstairs. There's clean bedding in the landing airing cupboard if you need it. Let me know if you need anything else,' she said, leaving him to it.

With that Clive slung his sports bag over his shoulder and bounded up the stairs. The front room was clean and tidy. It surprised him there was nothing to indicate Ali had used it. He half expected Ali to have made the room his own and put pictures of the desert on the wall or something. It was clean but bare. In fact he couldn't see any of Ali's things. When he pulled open the top drawer of the chest of drawers there were some clothes of Ali's there as he'd been told there would be. He scooped them up and they easily fitted in Ali's sports bag. An envelope was also placed in the bag. He stroked his hand over the items, kind of curious as to Ali's life, but wouldn't disturb his things further. That would be prying.

He put his own clothes into the bottom drawer which was empty, then threw his sports bag on top of the wardrobe, upon which there was a crash as something fell down the back. Annoyed, he couldn't immediately get his hand to whatever it was that had fallen. He ended up pulling the wardrobe out away from the wall to recover whatever it was. He could see it. It was a mobile phone, an Apple I-Phone. Nice, but not Ali's, surely. Ali had a phone, he saw him check it earlier. Besides, surely he wouldn't have left a phone on top of there. Perhaps it belonged to a previous occupant of the room.

Clive picked it up, turned it over in his hand, flicked it on, not really expecting it to be charged, but it was, and the time accurately displayed at 17.23. How strange, he said to himself. He slid the unlock and the phone screen showed a screen display picture of a lad on a bike.

'Well, that settles that, it's not Ali's phone,' he said to himself. He decided to switch it off to save the battery and then put it in his jacket pocket, intending to ask Flo about it later.

Turning out of the room, down the stairs, letting himself out of the front door, he set off toward Silver Street, giving Winston a call asking him to pick him up from home.

'I'm just dropping a bag off for a friend there, meet you in 15. I'll be outside. Dad's slung me out! Don't ask, I'll explain later!' he said.

As he left Flo and Bert's, Clive was observed. Charlie Spiller, once again drawing on his e-cig, was parked a few doors up. Again, he didn't give Clive a second glance, a local black lad off out for the evening, probably to a gym with a sports bag over his shoulder, nothing to note there. All this waiting around, surveillance work with nothing kicking off was shit. He hoped Sean would turn up early to relieve him. It had been a dull day.

Ali was feeling uncomfortable. Life was suddenly getting more risky. He was confused. How had he got so emotionally entangled with Kaylah, dragging her into his life? But, he told himself, his plan to get close to her had already helped him escape what he now felt was covert intelligence surveillance. She was proving useful to him and he needed to keep that thought up front.

He tried to think what had given him away to the authorities: a mistake by him or was it a regular sweep the security people were making, just watching anyone and everyone? He didn't know, had no means of knowing and it left him feeling edgy.

No, it couldn't be a general trawl, he reasoned, he'd been identified, but how? Was there a traitor somewhere? Abu perhaps? Not likely, but just how well did he know Abu? he asked himself. What's that man up to? Or was it the Drop In who were suspicious of him and that Ruth woman had been talking to those local police who called in? No, that wasn't likely either. He just couldn't fathom it out. He didn't like being in the dark.

But fate had been kind. Kaylah had actually helped him out just when he needed it. He didn't like the fact that he'd not been entirely straight with her, but he didn't have any choice, he told himself. Her family had provided him with a bolt hole just when he needed one.

He'd been touched by her kindness for him and didn't want to betray that trust. But if the security services were really on to him they could soon find out where he was. He had the sense that time was running out, he was feeling that stye were closing in, and desperation to get on with what he had come to do began to gnaw at his insides. He needed to act before it was too late.

Then he suddenly remembered something from his training back in Mosul. He'd been told how the locations of mobile phones could be traced. Yes, that had been fine whilst he wanted people to believe that it was Adam who was travelling back across Europe to London, but since he'd dumped Adam's bike, he should have ditched the phone too. He hadn't, he bloody well hadn't. It was still at Flo's. Now he couldn't get it. That's how they were on to him, yes.

It was fortunate he'd left the phone hidden at Flo's, otherwise he'd have been followed round to the Kone house. Things were getting very risky, he thought, feeling a surge of fear run through his veins. He needed time to think but felt he didn't have any; so, he excused himself by going up to Clive's room, saying he needed to 'freshen up.'

Clive had got so many bright clothes. A grey fleecy top with a US baseball team advertised on it caught his eye. It had a hood, now that would be helpful. Returning downstairs he asked Kaylah if she thought Clive would mind if he borrowed the grey top. He explained that he was feeling the cold and wanted to pop over to see 'a friend from the mosque.' Kaylah told him to help himself and said she would be preparing something to eat for later, 'would Italian be OK?'

'Great,' he replied, 'and quickly stepped out into the night.

He looked up and down the road. It looked all clear, nothing lit up on his personal survival radar. He pulled the hood up over his head. He felt safer now, his face hidden from sight. Safer too to be out of the house. No-one would know him as Ali now, a grey lone wolf. He strode off more confidently toward the Red Brick Estate to hold a crisis conference with Abu.

When he arrived ten minutes later, Abu wasn't pleased to see him. When Ali explained he was being watched, Abu flew into a rage.

'Then why the hell are you coming round here? Didn't they teach you anything? You're putting what remains of my life and what I do for the Umma at risk, you foolish man,' he chided angrily.

Anxiously, Abu leant out his front door, glanced up and down the street, then, grabbing Ali's arm, pulled him sharply inside. In the hallway Ali began to explain they were now on to him, how it was late October already and he was impatient to know when he would strike?

'Wait here,' Abu told him, pushing him into the front room. Ali heard Abu go into the back room, pulling the door shut behind him: then the hushed tones of a conversation. Minutes later Abu reappeared.

'Instructions from the CO. You will get a call at eight o'clock tonight. I don't want you to take your calls here. I don't want to be swept up in your jihad, I may have to fight another day. I've got my own business to attend to. Take his call: and take this.' He handed Ali a white envelope 'Do what your CO says, and God be with you, my brother.'

After Abu had looked outside to see the street was clear, Ali was shown the door and roughly pushed outside into the dark.

326

It was nearly eight, so he strolled round to the bins at the end of the block. It felt like a long wait. Then the call came through, no introductions, no politeness, just his CO's voice.

'It's go. Collect the bag containing all you will need from the Excess Baggage Company at Kings Cross Station in London. The Left Luggage is in the main station concourse. Abu will have given you the necessary paperwork to allow you to receive it. We weren't able to get all the things we'd hoped over to you, but there is enough. Take great care of it. All the instructions you will need are in the top, in the zipped compartment. Allah Akbar. We will watch the news to see your victory!' With that, his CO had gone.

Ali opened the envelope to find a collection ticket inside. He didn't take it out, just stuffed the ticket and the envelope in his jeans front pocket. His phone rang again.

'Something else?' he enquired grimly.

'Er, just to say spaghetti bolognese will be ready in ten minutes,' said Kaylah.

'Sorry, thought you were someone else, be with you in five,' he said.

Ali didn't say much over supper. The Kones tried to make polite conversation, but he wasn't in the mood and this didn't go down well with Kaylah who was keen that he should make a favourable impression. Next morning Kaylah had to be at College early, which Ali said suited him fine, as he had to go into London and collect something for a friend.

Getting to London was always a drag from Edmonton, no tube station nearby, so he agreed to accompany Kaylah up to Southgate and take the Piccadilly line in from there. Once on the hopper bus, he apologised for his behaviour the previous evening.

'Guess I have a lot of worries on my mind. The spaghetti was really good and I never showed my appreciation,' he said.

He was amazed at his chat lines being so warmly received. She liked what he said, and the warmth came back. Kaylah had her worries too; and, for some reason, was clearly

327

preoccupied about Clive and saw Ali as helpful. Ali just listened as she poured out her worries. She feared Clive was going to get himself into big trouble and there was nothing she could do about it. That makes two of us, thought Ali. He liked feeling they shared adversity together. Clive's troubles drew her closer to him, bonded her to him. So very useful, he thought.

Having said his goodbyes, Ali dived down the escalator at Southgate Tube Station promising to see Kaylah back there to chat more about Clive when her lectures finished at lunchtime. Having stepped straight on a train, thirty minutes later he was at Kings Cross Station. He found Left Luggage without having to ask anyone, the signage very clear.

At the tucked-away office, a testament to people's failure to remember things, he found himself unavoidably standing beneath a black circular cctv camera right in front of him with its eye looking straight into his. With his grey hood up, he handed his ticket in and in return, after just a few moments of anxious waiting, was handed a large dark blue rucksack.

'It's heavy mate,' said the uniformed assistant struggling to lift it down from the storage shelf and place it on the counter between them. 'Glad you've got to carry it and not me Guv.'

Ali said a polite 'thank you,' and hurried outside, terrified someone would tap his shoulder and apprehend him.

Once he was in what he thought was a safe corner, the first thing Ali noticed were the small padlocks locking the main storage part. Checking again to ensure he was well away from the eye of the cctv, he opened the top to find a sheet of lined paper with instructions in Arabic written on it; also the keys to get inside. Paperwork and keys placed in his pocket, he put the pack on his back and headed back down into the underground, just another person in the ant-like procession of thousands of fellow travellers. It bothered him that there were so many cctv cameras, all of which he was convinced were watching him.

But, so far so good. Today, fate was again on his side. No-one had stopped him. He now had his weapons and explosives, even though there had been difficulty getting him everything he needed, his CO had said. Even so, Ali reckoned things had now got a whole lot better. He was no longer homeless, he was armed and ready to go. After all the waiting, things were moving in the right direction again.

46

Before leaving the outskirts of Mosul, Adam spotted what could only be a checkpoint in the distance on the road ahead. Fortunately for him they had a light showing so that no-one came crashing into their barrier unawares. It gave him some precious seconds.

He had hoped to get further than this before any challenge. He was aiming for the nearest fighting he had heard, the explosions and firing to the north, but still he was surprised to have come upon soldiers so soon.

The IS guys in their dark fatigues and weapons clearly didn't expect many vehicles at this hour, only one guy having enough enthusiasm to start to show interest as he closed toward them. The man with his gun still casually slung over his shoulder had strolled from their guard hut to the horizontal road block bar by the time Adam was almost upon it.

Adam couldn't risk getting too close and, keeping his speed as steady as he could so as not to be too obvious, he turned into the last right turn before he would have been at the checkpoint itself. Quick thinking followed. I'm now heading east. East is also good, he told himself, but he needed to get out of Mosul without being stopped or that would be it. Perhaps every road out had its checkpoints. He just hoped he'd happen upon some friendly Kurds, but he knew his chances of doing so were slim indeed.

The city of Erbil lying somewhere to the east was a Kurdish city. It had been a seat of power for the Kurdish autonomous region for a generation. He could try heading there, though he had only the vaguest notion he might be going in the right direction. Not too far away, it may even prove possible to reach, provided he didn't get stopped.

Distance wasn't the issue. Erbil could, he speculated, only be a matter of less than one hundred miles away. The big challenge was not to get shot at or bombed by either side as he travelled. Allied drone attacks could take out any speeding vehicle on a main road or indeed any parked up vehicle if it was out of civilian areas. He felt he was anybody's target, so vulnerable, so exposed. There was nothing for it, but to keep moving. He had no choice.

The turn into the tight alleyway was an unexpectedly good move. The narrow road wound its way steadily east, houses pressing and constricting the lane, but because it was not a main thoroughfare there didn't seem to be any checkpoints. Going through residential areas also felt safer from attack and there was no-one about at this time of night to see him. However, after a few minutes, the number of houses began to thin and he was on the outskirts of Mosul and then he found himself very quickly in more open country where he felt once more very exposed.

He decided he had few options, so initially he chose to aim in a straight line out into the desert north east and then later zigzag south east, crossing what he assumed to be the main road to Erbil occasionally to keep track of his bearings. The starlight was now supported by moonlight, which felt like driving in conditions so bright everyone could surely see him. He pulled his makeshift towel disguise closer and tighter round his head. It felt comforting, rather like a cycle helmet did when racing downhill.

After an hour he pulled up under a palm tree, switched off the Toyota's lights and engine to take stock and have a drink, grabbing the water bottle in the door. The experience had given him a great thirst. He then went through the car to see what else he could find. He picked up the handgun again and found a box of ammunition with it. Looking around to see if there was anyone in earshot he decided to give it a go.

Opening the driver's door, he stepped outside and holding the weapon in two hands he pointed it toward the tree trunk ten metres away and pulled the trigger. The noise left his head ringing and he hadn't expected the recoil. Even though he felt safer having it and knowing that it fired, the noise it made had startled him and he glanced around anxiously. Fortunately there were no signs of life in any direction.

Going back to the Toyota, he found there was nothing else in the vehicle except a small bag containing a lighter, a camping stove and kettle. The dashboard clock showed the time to be two in the morning. Looking anxiously over his shoulder toward where he'd come from, he knew he had to press on. Any time soon, he thought, the chase would be on. He had no time to lose.

After another half hour of zigzagging which seemed to be working out, he heard what sounded like the noise of a plane's engine, and wound down his driver's window to see if he could spot where it was coming from. As the engine noise got louder, instinctively he grabbed the handgun, the box of ammunition, and the water bottle and threw them all in the small bag with the kettle. Quickly he moved away from his vehicle, trying to pinpoint where the noise in the sky was coming from. It was near, but he could see nothing. He headed further away from the vehicle and into some shrub he could use as cover, pushing his way in, before stopping again. This was a good move, the noise was definitely a plane of some sort.

Then there was a roar and the crushing penetrating force of a shock wave as he was thrown flat to the ground by an explosion that destroyed his transport in a flash of white light, leaving a column of smoke rising into the night sky. Shaken, it took an unexpectedly long time, or so it seemed, for his eyes to begin to adjust. He checked himself over to ensure he hadn't been hurt. Then all was quiet, so very quiet, there was nothing.

As quickly as he could he half-crawled, half-crept away from the scene, still moving east. He didn't want to be around when anyone came to inspect what was left of the Toyota. Walking on the uneven sand was slow. Roots and clumps of dry vegetation threatened to fell him and, with his mobility now greatly reduced, he felt his chances of escape had reduced too.

It was some hours later he found himself on the banks of a great river and his heart sank as his goal, he knew, lay on the opposite side. The night would soon end, but here at

332

least was vegetation. He thought he could hide himself in it, could rest up and come up with a plan. So very, very tired, he had, he thought, put enough distance between himself and his bombed-out Toyota to avoid easy discovery.

The first hint of daylight was beginning to show on the far horizon, Even in his desperation, he thought it a most beautiful sight. If only he wasn't in this spot of bother! He hunkered down and, as daylight came, dozed off. But it was not long before explosions and gunfire exchanges were shaking him awake. The fighting must be nearer than he thought. Looking round carefully, he tried to make out what was going on. Maybe the river acted as a kind of east-west boundary between IS and Kurdistan; it must be one of the great tributaries of the Tigris, but he could end up being shot by either side. In desperation he cried out, 'What the hell do I do?'

A short time later when the autumn sun was beginning to push the cold dawn temperature up to scorching for anyone out in the open, things were taken out of Adam's hands. He heard voices first. They were approaching and he decided to take the handgun out of the bag really carefully so that it didn't bang on the kettle. Keeping as low as he could he peeped out through the waterside vegetation. He had no intention of being taken back to Mosul.

There were two guys in black approaching, clearly on the wrong side, walking as if they hadn't a care in the world, and casting occasional wary glances across the river. They got within ten paces of him. He held his breath, but they kept looking away from him toward the river.

Then a cry, as he was discovered, the two men simultaneously swinging round in his direction, lowering their weapons from their shoulders, shots, noise. Adam, from his low and crouched position, had quickly raised his hand gun, pointed and fired, first at the man nearest to his left and then at the man on his right. Fast, must be fast, he told himself, trying to calm his rising sense of fear and panic. He fired and fired again until his gun just stopped. Both men in front of him fell, tumbling awkwardly backwards. Adam's lower leg hurt.

Not waiting to look at his attackers, he ran, staggering, limping, dragging his leg, dropping toward the river, instinct driving him to get away, survival only in his mind. He stumbled and fell into the water. He swam, slowly pushing himself away from the shore, so very slowly. The water embraced him, it was warm and taking him deeper into its grip. He let himself go, glancing back as he heard movement on the shore behind him.

One of his victims was struggling to get to his feet, injured, but still trying to lift his gun. Adam thought himself as good as dead and gave himself up to the water. He stopped swimming and drifted helplessly in the gentle brown current.

He waited for the shots to hit him, but none came. Not wanting to see the man in black getting up to ensure his shots were on target, his gaze drifted up to the blue sky above. Now drifting well out into the river Adam knew he was a sitting duck, but he couldn't do anything and a paralysing terror began to take hold of him.

Then he heard the splash of bullets ripping into the water around him and the rat-a-tat tat as his attacker managed to let off a round. Then came a crack of other gunfire, then another longer round; and, moving his head to see, he watched in surprise as his attacker fell back to the ground once again. In the confusion he had no idea what this meant. All he knew was the terror of the moment had moved into the terror of uncertainty and all the time the pain in his leg grew in intensity so as to be excruciating.

Adam drifted; maybe he was by now in the middle of the river. Water began lapping over his face, it was the end. He was fading, struggling now to keep his head above water. As the brown water entered his mouth, he could taste it, silt mixed with saliva, choking his airways. This would be the end, this was how his life would finish, in a few quick gulps of water and he would be gone.

A small group of Kurdish soldiers had observed it all. Their sniper had taken out Adam's would-be killer, their target throwing back a weapon-clutching arm, mimicking a famous Spanish Civil War photograph. When the platoon was sure it was safe to move into the open, they used an inflatable craft to pick up Adam's body from the water.

They dragged him, a motionless sack pulled over the side and into the bottom of the boat. Then they returned as quickly as they could to the safety of the shore and placed him none too gently on his back on the dry sand.

Whether this young man, whoever he was, was alive or dead it was hard to tell and though a little puzzled why he'd been shot, they were none too bothered. He wasn't one of theirs, just one more anonymous fatality of war. Leave him to die.

47

When Ali got back to Southgate with his rucksack, looking for all the world like just another student, he had time to kill before Kaylah would be out of college, so he wandered up towards MacDonald's just yards from the tube station exit. He noticed a boy and a girl had made up some tailor's dummy in weird costume and were yelling, 'Penny for the guy. Sir, please, penny for the guy.'

They had a box on the ground taking people's change. Some form of begging, Ali figured, how come they were not at school?

Once inside MacDonald's he ordered a Coke and parked up at a table. From the position he chose he ensured he could view the other customers as well as see the street outside. Carefully he lowered his rucksack to the floor: he'd explore it later. The precise make up of its lethal contents was not yet known to him, and certainly not to the blissfully unaware twenty or more people relaxing around him. How often we are all close to death but little realise it, he thought.

Looking at the Mercedes, BMWs and other four-wheel signs of affluence passing outside the window in the autumn sunlight, it was true what Kaylah had told him, Southgate was more aspiring than Edmonton, people dressed well, drove in upmarket cars and this MacDonald's had a better class of customer. There would be no confrontations with anyone here. He thought how out of place his own battered, well-used Toyota would look.

He felt calm, in control, his jihad now back on course, surely nothing could stop him now. Still, he thought to himself, he'd got to be careful. Being close to Kaylah was both good cover and a big risk, yet he also needed her, the warmth of her contact and her sexiness, it threw him all the time he was with her. He knew she was growing to like him, that suited his purposes; besides, he acknowledged to himself, he'd come to realise he was lonely when not in her company.

336

His phone went, a message. It was Mo. What could he want? Must be important. He opened the message, 'Bird has flown. Adam gone, some days ago, sorry.' That was it. He wondered how, where, and when. He knew he couldn't risk replying and he shook as he considered what reprisals might come to his family for letting their prize hostage escape. Things like that played out very badly. Well, Adam wouldn't get far he told himself. That just might save them. He worried for Mo and Maryam and their children, his sister Fatima, his uncle. What would happen to them now?

Part of him felt glad Adam had gone. Instinctively, he'd liked the lad. Why should this one more innocent victim be another sacrificial lamb for the party's blood lust? Good luck to him. He'd be hard pressed to survive outside the compound where we kept him, he thought. Now, on the out, he had a chance, like a gladiator in a ring. Maybe he'll get lucky and get out, probably he won't, but he'll have had a chance. Whilst he was my prisoner he had no chance. Fate will decide.

He wondered how often he put events into the hands of fate. Was fatalism something Islamic? He began to think it was. He raised his Coke to offer a toast to 'Adam' the guy whose name had given him his open road to England.

'To the memory of my English twin,' he said, 'we are both fearing discovery. We are more brothers than we know! The question is who will be dead first?'

Then he spotted her. In his imagination she looked to his eyes like every bit the virgin princess offered to the martyrs and maybe she was his. She seemed to be walking on air, and she was coming to him. He liked her shoes with heels, her long slender legs, her shapely body, her cheerful happy carefree face.

She's black, probably Christian, whereas I'm brown and definitely Muslim. His mind wandered speculatively. If we had children, what would they be? Have to be Muslim. Don't we just borrow all these identity markers and put them on and off like clothes?

Then she was here in front of him. As she came in he rose to greet her, couldn't help but smile and the two air-kissed. Ali aware of her scented perfume, sweet and floral. This was new, but nice and he knew he'd crossed the Rubicon when it came to how to behave. But it's OK, he immediately told himself, she's not a Muslim. He asked her what she would like and went over to get her a smoothie, telling her to watch his bag, but frequently turning round himself to both check it and watch Kaylah.

When he returned, she seemed relaxed. It was Friday, classes over, it was the start of a weekend. For a moment, Ali felt a surge of guilt; he'd missed Friday prayers yet again, but then told himself that he wasn't to be practising his religion too seriously so as not to attract attention. He still felt ill at ease with himself. He had the sense of floating between identities, who he was and who he might become. He feared liking what he might become more than who he was and he felt unsettled and confused, fearful his personality was undergoing a fundamental disintegration, some kind of metamorphosis.

She never asked him about the bag, which was a relief, he didn't want to lie to her again. Her mind was on something else. She wanted him to come down to Alexandra Palace, Ally Pally, she called it, tomorrow, Saturday night, to see the fireworks.

'A cultural event you should see,' she said. Some of the other students were also going to be there. He thought, why not?

'It's Bonfire night, haven't you ever heard, "Remember, Remember, the fifth of November, gunpowder, treason and plot?"' she said.

'No, never, what's that all about then? Anyway it's not the fifth until Monday,' said Ali.

'We were talking about it earlier at college. A man called Guy Fawkes and some Catholics tried to blow up Parliament on the fifth of November 1605. They very nearly did, but were discovered just in time. So every fifth November, up and down this land, people have firework

338

parties to remember the day the Gunpowder Plot was discovered and Parliament was saved. When the fifth doesn't fall on a weekend, like this year it's on a Monday night, the date isn't so good for firework displays what with work and so on, so big displays are usually moved to the nearest weekend, which is why Ally Pally fireworks are tomorrow,' she told him.

'Was that what the kids I saw by the tube station were doing? They asked for a "penny for the guy." Was that part of it?'

'Sure, I saw them myself, doing well they were. The guy represents Guy Fawkes. His effigy gets burned on bonfires, though there aren't so many bonfires these days. They are too unsafe, especially in big cities. Instead, people get together for publicly-organised firework displays, big ones. So you'll come then?' she pressed.

'OK, yes of course. But what was Guy trying to do? Was he a Muslim type of Catholic?' asked Ali.

She laughed, 'No way, but I guess you're kinda right too. He was a religious extremist. They're nothing new you know. He and his fellow conspirators, people like Fawkes' friend Catesby, wanted a religiously Catholic-led country. Catholic Christians hated the Protestant Christians. They argued over things, a bit like Sunnis and Shias, no offence. The Catholics saw Parliament as representing a total evil, deserving of punishment and very nearly succeeded in their plot to blow it up. Fawkes put barrel after barrel of explosives under Parliament itself. Come on, you need to learn some of our customs, say it, go on, say it with me, "Remember, Remember, the fifth of November, gunpowder, treason and plot."'

Ali said and memorised the words, in his head almost saying, the eleventh of November out-loud. He hadn't realised that religious freedom-fighters were nothing new in the UK and couldn't help but ask Kaylah more about them.

'What happened to the Catholics after the plot was discovered?' he said.

339

'I think, but don't know for sure, that there would have been an inquiry by the government and a severe clamp down on the Catholics, anyone they found to be linked to the plot; in those days they weren't too worried about proof, they'd have hung, drawn and quartered. It's so barbaric, don't ask, it's, it's just like IS do to people, chopping off hands and feet and things. You know we think of Guy Fawkes as of another age, nothing to do with us, but it still happens, doesn't it? I hadn't thought,' she said.

That got to Ali. He went quiet until Kaylah spoke.

'Do you like history then? You seem really interested,' she said, lightening up again.

'I guess I don't know as much as I thought I did. My country has had one long history of foreign invaders, different civilisations, most of them godless. It's only recently that it's become a proper Muslim-run country,' said Ali.

Then he realised he'd said too much and followed it quickly with a proposal.

'Let's go to the fireworks tomorrow. I think I'd like to get back now, drop off my stuff. When we go to Alexandra Palace, is it far? How do we get there?' he asked.

They chatted away about buses and times, Kaylah wondering if Clive would come with them. She sent a text to Clive. Then with a final slurp she'd finished her smoothie. Ali quite liked the idea of just being with Kaylah, the two of them out on a date, so was not disappointed when Kaylah's text exchange with Clive said, 'thx but busy tomorrow.'

As they walked back down to Edmonton and home together in the late afternoon, the incessant traffic noise made them raise their voices to hear one another speak. Ali was thinking of Guy Fawkes and thought Guy was a failure because he didn't plan, prepare and perform as he should have. It was not a mistake he intended to make himself, he thought.

For his part, Ali was now determined that he was going into the centre of London on Sunday morning to do his homework on Parliament, government, and the big international gathering the media were announcing. The build-

340

up had already began. Everyone was getting ready for the Remembrance commemorations. This weekend's rehearsal for Armistice Day the following Sunday the eleventh of November would give him chance to see exactly what they had in mind.

Ali told himself he was going to be no idiot like Guy Fawkes. He wouldn't be discovered at the eleventh hour! Ali had seen a sign saying that some bus services were not running in London on Sunday morning as rehearsals for the following Sunday were taking place. So he determined he would get himself into London early and see what was going to happen. Perfect! Now that, he told himself, is the perfect time to plan and prepare for a performance to shake the world in just one week's time.

Walking beside him, Kaylah was lost in her own thoughts, thinking of a shower when she got in, and what she would wear for a night out at Alexandra Palace tomorrow. It had been quite a week.

The sky was clear and as the sun dropped behind the houses there was a chill in the air as the temperature suddenly fell. She found herself shivering even as she moved closer to Ali.

48

The Kurdish unit was unsure what to do with the body they fished out the river. Their first assessment was this guy was a foreign fighter with IS and they should just let him die. But those who had seen what had happened on the far bank pondered further.

'But why, if he is some foreign IS supporter did he shoot up their patrol and try and escape them?' one of the men asked.

'Because he'd had enough,' another said.

'He was disillusioned and wanted out. They all get to feel like that, well most of them anyways. This guy knew he was with a bunch of losers in a losing war. He wanted to get home to the comforts of the west, to live to fight another day, to fight his war on another front. Leave him to die,' a third man said.

They'd dragged Adam's body out of the water and dropped it unceremoniously on the sandy shore line. Some flies were already feasting on the blood now smeared all down his right leg. The dropping of his body did something, pushed a spurt of water out of Adam's mouth, and set a choking gurgle in motion. One of the soldiers kicked Adam in the side, rolling him. More water flowed. He began to splutter, but no-one did anything except look on.

Adam's eyes flickered open to see a different sort of soldier staring at him. He tried to speak but could only splutter and cough, fighting to get air and clear the mucus from his mouth. He fought to get some air, then some more.

'English, I'm British, please help me. Escaped from Mosul.' One of those around him spat at him, another kicked him. They couldn't understand a word he was saying. Adam lay quiet just hoping they wouldn't hurt him more.

Then he was shaken by a slim guy who had bent down and dragged into a sitting position. He coughed more, his mouth was full of grit. He hurt. Another guy offered him a water bottle. He used it to swill his mouth and then to spit out. He knew he had reached another fighting group, but he had no means of knowing which, though he suspected and hoped they were Kurds.

'I was a hostage. I've escaped from Mosul. I'm Adam. Please help me,' he pleaded.

He thought he sounded pathetic. He found it hard to concentrate. He must stay with it. The guy in charge issued some sort of command and two of the men, one each side, scooped him up and began dragging him, half walking, half falling, away from the river. They didn't care about the pain in his side or in his leg. He began to feel very frightened, that even now he would be simply leant against a dusty wall and shot.

They got him to a military tent, camouflaged in desert colours. The inside was set up like an office with desk, chairs and computers. He was sat down, two of them, one hand to a shoulder each, holding him upright. Moments later a smarter man appeared and sat down opposite him.

'My name is Khaled, you are with the Kurdish forces. Please tell me your full name.'

'Adam James Taylor,' he said.

'Where are you from?' said Khaled, staring straight into Adam's eyes.

'London, England. I was cycling on a Gap Year and got captured and taken prisoner and held in Mosul, where I escaped from, yesterday evening,' he said.

'OK, OK. Hold on,' said Khaled, trying to write as Adam spoke.

He flicked through his sheaf of papers. He was in no hurry. Adam didn't know whether he could hold on.

'Hmm. Your name checks out with our intelligence reports. I want to notify British Special Forces working with us. Please wait,' he instructed.

He picked up his mobile phone, stood up and walked just outside the tent, beyond earshot. It seemed like an age but a few minutes later, he returned and sat down looking at Adam, curiosity in his eyes.

'Please to wait Adam, and please forgive me. Would you care for some coffee and something to eat? I will get our medical orderly to see to your leg. It looks no more than a bullet graze, but it may have done some muscle damage. If my troops were a little rough it is because they cannot take chances. We have paid the price for carelessness too many times,' he said.

Adam felt hope beginning to surge inside. His interrogator paused to call in another soldier who was given instructions which Adam couldn't follow and then the three soldiers left him. He was just left sitting there, alone. It was getting very hot in the tent even though the side flaps were open, the late October sun was getting up. He was finding it hard to stay sitting, felt so weary and his leg now really hurt, but a sense of elation at being free was dawning.

He fought hard to stay focussed though he just couldn't seem to order his thoughts. Every now and then he had a moment of panic as if he wasn't really free, as if it was all but a mirage, something unreal that would soon evaporate before his eyes.

Then he heard the sound of a vehicle approaching, and this unnerved him again. Anxiously he turned his head to see a Land Rover with three men in it pull to a halt, dust billowing from their slowing tyres. The man in the front passenger seat immediately leapt down and marched in. Adam could see they were British SAS forces with their silver winged insignias and berets, and his initial wave of panic began to subside.

'Hi Adam,' the man said in a very self-assured calm voice, 'Call me Steve. You're in safe hands. We will have you seen to and out of here presently as soon as I've had a chat with the local chaps,' he added.

In gentleman-like English fashion, he shook Adam firmly but warmly by the hand. Then turning to the Kurdish commander, words were politely exchanged, which seemed to Adam to be a formal handing over of Adam to the British.

As Adam sipped the last of his coffee, Steve walked over and said he was just going to look at Adam's leg. Taking a saline wash and gauze swab from a medical pack, he

344

washed and wiped the wound. Adam clenched his teeth with the pain. A dressing was applied and secured in place with some kind of tape.

Adam was asked if he had any belongings with him, and Steve then scooped him up bodily and carried him out to the Land Rover, asking 'Ash' in the rear to take care of him. With that they began moving away.

'Sorry for the bumpy ride,' said Steve, 'we'll be somewhere more comfortable in twenty minutes. Sounds like from what I was told you did well against those goons trying to get you. Shooting straight from low down, nice action. Want to join us?' he jested.

The humour was almost too much to bear for Adam, his emotions were all over the place. His body hurt in several places. He wanted to cry and he wanted to laugh, so he just sat there with no expression on his face, wearing the frozen mask of the traumatised. They drove into the outskirts of a town he was told was Erbil and pulled up at a small house.

'Our support team is here. It'll be said to you again, but you are not to say anything to anyone about seeing us or about our operation here. So far as anyone back home is concerned we don't exist, though every last newspaper seems to report our presence all the same. This isn't going on. It is really important that you understand this,' said Steve, a serious look on his face.

Adam simply nodded, he understood.

Once inside the house, he was given a more gentle and routine triaging of his leg injury, and supplied with some welcome pain killers which he immediately made use of. The initial assessment was correct.

'Only a deep graze,' the verdict.

He wanted to tell his parents he was safe, but this kept being delayed.

Then a female soldier came in and sat with him.

'We have reports that your identity was used to help get an IS operative into London. The work to discover who this is and prevent what he intends to do is ongoing and we have to consider who needs to know you are safe in order not to put

345

the operation to catch this man in jeopardy. Other lives are at stake here. Obviously as soon as he is apprehended, no problem,' she said.

'But I really would like my parents to know I am safe. They can be trusted to keep it quiet,' said Adam.

'It'll have to be checked out I'm afraid. But what I can tell you is that arrangements are even now being put in hand to see you are flown by military plane, first to Germany, and then on to Northolt, near London. I'm afraid you need to prepare yourself for a full intelligence debriefing en route. IS went to a lot of trouble to capture you, use your identity, and place someone in London. But that's enough for now. We don't have more than field amenities here, but the showers are good and the food tolerable. First, only because there is some urgency, can you just tell me right now what you know of Ali,' she asked.

'Well, he left the compound where he lived in Mosul as soon as I was captured and made prisoner there. It was his Toyota Hilux I stole to get away, but it won't be any use to him any more.'

'So that was yours. Thought as much. You were lucky we didn't fry you in it. You are one lucky guy. The gods must be on your side. We took it out of action, some local supportive action,' she said.

Adam talked freely sharing in rambling fashion anything he could remember about Ali and his time in Mosul that might be useful.

'Now is there anything else you need for now?' she asked him.

'A change of clothes, a shave, a sleep,' and with that, an overwhelming sense of tiredness began to roll over him. It wasn't something he could fight. 'I need some sleep first,' he said.

He was led into a side room with a bed. He later remembered the soft touch of the sheets and he was out like a light. Even so, he was conscious that he woke more than once, startled by flashbacks. At one point he was down a deep well, drowning in the water and an Arab looking guy, who looked like Ali, was looking down and laughing. Again and again it happened, until each time the weariness of sleep took over and shut out everything.

Whilst Adam was sleeping the lines were hot between British special forces Iraq, MI5 and MI6 in London's Vauxhall HQ, Israel's Mossad and contacts in the American FBI with an IS brief. There was one common urgent theme, one instruction given, 'find Ali'.

49

It was Saturday morning on the third of November and suitably grey, cold and misty. Kaylah was up and out of the house by nine-thirty. She wanted to call and see Ruth at the Drop In and knew she would be there around ten after taking the Morning Prayer service in church. She'd left Ali fast asleep, as far as she knew, and hadn't knocked on the door of his room before leaving. Plenty of time to catch up with him later, she reasoned. Clive, she had heard from Flo, was fine.

As she walked the few minutes it took to get to the Drop In, she saw her breath in the cool air. The mist was already clearing, it looked ideal for fireworks later.

She wondered how she was going to keep the news about Ali and Clive's domestic swap from Ruth. Sooner or later Ruth would know, and after what Ruth had said to her before about placement boundaries and inappropriate friendships, how was she going to take the fact she and Ali were, well, what were they? They were sort of good friends, though they hadn't described their relationship quite in those or any other terms. Yes, he'd moved into her house, though to read anything more into that would give entirely the wrong impression. She hoped she wouldn't need to discuss it, well it was too complicated and, let's face it, too embarrassing to talk about, she reasoned.

Ruth was there when she arrived. They hadn't been talking long when Ruth showed her what was in the envelope she was holding.

'I've been given some tickets for next Sunday's special Armistice Day parade,' she said, holding them up like precious, gold prize-winning tickets.

'It promises to be quite a sight. Just a small number of parishes have been sent tickets to send people to view the occasion from Church House Westminster's prime location. Their windows face directly on to the event. I was thinking you might like to go? I've got to cover church services here

348

on Armistice Sunday, otherwise I'd be down there. I can let you have a couple of tickets: you can take a friend. That'll leave me with three. I'll easily find three other people who want to go. It's a big thing, live TV coverage, world leaders coming, huge military parade - London showing off and at its best!'

'Great! Thanks, that.s really kind.' Ali would love to go, she thought; he seemed really interested in all the history stuff.

Ruth took two tickets out of the envelope and passed them over, explaining as she did so where the building was and how to get in through the reception desk in Church Yard.

Ruth seemed to have a lot on her mind. She had several people whom she needed to talk to today, she said, but before she hurried off she had time to ask Kaylah how she thought her placement was going.

Kaylah could truthfully say she was really enjoying it and Ruth for her part was pleased with the benefits Kaylah had already brought to the Drop In.

'Your ability to organise us to be more efficient has been appreciated by everyone, not least by myself. But what have you made of the business side? Have you had time to appraise it?' asked Ruth.

Kaylah thought for a moment before replying.

'You've got some problems. Everything is hand to mouth and dependent on a constant supply of goodwill and last-minute small individual donations. These are all very well and indicative of the generous local support and goodwill there is for what is being done, but what the Drop In really needs are a few larger grants, some more regular income, to ensure the bills can be met and the services you provide for the asylum-seekers are sustainable. If you had that, you'd also be able to offer more support services. At the moment, it's so, so on the edge of a crisis.' She paused before continuing.

'Have you thought of asking the London Borough of Enfield's Social Inclusion Unit for a grant, or maybe getting the Church Treasurer to make some funding bid applications to charities? It might also be worth seeing if you can partner a

349

couple of similar enterprises to see if you can gain by working closer together. I can suggest some places to try if you like,' she said, glad not to be talking about Ali.

'That sounds like music to my ears. It's just I've been too busy to attend to it,' said Ruth.

'Well, I don't mind starting on making a few enquiries next week if you want me to?' offered Kaylah.

'OK, just pass things by me before you submit them, and copy me in. Look, I'm sorry but I have to dash,' said Ruth, looking away, ready to go.

With that she moved briskly away leaving Kaylah clutching two tickets. Well, apart from the fare into London it won't be an expensive outing, she thought. But could she really begin to think of Ali and her as 'us,' more than just friends? Over recent weeks they'd really got on. She liked his company, she liked spending time with him. Tonight they were going to see the fireworks, that would take things in one of two directions. We could be 'us' by the end of today, who knows, she mused.

Kaylah spent a further hour in the church hall, putting freshly donated food items away in the store room Ali and she had reorganised. It was working much better through having been worked on.

She could see Abu was there. Now why didn't she like that man, she asked herself. She ought to be sympathetic to his personal loss, but he didn't seem to be touched even by such a great personal tragedy. He always seemed to be quietly cultivating every new Muslim arrival and she had an instinct that all his wheeling and dealing was a front to serve his particular soul-less Muslim cause.

One thing was certain, he had no time for her and in spite of her efforts to be friendly, not once had he responded with any warmth, just a cold brush-off. She remembered how Abu had spoken out at her college in the summer, with such an alienating view of other religions. He'd wound up and upset people then. She was sure it was one of Abu's friends who had hurt her friend Melissa. How conservative, how almost fundamentalist he had sounded.

350

It took one to know one, she thought, recognising her own Dad could sometimes sound so like Abu. Yet there was a difference, Dad had a forgiving and loving side, and in spite of everything she had a warm spot for her Dad, well most of the time. She hadn't seen anything of that in Abu. Whatever he was up to she didn't like it and she didn't like him.

After she'd finished, she took a bus up to Edmonton Green. She had a hair appointment, and whilst she was sitting there having her very African, tight curled, hair attended to in a hairdressers which understood these things, she decided she also had to have her nails done. Thinking about her hair set her thinking about Ali, and just how very different the two of them were. Black hair was such a distinctive thing. Some girls tried to straighten it and pass as white. She thought how the USA president's wife, had always straightened her hair and wondered how far she had sidestepped what it meant to be black in a white-dominated world, the straightened hair signifying some degree of capitulation rather than standing with the cause.

She just wanted to stay true to herself and part of her cared about black justice, she reminded herself. She aspired to hold her head up in the world with pride, one with her family and her people, she thought. How very strange, hair meaning so much.

She began to share her thoughts with Dee who was blowing her hair dry. It was hard to talk above the rushing hot air noise and anyway Dee never did causes. Other women she knew had tight corn rows like the woman sitting next to her, who was spending her whole time playing on her phone. No, that wasn't her, she wanted her hair somehow looser, more flexible.

Her eye caught the row of hair extensions on the side wall. Nah, she thought, not her either. There was a night out ahead, with Ali. How would he see her? And she decided she wanted to be just truly herself with Ali. Once she started thinking about Ali she realised she was finding it difficult to think about anything else. She liked him, yet she knew so little about him. They got on, but wasn't there also a huge

351

chasm between them waiting to swallow them both whole? Then Dee interrupted her day-dreaming.

'Who is the lucky guy then?' asked Dee smiling. Dee heard everyone's stories. She'd known Kaylah for years and just waited for her to spill the beans.

She hesitated and then told Dee everything. Listening to the love life of customers was something Dee excelled in. Nonetheless, the Kaylah-Ali story took her breath away. It made her day. Kaylah thought she must have sounded like an excited teenager, but Dee wanted to know every detail and Kaylah just couldn't stop herself talking. Was it anything or was it nothing? She didn't know, but both Dee and she guessed it would go one way or another soon.

Kaylah, returned home at six to find Ali sitting in the front room watching TV. It was the Al Jazeera news channel. It was kind of sobering to see him there sitting so still and attentive as she pushed open the front door. He swung round, and looked at her, then looked again. She wanted to read him. What did his eyes say? He was looking at her. What was his mind thinking? What would he say? A silence fell between them and it was Ali who dropped his eyes to the floor, before speaking,

'You look nice.' He said it so quietly she hardly heard him.

'Thanks,' she chipped in, inwardly pleased. 'Have you had a good day?'

'A quiet one. Didn't hear you go out. Didn't really know what to do. Are we still going to see fireworks?' he asked.

'Yes, our night out!' Give me a few minutes to get ready. Shall we say, leave at seven?'

'Fine by me. I'm ready when you are,' he said, turning his back to the TV.

'OK, it takes a girl longer,' she said.

She skipped off upstairs. A short while later she reappeared in tight trousers, a shiny pink top and short cropped black leather coat with small black purse clenched in her hand. She heard Ali take a deep breath and for a second time enjoyed his attention.

Ali had fallen into a deep ravine, he was still falling, hearing her voice as if it were from a distance. He liked, if not loved this girl. He desired this girl, but at this moment everything in his life was falling into this chasm with him, his family, his home, his people. All would be drowned as if he'd got into the Tigris river in flood. He felt as though suspended in water, pulled up by her toward the surface and the light, but at the same time being sucked down to where he felt his life still belonged. He had to breathe, he had to surface, he had to die. His confusion was disturbing him and he was fearful of being distracted from his mission. There was something so disarming and beautifully naive about her.

'You alright?' said Kaylah, taking his hand.

'Yes, just, just it's difficult to think. How lovely you are, how lucky I am. When I think of where I've come from, I feel transported into a different world,' he said. He took her free hand and pulled her toward him.

'I'm lucky to have you,' and then she wasn't sure how it happened but their lips touched, no more than touched, and fire flowed through them both. Kaylah now had a very clear idea what direction their relationship was taking! What he said was music in her ears.

A few minutes after seven they went out into the night, took a 144 red double decker bus from the nearby Cambridge Roundabout and twenty minutes later were walking the short distance to the fireworks with the crowds. Excitement was tangible, young children shrieked and squealed. Every now and then a bang was heard as some illicit firecracker went off. To Ali the sound was reminiscent of gunshots and weaponry, a reminder of his jihad intruding on pleasure.

In the dark, it was easy and natural to cling to one another to hold at bay the coolness of the night. Kaylah pulled out her phone, there was a flash.

'This selfie will be my new wallpaper,' she whispered.

Inwardly Ali felt as though part of his soul and hers had been taken away. She had no idea of the pain he could cause her, but this suited him fine, he was safely hidden by her and for now hidden in the night crowds.

353

'C'mon,' she said, playfully tugging him along, 'the display is just starting.'

Led by the hand, she knew he was hers. She wanted it that way, and as the opening mortars whooshed up and explosively lit up the heavens, her own heart felt lifted to a new plane. This was life, and no-one was going to stop her now.

Ali, for his part, knew he now had her tightly in his grip. For the present, in the dark, he was safe, hidden in the large crowd, Kaylah an extra layer of body armour, a distraction to anyone whose eye might look in his direction.

All the while, at the back of Ali's mind he was telling himself of the need to stay focussed. He would be no Guy Fawkes, caught out by Kaylah or anyone else. The clock was ticking and with little over a week to go, soon the world would know why he was in London.

50

It was Sunday morning. Ali woke up early. He was in Kaylah's bed. They were both naked. She was still sleeping, so he kept totally still, not daring to disturb what he saw. He looked at her smooth dark skin and thought of the soft curves of sand in the desert. He watched her gently breathing and was mesmerised, thinking of the stillness of desert dawn. At this moment, he had no wish to be anywhere else.

He gently touched her elbow and stroked his finger along her arm and across the back of her hand, stopping to look at her long finger nails. She seemed so at peace, and the evening had been bliss, even paradise. Never had he felt so content at what he'd been able to organise for himself. It was one of those rare nights he had not had a nightmare in which his dead father appeared, but he knew this fleeting moment of satisfaction had to be savoured for it was like a passing rain storm in a desert.

His sexual inexperience hadn't seem to matter. He had led her, a willing, yielding victim. She moved slightly, then stilled. He felt touched by her innocence and stained by his deadly mission. He felt the tug of her warmth and love and life, and had to reach deep down within himself to reconnect with why he was here. He began to tell himself over and over that his jihad was to inflict a deep blow on the evil government that was so hurting his people.

The pull of his people began to reassert itself, the training patterns and drills, the call to duty, to obedience, the long journey he had made, even the plight of his family back home.

He knew that time was running out. Soon they would be on to him, but Kaylah had given him shelter, another day of precious safety. He had no future other than what he had come to do. He told himself he had no choice, obedience was everything. He glanced at the red numbers on the illuminated digital clock. 07.32, it said. He glanced back at Kaylah, a knot of pain in his stomach. He stilled and steeled himself.

'Kaylah,' he whispered, 'can I ask a favour?'

'Mmm,' she said, turning sleepy eyes toward him, only the orange glow of the street light outside breaking through the ill-fitting curtain giving any light in the room.

'Thought I might take myself on a bike ride round London this morning and wondered if I can borrow the bike in your back yard? The exercise will do me good and besides I promised myself to do the sights sometime ago. I saw it yesterday. Is it yours or Clive's?' he asked.

'Clive's, but he won't mind. I think I'm having a Sunday lie-in. You'll have to watch out for Mum and Dad, they'll be up around eight and getting ready for Church,' she warned.

'Thanks. I'm off out before they start asking me questions. I'll leave those for you,' he said. He dutifully kissed her on the cheek and pulled himself up and out of bed. Kaylah snuggled down under the duvet. For some reason she dreamt of a TV advert where a man slipped outside to get his lover an early morning coffee whilst she lay in bed. She became restless as she couldn't remember the brand.

Ten minutes later, he was dressed, had quietly pulled Clive's bike from the back yard through the house and outside the front door. He quickly checked it over. It seemed fine, just the front tyre a little low, but that didn't matter. In blue jeans, grey T shirt and Clive's hoodie, he pedalled off, heading for Windmill Road, the A10 and the city. The bike had chunky mountain bike tyres and the soft suspension on the front was heavy, making it feel like some overloaded ship. But it worked, and it felt good to be in the cool November morning air. There was little traffic to worry about. He felt free and imagined Adam felt the same freedom when he rode. He wondered where Adam was now, concluding he was probably lying dead in the sand.

It took him over an hour to find his way to the Thames embankment. Once there it was really easy to navigate along the course of the grey river up to Parliament. He had to admit it, Parliament was really impressive, Big Ben's clock face, such a well known iconic landmark, indicating it wasn't yet nine o'clock. He couldn't help but notice the many policemen, some armed. There was also a small group of protesters who had gathered on the green opposite. Wouldn't happen at home, he told himself.

By Westminster tube station he found a shop, picked up a Coke, some wraps and a box of orange fruit pieces under a plastic film with a forked spoon device to spear them. Placing all in a plastic bag, he pushed his bike over to where the protesters were gathering, thinking he'd be less obvious in a crowd. Although it was still early on a Sunday morning he'd thought there would be more people about. To his mind the streets were too empty. They made him feel too conspicuous.

The people he'd joined were protesting at the lack of support for asylum-seekers and refugees. He blended in easily, couldn't be better; when he heard and then found a couple of guys from Iraq, his heart lifted. He began moving toward them, only to quickly pull himself back, remembering the solitude his mission required. Not for the first time, he felt the inner chill of being alone. Leaning on a lamp-post on the edge of the group, he ate his wraps and drank his Coke whilst observing what was going on across the way. No-one intruded on his space or tried to start a conversation.

Whilst at the firework display the previous night Kaylah had told him about the tickets Ruth had given her for next Sunday's Armistice Day commemorations. A Church House window, she had said, next to Parliament, with a good view. She really could be surprisingly useful to him, he thought. Such an unexpected opportunity had just fallen into his lap. Fate was dealing him a good hand and the thought lifted his spirits. He decided to check out where it was.

He could see Westminster Abbey from where he was standing, and once he'd finished eating, he ditched the fruit tray and the plastic bag and rode off toward the impressive stone Abbey. He soon found Church House and the street called Deans Yard. He couldn't think they were offering window viewing from the main building which he could see lay behind metal railings. It would have to be from the first-floor

357

corner windows facing toward Westminster Abbey and Parliament Square, but he couldn't be sure. This was information he had to know.

He decided to take a risk and, leaning Clive's bike against a wall, he went in the front entrance of Church House itself where there was some kind of conference going on. There was a concierge woman on the front desk. Telling himself to act confidently, he boldly walked up to her.

'Good morning, I wonder if you can help me?' he asked politely.

'We're here to help,' she replied smiling, 'are you here for the Eco-Congregations Conference?'

'Er, no. I'm coming down next week for the Armistice Commemorations, with a friend, and my friend has accessibility issues. She's got cancer of the spine. I'll be bringing her and wondered whether it would be difficult for her. Where exactly will people be viewing from? Our church was sent special tickets. That was so kind,' he said, trying to sound appreciative.

'Oh, I see. Give me a moment, my colleague will be back in two ticks, then I can show you. I'm sure it will be OK, we have a lift up to first floor. Anyway, the viewing windows are actually over above the Abbey gift shop on the first floor,' she said waving her arm over his shoulder to give direction.

'People don't realise, but the best view really is from there, where you and your friend will be watching from. You'll need to be here early because of all the security. Oh look, here she is now.' She turned to speak to a young woman whose shoes clicked noisily as she approached.

'Laura, I'm just taking this gentleman over to show him the viewing area. He's bringing a disabled friend, needs to check out access. We won't be five minutes, OK?' she said, not waiting for a reply.

She walked him round. Ali thought she was trying overly hard to be helpful, but that suited him just fine. He got chatting. 'So next Sunday, we come into the reception desk, as I did earlier?' he asked.

'Yes, then in return for your numbered ticket, we issue you with badges to show you are our guests. Then my colleague or myself, whoever's on duty, will walk you over to the viewing windows. Look, here we are. The rooms are quite small, so we're limiting numbers to just a few guests in each location. You see what I mean about the view, perfect isn't it?' she said, standing and gazing out of the window.

'We actually only have a small number of suitable windows, but the Dean thought it would be nice to make them available to parishes which have done a lot for people in poorer areas. "All the best seats go to the great and the good," he said, "so why don't we get some of the ordinary folk in." As you can see, it's a pretty good view. These rooms are just store rooms the rest of the time, so it's easy enough to make enough space. It's one window per two or three people from each church group. Now which one were you with?'

'Holy Trinity in Edmonton, north London. Think there will be five of us coming in all, us two and I don't yet know who the other three guests will be,' he said.

'This will be your window then and the room next door for the other three. We can get your friend in this way, up the lift, round this corner. Can she stand up?' she asked.

'She has a weak spine, but on pain killers, I think she can manage to stand. I can help her. She'll be fine leaning on me. A lot depends on how she feels on the day. Sometimes she can move pretty well normally, but other times she uses her wheel chair,' he lied, seeing this woman appreciating the 'carer' role he had described for himself.

'Well that's it. It was a good idea of yours to check us out a week ahead. It would have been so disappointing for your friend if she'd found she couldn't get up here. We'd better get back. My colleague's pretty busy this morning with conference guests. Do you mind?' she said.

'No, you've been most helpful.' Ali followed the uniformed concierge back toward reception, carefully noting the other rooms along the corridor and the layout of the floor.

'If you've got time on your hands before you head back, you could watch the rehearsals. They start in a few minutes.

But I'm afraid you'll have to do that from the street,' she added.

'I must just pop to the toilet,' said Ali, sliding quickly into the door marked 'Gentlemen' before his escort could say a word.

Once inside, he quickly opened the single small outside-facing window. No lock, good view, excellent, he surmised. He flushed the toilet, ran the tap and stepped back into the corridor. He'd seen all he needed to. His final plans had taken shape in his head.

'Thank you,' he said, 'I'm sorry to have delayed you. I realise you are very busy. You have been so very helpful.'

Moments later he was reunited with his bike and back on the street. So far he had found he had nothing to lose and everything to gain by being bold, so with his confidence boosted he went up to the nearest policeman.

'What's going on today? What are all these cones out for?' he asked.

The officer, already on his feet over three hours on a graveyard shift, so quiet he could count to one hundred in the time it took for Big Ben to move from one minute to the next, was only too glad to play the part of the helpful London Bobby. He loathed the negative press the Metropolitan Police had been getting. To his mind, here was another chance to earn some goodwill with the public.

Over the next few minutes, he gave Ali a most helpful description of the events planned for the following Sunday, so glad to have such an attentive, polite and interested young man to talk to. Ali of course, thanked him most appreciatively and, guided by the policeman, made his way over to Parliament Green to watch the rehearsals proceed before him.

A soldier figure appeared with a large compass which he used to spin in his hand as walked along the street. He was the first of the military men, his job to work out the paces for the marching regiments. Security men then appeared and these made Ali feel nervous. They had sniffer dogs and crowbars.

They lifted any drain cover they could find and with mirrors on sticks gazed in every recess, before glueing them down with black rubber strips. Others with clipboards looked at where the marquee was going up, trying to be sure who sat where as they faced the Abbey to see the procession march by.

To complete the roll-call of helpful people Ali met, a man in a yellow reflective jacket kindly told him precisely where the top dignitaries would be sitting. He seemed pleased to be in the know and delighted to let Ali have his exclusive insider knowledge; just an ordinary guy showing off, thought Ali.

Three kind people had told him all he needed to know. By now there were dozens of police and council officials nosing into everything. It was time to leave. Ali had seen enough, it was time to get back on his bike and to meet up with Kaylah. His double life had only a week to run, his planning session had been most encouraging. Everyone he'd met was so very helpful, Ali's mind was totally clear as to what he had to do. Now it was the small detail he'd attend to, the things that all too often tripped people up.

'Just watch what I'm going to do, Mr Guy Fawkes. Preparation you'll see is everything!' he said out loud as, with a smile on his face, he began his one hour cycle back to north London.

51

A military helicopter lifted Adam out of Erbil a couple of days later. They said these things took time to arrange. Adam didn't mind, he slept fitfully for much of the time, making up for hours lost and a crushing fatigue that had beset him. The Chinook headed south to a large military airfield, its noisy twin blades rhythmically slicing and pulsing through the air in tandem.

On arrival he was transferred to a desert camouflaged plane full of military hardware and unmarked containers. There was no less waiting around it seemed to him than in a commercial airport, but finally the flight to Berlin took off, a journey, he was told, that would take several hours.

No flight attendants or helpers were on hand when he arrived in the late afternoon. He was simply walked off the plane, limping slightly from his injured and still painful leg, supported by the same female officer who had interviewed him about Ali and looked after him in Erbil. It felt strange to be travelling with no baggage at all, as if stripped of identity.

She now accompanied him as he was shown into the spacious smart rear of a black Range Rover with dark tinted windows. Opening his door for him first, she then went round the other side and sat down beside him. Every now and then she would look at her mobile. The driver was smartly dressed with an ear piece for communication. He never once took an instruction or looked round.

In moments, the car powerfully moved away, its route avoiding the airport buildings and heading for a small barrier-guarded gate in the perimeter fence. The Range Rover hardly slowed as the barrier was raised and the car slid smoothly into the Berlin traffic flow. A little further on, he saw part of the old Berlin wall, now a museum piece and covered in graffiti and spotted signs to the Tiergarten and crowds hanging around the entrance to the zoo.

Judging by the direction of the setting sun, Adam deduced they were heading north and into Berlin's extensive outskirts. They weren't telling him where they were going, and once more he worked out the direction for himself, knowing that once already this practised skill had helped save his life. He observed the passing street names and found he was constantly reminding himself he was actually free, a truth that for some reason kept evading his conscious mind. Berlin indeed looked free, its people carefree and oblivious to the dark and dangerous world he had just left. Adam fell silent, lost in his thoughts, his companion likewise. He was the first to break the silence.

'No Border and Customs to worry about then,' he offered.

'No, we've taken care of that. Anyway, you don't have a passport, what would you do?' She smiled.

'We're nearly at the debriefing centre. Time for something to eat and drink in a couple of minutes. Debriefing shouldn't take long. We'll end up staying here overnight before getting you back to England. I'm sure it would be nicer for you to know more precisely what happens then, back in London, but, so far no-one there is saying anything to me about when you get to go home. Don't worry, I expect decisions will be taken before morning. They usually are. It might simply depend on available flights, nothing more to sort out than that,' she said, but Adam was not convinced.

They pulled up; metal gates opened and they drove noisily along a gravelled drive to a large secluded house where the driver brought the car to a halt adjacent to the front door. Without a word and with practised ease, he looked round, opened his driver's door and went to let his passengers out. Even as they moved towards the house, their driver was already taking the car round the back out of sight.

Two people, a man and a woman, not in uniform, were waiting at the door to welcome them in. Anonymously-suited civil servants, thought Adam. But they introduced themselves: Siobhan and Mark.

'Good trip I hope,' Mark enquired politely, not waiting for a reply.

As they moved into a comfortable spacious lounge, refreshments were provided by a young person much the same age as Adam himself. All began loading their plates with the slices of warm apfelstrudel und zahne and poured mugs of steaming strong coffee.

'Best to bring it straight through, no time to waste,' said Siobhan picking up for herself what remained of the plate of apfelstrudel.

Adam tried to imagine what form the questioning would take. Would they use drugs on him to stimulate memory or hypnotise him? He told himself his imagination was running away with itself, but then the whole trip was something else, nothing he might have anticipated.

As he stood up he winced slightly, his leg wound still troubling him. Having got himself moving, he followed his two new minders into a small library-come-study room. His companion on the journey excused herself, promising to catch up with him over supper. As she went out the door, Adam watched her raise her mobile to her ear and knew much more was going on behind the scenes than he was aware of. He had got used to having little say about his own destiny, but that didn't mean he liked it.

The remaining two settled him down in the best upholstered chair and invited him to tell them his story, right from the beginning. A low table supporting travel books stood between them. He hadn't expected this, neither the setting nor the line the conversation took. He thought they would go straight for the moment he was captured and want names and descriptions and vehicle numbers. But no.

'Tell us your story,' they invited, 'and take your time.'

Mark and Siobhan were a bit like a good cop, bad cop, double-act and skilfully fired open questions at him to get him to talk. He soon got into his story, how he'd left home in London on his bike for the Gap Year trip of a lifetime, riding ever further east.

They listened politely and seemed to get increasingly attentive as the narrative unfolded, leaning in toward him as he described how in a Nurnberg cafe a Bulgarian guy called, yes, Gezim, had got him to tell him his story of how he had cycled from England.

'But Gezim was part of it, I'm sure. He and a couple of Middle Eastern guys were watching me next day. Even took my photo now I think of it. That was the first time in my travels things felt, well felt not right,' said Adam.

'Gezim, can you describe him, what did he look like? The detail, think back. His clothes? Anything on his head? A beard? How long? He spoke English, but with what kind of accent? His own story, did he give you an idea of his history? From where? Sofia? Fled from Milosovic. A Muslim then? You had a head next day? Did he get you drunk or drugged? Think. Describe exactly your symptoms next morning,' they said, keeping Adam thinking and talking.

These guys didn't let up, he was taken into his memory palace, made to walk through and talk, talk, talk. At times he felt he was back there, re-living the journey again, and from time to time with an increasing sense of dread as it progressed.

Then he was back in Istanbul, the noise, the vast city, the sun and the smell of smoky charcoal, kebab street-sellers.

'When I got to Istanbul, looking back, I know they were on to me there. That's where I sent my last message home with a selfie picture outside the blue mosque. I remember now, it took ages to send. I needed a map of Eastern Turkey, so I found a map shop and it was after that I felt I was being spied on.' He fell silent as he pictured the shop scene in his mind.

'I remember wondering whether I was being paranoid. You get lots of people hassling you to visit their shop or stall, but there were these two guys, can't really remember what they looked like, except they were young and Arab-looking, they were different, they definitely had their eye on me. It was then I thought, I'm a foreign tourist in a foreign land, I'd best watch out. I took myself off, I thought I'd lost them as I cycled out of the city. I really pushed it to get away, maybe I didn't, get away that is,' continued Adam.

He went on to describe how he'd been skilfully kidnapped, after having been talked into joining a family for a party and ending up a prisoner. Then he recalled Stefan and Yusuf who'd taken him in their yellowing white van and handed him over to Ali in his Toyota Hilux. He described them both. It all came vividly back, the dusty white van and at the point of exchange how he had seen its registration.

'Their van was registered in Ankara, the registration number began TR06 and then ET, I remember that because of Extra Terrestrial and then 6898, yes 6898. I made a point of remembering it when they slipped up and I caught sight of it. Show me a map and I can probably re-live the journey they took me on.'

At this point he could tell they were impressed, or was it they were trained to make him feel he was doing really well?

There was a pause whilst more drinks were sent for. This time they found him a bottle of Suffolk Ale, so evocative, so refreshing. Adam looked up. The light in the study was soft, not like the bright light of the desert, the economy bulb diffusing a gentle light, not really bright enough to read the book titles by, but it felt cosy, safe, quiet.

A map of Eastern Turkey was spread on the coffee table, a table lamp switched on and Adam's fingers traced a route east from Istanbul. When he was sure, he showed them.

'Yes, this is the route I took and the garage was somewhere along this stretch of road,' he said.

'Bear with us a moment,' Siobhan said, halting the conversation. She flipped open her laptop, typed, and flicked round the screen. Something like Google Street Map appeared. He was immediately transported back to the road; and, as Siobhan moved the view along it, the garage appeared.

'That's it,' he said, 'the very place.' The visual image scared him, transporting him back to the very moment of his fall into captivity.

366

Then taking the laptop he followed his ride to Yusuf and Stefan's place.

'That's it, that's where I went. That's where I was kidnapped.' The detail was amazing, no ordinary Google imaging here, Adam thought.

'This is so very helpful Adam, and can you describe where you were taken in the van?' asked Mark.

'After all the cycling, I'd got quite good at judging direction and distance, so I knew they were heading east, always east and when they pulled up it must have been maybe a hundred and forty miles judging by the speed of the van, the height of the sun and the terrain. It was hell, my hands were tied and a sack was over my head, but I could see a bit through the weave of it. Then they drove on, stopping for the night. Maybe we travelled 300 miles, I guess,' Adam paused; he was uncomfortably close to the memory.

'Later next day, there was a lot of stopping and checking. They handed me over to Ali and two other guys were with him. An envelope was handed over to Stefan. My guess was they were paid off. They disappeared off and then it was a tense dark ride. If they were anxious, I was more! I guess it was as we made a border crossing things relaxed, especially so once we were in Mosul. Can your map call up Mosul? I think I can give you some idea where I was held?'

'Would it be here?' asked Siobhan turning the screen toward him. It was. Adam leaned in to examine the image more closely. He was surprised to see the courtyard and nearby mosque so sharply shown.

'How did you know?' he asked

'Your mobile signal was tracked,' Siobhan said.

Adam was weary and tired, but he asked, 'Can I ring home?'

Mark looked at Siobhan. 'One moment.' He stepped out the room, returning with another laptop open.

'FaceTime in two minutes, but first the ground rules,' he said.

Adam listened as Mark explained that there was the safety of a lot of other people to consider and, although he was going to be able to speak to his parents, both he and his parents needed to understand and agree to the news of his release not going any further for now. A private reunion for just the three of them would be arranged at a safe house in London shortly. His parents had already been told that afternoon that their son was safe and they had understood and agreed to the news embargo. Adam was asked if he also agreed, to which he nodded assent.

Mark leaned in and the laptop started ringing through.

There they were, his Mum and Dad. He didn't know what to say. He felt overcome and struck dumb. Eventually he controlled his emotions and spoke.

'Hi, I'm OK. How are you?'

Then words flowed, tears too, and for thirty minutes Adam felt huge emotional pulls and distance. Bonds of love and apron-string ties. He knew they didn't understand and never would. He knew he'd left home. Sadness and relief mixed to make confusion. It was an awkward conversation, so much they wanted to know and for him to tell, all so difficult to say, to find the words, to handle the raw emotion. Finally, Mark signed to wind up the call.

'Got to go now. See you very soon, love you both.' The screen went blue. Silence followed, the long spell no-one daring to interrupt such a significant moment. Then, emotions under control, the conversation was put behind him.

Mark and Siobhan wound up by asking about life in Mosul and his escape, but focussed most on what kind of person Ali was.

'Bit like me, but he's had a different kind of life experience. He's no freak, a normal sort of guy, speaks English well, educated at university. He'd be just another young person in a different life. He's living in a very different world to me, it makes people think differently,' said Adam, really not feeling he was explaining himself that well. Maybe, his hosts read this for things moved on.

'We've an RAF plane returning you to the UK first thing tomorrow, to Northolt. We'll get you to the airport after breakfast. When you arrive, a car will meet you and take you

368

to north London. There will be more debriefing there I'm afraid, and then, then you will see your parents. Can't say where presently, nor what time, but should be tomorrow, Monday.'

'Thanks,' was all Adam could think of to say.

'These past six weeks have been quite an ordeal for you. You've done extraordinarily well. We can offer some support, an advisor, counselling, that sort of thing, but you'll be told more about that in London. If your leg plays up, we can get the doctor in, but hopefully you'll be OK. Siobhan will show you where you're sleeping. Help yourself to anything to eat or drink in the kitchen. There's some rather good bottled German pilsner, oh and more of the Suffolk Ale. If you need anything else just give a shout, we're both somewhere in the house. There's a TV in your room, you can get the usual channels, so you can catch up on things you've missed, that should send you to sleep. I guess you'll find all that quite boring after what you've been through,' said Mark smiling.

Again Adam felt an overwhelming tiredness. He didn't need food, beer or even Eastenders, just the sleep of freedom or the freedom of sleep. Yet part of him dreaded putting his head down on a pillow for fear of re-living his torment. It was also somewhat unnerving to think his story wasn't completely over. He wasn't fully free whilst Ali was on the loose. Where now was his captor Ali? he wondered. Who was this lone wolf seeking to devour? Everyone seemed very worried at what could happen, he could sense it in their questions and in the behind the scenes communications he spotted out of the corner of his eye. Whilst Ali roamed, Adam knew he was still not free to roam himself. As he lay down in bed minutes later, his throbbing leg and unsettled frame of mind denied him the sleep he needed. He kept seeing Ali's face, tormenting him, provoking him, and telling him he was still his prisoner.

369

52

As a grey military Airbus Atlas Transport plane circled over north London's Monday morning rush hour, military personnel were being briefed and prepared for the coming weekend and last minute square-bashing and military band practices were being held ready for the following Sunday. At Edmonton Police HQ a mixed team of officers and Prevent specialists were attending a briefing ready for an afternoon house search.

Although Prevent, as part of the Home Office's Contest approach to address extremism and terrorism, had now been running many years, it was still not popular. Even regular PCs felt uncomfortable preparing a joint enterprise with Prevent's community spies, with their regional, rather than local, affiliations. Those engaged in the distinct Prevent and Pursue elements of the anti-extremism strategy often rubbed each other up the wrong way.

Too many Muslims felt alienated from the police and local PCs laid part of the blame on the big-booted, top-down, bureaucrat-led, Prevent approach. Only in Leicester, some had heard, were things being done differently, working with the grass roots, talking to people, Muslims themselves driving things along rather than being forever spied on as outsiders. Yet in spite of all the misgivings and tensions the Prevent Policy had created, those gathered had nothing else and an air of resignation rather than enthusiasm hung over the briefing. At least working together raiding a possible terrorist den was doing something, showing willing. No-one wanted a major incident to happen on their watch or in their patch.

The Inspector gave a call to order, it was time to move out. Two vehicles, two unmarked vans, four men in each, one of whom was PC Bob Steer, the local beat officer whose presence on this job, Bob himself was well aware, was a box-ticking exercise. Simply having him in the van was meant to demonstrate local working.

The fact he'd been asked to drive meant they'd get there directly and that Bob would be kept out of the way dutifully sitting, waiting, behind the wheel. There was also a specialist explosives man, and all of them were armed with Glock 17 pistols and kitted up, their Kevla body armour on. They had Tazers and pepper sprays, but they all knew that on this occasion it was a guns first mission and a couple of the guys had Heckler & Koch MP5 submachine guns, the ones that used hollow-point rounds, meaning that when fired the bullets didn't carry on killing by going through wall after wall. A camera sat awkwardly perched on two helmets. One heavy guy, Tony, always went on these house jobs with his big red key. He cradled the red door hammer in his arms like a baby. He took a personal pride on breaking through on the first blow.

Conveniently, both vans were able to pull up right out outside Flo and Bert's. It was early afternoon and quiet by Edmonton standards; being term-time on a Monday afternoon local kids were still in school for an hour or two yet. No-one wanted kids in the street when a raid took place.

The MI5 guy had said the man Ali was dangerous and from the moment they arrived, there was to be no messing, no doorbell ringing, no hanging by the gate wondering who was going in first. Radios on, Bob pulled up the van. Their Leader called them to action.

'Go, go, go,' commanded the radio and they were out of the vehicles and against the front wall of the house. Within five seconds Tony had forced the front door with one rending crack of his big red key that even Flo and Bert would have heard.

Two guys ran in to secure downstairs and the back door, to seal off any escape across rear gardens, the two drivers staying with the vehicles. The other four followed the well-oiled routine to take the front upstairs bedroom, covering for each other as they went upstairs. Door hammer Tony was in the middle of the bunch, his red key poised ready. Bomb squad were on stand by ten minutes away should they need to be called.

371

The bedroom door crashed flat to the floor from the blow given it. Tony grinned with satisfaction. The room was empty, and the searching began. Was there someone hidden, were there booby traps? The radio began to talk, the pressure began to ease, the guy downstairs called up to ask if Bob Steer could be called into the house from the van. The old couple downstairs seemed to know him and were rather shaken up.

'Would you believe it, they are asking if we wanted a cup of tea, Gov, and we've just smashed up their house,' exclaimed one of the officers sent out to fetch and relieve Bob.

Bob was called in by the officer in charge and he ended up being the lucky one who sat and drank tea whilst upstairs a fingertip search was going on. From nowhere, an overalled man in a white forensics van pulled up outside and came running upstairs. He began poking around, sticky tape here, fingerprint dusting there, putting things in bags with a pair of tweezers. He had a silver magician-like case out of which and into which items came and went. After a while, Bob, dispensing with his radio, called upstairs to the governor.

'Do you want to know what's gone on here? I think I've got the full picture,' he said, in a matter of fact voice.

The Governor came down and Bob gave him the story. Ali had indeed been living there until only two days ago, but had suddenly left and they'd been asked to take Clive instead. Neither had been any trouble, couldn't understand what all the fuss was about. They wanted to know how soon the police could make good the damage.

'Think in this case we should get straight on to it Sir, local goodwill being all important here,' suggested Bob. He was promptly told to see to it by the frustrated unit leader.

A few minutes later the vans were on their way back to HQ, nerves still high. It always took a while for the adrenaline to dissipate. Bob had been left behind, 'to make good on the collateral.' He settled back into the sofa, and called in the emergency repair contractor.

'Look, if you want to keep your contract, you'll be down here to do a top-class repair this very evening. Yes, someone will be available to sign it off,' he told the Met's preferred repair service provider. Then he called April.

'Emergency has cropped up, need you to come and sit with Flo and Bert until their house is made secure. I'll wait until you arrive. It's just the job for you.'

Whilst waiting, he took up the offer of a second cup of tea from Flo, who was describing the last time any damage like this had been done to the house.

'It was when a right wing fascist had a go when this was my Mum and Dad's house. Now who was the man, I don't remember?' Flo said, turning to Bob.

'Nick Griffin,' volunteered Bob.

'Nah,' said Bert, 'it was Adolf's Luftwaffe. Not sure we can keep having people to stay here if this is going to happen, not at our time of life.'

Sitting in her Israeli embassy car on the other side of the road, Lena had videoed and watched it all. She picked up her mobile.

'We've got a problem, the wolf has left his lair. He's still on the loose.'

She slipped the Volvo automatic into drive and quietly set off south back to the city, the West End and Kensington. Tonight would be a far less interesting part of her life, another of those cultural, wine and canapé receptions hosted by the Israeli Ambassador.

Perhaps she could persuade her boss Dan Abrahams to let her off so that she could make some further enquiries of her own. No Muslim terrorist was going to escape on her watch. With hands-free she made the call to Dan and got her wish instantly granted. She eased the Embassy's car into the line of traffic on the main A10 heading south. 'Ali Muhammed, you won't escape me so easily,' she said to herself.

53

Seeing the sights of London from the air in the grey of a late Monday afternoon in November, Adam spotted the white office lights on in the London Shard, and the London Eye winding slowly on the south bank of the Thames. The panorama below him made Adam realise just how long it had been since he cycled away from Muswell Hill five months ago. It felt so good to be back. Belonging, being rooted was not a feeling he'd registered before, but just now, seeing these familiar sights below, he understood afresh how much he belonged in London.

He wondered what he would be doing when he came down to earth. Surely he was too late for university this year. What would he do? He didn't think his folks would like him to go off on another cycle ride just yet. He chuckled to himself as he imagined what his parents' faces would look like if he ever dreamt of suggesting it.

His past life here seemed so distant and he thought of himself as if he were starting life anew. Not everyone was given a second chance, a new birth, he thought. He was a different person, and this once familiar place he now saw through different eyes.

The plane had been descending for some time and his ears played up as the air pressure built. Then they were shooting forward over the roofs of familiar yet endless suburbia. They were down, the roar of the propellers increasing as the mighty cargo plane slowed, the nose then turning toward its allocated bay, where finally the great noisy beast was silent and still.

When the stairs had been wheeled in place, the hatch door opened and Adam, along with around a dozen returning military personnel, made their way down onto the tarmac. Various vehicles were honing in to begin unloading the netted and crated military cargo. Adam observed none of the usual busyness of a commercial airport and a singular lack of people around. In the distance he spotted the mesh and barbed wire of a perimeter fence. For some reason the sight of it unsettled him.

An Asian young man, came half way up the stairs and introduced himself to Adam as Krish Patel. Hindu, Adam guessed. A young guy in a smart dark blue suit. They shook hands.

'I've been sent to fetch you and to take you to meet your parents,' he said smiling. In fact he never seemed to stop smiling. He was clutching a clear plastic folder of papers under his arm. 'Oh, and we'll need to go through one or two preliminaries en route. We can do this in the car. Just come with me. We'll be on our way in no time,' said Krish.

Adam was shepherded straight to a nearby shiny black Vauxhall, which had cruised up beside the plane unnoticed. In the military manner he was getting used to, its driver greeted him as 'Sir' and opened the rear door for him to climb in. Krish got in beside him and opened his folder. For twenty minutes Adam felt like he was back at school. All these rules, all these instructions - don't say this, don't talk to the press, don't use social media, the nation's safety was at stake, do this, do that, imperative it doesn't get out you are back, etc. etc. At the end of it all, Adam was feeling tired again.

'Is that clear? Any questions?' Krish finally said with a grin. The young man, for his part, had taken all these preliminaries in his stride. It had take a while and Adam noticed they had driven past the same streets in East Finchley twice.

'Then sign here please Adam,' Krish said, thrusting a biro into his hand. Adam did as requested, knowing the journey wouldn't end until he did anyway. Krish wasn't such a bad guy, if only he wouldn't smile so much!

Then they were in Highgate, passing the Woodman pub, swinging left off the A1 into Shepherds Hill. They were dropping down toward Crouch End, the familiar and strangely unchanged local streets Adam knew so well, when suddenly they swung left and pulled into a driveway. The front door where the car stopped could not be seen from the road. They were less than a mile from his own home. Adam hadn't really noticed the house before, then there was no reason why he should have, he told himself.

It was a typical detached brick house in well-to-do north London. A silver Renault Espace sat further round in the drive. His door was opened by the driver, Krish staying in the car, calling out final instructions.

'Just ring the bell,' he said, with a final smile.

The Vauxhall was reversing back into Shepherds Hill leaving him standing all alone as the front door opened.

'Mum, Dad,' he cried.

The three just stood there in the kind of long hug he realised he'd never be seen dead giving before he left. He belonged, he was missed, he was home. They moved without knowing into the front room and fell into easy chairs. All were on a high, so much so it was impossible to hold an ordered conversation. Hell, it was good to be back, but part of him felt a stranger in his own land. He felt older, responsible for how his parents would cope with him, and less sure of himself than he used to be, unsure whether he could hold his emotions together.

Food was brought in by another 'minder' who appeared without warning from somewhere in the back of the house. There was a large tray with plastic packs of snacks and cartons of apple and orange juice. Conversation became more strained when Adam and his Mum and Dad had to discuss the need to keep his presence low key for the next week. They had all been told it was a matter of national security, nothing more. The restriction became more bearable knowing it was temporary, and Adam was told he might be allowed out if particular requests were made and approved.

For now Adam would be staying at this 'safe' house and his parents could visit whenever they wished. With a zeal he'd not known before, they promised to get him anything he needed! Adam's Dad handed him a new phone with a pay as you go sim card.

'It's to be going on with. It's one they gave me for you,' he added when he saw Adam's quizzical look. When Adam brought it to life, the phone screen wallpaper had a message which simply said, 'Only For Calling Parents.' His Dad said they'd had to sign for it and was told it had to be returned when things returned to 'normal'.

'That's the only present we've had chance to get for you! We literally got picked up by car from home and brought here. Nothing more was said to us after we Face-timed you yesterday, right up until we were in the car. For so long we haven't known whether you were dead or alive. This is so unreal,' said his Father.

'I have got a present for you, Dad. You'll like this!' Adam said, with a sense of pride, reaching inside his jacket pocket. 'Here's 200 Euros which they never managed to take from me and which I never had chance to spend!'

Sue's mobile went off. She could see it was Ruth calling and knew she had to take it. They all looked at her. She said, 'Ruth,' and took a deep breath to still her excitement.

'Hi Ruth, how are you doing?' said Sue.

'How are you? Don't suppose there's any news yet or you'd have let me know. Anyway, thought you might like to have an outing. You could take my Phil along with you. I've got three grandstand tickets for next Sunday's Armistice commemorations outside Parliament. A good show has been promised, the PM, the military, an impressive parade, you'll have heard about it I'm sure. It's just that a few parishes have been sent five tickets each to view from Church House windows. What do you think?' Ruth asked.

Sue had to think fast. She didn't know what to say. It was kind of Ruth to think of them, but life had suddenly been thrown into chaos.

'I'm not trying to press you to take them. Look, I'll leave the tickets with Phil. Just give him a call when you've made up your mind. Got to go, thinking of you, bye.' And with that she had gone.

'Just your Aunt Ruth asking if your Dad and I wanted tickets to view the special Armistice Day event outside Parliament on Sunday. It's not important, but the PM's making a big thing of it. Oh, I don't know. I can't make decisions now,' explained Sue, shaking her head.

'I really want to go. Now Adam's back, it would be a kind of way for us to pay our respects to the military who helped get him home, don't you think?' Jim broke in.

'I'm going to ask my minders if that's an outing I can join you on. You never know, they might even provide us with one of their shiny cars to take us in! I'm sure we can persuade Uncle Phil to let me have his ticket,' suggested Adam.

The reunion conversation lurched from euphoric hysteria to moments of silent reflection and back again. There was no coherence or order to it. One minute Adam described life in Mosul, another his Mum was saying how she hadn't been able to feel alive for weeks. His Dad went on about the jobs he'd not done. Then Adam was completely thrown by his Dad's next remark.

'And your bike is still in the hallway, since forensics let us have it back,' he said.

'You what! My bike's here?' gasped Adam.

'Yes, it was left in our front garden weeks ago. When Mum came home from school one day, there it was. Police say it was because they wanted us to think you were back. At first we thought you must be, but couldn't quite see it. You would never have not got in touch. But then the story changed. The police said forensics had found Iraqi sand on it. Someone had brought it back and wanted us to think you were back, in order to mask their own presence. That's why they think something's going to happen, a terrorist attack,' his Dad said.

A chill went through Adam. IS know where his family live. They've been to his home. Ali has got here, he knew where he was and how to get to him. Any feeling he had of being safe again was running through his fingers as sand in the desert. His own home, known to Ali and IS, they weren't safe, the nightmare wasn't over. For some reason his body began to shake and tremble. His parents called for help. They didn't know what was happening to Adam and they were frightened.

Adam might be home, but he'd brought his nightmares with him. It took the rest of the afternoon for him to begin to calm down, his fears seizing him periodically. There seemed little, if anything, anyone could do to ease them. Adam had earlier thought about his future, maybe at university, but now he couldn't even think straight about the present. What tipped him over the edge was knowing Ali to be so close.

54

Flo and Bert stayed up late after the doors were fixed and April had gone. After what had happened they decided they were going to see Ruth first thing. Both of them were going to wander down to the Drop In after breakfast and tell her that they couldn't have people staying any more. At their age the unexpected excitement of the previous night was all too much. Tuesday mornings were when Ruth was certain to be there, so wrapping up well and clinging on to each other for mutual support they rocked and shuffled their way down to the hall, arriving as the sweet smell of coffee enticed them in through the front door.

'Busy as ever,' said Bert, nodding in the direction of the latest arrivals spilling out onto the pavement outside. Flo acknowledged she'd never seen it so busy as in recent weeks.

Spotting them arrive, Olive called Ruth over to Flo and Bert. Ruth noticed they looked crestfallen and frail. She knew immediately they were bringing their troubles, her minister's instinct was invariably correct on these things.

'How are you two sweeties?' she asked, 'so nice to see you both.'

They told her about the police raid the previous night, before hastily apologising.

'No lasting damage was done. Bob and April have been wonderful, made sure everything was left almost as good as new. But me and Bert, we can't do it any more. It's become a worry having people in the house. We're not as young as we were. You do understand don't you?' implored Flo, feeling she was letting Ruth down.

'Of course I do, I'll make sure we find somewhere else for Ali to stay. No problem,' said Ruth, already trying to think ahead.

'Ali, you say? No, he was the last one. We've had Clive since the beginning of the weekend. You should know Clive, he's Kaylah's brother. He's a dear. We never have any problem with any of the people you send. But you do understand, we can't do this any more, not after last night. Me and Bert, well we couldn't sleep, them breaking into our house,' said Flo.

'Ali's gone? Clive's there? I must have missed something. Don't worry I'll get on to it today. We'll tell whoever it is you've had staying, we will find them somewhere else. Can you cope if you give me a few days to sort things? It's just we've so many people to find somewhere for. Apart from putting your guy on the street, I can't just find somewhere else to take him today. But I promise I will find somewhere, and I promise we won't be sending you anyone else, for now at least. I really do understand, I'm just so sorry to hear that you've had so much trouble. What do you think it was all about?' asked Ruth.

'Well, we asked Bob and April that very question,' Flo said. 'Bob said they thought Ali would be there and just wanted to talk to him, ask him some questions. So I said, "was it because he was a Muslim?" And Bob said, "maybe." He didn't rightly know. So I said, "Why the bloody hell," excuse my french, "didn't they ring the front door bell like anyone else?"'

At that moment April Cooper came in through the door, looking as smart as ever in her black and white uniform and seeing Ruth, Bert and Flo together, she knew immediately what conversation would have been taking place. April walked straight over.

'How are you two today after all the unwelcome visitors last night?' she asked them.

'We're OK thanks,' said Bert, 'but like Flo was saying, we don't think we can cope with having people to stay any more.'

'That's a shame. I wouldn't for a moment think anything like what happened last night would ever happen again. A one-off. It was just your bad luck to have someone staying who the police wanted to talk to,' said April.

'But April dear, you're too young to understand. It's not them, it's us. We can't do it, we can't do it any more,' said Flo, taking April's arm.

Ruth stepped in; attention was being drawn to them and some of the Drop In visitors were looking at them warily. Abu had moved in close and Ruth decisively ended the conversation.

'Don't you worry, we'll have your guest moved on as soon as possible and thank you both, so very, very much for all your kind hospitality. It's people like you that reassure me that there is goodness, love and kindness to be had in the world.' Taking them by the arm she led them to the door and out on to the street, finally steering them with a gentle nudge back in the direction of home.

On re-entering the hall Ruth was confused. She touched April's arm to ask the one question that was troubling her.

'Was it Ali the police raid was about?' she asked quietly.

'Yes, but don't ask me why, I don't get told these things,' replied April.

'But Flo said, Clive Kone was staying there, not Ali. Doesn't make sense. I didn't arrange that,' said Ruth, 'I put Ali there.'

'That's what we heard too. Apparently Ali left last Friday and Clive arrived saying he needed somewhere and Flo and Bert simply agreed,' said April.

Ruth left it there, so much to do, more pressing matters had to take precedent, no time now for little mysteries. She'd left Aneni with the kids yet again and so needed to press on so she could get back to them herself. They'll think Aneni's their Mum, she thought ruefully. She watched April as she professionally wandered round the Drop In, mingling with today's crowd, a word hear, a listen there, before slipping out of the door to take a police radio call. Then she'd disappeared to attend to other matters, something more urgent, she guessed.

No sooner had she gone, than Kaylah wandered in with Ali in tow. They had a serious look on their faces. Ruth was still wondering what to do, to call back April, to quiz Ali about his room, to ask Kaylah how it was that Clive was at Flo and Bert's, but Kaylah got in first. She came directly across to Ruth.

'We've got a problem. You know Ali has escaped from Iraq. Well, he's had to move out of Flo and Bert's because people are spying on him and he's terrified they are after him. On Friday, your day off, he came to me to ask for help. He couldn't go back there, they'd get him you see. So he asked me for help. I didn't know what to do, but my brother Clive, you know Clive of course, well he and my Dad don't exactly see eye to eye and had had a bit of a falling out and Clive came up with this idea that Ali have his room and Clive move out and into his. A swap seemed to suit them both. Well, I went and spoke to Flo and she was OK about it. This is the first chance I've had to tell you. I hope I've done right,' Kaylah said, her speech getting faster and faster. She hadn't quite finished.

'And, you know you spoke to me about boundaries and friends, well it's all got rather out of hand and I thought we'd better both come and see you to help us sort it.'

Ruth was stunned. 'Help you sort it,' she repeated, feeling this was one too many a difficulty to manage in one morning, looking at her watch again and thinking anxiously of her children.

'Yes, I'm going to ask you a big favour. It helps me keep boundaries for my placement and helps the Drop In team help Ali with somewhere to stay, that is until the weekend, that's when Ali says someone he knows has a room he can use from Monday,' said Kaylah. Then barely pausing for breath, she came to the point.

'You know the balcony at the back of church, the one no-one ever uses or goes into except to store stuff, can Ali stay there until Sunday? He won't be any problem. He won't be around in the day time. It's just that he doesn't feel safe any more,' said Kaylah appealingly.

'But the police want to talk to him, Kaylah,' said Ruth.

'Oh,' said a surprised Kaylah, 'what about?'

383

'Don't know exactly, but they raided Flo's house to find him last night,' said Ruth looking across at Ali.

'Do you think I ought to take myself down to the police station then Miss Ruth?' asked Ali, trying to appear helpful, offering them a way forward.

Ruth thought that to be a good solution. She was getting increasingly impatient to get this all sorted out so she could get back to the vicarage and get the children their lunch. Aneni had been so unstable recently, she really mustn't leave the kids any longer, she told herself.

Ali's offer to report to the police was a godsend to which she quickly agreed. She felt Kaylah needed reassurance and so praised her for acting so professionally in what she had done and in bringing Ali into the Drop In to sort it all out this morning. The situation seemed to be resolving itself, but she suddenly had one final thought.

'What are we going to do with Clive?' she asked.

'Leave that to me. It's about time I spoke to my parents. My Dad will have cooled off by now, he'll be feeling sorry for himself and I'll see that Clive gets back home, don't you worry. I'll see to it, it'll get sorted,' said Kaylah firmly.

With that she and Ali moved off to help Olive with lunch refreshments for the waiting queue. Ruth, in a whirl of confusion, swept out of the door, almost running to the vicarage next door to get back to her children.

Ali and Kaylah didn't stay long. Kaylah could tell Ali was anxious, always looking over his shoulder. It was making being there uncomfortable for her too.

'Do you want to go, now?' she asked sensing his unrest.

In seconds, or so it seemed, they were out of the door leaving Olive serving solo. Ali just couldn't wait to be outside and in the street. The news of a police raid to find him, he knew had changed his situation. He was being hunted, they were so near to getting him, had just missed him; and he had no intention of being caught unprepared.

They walked hurriedly away from the Drop In before Ali's pace slowed. Kaylah sensed an atmosphere. Ali wasn't saying anything, Ali wasn't explaining anything and she

384

needed him to talk. This wasn't how it should be going, she thought. Anyway, who was this friend she knew nothing about who was going to put him up after the weekend?

'We'll need to pick up a church key for you later,' she said.

'Yep,' Ali replied, his eyes furtively looking up and down the street.

'You look like a hunted animal, what's up?' she asked.

'Nothing. They're out to get me, that's all. I need your help, I'm done for if I'm not really careful now,' he replied.

Kaylah explained this to herself as his very understandable paranoia and let it go at that. She tried another approach, picking up his hand in hers. At first he was unresponsive and she was fearful for him. Then he squeezed her hand.

'Let's go to MacDonald's before you go into college. We had such a good time there last Friday. I'll wait there for you until you come out after lectures and we can come back together,' he offered.

She agreed adding, 'but when are you going to the police, they wanted to see you?'

Ali promised her he would call and see them after they got back, saying it was best if he did it on his own. They walked up to Southgate, the stroll taking them an hour and they flopped into the chairs where they had sat so happily the previous Friday.

Ali was looking more relaxed by the time they'd had a burger and drinks. Thinking Ali was having a difficult day she leant over and kissed him on the lips before dashing over the road to College.

'See you later,' she shouted from the door over the noise of the Southgate traffic outside.

Things were back under control again, she thought. Ali's just been through a lot, 'He needs me, he's like my brother Clive, a lost soul, just needs a bit of loving, just like me,' she whispered to herself.

It was dark when they got back to Kaylah's house at the end of the afternoon. Ali had been glad to spend his time

385

hanging around in Southgate, one young person amongst crowds of others in MacDonald's. He felt more comfortable inhabiting the shadowlands, more in control again of his own destiny. He'd had some thinking time.

Once back at Cheddington Road, Kaylah found her Dad in the back room and he was, just as she'd told Ruth, all ready to welcome Clive back. Anyway Clive will have learned his lesson by now, Sam Kone reasoned. What's more, he told Kaylah, it didn't reflect well on a church family to have these things happen. Normal service needed to be resumed. So he agreed to Clive's immediate return. Ali went up to Clive's room, pushed his few things into his sports bag and swung his rucksack onto his shoulders, before returning downstairs ready to leave.

'Let's go and get that key,' Ali said to Kaylah, 'and thanks Mr Kone, for putting me up.' His thanks was acknowledged with body language which said, it was nothing; and with that, they were out of the door as Kaylah busily chatted on her mobile to Clive.

'You're back home in your own room again! No, you're not sharing it with Ali. It's yours. Oh that, I'll explain the police raid later,' she told him.

After Kaylah and Ali had collected a church key from Ruth at the vicarage, Kaylah needed to get back home and Ali made his way alone into the church and up to the interior balcony. I wasn't hard to find.

Despite his offer and what he had told Kaylah, he had absolutely no intention of calling in on the police. He knew he had just five days to go: and until then, his priority was to remain undetected. Kaylah had proved useful again, so very useful. He was still one step ahead of those hunting him.

It was dark, but he didn't dare use the church lights, there being just enough light from the church's outside floodlights coming in through the window for him not to need them once his eyes had adjusted to the gloom. He gently lowered his rucksack to the dusty floor beside his bag of clothes.

It was time to check its contents. He opened the security ties, and to his delight pulled out his own AK47 wrapped in its familiar sheet. He kissed it.

'How I love you,' he told his old friend, hugging it to him. 'We're going to have some more adventures together. Now let's see what other little presents we've got from our friends in Iraq.'

His hands pulled out package after package which he laid out in neat rows on the wooden floor, but he couldn't hide his disappointment that all the high explosives, all the detonation devices he'd trained to use, weren't there. Just ammunition for his AK and a handful of fragmentation grenades. Is this a refection of the pressure on IS these days, he wondered. It just gets harder.

Still, he reckoned he could do quite a lot of damage with these little beauties. His confidence lifted. Tomorrow was Wednesday. He had some more preparation in mind. No-one would find him. He told himself again, he was going to be no Guy Fawkes, getting caught at the eleventh hour was not part of the plan.

He decided to sleep cradling his AK. At first it made him feel safe, having the ability to defend himself, but then its physical presence kept giving him disturbing images of how it was used to kill his father. As he drifted in and out of sleep, he imagined the gun with a mind of its own, going off in his arms and the bullets ripping into him and all the while, his father looking on, laughing.

55

Ali slept fitfully on the wooden floor of the church gallery, but it felt quiet and safe in the building. The noise of traffic going by outside, especially the roar of London buses taking early commuters, every sound outside, carried through the single-glazed leaded lights. What with that and his nightmares, it was not a comfortable night.

He got up, washed downstairs and climbed back up the stone steps into his new bedroom. It was spartan, boxes of unused service books in decaying brown cardboard boxes, a Christmas crib and figures ready to be brought down into the church later in the year, gifts of all kinds for the next jumble or car boot sale. Decay and dust. Looking around him, he knew he wouldn't find it hard to hide his stuff before going out for the day.

He picked up a box here, and moved a roll of old red carpet there, looking for a suitable hiding place. The carpet roll against the far wall, untouched for decades judging by the layers of grime, offered a suitable place to leave his rucksack and sports bag well out of sight.

Once all trace of his presence was removed, his eyes scanned round for one last check. He could afford no last-minute mistakes now he told himself. Not knowing what time Ruth came across to lead her Morning Prayers, he didn't want to hang around and face more questions. Discovery was a real fear since the raid on Flo and Bert's. Even now they might be asking Ruth or Kaylah more questions. Best to lie low and avoid unnecessary contact. It was Wednesday, he told himself, just four days to go.

The morning was cool as he stepped out through the large oak doors into the quiet street, pausing briefly to gently close and lock them behind him before moving away swiftly in the direction of the Cambridge Road. He reasoned his best bet was to mix with crowds today and stay away from the Drop In.

There was some planning and some shopping he still had to do. He knew Kaylah had a full day at College which gave him a chance to get on with things. They'd exchanged mobile numbers to stay in touch, but he decided to keep his phone switched off until later in the day. It was one less thing to think about.

A red double-decker slid to a halt and Ali leapt on, making his way upstairs. It was crowded. He was just another face in the crowd. Looking around it was as if all London's faces were represented in the bus, a diverse mix of people as passengers squeezed in together. They hid him perfectly.

He'd heard about Wood Green Shopping City and he thought he might get what he needed there. It wasn't far, and alighting by the Tube Station where he and Kaylah had begun their walk to the 'Ally Pally' fireworks the previous Friday, this time he turned left instead and headed downhill with almost everyone else in the direction of the shops.

Some people were going to work, he could tell by their head-down focussed gazes, others who were more fraught, going to drop off children. There weren't any older people, too early for them to use their free bus passes, he told himself.

After half an hour searching, he eventually found an outside market stall in the High Road that had just what he wanted. The stall holder was still setting up. Fluttering in the morning breeze were small red, white and blue Union Jacks, alongside a colourful assortment of football banners and football scarves, mainly Arsenal and Spurs. He asked the surprised stall holder for fifty flags.

'Gor blimey, Sir, forgive me for saying so, but never took you for being so patriotic! Getting them for the children?' he asked. Ali nodded obligingly and accepted the offer of having them wrapped up and then put in a large plastic bag.

'Just the thing I need,' he said cheerfully, placing in the palm of the beaming stall holder fifty pounds in five ten pound notes.

'That's made my day already, God bless you Sir!' he said, as he pushed the notes into his market-trader purse.

389

Clutching his bag of flags, Ali moved down the High Road and saw the familiar sign of a MacDonald's. He needed something to eat and drink. It was already busy, people grabbing breakfasts, some taking them with them, most customers too busy to stop and eat. He saw there were children's pens and colouring sheets, so he helped himself to some as he picked up his Coke and pancakes breakfast.

Sitting himself down, as ever placing himself in a corner so he could watch what was going on, he began to draw on the blank back of the children's colouring sheet his memory of the rehearsal site outside Parliament he had visited the previous Sunday. He jotted down times and carefully estimated distances. He used the Wi-Fi to call up Google Street View so he could once again picture and virtually walk through the area outside Westminster Abbey and the parliament buildings. He then jotted down times for when he needed to leave Edmonton early on Sunday morning to be sure to get into place in time.

By now his chicken was cold but he ate it anyway. As he looked up, he was shocked to see there were two policemen in front of him and his heart missed a beat. He was in a corner, no escape possible.

'Is that your bag, Sir,' they asked.

Ali nodded, after discreetly turning over the children's drawing sheet.

'Oh, that's fine,' the officer said, noticing the flags protruding from Ali's bag and reaching to touch them.

'We don't often find such patriotism round here. Keep it close to you, you can never be too careful. Thank you Sir and have a nice day,' the same officer said, entirely satisfied Ali was no threat to anyone.

The officers continued to move round the tables, speaking to customers and chatting with them. A black guy on the next table whispered across to Ali.

'They don't normally act like this, must be worried about something. Good job I left my tool at home!' he confided.

Ali smiled politely back, before resuming his calculations. He needed to know how to get the best angles and the most effective trajectory. At the end of an hour he sat back.

'It's do-able,' he said out loud.

Having nowhere else to go, he ordered himself another Coke. Then the thought returned to him, that his chances of surviving this were negligible. He thought of himself as a condemned man who had been told he has just four days until his execution and for a moment found himself shaking uncontrollably. An image of his father flashed before his mind. Maybe soon he would be with him amongst the legion of the dead. After many weeks outside the violence of the Caliphate he saw again in his mind's eye a future world of violence and death.

With just four days of life ahead, he began to think how he might make the most of the time. In his inside pocket he still had almost all the two thousand pounds in sterling his CO had given him before leaving. I'm a condemned man with four days to live, why not live a bit, he thought. He felt his senses to be alert, mind sharp and resolved to enjoy the days as best he could. Then he had an idea. There was only really one person he could bring into his plans and he definitely didn't want to spend his time on his own. Somehow he needed her to help him keep beneath the security service's radar.

Leaving MacDonald's he searched until he found a restaurant serving Middle Eastern cuisine. Right in the middle of Wood Green was a Turkish restaurant, Gokuzu & Kervan. He noted their telephone number, phoned and booked a table for two at eight that evening. Perfect! Kaylah would love it. He needed her. She calmed him, took his mind off things, stopped him being so lonely and would help him pass the remaining hours left in safety. He sent her a message inviting her to a meal out. A reply came straight back. She was so looking forward to it!

Clutching his plastic bag of flags, Ali decided to wander through the shopping city until it was time to head back to Edmonton. Every minute undiscovered gave him encouragement. Then he sent Kaylah another text telling her of a change of plan. She was to meet him at the Wood Green

Tube station at seven. The new arrangement meant he could keep out of Edmonton that little while longer. She, of course, was delighted and excited. A night out, planned by Ali, what more could a girl want?

56

Clive was glad to be back home. Somehow it had worked out that he could be back with his head still held high. Dad had seemed easier, OK about his return. Anyway, he missed Mum's Jerk Chicken and rice, his own bed, his music, the comforts of his familiar room. Looking round it again he had no complaints. Ali had left it as it was.

Cool guy that Ali, and going out with his big Sis. Hmm, not sure he'd make it to be a brother-in-law though, he mused. Dad would go off on one if Kaylah got too serious about a Muslim. Christians and Muslims should stick to their own. He'd heard that any girl who gets hitched to a Muslim guy has to renounce everything, become a Muslim whether she wanted to or not. Kaylah would never go that far. She's just having fun, don't blame her really. All in all, he felt quite chilled about Kaylah and Ali.

Being back home still didn't made it any easier knowing what he was going to do that day. It stretched out before him as a white void, empty of meaning, empty of anything and everything. He didn't know whether life amounted to much more than a can of beans. Thursdays were usually nothing special, one more day hanging around, mainly in his room listening to music. So when Winston unexpectedly called him, the sun shone. Winston was upbeat, said he'd got a new motor from Dillon and would pick him up around three.

'Cool, that's fine, good by me,' said Clive.

Sure enough, Winston turned up, this time in a silver Alfa Romeo 1.4 Guiletta.

'You go for smart cars then?' said Clive, running his hand along the roof before getting in.

'Just feel the quality and get in,' returned Winston grinning.

'Dillon wants us over his place. Apparently Sunday's looking good, Dillon's all excited, can't stand still, can't stop taking pills, can't see any problems. Me, I don't like it. Spent my life staying one step ahead of trouble, like a surfer on the front edge of a big wave that could catch and swallow me whole if I make the slightest slip.'

'It's not my idea of fun to be swept along by Dillon and Will, but to be honest Winston, I don't rightly care. I've had a few nights chucked out of home, a few nights to think. My Dad's written me off, and he's right. Since dropping out of school I've done fuck all. What's more, I don't give a damn. There's nothin' I want to do. So hell, why not? Bring it on. Let's live a bit I say,' Clive said.

'Never heard you talk like that before brother, you scare me. We knows that us street kids have to get by, live from day to day, but we do, we do. Will said this was the one job to make us all rich, then that's it. Takes the pressure off for a bit, that's what we all need, the pressure off. Will's just pissed off with that Abu guy. He just won't lie down. He's busy taking back territory, fishing in our sea, doing new business right under his nose. Will is livid, man, he's just going to finish Abu, once and for all, but that's his business. I'm not getting into any of that violence stuff. Will's clever, getting Dillon and us to do his dirty work whilst he's above it all. After Sunday I'm out of it, staying low.' said Winston.

'I'm right with you on that,' said Clive.

They were in Muswell Hill in minutes, Winston struggling today for a parking spot, creeping along like some law-abiding citizen - all out of character.

'You become all legal with your parking now, the new Winston? I've never seen you looking round for legal parking places before, you scare me,' Clive mimicking and mocking his friend.

Winston grinned, that was more like the old Clive. Moments later they'd parked up and were in Dillon's flat.

Dillon was high, the room reeked of weed.

'Mind if I open a window mate,' asked Winston.

Dillon, waving his hand like royalty, simply said, 'Fine. Open it. Make yourselves at home. Excuse my bad manners. You boys want a drink, or perhaps a little smoke, you name it, or what about something stronger on me, got some Banging

Mandy, just in. Try one, I think they're greaaaat!' he roared, completely oblivious of everyone else in the room.

The small room felt overcrowded. Will was there, so was Woody still nursing his cut face, a patchwork of white bandage.

Clive didn't like this. He'd never really felt comfortable with drugs, never really done more than smoke a spliff at a party and not liked it. He never worked out whether it was the rum or the spliff, one or other or both had made him feel sick. 'Not for me Dillon,' he replied, flopping onto the leather sofa.

Dillon then went all serious, made sure everyone was sitting down and focussed. He stood there like a stork, all out of balance, leaning on one leg, yet upright. His singed hair and burnt face made him look a twisted grotesque. He and Woody gave the place the feeling of some oddball hospital corridor.

'Now listen here you mother-fuckers. I ain't ballseying around any more. Will says we definitely have a job to do Sunday morning. His Sis says it's a dead cert, isn't that right Will? She's there ready for the counting, but she won't have to count it this Sunday will she boys,' he chirped.

There were laughs all round.

'We count it for her! As sure as eggs is eggs, there will be a six figure bag of dosh on her desk which she will just drop out of her office window to us. She wants ten percent. She's not greedy. I'd be happy to give her more, being a generous big-hearted guy,' Dillon said.

He laughed again.

'But she can have her ten percent if she's happy with ten percent. The rest of you will also get ten percent, that's ten grand each at least.'

'But that means someone gets more, a full fifty percent,' said Clive, daring to speak up.

'Now who's the bright one,' Will replied, joining the conversation, swinging round to face Clive.

'So glad you're with us and not against us. Yes, I sure do get fifty percent, but it's money to run things round here. It's not for me. We have a contract to pay for, a business to expand, competitors to deal with. You're right, a full fifty percent to ensure a happy future. Now Dillon, mind if I take things from here,' Will instructed, indicating Dillon was to back off. Dillon steadied himself, his hand reaching and then resting on the wall, giving his attention to puffing on what remained of his spliff.

'Right, Sunday, we leave here at ten thirty sharp. That means bloody set your alarms you afternoon risers. Not there, no money, final. Clear?' said Will, staring at each in turn.

Nods all round.

'Winston, you pick up Clive our runner and bag man. Dillon, I want you to use this untraceable phone, no other, to talk to my sister when the time comes for her to do the bag drop. You're to be here and ready to leave at ten on Sunday after checking my sister has gone to work. Right, Hoodie, you are to be here for ten as well. We need you to stand on the corner of Seven Sisters Road. You are to use your sharp eyes and if there's a cop anywhere, if there's even one old lady that don't look right, you're to call me. In fact I want you to be talking to me every two minutes whilst we're down there. Dillon, you'll be in the back of the car making sure you idiots don't fuck up,' he said waving a hand airily in he direction of Clive, Woody and Winston.

'What you lot staring at? You got any questions?' Will added finally.

Winston asked Will where he wanted him to drive to after they'd got the money, which gained a curt reply.

'Back here, to Dillon's you idiot, to count the money. But you drive carefully and slowly. You park down the road, you walk the last bit to the flat, in ones and twos. You should be able to manage that,' said Will smiling.

Dillon laughed at Will's humour, as he eyed his now smoked-out spliff, his hand reaching down into his tight trouser pocket to find another.

'You get the money straight when it's counted; then you get the hell away from here, and anybody grassing gets burned. Any grasses get burned,' Will repeated, glaring round at each of them in turn, his eyes staring wildly. 'I will join you

396

back here after, just to see you count properly.' He looked across at Dillon who seemed to be losing it.

'Now where's my bloody lighter?' Dillon said as he began throwing cushions off the settee before spying a disposable red lighter on the windowsill.

Winston pulled Clive over toward the door. They slid out knowing the meeting was over.

'Let's go down to Cliff's Coffee in Bruce Grove, chew this one over,' said Winston.

'It's a mad house,' he added once they were out of earshot.

Back in the Alfa Romeo they moved off to the roundabout, down Colney Hatch Lane, right down Alexandra Park Road and into Tottenham's Bruce Grove. They hardly said a word.

'Will made everything sound too good to be true,' ventured Clive.

'Then we've got to talk this through. We're not being set up to fail just so Will gets off,' a serious-faced Winston replied.

Pulling into Bruce Grove and parking in the usual spot round the back, they were soon embraced by the cosy fog of Cliff's cafe. Time for a council of war, but both of them knew deep down there would be no backing out. Will had them where he wanted them.

Winston would be driving, Clive collecting the bag of money, Woody acting as look-out. Dillon would be the communications man with the mobile to step in if anyone fouled up. Any mistakes and it would be Dillon who'd be the first to call Will.

Clive knew that a day which had begun well with relations at home improved, had just turned sour. And he wasn't alone, he noted: Winston's usual cheerful disposition had totally deserted him. Both knew they had no way out without serious loss of face or worse, and both wanted to get clear of Will and Dillon who sooner or later would finish them all.

57

Ali and Kaylah had had a great night out in Wood Green, Ali turning the occasion into a romantic dinner with food that he had long missed enjoying. He'd bought Kaylah flowers, handing them to her in a little drama of his own making. Kaylah had loved the entire experience, and the exotically different Turkish and Middle Eastern cuisine. She felt it had been an illuminating window on Ali's world. He'd talked about far away places, hot sunshine, moonlit desert nights and stories of his childhood. He'd had her eating out of his hand. She'd loved it.

By the time they'd got back to Edmonton by mini cab, though, it was very late. Ali shared an idea he had been thinking through earlier in the day whilst at MacDonald's. Standing in the dark of Silver Street, the church flood lighting having by then switched off for the night, he hugged Kaylah and they talked holding hands on the street corner. His dusty church balcony was no place to take a girl back, he said, and Kaylah replied it wouldn't work out to go back to hers with everyone in the house.

So Ali, knowing this and having tested Kaylah, gently suggested something.

'If you are up for it, I'd like to take you to London for the weekend, a stay-over treat for the two of us. We've already got tickets for a special outing on Sunday. If we stayed Friday night somewhere nice, on Saturday you could show me the sights. We could explore London together, perhaps go on the Eye. I'd so like to know London better - would you do that for me, be my guide?' he asked her imploringly.

Kaylah's eyes lit up as she gazed at him.

'Do you mean it? But how can we afford it?' she said.

'Leave it to me. I've got some money I brought over with me. It's on me. I'd really like to, but only if you would?' he said.

398

'Oh yes, of course. I've no lectures Friday afternoon so we can leave at lunchtime. Catch the tube into town from Southgate. Where shall we stay?' Kaylah asked.

They used Kaylah's phone and together found a place near Kings Cross. It sounded fine, the Tavistock, in Tavistock Square. From there they'd be able to walk into London. Ali asked her to make the reservation on her card.

Ali knew that this hotel booking, barring fate, alleviated the risk of a last-minute chance discovery; he could keep himself in the shadows, out of sight of searching police and security personnel. Kaylah had been such a piece of good fortune, and he really liked her, which made him feel uncomfortably guilty more and more of the time.

No room for foolish sentiment he kept telling himself. She is not one of us. His sister Fatima would hate him if she knew, but then he always had to carry the hard things. He had to do what was required. Duty and obedience or failure and dishonour, he told himself. He steeled himself to manage his double life. Kaylah was only part of this in so far as she helped him achieve his mission, he tried to tell himself again. Above all else, he needed her to get him where he needed to be on Sunday morning.

Kaylah had noticed Ali's tendency to fall into deep silence and it bothered her. She'd challenged him on it more than once, but always he came up with some reassuring words. Instinctively, she knew he was troubled and put it down to his unspeakable past, telling herself this made her want to care for him all the more. After all, she reasoned, how could she begin to imagine what he'd been through.

She wondered if the weekend was wise; it seemed so extravagant, and where would it leave Ali, penniless? He didn't have work. All this generosity must be a sign of his deep affection for her and how cruel to reject it, she reasoned. It seemed churlish to try and argue, and anyway, he wouldn't hear of it. Then the deed was done, all booked on her credit card., Ali handed her a roll of notes to reimburse the cost incurred on her card.

'That'll cover it, take it,' he said forcing it into her hand.

'You're full of surprises,' she laughed as she slipped the notes into her purse.

'Look it's no good us standing all night on this draughty street corner, not that it's very comfortable inside either. It's time to say good night and sleep well!' he said.

He kissed her full on the lips and she responded pressing close. Then she was gone, walking up the road the few hundreds yards home, melting into the night, her fading silhouette captured by street lights.

Ali turned and unlocked the heavy church door to let himself in. It was cold inside as well as outside. He made his way in by touch, as much as by sight, up to the gallery. He didn't want to put on any lights to give his presence there away.

He almost jumped out of his skin when his phone loudly rang in the echoing vast interior of the church. At first he thought it must be Kaylah, but it was a call from Salim Ismat, his CO in Mosul. Suddenly language in his home dialect filled the air. Sound carried with alarming clarity in this empty space. There was urgency in Salim's voice.

'You copy me,' he said, 'you must succeed, for the sake of us all. You must cut off his head, you must remove the leadership of Parliament, our cause is under great pressure and we are relying on you to do your duty. Your family need you to succeed. For you there is greater reward than for us all, for in your jihad there is victory, your sacrifice will be richly rewarded. Now tell me, is there any problem?' asked an unusually on edge Salim Ismat.

'No, no, things are good. I have scouted the scene, I have measured it out, got my stuff, not all I wanted, but it will do. I've drawn up my plans and have a way to deliver the success we long for. But, but I think people are on to me. The house where I was staying here was raided by the police, so I've taken steps, moved out. I'm lying low. Enshallah, things are secure and on track. Salim, will you do something for me? Send a message to my family. Tell them they can hold up their heads with pride. Their Ali did his duty. Tell them please,' said Ali, thinking such a request would be to Salim's liking.

400

'Your name will be forever honoured. I will personally go and see them on Sunday. Goodbye. Allah Akbar my friend,' he replied before the phone went dead.

Startled by the unexpected call, Ali went through his few belongings one by one before settling himself down on the wooden floor for the night. Although he knew exactly what was there, to do so made him feel in control. His one fear was that a net would close around him before he could get into place in London on Sunday morning. Kaylah had said he was paranoid, but he wasn't. He knew they were on to him. Just over three days and it will all be done. But, he asked himself, what to do tomorrow, Thursday?

As he pondered his situation, he realised the risk of his discovery staying here in the church was increasing by the hour. He decided that at first light, he was going to take himself off to London on Clive's bike, but first he would call round to Abu and drop off all his things for safe-keeping. Yes, and much as he disliked the man, he was going to require him to put him up for Thursday night. It was absolutely imperative he stayed somewhere safe for twenty-four hours until he went to Southgate Friday lunchtime and headed into London with Kaylah for the last time. He picked up his mobile again and called Abu,

'Salaam Alekum, Ali here, need you to put me up tomorrow. OK?' he ordered, knowing he had the upper hand.

There was a silence at the other end, he could almost hear Abu thinking at the other end, then came a reassuring reply.

'It will be my privilege my brother. What time do you want to come?' said Abu.

It was arranged. All was quiet outside the church. Ali was terrified of every sound outside and could hardly sleep all night. In the grey light of dawn he gathered his things, posted the church door key through the vicarage letter box next door, walked round to Kaylah's and rang the bell. Sam Kone answered the door in his dressing-gown.

'There's no-one else up Ali, what you be wantin' at t'is early hour?' asked an irritable Sam Kone. Ali felt he'd interrupted something.

'Just to borrow Clive's bike today, Mr Kone, that is if he's not using it?' enquired Ali, politely as he could.

'No, he won't be usin' it. I try and tell him to get on his bike and find a job, but no, he won't be usin' it, I'm sure of it. Help yourself, it's in the back yard where you left it. Would you mind seein' yourself out, got a TV programme to do later,' said Sam, leaving Ali to it.

'Thanks,' said Ali, quietly taking the bike and wheeling it through the house to the street.

It was awkward cycling with a rucksack, bag of flags, and a sports bag. In the end he wheeled the bike the last few yards round to Abu's flat. Abu smiled as he opened the door.

'At last you know where to find a true friend,' he said.

Ali ignored the comment and hastily off-loaded his things. He had nothing to do but stay out of the way, but he certainly didn't want to stay in Abu's flat all day.

'I've got things to do, I'll be out on the bike, see you back here around seven after prayers, OK?' said Ali. As he spoke to Abu's expressionless face, he had the feeling Abu was glad to see the back of him.

Abu simply nodded. He was glad Ali would be out, the drugs business was picking up nicely again and he had a busy day of calls and visitors ahead of him and it would complicate things having Ali there.

'You do that, Ali, we are all right behind you,' purred Abu, 'I can feel the wind of success blowing our way.'

Ali pedalled along Silver Street, passing the Drop In and the Church for what he thought would be the final time. A day cycling in London, now what better way to be invisible, he thought.

58

'Thank God it's Friday,' said the PM to his PPS, 'and no more parliamentary questions for me this week.'

He'd handed this particular task over to his Deputy in order to welcome the first arrivals of foreign leaders flying into London later in the morning. He relished the role he'd planned for himself, greeting them all on his own turf, the world seeing an international leading statesman, a first among equals when all the foreign dignitaries lined up behind him. That's how he want to be remembered: leading the world internationally and providing a consistently invincible Tory leadership at home.

However, his immediate task was to chair a meeting of COBRA, so named because these emergency meetings originated in Cabinet Office Briefing Room A and someone's scribbling of the acronym had stuck. He was not sure why this emergency group had been called together today; he liked to know such things ahead of time, he needed to be in control and not being so made him edgy and uncomfortable.

He could feel himself beginning to look this way and that, irritability rising from somewhere deep inside. Surely they ought to know to brief him and get it right, after all he'd been PM for years. Besides, he had more than enough to deal with this morning without the need for this meeting. COBRA was supposed to be there to deal with emergencies and no-one had deigned to tell him of any emergency. For a moment he felt all this was beginning to make him feel old. One last big push, he told himself, trying to pull himself together.

Pushing open the cabinet-room door, he slipped easily into political gear, trademark smile in place, making polite noises to colleagues as he shuffled round to his usual place at the table. He thought to himself how tired a bunch they looked after years in government without any opposition worthy the name. But soon I'll be out of it, then they'll have to fight it out amongst themselves, he thought, eyeing briefly the leading man and woman heir contenders-in-waiting sitting to his left and right. He looked down at the Agenda papers to quickly scan what he was chairing, scouring them for a clue, anything. One phrase stood out, 'Lone Wolf in London'.

'OK,' he said, just loud enough to still their conversations and gain his attention. He lifted his eyes.

'Good morning everyone. Let's get to it. We have a busy weekend with London the focus of the world. Parliament, our Parliament beamed across the media, it makes me so proud to be British,' he said.

The Secretary of State was sitting looking too glum for the PM's liking. 'Now what's the Head of Joint Intelligence got to tell us about a Lone Wolf?'

'Sir, I'm sorry to say we have a young and highly trained IS operative in our midst in London. There is an ongoing inquiry to establish just how he got through, but we do know he got into the country using as cover the identity of a young British man, whom I am happy to tell you, though the public must not yet know this, is safely returned to British soil thanks to the efforts of our own superbly professional armed forces.' There were murmurs of approval around the table.

'The young man, Adam Taylor, has been able to fill us in on a terrorist we know only as Ali Muhammed, from Mosul, Iraq. Ali has used Adam's identity to get himself to north London. Unfortunately our police force and counter-extremist officers narrowly missed apprehending him in Edmonton on Monday afternoon, in the London Borough of Enfield; and, try as we have since, he's gone to ground and we haven't been able to pick him up. He's out there. He's dangerous, and as we are all too well aware, we have a major event here in London on Sunday morning, and we have every reason to believe that will be his target.'

The PM raised a finger and turned, all eyes following his gaze. 'Andrew, what do you know?' he said.

Andrew Baker, the experienced and respected Director General of MI5, who was sitting near the door, stood to speak.

'Thank you PM. Adam Taylor has indeed been most helpful. From information he has provided and through what

404

our allies have told us, especially I have to say our Israeli friends, we know this terrorist to be Ali Muhammed from Mosul. The description of a particular minaret near the house where Adam was held prisoner, the three family names he heard spoken - Fatima, Mo and Ali - have enabled us to ascertain with total certainty that this long serving IS soldier, Ali Muhammed is the man now over here in London.

'I'm afraid he is every bit as dangerous as my honourable colleague says. He has seen battlefield service, was integral to the IS taking of Mosul and has the ear of a senior IS CO in Mosul where he will have been trained and from whom he receives his orders. Ali is not infallible. He has already made mistakes, the most serious one from his point of view was to retain Adam's mobile phone without realising our Israeli friends had been monitoring its movements. Once in London, Ali tried to make us believe it was Adam who had come back, and that he was just not coming home. A deliberate smokescreen was laid, efforts to put us off Ali's trail. All this was a covert operation to deceive us and in this respect their mission has failed. We are on to them, but we still face a very real, clear and present danger,' Andrew stated.

'OK, enough detail. Where is this Ali now and what does he intend?' asked the PM leaning forward. 'Can he be a threat to events on Sunday?'

'We're very close to picking him up. We missed getting him in a security raid on a house in Edmonton, north London, but we think he's still in the area. Unfortunately we only have a grainy picture of what he looks like, one that Israeli intelligence gained from CCTV at a customs border point,' he said. Andrew passed copies around the table. The picture could have been of any young man with dark hair. He could see their disappointment but knew the grainy image would keep them on message, listening to what he would next tell them.

'Our guys have discovered that this same Ali has collected a large dark-blue rucksack from the Left Luggage at Kings Cross.' He then passed a clearer photo image around.

405

This picture was really sharp. 'Unfortunately, because he has turned off and not used Adam's phone since, we don't know his exact current whereabouts. We believe that his rucksack contains the weaponry he needs for his mission.'

'Have our eavesdropping facilities picked up anything?' asked the PM.

'Normally there would be messaging chatter from within IS, but because they are trying very hard to hide their lone wolf, we're not getting any helpful pings. One message, giving the command 'Go' was sent a couple of days ago. Truth to tell, in sum we have a trained and deadly jihadist here in London equipped for his work. We believe he will have a go at the commemorative events here on Sunday and we are stepping up our security arrangements best we can, but need political advice as to what you will change to make things less risky,' he said.

'Change, change,' said the PM's voice rose, 'It's too late for change. It's your task to make this event safe. It's our job to see through the best Public Relations event this party will have held in years. It's all about PR, is that clear Andrew?'

'Yes Prime Minister. We will do our best,' said Andrew, knowing the PM invariably got his way.

Anxious looks were cast around the table, but the PM was adamant. It was time for him to leave and meet the German Chancellor who would be arriving in thirty minutes and the meeting was terminated, Andrew immediately picking up his mobile to order a number of further house searches in north London.

Lena Bloom meanwhile had had a lucky break. Given permission to go out on a limb, she had just got hold of pictures of her own of Ali Muhammed sent through to her mobile. She had decided to brazen it out and visit the Drop In which she knew Ali frequented and just ask people about him. What had she to lose? Dressed down for the occasion and with ruffled hair, she went inside, introducing herself as Ali's sister. Her storyline was that she needed to find her brother whom she heard had escaped to London.

'Can anyone help me to find him?' she asked. She had put on her best crestfallen tearful demeanour and began with Olive. Bingo!

'Oh, such a nice young man, done so much to help here, reorganised our food store. I do think he has such a promising future in this country now he's safe. His English is so good. I always knew he was educated like, from a decent family like, and to know he has a sister who cares, you just don't know what it will mean to him to know you are looking for him. He seemed so, so alone. He'll be over the moon,' said Olive.

'But have you seen him Olive? How can I reach him?' Lena pleaded.

Olive took out the register list and looked through the records.

'Yes, here he is, Ali Muhammed, staying at Flo and Bert's house.'

Lena's heart sank, this was going nowhere.

'But, I've been there and he wasn't in,' she said.

'Oh, then I don't know what's happened. I can only suggest you talk to Kaylah Kone. She's been ever so helpful to Ali, with his forms to fill in, with finding his way around. Yes, talk to Kaylah,' she suggested.

'Where can I find her?' Lena asked, hardly able to contain herself.

'She'll be in Monday morning now I guess, always is, around ten You can see her then,' said Olive. Lena needed the information immediately and pressed on.

'But,' Lena pleaded, 'I can't wait that long to see my long-lost brother,' and pulled out a paper tissue, pretending to cry.

'Now, now dear, don't get upset. I'll give Kaylah a call now. I'm sure she won't mind,' offered Olive, pulling a chair across for Lena to sit down.

Though the call did not pick up, Olive was quite happy to give Kaylah's mobile number to Ali's 'sister'. Lena poured out her sincerely felt gratitude with true theatrical drama, before making her way out of the door. It was time to get out, she could see curious eyes gazing in her direction from around the hall. Swiftly she made her exit through the green door to the street.

She had a lead, Ali would be hers for the taking. A call was made to the embassy in Kensington and a car was sent to Cheddington Road to pick her up.

'Ali,' Dan told her, 'should be taken, alive if possible, dead if not. To date, cooperation to date with Britain hasn't yet dealt with the problem.'

With the Israeli Prime Minister flying into London tomorrow, direct action to effect a solution was the only option still open. Knowing now Ali had a helper and who she was, they'd soon track them down and get Ali. The race was on in earnest.

59

If this was freedom, then Adam Taylor was not a happy person. He told himself he was out of his mind with boredom being kept in a safe house, but underneath, it was the terrors that kept assailing him, so unexpectedly, that were making him desperate to get out. In his head, he was confused between being kept in a safe hose and a prison. Nights were especially difficult, even if he left the TV on all night.

The elation at being back home had turned into a doctor's waiting-room experience, followed by the sense he was incarcerated in some mental institution. He couldn't call his friends, he couldn't go out. How ironic, he thought, to feel like a prisoner in his own country, cast aside by the authorities, forgotten about and contained. He felt his hackles and then his fears rise in equal proportion.

After breakfast on the Friday, provided as usual at eight o'clock prompt, he decided he couldn't take any more of this. As a tactic, he'd fall back on his 'I've got choices' approach which had served him so well in his previous period of incarceration. He had toed the line since the beginning of the week. The point had come where he couldn't tolerate being in the house any more.

Today, he announced to his 'minder', who'd introduced herself as Chloe, that 'I'll be going out later.'

He'd decided he would be well-wrapped and wear a hoodie, it being November; he'd said he'd be 'taking a walk.' No-one would recognise him, his head hidden in his hood. Chloe looked surprised and re-stated the instruction she knew had been given that Adam was to stay quietly at the house out of public purview whilst the security operation was conducted; afterwards he'd be able to go exactly where he liked.

'It's not for much longer,' she said in a matter of fact voice, hoping to sway him to stay.

Adam heard it all twice more, and then said, 'I'll be going out of the door at eleven, I'll be taking a walk and I'll be back later in the afternoon.'

Something must have clicked with Chloe, that Adam meant it. She excused herself and stepped outside to make a call. On her return, she tried the same mantra again.

Adam's face was deadpan. 'I am not a prisoner here, surely?'

A silence ensued.

'I thought not. Look, if it's any comfort, I won't be selling my story to the papers or anything. It'll be fine. I just need some fresh air, I'll keep away from people, just take some exercise, take a breather, I must get out of here,' he said.

'Shall I come with you?' she offered.

'Are you some prison guard or something?' he said rather more unkindly than intended, then more quietly, 'I'll be going out alone.'

Adam called his parents and told them his plans. They offered to bring the car round and take him out in it, a kind of compromise. 'No offence,' he said, 'but I don't want to be driven around by my Mum and Dad. I'm a bloody adult!' he told them bluntly and then more coolly, 'thanks all the same.' He knew he was on edge, moody, unpredictable.

'Sorry about that. Just wondered if they're allowing me to go to London with you on Sunday using Aunt Ruth's tickets? Have you heard? Can you chase it up? Personally, how I'm feeling right now, they won't be able to stop me going, but it might be less hassle if you chase up their decision. They just can't keep me here for ever. We could have Sunday lunch somewhere together, a kind of family celebration. They won't be able to hold me now. If I can escape IS, I can escape here too,' he said, making it clear that he felt imprisoned.

His Mum could hear the frustration in Adam's voice, and she was only too happy to show her support.

'Now look dear, we just want you home again. OK I know you'll only want to stay until you're ready to do whatever

410

it is you are going to do next, but to tell you the truth, we don't like you being held in secret in Shepherds Hill one bit, not after what we've been through and of course what you've been through too. We can't wait to get you properly home. Well, we feel we're not trusted when they say you can't stay here with us. It's hard for us too you know,' she said.

Adam felt he had allies and he promised he'd be back in time to see them when they 'visited' later in the afternoon.

There was one further effort to dissuade him from going out when a policeman or security man called about ten-thirty. Adam wasn't exactly sure where the man was from. He never said. He began addressing Adam with a patronising air.

'Now look mate, I know how hard its been, but...'

Adam surprised himself by cutting him short and telling him 'Piss off!'

With a shrug, presumably duty done, the man turned and left. Adam guessed that much as they wanted to keep him inside, they knew they'd be overstepping the mark if they officially detained him, even using the Terrorism Act legislation they were so fond of calling upon, to get their own way.

At precisely eleven Adam stepped out of the door and pulled it firmly shut behind him. He'd asked Chloe to lend him a tenner before going out, which to his surprise she did, saying if he spent it, she could claim it back on 'expenses' anyhow.

Turning left at the end of the drive, after a watchful look left and right, he began walking down Shepherds Hill, having a very definite spring in his step. This is freedom, to walk the street without a care in the world, he said to himself. A little apprehensive he might bump into one of his friends on the street and then have some difficult explaining to do, he kept a careful watch, always trying to make out who was where and if there was any chance they might know him.

A few minutes later he was down in Crouch End and heading toward the Clock Tower. He looked in a few of the shop windows, then spotted a cafe-bar. It was well enough away from Muswell Hill and, he didn't see anyone in there he recognised, so he made his way inside and ordered a beer.

They must be idiots, the people minding me, he mused. All my friends will be away at Uni now, and anyone else would be at school or work at eleven-thirty on a Friday morning. Lacking anything else to do, he grabbed a complimentary copy of the Guardian. Anywhere else it would be the Mail or the Sun, but Crouch End, it's the Guardian, but it was thinner than ever, he thought. Like some fugitive in a movie, he thought he could always use the newspaper to hide behind if needed. He sat inside facing the window so he could see outside, his back to everyone inside.

It really was so stupid to think that even one of his friends like Seb couldn't be trusted to keep things quiet anyway, well maybe not Ryan nor Shaima, they always spilled the beans, but I'm just not going to see them. He'd have loved to get on to Facebook, Instagram or start sending Tweets, to express how he felt, that he was still being imprisoned with a useless phone when supposedly free in his own country.

In desperation for something to occupy him, he borrowed a biro and began the Suduko, quickly filling the boxes and completing it. As he looked up, a red London bus was sweeping past heading for Finsbury Park and the city and a group of young men was heading in the opposite direction, maybe to the YMCA. A lone cyclist was coming his way, slowing because the bus had almost stopped and obscured his way, the cyclist looked familiar; no, surely not! Could it be? It was. Ali.

Adam froze in his chair. No, double check, no, yes, he spilled some beer. The cyclist was still there. Forcing himself up, Adam moved up to the glass window and pressed his face against it to better see the cyclist's face, his hands to either side on the glass. He was fearful, feet glued to the spot, hands as if frozen to the window pane, he couldn't move, let alone decide what to do. His breath misted the glass. He wiped it, it was smeary.

Then the man was cycling again, looking so western, moving after the bus as it accelerated away, up the hill, on

412

toward Finsbury Park. Must see if it is really him, Adam thought, dropping the still open newspaper, pushing himself quickly to the door.

He rushed outside as if in slow motion, almost falling into the street. Now he had doubts. Was the man cycling after the bus up the hill toward Finsbury Park really Ali? As the cyclist disappeared into the distance, Adam, turned and told the barista to keep the change as he left Chloe's ten pounds in his open palm. Then he began to run, not after the cyclist, but in the opposite direction. He turned up Shepherds Hill and didn't stop running until, quite breathless, his leg hurting, he banged on the front door he had so recently left.

'Let me in, let me in,' he cried fighting for breath.

Chloe opened the door with a smile.

'It doesn't take you long to spend a tenner then, or had you heard, they said you can go to London on Sunday!' she said.

By then she could tell something had happened, her face switched to serious mode and seconds later she was listening to Adam's story. Adam was in a state of panic. He told himself the cyclist couldn't have been Ali, but being outside where Ali might be had unnerved him. He'd felt irrationally frightened again, yet he didn't want to show it to Chloe. He feared the terrors and flashbacks of the night were now entering his daytime too, and became anxious at the thought of losing control.

Even back in freedom nothing felt certain any more. Was he a prisoner, was his captor outside, were his friends his enemies? His mind was now playing cruel tricks on him. Making his excuses, he left Chloe wondering at his state of mind, as he himself went to put on some music.

As he tried to calm his frayed nerves, he wondered if he'd have enough confidence to go outside again. Going to the centre of London in two days time, even with permission, filled him with apprehension and dread.

60

Ruth saw the key. It had fallen through the letter box and onto the front door mat. She stooped and picked it up. It was still early and she was on her way over to Church to say Morning Prayer, a lifetime's habit, that kept her world in a kind of balance. It ordered her day, breathed in some peace, some quiet, some silence for a few minutes at least.

The returned key was thrust into her bag to be retrieved and placed in her desk drawer later. Ali must have been able to secure his new place early, she told herself, which is rather fortuitous for it wasn't ideal having him tucked away in the gallery. In fact on several fronts it was awkward and could only be viewed, indeed justified as an emergency arrangement. She was relieved not to have the complication of his continuing presence and possible Church Council questions she might have had to face had his stay been discovered.

As she was using her own key to open the heavy west end church door and make her way into its still dark interior, she turned her gaze back to the street as a car pulled up, wondering who it was. Two officials, possibly council officers, no, on second thoughts it was too early for them, approached her.

'Rev Churchill?' one of them called out.

'Yes, can I help?' she said.

'We hope so. We're from Edmonton police station, DI Josh Reynolds, this is my colleague Ian Mills.' Josh flipped open and held out his warrant badge with its metallic silver shine and leather fastening strap.

'Can we step inside for a moment and have a word?' he said, as the badge disappeared again somewhere inside his jacket.

'Well, it will have to be brief as I have prayers in five minutes and there are usually a couple of faithful souls who join me. They'll be along any minute,' she said, wondering what they wanted.

'Won't take long,' confirmed Josh.

They moved into the church and Ruth switched on a selection of lights from amongst the array of switches on the panel inside. The long-life bulbs began to glow, slowly piercing the late autumn gloom. Ruth placed her bag and papers on the table at the back of the church and turned to give them her full attention.

'We believe there to be a dangerous extremist in the area and we want to track him down before he does any harm to anyone. This guy is a Muslim, who arrived in this country from the Middle East some weeks ago but has made Edmonton his place of choice to lie low. You will have heard already no doubt that some of our officers tried to apprehend him at Bert and Flo Harper's house last Monday, but by the time we got there he had gone. The bird had flown.'

Reaching inside his jacket pocket he pulled out his phone and with a couple of taps showed her the image.

'Is this him, your Ali?' he asked, holding the picture before her.

'Yes, yes, no doubt, that's him. Oh, I heard about what happened at Flo and Bert's. In fact Ali, that's definitely his name, and our placement student helping with his care, Kaylah Kone, they both came to see me last Tuesday. Ali was worried. He felt people were after him. He led me to think it was not the police, but other people who were after him, because he'd fled from Iraq you know. But when I told him that it was yourselves who had tried to see him at Flo and Bert's house, he agreed to my suggestion that he would call at the police station later and see you himself. I'd have thought he'd have done that by now.'

There were negative nods from the two men. Ruth had a sinking feeling.

'Ali said that until he could find new accommodation with a friend this weekend he desperately needed somewhere to stay at night. I was at a loss, we can't have people sleeping rough, so where could we house him? All our spaces

415

were full. It was suggested he could come here; not so strange really, throughout history churches have always been places of sanctuary. I gave him the key and he's been staying in the gallery here in the church since then. He asked me not to broadcast the information. He seemed frightened people were after him. So it's only one of our helpers, Kaylah Kone and myself who would have known he was here,' she explained.

She began to fear she might be in trouble for harbouring a criminal. She worried that Kaylah needed a call from her and made a mental note to call her after the prayers.

'Might he still be here now, Reverend?' asked Josh looking around.

'Oh please just call me Ruth. Oh I don't think so. No, I just now found his key posted through my letter box and the church was locked up when I arrived. I thought he must have returned it because his new arrangement had come through. He said his friend had somewhere for him from this weekend,' she said.

'Please can you show us where he's been sleeping,' said Josh's colleague Ian.

Ruth led the way, the officers holding a hushed conversation and going up into the gallery pressing tight on the walls.

'There's nothing to worry about. The building's quite safe,' she said as she strode up the stairs ahead of them and on to the gallery platform.

The officers followed her. They seemed disappointed. The one called Ian stepped away from Josh and Ruth and began speaking into a radio. She couldn't hear the conversation.

'Well thank you for your help Ruth. We really do need to try and track this Ali fellow down. Have you any idea how we might find him? Any help would be useful. Did he by any chance say where he'd be moving to, who his friend was?' asked Josh.

'I hesitate to say this, but the person who knew him best was Kaylah Kone. She's a business studies student from

416

Southgate Community College, a local girl on placement with us here. She got on with him well. Are you sure he's a dangerous extremist? You see we never had any problem with him. In fact he helped Kaylah reorganise our refugee and asylum-seeker food store. He was always courteous, helpful and he speaks really good English. He worked really hard helping out. Yes, try Kaylah Kone. She won't be in today, it's Friday, she'll be at lectures, but if it's urgent you could call round at the Kone's house in Cheddington Road. Nice family,' she told them, trying to be helpful, but knowing the officers were neither persuaded nor satisfied.

The two officers lifted a few boxes and poked their fingers here and there, but not wanting to dirty their smart suits on all the stored church detritus, they turned as one and thanked Ruth before departing. Ruth swept up her bag and papers and began organising herself for Morning Prayer in the south chapel.

Once outside, Josh and Ian climbed back into their car and held a quick conference call with Edmonton and London. The only lead they had to go on was that Kaylah Kone might know where Ali was. To ensure risks were kept to a minimum they asked Beat Officer Bob Steer to keep a low profile watch on the Kone house until they could get back to HQ and organise a proper visit with a full team back-up. Josh hoped their two-vehicle team would have better luck this time. The Counter-Terrorism officers kept drawing blanks and desperately needed a break, perhaps Kaylah Kone would provide it. Time was running out.

PC Bob Steer was at the end of Cheddington Road by nine-thirty. He disliked what he called loitering with intent. It was so difficult not to be obvious, even more so in uniform. Around nine-forty-five the front door of the Kone's house opened and Kaylah walked out pulling a small pink suitcase on wheels behind her. Bob didn't know what he should do. At the very least he should offer her a 'good morning', before he reported the 'event' to police HQ. Kaylah looked cheerful and offered him a 'good morning' first.

417

'Can't stop, must get the bus or I'll be late for lectures,' she said, leaving Bob on the corner. As Kaylah disappeared down the street, the noise of her case wheels receded into the distance as they bumped on every crack in the pavement. Bob called Josh at police HQ moments later to give his report.

'No sign of Ali, but Kaylah Kone has gone off to college,' he said.

And for that he was immediately reprimanded.

'Couldn't you bloody well have held her? We need to ask her some questions. She'll have to wait until later. We're still planning on checking her home out, be with you later with the troops. Over and out,' said DI Josh Reynolds.

Bob continued to pace up and down the street. There were some parts of the job he loathed, but his conscience was clear. He'd not been ordered to detain her, so he was no way to blame. Anyway, for the life of him, he couldn't think a nice girl like Kaylah Kone should be held by the police. These boys from region, he thought, they just don't know the territory.

Kaylah switched her phone to silent as she went into the lecture theatre. She found she just couldn't concentrate on her lecture today. It was year two and important exams were lined up for January and a whole period was spent telling her what areas the questions would cover. She knew this whole dull but important lecture would be there on the student electronic blackboard which she could look at later when it suited her, so her eyes glazed and she drifted into her own imaginings.

After a short coffee break with her friend Melissa, and before lunch, there was a panel presentation by two 'successful' entrepreneurs, a woman who had set up a coffee franchising chain and a guy who had used e-selling to cut out the middle man and maximise profits in fashion babywear. This was more interesting and she was full of admiration for these role models, those who had, in her eyes, 'made it.'

At precisely one o'clock she wheeled her case out of college and looked up and down the street, exchanged brief conversations with her friends at the college gate and then began walking the short distance to Southgate tube station. She always marvelled at the iconic shape of tube stations, evocative of a bygone era. Southgate station was no different, it looked invitingly glamorous today, the gateway to an exciting weekend; and there was Ali, clutching his things, his rucksack and sports bag, looking somewhat lost, awkward, watchful even, but she knew he was waiting for her.

This was so, so exciting. Other people at the tube station also seemed to be thinking it was time to make off for an early weekend. Kaylah was only too happy to join the happy throng as she saw them. There was a kind of movie hug with Ali before they moved off.

Ali had already got their tickets and they glided down the Piccadilly line escalator and made their way to the city southbound platform.

'Why is it,' Ali asked, 'everyone stands still on an escalator, why don't they just keep walking like they do before and after? It's so unexpected.'

Kaylah smiled, his observations of what she took for granted amused her. The escalator took them down to the platform and in moments a train collected them up and sped them toward the city. Ali felt safer with his bags having Kaylah as company. No-one would suspect a thing.

Back at Edmonton Police HQ Josh was frustrated; it took forever to get his team together. In the end there was only one police van available, so everyone crammed into it, all irritable like him.

'Come on,' he urged the driver. Josh had just had a call from his Assistant Chief to tell him to get on with it, the words still ringing in his head.

'Get Ali!' he was told, 'or heads will roll.'

Fired up they pulled up outside the Kone's house. Usual procedure followed, the front door flying off its hinges in one hit from Tony's big red key, everyone piling in with shouts of 'police, police.'

There was much screaming from Mrs Shazee Kone, as her son Clive was forced to the floor by two burly guys in blue. Bishop Sam Kone was in the bath, being viewed by all the team in turn. He vainly tried to cover his expansive girth with a towel that didn't really do the job. It took only seconds to discover there was no Ali there.

Several minutes later, the three members of the Kone family were seated in the front room, the missing front door giving the curious neighbours opposite a direct line of sight at proceedings. Now wrapped in a dressing gown, Sam Kone could hear officers going through every last nook and cranny of their home. His blood pressure was rising fast. At first he was shocked and embarrassed, but now finding his voice he was incandescent with rage and Josh prepared himself for the blast to come.

'Racism,' was the word Josh heard first. His heart sank. The day was continuing where it had begun, going rapidly downhill.

Another public relations disaster was looming, he felt it crawling up his back. Clive was going on about police brutality and victimisation, though as far as Josh could see he looked fine. Shazee was clutching Sam's arm sobbing. The only way through was to tell them how it was, thought Josh.

'We're looking for an Islamist extremist, a most dangerous man called Ali, who must be apprehended before he commits untold atrocities, and we thought he might be here.'

'Ali, he isn't here, but he was,' said a more lucid Sam.

'He was?' queried Josh.

'Yes, he stayed here earlier in the week. My daughter Kaylah invited him back, and my son Clive and he swapped places to stay for a day a two at the beginning of the week. That's it, he's not been here since. He's not here now, and when are you going to get the door fixed?' asked Sam, waving at the empty void before them where once there had been a front door.

The search was concluding, each officer reappearing to shake his head and go back to the van. One guy held out a phone in a transparent plastic bag. 'This is of interest, Sir. It was in the lad's room. I switched it on, not his, belongs to a guy called Adam Taylor.'

'Ali must have left it when he was here,' offered a quick-thinking Clive.

'It was in the lad's jacket pocket, Sir,' looking at Clive.

'I was going to give it back to him, but I haven't seen him since,' responded Clive.

They seemed satisfied with that. The phone gave the police a kind of trophy that meant the raid was at least a partial success. Josh became more conciliatory and said he'd get a man organised to get the door fixed right away and thanked them all for their cooperation. He asked the family if Ali had said anything to them about where he might be going to stay next or indeed if they had any idea of his whereabouts.

Clive knew Kaylah was away for the weekend with Ali, she'd confided in him, but after two police raids on where he lived, a bruising from being thrown to the floor and sat on and his own weekend plans involving a certain Post Office, he was not going to say anything. With that the police left, their attention turning to what they were going to do next, leaving the Kones to pick up the pieces.

Clive ran upstairs and picked up his mobile. No reply.

'Hell Sis, why don't you pick up?' he said as he threw it on the bed.

By the end of the afternoon Ali and Kaylah had checked into the Tavistock and left their stuff in their room, Ali hanging the 'do not disturb' sign on the door before they both made off for the centre of London for the evening. Kaylah had lots of ideas where to go and Ali followed. This was exactly how he hoped things would go.

Kaylah though had one thing bothering her. Somehow since arriving in London she'd lost her phone and without it she felt part of her life was out of reach. It took the edge off her enjoyment.

When Ali simply said, 'forget it, enjoy yourself, it's your weekend, a time for us both to remember,' she accepted it wasn't so bad not getting calls. Ali worried in case she asked to borrow his, but she didn't.

They discussed a day of sight-seeing for the next day, beginning with the London Eye, and strangely, but because Ali wanted it, an afternoon at London Zoo. Almost the first thing Ali asked was whether she had remembered the tickets for Sunday morning; he appeared wide-eyed with excitement about it.

'Of course,' she replied waving them teasingly, 'I might have lost my phone, but not these.'

That night back at the hotel, they clung on to each other in bed, enjoying their freedom, each wondering what the future held for them. Long after Kaylah was slumbering quietly beside him, Ali was sitting up in bed going over and over in his mind what he had to do, what lay before him. It hadn't been easy taking Kaylah's phone to ensure another route for the authorities to get to him remained shut, but he told himself it had to be done. Yesterday, after his cycle to London, he'd left Clive's bike in Deans Yard by Church House, Westminster, along with all the other bikes. He hoped it was still there just in case, though somehow he doubted he'd be around to be able to use it ever again.

He needed some time to himself before Sunday morning to make last-minute preparations and had to plan how he might get that. Perhaps, if he offered it, he could persuade Kaylah to have a hotel massage after tomorrow's zoo visit, she'd like that. The Zoo, now he should be able to relax there. No-one would be looking for them in London Zoo, it would take his mind off things, it would calm him before battle.

422

61

After a thankfully uneventful Saturday strolling round London Zoo, making the visit last as long as possible, Ali woke at five o'clock on Sunday morning: not that he'd slept much. There was an orange glow from the street lights outside in Tavistock Square, filtering in throughout the thin gold cloth of the hotel room curtain, just enough light to see by. Kaylah slept like a top. He gazed upon her knowing that their life together would end in a few hours' time. Well, that's how it had to be.

Climbing out of bed quietly, he took the flags from their plastic bag and quietly laid them out on the floor. Most of them already had shortened sticks, reduced to around 10 cm. He'd cut them down in size earlier. Next he bound them together in little bundles with black cable ties. Checking Kaylah was still totally asleep, he slowly undid the top of his rucksack, opened the neck and placed all the short-stemmed bundles of flags in the centre. The rest he carefully inserted around the outside, forcing their long sticks down the inside between the hard packed centre and the outside.

Once done he surveyed his handy work. It looked good, his rucksack had to appear to be full of flags; it looked fit for purpose and he hoped his handiwork would be good enough to fool a casual search. He retained a couple of flags for Kaylah and himself to hold. They needed to look the part too and Kaylah's presence with him would help to convince anyone looking for a lone wolf terrorist that he wouldn't be found here.

After he had done, he rolled up the wrapping paper and squeezed it into the circular metal bin. Kaylah still slept on, so he crept back in bed beside her. Even then she still didn't move. It must be nice to sleep so soundly, he thought, an experience that invariably escaped him.

At seven Ali got out of bed again, this time to go to the bathroom; to begin a slow and careful washing of himself. It

423

was always something he'd carefully attended to, no more so than when his faith required it. Today he found himself reciting his prayers under his breath as he attended to his ritual. After he was clean, he quietly dressed and when he was sure he was ready, only then touched Kaylah, telling her it was time to get up, explaining they mustn't be late.

Kaylah was none too pleased at this summons. 'No way! Why so early on a Sunday morning?' she asked with a surly face. Then more sweetly adding, 'come back to bed, we have hours yet.'

She smelled warm and the invitation pulled on him, but he held back. It was that pause that woke her and she felt a chill of dawn as she knew the weekend was coming to an end. This was their last day and normal service resumed tomorrow. The dream always ends, she thought. Some of the romance and happiness seemed to seep out from what was a pretty dully-decorated, tired-looking, hotel room. She turned to look at Ali again. He was sitting there, dressed like he had somewhere to go.

'Hey, Ali, what's up with you, chill, don't you like holidays?' she playfully chided, puzzled at his appearance and manner.

Ali shrugged, he didn't know what to say. He didn't want to hurt her any more than he knew he would.

'Just keen we shouldn't miss out. Sorry,' he offered.

He gave her a kiss on her cheek. She smelled the acid yet fruity scent of soap the hotel provided. She was now fully awake. The bed no longer held her.

'Give me a few minutes to shower and dress and we'll go down to breakfast.' She disappeared into the bathroom, Ali's eyes following her.

'Nice touch, very thoughtful, more than enough for everyone,' she said, nodding at the flags protruding from Ali's rucksack. 'You've been busy.'

Ali smiled, if only she really knew how busy he had been. He knew Kaylah wasn't far away from finding him out, knowing what he really had in mind. Just hours, just a few more hours, that's all he needed. He hoped fate would continue to be kind.

By nine they had breakfasted and he'd paid in cash the remainder of the hotel bill. Some blazer-wearing British Legion members were clearly staying at their hotel with the same Armistice Day event lined up ahead. They filled the foyer with their excited chatter. Some older men in their navy outfits had unfurled British Legion flags, enjoying checking them over for use later.

By nine-fifteen the two had left the hotel, Kaylah dragging her pink case, Ali carrying his rucksack and sports bag. Ali was pushing the pace, Kaylah half-running to keep up.

'What's the hurry, Ali?' she asked him, again feeling her composure ruffled.

'Sorry,' he said again, slowing. 'Shall we take a bus into town?'

It was agreed. They crossed the road at the next stop and waited. A 91 bound for Trafalgar Square appeared minutes later.

'Perfect!' said Kaylah. Once inside, sitting next to a very subdued, preoccupied Ali, she sensed something wasn't quite right with him, but for now she couldn't for the life of her work out what it was.

At the same time as Ali and Kaylah were boarding their bus, an Audi saloon car pulled up in Shepherds Hill, Sue and Jim Taylor already inside in the rear. Chloe had indeed arranged the transport.

'As we still need to keep you under wraps until the end of today, the taxi is on us,' she had explained.

Adam felt as he imagined prisoners did when they talked about 'gate fever' before release. Since his walk outside on Friday he'd not been out since. He was almost frightened to do so, it felt so unsafe and Ali might be there. He knew that he was being irrational; he tried to persuade himself it most probably wasn't Ali he saw in Crouch End when he went out on his first walk of freedom, but he couldn't entirely convince himself. It was debilitating, depressing even, to know he felt the way he did, and he wasn't going to mention how agitated he was feeling today. He hadn't yet said anything to anyone when he came back to the safe house about who he thought he'd seen. He didn't want to make a fool of himself, reasoning they would only send him off to get counselling or put him on sedatives. The best thing was to let time heal, bravely stick it out, he thought.

Chloe waved them off after Adam had climbed in the front seat of the Audi next to the driver. Leaning between the front seats to speak to his parents in the back, he said, 'did I ever tell you about the last car I drove, a Toyota Hilux? It was Ali's. He won't be pleased to know what happened to it!'

As he spoke his upbeat moment crashed as he feared Ali might seek him out if he ever found out what happened to his car. The driver looked across at Adam with a worried face.

'It's a long story. Let's go, it can wait, I'm free at last,' he said, turning and settling back into his seat, his anxious eyes fixed on the road ahead.

The car made its way back to the Archway Road and headed left, down under the high bridge and straight for the city centre. Adam told himself once again it was good to be out, the house in Shepherd's Hill had been so claustrophobic, enclosing, almost stopping him being able to breathe. He'd made his mind up he wouldn't be going back there. But the nearer they got to London, the more he realised the problem wasn't just his being confined to the house, it was much bigger than he'd thought: his head was in a mess.

Winston had just picked up Clive, his first passenger of the day. Clive didn't quite look his usual self. Winston thought he looked haunted, with hollows under his eyes. He knew he had got his friend into stuff neither of them ought to be mixed up with and if it was doing that to Clive, he hated to think what was it doing to him. As usual, when faced with the negative, he tried to inject some cheerful concern. Often it seemed to work.

'What's up with you man? Out late last night on a bender or summit? Will won't be pleased if you ain't all sharp,' said Winston teasingly, trying to get alongside his friend.

'It's fine, cool, give me five minutes. It's my Sis, she's into deep shit. The guy she's with, Ali, well he turns out to be some sort of terrorist, but she don't know it and I can't reach her nowhere. I've tried calling her day and night, even had two police raids on my space in the last week. They're looking for him real hard. The cops keep calling me to hear if I've seen my sister. It's scary stuff man, can't deal with this right now; and it can't go wrong today.'

'Look, we've got to sort out this job, then we can sort out your sister. So far as Ali goes, the police don't seem to know what they're doing, but ain't nothing new there, now is there?' he said forcing a chuckle.

Winston offered him a can of Coke and told him to sit back and take it easy in the Alfa.

'It's all cool, we pick up the others at ten and we just wait for the call to collect the cash. It'll be so straightforward man, won't be a policeman outside the city all day. Dillon was right. As I see it, that guy Ali is doing us one big favour. Police looking for him won't be looking for us none,' said Winston trying to lift morale.

Clive wasn't so sure, but now wasn't the time to say it. Clive was right about one thing, he couldn't think about helping Kaylah until the Post Office job was out the way. He picked up his mobile and tried one last time to reach her. On two fronts he was one very worried guy.

Kaylah thought they'd arrived ridiculously early at Westminster. As she looked around her it seemed like everything was still being set up. There weren't even that many people about, only the one's who had jobs to do. Events in Whitehall at the Cenotaph weren't taking place until eleven, and then it wouldn't be until eleven-thirty things would start to happen where they were, she thought.

Ali still seemed preoccupied, hardly saying a word. This was weird, unsettling behaviour. The military processions after the RAF fly past, well that wouldn't start until eleven-forty-five her programme said. Just what was Ali thinking? He was obsessive about being at the heart of this thing, something she just couldn't get her head round. She realised there were things about Ali she just hadn't yet begun to understand.

Before she knew it they were at the Church House reception desk. Unsurprisingly, the lone receptionist and security man, were hardly ready for visitors yet; they were just checking the paper work and the day's diary. Kaylah announced their presence and waved their tickets.

'Need to check your bags first Miss, and you Sir, before I can take you through,' said the young woman. Ali was relieved that it was a different person on duty to the one he'd spoken to the previous Sunday. Hopefully, he'd be spared any tricky accessibility questions.

Kaylah lifted and placed her pink suitcase onto the desk, opened it and let the female receptionist run her hands through it.

'Do you want to leave it here whilst you're viewing from the window, dear, and then collect it after? It'll save carrying it upstairs, it'll be quite safe,' she said helpfully.

Ali's heart was missing a beat. Kaylah agreed and the case disappeared from view and into the back room. Ali dropped his sports bag on to the desk and the same woman unzipped it and did the same with his things, again asking him if he'd like to leave it with her. Ali nodded. It too disappeared. Then he was obliged to hoist his rucksack onto the desk. He placed his hand on the drawcord ready to open it, his heart in his mouth for fear of discovery.

At that precise moment the security man next to the receptionist had his attention diverted as his phone rang. With the interruption, everyone paused what they were doing, in case it was a call for them.

'A delivery of a wreath you say, mmm... Give me a moment madam,' he said. He turned to the receptionist with a look of, what do we do? Together the two began to run their fingers down a telephone list. All the while Ali's rucksack just sat there on the desk. The call had given him time to think. When the call was over and attention switched back to him, Ali pulled out one flag, then another from his rucksack.

'We'll all need one of these to wave,' he said cheerily, waving a Union Jack in both hands.

'Look we'll leave one for you and your friend so you don't feel left out. OK. I'll take the rest with me so we can wave them from the windows.' Ali smiled as he pulled the rucksack off the desk and on to his shoulder. There was a look of hesitation on the receptionist's face as if she had missed something, but it soon passed as she saw Ali grasp Kaylah's hand.

'You know where to go, just along there, second room along, up the stairs, above the Westminster bookshop. Can't get lost. Excellent view from there. We've left chairs out as there'll be quite a lot of waiting around; and help yourselves to soft drinks and biscuits on the landing,' the receptionist directed, raising her voice as Ali began leading Kaylah away.

They moved off and up the stairs to find their allocated viewing window. Ali's confidence rocketed, he felt nothing could stop him now. He kept forgetting he was supposed to be with Kaylah, his mind ratcheting up a notch as his adrenaline kicked in. Alert, ever watchful, he knew as they silently looked out the window in front of them that nothing could stop him now.

The Audi got caught in heavy traffic as it approached the city. The driver muttered in frustration under his breath.

'I'll drop you as near as I can, but there are so many road closures for security, it's making the trip difficult. I'll pick you up where I drop you at one o'clock. OK? Wait for me if I'm late,' he said.

A few more corners, traffic lights and he finally slowed to a halt.

'This is it. I can't get any closer. You can see Westminster from here, ten minute walk maximum, OK?' he asked with an air of defeat.

They got out and walked together. Adam was glad to be in the open air, but he couldn't help but look around him, to see who was near. There were so many people, too many faces to search. The demons kept coming back, but so far he was just about keeping them at bay. The walk would do him good, he thought.

Crowds had filled the pavements. It was almost ten-forty-five. It was getting difficult to get near the Houses of Parliament and their progress had slowed to a snail's pace. Already they had been stopped and frisked twice because of additional security called for by Andrew Baker.

'We need to get in place or they might not let us through,' said Jim, trying to get Sue and Adam to push through the gap he was making.

They shuffled forward as fast as the pressing crowds would allow. It was with some relief, as none could bear lateness, they eventually found their way to the Church House reception desk as Big Ben struck eleven. It was then they were caught by surprise. The obligatory two minutes' silence began. Nothing happened. Like everyone else they too stood still; then, in the silence, they could hear the sound of a bugle playing the last post some way off.

When they finally stepped forward, the Church House receptionist had a bit of a queue. They weren't the only latecomers and she was searching her list and allocating visitors to windows as fast as she could. By quarter past, they were through and taken by one of the Armistice Day Volunteers, identifiable by their red armband, up to their viewing window. The veritable army of these British Values Volunteers in their red outfits had made quite an impression as they'd walked in. There were a few doors off the first-floor corridor. They entered the third one along as directed.

'You're here, in this room. Help yourself to coffee or tea from the trolley down the corridor,' said the volunteer before strolling to the viewing window and adding, 'it'll all kick off down there in the next few minutes. You can see you're facing the main marquee from here and the processions come very near, so I'm told. You really will have the best view.' With that, he turned and dashed off.

They took in their room. It was a small room really, but the leaded-light window view was good. Adam needed to open the window, which thankfully he found went right back. He felt the welcome cool autumn air hit his face and heard the hushed noise of the pressing and expectant crowd below. They all squeezed in a line by the window, Adam between his parents. There really wasn't much space, he didn't like it much, but chose to suffer in silence.

Ali found himself sweating, his under arms were wet, his palms damp, his mouth dry. The waiting was unbearable. He was taut like a coiled spring. When the two minute silence arrived he'd been glad of the opportunity not to have to speak to Kaylah. She was beginning to get to him. It was all getting too strained between them. Her smile had gone, she looked at him strangely. He was frightened she might read his intention.

'Who are you going to give all those flags to?' she asked suddenly as soon as the two minute silence was over, one more puzzled expression on her face.

'Give me five minutes and they'll all have gone,' he said smiling, as he swung his rucksack to his shoulder and stepped into the passageway outside, Kaylah's quizzical gaze following him.

By now he was anxious to get away from her. She could be more liability than help from this point in. He turned, wanting to contain her, his biggest threat.

'Keep an eye on our viewing position, won't be long. They'll be lots to see, you wait,' Ali said from the doorway. Yes, she'd be watching a blood bath.

431

Then he was gone, leaving Kaylah standing motionless as the door closed behind him. He was pleased to be alone.

Three paces away down the corridor, Ali side-stepped into the toilet room next door. It too had a full view of the marquee with its banks of seats. Then he feared his small window couldn't be opened wide enough or propped up. It was a top window with a horizontal latch.

Looking at it again a week on, he realised it might be more awkward for him than he had anticipated. A tremor of panic rose. Lifting it open, he found it kept dropping down and the space for him to move in was very confined. However, a minute of trial and error later and he'd managed to get the window to stay open, one of his flags with its wooden stick proving to be just the ironic item to do the perfect job.

Next, he released the corded top and fully opened his rucksack, pulling out all the flags and placing them on the floor. He hoped standing on them wouldn't make him slip, but wiping his feet on them felt reassuringly appropriate in the circumstances. Peering out of the window carefully a second time, he judged the view 'just perfect.' If only the space were not so tight.

He sat down on the closed toilet seat lid as he silently pulled out his AK47 and rested it upright against the tiled wall before placing the ammunition box on the window sill and finally unwrapping the packs of cluster grenades. It had been a heavy load which he had tried to make look light and inconspicuous. With his weaponry spread out before him, he looked at each piece in turn, scrutinising, checking, aligning, so that nothing would fail, the grenades all in a line. He practised in his mind just how he would seize and throw each in turn and the trajectory spread of right to left.

He was almost ready, but frightened someone might disturb him even now and so tried to keep very quiet as he handled his gun, loading it under his jacket to mask any noise. He realised his armoury was small, so much smaller than he'd hoped; but then it was as well it was. Travelling light he'd been able to get within striking distance and he still had more than enough lethal force at his disposal to achieve his goal. Everything he had by him would be needed, all his armoury had to be used with ruthless efficiency.

He checked his phone: eleven-thirty. Finally, he unzipped the bottom pouch of the rucksack and pulled out a black silk cloth. On it were Arabic words in white. It was almost time to let the world know IS were in town. Time though for him to settle down and wait, find the calm, still the mission nerves, remember the training, it was only minutes to wait, 'Enshallah, Enshallah,' he repeated in hushed tones under his breath like a mantra. Finally, he was ready.

Winston drove carefully down to South Tottenham. It would have been all too easy to exceed the speed limit, there being no-one on the road. Those who weren't in central London, were probably at home glued to their TVs to watch this PM glory swansong. Everyone was obsessed by the event. That suited him just fine.

In the car, Dillon was unusually quiet, clutching his mobile tight and close to him, awaiting the call from Will's sister. The concentration was etched in his face. Woody was all set to be dropped off at the corner of Seven Sisters Road to keep look out, his recent injury now only masked by a thin tape on his face, replacing the big bandage of past days.

Then Dillon started fidgeting, one moment quiet, the next as high as a kite. Winston was glad Dillon was sitting in the back. He never liked driving with four guys in the car, it usually meant being pulled over, but not today. Everywhere was quiet as a grave. He glanced to the front passenger seat. Clive was looking pensive, lost, staring straight ahead.

By eleven they were in place and Woody was unceremoniously pushed out of the car by Dillon at the corner of the street. He ambled off to loiter a few yards further on, furtively casting glances this way and that. Woody would do his job. He drove on a short way and pulled into a drive where they could lay up. The waiting was already unbearable. Dillon took a call.

'Go,' he said quietly under his breath, then 'Go!' he yelled.

Winston told Clive to start walking with his bag, giving him a gentle prod as if to say, it's alright. Clive stepped out and onto the pavement and began walking.

The two hundred metres seemed a mile to him and he felt his heart beating ten to the dozen. He thought he ought to look as if he were strolling back from the gym or something, but he couldn't fool himself into thinking like that. He was not ten paces away from the drop zone and wondering what the fuck to do if the window in front of him didn't open and nothing came out. He didn't want to slow, but he did, he had to, for nothing was happening, there was no dropped bag! He knew he shouldn't, but he looked back at the car.

Then a crash above his head. He looked up, a window was pushed open, up and wide, right by him. He saw an arm, an elbow, and then a grey sack with metal clasps fell, fell to the ground at his feet. He struggled, knowing he must get it into the sports bag, he fumbled, it wouldn't go, did he do the zip up. He looked round, 'where's the fucking car?' he muttered desperately.

With the sports bag awkwardly cradled under his arm, the cash bag sticking very obviously out of the top, he'd started walking before he heard the reassuring sound of the Winston's car engine start up. Then Winston was cruising alongside, the passenger door swinging open as he leant across to release it.

'In, in, get in,' Winston shouted, and moments later they scooped up Woody the Hoodie at the corner and slipped back into Tottenham High Road, this time heading north, every moment taking them further away and nearer to safety. No-one could say a word except Dillon, who began singing.

'If I were rich man...'

Winston told him to 'shut it' and to 'give Will a call with the news he'd be waiting to receive.' As they drove past Tottenham Police Station in the High Road, Dillon couldn't resist making a two finger gesture, whilst with his other hand reaching for his mobile.

'Trouble is,' said Dillon, 'there isn't a single fucking policeman there to see that!' Popping another pill, he eventually managed to call Will. Putting the phone on speaker, they all heard him.

'You boys have had a successful morning shopping, so pleased to hear it.' Rarely was Will ever heard to make a compliment, it was as well they all listened in so not as not to have missed it, thought Winston.

The Prime Minister and those with him walked slowly side by side down Whitehall. His wife, Tabitha, walked beside him, with the presidents of the United States and France and their partners either side of them. The Royal family were well represented, at this point by the royal princes who passed by in ceremonial military dress. They, unlike the PM, had found their popularity over the years remained undiminished, if not enhanced.

Slowly, very slowly, the dignitaries progressed, the leading group of six now in a single line across the width of the road. Down into Parliament Square the group moved ever forward with quiet and solemn dignity. When they arrived they were escorted to their respective places according to rank, slowly finding their seats in the open marquee.

More leaders and dignitaries were following on behind, first key commonwealth and European friends, then many others. It would take some time to seat them, but all was choreographed and no-one would be allowed to be late.

The military march past was about to commence with the massed bands of the services' regiments joining the commemorations. As it passed by, the air was filled with the melodious and atmospheric marching rhythm, the sound of feet hitting the ground in scraping synchrony. Following them were the Scottish bagpipes, the stirring, reedy, swirling melody moving the silent crowds to lean forward to catch a glimpse. In places the gathered masses were more than fifteen deep, with red-suited volunteers adding to their numbers and though not everyone could see, all could hear and could not help but be moved by the occasion.

As the PM looked round him, he knew in his heart he had pulled off a masterful political coup. Today his name would be talked about, forever linked with national pride. He looked straight ahead, his heart joyful beyond belief at having pulled it off. The look on his face however, as befitted the sombre occasion, showed none of this.

Ali watched it all in stolen glances from his window. He was trying to judge when to strike and when to fire and he didn't yet know. He kept raising and lowering himself to look out, fearful of being spotted, of drawing attention to himself.

It felt like he was once again back in one of the early IS street battles for Mosul, where shattered windows and holes in walls were where the cause was fought out. Pictures of past city street fights flashed before his mind. He hadn't dared to look out then for fear of being seen and shot.

This was no different he told himself, another piece of military action; he clutched his old friend, his AK47 ready-loaded, in the cradle of his right arm. Keep cool, wait for the best time for a shot, he kept telling himself, hold on. Again, for the umpteenth time, he stepped back from the window and out of sight. He didn't want to be spotted now.

Then someone tried the toilet door. There was a voice outside the door. Ali couldn't move for terror.

'Anyone in there?' a man called.

It was, no, it couldn't be, it was Adam! Ali tried to disguise his voice.

'Gimme five minutes man,' Ali muttered through his sleeve.

He heard Adam's footsteps retreat. Then just as he was settling down again he heard more footsteps, this time it was Kaylah.

'Ali, Ali, you in there?' she said, evident concern in her voice.

'Yes, just tummy trouble, be with you soon. I'm OK,' he said, trying to keep calm.

Her footsteps also retreated down the passage. Ali realised his window of opportunity was running out. He could be discovered any second. He looked out again. At last, now he could see it was time. Everyone was sitting in their allotted places. He double-checked carefully to see who was there. There was the PM in the centre, where else, he thought. Around him like multi-coloured jewels, all the political and military leadership from around the world sat all ready to see the first of the military bands pass by. Rather than talk to each other, all were sitting still, solemnly, silently, like sitting ducks. In the distance, lining up as far as he could see in the approaching streets behind the marquee were the dress uniforms of the military ready for another march past.

Not daring to wait any longer, and taking a deep breath, Ali pulled his AK up to his shoulder. It was awkward in the tight space, the wall angle was all wrong to support him. His trigger-finger tightened, ever so slowly; and then there was the huge noise of the ratatatatatat as he let rip. The recoil against the angled wall forced him back.

As he moved forward again into position, he looked out to see figures beginning to move from the marquee. Some fell over. However, the PM was still standing, he'd missed him. Lining up his AK again, he hesitated as, crouching low thePM was being escorted down below him by flanked minders from the banks of the now-emptying seats.

As Ali paused to take stock, there were shouts, screams and commotion in the corridor outside. He didn't really know what he should do next, whether to let off another round or throw some grenades out; but, he opted to hang out the IS flag, the other end of which he'd already tied to the toilet cistern to hold it in place.

Ali immediately realised it was a mistake. The initiative that had lain with him was now lost. They already knew where he was and he wouldn't have another crack. The crash and thud of shots now piercing his window and penetrating the plaster wall above him were being directed at him.

437

Instinctively Ali moved back, one hand reaching for the door lock, the other grabbing a grenade from the window sill. His AK lay by the pan. Leaving it there, he pulled at the door, panic seizing hold. He didn't want to die, to be a martyr, he wasn't ready for that just yet.

One grenade in his hand, he stepped into the corridor. He had to move quickly for more shots were hitting his lair, driving him still further into the corridor. Another shot fired and the last piece of his toilet window shattered, falling out, leaving a gaping hole and Ali with nowhere to hide. At the sound and then sight of people who were, like him, stepping into what they thought was the safety of the narrow corridor, he yelled out loudly at them.

'Get back, get back,' as he moved out of the tiny toilet into the corridor.

As he grabbed the pin of the grenade, the curious and frightened faces of those facing him realised what he held and instinctively tried to back off, pushing each other and casting scared glances, frantically searching for safety. But they didn't know where to go. They were sheep trapped by the wolf.

Did they move away from the immediate danger Ali presented or back into their rooms where they feared they'd be shot at by the guns outside? Panic and indecision froze them in their tracks.

At that moment Ali saw Kaylah, open-mouthed, a silent scream on her face. And he saw Adam behind her, watchful, staring, looking at him, standing still, poised even; whilst others behind them in the corridor in their panic and confusion were now moving again, trying to push forward, some trying to go one way, others a different way in their terror.

It was at that precise second Ali chose to release and throw his grenade, reasoning it was him or them. As the grenade flew up and out, it almost touched the corridor ceiling. Eyes were watching its rise and the arc it made. It was going to land right by Adam which suited Ali just fine. As it flew, Ali swiftly turned to make good his escape.

Then Adam's hand reached high, caught the grenade and in a single fluid move propelled it on as if it were a cricket ball aimed at the stumps. Using its momentum he helped it on, diverting its path, his own aim true, and he watched it go, flying on its way up and out through the open window, out of the room he had just left, to fall down into the street below.

Outside there was an immediate flash and thundering explosion, glass shattered, the reverberating sound and feel of the blast so nearby shaking everyone inside. As he'd thrown his one grenade, the now unarmed Ali was already running. The shocked group in the corridor were motionless, paralysed as to what to do, and he doubted whether any would give him chase. He ran down the stairs at the end of the corridor, turned and raced across to reception. No-one saw him coming.

They were all trying to look outside, not to where he was coming from. There was chaos in the street. Something terrible was happening, they thought, but they didn't know what it might be. Something was very wrong and it paralysed them. Ali slowed to a walk.

'Can you see what's going on? I just need to get some air,' Ali said to the receptionist, reaching into the back room to retrieve his sports bag.

She barely turned her head. Together with the Security man she was more interested in trying to see what was happening out in Parliament Square than worry about here in Deans Yard. They weren't interested in him, Ali couldn't say he'd even been noticed.

He quickly turned into the street, to where all the bikes were. Clive's bike, unlocked as it was, was still there where he had left it two days ago. He climbed on and began pedalling slowly, all the time moving away from the commotion behind him. He gradually increased his speed. Sirens were wailing, the band's playing had stopped. Moments later he was out of Deans Yard and into Tufton Street. Then he turned across Millbank and pointed his bike toward the east end of

London. In just half an hour, he considered himself to have got away.

'How did I get out of that?' he asked himself, 'But it doesn't matter. I've failed, totally failed. I hardly got one round off. All that effort, wasted! I'm finished.'

Armed police were the first to go into Church House, systematically running through, covering for one another. The AK47 was found almost immediately. The unused grenades on the window sill took precious minutes to check for safety as did the scout around for any booby-trap explosives left for them.

Once declared 'safe,' forensics were called in to make an initial rapid assessment. Those with more experience instinctively knew the bird had flown, but procedures had to be followed, not instincts. In the meantime it was lock down, no-one could go anywhere as the long process of checking people and places began and endless security protocols were followed. It would take a lot longer to analyse what the multitude of CCTV cameras and mobile images had to offer.

It was slow and safe, but oh so slow for those who wanted to find Ali. As procedures were followed, the sound of crying was drowned by the sirens of the emergency services. Blue and white tape was being rolled out to control the movement of people eager to get away. The seconds became minutes and the minutes an hour.

Leading dignitaries and military personnel had to be withdrawn to safety, the carefully worked out contingency plans for such an eventuality put into full swing. Remaining senior figures were cocooned by personal security personnel. British Values Volunteers in their red outfits, recruited for the event, were were moving through the crowds looking like channels of blood. Diplomatic cars were shunting backwards and forwards picking up leaders anxious to get away from the area.

Reporters and cameramen were having a feeding frenzy, whilst thousands of policemen, one minute making a human barrier behind which the public stood, now didn't know what to do and simply waited to be told. Bewilderment was rife. Fear and uncertainty were written on everyone's face. Uncertainty meant many people were asking if worse was yet to come. No-one knew. Dark rumours were already circulating. Would there be further attacks?

In front of the book shop where the last grenade had fallen, there had been serious casualties and shrapnel had spread widely. The contingency plan which had first been put into operation was to move the PM over to the safety of the nearest buildings and into the ground-floor book shop, below and in front of Westminster Abbey. It was the nearest solid structure, the designated place of sanctuary and safety.

But he never made it. He lay dying, held in the arms of his wife who was urging him to hang on.

'Please, Dear, just hang on a little longer,' she whispered in his ear, her tears falling on to the wet blood and tear stained road.

An elderly military man with medals on his chest, a young policeman and an unknown female lay dead on the pavement nearby. Four dead. Attention was being given to those still living. Amongst the sixteen injured, some were lying prone, others sitting or if they were fortunate standing, waiting to be stabilised, before being fed into the stream of waiting ambulances and then whisked away.

At five past midday, lying where he fell, in line with the chequered grey stone squares of a London pavement, the Prime Minister died, his blood pooling red and filling the cracks as it spread. He would forever be remembered for today, but not in the way he had intended or expected.

Inside Church House it was pandemonium. Reception were making calls to senior church officials to explain what they thought had happened. One of the Archbishop of Canterbury's chaplains was advised the Archbishop needed to be urgently briefed. It would appear a terrorist had accessed Church House. Questions would be asked of the Church of

441

England at the highest level. At the same time the Archbishop was being told by a Cabinet Office official that the PM had died. In the short term, it was going to be difficult for the Archbishop to know where his priorities lay.

Later that day, the Archbishop learned that Church House had issued invitations through local clergy and there was no longer any doubt, it was his own people who had arranged for an extremist to use his church buildings to kill the PM. The early-warning signs were already there, a catastrophic public relations disaster was looming, one he knew that not even his best advisors at Lambeth place could help him overcome. The Archbishop knew it was time for him to pray.

In the first-floor passageway, senior police investigators were checking out individuals, who they were, where exactly they were positioned when the attack came and what happened as they saw it. As they did so, rumours of a second or third accomplice were putting everyone on edge and this was interrupting their progress as each danger had to be explored.

Adam and Kaylah stood silently next to each other waiting to be interviewed. Kaylah felt utterly betrayed, hollowed out and empty. Her ears were ringing from the exploding grenade. Distraught, her tears flowed. Just how had she helped Ali come and kill the PM she asked herself again and again. He'd wrecked her life. Ali had betrayed her in life and in love. Who, she asked, as the tears came, can help me now?

Adam was in shock, terrified at his action. How was it, in trying to save his own life and the lives of those looking on around him, he'd thrown the grenade that killed and injured people outside?

He heard someone in the corridor with a mobile saying the explosion had killed the PM. Could it be true? thought Adam. It was impossible to believe. He had survived when he ought to have died. He began shaking. 'What have I done?' he asked himself in terror.

All were asking themselves questions, but the answer everyone wanted to know was, where was Ali now? Adam knew, wherever Ali was, whether dead or alive, he would continue to haunt and pursue him for ever.

62

It wasn't until late afternoon they searched Kaylah's pink suitcase again before returning it to her. Her missing phone had been found. Ali had hidden it inside the case's inner zipped liner. Another betrayal. She was insistent she hadn't put it there. Its welcome return did nothing to change her feeling that Ali had taken a precious part of her soul, her inmost life and Kaylah wondered if women who'd been raped or abused felt such shame and exploitation as she felt now. She felt foolish, guilty and so, so vulnerable. Her usual self-confidence had evaporated like the autumn morning mist. In a moment she had become but a diminished version of her former self, with her light of life barely flickering within.

Her phone once more in her hand and desperate for a friend, Kaylah picked it up to see a string of missed calls from Clive. It made her cry again. She called him back in desperation. She could barely string two words together. It sounded like he was at a party. He told her to hold whilst he stepped outside so he could hear her.

When she picked up again, she told him everything she could get out between tears. Words came to a halt and Clive told her he was getting Winston to drive him straight down; they'd be picking her up within the hour.

'Hold on there Sis,' he said comfortingly, 'we're on our way.' It was all she needed to hear.

Jim and Sue could see Adam couldn't face any more of the flashing cameras or the incessant questioning and after all the intercessions made on his behalf, he was finally allowed home in the evening, their Audi taxi replaced by a BMW police car and a high speed ride back to Muswell Hill.

Adam was both victim and hero, a brave warrior and a beast, a contradiction no-one, including himself, knew how to handle. He would go down in history as the man who killed

444

the PM, even though many months later the courts and the inquiry would exonerate him. There was no way, they said, he could have known that an initial act of bravery would have had such tragic consequences. He could in no wise be held to blame.

Some questioned whether he was an accomplice all along. Haunted by self-accusation, Adam often blamed himself. His parents tried to reassure him, put their arms over his shoulders, told him they would take care of him back at home now. That wasn't what he wanted.

But the nightmare wouldn't end, guilt pressed down squeezing the very air from his lungs. The grenade looping through the air and into his hand kept playing before him. This and other nightmares continued, sometimes dreams were of prison or drowning and always, always, there was Ali taunting and torturing him. His sleep pattern got so bad he started using medication from his GP. Ali had stolen his identity, his name, used him and abused him.

Ali got lost in East London. Just cycling away, on and on, taking all the back doubles he could for fear of leaving an obvious cctv trail. He hadn't dared ease his pedalling. By early evening he'd ended up in a Walthamstow kebab shop. Ordering a Doner Kebab from the young Turkish guy behind the revolving meat tower, dripping hot fat into the tray beneath, he glanced up at the TV behind the counter to see the rolling red banner's breaking news. Waiting for his food, his eyes followed the text.

'PM dies in Armistice Sunday Commemoration terrorist attack.'

He stared uncomprehendingly. How? he asked himself. The same words streamed across the screen again. Just then his mobile rang. It was his CO.

'You're still alive!' he said, as if he were surprised.

'Wait, I'll go outside,' Ali said as he pushed open the glass door with one hand, clutching the polystyrene kebab box in the other.

445

The poster on the door advertised a forthcoming Russian circus visit. He stopped. He hadn't paid, he waved to the lad who had served him to indicate he wasn't running off.

'Yes, still alive, I'm heading for a friend with a boat, but when I get to Calais, what do I do?' asked Ali.

'You are a hero, your name and that of your family will be held in highest honour for eternity. I will have our friend meet you in Calais. Let us know when you arrive there. Have no fear, we will get you home. Take care my hero, God be praised, Allah Akbar! Allah Akbar! We have seen pictures. Everything will change now.'

Ali went back inside, paid for his kebab, the grease oozing through the bread and dropping onto his trainers. Stepping outside the kebab shop once again, he wondered how on earth did he get to Blackwater, to Dave and his boat once more? What if Dave wasn't there when he arrived? Well, he told himself, he'd need to lie up somewhere and just hope for the best.

His confidence much restored by his CO's call, Ali pushed all the things he didn't understand to the back of his mind: how the PM had actually died; and why Adam Taylor was there,. These details could wait. Keeping moving, putting London further and further behind him felt better with every mile.

He climbed back on his bike and cycled on until it was getting quiet. He reasoned that if he was the only one on the road he'd be more likely to get noticed and picked up. There was a right time to stop and rest up. Then he found a bus shelter and dragged his bike out of sight round the back. He lay down, sports bag under his head on the wooden bench seat and fell asleep. Waking with a start, he found it was only midnight. It was cold and he didn't sleep again, just shivered uncontrollably. Autumn was no time to be a fugitive, he thought. After a long night, he saw the chill light of a new grey dawn was breaking.

It took Ali ten days to track down Dave, who never followed the news and in any case never questioned this nice lad who'd enjoyed his sail with him once before.

'Of course I'll give you another crossing,' he said, 'come on board.'

Dave still hadn't fixed the radio. This time the boat's many other faults seemed less alarming to Ali. It only finally clicked that he may have slipped the net of his pursuers when he took his turn at the wheel. The rhythmic movement of the boat and the open vastness of the sea soothed him. Dave, as before, had asked him to steer while he had his break, reappearing periodically from below deck to resume control as the French coast slowly came into sight, the grey autumn mist shrouding where sea met land.

Ali was back in Mosul five days later to a relatively quiet hero's welcome. IS leadership were worried that too much attention on Ali would lead to yet another drone execution and celebrations were restricted solely to the time of his arrival in Mosul. Territorially things were going badly for IS, notwithstanding Ali's success. There would be greater reliance in future on destabilising acts of terror in the nations of the infidel. It was all they could do.

Unfortunately, the air and drone attacks had kept increasing and Ali's home had already been destroyed by one such night-time drone attack, killing Fatima and injuring one of the children in the house at the time. Ali wondered, in the half-life that he lived, whether all he had been through had been worth it; and every time he thought he found peace and quiet, the image of his father, sometimes laughing, sometimes crying, would come to him. Ali would see him dying again and again before him, on that dusty road. Just occasionally he would think of Kaylah, but then dismissed the thought, thinking she and fate had served him well. It didn't do to dwell on sentiment.

Ruth took a call from Sue late on Sunday afternoon. Earlier she had taken part in the Holy Trinity Church and Edmonton Green Public Armistice Day services and was just back in the vicarage kitchen making a pot of her favourite Earl Grey tea. As she listened to her sister Sue recounting what had happened to them in London, Ruth began shaking. She grabbed a chair back and lowered herself gently down on to its cushioned seat, feeling utterly deflated.

'No, no,' she kept saying over and over. 'No, he didn't. He didn't, no, no, no. Sue I need to talk to someone, to you. I've just realised I've been really stupid, I don't know how I'm going to cope. Ali Muhammed was looked after by me! I should have known, I should have seen it coming, I might have stopped all this. Sue, please, I need help. I need to know what to do,' said Ruth in tired desperation. Her sister Sue was equally in need of a sisterly shoulder to cry on.

'I don't know what to do either. We've just arrived home to find the world's media camped outside, even two press people in the back garden on the patio poking their cameras through the kitchen window. If I leave they'll follow me, I'm sure. If you come, they'll be on to you too. Adam's in such a state, I can't leave him. He says he keeps getting flashbacks and I've got the GP coming as soon as he can. He's sitting on the stairs with his head in his hands. I can't do anything with him.'

Then Sue had an idea, 'I know, I'll ask the policewoman sitting in with us to get you to us safely, will that be OK?' she asked.

It was agreed, and one hour later Ruth was embracing, clutching her sister for dear life in the hallway of their Muswell Hill home. Jim was trying to talk to Adam on the stairs but getting little or no response. As she looked and listened, the scope of the unfolding tragedy became ever clearer, Ruth knowing she would have to explain her actions, maybe even to the Archbishop of Canterbury, but most of all to herself.

Gradually, Ruth's early panic began to subside, she found some inner peace from somewhere. As she and Sue talked and drank more tea, they both gained more perspective and calmed each other. They were both normally very level headed people. Finally, Sue asked if Ruth would like to stay over; and, after a call to Phil to get Aneni to help with the children' supper and bedtime, it was agreed. Phil reported

448

that Aneni and Joseph were already round at the vicarage as they had got their leave to remain letters through. However, this long-awaited good news passed over Ruth and Sue's heads. Their thoughts and concerns were elsewhere. Neither of them yet knew what to do to help Adam, who was still cringing helplessly like a cowed animal on the stairs.

Although Winston didn't want to drive again so soon after the heist, on Clive's insistence he agreed to do so and they made their excuses to their celebrating friends, now high on rum, skunk, and whatever else they'd been able to lay their hands on in the space of three hours. They bid their farewells, each clutching their own large padded white envelopes, their names written in black felt tip on the outside, both envelopes fat with £7,525 in notes each.

Yes, it was far less than they'd expected, but it was pay day and it had made everyone uncontrollably happy once they'd got back to Dillon's place and counted it all out. The task had taken ages. Notes were counted and stacked time and again on the floor, checked and rechecked until everyone was satisfied. Will had joined them to oversee the counting and collect his larger share. For once, he was more relaxed and expressed his satisfaction in what they had done.

'Now,' he told them, 'it is we who is running the show in north London.'

Once outside, Winston and Clive looked at each other. They realised they were glad to be away. Winston could see the worry in Clive's face for his sister. As the Alfa moved off toward Archway and the city, Clive told him the story Kaylah had relayed to him. It sunk home and Winston registered its seriousness and significance.

'God! My God! Never! Let's get down there brother, let's pick her up. Poor kid. Look we need to make sure these envelopes are put somewhere safe, push them under your seat will you,' said Winston.

Much to his dismay, Winston wasn't allowed to drive anywhere near where he wanted to get to. The whole

Westminster area was a crime scene with lines of blue and white police tape stopping people every which way they turned and tried. The one good thing was the police definitely weren't interested in Clive or himself today, they clearly had more important matters to follow up.

In frustration, after one more failed attempt to get through, Winston got Clive to call Kaylah and told her to pull her pink case across Westminster Bridge where they were eventually able to pick her up on the south side of the Thames. When Clive saw Kaylah's face, he knew she was suffering as he'd never seen her suffer before. He needed to get her home.

Wordlessly, Clive put Kaylah's case in the boot, opened the rear door for her. Then he went round and got in the back to sit next to her. She leaned over to Clive, reached right round him and cried and cried, deep sobs, retching sobs that Clive felt shaking right through him.

'It's OK Sis, it's OK,' he kept repeating, 'let's get you home.'

Winston could be sympathetic sometimes, and leant over with a pack of tissues.

'You can use these,' he said kindly.

'Thanks, bro. She's got a lot to get over after what she's been through,' said Clive, knowing that his own story was one he would not be able to tell. More than that, he knew he hadn't yet begun to think about redirecting his own uncertain future. Was he just becoming like Winston, living on the edge, at the margins, in the now, after what they'd done earlier? Could he ever climb back into the mainstream or was it too late? These thoughts had to wait. The one thing that meant most to him right now was that his sister Kaylah needed him and he had to be there for her.

Lena Bloom had been busy in the intelligence world. Earlier in the week she'd watched discreetly as, following the unsuccessful raid on Flo and Bert's home, the raid on the Kone's home had subsequently taken place. Like many people that Sunday, she heard news of the Armistice Day outrage in a news feed on her mobile phone. The shock of it had her immediately disappointed that they hadn't got to Ali, but then she was very quickly thinking about damage limitation. What had happened could have a bad impact on her diplomatic career. Opening up her laptop she began reconstructing the report she had begun writing earlier. It would need to be changed here and there. Barely had she begun when her phone rang. It was her boss.

'Too little done too late,' she crisply and succinctly reported back to Dan Abrahams at the Israeli Embassy before he got in a word.

'Agreed, but tell me, what's anyone doing about Abu?' asked Dan. He didn't wait for Lena to answer. 'Nothing, so far as I can see, but that's one guy who needs checking out. Don't you agree?' he asked.

'Good idea,' she acknowledged.

'Leave him to me. We'll need to have a full debrief later, my office nine o'clock Monday,' said Dan ending the conversation.

At once, Dan made a further call and later that afternoon Abu found he had two unexpected visitors at his door on the Red Brick Estate. They didn't wait to be invited in, they simply pushed him back inside and tied him to a chair. He knew inside a minute they were Israeli and a cursory look round told them his drugs money was being fed through to support IS.

They soon knew he had put up Ali on Thursday night, but when they asked him what Ali's plans were he wouldn't tell them. Abu went quiet. Frightened that neighbours on the Red Brick Estate with its paper thin walls might be curious at any noise, the two men gagged Abu's mouth with tape and stuffed a pen in one hand and a clip board in the other.

'Now you write down answers to our questions,' they told him with determined menace.

They couldn't know Abu was fighting to breathe through his nose, that he was panicking. As they looked they saw he was turning blue and leaning forward he fell to the floor, pulling the chair over with a clatter. At first they thought he was play acting or maybe frightened and they didn't read the signs until it was too late.

Only then, failing to find a pulse did the two guys unwind the tape from Abu's mouth, check again for any flickering pulse and, finding none, called a halt. After quietly looking round they made to move quickly away and pulled the front door shut after them.

On one thing they were agreed as they left, that there was now one less problem in the world to be concerned about. Abu Tariq was dead. Glancing around, they climbed unobserved back into their four-wheel drive and headed south and away, confident no-one would be asking them any questions. Before they had gone a mile, the man in the passenger seat made a call to Dan Abrahams.

'IS funding in north London has just closed down,' he said.

'Excellent news,' said Dan and closed the call.

In the coming days, Adam Taylor knew he needed to get right away from the claustrophobic world of Muswell Hill. He wanted a completely fresh start and began looking for what he might do. Though he was a full term late in starting, Exeter University with their Institute of Islamic and Arab Studies wanted him there and were willing to allow him late entry. Unknown to him the British intelligence services had asked the Vice Chancellor to facilitate a place for him, 'in the national interest,' and it was arranged that from the beginning of the Spring Term, Adam had a no strings attached 'sponsored' place open to him. It was his for the taking.

Adam was not going to miss out on this opportunity, in spite of his continuing nightmares, difficulty in concentrating, the impossibility of 'small rooms and waves of crushing guilt. As the weeks passed, he desperately wanted to be fluent in Arabic and know the Islamic world better, before returning there one day. There was a side of him that was driven to know and understand the Muslim and middle-eastern world. It was the one thing that gave him energy and motivation.

At this stage he wasn't going to tell the security services where to put their sponsor money, they who'd so dropped him in it. He'd take it, every last penny. They didn't know it, but the last thing he intended was to be working for them.

His GP told him he was young and time would heal and to help the process he gave him some medication for the coming three months. Adam wasn't convinced by the GP's optimism and the flashbacks and nightmares continued whenever he stopped taking the tablets. Even so, Adam was resolved and started making plans to get himself to Exeter after Christmas. He figured physically moving away from London, away from the now suffocating embrace of his parents and all his bad memories, would give him the best chance to finally put behind him all the events since he set out on the summer's fateful Gap Year cycle ride.

It took Kaylah until the New Year to return to her course at Southgate Community College. Somehow she had found a new determination to take on the world. Once she'd completed her course the following summer, she thought she would set up and run her own business.

Surprisingly, because it had been cut short, her placement assignment and report for her work at the Drop In had still given her an 'Excellent' mark. This had greatly boosted her flagging confidence and Ruth's support and feedback to the college really helped.

Clive had been great, supporting her, walking with her, talking and most of all listening to her. He'd decided to enrol for college himself in the coming Autumn, though he hadn't yet decided where. Soon, he'd bought himself some new clothes and looked quite the cool dude.

'I've been thinking it's time to take on the world like my big Sis. I'm not sure I'll do business studies like you - seems to have got you in a load of trouble,' he joked. 'No, maybe, I'll do something else, working with people perhaps, but I'll need qualifications along the way. I'll see what they suggest.'

'Clipper, I'm so pleased you said that,' and she gave him an unexpected sisterly hug.

About a month later, as Kaylah was walking to college in December, on her way to see her tutor and agree with her a January return, a car pulled up ahead of her and a smartly dressed young woman stepped out, walked toward her and introduced herself as Lena Bloom.

'We wondered if you'd like to do some work for the Joint Intelligence Services,' she said. 'You could help us reach a guy called Ali Muhammed. We need to find him for what he's done. Will you help us?'

On that occasion Kaylah had said, 'no,' but Lena was insistent and she left her card and number anyway which she stuffed away in her pocket. At the time, Kaylah thought nothing further of this pushy woman.

It was late January, a Friday lunchtime and Kaylah was leaving college for the weekend. She was outside MacDonald's with her friend Melissa when her phone rang. Her screen showed a number she didn't know, but she took it anyway. Her heart stopped. It was Ali.

'I'm sorry,' he said.

Before he could say another word, she replied, 'Go to hell!'

'Please,' he called out, 'things are bad for me here, don't hang up. I am really sorry.'

'I don't want to talk to you,' she said loudly, shaking her head defiantly.

Then, feeling Lena's card in her pocket, she calmed herself before having the last word.

'But, call me in a week or two, we've got a lot to catch up on.'

ISTanbul

J E Hall

Want to know what happens next?
Flashbacks is the first novel in a trilogy.
In the second, the central characters
find themselves in Istanbul,
caught up in an IS terrorist plot.

IStanbul is scheduled for publication early 2017

Harry's England

J E Hall

The final novel in the trilogy moves the action
to the south west of England where a right wing
extremist decides to stand
in a Plymouth parliamentary by-election.

Harry's England is scheduled for publication late 2017

A Fitting End

Making the most of a funeral

Hugh James

CANTERBURY
PRESS
Norwich

First published in 2004 by the Canterbury Press Norwich
(a publishing imprint of Hymns Ancient & Modern Limited,
a registered charity)
St Mary's Works, St Mary's Plain,
Norwich, Norfolk, NR3 3BH

www.scm-canterburypress.co.uk

British Library Cataloguing in Publication data

A catalogue record for this book is available
from the British Library

ISBN 1-85311-602-5

Typeset by Regent Typesetting, London
Printed and bound by
Biddles Ltd, www.biddles.co.uk

Contents

Acknowledgements   v

Foreword   vii

Introduction   ix

1   Making Sense of Death   1

2   Theology and the Funeral   25

3   What Makes a Funeral?   44

4   Whose Funeral Is It?   62

5   Institutions and Organizations Involved   81

6   Some Social Influences   94

7   Contemporary Issues   109

8   Difficult Funerals   128

9   Remembering the Dead   149

10   Tying Together Loose Ends   159

Appendix 1: Further Reading   164

Appendix 2: Websites   168

Appendix 3: Addresses   171

Index   177

Acknowledgements

This book reflects much of my experience as a parish priest and research for a higher degree on the subject of funerals. There are a number of individuals who have helped me in specific ways. They include: the Reverend Peter Jupp, Director of the National Funerals College, who gave me much helpful advice when I first embarked on the research; the Venerable Hywel Jones, Archdeacon of Cardigan; the Right Reverend D. Huw Jones and the Right Reverend Carl Cooper, successive Bishops of St Davids who have encouraged me at various stages of the project; Rabbi Alexandra Wright who made several suggestions and circulated questionnaires to a number of rabbis; and those priests who answered similar questions; the Reverend Tim Alban-Jones, for his helpful comments and agreeing to be quoted.

The University Libraries at Lampeter and Cardiff, and the National Library of Wales at Llanbadarn Fawr, near Aberystwyth, have provided me with access to much reading material. Their staff have always been most helpful.

I am particularly grateful to those who people who have read and commented on all or part of the manuscript: the Reverend Wyn Beynon, Mrs Kirsten Canning, Mrs Lynn Chambers, Dr Ann Jay, Mrs Gwenllian Kidd, Mr Malcolm Porter, Ms Christabel Russell-Vick, Mr Iliff Simey, Mr David West, and the Reverend Mandy Williams-Potter. Their suggestions have helped shape the final document.

I have appreciated all the comments from staff and students at St Michael's Theological College, Llandaff, fellow research students at the Centre for Ministry Studies of the University of Wales, Bangor, clergy of St David's Diocese, and others who

A Fitting End

have heard me lecture on the subject. I have valued the assistance of the staff at Canterbury Press, especially Ms Christine Smith and Ms Mary Matthews, whose guidance through the pitfalls of writing a book has been invaluable.

My thanks and gratitude are due to my parishioners and colleagues who have supported my study and writing, although it has sometimes kept me from parish projects which might otherwise have been completed more quickly. I only hope that they will value the difference it has made to my conducting of funerals, and that it may help others in other places. Where I have referred to a specific funeral, I have changed details in order to preserve individuals' privacy. In particular I must mention the help I received from the Reverend Noel James, the Reverend Janet Robbins, and the Reverend Canon William Richards who maintained services in my group of parishes while I took a period of extended study leave to write this book.

Above all I have to thank two people: first the Reverend Professor Leslie J. Francis, Director of the Welsh National Centre for Religious Education and of the Centre for Ministry Studies, and Professor of Practical Theology at the University of Wales, Bangor, whose friendship and supervision has guided my research. He has made so many helpful suggestions over the years that it is impossible to imagine this book without his help. Second, my wife Susan, who has lived with this project for so long. She has patiently supported my work, often putting up with my absence, and provided many insightful suggestions, as well as correcting my spelling, grammar and logic. Without their support this book would never have seen the light of day.

Hugh James
Cydweli, 2004

Hugh James is a parish priest and former Area Dean in West Wales. He studied funeral practices for a higher degree from the University of Wales and is involved in pre- and post-ordination training in this aspect of pastoral ministry.

Foreword

The crematorium and the cemetery remain at the centre of ministry for many clergy. Funerals bring clergy closer to members of their core congregation and introduce them to individuals and to families who live most of their time far removed from their local churches and chapels. In the twenty-first century death remains inevitable and largely undiscussed. Funerals bring clergy face-to-face with the depth of human emotion, negative as well as positive. Here is combined the ministry of pastoral care, Christian teaching, and evangelization.

In this carefully constructed and well presented analysis, Hugh James invites his fellow clergy to stand back from their personal experiences of funerals and to reflect on the underlying issues. His chapter structure raises profound and puzzling questions: What is death? What is a funeral? Whose funeral is it? Clearly the way in which we conduct funerals reveals our fundamental assumptions about these questions. Pausing to reflect rationally on these questions may change our minds and influence our practices.

Unlike so much in life, we do not get a second chance for a funeral. Each funeral is unique, specific, and utterly final. Clergy are committed to making the most of every funeral, and to seeing that all who are entrusted to their ministry are offered a fitting end. This book helps us to fulfil that important ministry.

Leslie J. Francis
Priest and Professor of Practical Theology
University of Wales, Bangor

Introduction

I began to form the idea of writing *A Fitting End: Making the most of a funeral* after moving to Llanfihangel-ar-Arth as vicar in 1992. Llanfihangel is a rural, mainly Welsh-speaking part of West Wales, and I discovered that my parishioners' expectations of funerals were somewhat different from my own. I was once asked to attend the funeral of a parishioner's elderly relative. I had never met the deceased and the funeral was to be conducted by the vicar of a neighbouring parish, and so I was puzzled as to why I was being asked. People would talk about funerals being public, private or strictly private. I had never before heard such terms used in this way. It took time to realize that such descriptions gave neighbours and friends clear messages about whether or not they should attend. Often when I arrived at church to conduct a funeral I would find up to eight other clergy, of various denominations, waiting for me in the vestry. They would all have some connection with either the deceased or close relatives of the deceased, and would all be expecting to take part in the service. It was very different from my experience in another part of Wales, where I had nearly always been the only cleric taking the service. It frequently proved impossible to conduct it in the way I had intended, as others did things in their own ways. Clergy who came from the area, however, were surprised when I talked to them about this; they had never known anything else. It then struck me that although the Church had helped me prepare to minister in my second language (Welsh) it had, apparently, not considered helping me prepare for this aspect of ministering in a new area. The difference in culture was far more than simply speaking a different language.

Experiences such as these prompted me to ask wider questions about what we are doing when conducting funeral services. What is a funeral for? Who is responsible for deciding what occurs during it? Who should take part in it? Who may or may not attend? Who are the appropriate people to decide who may or may not attend? Whose funeral is it? I discussed the matter with Professor Leslie Francis and the result was my spending some years researching for a higher degree.

I reflected on my own training for funerals. It had consisted of walking round the college grounds with some of my fellow students, playing the parts of minister, bearers and mourners. When it came to my turn to be the minister, I led the coffin to the graveside and stepped on the blanket which had been folded to represent the grave. I was told that if I did that in a real funeral I would fall into the grave. It must have had a powerful effect, as I have never since fallen into a grave while conducting a funeral! Nevertheless, it prepared us for only one model of funeral: burial in the churchyard immediately following a service in the church. There are so many alternatives. It taught us nothing about the differences between cremation and burial, about taking a service in a house before the funeral, what to do when the service is to be held in a force-eight gale, how to give of one's best at the tenth funeral in a week, or when the two wives of a deceased bigamist, only recently aware of each other's existence, are unable to agree on the hymns.

Despite the pressures of parochial ministry, I received much guidance from my training incumbent and fellow curates, but regretted that I had not been given more practical preparation before ordination. As the years went on I realized that I was also unaware of the theoretical knowledge which would have helped me understand why I was there in the first place. Academic theology, pastoral and liturgical studies, anthropology, sociology and psychology have much to offer, and, in my view, we fail our clergy by not relating these disciplines more closely to the funeral ministry. Of all the occasional offices, that of the funeral brings us most closely into contact with all sorts and conditions of men and women. Only a small number of people come to the churches for baptisms and weddings but the vast majority still do for funerals, and we meet them at a time when they are at their most vulnerable. The potential for a positive and helpful ministry is huge, and clergy meet the challenge with a high degree of professionalism and pastoral skill. Nevertheless, the possibility of disaster is equally huge. We live in a rapidly changing society where consumer choice is now viewed as a right and increasingly mourners are seeing funerals as a commodity to be purchased. The Christian churches need to take this far more seriously than they do, before they discover that unsatisfied mourners take their custom elsewhere. It is not that I believe that the Church should operate as a commercial organization, but that we need to realize that we operate in a world led by considerations of supply and demand. In an average week the number of people attending funeral services conducted by Christian clergy will be in the millions. The funerals we conduct form a shop window for the Christian faith which is seen by far more people than almost any other activity in which we engage. It might be argued that the long-term impact of the churches on our society will, to a large extent, be determined by how effectively we perform that ministry week in, week out.

As I began to realize how brief the preparation had been for this part of my ministry, I resolved that what I have learned should be shared more widely. It is my hope that this book will help clergy and others who arrange and conduct funerals to do so in a way that is better informed, producing funerals which more people find helpful and which leave the clergy themselves feeling they have been of more use to the Kingdom of God.

Making Sense of Death

Death is an abstract concept with a negative content for which no unconscious correlative can be found.

Sigmund Freud[1]

'What is death?' At first sight this question might appear rather odd. Yet over the generations society has chosen to define death in different ways. Sometimes it has been from a theological perspective, sometimes from medical, legal and sociological points of view. People have variously seen it as part of an ongoing process or merely a single event. How has death affected our relationships? Over the centuries it has done so in differing ways. The wars of the twentieth and twenty-first centuries have had a significant influence on our thinking about it. What place has bureaucracy in death? Record-keeping, statistical analysis, and the administration of modern life make demands on the way we handle death, which previous generations did not face. These are some of the issues addressed in this chapter, and before going on to look at the funeral we will examine various ways in which death has been understood, reflect theologically on its meaning, and look at recent research into popular beliefs regarding death and life after death.

Defining Death

During the eighteenth century, a change took place in the way death was perceived. The spiritual gave way to the medical. Until that time, the primary role of the doctor had been seen as that of predicting the time of death, so that a dying person might organize his or her last hours and prepare to meet the Creator.

During the eighteenth century the doctor's role changed to one of relieving pain, sometimes keeping knowledge of death from the patient in order to relieve suffering. Thomas Sheridan commented on this in the 1760s: 'Very few now die. Physicians take care to conceal people's danger from them. So that they are carried off, properly speaking, without dying; that is to say, without being sensible of it.'[2] Previously death had been seen as a religious event: God calling a soul forth from this world into the next. Now it was becoming a medical event caused by any one of a host of germs and diseases. It was ceasing to be primarily a spiritual passage and becoming a natural process overseen by doctors. Accordingly it became normal to call the doctor, rather than the priest, to the bedside of the dying. There is still, however, an expectation among clergy that they will be called to minister to dying parishioners. My experience is that this does occur, but less often than I expected. I have frequently been surprised by how many devout and regular churchgoers choose to die without the ministry of their priest. Are clergy still being trained to expect a role that largely disappeared more than two centuries ago?

Today a death must be certified by a doctor before it can be registered, and in some circumstances more than one doctor's certification is required. When a patient dies at home a doctor may issue a death certificate provided he or she has seen the patient during the previous two weeks and knows the cause of death. If the patient has not been seen or if there is no known medically accepted cause of death, the coroner must be informed and, if there is any possibility of crime, the police also. In practice the police are often involved if the death is sudden or unexpected. If the deceased is to be cremated then the doctor must discuss the death with a second independent doctor who has been fully registered for at least five years. The fact of death is not, there-fore, legally recognized until the medical profession has con-firmed it. What criteria do doctors use to decide whether or not death has taken place?

The situation today is rather more complicated than it was thirty-five years ago. In 1968, *Black's Law Dictionary* gave the following definition of death: 'The cessation of life; the ceasing to exist; defined by physicians as a total stoppage of the circulation of the blood, and a cessation of the animal and vital functions consequent thereupon, such as respiration, pulsation, etc.'[3]

That definition has since proved inadequate for the medical profession as it does not take into account the concept of 'brain death'. In the 1950s, a relatively simple invention, the respirator, helped keep alive many patients who had no chance of recovery from a state of permanent loss of intellectual function. In December 1967, medical science took another step forward when the first heart-transplant operation was performed. Such an operation, not surprisingly, involves certain difficulties, some of which are exacerbated if the donor heart has stopped beating, as it is then liable to damage. The same applies to some other organs: they need to be taken from the body of the donor before the heart stops. This raised difficult moral questions: When have a person's 'animal and vital functions' actually ceased? If the heart has not stopped, can we say the donor is dead? If it is still beating, then does removing the heart constitute murder? Should doctors have to wait for the heart to stop before using a 'dead' person's organs for transplant? As a result of these and other dilemmas, the Harvard Medical School set up an ad hoc committee to examine the definition of death. The committee's report defined death as 'irreversible coma' and referred to 'permanent loss of intellect'. This definition became known as 'brain death' (although in fact some functions of the brain do continue) and has since been adopted by nearly all developed nations.

The now-established concept of 'brain death' is not without its own ethical difficulties, as in the cases of pregnant women pronounced 'dead' but kept 'alive' until the birth of the child. Such ethical questions are beyond the scope of this book, but I mention them here in order to make the point that the understanding of death is, even today, not always a straightforward matter. Most people do not think about death at all until a loved one dies. When that occurs they are forced to think about it. Lay people have not usually had to analyse death in the way the legal and medical professions have, and when faced with it there may well have been considerable heartache and soul-searching. Questions, such as whether a life-support machine should have been turned off, or why a patient was kept alive 'artificially' for so long, may have been asked. The task of conducting a funeral following such circumstances will be very different from, for example, the situation where an elderly person has died quietly at home in bed, surrounded by family.

Later in this chapter we will see other ways of defining death, which have been used at different times in our history. Different ways of thinking about death and the theological and practical implications of them will become apparent. For the moment, it is enough to note that the way death is officially defined in our culture has undergone a significant change within the last few decades, although lay people's understanding has not always caught up with that of the medical and legal professions

The Theological Language of Death

Traditionally, theological language about death has spoken of the separation of the soul from the body. A common illustration has been of the envelope and the letter. When we die, it is suggested, our body is like the envelope. It has served its purpose, whereas the soul (the letter) survives. So long as we accept that a human being consists of a body and a soul, this illustration is useful. What if we are not like that, however, but bear more resemblance to a postcard? In other words, an individual is understood to be not body and soul but simply one discrete person: this is a unitary rather than a dualist understanding of human identity. How do we speak of death if we adhere to a belief system that is unitary rather than dualist? Other disciplines and much of modern theology are uncomfortable with the idea of a body–soul dualism, and the unitary view of an individual as a single person is more acceptable to them.

Jewish, or Hebraic, writers before the time of Jesus were essentially unitary, not believing in a body–soul dualism.

Dualism resulted from Greek, or Hellenistic, ways of thinking, particularly those of Plato and Aristotle who understood human beings to be both body and soul. In early Christianity there was a tension between these two ways of thinking, as the Hellenistic understanding was imposed on the Jewish, or Hebraic, world. This change in understanding was taking place at the same time as the early Church was developing its own identity separately from Judaism. It clearly influenced the writing of the New Testament, and it is difficult for us to know to what extent Hellenistic influences affected the thinking of Jesus and the apostles, and how much of what is ascribed to them was influenced by New Testament authors writing at a later date. The same ideas also influenced the development of rabbinic Judaism as it struggled to come to terms with the destruction of the Jerusalem temple. The relationship between Jewish, Christian, and other philosophical views in this period is a highly complex one.

There is a similar and related dichotomy between resurrection and immortality. The Hebraic, or Jewish, understanding of resurrection is that the whole person dies and is resurrected albeit with a different kind of body. This is, however, quite complex as the belief in resurrection in classical rabbinic Judaism manifests itself in different ways, from those who see the reconstituted body being resurrected in the land of Israel, to those, such as Maimonides (1135–1204), who explain that we cannot understand the notion of resurrection as it is miraculous and wholly spiritual. The Hellenistic, or Greek, idea of immortality of the soul is that the body dies but the soul, being immortal, does not die but survives. A belief in resurrection assumes a unitary viewpoint, whereas a belief in immortality requires a dualistic understanding. Christianity has often tried to hold these two concepts together, giving rise to a number of conflicting questions.

Paul Sheppy argues that a 'unitary anthropology', not seeing people as divisible into body and soul, is consistent with biblical revelation and the writings of the early Church fathers.[4] His understanding of death and resurrection challenges the body–

soul anthropology which has so commonly been assumed in Christian theology. Language that speaks of commending the soul to God and the body to the elements loses its place, because the whole person is dead and all must be 'released' to God. So a unitary anthropology affirms resurrection as being the act of God in response to death.

This has important implications for funeral liturgies and the language used. Historically most funeral liturgies have used the traditional language of commending the soul to God and committing the body to the elements, but increasingly there are ministers seeking to use the language of 'release'. If such language is to be used it should achieve two ritual functions: declaring that the living have no further claim on the dead, and also declaring that the dead have no further claim on the living. Ministers who try to adopt this understanding in the wider context of their whole ministry are seeking to find ways of speaking about death and resurrection that do not allow it to appear that the soul escapes the body, but link resurrection with God's action in raising Jesus from the dead: we do not escape death; we are delivered from it. Some modern funeral liturgies have tried to meet the needs of both those who use this unitary terminology and those who use more traditional language. Compare, for example, the following prayer from a modern liturgy with those from the various books of common prayer quoted in the section on commendation in Chapter 2:

From the dust you made us, O God;
to the dust we return.
Awaken your *daughter N.*,
whom we release to you,
from the sleep of death,
and feed *her* at your table with life eternal.[5]

A Theology of Death

The development of Christian beliefs about death and future life has its roots in pre-Christian Judaism, and our contemporary understanding of dying, death and the disposal of dead bodies has been powerfully shaped by what the Christian faith has had to say about death and the hope of a life beyond the grave. These beliefs are expressed in our funeral liturgies. To understand them we have first to recognize that they have undergone a complex evolution, and that Christian eschatology, or the study of 'last things', is by no means simple.

We have already seen something of the dichotomy between resurrection and immortality. Yet if, in addition to that, we give more thought to resurrection, we will discover a further conflict between a sense that resurrection takes place almost immediately after death, and an understanding that it will take place at the end of time. Thus, Christian eschatology straddles, somewhat uneasily, a sense of sharing immediately after death in the worship of the heavenly places, and a waiting for the fulfilment of resurrection at the end of time.

Turning to the question of immortality, it is not only Greek but also Roman and Egyptian mythologies that have influenced the development of Christian theology, bringing with them the conflicting belief in the existence of an immortal soul. Whereas the Hebraic understanding speaks of the death of the whole person, followed by resurrection *at a later time*, the Hellenistic idea speaks of an immortal soul that survives the death of the body and *immediately* moves to eternal life, possibly through a number of intermediate stages. This notion produced the medieval beliefs in purgatory and the Reformation reactions to them.

During the nineteenth and twentieth centuries further secular influences altered the way death was viewed. The growth of cemeteries under secular control and the practice of cremation played their part in this and in the changing patterns of burial and disposal. This was accompanied by a decline in membership of the institutional churches. Western societies have also been changed by the presence of other world faiths, and the latter part of the twentieth century has produced, even within the Christian churches, a variety of beliefs about death and future life. There are individuals within the Christian community who, rather than looking for a future life beyond the grave, hope for a social and political transformation of this world. Indeed, scientific materialism has, for some, eroded the hope of life beyond death. Yet, despite secular agnosticism, when the Church of England's Doctrine Commission produced its report, *The Mystery of Salvation*, in 1995, the secular media criticized it mainly for its suggestion that hell might be better thought of in terms of a second death of total non-being, rather than of flames. Criticism was centred almost entirely on just a few pages of what is an extensive report.[6]

Most modern Protestant theologians would prefer to accept the idea of death and resurrection rather than immortality, although they would reject quite firmly a belief in the resurrection of the actual physical frame that is laid in the tomb. The differing understandings of academic theologians, people in the pews, and the population in general is something we will return to in the final section of this chapter.

Death and the prospect of its approach can be devastating for any person. Religions have always struggled with the human need to find meaning to the questions raised by death and have tried to place our understanding of it in a much wider context than that of the individual's demise. The valuing of human life includes the reality of death, maybe as the last enemy, but also as a necessary condition of life. Attempts to evade death or to pretend that it is not serious or to deny its necessary place in the ordering of life have almost always been regarded by the major religious traditions as false, dangerous or subversive of truth. It is suggested that enterprises such as spiritualism, by trying to communicate with the dead, give the impression that death is comparatively insignificant or unimportant, and they are, therefore, regarded by most religions as denying a truth about ourselves.

It is often argued that religious traditions came into being in order to reassure those who could not face the inevitability of their oblivion. The argument is that the idea of God was invented as a super-powerful being who provides a life for us beyond the grave, a kind of 'pie in the sky when you die'. This is not consistent with what is said about death in the early history of the major religious traditions, both East and West, where there is frequently a clear concept of death being necessary in order for life to exist. Death is necessary so that one generation can make space for the next; the processes of growth and development depend on generations succeeding one other. Death is therefore the price that has to be paid if there is to be self-replicating, self-conscious life within our world. If we ask why it occurs, part of the answer is that life could not exist in any other way. For Christians, the death and resurrection of Jesus are the events that initiate the new creation. The crucifixion is a statement that there cannot be new life without death and that God, in drawing us freely to himself, has accepted the necessity of death into himself. But the resurrection is equally a declaration that death does not exist without the consequence of life. You cannot have life without death; but where you do have death, you can have life.

It is one thing to philosophize on the meaning of death, and another to be faced with its imminence. In October 1983, at Trinity College Chapel, Cambridge, Bishop John Robinson said in his last sermon, preached some months after he had been diagnosed as having an inoperable cancer:

> Two years ago I found myself having to speak at the funeral of a sixteen-year-old girl who died in our Yorkshire dale. I said stumblingly that God was to be found in the cancer as much as in the sunset. That I firmly believed, but it was an intellectual statement. Now I have had to ask if I can say it of myself, which is a much greater test.[7]

The rest of the sermon consists of reflection on how one deals with the diagnosis of a fatal illness, the meaning of death, life and resurrection, and our resources as Christians for dealing with death. It is a powerful reflection from one of the most noted of radical theologians and ends with a reference to St Paul's words, 'For me life is Christ, and death gain' (Philippians 1:21). Any preacher may face a similar question: how to help a congregation find meaning in the circumstances of a particular death. The difficulty is often how to condense the complex arguments of theology into a short funeral address without being patronizing or insensitive.

Changing Perceptions of Death

Today we are accustomed to thinking of death as one single event which brings an individual's life on earth to an end. Such an understanding is by no means universally held, either within other cultures or during other periods of our own culture. Medieval man would have understood death as a process, of which the act of dying was but one part. Hence it was considered effective to serve a legal writ on a corpse as it was carried to its grave. The soul and its destination were affected by the actions of those left behind and it would be considered effective to exhume the body of a criminal and exact punishment upon it. Masses for the departed soul could secure a place in heaven or at least alleviate the sufferings of purgatory. As time passed, this sense of connection with the deceased became less and this was mirrored by what happened to the physical remains. After burial, decay set in and in a number of years (between 5 and 15, depending on local conditions) only bare bones would be left. In many cultures these would be moved to a separate place and the grave space re-used (as is still the case in several European countries today).

In the Middle Ages the inhabitants of Europe were haunted by death as a random, feckless and capricious evil that could strike any person down at any time, without warning. By the late nineteenth and early twentieth centuries that perception had changed. Medical improvements, better standards of public health, improved housing conditions, higher wages, shorter working hours and a more nourishing diet all played their part in taming many ravaging diseases. Mathematicians and statisticians now turned their attention to death, resulting in tables of death and actuarial analyses that created a concept of life expectancy. Life expectancy might vary according to the area in which one lived or one's occupation; nevertheless, people began to expect that they would live for so many years at least. Unexpected death began to be seen as an effect of illness and something that in time would be overcome.

The recording of official statistics relating to death has also affected the way death is perceived. The modern death certificate is accompanied by rules and explanations:

'Rule 1. Death is a product of pathology.' That is to say, the cause of death will always be a disease that is evident in the body. For every death there will be a pathology.

'Rule 2. Death is a physical event.' Consequently, the cause of death can always be located in some part of the body.

'Rule 3. A cause of death is a visible thing, susceptible (in theory at least) to detection by sense data.' In other words, one ought to be able to see the diseased anatomy at a post-mortem.

'Rule 4. A cause of death is always a singular event, (although it might exist as part of a sequence).' That is, the cause of death is always identifiable as one specific event.

'Rule 5. A pertinent cause of death is usually one that is proximate to the event.' This means that the cause of death is normally present at the moment of death.[8]

Some of these principles and assumptions are unrealistic in the sense that they fail to reflect the complications of individual deaths. They attempt to reduce death to its pathological essentials and it is this process that is called 'the deconstruction of death'. Death is now explained as a result of one of a number of diseases, generating the illusion that it can be controlled. Since all disease is, in theory, conquerable, then death itself may be overcome. It is perhaps a small step to believing that, once we have fathomed out and overcome the causes of cancer, pneumonia and wasting diseases, we will have overcome death itself.

This line of reasoning is most forcefully expressed in late

twentieth-century public health discourses, often characterized by two themes: first, that ill health and early death are avoidable; and second, that the key to good health lies within the grasp of individuals. Death and misfortune can be avoided if people behave appropriately. Death, it seems, now stalks only those who are careless. We forget, however, the effect of war and terror, and even the fact that we all one day die, and it is when our expectations of life are defied (for example, with the deaths of children or young adults) that we are shocked at death's capacity to strike in its hitherto random and senseless fashion.

It could, of course, now be argued that the dramatic images of the World Trade Center's twin towers collapsing on 11 September 2001 and the Madrid bombings of 11 March 2004 have created a new awareness in Western nations of the horror of sudden and unexpected death. In addition, the emerging patterns of terrorism and threats of terrorism, in places where these were never previously considered likely, may engender a new feeling of insecurity. It is, perhaps, only under such conditions that we, in the modern Western world, can even begin to glimpse the image of death which once haunted the inhabitants of pre-capitalist Europe, and which still haunts our contemporaries in developing countries.

The Effect of Wars

At a personal level we are brought into contact with our mortality by the death of a person with whom we are closely connected. There are, in addition, large-scale events that simultaneously bring a whole community or nation into such contact. The two world wars of the twentieth century both, in different ways, changed the way death was perceived.

In the First World War thousands of young men from all over the country and all social classes died over a four-year period, with the national press quickly making the widespread nature of the sacrifice clear to everyone. The loss became national and, above all, the dead were not career soldiers but volunteers or conscripts. In one sense, both during and after the First World War, there were two nations: those at the front, who saw and purveyed death, and those at home, who saw no death, no carnage and no corpses, but who experienced bereavement.

Against the background of such a war, the churches' teaching about life after death had a political as well as a pastoral significance. Believing in heaven could nerve soldiers to face death and induce families more readily to accept the sacrifice of their loved ones. This led many Christians to a more inclusive view of salvation: not even the most conservative pastor would be likely to tell a dying soldier or his bereaved relatives that he was destined for hell. Most soldiers thought that the churches offered only heaven or hell, that heaven was primarily a reunion of friends and relations, and that hell could usually be discounted.

The Second World War was different. By the end of 1940 a considerable number of people had been killed in air raids. Funerals caused by the First World War had been conducted mainly by military chaplains at the front whereas in the Second World War funerals were also conducted at home. The scarcity of resources and the need to engage in the war effort caused some simplification of ritual, and there was a greater sense of having been involved in a clear struggle against evil; consequently the sacrifice needed less justification.

The casualties of the First World War blighted the inter-war years, but the years following 1945 have been haunted by the Jewish Holocaust and by the spectre of nuclear war. Death on such a scale confronts all human beings with the darker side of human life and forces believers to face uncomfortable and difficult questions about a God who appears uncaring in the face of human suffering and misery.

Attitudes to death, then, evolved considerably during the twentieth century as a result of the two wars. Many of those raised before the First World War always acknowledged their mortality. Between the wars there was an obsession with death and the inter-war generation grew up with a horror of morbid ritual, perhaps in reaction to this. This generation was then plunged into the Second World War and some of its children have subsequently criticized it for 'denying' death. The post-1945 generation has grown up under the abstract shadow of the Bomb, but also with low mortality rates, death increasingly occurring in hospital rather than at home, and families remaining intact for many years without direct contact with death.

Accordingly, those who face the death of a loved one for the first time are often less emotionally prepared than they might otherwise be. This raises the question as to whether part of the Church's role is to remind people of their mortality and the fact that they, and those around them, will one day die. The whole tenor of the burial service in the 1662 Book of Common Prayer was precisely this: to remind the congregation of their own mortality and to exhort them to godly living. Modern funeral liturgies have discarded this in favour of commending the deceased into God's hands, celebrating the life of the deceased, and praying for the comfort of the bereaved. In doing this I wonder how much we have rejected something important, and how much of that we need to recover. This not only applies to our liturgical language but also the things we say in pastoral care of the bereaved and those approaching death, and in the more general area of our teaching and preaching.

It is worth noting the changes in approach to the burial by the British armed forces of those killed in action. In the past, dead soldiers used to be buried in the country where they died and there are British military cemeteries in many parts of the world. The Americans, by comparison, used to bring their dead home wherever possible. Indeed the sight of body-bags being taken home from Vietnam is generally accepted to have been one of the causes of pressure to end the war there. During the Falklands conflict in the 1980s, however, British practice changed and bodies of fallen soldiers were brought home. The same has occurred in respect of those killed in the invasion of Iraq in 2003, and those killed later, although in Britain no filming of the repatriation of bodies is allowed, in order to protect the privacy of those bereaved.

A Bureaucratic Nightmare

Since 1837 it has been a requirement that all deaths in England and Wales be registered, and the compilation of mortality statistics has thus become possible. The image of Death, personified by a skeleton tugging at an individual's coat, has been replaced by life-expectancy tables. They enable actuaries to calculate pension premia, and health-care officials to correlate mortality with the environment, nutrition, income, class background, and ethnic origin, to name but a few. The task of public officials is 'not to pray over the corpse, but to register, categorise and sanitise it', to quote Tony Walter.[9] Our modern laws require a death to be explained. When there is any doubt about the circumstances, a post-mortem examination is conducted, often causing considerable distress to relatives, while the funeral is delayed until the coroner releases the body. Scientific examination takes precedence over religious requirements and the personal sensitivities of the bereaved.

We have already seen how death ceased to be viewed as a primarily religious event and was seen as a medical one. It can now also be regarded as a bureaucratic one. The point is well illustrated by a booklet *What To Do When Someone Dies*, published by the Consumers' Association.[10] It says nothing about preparing the soul for the next life, or about the emotions one may feel; it is almost entirely about forms that must be filled in, and the bureaucratic procedures involved in disposing of the body. Its foreword states: '[This book] makes no attempt to deal with the personal or social aspects of death such as the psychology of grief and shock or the conventions of mourning, nor does it trace the historical development of rituals and attitudes to death.' I also notice that, although this booklet states that it 'deals with the formalities and procedure in England and Wales', and refers to important differences which apply in Scotland, it makes frequent reference to the Church of England without once mentioning the Church in Wales, which has different rules and regulations, even though my edition of the booklet was published forty-nine years after the disestablishment of the Welsh church.

In North America cremation has recently become more common and now accounts for around a quarter of US funerals and almost half of Canadian ones. It has been the norm in the United Kingdom for several decades, where its expansion in the latter half of the twentieth century was driven mainly by the financial and administrative concerns of local authorities, not by the requirements of religious ritual or the needs of mourners. Funerals are scheduled to fit into convenient time-slots made available by crematorium staff, the convenience of mourners sometimes being a secondary consideration. Those arranging and conducting the funeral have therefore to wait and work within the restrictions placed upon them. More will be said about this in the section on cremation, but one thing is clear: modern death is surrounded by bureaucracy on a scale that our forebears would find totally incomprehensible. When a funeral takes place today it comes in the midst of many new and confusing demands for the mourners. The minister's skills may be tested to the full in attempting to make it a helpful experience, rather than one more ordeal that must be faced.

Sociology of Death

In the 1970s, American sociologists devoted a great deal of study to death in American society, so much so that Robert Slater wrote that sociologists of the future would look back at the 1970s and say it was the decade of death, just as the 50s was the decade of sex, and the 60s of drugs.[11] That may have been so in America, but not in Britain. With the exception of medical sociologists, British sociologists have written little on the subject of death. Until the late 1980s, even sociologists of religion were largely silent on the subject. One reason put forward for this is that death has been perceived as a medical rather than a social or religious event and that sociologists have themselves held this view. Whatever the reason, one effect of it is that we know more about funeral rites in many pre-modern societies than we do about those within our own country.

In 1989, Ralph Houlbrooke considered how death had become a marginalized concern. In his introduction to a collection of essays on *Death, Ritual and Bereavement*, he reflects on the view that a longer life span greatly reduces society's concern with death and the hereafter. The most important single stimulus for interest in the subject was provided by Geoffrey Gorer's *Death, Grief and Mourning in Contemporary Britain*, published in 1965. Gorer claimed that the drastic simplification of funeral and mourning customs during the twentieth century was symptomatic of a desire to ignore death. Grief itself, deprived of the supportive framework of mourning, was discouraged, while the terminally ill increasingly died alone in hospital rather than at home surrounded by family. Gorer's work has provoked a continuing debate about British attitudes to death and whether or not it is a taboo subject.

There is a conventional wisdom quoted among sociologists in recent years that 'death is publicly absent but privately present'.[12] They argue that death is institutionally repressed and hidden away from the major areas of modern life. Some would argue that this is partly due to the demise of a generally accepted religious language in which the symbolic meanings of death can be articulated within our society. There is, however, another and opposing view that death is very much present in the public sphere. Our concerns with health and diet, medical and life insurance, and the active steps we take to live as full a life as possible until we die as peacefully as possible in old age are not a denial of death but a mode of accepting the reality of death. Much of public life, it is argued, is based not only on an acceptance of human mortality but also on scientific assessments of mortality risks. This is most clearly seen in the actuarial basis of pension funds and health-care planning. The dying are cared for in public hospitals. The disposal of the dead is arranged by commercial funeral directors and crematoria. All of this could be interpreted to suggest the opposite of the conventional wisdom, namely, that death is publicly present but privately absent.

Others suggest that, whereas religious narrative once sustained the hope of individuals as they approached death or contemplated the death of others, other opportunities to construct meaningful narratives are still available. For example, the medical profession has become more open to talking about death, which is now more commonly discussed with the patient. A 'heroism involving emotional expression and self-sacrifice' is offered to the dying person. The talk, in place of silence, by nursing and medical staff is seen as providing the means for the dying to embrace their death in heroic fashion, different from traditional male heroism as it includes the 'female' values of caring. The sense of companionship on the journey from those who talk and share with them is seen as being of particular value to those who are aware of their impending death and open about its approach. I have certainly found this to be the case in my own pastoral ministry and on numerous occasions have lent books, such as Norman Autton's *Peace at the Last: Talks with the Dying*, to parishioners. They nearly always come back well-thumbed.

In his influential book, *The Hour of Our Death*, Philippe Ariès highlights a shift from concern with an individual's own death to that of those close to him or her: 'from *my* death to *thy* death'. In the Middle Ages people had been concerned with what would become of their own souls when they died. By the nineteenth century they were more concerned with how they would manage when their loved ones died. Bereavement, rather than one's own demise, became the great fear, resulting in changes in religious rites. At a person's deathbed, concern about the destination of the departing soul became eclipsed by the survivors' grief, and the hope of an afterlife became reunion with the beloved rather than union with God. This still appears to be the major form of belief in an afterlife in Britain today and creates something of a challenge to choose biblical passages for a funeral that do not leave people feeling bewildered by talk of resurrection in terms that differ from their own expectations.

In cases where the deceased is a child such a hope can be even more poignant, not least because infant deaths are now relatively uncommon. Most people who die in Britain today do so when they are old and retired. Their children have grown up and support themselves economically. In previous generations the rates of infant mortality were extremely high. In pre-seventeenth-century Europe this produced a situation in which children under five were essentially regarded as non-persons, their deaths receiving the scant attention that today might be given to a dead pet. This would be unthinkable today, when stillborn children receive the kind of funeral that, a generation ago, would never have been considered. I have buried a stillborn child on several occasions, only to be approached afterwards by older mourners who now feel guilty that they didn't hold a funeral in similar circumstances twenty or thirty years earlier. Perhaps we should make some liturgical provision for this need.

In previous generations, a much higher percentage of those who died were breadwinners, younger mothers, and otherwise active members of the paid work-force. Today, life-assurance policies can help cushion the family from the impact of death, and the economic life of factories and offices continues relatively untouched. One sign of this change has been a split between public and private, between the world of employment and the world of family. Death and the funeral have ceased to be public spectacles and have become private, family experiences.

Economic life may be less affected by death but relationships are different. A marriage or a parent–child relationship may exist for far longer than in previous generations. Forty or fifty years is not uncommon, and so the death of a spouse, parent, or child may have a much greater emotional impact than ever before. The modern era may well have dealt with many of the economic and social problems of death but it has perhaps brought enlarged emotional ones. In previous generations many marriages that were under considerable strain ended with the death of a partner. Today such unhappy relationships may continue for many years longer. Many such marriages will end in separation or divorce; in fact, about the same number of marriages which today end in divorce were formerly ended by the death of one of the partners. As a naive and idealistic young curate I once said to a newly widowed woman that she must be feeling a great sense of loss, and I was completely taken aback when she replied, 'To tell you the truth, Vicar, I'm bloody glad he's gone!' Had I known then what I know now about the high rates of domestic violence, I would not have been so lost for words.

Attitudes to death and mourning depend on the cultural values of the local community. Mourning in the British Isles has been broadly divided into English versus Celtic; the one placing great importance on emotional privacy, the other on communal ritual. Yet the diversity of funeral customs within modern Britain is far more complicated and, in my view, has not been sufficiently addressed by academics. A contemporary sociological under-standing of death should incorporate the wide variety of views held by different national and ethnic groupings. An awareness of this would, no doubt, cause a cleric's approach to the bereaved to differ from one place to another.

Contemporary Beliefs in Life after Death

Churchgoing in Britain has declined so that many of the people to whom the Church ministers do not regularly attend worship. This means that fewer people have a consistent religious way of looking at life, so that their understanding of what occurs at death is less clear. Fewer people now attend worship than are buried in church ceremonies but a vague notion persists that the deceased go on to a better place.

The complexity of human life means that matters of belief are not simple and those concerning life after death are no exception. Some individuals will hold clear beliefs whereas others will change their minds with ease or hold only tentative views. Some religious institutions demand acceptance of sharply formulated doctrines while others foster a variety of beliefs among members. Indeed, religious groups may hold attitudes that differ widely from the beliefs of their adherents, some viewing firm dogma as a sign of deep commitment, others seeing it as an immature stage in the journey of faith.

In this section we are concerned with belief as it is held by the population in general, rather than the officially-held doctrine of religious institutions. Various social studies of the population have obtained information about a wide spectrum of belief but it is not easy to assess the findings, as responses depend very much on the way questions are asked. Information from one survey was published by Professor Douglas Davies in 1997.[13] For this survey, some 1,600 individuals were interviewed at length in their homes on matters concerning funeral ritual. They were shown cards indicating a list of possible attitudes towards life after death and asked whether they 'agreed', 'disagreed' or 'did not know what to think' about each of the following statements:

1. Nothing happens, we come to the end of life – 29 per cent.
2. Our soul passes on to another world – 34 per cent.
3. Our bodies await a resurrection – 8 per cent.
4. We come back as something or someone else – 12 per cent.
5. Trust in God, all is in God's hands – 22 per cent.

What was particularly interesting, however, was that the great majority (79 per cent) of those interviewed chose only one of these options, suggesting that these options reflect popular views fairly well. It also means that the majority had some sense of life as not entirely bounded by death.

Analysing the data, Professor Davies came to some surprising conclusions. We might have assumed that atheists would neither believe in an afterlife nor agree with statements involving the name of God. The survey revealed a more complex picture: 18 per cent of atheists and 15 per cent of agnostics accepted an afterlife – 'the soul passes on to another world'. Furthermore a smaller number of each group (7 per cent of atheists and 5 per cent of agnostics) also accepted the idea that 'we come back as something or someone else'. These results were surprising because reference to souls or the afterlife is normally assumed to involve some reference to God. The results suggest that such an assumption is not necessarily wise. Unsurprisingly, no atheist or agnostic said 'all is in God's hands', although two atheists agreed with ideas of resurrection. Another survey, by William Kay and

Leslie Francis,[14] provides supporting evidence for this view: 'Surprisingly, about a quarter of atheists do believe in life after death.'

If we compare the beliefs held by people in general and the official position of churches, it becomes clear that formal theology is not always reflected in the popular religion of active church members, let alone those who attend church only periodically. The majority of those claiming church allegiance in Britain also claimed to believe in an afterlife, yet a substantial minority did not. Surprisingly 14 per cent of Catholics, 30 per cent of Methodists and 32 per cent of Anglicans said they thought life came to an end at death. Given the emphasis upon eternal life in those denominations, it seems odd that just under a third of Methodists and Anglicans appear not to believe in an afterlife.

Professor Davies also noted the gender of the respondents and discovered a clear difference between men and women; women are far more likely to believe in life after death.

This research contains many points of relevance to those who conduct funerals or minister to dying and bereaved persons. It indicates that there are widening varieties of belief among the people sitting in the congregation: the widower is less likely than the widow to believe in an afterlife; the middle-aged and younger are less likely than the elderly to believe at all; even regular churchgoers may hold firm beliefs about reincarnation or the finality of death. This has implications for the plausibility and relevance of what is said at a funeral service. Those conducting them may need radically to rethink the content of sermons, readings, prayers and gestures at funerals. That is, of course, less easy for clergy who are bound to use set forms of liturgy. Careful and sensitive contact with the mourners beforehand is one way in which we can articulate and express the Christian message so that it speaks to them. This will prepare both the congregations and ministers for the service and, one would hope, result in a funeral perceived by mourners as far more relevant and personal.

New Age movements speculate on what happens at death, producing publications and seminars rife with speculation and assertion. Discussion of near-death experiences, belief in reincarnation and channelling (communication with the dead) are part and parcel of the New Age scene. Browsing a book shop may well reveal the conventional religion shelf to contain nothing on the afterlife, while the New Age section may include several publications, such as: Annie Besant, *Death and After*; (1906), Anthony Borgia, *Life in the World Unseen* (a former priest's findings as a medium, 1970); Arthur Ford, *Unknown but Known* and *The Life Beyond Death* (1969); Jane Sherwood, *Post-mortem Journal* (communication from T. E. Lawrence, 1964); M. H. Tester, *The Bewildered Man's Guide To Death* (a statement of spiritualist belief, 1970); and *The Tibetan Book of the Dead*.[15] It is not my intention to summarize their views here; merely to note that they exist and that the churches and their clergy ought to be aware of their existence, and that a sizeable number of people read them. Those who do so may also distrust church dogma and revelation. Unless we are sensitive to the varied belief systems held by members of the congregation, the manner in which we speak at a funeral, as well as the words we use, may serve to alienate some still further from a church they already distrust.

This chapter has summarized the ways in which society's perceptions of death have altered and how such change has affected the beliefs of individuals. Now we move from trying to make sense of death to the funeral, looking first at some of the theological questions it raises.

NOTES

[1] See Enright, D. J. (ed.), *The Oxford Book of Death*, Oxford, Oxford University Press, 1983, p. 1.

[2] See Porter, R., 'Death and the Doctors in Georgian England', in R. Houlbrooke (ed.), *Death, Ritual and Bereavement*, London, Routledge, 1989, p. 89.

[3] Singer, Paul, *Rethinking Life and Death*, Oxford, Oxford University Press, 1995, p. 21.

[4] Sheppy, Paul, 'The Theology of Death and Disposal', in Peter Jupp and

Tony Rogers (eds), *Interpreting Death: Christian Theology and Pastoral Practice*, London, Cassell, 1997.

⁵ Sheppy, 'Theology of Death', p. 50.

⁶ Church of England Doctrine Commission, *The Mystery of Salvation*, London, Church House Publishing, 1995.

⁷ Robinson, John, A. T., 'Learning from Cancer', in *Where Three Ways Meet: Last Essays and Sermons*, London, SCM Press, 1987, pp. 189–94.

⁸ At the time of writing these were the rules in use. Certification of death, however, is currently in the process of undergoing a major review, as a result of the Harold Shipman case in 2000 when a Manchester doctor was responsible for the deaths of several of his patients. This review is likely to produce far-reaching changes to the system of certifying death. It is not yet clear what those changes will be, although they are likely to involve more, rather than less, bureaucracy. Concerns have been expressed in connection with this, including the amount of time that doctors spend certifying death, rather than curing the sick, and the rules of some religions which require a body to be buried within a certain time of death.

⁹ Walter, Tony, *The Revival of Death*, London, Routledge,1994, pp. 9–10.

¹⁰ Rudinger, E. (ed.), *What To Do When Someone Dies*, London, Consumers' Association, 1967.

¹¹ Draznin, Y., *How To Prepare For Death: A Practical Guide*, New York, Hawthorn Books, 1976, p. viii.

¹² Walter, Tony, Littlewood, J., and Pickering M., 'Death in the News: The Public Invigilation of Private Emotion', *Sociology: The Journal of the British Sociological Association*, Vol. 29 (4), 1995, pp. 579–96.

¹³ Davies, Douglas, 'Contemporary Belief in Life after Death', in Jupp and Rogers (eds), *Interpreting Death*, pp. 131–42.

¹⁴ Kay, William and Francis, Leslie, 'The Young British Atheist', *Journal of Empirical Theology*, Vol. 8 (2), 1995, pp. 5–26.

¹⁵ See Walter, Tony, 'Death in the New Age', *Religion*, Vol. 23, 1993, p. 127.

2

Theology and the Funeral

At his wife's funeral, Robin Meredith was asked by a woman in a paisley headscarf, whom he didn't immediately recognize, if he wasn't thankful to know that Caro was now safe with Jesus. He, summoning all the courtesy he could manage at such a moment, said no, he didn't think so. He then went out of the church into the rain and looked at the black hole into which Caro was to be lowered.

From *Next of Kin* by Joanna Trollope[1]

In May 2000, at the turn of the second millennium, the first Funeral Services Exhibition in Britain was held in Birmingham. A vast array of items was on display, ranging from battery-powered CD players to be placed in the coffin ready to play the deceased's favourite music and posters of favourite football players which could be placed always in front of the deceased's eyes on the inside of the coffin lid, to coloured lamps to stand beside the coffin while it awaits burial, and specially designed black gloves embroidered with the deceased's name, to be worn on the day of the funeral. One commentator[2] was struck by the way the meaning and purpose of a deceased person's life can be seen solely in terms of past achievement or in association with football teams or pop stars, and how the funeral may be dominated and surrounded by ultimately meaningless and sentimental trivia. An internet search for the word 'funeral' will allow a glimpse of the kind of merchandise available, or a visit to a website dedicated to 'providing for all your funeral needs', such as www.funeralshop.co.uk which describes itself as 'the UK's most popular funeral website'.

Had a funeral services exhibition been held a thousand years earlier, at the turn of the first millennium, it would have been far simpler. It would have been local, not national. Everything would have been made locally, using local products. There would have been no coffins or caskets except, perhaps, for the extremely wealthy. Instead, shrouds and simple stretchers for carrying the body to burial would have been displayed. Holy water to remind mourners that Christians die with Christ in baptism, candles, crosses and a service book with prayers commending the departed to God and the bereaved to his comfort, would all have been on prominent display.

Our culture has changed beyond recognition and, with it, the liturgies that we use for burying the dead. The Christian Church is called to minister to the bereaved and to officiate at funerals within a culture that is highly individualistic and places a great emphasis on choice. Many can only look backwards in the face of death, and this provides a challenge for the Church. Somehow we have to find the language to speak of Christian hope, and of the God who shared in our dying to call us to new and eternal life. If there is one thing that encourages me, it is a deep-seated belief that there is no other understanding of life and death that compares with the Christian gospel of resurrection.

In this chapter we will look at aspects of the funeral that are primarily theological in nature, such as the character of funeral liturgy, the commendation of the deceased into God's hands, the proclaiming of faith in the presence of death, the nature of the funeral congregation and the use of scripture in the funeral. In the following chapter we will look at more general aspects of the funeral, such as the disposal of a corpse, the marking of a death, the celebration and affirmation of the deceased's life, the process of grieving, and mirroring of cultural values.

The Character of Funeral Liturgy

In recent decades nearly all churches have made huge and far-reaching revisions to their liturgies, including to burial and funeral services. The *Series Two* service, produced by the Church of England in 1966, as part of the series of experimental liturgies culminating in the *Alternative Service Book* of 1980, was accompanied by a long introduction asking, among other questions,

'What ought we to be doing at a burial service?' In their answer, the Liturgical Commission described five tasks: to secure the reverent disposal of the corpse; to commend the deceased to the care of our heavenly Father; to proclaim the glory of our risen life in Christ here and hereafter; to remind us of the awful certainty of our own coming death and judgement; and to make plain the eternal unity of Christian people, living and departed, in the risen and ascended Christ. They stated that, although it would have been natural to add the consolation of mourners, they believed this would arise as a natural consequence of fulfilling the existing five tasks. Their report also set out the following aims: that the rite should not assume the soul of the deceased to be in any particular place or state; that the congregation should be given a more active part; that as little as possible of the service should be required to take place out of doors; and that one burial service be used for all baptized persons (including suicides) but with an exception for children.

In the 1980s, the Roman Catholic Church introduced *The Order for Christian Funerals*. This also prompted a great deal of thinking about what we do in a funeral. The emphasis of this rite is that for the Christian death is not just the ending of life. As it says in the funeral Mass, 'For your faithful people life is changed, not ended'. While recognizing the need for the new Order, some commentators raised concerns about the ways in which it might prevent people from expressing important negative feelings which often surface in the face of death.

Before these reforms, funerals and the other rites of the dead were certainly sombre affairs. Vestments and altar-hangings were purple or black and the liturgy drew on passages of scripture that emphasized the fear of judgement, the terror of death itself and the need for mercy. It could be argued that this was a negative approach as it encouraged mourners to be afraid of their redeemer and to focus on their own sinfulness rather than the grace of God, and it made death harder to accept. The new liturgies have swept much of this away and try to console the living by a trusting faith in a God who has shown himself to be a God of love. The scripture readings emphasize trust, hope, the mercy of God, and the joy of resurrection. There are those who feel, however, that something important has been lost, that the new rites dilute the liturgy, that something of the complexity and depth they used to possess has gone. There is a danger of depriving the liturgy of a universal appeal by expressing only a small range of responses to death. There needs to be a place for the expression of anger, complaint and protest in funeral liturgy so that we can pray all our thoughts and feelings, to acknowledge before God what we really are and not suppress our innermost selves. A bitter note of protest is one of the most basic human responses to death, and one of the most legitimate. It is echoed in the cry from the cross, 'Why have you forsaken me?' We need to acknowledge that our redeemer lives, yet we need also to rage against the dying of the light. It is argued by some that the old liturgies did allow for both, but that the new ones do not.

In fact, there is some evidence to suggest that it is not the liturgy alone which curbs the expression of feeling at the funeral. In 1992 and 1993 Jenny Hockey published studies of funerals in the Sheffield area,[3] including interviews with clergy. Interested in how emotion is expressed in funerals, she portrayed the clergy as seeing themselves in control, using various means to regulate the amount of grief publicly expressed during the service. This may or may not be desirable, but the handling of grief and anger in a public service is not an easy matter, particularly when the crematorium clock is ticking and we know that another funeral cortège will shortly arrive. It is a subject to which we will return in a later chapter.

In 2000, the Church of England published *Common Worship*, a replacement for the *Alternative Service Book 1980*. Its funeral services are contained in the volume *Pastoral Services* and reflect another, very different, approach to funeral services from that traditionally adopted in Anglican churches. The introduction to the book states:

From the eighth century or earlier, the funeral rite was a con-tinuum, broken by movements from place to place, from home to church, to the place of burial and back to the home. This

pattern was severely truncated at the Reformation, but today's
pastoral needs suggest a return to it. As grieving is a process
marked by different stages, we believe that one helpful contribution the church can make pastorally is to have a series of
services and resources in which some of these different stages
can be recognised, spoken of in advance or recapitulated.

This wide variety of services and resources allows for great flexibility and therefore choice, and more will be said about this
particular approach in Chapter 7, on contemporary funeral
practices.

The titles used for funeral services say a great deal about how
their authors expect them to be used. Anglican liturgies have
variously changed from *The Order of the Burial of the Dead*
to *Pastoral Services* to *An Order for Christian Funerals*. The
different emphases are clear, but I do question the use of *An
Order for Christian Funerals*. The Anglican Church has traditionally taken responsibility for the funerals of all who turn to
it, whatever their background. It can be argued that a church
funeral service, or one conducted by a Christian minister anywhere else, is indeed a Christian funeral, whatever the faith of
participants. It might however be deemed more sensitive to some
mourners not to proclaim this on the front cover of the service
book. I remember clearly a long discussion I once had with a
devout churchgoer's next of kin, who was anxious that his sister
should have the Christian funeral she would have wanted. He
was also concerned, on the other hand, that I should know that
he did not believe in Christ. He felt he had to be there to honour
his sister's memory but felt deeply uneasy at appearing hypocritical, given his strong and well-known atheistic beliefs. I was
glad at the time that the service book we put in front of him was
entitled *The Burial of the Dead* and not *An Order for Christian
Funerals*. It made it easier from him to take part in an act of
Christian worship and maintain his own sense of integrity. It
did not feel right to use his sister's funeral as the occasion to
challenge his beliefs and proclaim my own; that discussion was
left for a later date.

The Commendation of the Deceased

The Church conducts a funeral service using a liturgy specially written for this purpose, but the words of that liturgy have varied greatly over the centuries from place to place and from one denomination to another. The rite with which I am most familiar is that contained in Volume Two of the *Book of Common Prayer for Use in the Church in Wales*. This liturgy makes greater use of the term 'commend' than most other contemporary liturgies. The body is brought into church and the minister says 'We have come together in the presence of God to commend our brother/sister N. into the hands of God our maker and redeemer.' In the penultimate prayer, which is called 'The Commendation', the verb to 'commend' is used twice. Its usage is much less prevalent in the comparable liturgies of the Church of England, the Episcopal Church of the United States of America, the Church of Canada, the Church of the Province of Southern Africa or the Church of the Province of New Zealand (or Aotearoa). It is also less evident in the liturgies of other communions. In commending the deceased to God we are saying that we entrust this person to God, that the deceased no longer has any claim on us, nor we on the deceased. He or she has moved on to a new existence in God's Kingdom, and we pass over to God any responsibility we held for the deceased.

The use of the commendation may seem very natural today but over the years it has been a matter of great controversy, reflecting the turbulent debates of the Reformation, when there was a reaction against medieval Catholicism, and prayers and Masses for the dead which had previously been commonplace were not included in the first Book of Common Prayer published in 1549. This reflected a general trend among the reformers to purge references to prayers for the departed, since they held that one's fate was determined at the time of death and could not be affected by the prayers of others. However the political climate of the 1540s was very confused, and in England the Reformation was a complicated alliance of those motivated by religious ideals and those seeking political freedom for Henry VIII and the

English crown from Rome and the Pope. Henry VIII had been a defender of the Catholic faith but he had split with Rome over the question of his first divorce and remarriage. He died in 1547 and the 1549 Prayer Book was published early in the reign of Edward VI. The more zealous of the Protestant reformers had not, at that time, reached the heights of their later influence. The effect of all of this on the burial service was that, despite the reaction against prayers for the dead, words of commendation were still retained in the prayer of committal:

> I commende thy soule to God the father almighty, and thy body to the grounde, earth to earth, asshes to asshes, dust to dust, in sure and certayne hope of resurreccion to eternall lyfe, through our Lord Jesus Christ, who shall chaunge our vile body, that it may be lyke to his glorious body, accordyng to the myghtie workyng wherby he is hable to subdue all thynges to himselfe.

In 1552 a further revision of the Book of Common Prayer was produced, when even more material was deleted from the service and the prayer of committal became simply a committal of the body to the ground with no commendation of the soul to God:

> Forasmuche as it hathe pleased almightie God of his great mercy to take unto himselfe the soule of our dere brother here departed: we therefore commit his body to the ground, earth to earth, asshes to asshes, dust to dust, in sure and certayne hope of resurreccion to eternal lyfe, through our Lord Jesus Christ, who shal chaunge our vyle bodye, that it maye bee lyke to his glorious bodye, according to the mightie working wherby he is hable to subdue all thinges to himselfe.

Six months after the introduction of this prayer book, Edward VI died and England returned to Catholicism under Queen Mary, who outlawed the use of the Prayer Book, restoring the Latin Mass. England later reverted to Protestantism with the accession of Elizabeth I to the throne and another Book of Common Prayer

was introduced in 1559. The prayer of committal remained
unchanged, apart from the spelling:

> Forasmuch as it hath pleased Almighty God of his great mercy
> to take unto himselfe the soule of our deare brother here
> departed, we therfore commit his body to the ground, earth to
> earth, ashes to ashes, dust to dust, in sure and certain hope of
> resurrection to eternall life, through our Lord Jesus Christ,
> who shall change our vile body that it may bee like unto his
> glorious body, according to the mighty working, whereby he is
> able to subdue all things to himselfe.

Thus there was no longer any prayer for the deceased in the
Church of England. There were minor changes under the
Stuart kings but, in any event, under the Commonwealth the use
of the Book of Common Prayer was forbidden by Oliver
Cromwell, when extreme Protestantism held sway. Following
the restoration of the monarchy the Book of Common Prayer
was re-introduced in 1662, moving the Church of England in a
more catholic direction. As far as the burial service was concerned, further changes were made by the addition of rubrics
forbidding the use of the service for 'any that die unbaptised, or
excommunicate, or have laid violent hands upon themselves',
and that prayer book made no provision for such circumstances.

Throughout this period of considerable political and religious
change, it is difficult to know what actually happened in parish
churches throughout the country; there must have been a variety
of practices, but after 1662 it appears that there was a long
period of stability and a comparative consistency of practice.
There was no wide-ranging liturgical revision until the production of the 1928 Prayer Book. The intervening period had
seen the Oxford movement and the development of Anglo-
Catholicism in the Church of England, and the disestablishment
of the Church of Ireland and the Church in Wales, creating
Anglican provinces within Britain which were not under the
authority of Parliament. Accordingly, although parliamentary
approval was withheld from the 1928 Prayer Book, it could still

be legally used in those provinces. It was also certainly used in many English parishes as well as in those beyond England. That prayer book restored words of commendation in an alternative prayer of committal:

> Unto Almighty God we commend the soul of our *brother* departed, and we commit *his* body to the ground; earth to earth, ashes to ashes, dust to dust; in sure and certain hope of the Resurrection unto eternal life, through our Lord Jesus Christ; at whose coming in glorious majesty to judge the world, the earth and the sea shall give up their dead; and the corruptible bodies of those who sleep in him shall be changed, and made like unto his own glorious body; according to the mighty working whereby he is able to subdue all things unto himself.

Further significant liturgical revision did not take place until the 1960s when the Church of England produced the *Series One* and *Series Two* revisions. The *Series One* provision, published in 1966, included the 1928 burial service quoted above.

The *Series Two* funeral service did not receive official approval but it did include a prayer of commendation, which is very similar to that which would later be introduced into the Church in Wales rite approved in 1974. Unlike their predecessors these services separate the commendation, which is read in church, from the committal, which takes place at the graveside or crematorium:

> Let us commend our *brother* N. into the hands of God our Maker and Redeemer.

> O God our heavenly Father, who by thy mighty power has given us life, and by they loving-kindness has bestowed upon us new life in Christ Jesus: we commend to thy merciful keeping N. our *brother*, through Jesus Christ thy Son our Lord, who died and rose again to save us, and now lives and reigns with thee in glory for ever. Amen.

In the faith of Christ, and believing that our *brother* is in the hands of God, we commit his body

> *(at the grave)* to the ground, earth to earth, ashes to ashes, dust to dust,
> *(at cremation)* to be cremated,
> *(at sea)* to the deep,

in sure and certain hope of the resurrection to eternal life, through our Lord Jesus Christ; who shall change our corruptible body, that it may be like unto his glorious body, according to the mighty working whereby he is able to subdue all things to himself.[4]

The 1970s saw the introduction of the *Series Three* services, which ultimately appeared in the *Alternative Service Book 1980*, and these followed the same line of thought.

The closing decades of the twentieth century brought with them new expectations of funeral liturgy. Concern has been widely expressed in recent years regarding the archaic nature of the language in the services, about the lack of prayers appropriate to particular circumstances and the omission of readings that are often used at funerals. The services provided in the Church of England's *Common Worship Pastoral Services*, published in 2000, do much to meet these criticisms and, as was mentioned in the previous chapter, provide for a far broader range of services making liturgical provision for a wide variety of situations outside of the formal funeral service. The flexibility for their use is increased by their availability on the internet. They can be downloaded from the website www.cofe.anglican.org/commonworship, and parishes are encouraged to use them in ways appropriate to their own situations and to produce their own booklets.

In 2002 the Church in Wales published *An Order for Christian Funerals*[5] which contains a considerable amount of useful material additional to that of its 1974 service. It is intended to bridge the gap while an alternative service is prepared but it does not, at this stage, make the radical changes in approach that *Common Worship* has done.

The focusing of the funeral into one short service has been normal, at least for Anglicans, since the time of the Reformation. Most modern burial service revision has begun by examining the prayer book service of 1662 and trying to improve upon it, taking into account the main theological debates of that period, such as prayer for the dead. Work done in the last decade has, however, started from a different position, asking questions about what we are doing and why. It has looked much further back in time and more widely and ecumenically in its theology, putting prayer for the departed into a wider context, and seeing the funeral rite not as one isolated service but, as previously mentioned, as a continuum broken by movements from place to place. The basic structure has been determined by the emotional and spiritual need to move: from the place of dying to the place of worship, to the place of burial, and onwards into life.

Proclaiming Faith

We quoted earlier the Church of England's Liturgical Commission,[6] which stated in 1966 that at a funeral we ought 'to proclaim the glory of our risen life in Christ here and hereafter' and 'to make plain the eternal unity of Christian people, living and departed, in the risen and ascended Christ'. This proclamation has two differing aspects, a celebration of that faith for those who share it and a proclamation to those who do not. Almost any congregation will include people of both categories as well as those who might not be sure where they fit. Funerals and other rites of passage have a potential for evangelistic contact with people who rarely or never attend church, but who are favourably disposed towards institutional Christianity. It is possible that this kind of evangelism has a particular appeal to those who would be offended by a more overt, potentially confrontational style. Some would describe this as 'pre-evangelism', building bridges between the Church and the wider population, hallowing significant moments in human lives, commending the Church and the Christian faith to those with little knowledge of it. It is unlikely that anyone will come to faith by attending a funeral, however well it is conducted. It is much more likely if a process of other contacts, before and afterwards, is available.

In some areas there is a tradition that on the Sunday following the funeral the bereaved family will attend the main Sunday service at the church or chapel where the funeral took place. A deceased woman's father, who came from another part of the country, once asked me if I had a 'following'. It took some time for me to understand what he meant. It happens in West Wales but the terminology is different: the bereaved family will traditionally sit in the front rows on the north side of the nave and will remain seated throughout, not visibly taking part in the service. Most have modified this practice, but one of the first occasions I experienced it was when I had planned the first of a series of discussion groups in place of sermons during Lent. Four full rows of people, dressed in black at the front of the church, who remained silent and motionless throughout, disconcerted me and had a clear effect on the congregation's discussion.

In some churches there is a clear strategy of following up the contacts made during funerals. This variously includes visits from the clergy or lay visiting teams and invitations to special services on All Souls' Day or Easter. In one church there is a quarterly requiem Mass, when those whose funerals have taken place in the last three months are remembered by name, and their families are specifically invited to attend and light candles in their memory. Another church holds an informal monthly service of prayer for healing to which the bereaved are invited, at which they can be prayed with individually and privately. It is followed by tea or coffee and a chance to talk with others in similar circumstances or with a trained grief counsellor.

Jenny Hockey's study of funerals in the Sheffield area[7] revealed that some clergy found difficulty conducting funerals for people without Christian faith, particularly when they were required to declare that the deceased had taken up a new position 'in the hands of God'. One cleric said that the greatest difficulty was how to be true to the New Testament and still be kind to people in bereavement.

There is a dilemma faced by the preacher at a funeral: is he or she there to help the bereaved through this ancient rite of passage, or to bring the good news of God's eternal purposes for us? Most clergy will probably see themselves as doing both, proclaiming the hope of resurrection in Christ but doing so with regard for the context in which they speak. There are two commonly held views in our society: first, that there is nothing after death, and second, that there is some sort of survival beyond the grave. The hope of most mourners centres upon the expectation that the deceased will joyfully rejoin loved ones in a life similar to the one they have already known The gospel message of resurrection is different, however. It has significance, not so much for the individual, as for the whole people of God who will live again and come into their own true home. It is not some kind of survival from this life to be reunited with our loved ones, but a total transformation to become like Christ and to be united with all who love and serve him (Matthew 22:29–30; 1 Corinthians 15:51–52; etc.). The challenge for the preacher is to help people move on beyond their immediate grief to grow in faith and love of God. It is a challenge not just for the funeral sermon but also for the whole of preaching and pastoral care.

Some ministers see the funeral as an opportunity to preach the gospel, a chance to present Christian doctrine and the words of scripture to those who never hear them; many mourners, however, perceive the funeral differently. They may not wish to have Bible readings and prayers because they do not understand life and death in such language. Or they might wish to pray, but in a simple and direct way and not in archaic prayer-book language. The mourners will look to the cleric to bridge the gap between their differing ideologies, to find words that will express the spiritual instincts of those mourners who believe, without betraying the deceased's viewpoint. Most mourners will not feel confident or emotionally composed enough to plan and conduct a funeral service themselves and they need someone with the clergy's training in leadership of public ceremony; but even in this largely post-Christian age there are very few others who can fulfil the same role. So mourners turn to the clergy to fulfil a priestly role, as persons representing mystery and solemnity, and expect them to lead the ceremony competently and compassionately as they lay their deceased relatives to rest with dignity and tenderness.

The mourners may well feel that they have paid a fee to engage the services of a professionally trained public figure to conduct the funeral, and it will seem reasonable to them that they should expect such a professional to take care in considering their ideology and emotional needs. As for preaching the gospel, there are more ways than one of doing that. The mourners will know that the minister is a Christian and it will be his or her attitude and behaviour which will be the sermon, not the words alone. The courtesy of hearing and understanding others' outlook on life, humbly helping them to make their farewells as they, rather than the minister, need to do, will in itself preach the gospel. Perhaps the professional help of a minister who hears, who understands, who uses his or her skill with words and ritual, may do more than reading of the prayer book ever can do to speak of Christ's love.

The Funeral Congregation

In the past, the funeral congregation was a natural one in the sense that the people who came knew one another on a day-to-day basis. The family did not return from 'away' but lived near one another and were joined by friends who were also neighbours. They were a community before they came into the church. There was, therefore, no need to bind them into a community at the start of the service. This is of course an idealizing of the past, but the service could, on the whole, proceed on the basis of that shared sense of community. It was a natural congregation too in the sense that there would have been a common faith and a common religious observance. Even when some of the people did not go each week to that particular church, they did go to some church or chapel. They were on familiar ground, and they were not without knowledge of the basic tenets of the Christian faith.

Most of our rites assume that sort of community: Christian people of faith, at home in church, and constituting a natural community. Today things are very different. The family will come from many different places, and might not know each other very well. The friends will be equally widespread. The neighbours might not be there. There will be a wide range of religious attitudes, from deeply Christian, to perplexed and doubtful, to unbelieving, to adherents of other faiths. The service and those who conduct it have to take all this seriously and create very quickly a shared sense of belonging, a relationship with one another and an atmosphere of worship. There is always one thing in common: everyone is somehow connected with the deceased. It is on that that the minister must build. I once buried a man who had been born to parents of different nationalities. He had met his wife in another country, seen each of his children born in different parts of Europe and finally retired to Wales. His family was extremely disparate. A large part of the address was taken up with explaining where he had lived and when. All of his family knew a part of the story whereas only his wife seemed to know the whole of it, and several of his relatives commented afterwards on details that they had not known about him before.

A change of emphasis is clear from the way those presenting the *Common Worship* services describe them. Instead of beginning with the service, their description starts with the context in which the service is to be used. Each death is unique and the funeral should reflect this. For example, grief is present in nearly every bereavement but it does not always dominate; thus the funeral of a Christian who dies peacefully in old age can reflect thanksgiving and rejoicing for one who has 'gone to glory'. Another death may come after years of pain and suffering, and the funeral might reflect feelings of relief that this is now a thing of the past. Many deaths are experienced as untimely and unfair and the funeral service needs to acknowledge and respond to feelings of outrage and shock.

In conducting a funeral, are we ministering to the whole congregation or a part of it, or even to different groups within it at different times? This is a question to which we will return in Chapter 4, 'Whose Funeral is it?' For the moment we might usefully bear in mind that when we address the congregation, some mourners will be so grief-stricken that they will not take in a word we say. Others, whom we might not expect to be deeply affected, will be reflecting on the recent death of a loved one that we know nothing about. Others will be using our words to help make sense of a bereavement that might now be quite distant in time but of which they are only now beginning to make sense. In preaching at funerals in a closely-knit village community I have often had the feeling that my words are being listened to intently by those whose close relative I buried two, three or four years earlier.

The Use of Scripture

We have considered the character of funeral liturgy, how we commend the deceased, proclaim faith, and the nature of the funeral congregation, but have said little about the use we make of scripture in the funeral. Most liturgical revision has taken for granted that scripture will be read, without giving a great deal of thought as to what should be read and why. In this section I consider why we use scripture and what we hope to achieve by doing so, rather than give a list of readings suitable for different occasions. (For those who would like such a list, there are many excellent books which contain them, such as Paul Sheppy's *In Sure and Certain Hope*, or the website www.cofe.anglican.org/commonworship.)

Is it possible to take words that were written almost two millennia ago (or even far longer) and expect their meaning to be understood in a very different age and culture? Given that regular churchgoers will have heard scripture read and explained Sunday by Sunday, that would not seem an unreasonable expectation in their case, although any parish priest could relate horror stories to show that the contrary is sometimes true. We are concerned here, however, with the non-churchgoer to whom the Bible has been a mainly closed book. In choosing passages to be read, it is important to take care over what is chosen and about how it is introduced so that the hearers are not left bewildered and justice is done to the text. The service from the 1662 Book of Common Prayer made very extensive use of scripture. As the body was carried into church, verses were read which were realistic about death, but also confident about life beyond the grave for believers. 'I am the resurrection and the life, saith the Lord: he that believeth in me though he were dead, yet shall he live: and whosoever liveth and believeth in me shall never die.' The only lesson set was 1 Corinthians 15, where Paul speaks of death and the certainty of resurrection. The preacher would expound such a text, not eulogizing the dead, but speaking about the Christian expectation of resurrection. What would people make of such an approach today? Many would not be so familiar with the scriptures. They might not know who Paul was. When the lesson is announced as being from the first letter of Paul to the Corinthians they may not even know that it is from the Bible. The terms in which it talks about death may sound strange and puzzling to a person raised on a diet of soap operas and reality television shows. Nevertheless, I do believe that such difficulties may be overcome by sensitive introductions. For instance, one might explain that the congregation is going to hear a passage from the Bible in which St Paul talks about the Christian expectation of resurrection, that the way in which it is written may seem strange today, but that it has been a great comfort to many people over the years, and one hopes that it will be of help to them as well.

There is, however, one matter that worries me more than whether or not the words are understood and that is the authority, or lack of it, which mourners attribute to scripture as a whole. Christians vary, of course, in their understanding of how scripture is inspired but would all agree that somehow and to some degree God uses it to speak to us, although non-Christians do not necessarily accept that. Alan Billings describes a service where various relatives and friends of the deceased read tributes they had carefully prepared in advance. The young man who had died was described by different mourners as 'a star shining in the night sky', 'the wind at your back', 'the rain on your face', and 'the flowers that turn towards you'. These images helped the mourners come to terms with their loss but they were contradictory; he could not possibly have been the star, the wind, the rain, and the flowers all at the same time, and the readers had not meant them to be taken literally. People were speaking figuratively. Are the words of scripture anything more than mere metaphor to such people? Do they speak words of eternal significance? Or are they seen as just another figurative image, which might be helpful to a person in mourning, but are not to be taken too seriously? When the clergy talk about resurrection, are we heard to be speaking of God's eternal plans for and love of humankind or are we seen as just another visitor, friend even, trying to say something helpful? As our society moves further away from being the devout church-going community of former days, it is necessary to realize that what we say will not be accepted as having the authority with which it was once automatically endowed. People today are taught to question authority, to make up their own minds, to feel that their own views – however bizarre and extreme – are as valid as those of anyone else. When we choose a reading from scripture it will increasingly be required to contain its own authority, to convince by the strength of its own argument; we will not be able simply to rely on the fact that it is from the Bible.

In the light of all this what are we to make of requests for non-scriptural readings to be included? Would we wish to include them ourselves? This is clearly related to the questions we will discuss in the chapter 'Whose Funeral is it?' as it is connected with who decides what does or does not take place. There are, of course, different reasons to include other readings. Many people have been helped by hearing the experience and reflection of others, whether it is through a poem such as 'Footprints in the Sand'[8] or Bishop Brent's 'What is Dying?'[9] or even the lyrics of a piece of modern music. Sometimes the item is of comfort not because of its religious value, but due to the simple fact that it was, for example, the deceased's favourite song. This brings us to the question that introduces the next chapter: 'What is a

Funeral?' If it is, at least in part, a celebration of the deceased's life, how can we say that the poem his daughter has written is inappropriate? Perhaps its words appear trite and the poetry is something at which we are embarrassed, but if it expresses her sorrow at her father's passing, then who can say it should not be used? There is also the question of helping people to feel comfortable in the liturgical setting. This is not a problem when the mourners are themselves regular churchgoers and in their own church; they will already feel at home. When, however, we are dealing with those who seldom or never attend church that may not be the case at all. It is my view that one reason why secular readings and particular pieces of music are requested is a need for something familiar in the service. It helps mourners identify with what is happening and that will, it is hoped, make it easier for them to hear the message that the Church is trying to proclaim to them.

NOTES

[1] Trollope, Joanna, *Next of Kin*, London, Black Swan, 1996, p. 7.

[2] Rowell, Geoffrey, 'Tucked up for Eternity', *Church Times*, 2 June 2000.

[3] Hockey, Jenny, *Making the Most of a Funeral*, London, Richmond upon Thames, Cruse-Bereavement Care, 1992, and Hockey, Jenny, 'The Acceptable Face of Human Grieving? The Clergy's Role in Managing Emotional Expression during Funerals', in D. Clark (ed.), *The Sociology of Death*, Oxford, Blackwell, 1993, pp. 129–48.

[4] The Church in Wales, *The Book of Common Prayer for Use in the Church in Wales Volume II*, Penarth, Church in Wales Publications, 1984, pp. 788–90.

[5] The Church in Wales, *Trefn Angladdau Cristnogol / An Order for Christian Funerals*, Cardiff, Church in Wales Publications, 2002.

[6] Church of England Liturgical Commission, 'The Burial of the Dead', in *Alternative Services: Second Series*, London, SPCK, 1966, pp. 101–41.

[7] Hockey, 'The Acceptable Face of Human Grieving?', pp. 129–41.

[8] See www.footprints-inthe-sand.com/

[9] See www.eade47.freeserve.co.uk/files/funpoems.rtf, where the poem is attributed to Victor Hugo from *Toilers of the Sea*, rather than to Bishop Brent to whom it is often attributed.

3

What Makes a Funeral?

> For many bereaved people, the funeral is an ordeal to be endured. For others, not immediately bereaved, it is a rip-off. For clergy, it is a time of committing the deceased to God's care. Psychologists say it is a minor part of the grief process. Funeral directors, especially those in Australia and the United States, say it is a major part of the grief process; though for them it is also a way of making a living. For anthropologists, it affirms or creates social structure. In the eyes of some sociologists, it is a display of status and an atonement for guilt.
>
> From *Funerals and How to Improve Them* by Tony Walter[1]

Nearly all human societies possess some formalized rites along-side the disposing of a body, suggesting that funeral ritual fulfils some very positive function in human life. If not, these rites would have been abandoned long ago, even though in many instances mourners talk of 'surviving' the funeral, which is a complex ritual which meets, and sometimes fails to meet, the needs of a whole range of different participants and onlookers. They will all have their own reasons for being involved and might hold different expectations as to its purpose. In this chapter we will be looking at the nature of a funeral by consider-ing its different elements. We have already considered two of these in the previous chapter: the commendation of the deceased and proclamation of faith. The others I propose to look at are: disposal of a corpse; marking a death; affirmation of the deceased's life; part of grieving; and the funeral as a social phenomenon. In my view there is no one element that is of primary importance, but all seven are essential, although the emphasis on each will vary from one funeral to another.

A funeral is often seen as unsatisfactory if it fails to address one or more of these constituent parts (even though the reasons why it is perceived as such may not be clear to those involved). In some cases the funeral is reduced to only one of its aspects. For example, it is possible so to emphasize the joy of the deceased in God's presence that other elements of the funeral may be forgotten and the grief of the mourners may be inadequately acknowledged. In order to consider their relative importance, I propose to look at the constituent parts individually, thus focusing on the positive features of each.

Disposal of a Corpse

Every culture has its own methods of disposing of corpses. Tony Walter described some of the ways in which this is done in several different cultures.

> Masai tribesmen leave their dead out for the hyenas to eat. Parsees leave theirs in towers for the vultures to pick at. Hindus burn their dead on open pyres. The British too burn most of their dead, but indoors – maybe because of the rain? Like many other Europeans, the British used to leave their dead three feet under the flagstones where they stood to sing psalms every Sunday morning, but then the smell got too bad. North Americans like to embalm their corpses and then bury them in everlasting lawn cemeteries. Belgians bury theirs, but dig them up after a few years so they can use the grave again. Neapolitans store their corpses in lockers, and take them out every now and then to see how they are doing. The Jivaros of the Eastern Andes bury their women and children under the floorboards of the family hut, but males they place in a sitting position and then set fire to both corpse and hut. Some hunter-gatherer tribes just leave their dead behind, up camp, and move on. Elsewhere they eat parts of their corpses and are then sick; or place them in caves, as they did Lazarus and Jesus; or weight them and sink them in the river.[2]

In some cultures disposal will be carried out quickly because of the climate; in others it will be more leisurely. In Britain there are two main methods: burial and cremation. Traditionally burial has been predominant but, since its introduction, cremation has gradually become more popular. In England and Wales the number of cremations exceeded that of burials for the first time in 1967 and it was estimated that cremations constituted about 70 per cent of funerals in 1990.[3] There are several reasons for this change, which will be looked at in more detail in Chapter 7, 'Contemporary Issues'. This trend has created changes in funeral patterns, partly because of the distances involved. A traditional funeral procession would have left the deceased's home, gone to a local church or chapel, and the body would have been buried there: all local. A cremation, on the other hand, might involve the cortège travelling for an hour or more with the result that some mourners may not make the journey. Sometimes two services are held: one locally, and the other at the crematorium.

Whereas in a burial the disposal of the body is completed, the mourners leave and the grave is filled in, disposal of a body is not completed by cremation as ashes remain. Some families take them away for burial in family graves, but the pattern that initially developed in Britain was for them to remain at the crematorium and be disposed of in a variety of ways: burying in caskets in miniature graves, placing directly into the ground, scattering on the ground or in grass, or placing in a columbarium. A report from the Federation of British Cremation Authorities gives the disposition of cremated remains for 1987 as follows: strewn in crematorium grounds (57 per cent), interred in crematorium grounds (14.2 per cent), placed in graves or niches (3.6 per cent), taken away by representatives (23.7 per cent), and retained pending instructions (1.5 per cent).[4] Increasingly ashes are disposed of in bizarre ways. Fans of Star Trek will know that a small part of the ashes of its creator Gene Roddenberry were launched into space after his death in 1991. The Celestis website[5] will explain how this can be done for a mere $12,500. There are other more glamorous methods of preserving ashes. For instance, in 2002 a Chicago company[6] announced plans to turn cremated remains into diamonds: this is now a reality and the company has three offices in Europe. Whereas burial in Britain is governed by several Acts of Parliament, there is virtually no legislation about the disposal of cremated remains. One of my parishioners recently asked my advice as to what he should do with a miniature urn that had arrived in the post. It contained a small portion of his cousin's ashes and had been sent by the man's widow. She had apparently sent a similar urn to all the members of her husband's family. More commonly I have had many conversations with families of a deceased person about how to dispose of cremated remains. Many have chosen to bury them locally in family graves but it has surprised me how many have not realised that they could do this. I have also noticed an increasing number of people wanting to take their partner's remains with them when they move and have them re-interred near their new home. The traditional idea of the bodies of the dead being laid to rest and left in peace seems to be changing to one of keeping their remains near one.

Traditionally the British churchyard has always been central to its community and people have passed through it or by it constantly, being always reminded of their own mortality by the presence of family graves. The Burial Acts of the 1830s changed the pattern of burial in Britain by introducing the idea of the grave as a permanent resting place which would be left un-disturbed in perpetuity. Graves were not re-used, as in previous generations, and permanent stone memorials became common-place. The result was that churchyards became full and new cemeteries were built. Because of the availability of land, these Victorian cemeteries were often built on the outskirts of cities, rather than in the centre of communities, but were usually set on high ground to be visible and so remind everyone of their final destination. Today new crematoria are placed out of sight and people are unwilling to allow a funeral parlour to be built next door. We have chosen to hide death away on the fringes of our communities. This has implications for the way we mourn our dead and the ease with which we can visit the graves of those close to us. It is perhaps time, now that cremation accounts for the majority of funerals in Britain, to consider the location of crematoria. At present it is mainly local authorities who build and administer them, although a small number are run by private companies as commercial enterprises. Might they not be better placed within local communities, attached, for example, to churches, chapels or civic buildings? This is not something to be undertaken lightly. It could well change the ministry of an individual church and its priest or minister, or change the way a church or chapel is perceived by the local population. A significant difference between a crematorium funeral and one held at a church or chapel lies in the fact that crematoria are used only for funerals and people associate them only with death. By contrast, the church is also used for other celebrations: baptisms, weddings, harvest thanksgivings and regular Sunday and week-day worship. Mourners' previous experiences will affect their feelings about being there, both for the funeral and afterwards. For some there will be good associations and they will feel at home but for others it may be very different. I have noticed how helpful it is for a number of people, particularly widows and widowers, to attend Sunday worship at the church where the funeral took place. It seems to bring a sense of closeness to the departed and a sense of belonging to that congregation. This is clearly not possible at a distant crematorium.

Whereas the majority of people agree that churches and churchyards are sacred places, research suggests that only about 50 per cent regard crematoria in the same way.[7] Experience is often cumulative, however, and it is possible that, after several years crematoria will come to be perceived as sacred.

There are many issues surrounding the choices people make between burial and cremation on which we have not yet touched. These include the influence of national and local government policies, the availability of space for burial, the various approaches to the re-use of burial spaces, different approaches to cremation and burial in other countries, and the environmental issues surrounding cremation. These will be addressed in Chapter 7, 'Contemporary Issues'.

Marking a Death

It is hard to imagine a funeral not being closely preceded by a death, but is death always followed by a funeral? Some would argue that to deny a person a funeral is to deem him or her inhuman.[8] During the seventeenth and eighteenth centuries, bodies of executed criminals in England and Wales were dissected by an anatomist. This denial of a funeral was a deterrent more feared than capital punishment. When the 1832 Anatomy Act allowed the bodies of those dying on the parish to be used for dissection, it was seen as a punishment for poverty rather than crime.[9] In previous generations stillborn children and aborted foetuses were hardly ever afforded the dignity of a funeral and their bodies were normally disposed of without ceremony. Today it is increasingly common that they are treated as having possessed human life and given a funeral.

There are occasions when there is no body and relatives might be uncertain as to whether or not they may organize a funeral or memorial service. Such instances might include a person who has gone missing. The uncertainty as to what has occurred might always persist if the person is never found, but from seven years after the disappearance the missing person may legally be assumed dead. Sometimes it will be known almost immediately how he or she went missing, for example, if lost at sea or in an aircraft crash, or there might have been witnesses to the event but no body ever recovered. Alternatively some time might elapse before the facts become clear, as occurred following the bomb blasts in Madrid in March 2004, when the official number of those killed varied over several days. This was due to the effect of the bombs: not only did rescue workers have to establish the number of bodies, but they also had to decide which body parts belonged together. On the other hand the truth might be discovered only years afterwards, as in the case of the King's Cross Underground disaster: it was only in January 2004 that the last victim was identified, almost seventeen years after the event. Alexander Fallon had been living rough in London and his family had had no idea he was in England, let alone at King's

Cross. The circumstances in which a person has gone missing, then, may vary considerably. It is my view that the provision of appropriate liturgical resources for situations such as these would be useful, whether they be to commend the deceased finally to God or, even, in the event of his or her being found, to give thanks for a safe return.

A further situation of there being no corpse arises when the body is donated for medical research. If an individual is thinking of doing this, it is first worth enquiring of the medical school concerned whether the body will be accepted, and in what condition it might be unacceptable. That way the family will be more ready to deal with its possible rejection, which might be for a number of reasons including damage caused by a degenerative illness. Of course relatives of the donor might find the idea of a loved one donating his or her body upsetting and even when they are prepared, they might nevertheless feel that the death has not been properly recognized if no funeral has taken place. It might, therefore, be appropriate to hold a memorial service around the time of donation.

In 1981, Eric Tinker was approached by Her Majesty's Inspector of Anatomy about how to dispose of such bodies after the medical schools had finished with them. Together with teachers of anatomy and chaplains of teaching hospitals they devised a suitable liturgy and held a service to which relatives of donors were invited. This has now become an annual event which meets a need for a great many relatives and friends, giving them an opportunity to recognize publicly their bereavement in a liturgical setting.[10]

In many parts of the world the funeral appears to be something very basic to human dignity, and poor people go to extraordinary lengths to ensure a suitable funeral. It indicates that something of great importance has happened, that a particular human life has ended, and it interprets that event. One of the reasons why people express disappointment about the way a funeral is conducted is that one would never have guessed that something significant was being marked. A funeral, then, marks the fact that a human being has died.

Affirmation of the Deceased's Life

'Life-centred funerals' is a phrase used in Australia to describe a development intended to meet the needs of mourners unhappy with what they perceive as empty religious ritual. They are seeking a ceremony conducted with dignity, but which will celebrate the life of the deceased rather than the beliefs of the priest or minister. Sometimes the celebrant will conduct a funeral in cooperation with a priest or minister, reflecting that a person's religion was an important part of his or her life.

In Britain the alternative to a religious ceremony is the 'secular funeral', but the people to conduct them are few and far between and the extent to which these ceremonies are personalized varies enormously. It is not unknown for a secular celebrant to come from fifty miles away and to be as impersonal and ill-informed as any minister on a crematorium duty rota. Another important difference from Australia is that most secular funeral celebrants come from a background that has rejected Christianity, which can result in a refusal to include prayers, hymns or Bible readings.

The growth of life-centred and secular funerals should encourage churches to think again about how they celebrate an individual's life. There is an attitude, strong in some Christian traditions, which views the identity and individuality of the deceased as of little importance, and places an emphasis upon sin, divine mercy and an afterlife in heaven. This has tended to devalue earthly life, and forgiveness for the past – rather than thanks for its enjoyment – has sometimes taken ritual precedence. The 1662 Book of Common Prayer, for example, reflects a common trend of the Reformation. It included no prayers for the deceased, no memorial of his or her life and no commendation of the deceased to God; merely a committal of the body to the ground. Its emphasis was an exhortation to the congregation to live a godly life. Yet an important element of a funeral is giving thanks to God for the life of the deceased person and celebrating that life. This can involve sharing of memories and a description of the deceased's life and can be powerfully personal. In her study of the views and experiences of recently bereaved people and their ministers Jenny Hockey discovered a common theme in every interview conducted, that is, a desire that the funeral should be as personal an event as possible and should reflect the unique individual's human life.[11]

In a World of Wonder programme, broadcast on Sunday 30 January 2000 by HTV, funerals from a particular area of Ghana were shown. The coffins were all made according to individual designs, which reflected the deceased person's life. They included coffins made to look like a fishing boat, an iron and a gigantic chicken. It is increasingly possible to have an individually designed coffin made in Britain, although it is not something I have personally come across, except for cardboard and wicker coffins. In March 2004 a second edition was published of *The Dead Good Funerals Book*. This guide to arranging funerals was written by Sue Gill and John Fox 'to empower you to take control of the funeral process' and arose out of dissatisfaction with what is frequently seen as the conveyor-belt approach of much of the funeral industry. Many clergy do now individualize funerals within a framework that is broadly Christian. Readings, tributes and prayers can all be carefully chosen or written to reflect an individual's life, and appropriate people are sometimes asked to deliver them. The music used may also be a way in which the funeral can be personalized and this is the area about which people feel most confident, in my experience. More and more families are anxious to suggest suitable music for before and after the ceremony. Often the suggestions are of 'secular' music. This may prove challenging for the church. Some ministers 'solve' the secular music 'problem' by suggesting that this choice be played during the time at the crematorium. It is perhaps wise not to have a hard and fast rule. A pop song, for example, carefully chosen and consistent with Christian belief, can be both appropriate and intensely moving.

A number of clergy, however, would have reservations about personalizing funerals and would be wary of sentimentality, even triviality, and a loss of integrity on the part of the funeral celebrant. They would be concerned not to lose sight of the significance of human death in the light of the death and resurrection of Christ and in the context of the community of faith. A willingness to allow friends and relatives a large degree of freedom led, in one case, to an hour of heavy metal music. Clearly a balance needs to be struck and extremes avoided.

There are examples of people who have been encouraged by their clergy to think ahead and indicate what they hope might take place at their funeral. Sheffield Cathedral promotes this practice and encourages people to complete a 'my funeral planning sheet' form, which is kept on file. When parishioners have talked to me about their desires for their funeral I have encouraged them to commit their thoughts to paper and discuss them with their next of kin. Sometimes they have asked me to keep a copy of what they have written.

Part of Grieving

Rebecca Abrams, in a book written for those learning to live with the loss of a parent, says,

> Even the most well-planned funeral will be upsetting on the actual day . . . The day of the funeral is painful, it is supposed to be: it is the first moment since your parent's death when you can focus fully on the fact that he or she is dead. One of the most crucial functions of the funeral is precisely this: to allow you to feel your loss and your pain. The formal emphasis of the occasion may be committing your parent to God's care; it may be to comfort the bereaved; it may be to make some sense of death itself, but the private function of the funeral is to let you concentrate for a while on your loss. Then having recognised that something has been lost, you can hopefully begin to find ways of living with that loss.[12]

There are many opportunities that present themselves for the priest or minister to help mourners by praying with them or reading scripture, or to mark particular moments with ritual actions, and handbooks of advice on pastoral care often suggest this. Readings drawing on the experience of other bereaved persons and from non-scriptural sources could be included in the service, or in pastoral contact with the bereaved both before and after the funeral. Church in Wales Publications once published a collection of articles by a bereaved woman because of the response to them when they had appeared in the *Welsh Churchman*, to help those dealing with a similar experience.[13] It is not only those most closely bereaved who suffer grief, however, and we can make the mistake of focusing most, if not all, of our pastoral attention on them. While acknowledging that they are the primary recipients of pastoral care, some of our attention should be given to the wider community, which will include people recently bereaved and others more distantly so. Readings, sermons, tributes, prayers and hymns should all be chosen with awareness of this much wider 'audience' and try to help some people at least to articulate questions about the meaning of life for them, and to begin to explore some answers.

An important aspect of funeral liturgy is to help turn our thoughts, at a time of deep grief, away from feeling sorry for ourselves and towards the praise of God, where we can rediscover the right place of the deceased, ourselves and the community, in the kingdom of God. One purpose of the sermon is to proclaim the gospel in the context of the death of this particular person, and the service should not be so constructed that it reinforces bland assurances of comfort and leaves no scope for challenge, or an exploration of the deeper questions that some people will be addressing.

A great deal has been written in recent years about 'stages of grief'. It is useful to be aware of these stages, although there are dangers in applying them too rigidly. It can create the impression that the bereaved will go through these stages in order, one after the other. In my experience people grieve in different ways, many of which are culturally conditioned. How else can one explain the difference between Welsh men who may well cry at a funeral and their English neighbours who keep a stiff upper lip, albeit one which will tremble when deeply moved? That is not, of course, to imply that their grief is in any way insincere but that its expression is culturally affected. Rather than talk of stages of grief I would prefer to follow Alan Billings' lead and speak of 'aspects of grief'. In his book *Dying and Grieving* he considers ten such aspects: shock, disorganization, denial, relief, guilt, depression, anger, anxiety, resolution and re-establishment, and loneliness.

It is perhaps helpful to mention here the effect on the pastor of continually listening to stories of other people's loss and supporting them through those experiences. Most people do this for close friends and relatives on a number of occasions during their lifetimes. The priest or minister may do this several times a month and it is potentially very draining emotionally and spiritually. He or she will need to find appropriate ways of dealing with this. I have found it helpful to have the support of a spiritual director; this is a person who knows me well, who will listen and understand without being judgemental, but who will also challenge me when necessary and help me discover the spiritual resource which God provides for me. This applies, of course, to all aspects of ministry, but I have found the emotional and spiritual cost of funerals to be particularly high. All ministers will have their own methods of finding support and I believe this to be important; otherwise, despite the need for a degree of objectivity, there might result a kind of cold professionalism which keeps the bereaved at a safe distance.

A Social Phenomenon

The funeral and the events surrounding it do not take place in a vacuum but reflect cultural aspects of the community in which they occur, and, in turn, act on that community.

In medieval England the death of a nobleman had enormous repercussions for the community. A power vacuum was created and it was important to the nobility that their influence be quickly reasserted. The funeral was used to show the significance of the deceased's successor by placing him, rather than the deceased's widow, in the position of chief mourner. Through its display of pomp and ceremony the funeral was used to re-establish the power of the ruling class and quickly to suppress any thought of rebellion.[14]

This is an extreme example of what is happening in funerals all the time. Old dependencies are disappearing and new ones are established. This is as true of the local doctor or vet today as it was of the medieval monarch. In the case of a valued member of the community who dies, members of that community need to feel that those things that are important will continue. The funeral, by demonstrating changes in social structure and ritually endorsing them, can bring security at a time of change. This is also true within the family. When, for example, the person who draws the family together dies, a new figure often emerges to take on the role.

Sometimes the values of the wider community will not be moulded or reinforced but, rather, challenged by the funeral as, for instance, in the funerals of activists in the South African struggle against apartheid. At the funeral of Frikkie Conradie held in March 1982 in the Alexandra township of Johannesburg, Bishop Desmond Tutu said in his sermon:

> Can you imagine the unimaginable in this country of separation, of bitterness, of suspicion and hatred: can you imagine an Afrikaner, a DRC [Dutch Reformed Church] dominee of all people, leaving his own community to identify himself so closely with the downtrodden, the poor and the suffering, a White man giving himself and his family to a Black community, to be their servant and to work for justice and reconciliation and to work under a Black minister? It is unbelievable and yet we saw this miracle of God's grace working here in Alexandra Township, here in South Africa.[15]

Turning to a different society, one may consider the effect of President Kennedy's assassination on America, in particular the way in which the president's widow handled her grief, which was controlled and disciplined. Not only did this suggest that part of the role of the funeral is to reinforce the values of the society in which it takes place, but it also reflected values considered important in that society.

Closer to home, rural communities in Wales provide an example, with which I have become very familiar, of how funerals reflect the differing attitudes within the society. It is made more interesting to me by the interactions between two linguistic groups within the same society: the one Welsh-speaking, the other English-speaking. Within both groups, sympathy for the bereaved and respect for the dead are considered important but these values are expressed in different ways, and on occasions some people from one group will not realize that their ways are different from those of their neighbours. When the funeral is announced within the Welsh-speaking community it will normally be described as 'public', 'private' or 'strictly private', and people will have a very clear understanding of what is meant by those terms. A strictly private funeral will be for close family, and only those that are invited will attend. A private funeral will be similar but the circle of people invited will be wider, and friends and neighbours will feel able to ask if they might attend. By contrast a public funeral will be open to anyone and there will be an expectation that members of the community will be there. Friends and former residents may come from considerable distances and the refreshments afterwards may take on the character of a reunion. These very commonly used terms mean little to most English neighbours who do not normally use them unless they have been resident in the community for a long time. To me, the very clear understanding of what is expected at a funeral among the Welsh-speakers shows the relative importance that is attached to the rituals surrounding death, in contrast to the apparent uncertainty regarding how one should arrange a funeral, which may be detected among the English who have moved into the area. A colleague of mine, who comes from the north of England and whose first parish was in Ceredigion, described how a teenage girl asked him 'Ble rydych chi'n claddu?' ('Where do you bury (your dead)?'). He was surprised that a girl of that age should have been aware of a relationship between her family and a particular piece of land. For him it was simply not a question he had ever thought about. Whereas she was well aware of funerals she had attended and which had been conducted in her village, he had never attended one until he was ordained.

Sometimes the culture reflected by the funeral is that of the deceased's circle of friends and acquaintances. A few years ago I attended a biker's funeral, during which his friends, clad in their best leathers, escorted his coffin to the crematorium on their Harley-Davidsons. It was very different from the usual, as they stood solemnly listening to the strains of Led Zepellin's 'Stairway to Heaven', in contrast with some respectably be-suited members of the community who whispered all the way through the sermon.

The clergy have a key role in making arrangements for funerals and it is important for them to understand what is happening in the community, be it large or small. The funeral is not the property of the Church but a ritual in which the whole of society has a role to play. Jenny Hockey's study of Sheffield funerals,[16] however, shows that many clergy find this difficult to accept in practice. Reservations about the contribution of outside groups were expressed in terms of a concern that they might 'take over', thereby undermining the Christian framework within which the service as a whole was couched. I, personally, find it useful to remember the following advice given by the Anglican Church of Canada in its preface to funeral services: 'It is important for Christians to be aware of the universal dimensions of funeral practices.'[17] We are privileged that a very wide cross-section of our society turns to us to conduct their funerals and it is reasonable to take the view that we bury the dead on behalf of the whole of society. That view might not be shared by all clergy, of course, and I have sometimes attended funerals in churches and chapels when all the tributes and prayers have focused solely on the deceased's contribution to that church or chapel. Yet it is my feeling that, as a Christian church, we should be celebrating the whole of a person's life and not simply that part of it with which we ourselves are closely connected. The concerns of a specific society or club, of which the deceased was a member and who wish to pay tribute, might be different; the Church, on the other hand, should have its eyes and ears open to the whole of life and my concern is that we should not give the impression of being merely an exclusive club.

In Chapter 3 and parts of Chapter 2 we have considered the importance of seven elements of the funeral, noting that the appropriate emphasis for each is not readily apparent. Consequently it is important for clergy and others who arrange funerals, not only to be aware of these, but also to be able to assess, in any given situation, the emphasis that should be given to each of them. This is not to commend a slavish adherence to checklists every time we deal with a bereavement, as the more experience we gain, the more instinctive the assessment will become. There is nevertheless a concern that, if thought is not given to these elements during the ministry of a cleric, mourners will not experience what might otherwise have benefited them.

Surprisingly little work has been done on analysing the effects of funerals on mourners and there has been relatively little work done on comparing the form and role of funerals in different parts of the world. In this area, our understanding of death remains wide open for research. All kinds of evidence about the effect of funerals upon mourners are of value, however anecdotal. If it were possible to collect such evidence without changing the quality, and hence the accuracy, of the experiences being reported, we might draw useful conclusions about the relative benefit of particular kinds of funeral and of various factors involved in any one approach. We should ask particularly about the relationship between depression and funerals and how it varies as the expression of grief is inhibited or discouraged.

This chapter has attempted to analyse the funeral by looking at its constituent elements and asking what makes a funeral and what is essential to it. In Chapter 4 we will look at funerals from a different perspective and ask the question 'whose funeral is it?' In other words, who can decide what does or does not take place, who may or may not be there, and other related questions.

NOTES

[1] Walter, Tony, *Funerals and How to Improve Them*, London, Hodder and Stoughton, 1990, p. 109.

[2] Walter, *Funerals*, p. 18.

[3] Jupp, Peter, *From Dust to Ashes: The Replacement of Burial by Cremation in England 1840–1967*, London, The Congregational Memorial Hall Trust, 1990, p. 1.

[4] Saunders, K. C., 'Service Without a Smile: The Changing Structure of the Death Industry', *Service Industries Journal*, 1991, Vol. 11, pp. 202–18.

[5] www.celestis.com.

[6] 'Life Gem Memorials, www.lifegem.com, a Chicago company, caused quite a stir in August 2002 after it announced plans to turn dead people into diamonds. Company spokesman Mark Bouffard said the business concept was simple: Humans are made of carbon, diamonds are made of carbon. Why not make diamonds out of humans? Using a patented process, they tested the concept on a pig, got dazzling results, and started taking orders for people. "The average person has enough carbon in them to produce between 50 and 100 diamonds," said Bouffard, adding that the company has gotten "hundreds" of requests for information from people interested in turning themselves, their relatives or their pets into jewels. The company expects to finish its first human diamond in 11 weeks. LifeGem's least-expensive product is a $3,950 quarter-carat diamond. At the moment, the company is only taking orders for blue diamonds, which are irradiated in a lab to achieve the same hue of the famous cerulean *Hope Diamond*. And if Grandma gets lost or stolen, don't worry: The company stores extra carbon so she can become a gem again.' Reported by Julia Scheeres, Lycos Inc., 19 Sept. 2002. It is now a thriving commercial venture with three European offices, one in the United Kingdom.

[7] Davies, Douglas, *British Crematoria in Public Profile*, Maidstone, Cremation Society of Great Britain 1995, pp. 8–9.

[8] Walter, *Funerals* , p. 111.

[9] Richardson, Ruth, *Death, Dissection and the Destitute*, London, Routledge and Kegan Paul, 1987.

[10] Tinker, Eric, 'An Unusual Christian Service: For Those Who Have Donated Their Bodies for Medical Education and Research', *Mortality*, 1998 Vol. 3 (1), pp. 79–82.

[11] Hockey, Jenny, 'The Acceptable Face of Human Grieving? The Clergy's Role in Managing Emotional Expression during Funerals', in D. Clark (ed.), *The Sociology of Death*, Oxford, Blackwell, 1993, pp. 129–48.

[12] Abrams, Rebecca, *When Parents Die: Learning to Live with the Loss of a Parent*, London, Harper Collins, 1995, p. 27.

[13] Hughes, J, *Coping with Grief*, Penarth, Church in Wales Publications, 1979.

[14] Gittings, Clare, *Death, Burial and the Individual in Early Modern England*, London, Croom Helm, 1984, particularly chapter 9.

[15] Tutu, Desmond, *Hope and Suffering: Sermons and Speeches*, London, Collins, Fount Paperbacks, 1983, p. 132.

[16] Hockey, 'The Acceptable Face of Human Grieving?', p. 22.

[17] Anglican Church of Canada, *The Book of Alternative Services of the Anglican Church of Canada*, Toronto, Ontario, Anglican Book Centre, 1989, p. 565.

4

Whose Funeral Is It?

'Good afternoon,' Father Crompton said with such ill-will that I felt the bell and the candle were not far away.
'Mr Bendrix has helped me a great deal with all the arrangements,' Henry explained.
'I would have been quite ready to take them off your hands if I had known.'
. . . I said, 'You could hardly have done that surely. You disapprove of cremation.'
'I could have arranged a Catholic burial.'
'She wasn't a Catholic.'
'She had expressed the intention of becoming one.'
'Is that enough to make her one?'
Father Crompton produced a formula. He laid it down like a bank note. 'We recognize the baptism of desire.' It lay there between us waiting to be picked up. Nobody made a move.

From *The End of the Affair* by Graham Greene[1]

In recent years there have been great improvements in the pro-vision of bereavement counselling and hospice care, but those involved in funerals are still largely left to their own devices to decide what they are trying to achieve. As a parish priest I have been very conscious that my own training for the ministry included only one session on funerals. After ordination I was very fortunate in that my incumbent gave me much valuable help; not all clergy are so lucky, however, and a number are expected to conduct funerals with little practical or theoretical preparation. One survey revealed that a frequent and unexpected experience for newly ordained clergy was their being invited to view the deceased in the front parlour or upstairs.[2] For the majority of them this was their first encounter with a corpse. There are many other things of which the newly ordained should

be aware. For instance, during one of the first funerals I conducted some of the mourners jostled each other as they walked
into the crematorium chapel, two of them clearly trying to
gain the position of chief mourner in the front row. I had not
previously met any of them, as I had been informed that there
was no family living locally, and had spoken at length on the telephone to the man's brother. It was only afterwards that I discovered the existence of a woman who had lived with the
deceased for over forty years. They had never married and his
family disapproved of her. His brother was the next of kin and
responsible for the arrangements. Neither the undertaker nor I
was aware until after the funeral that the deceased's partner
existed, and she had not been informed of the funeral arrangements. Knowing about them only from the newspaper, she therefore tried to push her way in. By that stage it was too late for me
to do anything about it but, had I known in advance, what
should my response have been?

The funeral seeks to meet the needs of different individuals
and groups and the aim of this chapter is first to attempt to
identify those people and then to consider whose role it is to take
responsibility for the various parts of the rite. In this, there will
be conflicting wishes and interests and later in the chapter we will
consider possible approaches to these conflicts.

To whom does the funeral belong, with whom do we make
arrangements, and whom are we addressing at its various stages?
We will start by considering the role of the deceased person,
before moving on to consider the closely bereaved, family
members, the undertaker, the clergy, and the wider community.

The Deceased Person

In ordinary speech we refer to 'John's funeral' or 'Mary's
funeral' and we mean that John, or Mary, is to be buried or
cremated. In taking the service, however, the cleric does not
normally address John or Mary (although some liturgical revisions have made this possible) but, at different times, speaks to

the closely bereaved, the immediate family, the wider family, the local community, and God. It may be that we do address the deceased directly during the service to say a goodbye, especially if the circumstances of the death were such that there was no opportunity to do so. Even if we do not, mourners may well be doing so privately during the service, and certain prayers that address the deceased directly may usefully be used, such as:

> (*Name*), go forth from this world:
> in the love of God the Father who created you,
> in the mercy of Jesus Christ who redeemed you,
> in the power of the Holy Spirit who strengthens you.
> May the heavenly host sustain you
> and the company of heaven enfold you.
> In communion with all the faithful,
> may you dwell this day in peace.
> Amen.[3]

Some theologians would state that a funeral asserts that death, like life, is in God's hands and that the rite gives a clear message to the dead: that is, being now in a different existence, they must maintain a distance from the living. To quote Jesus' parable of Lazarus and Dives, 'There is a great gulf fixed between us; no one can cross it from our side to reach you, and none may pass from your side to us' (Luke 16:26). The funerals of many other cultures send the departed on their way with a series of messages whose meaning is clearly, 'This way only.' As we have already seen, the Reformation changed the emphasis of funeral rites in the Church of England; the dead were no longer prayed for and an emphasis was placed on the exhortation of the mourners. All this has resulted in a perception in some quarters that funeral liturgies exist mainly to comfort the living, so much so that in some chapels the coffin will not be brought inside for the service: the family will arrive with the coffin and enter the chapel while the coffin is taken directly to the grave. At the end of the service the mourners will leave the chapel and walk to the graveside for the committal.

It is often said that funerals are for the living and not the dead, yet it seems to me that, both liturgically and pastorally, this is to lose an important element. I have sometimes commented during funeral services that this is an occasion to say 'farewell' and numerous mourners have remarked later that this thought was particularly helpful to them.

An individual might be involved in his or her funeral in its planning. The deceased's wishes for the funeral have no legal standing but will normally have a strong influence on those arranging the funeral. I have frequently heard the bereaved say such things as, 'If only we knew what she wanted.' Many funeral directors now have pre-paid schemes which enable people to make arrangements in advance. Some people will simply leave instructions in a will or with their relatives; others, of course, will not wish to discuss this at all, considering it morbid to think about death or not wishing to cause their relatives added pain. It is clearly an extremely emotional and, for some, distressing topic. It is worth letting it be known among the members of one's congregation that, if they are planning their funerals, it is helpful to talk to one of the clergy about this at an early stage, mainly to check that what is proposed is practical. I do have to admit, however, that as a result of such a policy I had to spend considerable time explaining to one parishioner that I would not be prepared to exclude a particular individual from her funeral service. My point that she should seek to be reconciled before entering into eternal life rather than perpetuate division for eternity was not accepted. She decided that her funeral would be held elsewhere and be conducted by a more reasonable vicar.

The way an individual is remembered will be influenced in part by the way in which that person has prepared for death. Planning a funeral, giving mementoes and trying to create happy memories are all ways in which the dying contribute to the way they would like to be remembered. In 1996 Ned Sherrin, the popular media presenter, edited a book of 'Readings, Prayers, and Music chosen for Memorial Services'. It is entitled *Remembrance*[4] and contains biblical readings and traditional hymns alongside excerpts from novels and established classics. It includes memorial services that have been used for distinguished people, and services that other public figures, still alive, have devised for themselves. It shows that individuals increasingly wish to shape the final words on their own life and death and not necessarily accept those provided by traditional religion.

A tribute at a funeral could well form part of the process of remembering, and may be the source of much anxiety for the person writing it. What do we say about a person who was thoroughly disliked by others? Is it possible always to be truthful and not to cause offence or embarrassment? How do we resist the temptation to make every deceased person appear a saint, given that not all of us are? My own rule is that I do not say anything unkind or condemnatory of the deceased and that I never knowingly say anything that is untrue, however much others may wish me to do so. On occasions families give me a piece to read, or express the desire that a particular friend or relative should speak, and this may need careful handling. I will always discuss the contribution with the person who has written it and, if necessary, explain why I would prefer to omit or change some part of it. The limited time available at a crematorium can be a tactful excuse but on balance I think it is kinder in the long term to be truthful.

When describing a person and, to some extent, summing up a life, it is helpful to remember that we give thanks for the whole life. Some mourners are likely to remember an elderly person as a young girl and as a middle-aged woman as well as the old lady we have more recently known. Each mourner will of course remember the deceased in different ways and I have often noticed how surprised adult children are to hear of a parent's earlier life.

The Closely Bereaved

We might not always be dealing with one congregation alone since at each stage of the rite those present might differ. There may be a small and intimate group, for example, the immediate family or close friends at the bedside of a dying person, or a slightly wider group receiving the coffin as it is brought to the church the evening before the funeral. At other times the congregation could be composed of a variety of groups, each with a different relationship to the dead person, as occurs in the main funeral service. There will, however, nearly always be a small core of people who will be there at each stage: immediate family and close friends. These are the people I have in mind when referring to the 'closely bereaved'.

I have tried to draw a distinction between the two terms 'closely bereaved' and 'family', as the closely bereaved are not always family. I think, for instance, of the elderly spinster who constantly refers to 'my friend'. They had trained together as nurses and worked in the same hospital for almost forty years. Throughout that time they had shared a house and gone on holiday together. They were the closest of friends but they were not family. They continued to share the same house in retirement until one of them died, and her friend was obliged to ask the next of kin's permission to arrange the funeral. In that case it was gladly given but that is not always the case.

There was the father whose daughter was killed in a car accident. She had asked her solicitor to ensure that, in the event of her death, her lesbian partner should arrange the funeral. Her father was devastated by the news for it was then that he learned of his daughter's sexuality. Her partner was also distraught, torn between fulfilling her partner's wishes and hurting her partner's family.

I have known several instances of couples who regard themselves as married in all but name and have had children together but who have never married. When one dies, the partner discovers that he or she is not the next of kin and that others will organize the funeral and possibly inherit property if there is no will. This is an area where the law is likely to change over the next few years.

Where there is a dispute between the parties, it may reflect years of disagreement, and most clergy sooner or later learn to their cost how complicated and bitter those disagreements may be. There are, in my opinion, three questions to bear in mind. What is legally permissible? What is morally right? What is practically possible? Sometimes the answers to all three may be very different. At the end of this chapter I will return to this and try to establish some further helpful questions.

The closely bereaved, therefore, are not always family, yet mostly they are. The distinction I drew earlier will normally be very blurred and consequently the content of this and the following sections are often interchangeable.

It is now widely accepted that there is no one correct way to grieve and that individuals will mourn their dead in different ways. Neither is there one way to arrange a funeral and compromise might be called for among the immediately bereaved. Support organizations have commented that some mourners worry that their emotions are abnormal and they fear they are going mad. They need reassurance that this is not the case.[5] When they have freedom to do whatever they like, mourners will often feel at a loss and will look for a model to copy. On occasions, a visit to a bereaved family will be spent assuring them that what they are arranging is perfectly normal or that they are entitled to do it that way, even if it is a little unusual. While acknowledging this, it is important to note that there are those who do not accept grief to be a matter of personal inclination, and bereaved people are from time to time criticized for behaving in what others regard as inappropriate ways or for arranging the funeral in a particular way.

Many Jews will follow mourning rituals that relate to many details of everyday life, with clear prescriptions set for time and place. A survey conducted in Britain almost forty years ago revealed that all the Jewish participants found such concentrated and overt mourning therapeutic.[6] Its effect was to prevent their hiding their grief and they valued this. They also appreciated the fact that the period of mourning ended at a certain date. Given the comfort and consolation that mourners appear to find through such rituals, it might be appropriate for churches to be developing more home-based and family-centred practices to help the bereaved express and come to terms with their loss. For example, one church specifically invites bereaved families to attend a requiem Mass on the All Souls Day (2 November) following the funeral. There are also liturgical resources available for use at the end of a period of mourning, which might be helpful.[7]

Family Members

Just as the closely bereaved are not always family, so family may not always be closely bereaved. I think, for example, of a woman who arranged the funeral for a sister to whom she had not spoken for seventeen years. Families are now more likely to include an estranged, but not divorced, marriage partner whom the rest of the family feel is not the most appropriate person to handle the arrangements. Most of the time, however, we will be dealing with more conventional situations. Nevertheless, conflicting ideas as to who is part of the family do arise every so often concerning, for instance, the new but unmarried partner, the recently divorced spouse, the stepchildren brought into the family by a second marriage, or the homosexual partner. All of these will possibly feel awkward and wonder if they should be present.

Since people have their own preferred style of grieving, this will possibly make it difficult for other family members who have a different style. One might wish to go out and be with friends but finds that the partner thinks this inappropriate. One will wish to talk at length; the other would rather go for long walks and visit the grave alone. Partners who thought they knew each other begin to find each other behaving in unexpected and unfamiliar ways. A parent may remarry before the children have recovered from the loss of their other parent. If there is a general expectation of freedom to follow one's personal inclination, this does not mean that the bereaved are free from social influence: it is common for them to need affirmation or to receive unasked-for, and sometimes unwelcome, advice or criticism. Thus they will discover that freedom does not exist in a social vacuum.

We have referred earlier to the increasing variety of ways by which cremated remains can be disposed. This is one area where families are permitted to make their own decisions without bureaucratic control, and some would see this as the bereaved family's way of gaining control over at least part of the funeral rite.

Sometimes family and close friends will wish to view the body and this may facilitate their acceptance of the death. People have differing opinions and some react almost with horror to the suggestion, but if people wish to do this I believe they should be encouraged. If the body is in a hospital morgue, the chaplain may be of help in arranging a visit, or a local priest or minister might accompany the family and lead prayers. At other times the mourners would rather be left to themselves.

It is also quite common for families to ask the minister to conduct a short private service in the deceased's home before going on to the main service elsewhere. Such services vary enormously but the atmosphere is likely to be highly charged, as those present are very closely connected with the deceased. It may also be the only part of the proceedings attended by an elderly or sick relative who is perhaps housebound. I once arrived at a house to conduct such a service, to find the deceased's widow speaking on the telephone. She was explaining to the caller that the vicar had now arrived and that he was about to start the service. She showed no sign of finishing the conversation and, as I tried to hide my anxiety that we were being delayed, she asked if I would like to speak to the caller, who turned out to be the deceased's son. He lived in Australia and had been unable to obtain a flight home for the funeral. Throughout the service his cousin held the telephone in front of me, so that he could hear my words and share in that part of the service. When we went to the church the same cousin used a tape-recorder so that he could send him a copy of the service. After the burial we were asked to pose at the graveside for some photographs to be taken and these were later sent to the son. It reminded me of taking wedding photographs, yet none of us knew whether we should smile or remain solemn. It was a novel way for people who, for good reason, could not be present to participate in the service, and I have since thought that web cameras and the internet would make a live link possible in similar circumstances. There are other ways of making people feel that they belong to a funeral that they cannot attend. Some clergy call at the house of housebound people on the way home from burying an elderly relative to say prayers with them. On such occasions I deliberately choose some of the same prayers used at the cemetery. Not infrequently, a priest or minister will conduct a short service with those relatives unable to travel to a distant funeral and will arrange the time to coincide with the funeral – not a practicable timing when it is in New Zealand.

Thus far I have made no distinction between the needs of bereaved adults and children. The first funeral I attended, at the age of thirteen, was that of my mother. Six months later my father was also cremated, and those experiences made me particularly aware of the ways in which adults try to protect children from grief. Children are going to feel the loss of any significant person in their lives, and although they may not have reached an age when they have the vocabulary to express their grief, this does not mean that it does not exist. It is possible to help children find appropriate ways of expressing grief but we cannot prevent it. These days children have far more say in decisions that affect them, and whether or not they attend a funeral will no doubt depend on many factors, for example, their ages, what their siblings are going to do and the traditions of their family. It is my view that a major factor to be considered should be the wishes of the child. He or she may wish to go to the whole of the rite or perhaps only part of it. The child might even express a desire to contribute to it. A few years ago I read a poem in a funeral service by a ten-year-old girl on the death of her grandmother. Some members of her family had taken the view that she should not be present, but she was given the choice. She decided to attend, wrote her poem, and asked to be allowed to read it at the service. Later, before we went into church she changed her mind and asked me to read it for her.

If children are to make these kinds of decisions, it is important that they know what to expect and I am often surprised to discover that the day's proceedings have not been explained to them in advance. As a result, whenever there are children involved I now make a point of describing to them the events in some detail. In doing so, I have come to realize how many adults are also not familiar with funeral procedure.

The Undertaker

Undertakers vary enormously. At one extreme is the village carpenter who would traditionally have made the coffin but now acts as a part-time undertaker, buying his coffins elsewhere, whose main income is derived from other sources. At the other extreme are the national and multi-national chains of funeral directors committed to expanding their share of the market and maximizing their profits. This chapter concerns the individual funeral director and his or her involvement in particular funerals. The development of the undertaking profession and the changes that have come about within it will be considered in the next chapter, but there are some trends to consider at this point.

First, funerals are now organized not so much by the close relatives of the deceased as by professionals employed to do so on their behalf and this greater responsibility has resulted in undertakers being referred to as 'funeral directors'. The use of this title can, in some instances, lead to an attitude that the professional 'directs' the funeral and dictates to the mourners, rather than 'undertaking' to carry out their wishes. Second, funeral directors have sought to control more aspects of the funeral industry. The building of chapels of rest to house the corpse before burial or cremation and the organizing of transport for the occasion are examples of this, together with the growth of the practice of embalming. It is natural that any business will seek to expand; nevertheless there is a danger that mourners are pressurized into paying for services which they did not desire, as an unscrupulous undertaker exploits their vulnerability. My own experience is, happily, that most undertakers, including those who are not formally members of a professional association, are highly principled and abide by codes of conduct.

There is sometimes a tension between clergy and undertakers, with both sides failing to appreciate the value of the other's role or the pressures affecting it. A good working relationship is very necessary and the two professions can be most helpful to one another. The undertaker is more likely to be on the scene before the cleric and will have to deal with difficult situations immediately. In my experience most take a pride in their pastoral skills and know that if those are not developed they will quickly lose business, especially in small or close-knit communities. They are also under pressure to make arrangements efficiently, rapidly and professionally, for what may be one of several funerals in a short period of time. They will provide the cleric who does not know the deceased with basic information, although it is always crucial to check facts, such as the name by which the deceased was known. I remember once using a name that the family had given me and, after the burial, looking more closely at the registrar's certificate to find forenames other than the one I had just used in church and at the graveside. My first reaction was to worry if I had buried the wrong body; it was, however, simply that this elderly lady had always been known to her family by her nickname and they had not thought to explain this to me.

Undertakers increasingly find that they are being asked to provide for a wider variety of needs. It is no longer sufficient to ask, 'Which minister would you like?' There are several reasons for this. We are now a more cosmopolitan society and people from more varied ethnic backgrounds are asking for their traditions to be included. I conducted one funeral in Wales where a foreign family was particularly keen for wine to be served at the refreshments afterwards. Those responsible for serving them found this puzzling and said to me, 'But they'll still want tea, won't they?' The Welsh teapot was there ready alongside the bottles and glasses but none of the family could understand why. In addition to variations in custom, the number of religions practised in this country is greater than ever before and the emergence of 'secular' and 'alternative' funerals calls for different approaches. The easy availability of good quality audio equipment means that mourners can expect to play favourite pieces of music, and increased wealth allows for more expenditure on elaborate proceedings.

The mass media have also influenced change, heightening public awareness of what might occur at a funeral. Following the funeral of Diana, Princess of Wales, and other highly publicized funerals, a number of undertakers have found that they are more often asked to include particular pieces of music. These are not necessarily the same as those used at the high-profile funerals but the requests are made because it is now acceptable to ask. It is also now clear to mourners that it might be appropriate for someone other than a cleric to give an address during a church service. All of this has made the job of an undertaker more varied and it is perhaps more difficult for the part-time builder in a village to compete with the large firms. Nevertheless, larger businesses rarely offer what is the small firm's most competitive asset: the undertaker is local and probably knows the family.

The Clergy

We have already seen in Chapter 1 how the roles of the doctor and the clergyman changed in relation to death during the eighteenth century. This marked the beginning of a gradual loss of influence by the clergy in different areas of life, yet the one area in which a cleric's authority is still thought to be prominent is the funeral, and it may be argued that we are currently witnessing a struggle by clergy to maintain that control. Many people regard the cleric as a professional engaged to do a job in much the same way as they hire a solicitor and they would no more look for a continuing relationship with the cleric than with the others. This attitude sometimes puts the cleric in an awkward position. One of my colleagues was asked to hold a funeral service in his church without including any religious content. Neither the deceased nor the family were Christians and they wanted him to lead a secular service. He explained that he was a Christian minister, that it was a Christian church, and that any funeral held in the church, as opposed to the churchyard, would have to be conducted according to the rites of the Church in Wales. He also offered to let them use the church hall for a secular ceremony and to help them find a suitable person to lead it, as he did not feel he could do so. The family, unfortunately, were indignant and considered that he was being unreasonable. That is obviously an extreme example, but we do find ourselves asked to allow others from very different backgrounds to contribute to the service and on occasions to take part in situations where we may feel uncomfortable. Those requests will come with little notice and we will not always have much time to consult and consider them carefully, although it would be unreasonable of mourners to expect a cleric to respond instantaneously without taking time to consult the bishop, archdeacon or church officers, as appropriate.

This perception of the cleric as a professional hired to do a job, rather than a pastor, is unlikely to be countered if one considers the amount of time given to funeral visits by clergy. One study showed that most pre-funeral visits by clergy lasted between thirty minutes and an hour and only one per cent of clerics returned more than once.[8] It would seem that, in failing to visit the bereaved, we are missing an opportunity, especially when they are not churchgoers. In recent years the increased size of pastoral charges, extra-parochial commitments, reduced numbers and lack of time have all combined to prevent the clergy from doing all they would like, resulting in only minimal follow-up after a funeral, although many church members would expect such contact.

Reference has already been made to a study of funerals in the Sheffield area which highlighted one aspect of the minister's role, that is, as a manager of emotion. It portrayed the clergy as seeing themselves in charge and using various means to control the grief expressed during the funeral service. Nevertheless, training and personal experience have led many clergy to the belief that, although bereaved people may well need to express very powerful feelings, the formal structure of death ritual in Western society does depend on the congregation itself exercising a degree of self-control. When leading the service it is easy to feel uncomfortable at events beyond one's control, such as a mourner clinging to the coffin refusing to let go, the bereaved husband wailing loudly and crying inconsolably through the prayers, and later looking as though he will throw himself into the grave during the committal. There is little we can do to prevent the unexpected, but, as clerics, we are not alone. Undertakers will feel similarly awkward and will be there to assist, as we in turn will sometimes come to their aid. Perhaps the golden rule is that, whatever we do, we should do it in a dignified way that is kind to those involved.

A social gathering is held immediately after most funerals, perhaps at the home of a relative or friend or in a hall booked for the occasion. Traditionally the cleric would have been included in such a gathering as an important and well-known member of the community. Today many clergy still attend, often feeling honoured to be included 'as part of the family' and aware that not attending might give offence. In comparison, other clergy feel that pressure of work forces them to make difficult decisions about how their time can best be spent, and do not attend. This could also be due to their feeling awkward in attending what they see as a family gathering. I wonder how much of this is actually caused by pressure of time, or by an unrecognized response to the emotional demands that funerals place upon clergy. In studies that have taken place little evidence has been seen of clerics employing any strategy to manage that stress and remain loyal to the calling of an involved and caring pastor.[9]

Practical support for the dying and bereaved is of course important and is looked for from both family and friends. Spiritual support, however, is also significant, and mourners may well ask difficult questions, such as why 'God' should 'choose' to 'end' a particular life at a particular time. Elisabeth Kubler-Ross is well known for her studies of death and dying. She has been a pioneer in helping doctors, nurses, clergy and families of the dying to hear what the dying have to teach. In the seminars which she has conducted she describes the important role of clergy but also comments: 'What amazed me, however, was the number of clergy who felt quite comfortable using a prayer book or a chapter out of the Bible as the sole communication between them and the patients, thus avoiding listening to their needs and being exposed to questions they might be unable or unwilling to answer.'[10] Anglican clergy have the privilege of being called on to conduct most of the funerals in this country, especially when there is no religious affiliation and when mourners do not know where else to turn. They will frequently be expected to provide spiritual support to all kinds of people, together with some 'answers' to these ultimate questions. It is not an easy calling, and clergy need courage and insight in order to respond adequately.

The Wider Community

Very rarely does death take place in complete isolation. Nearly everyone is part of society and an individual's death will have an effect on the wider community, even if that effect is only to raise the question of how an elderly person could die alone and untended and the body lie undiscovered for a lengthy period. The first funeral of which, as a curate, I was given sole charge was for a reclusive elderly lady. She had, apparently, no friends or family and the only people present apart from myself were the undertaker and her solicitor, who felt that 'somebody ought to be there'. The majority of people, however, will have friends and neighbours beyond their immediate family who will wish to be part of the funeral. The number might be very large as, for example, in the case of a public figure such as a local doctor, or councillor, and there might be pressure from different groups who feel that they should be represented in the funeral. A club or society to which the deceased belonged might expect to provide the flowers, have some of their members carry in the coffin or host a reception at their premises afterwards. Normally such requests are made simply as offers of help, but on occasions they might not be welcomed by the family. I have learned over the years to be wary when dealing with requests that are made of me as vicar and to discuss them carefully with those arranging the funeral before agreeing.

The media can be particularly intrusive and we will look at their effect in Chapter 6, 'Some Social Influences'. On those occasions when the national media wish to report on, and perhaps broadcast, part of a funeral service, it is important to retain a firm hand. A denominational media-officer may be of help and we may well benefit from a standard denominational approach to such requests; thus the media will also know that their requests are being treated fairly. Nevertheless, a media presence will almost inevitably prove to be an added stress to what is probably already a very fraught situation.

Families vary in their response to media requests. Some will regard them as intrusive and wish to avoid contact as much as possible and one might question why the public should need to know about a given funeral. It is surprising to note the lengths to which representatives of the media will go. My car was once followed by a newspaper reporter for an afternoon while she tried to discover where the husband of a deceased person lived. I had already told her that I was not prepared to give her that information and at that point I had not even been asked to conduct the funeral, as the deceased had died only a few hours earlier. She therefore followed my car for the rest of the day, not realizing that she had sat in vain outside the church hall for two hours, since I had left by the back door and walked round to the deceased's house, returning by the same route.

By contrast, other mourners will welcome the interest of the media, particularly, it seems to me, in societies where a high attendance at a funeral is seen as a mark of respect. The presence of the television cameras will be welcomed as showing the respect and sympathy of a great number of people.

In this chapter we have looked at various groups of people who have an interest in controlling the funeral, or in the way it is conducted. Often there may be conflicting views between the groups;

we will not always know the families whose funerals we are going to conduct, and accordingly we will not know what awaits us on the other side of their front doors. What are the typical sources of conflict?

Situations where the wishes of the deceased differ from those of the bereaved might cause problems, for instance, where a devout church-going widow wishes to arrange a church service with burial for a husband who did not believe in God and was aggressively anti-church. There might be division between the close relatives: one son wishes his father to be buried, the other favours cremation. It could be a long-running family feud, or a person close to the deceased being prevented from participating in decisions. An undertaker might try to make arrangements that produce maximum profit. Perhaps the timing of the funeral is difficult: the undertaker wishes it to fit in with other funerals, the vicar can not arrange to be free because of a diocesan committee, and one of the family is hoping to avoid taking a day off work.

The list is endless and it is beneficial to have some questions in mind when faced with such division. We have already mentioned three:

- What is legally permissible?
- What is morally right?
- What is practically possible?

The following are further examples of the type of questions that I keep in the back of my mind:

- Is the request reasonable?
- Is it putting any individual at a disadvantage?
- Who is trying to promote his or her own interest above that of other people?
- Is any person being exploited unfairly?
- Is any party taking advantage of another's grief?
- Is there a relevant factor that the person being seemingly difficult has not appreciated?
- Did a mourner fail to take in information while upset?

- Is it possible that I have not been given all the information I should have received?
- Is there anything I can suggest to ease the situation?
- Would it help if I offered to find another person to take the service or to contribute to it?
- Am I being unreasonable in any way?

NOTES

¹ Green, Graham, *The End of the Affair*, London, Penguin Books, 1962, pp. 149–50.
² Hockey, Jenny, *Making the Most of a Funeral*, Richmond upon Thames, London, Cruse-Bereavement Care, 1992, p. 4.
³ From *Common Worship Pastoral Services*, Ministry at the Time of Death.
⁴ Sherrin, Ned, *Remembrance: An Anthology of Readings, Prayers, and Music Chosen for Memorial Services*, London, Michael Joseph, 1996.
⁵ Tony Walter, 'Emotional Reserve and the English Way of Grief', in K. Charmaz, G. Howarth, and A. Kellehear (eds), *The Unknown Country: Death in Australia, Britain and the USA*, London, Macmillan, 1997, p. 130.
⁶ Gorer, Geoffrey, *Death, Grief and Mourning in Contemporary Britain*, London, Cresset Press, 1965.
⁷ E.g. *Common Worship Pastoral Services*, and Paul Sheppy's *In Sure and Certain Hope*.
⁸ Hockey, *Making the Most of a Funeral*, p. 14.
⁹ Hockey, *Making the Most of a Funeral*, and Hockey, Jenny, 'The Acceptable Face of Human Grieving? The Clergy's Role in Managing Emotional Expression during Funerals', in D. Clark (ed.) *Sociology of Death*, Oxford, Blackwell, 1993, pp. 129–48.
¹⁰ Kubler-Ross, Elisabeth, *On Death and Dying*, New York, Touchstone, 1969, pp. 255–56.

5

Institutions and Organizations Involved

Soames had often noticed in old days how much more neighbourly his family were to the dead than to the living. But, now, the way they had flocked to Fleur's wedding and abstained from Timothy's funeral, seemed to show some vital change. There might, of course, be another reason; for Soames felt that if he had not known the contents of Timothy's Will, he might have stayed away himself through delicacy. Timothy had left a lot of money, with nobody in particular to leave it to. They mightn't like to seem to expect something.

From *The Forsyte Sage* by John Galsworthy[1]

In recent decades there have been many changes to the ways in which people die and in which their deaths are marked. In the 1950s, over half the deaths in England and Wales took place at home in bed. By the end of the century only a quarter happened at home, over half in hospital, and the rest in residential homes, nursing homes or hospices.[2] Institutions have increasingly become the place of death, and families have experienced a loss of control and participation in the dying of their relatives. The purpose of this chapter is not, however, to examine how hospitalization has changed the way death occurs but how institutions and their agendas have in general affected the funeral. In particular we will look at five institutions or organizations: government, the undertaking profession, the church, society, and the family. In the previous chapter we considered how individuals affected any particular funeral. For example, I, as a vicar, might have a reputation for taking a funeral well or badly and that will affect the choices people make about the individual funerals they arrange. The Church in Wales, of which I am a member, on the other hand, might affect all the funerals in parish churches throughout Wales through its liturgies. Discussion of that kind of issue therefore belongs to this chapter.

Government

Until 1850, the Anglican Church owned the majority of burial grounds in Britain. Since then, changes in legislation have allowed and encouraged the development of public cemeteries (owned and managed by local authorities), and crematoria (both publicly and privately owned), as well as graveyards attached to the places of worship of other denominations and other faiths.

Over the intervening years many churchyards have become full and have been closed. The Cemeteries Order of 1997 permitted parochial church councils in England, but not Wales, to entrust the maintenance of their closed churchyards to the public purse. Many churches took advantage of this and, consequently, the local Christian community had less control over the churchyard, but the Church has gradually realized that it is correspondingly harder to promote doctrines about life and death now that it no longer directs the burial process.

At the same time, the involvement of local government in burial provision brought about a great change in the disposal of the dead. The new cemeteries were spacious, nondenominational, increasingly difficult to maintain and, above all, secular. Local government having largely taken over control of burial (and cremation), decisions have increasingly been made according to economic criteria. Local authorities now face the same pressure that many church burial grounds faced at the end of the nineteenth century. They are becoming full and their maintenance is a growing burden on local government finances.

In July 1995, the Department of the Environment initiated a Private Finance Initiative which encouraged local authorities to sell their crematoria to private companies. Some authorities regarded this as a way of solving a financial problem and funeral directing firms made some of the purchases. The Department of the Environment's decision conflicted with a report published two months earlier by the Department of Trade and Industry, which stated that the joint ownership of crematoria and funeral directing outlets by a common company threatened to create a monopoly, which was not in the best interests of bereaved people purchasing their funerals. The current commercialization of the funeral industry has resulted in the growth of pre-paid plan schemes and companies acquiring crematoria. It would only require the additional acquisition of a nursing home for a company to achieve the complete commercial control of the whole process of death, and to turn what was once considered merely a nightmare scenario into reality.

A funeral is a purchase by distressed people who are not equipped for the task. It is sometimes referred to as 'the third most expensive purchase' we may make in a lifetime and it is often made at short notice with little research and preparation. It is a cause for concern that people should be adequately protected by legislation at a time of great vulnerability. Mourners will not necessarily know what is standard practice and may feel that they are in the hands of the funeral industry. It is not unfair to say that they are on occasions at the mercy of the unscrupulous. Our society's expectations that one will do one's best for the deceased and a desire not to appear penny-pinching when arranging a funeral for a person who might have been generous to one through a bequest all add to this vulnerability. One role of government is to protect citizens and it should be possible for funerals to be affordable and conducted with dignity and respect in ways appropriate to people's needs, wishes, and religious beliefs. Those professionals who arrange funerals ought to be accountable to appropriate public bodies, and mourners should have opportunity for redress if necessary. To some extent this occurs through self-regulation within the funeral industry but it is not always sufficient. The cleric will not be directly involved in the financial arrangements and will not normally be aware of the charges being made for a funeral, although one might sometimes consider it appropriate to question whether mourners wish to incur the costs of some of the proposed arrangements, and occasionally point out that a particular expense is not usual. My experience is that most mourners appreciate the concern and I see part of my pastoral charge as helping to guide the bereaved through what is normally a difficult experience. Guidance as to what might be considered reasonable practice is also available from undertakers' professional associations, the National Funerals College, and the Consumers' Association.[3]

The government's role should not end there, however. Legislation and policy decisions governing other areas affect the way a funeral may be arranged. We have talked earlier about bureaucratic restraints on funerals. While this is useful in protecting the rights of vulnerable people, it can sometimes cause them to feel trapped and frustrated. Officials do not always realize the implications of their decisions. When the management of a cemetery or crematorium is located in a local authority's department for parks and leisure facilities, the officers responsible might well see other priorities such as providing leisure centres and bowling greens as more pressing than, for example, weeding cemetery flowerbeds. Consequently, the government's role should also involve the monitoring of legislation in general and its effect on funerals.

Questions concerning the environmental effect of burial, embalming and cremation and the availability of suitable sites also need to be addressed by government. Land use in Britain is a more pertinent issue than in most other European countries, as the difficulties raised by using large areas of land for burial are more acute than in mainland Europe or in North America. It is arguable that the decreasing availability of land is the main reason why cremation has become more common than burial and why that has not been the case in other industrialized countries. Most of us assume that, if we choose cremation rather than burial, it is our choice and we are surprised to realize that the decision has been strongly influenced by successive government policies in connection with land use. More will be said about this in Chapter 7, 'Contemporary Issues'.

The Undertaking Profession

The British undertaking industry has an annual turnover of £500 million. Disbursements including burial and cremation fees, medical and registration fees and clergy and church fees will probably add another third to this figure.[4] The costs of monumental masons and the erecting of gravestones are another related expense. Funerals in Britain are indeed big business. The growth of the undertaking profession has been well documented elsewhere[5] but our concern here is to note that parts of the funeral profession in Britain are now beginning to promote an idea, which their American counterparts have been proclaiming for years, that funerals are 'good for grief'. Without adequate research, however, one suspects that this thesis might be mere sales pitch.

During the 1960s and the 1970s, there were four main types of funeral directors in Britain: small part-time undertakers also engaging in some other activity who were situated mostly in rural areas; full-time funeral directors operating from a single location, normally owned and managed by one family; medium-sized firms with up to ten branch offices, usually owned and managed by a single family, with some branches acquired non-aggressively from other businesses; and large firms which operated a centralized system and which were often part of the Co-operative Movement, frequently urban and covering a considerable geographical area. Of this last type of organization, the privately-owned firms grew predominantly through acquisition although the Co-operatives expanded mostly by opening new branches. During the 1980s, there was a reaction against the large organizations and in 1989 the Society of Allied and Independent Funeral Directors (SAIFD) was formed to protect the interests of family-owned and family-managed firms who believed that the existing National Association of Funeral Directors (NAFD), which embraced the key large organizations in their membership, did not represent their interests. In 1993, the Funeral Standards Council (FSC) was established following concern over the way the NAFD monitored its Code of Practice.

A significant proportion of Co-operative Societies subsequently resigned from the NAFD and joined the FSC. The SAIFD has reinforced the sector's independent identity by providing appropriately worded advertising copy and in 1997 instigated a 'Campaign for Fair Funeral Practices'. During the late 1980s and the 1990s, a number of new independent firms entered the market, including several that specialized in funerals for specific groupings such as the Afro-Caribbean, homosexual, Hindu or Muslim communities. Surprisingly some of the large groupings have disintegrated as smaller firms have appeared to reclaim a sizable share of the market. The reasons for this are as follows: a large firm absorbs smaller businesses, eradicates competition and rationalizes staff and services. This increases the cost of funerals owing to mounting overheads and creates a greater element of impersonality. As a result the small funeral director's reputation for a more congenial funeral is enhanced and mourners revert to the small family business. Demand grows and more of the large companies' experienced managers, retirees and their offspring establish new small businesses to meet it, drawing custom away from the larger groups. These groups then diversify in order to survive.[6]

Some commentators predict certain developments in the funeral industry over the next few decades. These include a growth in prepaid funerals and this is likely to favour the large firms, which operate at a nationwide level. There is a tendency for the elderly to retire to one area from another, particularly following the death of one partner, and employing this kind of company will ensure that the prepaid scheme will be effective in any locality to which the individual has moved. In addition, despite the recent re-appearance of a number of small firms it is predicted that this is a temporary change and that in time they will largely disappear, to be replaced by large companies, especially in urban areas, where local reputation is not so vital to the survival of the business.

For generations, women traditionally played an important role as 'layers-out' in preparing a body for burial but from the 1920s onwards this task shifted to the largely male-dominated world of the undertaker. More recently, however, women have begun to resume their place in mortuary practice as funeral directors, assistants, administrative workers, cemetery and crematoria managers and embalmers and it is predicted that in future a higher percentage of funeral directors will be women.[7] Some analysts expect formal regulation of the funeral industry by government, or other public bodies, particularly as a result of the growth of prepaid funeral plans.

In all of this we have said little about the ownership of the large funeral firms. A major concern in recent years has been the infiltration of the British funeral industry by substantial American and multi-national companies through the purchase of high-street funeral directors. The significance of this change may sometimes be noticed by the mourners only when they receive the bill. More will be said about this in the section 'American Influences' in Chapter 6, 'Some Social Influences'.

Christian ministry for the dead and bereaved has now to take account of these changes in power and control over funeral arrangements. The churches, however, are themselves part of this financial picture. According to the Church Commissioners' estimate, the Church of England conducts around 70 per cent of funerals in England and receives an annual income from them of at least £11 million.[8] This leads us to the next section, in which we consider how the Church at an institutional level affects funeral practice.

The Church

We have already discussed the argument that in recent decades the Church has lost the control that it previously held over many areas of life, except for that of death and its associated rituals. It is sometimes assumed that even here the Church is losing its position and the reason given is secularization, but this is perhaps simplistic. Even in the 1950s, Gorer's research found the British to be highly unorthodox in their afterlife beliefs and found little or no evidence of religious comfort in bereavement.[9]

This might suggest that the Church's role was not as key as one might have expected. In addition British society is now multi-cultural and a significant factor is the more obvious presence of non-Christian religions, due both to immigration and to interest in New Age and Buddhist death rituals. These trends imply new challenges to the churches, arguably met by the Roman Catholic Church through the *Order of Christian Funerals*, and the Church of England similarly through *Common Worship Pastoral Services*. These new rites include a greater variety of orders of service and permit far greater flexibility through the creation of ritual suitable for different settings. They are resources rather than liturgies to be performed in all circumstances. For example, one section of the *Order of Christian Funerals* contains forty-seven prayers for the deceased, addressing all sorts and conditions of person, and circumstances of death, and there are also fifteen prayers for mourners, over half of them concerned with the death of a child or infant. The concern that there should be sufficient options obviously arises out of the pastoral experience of those taking funeral services and it is also apparent within other denominations, for instance, in the production of supplemental resources by the Church in Wales in 2002, which included a greater choice of prayers and readings. In addition one publisher of liturgical resources informed me that prayers and liturgies for funerals are among their best-selling titles.

A funeral visit might well result in discussion about God, faith, resurrection and the afterlife. Such matters may well be discussed in language not traditionally used by the Christian church, and clergy need to be equipped to play their part in discussions with those of increasingly cosmopolitan and secular backgrounds. They require forms of in-service training which will give practical and theological backing to their response and ensure that they are familiar with the ways in which others view the world and our existence in it. It is an important call on the Church's resources to support these needs in what is a major meeting point between the Church and the wider society.

Society

Until the 1960s, it was possible to talk of a 'natural funeral congregation'. On the whole this would have consisted of the deceased's relatives and friends and members of the local community. Many of the community would have known the deceased and the family all their lives and they would also know each other. The congregation would include those who were originally from that community but had moved away. They would be returning for the funeral of a life-long friend and would be sitting with their family, who would also be life-long associates of the deceased and the family. In the villages where I have been a vicar one still conducts such funerals quite frequently, yet as the community changes they are becoming the exception rather than the rule, and this trend is greater in places where the rate of change has been faster. There are many reasons for this, including factors such as the following. People move away to find employment or because an employer wishes them to move. Perhaps a young person has gone away to college (possibly the first person from a family to do so) or met a partner from another part of the country and settled elsewhere. Others decide to retire to a new area of the country. Such demographic changes are more pronounced than they were fifty years ago and recent decades have seen a growing trend away from the 'natural funeral community'. The majority of funerals I have conducted in recent years have been attended by a different kind of congregation. It includes the family, of course, but they are not relatives who see each other every day and whose children go to school together; they come from a distance and rarely meet as a family. How often do we now hear it said that we meet our families only at weddings and funerals? The friends present will include a number who have known the deceased for many years but will not necessarily know each other, as they belong to different periods of that person's life and possibly come from different parts of the country. There will be other friends who will not be able to be present because of the distance at which they live and they might not have heard of the funeral in time to make arrangements to travel. Local friends will no doubt know each other but will be acquaintances of a few years rather than life-long friends; they share a drink in the same public house rather than share a common schooling. Very often the only factor uniting the funeral assembly is the particular individual who has died, who will have been significant to all of them, although probably in quite different ways.

Liturgy, and those leading it, must recognize and respond to these changes in society. Perhaps the most serious and sometimes perplexing change for the cleric is the wide range of religious beliefs that will be represented even at the funeral of a regular and committed churchgoer: from deep faith to resolute atheism, from Christianity to other faiths. The funeral service has in some way to respond to this and to take into account these diverse needs. The person leading it must somehow, very quickly, create a sense of community out of a very disparate funeral assembly in order to celebrate the life that has been lived and to assist in coming to terms with the death, seeking a careful balance between joy and grief, allowing the mourners, whether Christian or not, to mourn and at the same time to retain hope for the future. Yet the service must remain true to the Christian gospel and relate the death of the individual to the death and resurrection of Christ.

Over the years society has increased the number of locations where a funeral may be held. When a churchyard has become full it will either close or extra land will be purchased for burial. On occasions that land will not be immediately near the church. If the churchyard is declared closed, burials will still take place in existing family graves but new burials will be carried out elsewhere. There might still be space for cremated remains to be buried and there will be those who would otherwise have chosen burial but who opt for cremation because they wish their remains to be placed in that particular churchyard. If burial is to take place elsewhere, it will possibly be as far away as a neighbouring village where the public cemetery is located. The funeral will consequently have to move from church to cemetery and this movement will create a different atmosphere. On the first occasion I led a service in church followed by burial elsewhere, I concluded the service and immediately drove to the cemetery, not stopping to greet anyone, anxious that I should arrive there before the hearse. I had not realized how long it would take for mourners to leave the church, greet appropriate people, find their cars and travel to the place of burial. I was new to the area and waiting on my own. The bearers were travelling in a car behind the hearse, and the grave-digger was out of sight, sheltering from the rain. By the time the cortège arrived I was beginning to panic, worried that I might be in the wrong place. I now make very sure that I know exactly where the burial is to be.

The style of public cemeteries will differ from place to place and this is of significance. In a simple field on the edge of a village, where only one burial is to take place, the grave is likely to be clearly visible on arrival. The local grave-digger, who is well known certainly to the cleric and often to the family as well, will be available to assist. On the other hand, in a large city one might be required to register one's arrival at the manager's office before being conducted to the grave by an attendant and there could be a queue of other funerals waiting their turn. Such a cemetery may well have a chapel for services and there might even be a crematorium on site, which will cause a constant stream of funeral cars.

Different cemeteries and burial grounds employ different rules and regulations governing memorials. Many people expect to be able to place whatever they choose on a grave for which they have paid. They can be very distressed when they later learn that they cannot, for instance, plant a tree, install a heart-shaped gravestone, or bury the beloved family dog in the same grave as its master. I have on occasions found myself wishing that I had given this kind of information to a family beforehand. Some clergy leave a printed leaflet with bereaved families when they first call, mentioning several matters which the bereaved might not have taken in. In these days of computers and photocopiers it would be very easy for a parish to produce a tailor-made version of such a leaflet. More will be said about the question of memorials in Chapter 9, 'Remembering the Dead'.

The Family

Over the last few decades there has been a growing interest from different viewpoints in death, grief, funeral customs and bereavement support. Historians have considered changes in European social attitudes to death and how these have altered over the centuries. Psychologists have examined grief and how people deal with bereavement. Sociologists have been concerned with the ways society attempts to conceal, deny or embrace death and some have sought a more popular debate about funerals and death. In 1995, a report was published examining the possible re-use of graves.[10] Its authors had conducted a survey asking extensive questions about attitudes to this issue. One chapter entitled 'Death in the Family' is of particular interest as it examines attitudes towards death and how this is related to the institution of the family. Many studies have seen the family as the central setting for death and grief in contemporary society. Death is an occurrence which, perhaps more than any other, activates bonds of kinship between people, making the family visible as a distinct, physical group of related individuals. One of the distinctive features of the 1995 survey was the extensive information it contained on the history of death within the families of those participating. A series of questions gathered information about who had died, when that death had taken place, whether it involved burial or cremation, the location of the funeral and of any memorial, along with information on visits paid to the memorial site. To me some of the results of this survey were surprising. For example, almost a quarter (23 per cent) did not know if their mother's mother was buried or cremated and even more (31 per cent) did not know this information pertaining to their father's father. About a third were unaware whether or not memorials to various grandparents existed. The original study was made in only a small number of areas and these figures do not reflect the situation as I would have expected it in the communities where I have served as vicar. Nevertheless, the general picture conveyed by the Davies and Shaw survey is one that shows the family as becoming more fragmented than in previous generations and rarely gathering together.

In this chapter we have considered how a number of institutions and organizations have influenced the way funerals occur. In the next chapter we will examine the impact of certain social issues.

NOTES

[1] Galsworthy, John, *The Forsyte Saga*, London, The Reprint Society, 1949, p. 713.
[2] Jupp, Peter, 'The Context of Funeral Ministry Today', in Peter Jupp and Tony Rogers (eds), *Interpreting Death: Christian Theology and Pastoral Practice*, London, Cassell, 1997, pp. 6–7.
[3] SAIF, NAFD, etc.
[4] Jupp, 'Context of Funeral Ministry Today', p. 10.
[5] For example: Howarth, Glennys, 'Professionalising the Funeral Industry', in G. Howarth and P. Jupp (eds), *The Changing Face Of Death: Historical Accounts of Death and Disposal*, London, Macmillan, 1997, pp. 120–34.
[6] Parsons, B.,'Yesterday, Today and Tomorrow: The Lifecycle of the UK Funeral Industry', *Mortality*, 1999, 4 (2), pp. 127–45, and Saunders, K. C., 'Service Without a Smile: The Changing Structure of the Death Industry', *Service Industries Journal*, 1991, 11, pp. 202–18.
[7] Parsons, 'Yesterday, Today and Tomorrow', p. 140.
[8] Jupp, 'Context of Funeral Ministry Today', p. 11.
[9] Gorer, G., *Death, Grief and Mourning in Contemporary Britain*, London, Cresset Press, 1965.
[10] Davies, Douglas, and Shaw, A., *Reusing Old Graves: A Report on Popular British Attitudes*, Crayford, Shaw and Sons, 1995.

6

Some Social Influences

Show me the way a nation disposes of its dead and I will measure . . . the
level at which their society exists.

William Gladstone[1]

In Chapter 1 we considered how sociology had historically made
little attempt to study death in our society. This has changed in
recent years and sociologists now have much to teach us. In this
chapter we will be looking at some social issues which sociologists and others have studied, the way they impinge on our perceptions of death, and implications for the way in which we
conduct funerals. In particular we will focus on some effects of
the changing role of women in our society, the impact of AIDS,
the mass media and especially their treatment of high-profile
funerals, the consequences of American influences and finally,
issues of language and culture.

Gender and Funerals

Funeral and mourning rituals in both traditional and modern
societies have required men and women to behave in significantly
different ways. To my knowledge no thorough analysis of death
rituals in terms of gender has yet been attempted. In general
terms the shift in understanding death as a medical rather than a
spiritual event gave increased power to men rather than women,
doctors (mainly male) making decisions over nurses (mainly
female) and the development of funeral directors (normally
male) leading to the demise of the traditional layer-out (normally
female). This trend has seen some reverse in recent years as the

94

hospice movement has developed, led by women such as Cicely Saunders, Elisabeth Kubler-Ross, Mother Teresa, and Margaret Torrie (who founded CRUSE), who have pioneered alternatives to technological approaches to dying, which are predominantly male. One might also make a similar comparison if one considers the shift which has occurred in the care of the bereaved from the influence of clergy (traditionally male) to bereavement counsellors (mainly female). Mention has already been made, in the section on the undertaking profession in the previous chapter, of the growing numbers of women undertakers.

If this reflects a general trend it would be relevant to examine the impact of the ordination of women on funeral practice. During the period of debate over the ordination of women priests I frequently heard the remark, 'I wouldn't like a woman to take my funeral, Vicar.' More often than not this was made by women who were in favour of ordaining women but who had not directly experienced the ministry of an ordained woman. Occasionally, I would make light of it and reply, 'Well, you'd better make sure you die while I'm still around, then.' Usually, however, I would try to find out the cause of the anxiety. The reasons were sometimes vague and, in my view, ill considered. For instance women, I was told, were emotional and might break down. This ignored the possibility that I might also do so. It was argued that women's voices did not carry the same authority as men's, but anyone who has heard Margaret Thatcher speak knows that such a view holds no credence.

Within the Anglican Churches in the United Kingdom the ordination of women to the priesthood (and the episcopate) has been justified as necessary to provide a 'whole' ministry. The underlying assumption is that women offer a different approach since they possess different gifts and that only with the presence of both men and women can the priesthood be fully representative. How far this has been held to be true by women clergy themselves was not examined until, in 1998, a study was published which surveyed clergywomen's perceptions of themselves as a group and how they perceived their ministry in comparison with that of men. It found that almost two thirds of the women believed they possessed gifts other than those offered by men. It was only a much smaller proportion, however, who took this to imply their being more competent at specific aspects of ministry.[2] Further research would be necessary to ascertain if this perception is shared by those among whom they minister. Of the women clergy responding to the questionnaire, more agreed than disagreed with the two statements: 'clergywomen tend to be better at bereavement counselling' and 'clergywomen tend to be better at conducting funerals'.

With this in mind I conducted a brief survey of a number of women priests I knew. The impression I gained was that whether the funeral was conducted by a man or a woman was not a matter of concern to them. They tended to the view that mourners' first experience of a woman taking a funeral had been an anxious time, although afterwards their ministry had been much appreciated. They put it down to its being simply a new and unfamiliar experience at a particularly stressful time. One woman described how she had felt 'on trial' during the first funeral she conducted in her parish. It had been an all-male event at which she was the only woman present. Others said they had encountered some opposition to their taking particular funerals mainly arising not from mourners, but from male colleagues, particularly retired clergymen.

It is not only in the Christian Church that this sentiment is expressed. A woman rabbi of the Reform tradition writes: 'Anyone who has been in a house of mourning or at a funeral where there are no male close relatives will notice how a daughter or widow is passed over in the search for a male to recite Kaddish.'[3] I wrote also to a number of women rabbis asking questions similar to those I had put to the women priests. Their replies, as those of the priests, indicated that they had not viewed their gender as a significant issue; nevertheless, like the priests, they had encountered a wariness on the part of those to whom they were strangers. One of them, describing how she joined a new synagogue as its rabbi, explained how one gentleman agreed with her appointment on condition that a male rabbi would be provided for his funeral. One year later and knowing her a little better, he agreed that she could give the address. Two years later he agreed to her conducting the whole service.

In both groups, women priests and rabbis, there were some who had had experience of mourners actively seeking out a woman minister. They were perceived, by some at least, as being more capable of empathizing with the congregation and of sharing the emotional experiences of the bereaved. One woman rabbi described how one mourner, whose aunt had died, felt that her aunt would have been delighted by the fact that her funeral had been conducted by a woman who could do all those things that she would have wished to do but had never been allowed the opportunity.

The issue of gender and funerals concerns not only the officiant but also those who attend. Many cultures have differing codes of behaviour in respect of male and female mourners. In some settings, such as Roman Catholic Churches in Holland or Majorca, men and boys will sit on a different side of the church from women and girls and they may be expected to show their grief in different ways. In other places, including many mining communities in South Wales, only the men attend the funeral while the women stay at home and prepare the refreshments. When one asks why this should be, it is hard to find answers. One may be told that it is the tradition, yet there are no reasons given for the existence of that tradition. It is not so long ago that mourning customs in Britain were far more restrictive of women than men. A Victorian gentleman would have been expected to wear a black mourning suit, but he would have worn black at his place of work in any event. His wife, in contrast, would have been obliged to wear cumbersome and ungainly garments and to stay at home, severely curtailing her social life, while her husband was hardly affected.

In the majority of societies it is traditionally women who nurse the dying and attend to the messiness of death. Some have argued that when men become involved they require this to be hidden, yet at the same time keeping a firm control over the women's role.[4] One questions how much of this is due to patriarchal attitudes, a perceived need to keep women in their place, to control their sexuality and protect men from too great an involvement in the emotions which death triggers. In any case it is clear that, as women gain a greater degree of emancipation, so the traditional separation of women and men in bereavement declines and, no doubt, we will see in the next few years whether or not women's ordination has had any long-standing effect on funerals.

AIDS Funerals

From a worldwide perspective it is evident that AIDS has spread through many countries and devastated sections of the population, particularly in parts of Africa. The strain placed on the older generation and the wider society by the vast number of AIDS orphans has been enormous. The scale of death is something which we in our society can hardly even begin to imagine. Not even the slaughter of the World Wars of the twentieth century can compare, since these affected, in the main, men away from home. Perhaps the experience of the Black Death or Bubonic Plague is the nearest experience in Western Europe, although those diseases would have struck down people of all ages in a way that AIDS has not. The AIDS epidemic has challenged our assumption that it is mainly the elderly who die, since the majority of AIDS-related deaths have occurred among younger people, many of whom have been in the twenty-five to sixty age group, which represents the most active and influential group of any society. That much is as true in the West as it is in Africa.

The significant difference in the West is that the spread of AIDS, at least when it first became apparent, was seen as being more concentrated amongst homosexuals. Some Christians have claimed this as a judgement from God on their lifestyle, a position which, in my view, reflects an unfortunate understanding of a God of loving forgiveness. There have been a number of high-profile victims (such as Rock Hudson) and media attention has often focused on them and on homosexual males in general. On the other hand the extent to which AIDS has spread among heterosexuals is a topic on which the media are mainly silent. Owing to its transmission through sexual activity (among other ways), however, AIDS does affect heterosexuals as much as homosexuals, as the African experience shows.

AIDS has raised questions about the kind of funeral a person desires for him or herself. The uncompromising attitude of some groups has sometimes engendered an antipathy towards religion, in that many victims have felt the Church and Christian community to have been prejudiced against them and consequently they have not wished their funerals to be conducted according to Christian rites. During the mid-1980s, homosexuals with AIDS in London developed their own approach to planning a funeral, which involved discussion between the dying and those close to them. This was frequently not an easy process as it involved accepting issues of sexuality and lifestyle which an older generation would have largely preferred to ignore. It was an expression of a desire to celebrate openly a life and lifestyle that was valued rather than to pretend it did not exist. In the recent past such funerals might have been arranged by an unsympathetic family, committed to underplaying a 'deviant' lifestyle, and the formal trappings of a conventional funeral would have prevented friends of the deceased, and especially any same-sex partner, from creating the kind of celebratory rite that was now being proposed.

At the same time AIDS sufferers were stigmatized and this impinged on relationships with friends and family. A poster advertising the services of one support organization read: 'Derek lost his entire family to AIDS. One year later, they are still not talking to him. That's why he called us. We always listen. We never judge. We know that family rejection can sometimes be more distressing than the illness.'[5] The effects of stigma may be more wide-ranging than expected. We have already mentioned the certification of death and the way in which the cause of death is described. There are occasions when the official cause of death is not HIV infection but another disease to which the person was susceptible as a result of AIDS. In these circumstances doctors will fulfil their public duty in reporting the HIV infection to the

Centre for Communicable Diseases, but HIV will not be mentioned on the death certificate. This issue and people's natural embarrassment when talking about illness cause AIDS among heterosexuals to be a hidden subject.

Difficulties which might arise in connection with any funeral might be highlighted when the deceased had AIDS and where homosexuality has been a factor. The practice of leaving detailed instructions for one's own funeral after having experienced the death of close friends from AIDS challenges the attitude commonly found in our culture which attempts to deny that death occurs. Relationships between those who are most closely bereaved by such a death may be awkward or strained. There might well be a homosexual partner, for instance, whom the deceased might have considered more important than family. These kinds of relationships involving parents and partners, blood relatives and adoptive communities ought to be recognized, and the cleric must be prepared for a wide range of emotional responses including anger, shame, a desire for forgiveness or sometimes for vengeance.

Involvement in such funerals will challenge one's pastoral skills to the full; nevertheless, they will also give us opportunities to reach out to a sector of society which has often felt alienated from the Church. If we adopt a liberal view we might be rejected by some within the Church who do not accept homosexuality. If we take a firm view against it, we run the risk of rejecting those who come seeking the ministry of the Church. Either way we might be forced to take a stand, which we would rather not have to take, in a debate which is proving deeply divisive throughout the worldwide Church and particularly within the Anglican Communion. Equally, on a day-to-day level, one might face a dilemma between conscience and pastoral responsibility, remembering that those who die from AIDS-related illnesses, and their relatives and friends, are individuals, each of whom is as important to God as any other person. Such dilemmas might, of course, also arise in all sorts of situations other than those involving homosexuality, for example the funeral of a rapist or other violent offender.

AIDS, as is well known, is transmitted by means other than through sexual contact, such as intravenous drug use or blood transfusion. It is also passed to babies who are born to infected mothers. The challenges involved in preparing for and conducting a funeral in these circumstances may then be very different from those outlined above.

Media Influences

Towards the end of 1999, *The Times* published a series of special supplements to mark the new millennium. The topic covered by issue number five was death. A cursory glance through it strengthened my suspicion that the written news media are primarily interested in death only when it is likely to sell more copies of the newspaper. The articles examine, among other things, death rites around the world, days in the lives of those whose work is connected with death, terrorists, bodily decay, what happens after death, and near-death experiences. Fifteen pages were devoted to death, of which six dealt exclusively with terrorism, death in war zones, and weapons of mass destruction, in addition to the references to violent death which appear on the nine other pages. This could only be seen as a highly disproportionate amount of space to give to violent death in a publication which purported to reflect 'The World at the Millennium'.

The coverage of death during and following the terrorist attacks on the twin towers of the World Trade Center in New York was similarly disproportionate, in comparison with the reporting of unnecessary death which is caused globally by poverty, disease and warfare. On 11 September 2001, I was in Spain watching the events on two adjacent television sets. One was tuned to the main Spanish channel (TVE), the other to a satellite channel based in England. It was fascinating to observe the differences in the presentation on each channel, both of which had presumably been receiving the same pictures from America. The English station did show people jumping from windows to their deaths, but from a distance. The Spanish showed more close-up scenes. This prompted me to reflect on how different cultures regard death and how decisions are made as to which images are acceptable for television.

Only a small minority of deaths are reported in news and documentary programmes and they fall mainly into two categories: that of a public figure and that which is deemed newsworthy for some reason. A study commissioned by the Broadcasting Standards Council in 1989[6] concluded that television close-ups of the dead were not acceptable on the grounds that relatives might be watching. An exception was those deaths that occur in distant places, where any direct link between a viewer and the deceased would be unlikely. The timing of such portrayal was also considered, taking into account the fact that children might be watching.

The media, particularly television, have a powerful influence on the way both world events and ordinary topics are understood. In what way has media representation of, for example, the assassination of President Kennedy, the deaths of Princess Diana and the Queen Mother, and a number of child murders influenced our awareness of death? Consequently how has media coverage of their funerals changed our expectations of what takes place at a funeral?

A great deal more research is required to understand this phenomenon and current analysis focuses mainly on accounts of disasters, revealing a particular media interest in displays of grief. Some of that research, undertaken by Tony Walter, discusses reactions to the Hillsborough disaster where ninety-five Liverpool football fans were crushed to death in April 1989.[7] It is a commonly stated assumption that death is a taboo subject and Walter's research challenges that. My experience of writing this book inclines me to agree with him. When people ask me what my subject is, I rather sheepishly reply 'funerals' and expect an awkward silence. The exact opposite occurs, however, and people begin to relate their experiences of particular funerals, sometimes at length.

This casts doubt on the frequent assertions that people today do not know how to respond to the bereaved, that public mourning has been more or less abandoned and that the decline of local communities has eroded any funeral tradition. Moreover, it is often presumed that those who know how to handle bereavement are professionals trained to do so rather than ordinary lay people. Tony Walter's research draws attention to four ways in which these assumptions were proved wrong in the aftermath of the Hillsborough tragedy. A debate was conducted in the national papers as to how the world of football should mourn. The press looked for leadership in this, not to bereavement counsellors or clergy but mostly to professional football players. Liverpudlians, many of them young working-class adults who had not previously experienced bereavement, organized mourning rituals apparently spontaneously and with considerable organizational flair. Far from the bereaved being isolated, a whole city mourned together, at least in the first two weeks. Walter found evidence of wide discussion of the subject and a demonstration of remarkable resourcefulness on the part of ordinary people in coming to terms with bereavement. Thus, he argues that we are in fact emerging from a taboo period and beginning to recover a public awareness of death that was repressed in the mid-twentieth century.

American Influences

In an earlier section on undertakers reference was made to concerns about American companies taking over funeral firms in Britain. In 1997, it was estimated that Service Corporation International (SCI), a mainly American-owned organization, controlled 17 per cent of the United Kingdom's funeral trade and also owned over one third of privately-owned crematoria. The National Funerals College and the Society of Allied and Independent Funeral Directors (SAIFD) have both been concerned at the speed and scale of this take-over. They claim that the traditional values of a British funeral could soon be lost.

Jessica Mitford campaigned against the commercialization of the American funeral trade and is well known for her books *The*

American Way of Death and *The American Way of Death Revisited*, in which she described how SCI had taken control of a large section of the American funeral industry. Their approach has been one of clustering, acquiring existing firms but maintaining the appearance of the original company. In many cases the former owner will be employed as a salaried manager in order to ensure a sense of continuity and goodwill. The customer may be unaware of the strategy because of SCI's policy of anonymity. Everything will, to all intents and purposes, appear the same, until the bill is received.[8]

In the earlier 1963 version of *The American Way of Death* she included a section on funerals in England, in which she described a visit to a London undertaker, a Mr Ashton, declaring that if he was typical of English undertakers, traditional English attitudes towards the dead might be safe. This section is reproduced in the later version, *The American Way of Death Revisited*, along with a footnote explaining that the same firm is now owned by SCI.[9]

One cause of disquiet is the way in which companies owned by SCI are changing the nature of the funerals they provide. Another is the way in which SCI has hidden behind traditional English names and this is expressed in a report from the Monopolies and Mergers Commission in May 1995: 'We also have concerns about the degree of transparency of funeral directors' charges, the lack of transparency of ownership of funeral directing outlets and the ability of funeral directors unduly to influence the choice of funeral arrangements.'[10]

It is not only the ownership of firms that is being changed by American values but the way bodies are treated, for example, in the increased use of embalming. From my own unmeasured observations of the funeral businesses I deal with I have noticed this trend, although very few undertakers in the area have staff qualified to practise embalming. According to one local undertaker the demand comes mainly from English people who have moved into the area and who are used to the idea. He sees his training in embalming as an investment for the future, when he will be able to offer services with which his competitors will not be able to compete.

Perhaps of more long-term concern is the increasing American practice of 'immediate disposition'. This term describes what occurs when the body is removed from the place of death and cremated or buried without any ceremony. The family is not present, does not normally view the body and arranges no act of memorial, although one might be arranged at a later date. In 1991, according to the National Funeral Directors Association (an American organization) approximately 5 per cent of all deaths in America involved immediate disposition. Can one imagine such a thing occurring in our country?

Other practices are being transferred across the Atlantic. When a funeral service is held in America, the normal manner of cremation is for the body to be removed from the church to a 'crematory' (crematorium) where there will be no service and no mourners. It is a practice not unknown in areas of South East England. (More will be said about different countries' approaches to cremation in Chapter 7, 'Contemporary Issues').

It is not fair to assume, however, that all American influences are negative. In Britain, public crematoria have traditionally allowed clergy twenty minutes for a funeral service and woe betide the cleric who takes longer. Some of the privately owned crematoria, on the other hand, have now started to provide a standard length of forty-five minutes. The charge might be higher but several clerics have remarked to me that they no longer feel under pressure either to rush through the service or to curtail the number of items included in it.

Language and Culture

It seems to me that this is the area where the distinctiveness of West Wales is especially apparent in regard to funerals. The casual visitor to the area might think that it is simply a matter of which language is used or the manner in which the two languages are combined. This, however, is too simple. The Welsh language is used by those from a very distinctive background and reflects a culture that is different in its values from that of the English inmigrants[11] of recent years, and indeed from the culture of English speakers who have lived in Wales for many years. Gwynfor Evans, the first Plaid Cymru Member of Parliament, and a leading figure in Welsh nationalism, writes:

> The Welsh language is infinitely more than a means of communication. It is the factor which unites in partnership the generations who for a millennium and a half lived their life through Welsh. Language is the vehicle of a culture; it transmits values from generation to generation. It has dynamic power. It can revitalise a decaying way of life. It can create or recreate a culture as Hebrew has done in Israel. In recent centuries the gwerin of Wales – 'working-class' is not the equivalent – shared a unique popular culture the like of which was not to be found anywhere else. This, the greatest glory of Wales, was bound up indissolubly with the Welsh language, and where the language died this intellectual culture died with it, usually giving way to the trivial culture of the admass. The language is the lifeblood of the national community, the factor on which national survival must depend.[12]

I have reproduced this quotation at some length as I believe its emphasis on how language embodies culture may help one to understand why the atmosphere of a Welsh funeral is different from that of an English one. It is not only the language but also the cultural understandings that accompany it which make the difference. It may be typified in an over-simplified way by the comparison between a twenty minute English-only service at the crematorium, and the full-blown Welsh ritual. This frequently comprises a private service in the house followed by a public service in church or chapel and interment in the churchyard or cemetery, after which refreshments will be served, on occasions a vast affair in a local hall for the whole community. The ritual will not be complete, however, until the family and other close mourners have attended the main service on the following Sunday at the church or chapel where the funeral took place. Strict rules apply to the way they participate in that service although these are now becoming more relaxed. They will sit throughout the service, usually at the front, and not join with the rest of the congregation in the singing and reading. They will remain seated when others stand and the minister will be expected to greet them with some appropriate words of sympathy at the start of the service.

Welsh culture has felt under threat from an inmigration of English speakers into Welsh-speaking areas in recent decades and this is particularly pertinent in the Welsh-speaking heartland – *y fro Gymraeg* – of Gwynedd and Dyfed, which have experienced a steady influx of first-language English speakers. One result of this in West Wales is that members of the traditional Welsh-speaking community now have many English-speaking neighbours who will naturally enough come to their funerals. The result is a congregation composed of two groups who have different expectations and which often do not realize that they have such differing outlooks. This requires patience and careful handling on the part of the person leading the service.

I have referred to my own local experience but I believe that similar phenomena are present in many other communities. The language elements may not always exist, although inhabitants in many areas of rural England are concerned at the disappearance of local dialects and ways of life as townspeople move in, but the impact of removal from the city to the village and the inmigration of people from another culture is an important topic which is not always addressed. Language emphasizes cultural differences in Wales, by distinguishing two groupings of people, yet at the same time it can hide the impact of cultural diversity by becoming in itself the sole focus of attention.

We have examined some social influences on the funeral in our society. There are, however, social phenomena which have emerged as a consequence of changes in technology and a growing awareness of environmental concerns. These matters will be discussed in the next chapter, 'Contemporary Issues'.

Notes

¹ Weller, S, *The Daily Telegraph Lifeplanner Guide to Funerals and Bereavement*, London, Kogan Page, 1999, p. 13.

² Robbins, Mandy, 'A Different Voice: A Different View', *Review of Religious Research*, 40, 1998, pp. 78–9.

³ Wright, Alexandra, 'An approach to Jewish Feminist Theology', in S. Sheridan (ed.), *Hear Our Voice: Women Rabbis Tell Their Stories*, pp. 152–61, London, SCM Press, 1994, p. 155.

⁴ See for example Tony Walter, *Funerals And How To Improve Them*, London, Hodder and Stoughton, 1990, pp. 52–9.

⁵ Small, N. (1997), 'The Public Construction of AIDS Deaths', in K. Charmaz, G. Howarth, and A. Kellehear (eds), *The Unknown Country: Death in Australia, Britain and the USA*, London, Macmillan, 1997, pp. 160–1.

⁶ See Docherty, D., 'A Death in the Home', *Sight and Sound*, 1990, 59 (2), pp. 90–3.

⁷ Walter, Tony, 'The Mourning after Hillsborough', *The Sociological Review*, 1991, 39 (3), pp. 599–625.

⁸ Mitford, Jessica, *The American Way Of Death Revisited*, London, Virago Press, 1998, p. 191.

⁹ Mitford, *The American Way Of Death Revisited*, pp. 219–20.

¹⁰ Mitford, *The American Way Of Death Revisited*, p. 231.

¹¹ In this chapter I have used the terms 'inmigrants' and 'inmigration' when referring to people who move into an area of the same country or state rather than 'immigrant' or 'immigration' which refer to movement from one country to another. The word 'inmigration' is normally used to translate the Welsh word 'mewnlifiant', which has been used to describe this phenomenon of English-speakers moving into areas which are traditionally Welsh-speaking.

¹² Evans, Gwynfor, *Wales: A Historic Community. Who Are We? What Are We?*, Aberystwyth, Plaid Cymru, 1998, p. 3.

7

Contemporary Issues

It's about time someone corrected Napoleon. We are no longer a nation of shopkeepers; we are a nation of shoppers. And how good at it we have become.

John Humphrys[1]

The purpose of this chapter is to examine contemporary practice and to ask what the Church can learn from its relation to and its current approaches to the funeral ministry. We will be looking specifically at music and secular and alternative funerals before concluding with issues surrounding cremation and burial.

Music

Music is powerful; it can arouse, soothe, inspire, depress or console. Something so compelling should have a significant place in human rituals, especially those of death. Music may also be used to mark death outside the Church's liturgy. Songs, chants and laments are well-established customs in other countries such as Greece where there is a wide variety of popular laments. Their words are well known, although they vary from one locality to another, and are constructed so that details of a particular death can be inserted to render them more personal.

In a British funeral it is hymns that are usually sung and frequently great care has been taken in choosing them, although this is not always so; every cleric must occasionally hear 'Abide with Me', 'Mi Glywaf Dyner Lais', or 'The Lord's my Shepherd' chosen automatically and sung with little feeling, if any. *The Order of Christian Funerals* aimed to restore lost dignity to Roman Catholic funerals and it recognized the vital role of music, as did other new rites. Guidelines for using *The Order of Christian Funerals* discussed what could be sung, where different hymns, psalms, canticles and chants would be appropriate and how to deal with requests for 'music that is wildly inappropriate to a liturgical occasion but has great meaning for the bereaved or the deceased'.[2] Yet most of this discussion considered only sung music. There was scarcely any consideration of pieces for the organ or other instruments or the use of recorded items other than that intended to accompany congregational singing.

On 23 August 1996, *The Guardian* published a list of the top ten funeral songs based on research conducted by the *Funeral Services Journal*. They were, in order of preference: Whitney Houston, 'I will always love you'; Frank Sinatra, 'My way'; The Righteous Brothers, 'Unchained Melody'; Bette Midler, 'Wind Beneath My Wings'; Barbara Streisand, 'Memory'; John Lennon, 'Imagine'; Glenn Miller, 'In The Mood'; Aled Jones, 'Walking In The Air'; Louis Armstrong, 'Wonderful World'; and The Platters, 'Smoke Gets In Your Eyes'. In 1996, *The Times* reported a survey which showed that almost a third of funeral services in a particular area included a pop tune, an increase from only 2 per cent ten years previously.[3] This trend has been accompanied by the growth of an unapologetic consumerist attitude among the public. Since they are paying for the funeral they wish to call the tune, and with high quality, easily portable equipment available a wide variety of recorded music can easily be reproduced. The result is that at some funerals the organ might simply 'top and tail' the service and perhaps accompany one hymn. The funeral might be that of a devotee of a particular musical style, which is reflected in clothes and hairstyles that friends will wear to the service, considering it sacrilegious to ignore them or to make a mistake in the detail. Older people may have a favourite 'classical' tune, although it may be played in a manner and on instruments not considered orthodox by the purist.

Music is identified strongly with the way in which it is presented, and the cleric, in helping to make choices for a funeral, is faced with a wide variety of musical styles. One might assume that music chosen from a secular source will be devoid of 'religious' content. My experience, however, is that those who do so normally choose it with an instinctive feeling for what is suitable, although I do remember discussing with a fellow curate how he should respond to a widow's request for 'Happy Days are Here Again' at her husband's funeral because 'it was his favourite song'.

To me it is regrettable that much of our musical tradition, vocal and instrumental, appears to be neglected, when it could make a significant contribution. Historically a large proportion of our music has been written for use in sacred settings and composed under church patronage. Such ecclesiastical music could add much to many funerals although it is not only this type of music that I am referring to here, as many items composed for other settings are equally appropriate. In the twenty years or more since my ordination I have often had requests for recorded music and this has nearly always taken the form of renditions of popular modern songs, whereas there have been only a handful of occasions on which I have been asked for particular organ music and very rarely any classical orchestral piece.

Sometimes practicalities will affect the choice of music. When the congregation are expected to sing, it is useful to bear in mind that many funerals are attended only by mourners whose knowledge of hymnody is limited. Every cleric has experienced a hymn of several verses, each played at a different volume and tempo and with only his or her own voice audible. This is not always desirable: as one crematorium supervisor once reminded me, 'You won't be winning any *eisteddfodau* with your voice.'

Some would view the reason for our singing hymns at funerals to be the proclamation of the Christian faith, yet music does serve other purposes, such as the celebration of the deceased's life, and the provision of a familiar focus for mourners during the service. A young person's favourite pop song or an operatic aria might therefore well be deemed as appropriate as the hymn which an elderly aunt always loved.

Crematoria, churches and chapels are alien places to many people. The cleric is on familiar ground and might be seen casually chatting to the staff; mourners, however, are likely to need time to adjust. A hymn near the beginning of the ceremony may provide them with the opportunity to look around, settle down and take in this new environment. Choosing familiar and undemanding music at this point is often a kindness, creating the atmosphere for the rest of the service and giving mourners a chance to focus on their own thoughts, such as memories of the deceased and perhaps their own mortality. Hymns and other music have the advantage of providing welcome pauses where the mourners are not assailed by the spoken word. I have sometimes longed for a hymn or a recording when conducting a service in which only my voice is heard, feeling it would be easier for the bereaved and would allow them a chance to take in what has been said and to prepare for the next part of the service.

Do-It-Yourself Funerals

In California there is a law that a body must be delivered to a crematorium by an undertaker. It is argued that this is part of the American funeral industry's efforts to ensure that they control the whole process and it results in one's being unable to arrange a cremation without a funeral director. There is no such law in Britain and it is feasible to arrange the whole affair without the involvement of the undertaking profession. In *Funerals and How to Improve Them*, Tony Walter describes how odd a certain undertaker looked dressed in black amidst the uniforms and clerical robes of a military funeral and he asks why an undertaker should be necessary.

> A military unit capable of transporting personnel and equipment half way around the world at a moment's notice, capable of thrilling the world with the pomp and circumstance of a Royal Tournament or an Edinburgh Tattoo, and which incorporates a medical and nursing unit able to care for the wounded . . . is surely capable of transporting its own departed from deathbed to grave, with dignity and decency? Yet even here we find the funeral director . . .[4]

The point is that it is not necessary to engage an undertaker, although unless one does there will be many difficult decisions to be made. It is possible to arrange everything oneself, nevertheless unless it has been carefully thought out beforehand it will not be easy for a grief-stricken relative to foresee all the eventualities, which is why cemetery and crematorium staff and clergy are generally apprehensive about such funerals. In addition 'do-it-yourself' funerals give scope for the unexpected which could take staff and mourners unawares. An acquaintance of mine was once asked to speak at a friend's funeral and was informed that she should do so for about ten minutes. She arrived at the crematorium expecting to meet a minister and to ask at which point in the order of service she would give her tribute. She discovered, however, that her contribution was all that had been arranged. As she finished, the deceased's son raised his arm as a signal to the crematorium superintendent that the curtain should be drawn across in front of the coffin and the congregation then filed out.

There are, on the other hand, various understandable reasons why people will choose to arrange the service themselves. These include: a decision not to use the conventional church or chapel setting but instead, for instance, to hold the service in the open air, in a hotel lounge, or a local hall; a desire that everything should be done by individuals who knew the deceased; or a concern that everything be arranged in a way consistent with the deceased's values or those of the mourners. Specifically, this often reflects a desire that there be no religious service as this might appear hypocritical. The difficulty for the bereaved, however, is deciding what alternative might be arranged as the phrase 'do-it-yourself' covers many eventualities when applied to a funeral, in addition to managing without an undertaker. A period of silence might be observed during which mourners reflect on their own memories of the deceased and which is brought to an end by an appropriate person reading words of committal to conclude the ceremony. Sometimes silence is broken by people who wish to share their reflections with the congregation. One approach might be to arrange a number of different items, such as a tribute or musical items. Mourners might choose to have no minister or other outsider as officiant, although they will probably choose someone to act as a master of ceremonies. Experience suggests that it is best that this person should not be too closely connected with the deceased as this will allow a greater objectivity. It is one thing for the next of kin to read a poem whereas it is a much greater strain to conduct the whole ceremony, and that might prevent one from benefiting as a mourner.

All of this raises questions about the design of crematoria chapels, most of which resemble a place of Christian worship. For instance, it might be more appropriate for mourners who wish to share memories to be seated in a circle rather than rows, with the coffin possibly taking up part of the circumference of the circle. Other authors have suggested that the coffin should be placed on a low plinth in the centre of the room to enable mourners to gather around it. In such circumstances they could file out past it rather than arranging for it to be removed by mechanical means. Such ideas are not reflected in any crematorium that I know of in Britain but there have been experiments in other countries such as America and Australia.

For those who do desire to organize everything themselves there is help available from a number of organizations such as the Natural Death Centre, a charity pressure group encouraging and enabling people to create a do-it-yourself funeral economically and without the aid of a funeral director.[5] Another development which should be mentioned here is the funeral supermarket – a French idea which was copied in 1995 in Catford. It was a large, well-lit store with piped classical music and no interference from sales staff, where customers were encouraged to browse and select whatever they required. Everything was on open display including flowers, tombstones, memorials, statues, urns, and coffins, and could be handled by the customer. Prices were clearly shown and everything necessary for a funeral could be purchased for, it was claimed, considerably less than an undertaker's price. The experiment was not a success and the supermarket has been replaced by 'The

Funeral Centre' which is a funeral home and memorial show-room, the staff of which includes a traditional funeral director. The same philosophy of presenting every product on open display and allowing customers freedom to browse still exists but there are now staff available to help, and a traditional or non-traditional service can be arranged in their chapel.

Alternative Funerals

Most people probably have an image of a typical funeral: a service in the parish church followed by a burial outside in the churchyard. Such funerals do still occur today, particularly in rural areas, but they are far from typical, as most take the form of cremations. In June 1996, an article was published in *The Guardian* which described most cremation services as 'dismal affairs . . . [in] which the mourners were hurried out of the crematorium at the end'. The author referred to three main failings: impersonality, the time being badly used and the shortage of time available.[6] It is true that often the expectation and the reality of the funeral do not match up and this is causing increasing numbers of people to seek alternatives. They do so in varied ways. Horse-drawn hearses and mourners' carriages are enjoying a revival. Around a hundred woodland burial sites were established during the closing five years of the twentieth century. Cardboard coffins and shrouds have appeared on the market. Some people manage without a funeral director, making all the arrangements themselves. Others deliberately seek a non-Christian alternative and arrange for a secular celebrant from, say, the Humanist Association. Cremated remains have been sent heavenwards as fireworks and rockets, blasted from shot-guns, sprinkled from hot air balloons, boats and planes, launched into space, and, in one notorious case, scattered by a widow over her deceased husband's mistress while she was dining at a restaurant.

'Alternative funeral', therefore, embraces many different approaches and these rituals may be chosen for differing reasons, of which the most prominent appear to include: a wish to arrange the funeral oneself, environmental issues, an unease with appearing hypocritical in a Christian setting, or even a desire to be showy or eccentric.

Cremation was originally promoted as a clean and hygienic way to dispose of a body; today's environmentalists, however, take a different view. Each year approximately 400,000 coffins, normally chipboard, are burned, polluting the atmosphere with dioxins, hydrochloric acid, hydrofluoric acid, sulphur dioxide, carbon dioxide and even mercury released from teeth fillings. In addition large quantities of fuel are used, usually natural gas in Britain. By comparison, burial does not contribute to the green-house effect. Cemeteries and churchyards can become places of refuge for wildlife and plants and provide opportunity for peace-ful recreation, thus saving the land for the living. Sometimes this will involve congregations keeping the churchyard a little less 'tidy' in order to encourage wildlife.

There is unease also at the number of trees cut down to make coffins, whether for cremation or burial. Chipboard is seen as an unacceptable alternative since it contains resins which are released into the atmosphere when burned or are leached into the ground when buried. The Green Movement has, accordingly, encouraged the use of coffins of cardboard, wickerwork, recycled timber and other environmentally-friendly materials. Woollen shrouds complete with board support and cords are also available, although not all cemeteries will permit their use and most crematoria insist that a body be cremated inside a coffin. A further problem for environmentalists is the use of chemicals in embalming, as it is thought that formaldehyde injected into the body can be harmful as it leaches into the soil or is released into the atmosphere.

There is a growing movement for farmers, local authorities and wildlife charities to establish Natural or Woodland or Green Burial Grounds often with commemorative trees instead of head-stones. In 1994, The Natural Death Centre launched the Association of Natural Burial Grounds to assist schemes of this type. Two hundred such sites are now open or planned around the United Kingdom and a complete list is contained in the *Natural Death Handbook*. The Association provides a code of practice for its members in order that those considering using such a burial ground may be assured that it reaches certain standards and the Association provides support and information for its members.

Many of these sites are excellently run and maintained by people of integrity and commitment to the ecological movement, and the green credentials of woodland burial sites have been marketed with enthusiasm, although some commentators[7] do question whether some such sites might be laying down future problems. To begin with, second interments in a given grave, normally expected for a spouse or a partner, will possibly necessitate disturbing the root structure of trees, although this should not cause difficulty in the first few years after the first interment. Next, ground upheaval caused by the uprooting of trees in gales is another potential hazard, although this is not likely to be a serious issue for at least fifty years. There are also potential management problems: despite the fact that advertisements sometimes create the impression that a tree will be planted over every grave, this would result in the trees being too close to each other for sustained growth and they would require drastic thinning after some ten years. Moreover, if the aim is to create a native woodland, natural selection will eliminate the weaker trees enabling the more dominant ones to grow, although this system will not be achieved by customers all selecting their own choice of tree. In addition it will not allow for a tree over each deceased person's grave as perhaps had been planned. There is, perhaps, a need for clarity from site managers here. Woodland sites are intended to be long-term ventures, yet, as in the case of Victorian cemeteries where plots were sold in perpetuity, after the final plot is sold there will be no further income. Without it there can be no effective management and consequently the land might not emerge as mature woodland. Anyone considering burial in a 'woodland' cemetery would, therefore, be well advised to investigate carefully the claims that are made to discover whether or not the financial provision is sufficient. It is not unrealistic to suggest that some of the companies who own these sites might have ceased to exist long before any woodland has matured. Cemeteries and churchyards are long-established and mainly owned by churches or local authorities. Ownership of woodland sites, however, can vary considerably from individuals concerned about the environment to large companies seeking only to make a profit.

For some it is distressing and even distasteful to hold a religious service for a person who had no religious belief. Our now secularized society has become familiar with weddings at venues other than churches and this has increased the demand for non-religious funerals which, in turn, has presented the humanist movement with the challenge of finding enough people to act as officiants at secular funerals. In a published collection of 'portraits' of individuals involved in the funeral trade[8] one woman described how she became an officiant for humanist funerals. She had found that after her father died she had had to deal with the practicalities of not believing in God. Although her father's death had been expected it was only when it occurred that she began to consider the funeral. She knew which aspects she did not wish to include but had no clear picture of what she did wish for and accordingly discussed the matter with a friend who was a vicar. She felt that the eventual compromise suited nobody and, as a result, began offering her services to others as a secular officiant.

In revising funeral services during recent decades the churches have sometimes discussed whether or not they should prepare different orders of service for believers and non-believers and have mostly decided against the idea.[9] One aspect of the dilemma has been how to decide which order is suitable for which occasion. For instance, which rite is appropriate in circumstances where a believer wishes to arrange the funeral of an unbelieving spouse or parent?

Perhaps the important point we should note, however, is the trend towards a secular alternative. This is not always available to mourners and, even if it is, they do not necessarily realize this until too late. In many cases they have asked for the vicar to take the service because they are not aware of any alternative. In Britain the main secular alternative to the Christian funeral is humanist, which will be atheist; this is perhaps equally unfair to those with divided loyalties. A middle road might be more appropriate where both humanist and Christian (or other faith) perspectives can be acknowledged and provided for in much the same way as in the case of an Australian 'life-centred' funeral. This is conducted by a secular celebrant who, rather than proclaiming a religious or atheist faith, will celebrate the whole life of the deceased and be prepared to work much more closely with clergy and others to do so.

Burial

The Burial Acts of the 1850s absolved the Church of England from sole responsibility for burying the dead. Instead of over-crowded local churchyards urban burials began to take place in spacious new cemeteries on the outskirts of centres of population and most new urban churches have subsequently been built without burial grounds. Churches ceased the centuries-old practice of re-using graves so that many churchyards, even in less populated rural areas, became full and during the twentieth century were closed. Subsequently burial ceased to be local and mourners frequently had to travel to visit a grave. This has produced a situation very different from that of most of mainland Europe where the re-use of graves is widespread and local burial the normal pattern.

It is often assumed that the main changes to funeral rites in Britain have occurred as a result of cremation. This is only part of the explanation. During the nineteenth century the practice developed of leaving a grave undisturbed as a permanent and unmoveable memorial. The sharing of a grave by a spouse or other family members might be envisaged but certainly not its re-use by strangers. In many cities this has resulted in vast cemeteries, some of the older ones now being already full and others soon to become so. Consequently some local authorities have started to consider whether they might re-use graves where there appears to be no continuing family interest in maintaining them.

Our society's understanding of the permanence of a grave is now being questioned and during the 1990s certain local authorities commissioned a survey on the subject.[10] In answering questions concerning the maintenance of graves, over 50 per cent of respondents saw this as the responsibility of the local authority. Less than 40 per cent considered family or friends to be responsible and less than 1 per cent thought responsibility lay with the Church, although it should be noted that these answers appeared in a section of the questionnaire dealing mainly with local authority cemeteries. The interpretation of some of the results is problematic, as the questions dealing with visits to graves by relatives of the deceased do not make reference to the length of time that has passed since the death. It would be reasonable to expect such visits to decline over time. It has traditionally been assumed that families will maintain their relatives' graves, although this is not necessarily so and therefore the question of maintenance does now need to be addressed. In the case of churchyards this is clearly a problem for small churches with ageing congregations and declining financial resources. In some North European countries, such as Belgium and Holland, cemeteries and churchyards are smaller than their British counterparts and well maintained: the gravestones are neatly aligned and decorated with flowers. This is because the graves are re-used every fifteen years or so. There are therefore no problems comparable with those of our vast British cemeteries with their decaying monuments which often cannot be removed.

The questions in the Davies and Shaw survey, which was referred to above, were designed to discover people's attitudes to the re-use of graves and in particular the length of time that should elapse between the original burial and the grave's re-use. There are those who anticipate a time when there will no longer be family members to tend or visit graves and the idea of re-using them is attractive to these individuals. It also appears that there is little desire to perpetuate a grave without ongoing family support. Yet there exists another group of people who possess a strong sense of being attached to a particular grave and who object to re-use particularly for strangers.[11]

Furthermore, the survey demonstrates the need for caution before assuming that attitudes will be similar in different parts of the country, as regional variations were substantial and the survey covered mainly urban areas. Participants were not asked to give one clear answer in support of or in opposition to the re-use of graves. Instead they were asked: 'What do you think would be a respectable time lapse before an old grave might be used for new burials by a different family?', and further questions were posed regarding the maintenance of existing cemeteries if one assumed that graves were not to be re-used.[12] The results were published as follows: 55 per cent were likely to support re-use, 30 per cent likely to oppose it and 15 per cent were undecided.

This book is not the place to consider in detail why people support or oppose the re-use of graves, although reasons given for the antipathy towards re-use are revealing. Respondents felt the following: the dead should be left to rest in peace; families had connections with the grave or had paid for it; the idea of strangers in the family grave was objectionable; re-use contravened religious beliefs; and old graves were historically significant.

Earlier chapters of this book have included references to the place of burial. Yet little research has been conducted into the different elements which define a cemetery, and some academics[13] are concerned that many common assumptions regarding burial are untested. A public cemetery differs from other places of burial such as churchyards, burial grounds for specific minority groups, mass graves and war cemeteries. Although there are certain features in common, there has been little research into the differences and their significance. For instance, churchyards tend to be located at the centre of communities rather than on their periphery, tend to be smaller in size, are governed by their own denomination's rules and regulations, have different patterns of ownership and usually contain a church. These matters will affect the use and appearance of a burial ground in terms of, for instance, the shrubs and trees and type of monument allowed on graves or elsewhere. There will also be implications regarding who is and is not permitted to place flowers or other items on a grave and who may be entitled to remove them. I have, on occasion, had the awkward task of explaining to people that they should not have planted a tree or placed a bench in a churchyard without first seeking permission, and a colleague once found a man digging a hole in the churchyard in order to bury his dog. He claimed to be unaware that he could not simply go to the churchyard and do so.

Current rules are designed to ensure the safety and adequate maintenance of a burial ground. Whereas a modern cemetery normally has a smooth, lawn-like surface with graves set in neat rows at regular intervals, a churchyard may well have been used in a much more irregular way for centuries before the days of health and safety legislation. Consequently they frequently contain unexpected hazards such as two-inch high footstones hidden in the grass. I have learned to ensure that, before any burial, I know exactly how to reach the grave. Shortly after my ordination I was required to lead a procession towards a churchyard grave. I had taken steps to familiarize myself with the route beforehand. The procession, however, consisted of an undertaker, six men wheeling a coffin on a trolley, a crucifer, a robed choir, other clergy and mourners, some of whom were unsteady on their feet. What began as an orderly procession quickly become a disparate mass of people trying to pick their way through a medieval churchyard, some following me and others the coffin, since my route had failed to allow for its size.

Turning to the question of who is entitled to be buried in a particular cemetery, the regulations of the Church in Wales allow those resident in the parish or who die there to be buried at the parish church. The same rules apply within the Church of England. I once came across an entry in a parish register from the 1880s, which recorded the deceased's address as '*Ochr arall y mynydd*' ('The other side of the mountain'), and I wondered about the story behind this man's burial. Perhaps he was a tramp who died on the road or he might have been carried over a parish boundary so that the cost of a pauper's funeral would fall on a neighbouring parish. A colleague whose parish includes a particularly attractive rural churchyard not far from a large city has a steady stream of requests for burials there from people from outside the parish. He has a discretionary power to allow such burials but is aware that, should he use it, the space will not be available for local residents in future years.

Cremation

Since the majority of British funerals involve cremation, it is worth asking why people opt for a short service in a crematorium, given that it may be a long way from home and they might feel rushed through it. Perhaps the funeral director has advised it or it is cheaper or the mourners do not wish to have to endure a longer service. They might feel hypocritical using a church they rarely, if ever, attend, or perhaps their earlier experiences of church funerals have proved no more worthwhile than their experiences of crematoria. Given the resources of liturgy, language, buildings and settings at their disposal, parishes and their clergy ought to be able to conduct a funeral in such a way as to prompt the response, 'That's what I would like for my funeral.' If the Christian churches are to minister to a wider constituency, they will frequently be obliged to use the twenty-minute slot that is provided at most crematoria, for of all the industrialized countries Britain which has witnessed the greatest growth of cremation in the twentieth century.

There are significant differences between a crematorium service and the traditional burial. The timing will have been arranged to suit the demands of the crematorium rather than those attending the funeral. Mourners will be conscious that they are normally following one funeral and preceding another, that theirs is one of several that day and that constraints are therefore placed upon them. If an important mourner is late, they cannot wait as they might at a burial.

In the cemetery or churchyard the deceased's relatives and friends watch as the coffin is lowered into the grave. On the other hand, at a crematorium mourners are not likely to witness the actual placing of the coffin in the incinerator or to watch any part of the cremation process itself, even though a small number of them are entitled to do so. Unlike the burial which feels open and evident for all to see, cremation feels somehow hidden, since even smoke and the smell of burning are avoided as far as is technically possible. This is very different from the custom in India, for example, where cremation traditionally has taken place in the open air. Hindu mourners in Britain would prefer to see the smoke rising as it would have done from their traditional funeral pyres but in some modern British crematoria the technology hides it from view.

As a result of the demand for cremation many crematoria were built over a comparatively short period of time. There was thus little opportunity to reflect on their differing designs and the ways in which they had been and might be used. One feature which distinguishes most crematoria from churches, in Britain at least, involves using one door for entering and another for leaving the chapel. This developed to increase the rate of flow of congregations through the chapel. Some would argue that this has contributed to a perception of the cremation ritual as an impersonal conveyor-belt but others would take the view that, for those too upset to notice where they are going, it is a useful means of preventing mourners from meeting those entering for the next funeral and is likely to contribute to a more personal atmosphere.

The mechanics of a cremation service vary considerably from one crematorium to another and substantially different approaches may be observed in other countries. In Britain, there are four main ways in which the coffin is removed from the chapel: in about 75 per cent curtains are drawn or a gate is closed, so that the coffin is no longer visible or is only partly visible; in about 20 per cent the coffin descends out of view, imitating burial; in about 6 per cent the coffin itself is moved out of view horizontally on a system of rollers; and in about 17 per cent the coffin is left in full view as, in some cases, the congregation files past it, although they do not always do so if the coffin is out of reach or away from the exit.[14] Normally the coffin is removed automatically after the minister has pressed a button which is hidden from the sight of the congregation. These procedures seem mechanical and anonymous to some, and may be a cause of uncertainty as to what becomes of the coffin after it has disappeared. Other commentators[15] state that mourners are now asking for the coffin to be left where it was placed at the start of the service, although I have not personally received such a request.

Mechanical removal of the coffin from view seems to be a British innovation, confined to Britain and its former colonies. In the Netherlands, Finland and the USA, the chapel will be more reminiscent of a church. The coffin will be placed on a low plinth in front of the first row of seats. Thus mourners may file past it on their way in and out, which is normally through the same door. On their way past they may pause beside it, touch it for a moment or place flowers or mementoes on it. The final exit is not of the coffin from the mourners but of the mourners from the coffin. As previously mentioned, in some parts of the world such as in Sweden and parts of the USA a funeral service will be held in church, after which the mourners will return home while the coffin is transported to the crematorium, there being no further ceremony or ritual.

In Belgium people leave the chapel, which is more likely to be described as a 'ceremony room', and enter another room where condolences are offered by those who are leaving. The family and close relatives will then remain in a reception room at the crematorium, drinking coffee and eating sandwiches while they wait for the completion of the cremation, which will normally be within two hours. They then accompany a member of the crematorium staff to scatter the ashes on a lawn or place them in an urn in a colombarium or bury them in a grave.

We discussed in Chapter 2 the final disposal of ashes and the numerous ways in which this is being done. Many people, however, will leave the ashes at the crematorium and this practice has begun to invest these places with a sense of the sacred. It is becoming more usual in Britain for crematoria to hold annual open-air services of remembrance. Relatives of those who have been cremated there are invited and they are sometimes led by church choirs and clergy, with scriptural readings and hymns included. As many as several thousand people might gather together to remember their dead and to engage in a shared act of worship. They are, for a short period, united in their bereavement, and this in a society where bereavement tends to be more hidden than publicly announced.

This chapter has examined what the Church may learn from changes taking place in the use of music, the growth of do-it-yourself and alternative funerals and developments in burial and cremation. The next chapter will consider the reasons why clergy might find certain funerals difficult and ways of managing stress.

NOTES

[1] Humphrys, John, *Devil's Advocate*, London, Arrow Books, 1999, p. 103.

[2] Dean, S., 'Music in the Order of Christian Funerals', in S. Dean (ed.), *The Parish Funeral*, Great Wakering, Essex, McCrimmons, 1991, p. 61.

[3] Gledhill, Ruth, 'Funerals and Music', *The Times*, Saturday 9 April 1996, p. 4.

[4] Walter, Tony, *Funerals and How to Improve Them*, London, Hodder and Stoughton, 1990, pp. 80–81.

[5] Natural Death Centre, 6 Blackstock Mews, Blackstock Road, London N4 2BT. Telephone: 0871 288 2098.

[6] Young, M., 'Ashes to Hashes', *The Guardian*, Thursday 9 June, 1994, p. 22.

[7] See, for example, Weller, S., *The Daily Telegraph Lifeplanner Guide to Funerals and Bereavement*, London, Kogan Page, 1999.

[8] Grant, L., *A Way of Life: Portraits from the Funeral Trade*, Manchester, Len Grant Photography, 1999, p. 23.

[9] See, for example, Church of England Liturgical Commission, 'Burial', in *Alternative Services: First Series*, London, SPCK, 1966, pp. 85–91.

[10] Davies, Douglas and Shaw, A., *Reusing Old Graves: A Report on Popular British Attitudes*, Crayford, Shaw and Sons, 1995.

[11] Davies and Shaw, *Reusing Old Graves*, pp. 30–31.

[12] Davies and Shaw, *Reusing Old Graves*, pp. 39–41.

[13] See, for instance, Rugg, Julie, 'Defining the Place of Burial: What Makes a Cemetery a Cemetery?', *Mortality*, 2000, 5 (3), pp. 259–75.

[14] The figures total more than 100 per cent as some crematoria employ more than one means of removal.

[15] Walter, Tony, 'Committal in the Crematorium: Theology, Death and Architecture', in Peter Jupp and Tony Rogers (eds), *Interpreting Death: Christian Theology and Pastoral Practice*, London, Cassell, 1997, p. 204.

8

Difficult Funerals

Faith has given man an inward willingness, a world of strength where-
with to front a world of difficulty.

Thomas Carlyle[1]

In one sense every funeral is difficult. A death has occurred, and
people are in trouble. The circumstances may not be particularly
dramatic, and the death might even be welcomed in some ways;
nevertheless, for some mourners it will not be easy. In this
chapter, however, I have in mind a different kind of difficulty: the
funeral that is problematic for the minister conducting it. There
are certain types of funeral that I find hard to conduct, partly
because of my own past. When I see teenagers mourning their
parents, it reminds me of events in my life which occurred over
thirty years ago, but which can be recalled very easily and sometimes unexpectedly. I do not suppose that most other clergy
would react in the same way as I do when ministering to
bereaved young people, yet for each cleric there are likely to be
particular circumstances which prove challenging. Over the
years I have developed my own methods of meeting the situation
and have wondered how others do so. With this in mind I wrote
to some thirty clerics, most of whom I know well, and asked the
following questions.

> What makes a difficult funeral difficult? Do you have diffi-
> culties conducting particular (types of) funerals? If so, which?
> Can you identify why those funerals were difficult? What were
> those particular difficulties? How did you cope with them at
> the time? Have you put in place any particular strategies that
> help you cope with such difficulties in the future? And would

you like to share any of those with others? Is there anything that your church / denomination / organization / support networks / etc. do, or could do, to help you cope with those difficulties?

The replies varied greatly and covered a wide range of topics, which I have tried to reflect in this chapter. In the first part I have tried to identify those types of funeral which are perceived as 'difficult' and then move on to examine the strategies that have been adopted to deal with the situation.

Categories of Difficulty

The reasons vary as to why a particular funeral might be difficult for a cleric to conduct but they do fall into similar categories.

Problems might spring from the cleric's personal circumstances: he or she might be ill or anxious about an unrelated matter, or the funeral might echo previous experiences, bringing to mind painful memories, sometimes unexpectedly. One priest recalled returning home from her son's funeral to find she was being asked to take the funeral of a man who had been approximately the same age as her son. All involved knew of her tragedy and were very supportive and she was aware of God's grace through it all. Perhaps mourners benefited from the knowledge that this particular priest identified so strongly with their own situation.

On occasions the difficulty will be due to circumstances beyond one's control. A colleague described the chaos which ensued when a mourner collapsed and died during the service he was conducting at a crematorium. Another colleague discovered some time after a funeral that the wrong body had been cremated and was faced with agonizing decisions as to the best course of action: whether or not to repeat the service with the correct body, what theological and pastoral insights could she bring to bear on this situation, how to deal with the anger expressed by different groups, not all directly involved, and how to relate to the family of the person whose body she had mistakenly committed to the flames.

Complications might arise from time to time as a result of the wider society in which one ministers as in the case of a coroner being unable to release a body for burial. Bureaucracy surrounds much of death and often produces a sense of frustration and bewilderment among the bereaved. Particular activities and ways of behaviour might result in stigma directed towards the deceased and his or her funeral as, for instance, in the case of a convicted paedophile who has suffered harassment from local residents.

At other times obstacles might be created by the mourners. Death not infrequently causes people to become muddle-headed, irritable or awkward. There might be conflict between different relatives over the arrangements or an individual might behave unreasonably. One priest described how she had agreed to the deceased's aunt giving a testimony following his suicide. It began well but deteriorated into a tirade of abuse blaming the boy's mother for the tragedy. My colleague decided to intervene and bring the 'tribute' to an end, wondering as she did so if her intervention would only serve to make matters worse.

Finally, the predicament might have been caused by the deceased, for example, through instructions left in a will, or words or actions when alive. We have already referred to the newly-widowed woman who had just discovered her husband to be a bigamist. She and the 'other wife' had both been unaware of each other's existence. In such a case it could take some time to clarify the legal position and it might be necessary to deal with the effects of a legal decision which might not appear to be morally justified.

Sudden Death

From the replies I received to my questions it was clear that a funeral following a sudden death featured frequently on the lists of 'difficult' funerals. Accidents are a major cause of sudden death and most occur at home, over 3,000 of them proving fatal annually. Every year approximately 1,500 over-sixty-five-year-olds die following a fall in the home in the United Kingdom.[2] In 2002 there were 3,431 people killed in road accidents, 560 of them in drink-related incidents.[3] It is likely, then, that a cleric will sooner or later have to conduct a funeral following an accident. A significant number of clergy mentioned that they find the funeral following a road accident among the hardest to conduct, particularly when it is caused by careless or drunk driving or by so-called 'joy riding'.

Accidents are not, of course, the only cause of premature death and the phrase 'sudden death' might be defined in more than one way. There is the almost instantaneous and totally unexpected event, such as the case of the acquaintance in his late twenties who died suddenly while playing tennis. He had seemed to be in perfect health but was found to be suffering from a rare genetic disorder. Fifteen years later his daughter also died unexpectedly while playing hockey, the same condition having been passed unknown and unrecognized from father to child. His other children have been told categorically by one doctor that they do not have the condition and by another that it cannot be diagnosed. Consequently they no longer feel they can trust the medical profession and live with the fear that one day they might suffer the same fate.

Looking back over the list of funerals that I have taken, I am struck by how many have occurred in the weeks leading up to Christmas. A large proportion of these have been middle-aged men dying of heart failure, such as the man who had a heart attack during the week before Christmas. He left teenage children in the care of a step-mother to whom he had been married less than a year, his first wife having died some years earlier. Those children, like other people bereaved at that time of year, will always associate Christmas with the death of a loved one. The distress felt by the bereaved at Christmas is compounded if the funeral must be delayed until after the New Year celebrations since crematoria, cemeteries and coroners and others are not readily available.

A sizable number of funerals occur early in the New Year. At this time it appears more likely to be the elderly who die from long-term illnesses, possibly owing in part to the change in climate. The routine of nursing a loved one, constantly looking in on that person and arranging one's life to suit, is liable to make the carer feel as though it has always been this way. As a result, when the patient dies the death may feel sudden to the exhausted carer even if it has been expected for some considerable time.

A small number of people live in the knowledge that they have only a short time to live. This is a kind of 'sudden death', albeit not as dramatic as the instantaneous event. That knowledge, however, will in many cases have come suddenly. Relatives and friends will have had no time to prepare themselves for the sudden death of a loved one and will be struggling to find explanations. This may become apparent in a desire to apportion blame. Members of the medical profession will be aware of this response as they are occasionally the undeserving recipients of it. I remember hearing an irate middle-aged man telling a young hospital doctor that she and her colleagues must have been responsible for his father's death as he had been too young to die. The father had in fact been a very elderly person in a geriatric hospital. When there is no one to hold responsible the blame is often transferred to God. As his representatives the clergy sometimes receive the full force of a person's anger and this is one reason why clergy find funerals following a sudden death so difficult. It is helpful to remember that such aggression is a common response and that it is rarely directed at us personally; people frequently say things they do not mean as a result of the strain they have been suffering. By distancing ourselves and recognizing what is taking place, I believe we will be more able to help the bereaved person through the experience.

Violent Death

One of the most difficult forms of death to accept is violent death. Some individuals live from day to day with the possibility that their lives may be ended violently at the hands of others, for instance, captives held by violent regimes or by kidnappers, those living in war zones or trouble spots, military personnel on active service and the chaplains who minister to them. Violence might, however, be unexpected as in the case of terrorism or murder. Most of us in Britain do not expect to encounter these forms of violence personally, taking it for granted that they will affect others, although the terrorist threat in Northern Ireland has been a longstanding issue within British society. Yet terrorism does seem increasingly likely to encroach upon all our lives in the twenty-first century; it has already had the effect of reducing the number of American visitors to Europe. As far as murder is concerned, it is difficult to present accurate statistics on numbers of homicides occurring in a year using death registrations unless one is prepared to wait a considerable time following the year. The reason is that these deaths are usually handled in a series of legal processes which may take many weeks or months, beginning with the period of police investigation before a suspect is charged, followed by the trial and the appeal which may follow, in addition to the preliminary procedures involving a coroner and the time which may elapse after the trial before the coroner completes the registration. Over the period from March 1999 to March 2002, the number of homicides in the United Kingdom varied between 760 and 891. The figure for the twelve months from March 2002 to March 2003 was higher at 1,048, although the increase was largely due to 172 murders attributed to Dr Harold Shipman.[4]

For the cleric responsible for the funeral following violent death, one of the greatest difficulties is, perhaps, the sermon. A colleague was asked to take the funeral of a murdered mother and daughter. For him the task of speaking publicly at such a time was daunting and his anxiety was heightened by his desire not to let the family down. One has little time to prepare for the funeral unless of course the coroner does not release the body for a lengthy period. Even so, violence must exacerbate the situation as the bereaved are likely to be doubly shocked. They might, for instance, face the strain of waiting for news of a loved one or of receiving the victim's belongings. The involvement of bureaucracies such as police and coroner are foreign to most people's experience and, added to this, media representatives might be focusing on the event.

The presence of the media will inevitably raise the profile of the funeral, especially if children are involved. However sensitive the media might be, this will be stressful for mourners and clergy alike. A vicar who is well known in a small community could well find him or herself in the spotlight of publicity, with seemingly the whole community seeking counsel. This occurred at Soham when two ten-year-old schoolgirls, Holly Wells and Jessica Chapman, were murdered in August 2002. As a principal target of media attention the vicar, the Reverend Tim Alban-Jones, was scrutinized as he comforted families and friends and led Sunday worship. The churchyard became awash with flowers brought from near and far and visitors arrived in busloads to place bouquets at a shrine created inside the church. The vicar's telephone was in such frequent use that it failed, and the Town Council's offer of whatever help was necessary was accepted in the form of a new telephone. One can easily imagine being interviewed at such a time and later hearing one's own remarks broadcast on the national news, edited and possibly repeated out of context, now with a meaning never intended. Tim Alban-Jones later stated that at Soham only a few journalists had behaved badly, one reporter writing an account of an interview which bore no resemblance to what had been said; most, on the other hand, had acted professionally. Broadcasters had been more sensitive than print journalists and in general the British media had behaved more responsibly than some of the foreign journalists who had come to cover the story.[5]

The ramifications of a crisis such as this are likely to extend beyond the immediate situation. It is entirely possible that as a result of a single episode in one's ministry one is pushed in new directions in such a way that new aspects of ministry develop. Since those tragic events at Soham, Tim Alban-Jones has been asked to speak at conferences, to advise others finding themselves in similarly prominent positions, and to give further media interviews. The implications of this in respect of the workload of a parish priest could be far-reaching.

Most murders in the United Kingdom are not committed by a stranger but by an individual well known to the victim. They frequently occur behind closed doors between long-term domestic partners.[6] Domestic violence is widespread in our society and often results in serious injury or even death. The Metropolitan Police have stated that in London in 2001 a victim of domestic violence contacted them for help on average every six minutes.[7] According to the Home Office much domestic violence goes unreported, whereas their research shows that it claims 150 lives each year, that it accounts for a quarter of all violent crime, that it has more repeat victims than any other crime (there being on average, thirty-five assaults before a victim calls the police), and that in the United Kingdom it claims the lives of two women each week.[8] Sooner or later a cleric, then, might well find that he or she is called to conduct the funeral of a victim of domestic violence. The police will be involved and it may be that the situation will be unclear and complicated. How does one begin to discuss the arrangements for a funeral with, for instance, a man who is suspected of killing his wife? With whom should one be dealing when it is unknown whether the husband has murdered his wife or is the innocent victim of a terrible suspicion? One might also spare a thought for the police officers involved. I remember the funeral of a frail and elderly man who had died after falling downstairs. His wife had been upstairs at the time and the police, on their arrival, asked her to leave the house for twenty-four hours in order for them to investigate. What is the effect on a grieving person of being treated as a murder suspect? How does a police officer feel when obliged to carry out such an investigation?

The Death of Children

A hundred years ago the death of a child would have been relatively commonplace, as would have been the death of a woman in childbirth. Today, at least in the West, both events are rare, with the result that we are stunned when faced with them. Yet still-births, cot deaths and the deaths of young children do occur and my experience as a parish priest has led me to conclude that their incidence is higher than most would imagine, so that we feel those kinds of death to be an outrage in a way which would have perplexed our forebears. This sense of anger is felt as much by clergy as by the rest of society. Indeed, it might be felt even more keenly by Christians because the tragedy has been allowed by God who, it seems, did nothing to prevent it. We believe God to be omnipotent and caring and to be a God who hates injustice yet who does not intervene and who appears to be powerless in the face of unjustifiable suffering. The child's parents and other relatives question how this can be and, because they turn to us as representing the Church or God, they demand answers which we might feel unable to give. Often it is not that we have no answers but that those answers are complicated and difficult to explain. We are usually capable of expressing them through the language of theology but we cannot always easily put them into words that make sense to a grieving parent. What is communicated might then sound either obscure and unhelpful or seem to be a patronizing truism. We are left with a dilemma of how to bridge the gap between theology as studied in universities or theological colleges and the understanding of that theology among lay people in church congregations and also those who never attend worship. It may also be that an individual cleric has not yet developed his or her own understanding of the issue sufficiently well to respond to the questions posed by others. In such a case any media interest will serve to heighten any feelings of inadequacy and will be likely to increase the stress.

In speaking of the death of children one has in mind mainly young children; we know, however, that adult children also die. Nevertheless, we normally expect to outlive our parents and our parents expect to die before us. Today natural disasters, heart attacks, AIDS and other illnesses may be the major causes of death among those who are not elderly, but they do not occur at such a rate in the West that they change our expectations. Hence, when a person under retirement age dies, we are shocked by the 'early death' and less able to come to terms with it. Those whose adult child dies might also be confronted with the added strain of looking after their orphaned grandchildren. Visitors to countries such as Lesotho where AIDS has become widespread have commented that the strain on families is enormous. Much to the surprise of the authorities there, parents who are not infected with AIDS have begun to demand for their children the same provision that is being made by the state for those who are orphaned, adding to the strain on the limited resources available to a developing country.

Suicide

When a person has taken his or her own life, there are always questions. Was suicide the intention? Could it have been avoided? Those left behind may be feeling guilty, possibly wondering if they could have prevented it, or feeling that they were the cause. They might be angry, especially any partner or children, wondering why their relative has done this to them and blaming the suicide for inflicting pain on them. It is always possible that, as their pastor, the minister may also experience those feelings.

I have been surprised at how many people still consider suicide a sinful act which should be punished by the Church's withholding a normal funeral and insisting on burial in unconsecrated ground. While travelling back from a crematorium, an undertaker once told me that the deceased's family had asked that I be not told until afterwards that their fifteen-year-old boy had committed suicide. They had been afraid that I would refuse to conduct the service. I asked the undertaker why he had not assured them that I would, as he surely knew me well enough to know that I would not have refused. He replied that he had tried to do so but the family were not prepared to take the risk: some ten years previously one of my predecessors had, apparently, declined to bury a suicide in the churchyard.

There is some debate as to why suicide has been regarded as a sin and the burial of suicides has not been permitted in consecrated ground. The Christian Church's condemnation of suicide appears to stem largely from the teachings of Saint Augustine of Hippo and Saint Thomas Aquinas. They both base their reasoning on the works of two Greek philosophers: Plato and Aristotle. The two saints argue that the Sixth Commandment ('Thou shalt not kill') includes suicide and that it violates God's prerogative to decide the duration of one's life. The basis of Saint Augustine's opposition to suicide in *The City of God*, however, was to demonstrate the heresy of martyrdom-seeking sects, such as the Donatists, who would goad magistrates, pagan temple priests and other authorities into executing them, believing that as martyrs they would go to heaven. There are biblical references that support the view that suicide is not a sin, such as the book of Judges which presents the suicide of Samson as the act of a saint (Judges 16), and the Church has from its earliest days honoured certain Christians who, faced with persecution, committed suicide. Augustine and Aquinas assert that God must have secretly commanded these suicides. Other suicides in the Hebrew scriptures include: Abimelech who ordered his armour-bearer to kill him in order to avoid the potential shame of being killed by a woman (Judges 9:54); Saul who fell on his own sword after being defeated in battle with the Philistines (1 Samuel 31:3–6); and Achitopel (or Ahitophel) who hanged himself after his plot to overthrow his father, King David, failed. Far from being refused burial in hallowed ground he was buried in his own father's sepulchre (2 Samuel 17: 23).

When Paul persuaded the jailer at Philippi not to kill himself he did not state that suicide was sinful but that the jailer was acting under a misapprehension in believing his prisoners to have escaped during an earthquake (Acts 16:26–29). In all four Gospels Jesus himself is portrayed as choosing to provoke the authorities into crucifying him and explicitly states that his life was not being taken but that he was voluntarily choosing death: 'No man taketh it from me, but I lay it down of myself' (John 10:18). Some will insist that this does not amount to suicide. Nevertheless, it could be said to be tantamount to it.

The first comprehensive legal code to be promulgated during the Christian era was that of Justinian, approximately a century after Saint Augustine. It did not punish suicide if the person had a good reason for it. Such good reasons included: impatience of pain or sickness, weariness of life, lunacy, fear of dishonour, or 'another cause'. Suicide did not become a crime under English Common Law until the tenth century and later a rubric was inserted into the 1662 Book of Common Prayer which stated that the burial service was not to be used for excommunicates, suicides and those that die unbaptized. The same book made no liturgical provision at all for their burial. It has been argued that this had more connection with the claims of king and nobility upon the service of their subjects than with duty to God. A suicide would be guilty of denying his earthly master the right to his life-long service and such a crime would be punished with the full force of the law, even to the point of refusing the 'criminal' a Christian burial. As the highest authority in the medieval feudal system was, of course, God, suicide came also to be regarded as a crime against God. It is relevant that the prayer-book rubric forbidding the burial of suicides first appeared in 1662 after the restoration of the monarchy, at a time when the Stuart kings of England had placed great emphasis on their divine right to rule. It had not appeared in the previous editions of the Book of Common Prayer published in 1549, 1552, 1559 and 1604, although it is clear that the views reflected in the rubric were certainly held by some in Elizabethan England. This is shown quite clearly in a conversation between two gravediggers in Shakespeare's *Hamlet*. There, they discuss whether or not Ophelia should be given a Christian funeral as she has taken her own life.[9] At the time this was written, a decision on such a matter would have been made by a coroner, whose decision the priest would, in the main, have been obliged to follow. In *Hamlet* the first grave-digger asks if Ophelia's grave should be made straight, referring to the custom at that time in some parts of England of burying suicides in a 'crooked' grave, that is, one which lay in a direction other than the East–West axis along which the church would have been built.[10] In this play it seems that Shakespeare assumed the law of England, rather than Denmark where it is set, but his knowledge of that law was very thorough. Some commentators suggest that the Church of England was mainly responsible for the later moderation of this position through allowing suicides to be buried in churchyards, albeit on the North side and in the shade rather than the sun. England finally decriminalized suicide in 1961 upon the advice of a committee established by the Archbishop of Canterbury, being the last European nation to do so.

A contemporary view of Christian approaches to suicide is given in the following quotation from a publication produced by the Church of England's Board of Social Responsibility:

> Traditionally the Christian Churches were very severe on suicides and attempted suicides, refusing the former burial in consecrated ground, since it was argued that the person who committed suicide was expressing his or her total lack of faith in God.
>
> Nowadays, Christians generally recognise that suicide is not so much a deliberate rejection of life as an expression of dissatisfaction with the particular life the person is leading, and in many cases is a cry for help. To take your life is obviously a muddled and unsatisfactory way of responding to an unsatisfactory personal state of affairs, but seeing things in this way has led Christians to treat suicides and potential suicides as they would treat people who were depressed or sick in other ways, i.e. by seeking to help them where possible, and certainly not to engage in moral condemnation of them. This shift in attitude led this Board to produce *Ought Suicide to be a Crime?* And to press the Government to change the law so that suicide should no longer be treated as a crime. This change came about in 1961.[11]

Family Feuds

Probably every family has skeletons in its closet which are mostly kept well hidden but an event which disrupts family life can bring them out. Rarely does anything do so more effectively than a death in the family. Sometimes a family feud is well known, even dividing a whole village. How, then, does a cleric deal with being pulled this way and that by different factions, both of which may expect one's loyalty? We have already referred to the dilemma of who decides what should take place; how should one respond when one feels the arrangements made are unjust or in some other way wholly unacceptable? On one occasion I refused to allow the exclusion of certain relatives from the church service, as the next of kin had wished, but I was powerless to insist that they be invited to the private service at the deceased's home beforehand. Afterwards I agonized as to whether or not I should have conducted that private service. My difficulty was exacerbated by the fact that, although I knew much of the background to this feud, I could not understand it as it appeared to have started several generations earlier and I suspect that those involved had long forgotten its origins.

On other occasions one might know nothing of the feud until the day of funeral. Even the matter of the refreshments after the service can be a source of friction as a colleague discovered when asked just before the service to invite the congregation to tea on behalf of the family: a simple request, except that he was asked by two different people to invite them to different venues. For my part I have experienced a situation in which two parts of the family have remained in different rooms, neither faction speaking to the other, the food having been set out in the hall so that they may avoid as far as possible having to meet each other.

Occasionally I have been concerned that family relations might deteriorate into physical violence at the church and have taken the step of asking the local police to come to direct the traffic in case they should be needed for other reasons. I should add that there have been other occasions when I have asked the police to be present simply because of the large volume of traffic expected.

Close Friends and Relatives

There will come a time in almost every cleric's ministry when we are asked to conduct the funeral of a person we have known well. It could be a parishioner with whom we have worked closely, or a life-long friend, or a member of our own family. We might rather another person conducted the funeral and at times it will be possible to say so, perhaps offering to contribute to the service without actually leading it. There will be, however, occasions when it is not appropriate to make that request, perhaps because others might not understand and might be hurt by what they perceive as a refusal to help. Whatever the circumstances, we will be required to carry out differently a task we do regularly. The prayers we read and the words we use may be exactly the same as always but our emotional involvement will be different. We might feel overcome with emotion but there are times when we simply have to persevere, relying on our professionalism and experience to enable us to do so. A colleague told me that after a particularly traumatic funeral a parishioner commented that it was the first time she had seen him read his address. He remarked to me that it had been necessary to read it; otherwise he would 'have lost it, along with every one else'.

There is no guarantee against breaking down. How is one to deal with this? Each cleric will no doubt have particular ways of meeting the challenge but the following thoughts might be of use. When another minister is contributing to the funeral he or she could step in. I once continued a prayer in mid-sentence when a colleague stopped abruptly. A prior arrangement with an organist who is prepared to be flexible as to when the hymns are sung might allow a breathing space. If, however, one is taking the service single-handedly it is naturally more difficult. On most occasions there is some warning of an approaching wave of emotion and a deep breath or two taken at a convenient full stop might be helpful. If the worst happens, perhaps it is wise to accept one's humanity. The greatest damage will probably have been to one's professional pride. Clergy seem to worry that, should they break down, the whole congregation will follow suit, but perhaps that is no bad thing. I would let it occur, compose myself, make a brief apology and carry on. If the service is in a crematorium it might be necessary to omit a prayer in order to keep within the allotted time.

The ways in which we are close to others take different forms. To conduct the funeral of a close parishioner will be demanding, because the congregation will include people who know both cleric and deceased well and one will feel more emotionally involved. A different kind of relationship exists, however, within family and officiating at the funeral of a relative will potentially affect one differently. A cleric's own family will have known both deceased and cleric well and some will have known both all their lives. This creates a different kind of stress as one is experiencing the event as both close mourner and officiant simultaneously.

Common Threads

Throughout the responses I received to my enquiries of other clergy two common threads recurred several times. The first was the stress that results from being required to conduct large numbers of funerals. The number varies considerably from parish to parish according to the size and type of population. There will naturally be more deaths within a greater population, and an area to which large numbers of people retire will contain an ageing population, inevitably causing more funerals. If the Anglican church is the only place of worship, the vicar will probably take proportionately more funerals than would be the case in other similarly-sized communities. A crematorium situated in the parish may result in an increased number of funerals because families will not know whom else to ask. A high number of funerals will create a greater degree of stress unless there are correspondingly more people qualified and available to conduct them. The dilemma for many clergy is how to maintain an appropriate degree of detachment but nevertheless to remain sensitive to the needs of the bereaved. Some clergy approach this by constantly reminding themselves that each bereaved person and each deceased person is created in the image of God, and of infinite value to God, allocating a particular space in their prayers to pray for each by name.

An efficient system of handling paperwork is an advantage, in my view. I always use a separate sheet of paper for each funeral, on which I write the names of the deceased, the chief mourners and the time and place of the service. I use that sheet of paper when saying the daily office. I have learned to type the list, having once prayed publicly for a person using the wrong name because of poor handwriting. The paper is of such a size that it fits easily into an A5 ring-binder which contains a copy of the funeral service and any other resources that will be required. I always keep everything in the same ring-binder so as not to leave a vital piece of paper behind when, for example, arriving at the crematorium. Afterwards I will file the sheet along with any hymn sheet that was used. Over the years the file has become a helpful reference when taking another funeral in the same family.

I once walked into the chapel at a funeral home to conduct the eighth funeral out of ten that had been arranged for one week. I had visited all ten families, who were all unknown to me, and when about to start the service I looked up and saw what I believed to be the Jones family sitting there. My paper stated that they were the Davies family, yet I was certain in my own mind that they were the Joneses. Unable to decide whether to trust my paperwork or my memory, I decided to read the opening passage of the service from beside the coffin, in order that I could look at the nameplate. It was covered by a wreath. That funeral was the only one which I have begun by picking up the family's wreath and blessing it, and as I did so I saw that my paperwork had been correct and that my memory had been playing tricks.

Any vicar, rector or minister will face pressure from many

different directions including church, community and wider commitments. Some will arise out of the occasional offices: they take time and will possibly involve rearranging other appointments, especially in the case of funerals. There will be the stress, felt by many clergy, that we have no particular professional skill to offer, although that is perhaps what makes us so effective. Having to attend a funeral can force all of us to face the fact of our own mortality. To be obliged to meet these kinds of strain several times a week must create its own emotional pressure which needs to be acknowledged and dealt with. If it is ignored it will surely persist and might result in a withdrawal from emotional contact with the bereaved which will help neither them nor the cleric involved.

The other common theme relating to why clergy find some funerals difficult appears to be the need for forgiveness on the part of various parties. It might be that the family need to forgive the deceased or that an individual mourner never forgave the deceased and now feels it is too late. Equally perhaps the deceased appeared to die unrepentant and bearing grudges against others. Mourners might need to forgive a person or persons who were responsible in some degree for the death, either deliberately or by accident, or individuals who have aggravated the situation since the death occurred. Many of the examples that have been quoted in this book point towards the question of forgiveness, and the dilemma is that forgiveness is a central theme in any system of Christian doctrine, yet people fail to live up to this. A prominent lay member of a church once said during an interregnum, 'When we get our new vicar, I hope he won't preach about forgiveness.' I was taken aback by this as I could not conceive how a life-long church member could expect anything else. Many of Jesus' sayings link one's own receiving of forgiveness to forgiving others. How, then, does one deal with people who are bitter, resentful, sometimes deeply hurt but not prepared to forgive? When one's calling includes confronting the failure to forgive and encouraging forgiveness how can one ignore it? Yet is this the right moment? It seems callous and uncaring at a time of grief even to raise the matter. I have no answer to that, except to pray for those concerned and to take opportunities as appropriate for discussion with them. This may be possible when paying a visit to follow up the funeral at a later date.

Managing Strategies

It is important to be able to handle difficulties such as those described above. If one is going to be of help to mourners one must give of oneself. Giving at length without at the same time receiving, however, takes its toll emotionally and spiritually and must eventually be unsustainable. This is true of any ministry but it seems to me to be particularly so in the context of a consistently large number of funerals.

How does one go about restoring one's own spiritual resources? I would suggest primarily by making one's own spiritual growth and development a priority through a rule of life. Exactly how that process is structured will vary from individual to individual and we each need to discover what is effective for us. My own experience is that my rule has changed considerably over the years depending on the circumstances. There are certain elements, however, which are always present and these include: receiving communion, regular reading of the scriptures, theological reflection, intercessory prayer, types of prayer which allow one to listen to God, and spiritual direction. Other elements which at any rate in my case come and go include: making one's confession, going on retreat and prayer for healing. I have also found that my understanding of my own faith and an appreciation of the traditions in which I was raised have developed as I have shared in discussion with those of other faiths. It has made me realize how much I take for granted and I am learning how to express my belief to those who use a very different language of faith. All religions have to deal ultimately with questions concerning the meaning of life in the face of death, and I have discovered that we can learn about our own faith by understanding the ways in which others phrase their questions and the practices they adopt, even if we have to disagree profoundly with some of their answers.

Clergy will find different forms of support and some will benefit more than others from the systems provided by their denomination. For Anglicans these include deanery chapter meetings, when the clergy of a particular area meet together to discuss business and share fellowship; any other meetings of clerics who work together; review procedures to consider one's ministry either with peers or a member of the hierarchical structure; or continuing ministerial education provision which may involve lectures, discussions, structured courses or an individually tailored programme. Some find their support through family networks. For several generations nearly all the men on one side of my family were ordained. My father's 'clerical support group', although he would never have used such a term, would at various times have included his father, his uncle, his cousin and his two brothers. I am the only one of my generation that has chosen to follow in their footsteps and I have often thought how much I would have valued that level of family support, as family members would know the pressures from first-hand experience. Today fewer clerics come from clergy families and that is probably why there is more emphasis within the profession on creating support networks than in previous generations.

Many clerics find that, rather than using officially provided channels of support, they gain more by developing relationships of their own choosing. These might involve membership of an organization, fellowship, guild, or order, perhaps one that encourages a common rule of life; maintaining contact with a group of friends with whom one trained; meeting regularly with a spiritual director or work consultant; or simply spending time with one or more fellow clerics in a constructive friendship.

Without developing some means of support and encouragement for one's ministry, one can face loneliness in the ordained ministry of any church, and this is of great significance for the whole of one's ministry and not just for the conducting of funerals.

NOTES

[1] Wood, J. and Haydon, A. L. (eds), *The Nuttall Dictionary of Quotations*, London, F. Warne, 1930, p. 99.

[2] Department of Trade and Industry: see www.dti.gov.uk/homesafetynetwork/gh_intro.htm

[3] Dept of Transport information: see www.thinkroadsafety.gov.uk/statistics.htm

[4] www.murderuk.com

[5] Information found on the website for The Dart Center for Journalism & Trauma: a non-profit organization based in Seattle, Washington, USA. It is funded by the Dart Foundation of Mason, Michigan, under the supervision of the University of Washington School of Communication. The quotation has been amended after discussion with the Reverend Tim Alban-Jones.

[6] www.chrisbryantmp.co.uk

[7] www.met.police.uk/enoughisenough/

[8] www.homeoffice.gov.uk/crime/domesticviolence/ as at 4 May 2004.

[9] Hamlet Act 5, Scene 1.

[10] A lecture by R. A. Guernsey on *The Ecclesiastical Law in Hamlet* refers to the play as containing 'allusions and statements showing the most thorough and complete knowledge of the canon and statute law of England, relating to the burial of suicides that has ever been written'. For a detailed discussion of the burial of suicides as described in Hamlet, and the laws to which it relates, as well as the differences between the different editions of the play, see www.sourcetext.com/lawlibrary/guernsey/00.htm for this lecture which was originally presented before The Shakespeare Society of New York, 9 June 1885, and subsequently published by Brentano Bros., New York, 1885.

[11] Taken from 'The Church of England's View on Medical Ethics and Issues of Life and Death', available at www.cofe.anglican.org/view/medical.html

9

Remembering the Dead

When I started for Cefyn y Blaen only two or three people were in the churchyard with flowers. But now the customary beautiful Easter Eve Idyll had fairly begun and people kept arriving from all parts with flowers to dress the graves. Children were coming from the town and neighbouring villages with baskets of flowers and knives to cut holes in the turf. The roads were lively with people coming and going and the churchyard a busy scene with women and children and a few men moving about among the tombstones and kneeling down beside the green mounds flowering the graves.

From *Kilvert's Diary* entry for
Saturday, Easter Eve, 16 April 1870

In this chapter we are concerned with the different ways in which families and other groups create memorials to their dead, be they permanent memorials such as stained-glass windows or grave-stones, or impermanent such as memorial services and notices in newspapers. It is not only families and friends who create memorials, however, as it is sometimes the deceased who will do so during his or her lifetime. The nature of this kind of memorial may say a great deal about the values of the deceased and be of lasting benefit to others. A clause in a will may, for instance, provide for a stained-glass window to be placed in a church or a scholarship to be created at a school or college in memory of the deceased, and the creation of the memorial may generate a sense of purpose and pride as well as the satisfaction of knowing that one's wishes have been fulfilled.

Mention has already been made of Davies and Shaw's survey of 1995[1] which examined attitudes towards the re-use of graves. This survey asked questions regarding different types of memorial, and concluded that memorialization could be viewed from different angles. There is first the perpetuation of the individual's own sense of identity after death. Second, closely linked to this is the family's memorial which perpetuates their memory of the deceased rather than his or her own sense of identity. Other memorials such as war memorials will be created by a wider community, or even a nation, and often linked to particular disasters or events.

Davies and Shaw identified three main forms of memorial in Britain: graves in churchyards or cemeteries; plaques and columbaria at crematoria; and plants or trees, which may be planted in a place of personal significance such as a garden or park. The survey had asked what kind of resting place respondents would choose for their remains and revealed a preference for sites near to home and family and places that were well looked after. It revealed a growing appreciation of gardens of remembrance, linked to the decline in burial and the rise in cremation. An exception to this trend was the death of children, when the parents' desire for a grave to visit meant that many chose burial in preference to cremation. One surprising result was the large number of respondents who said that many of their relatives had no memorial. This perhaps has implications for historians and future generations as it suggests that details of family funeral history are more likely to be discovered from registers rather than gravestones. It was also noticed that for the majority of Britons photography played no significant part in memorials to the dead, whereas some East European and Indian families will photograph aspects of the funeral rites.

In the sections that follow, consideration will be given to permanent memorials and customs connected with the place of burial or disposal of ashes, practices which churches might adopt to help the bereaved to come to terms with death and to make the transition back into everyday life, memorial services, and other contemporary forms of memorialization.

The Site of Burial or Disposal

The need for somewhere to mourn is a recurring theme in much literature about grief. The grave is often a focus for this and particular items may be buried with the deceased. The gentleman who used to help children cross the road on their way to and from my primary school was buried with the 'Stop : Children' sign which he habitually carried. For generations of children from that village it summed up their memories of him as a caring man who was always available to help them. Sometimes items of special significance are placed on top of the coffin during a funeral service; this has the advantage of enabling mourners to realize the significance of what has occurred in a way that a bare coffin might not. Mementoes such as a person's military medals, when used in this way, normally hold particular memories and it will generally be clear to all those present why they were chosen.

At a later date people will leave flowers and other mementoes on the grave, perhaps even letters they have written to the deceased. Whilst recognizing the pastoral value of the practice, I am concerned that it might encourage the bereaved to suppress recognition of the death and, almost, to pretend that the deceased is still alive. Sometimes the action demonstrates a need to show others how much the bereaved person loved (or even hated) the deceased or to express guilt felt over a matter which to others might even seem trivial. An appropriate response might vary, depending on the circumstances, from a gentle affirmation of the bereaved to the hearing of a confession and pronouncement of absolution.

In most of Britain the maintenance of a grave is a personal act carried out privately by those most immediately bereaved, although it is becoming easier to make an arrangement with monumental masons for this service. In some cultures, however, tending graves has a communal aspect and in, for example, Hong Kong and Mexico a whole community will tend their graves on the same date, taking a picnic and spending the whole day, the cemeteries filled with people of all ages eating and talking together. There are perhaps parallels to this in the custom of dressing graves and in Welsh-speaking areas on Palm Sunday churchyards and cemeteries are a mass of bright colours. The day before, many people will have been tending family graves, laying flowers on them and visiting relatives while in the area. In the Welsh language, although Palm Sunday is translated as *Sul y Palmwydd* in the Church in Wales' Book of Common Prayer, it is more commonly known as *Sul y Blodau*, which means 'Flower Sunday'.

In a churchyard a gravestone is erected by a monumental mason and the vicar is involved only administratively to give permission and to approve any inscription. This may occur at any time after the funeral, although most masons will encourage people to wait for some months until the earth has had time to settle after being disturbed. The Jewish customs surrounding burial, however, include the placing of a stone on a grave on the first anniversary of a death and the rabbi will be there to pronounce a blessing. It is seen as a religious event and this 'Yahrzeit' or 'Year's Mind' will also mark the end of mourning and a return to normal life. Perhaps the Christian churches could learn something from this in relation to the usefulness of particular time periods or anniversaries and the likely need to mark a return to normality. Some churches do commemorate the departed in prayers on the Sunday nearest the anniversary of a death but rarely have I observed this being used specifically to help people move on to the next phase of their lives.

The lack of any grave to visit to express one's grief is a feature of studies on cremation. Some mourners have already made arrangements and, having buried the ashes in a churchyard or cemetery, possess such a grave. Others have left the disposal of cremated remains to crematorium staff and might later regret not having a grave which they may visit. Their pastoral needs might be partially met by creating a personal 'shrine', using a corner of the garden to plant a favourite shrub, keeping a treasured possession of the deceased as a 'keepsake' or going to a place of shared memories. Most crematoria make provision for individuals to be remembered in a book of remembrance or by way of a gift such as a bench or kerbstone. It should be noted, however, that, whereas most of these memorials will be permanent, some crematoria will 'lease' them to the bereaved for a limited number of years depending on how much money is paid. Reference has already been made to the variety of means by which ashes are disposed of nowadays[2] and one is always aware of the dangers of commercial exploitation of mourners' grief.

Practices which Aid the Bereaved

Alongside the development of cremation a new ritual has developed: the annual memorial service held at crematoria. In some cases these services attract several thousand people, which contrasts with the relatively small number who attend an ordinary cremation service. People see that thousands of others are in similar circumstances to their own and they share their grief collectively. It has been suggested that this sort of gathering fulfils some of the same needs as the customs of Roman Catholic countries associated with the Feast of All Souls on the second of November, by providing an annual occasion on which the departed can be remembered.

Observing the Feast of All Souls is by no means limited to Roman Catholics. Many Anglican churches hold requiem Masses during which the names of the departed are read out. Congregations are normally asked in advance if they would like to place the names of relatives or friends on the list. Some clergy use this occasion to remember in addition all those whose funerals they have conducted during the past year and they write to the relatives inviting them to attend. Some churches hold requiem Masses more frequently than annually, perhaps every three months. Alternatively, congregations remember the departed by mentioning them by name during the intercessions at the main Sunday Eucharist following the funeral and in following years on the Sunday nearest the anniversary of the death.

Many people find it of great comfort to pray for the repose of the soul of those they mourn, and others, especially perhaps the housebound, will be comforted by simply knowing that the Church has not forgotten their departed but that they are remembered before God.

There is, however, a dilemma here for some Anglicans who come from Protestant traditions and who believe that a person's fate is sealed at the time of death and that it is wrong to pray for the departed. This matter was a subject of great controversy at the time of the Reformation and was raised again by the Church of England during the revisions of the funeral service in the 1960s.[3] Subsequent revisions have been closely scrutinized for any shift in doctrinal emphasis. This appears to be a particularly Anglican problem, as prayer for the departed is taken for granted by Roman Catholics and does not give rise to much debate in the Free Churches. I would personally find it difficult to refuse prayer for the dead as I am aware of how much consolation it can give bereaved people and I would be concerned at not meeting their need in that way. Other churches will try to meet the needs of the bereaved by inviting them to a healing service and offering them the opportunity for individual prayer and counselling either during that service or privately by appointment.

The bereaved might also be assisted in unexpected ways including by ritual actions not directly associated with death. For instance, it is the custom in many churches for children to present their mothers with flowers on Mothering Sunday. In one parish these flowers were given to every member of the congregation, not only to children whose mothers were present. I hesitated slightly when a middle-aged woman whose mother had recently died came forward to receive a posy. After the service she placed the small bunch of daffodils on her mother's grave and I noticed several other people doing the same thing at their own family graves. A ritual action, which I had expected to be carried out by children whose mothers were either present or at home, had been interpreted more widely by the congregation.

Memorial Services

It used to be that memorial services were held only for public figures; in recent years, however, I have noticed that they are often arranged for other people. The term 'memorial service' may be used to describe a service held on the same day as a cremation but later on at a more convenient time and in a more convenient location. In such circumstances it is very similar to a funeral service except that there is no body. Sometimes the 'memorial service' will be held some days or weeks after the funeral and when, for example, mourners have to travel from many different areas, even different countries, it makes sense to do this. The degree to which a later memorial service differs from a funeral will depend, in part, on how much time has elapsed between the two events. In the case of a few months' gap there will be more time to prepare. It will no doubt be easier to ask different people to take part and they will have more time to consider their contribution. The shock of hearing about the death might have passed and the depth of the emotional response might have changed over time. On the other hand, where the period between the funeral and the memorial service is short it is not so easy to make a clear differentiation between them: the normal constraints of time will apply and mourners are still likely to be deeply affected. I once attended a memorial service for a friend following her sudden and unexpected death. A funeral attended by only her immediate family had been held a few days earlier. According to the preacher, her relatives' grief had been expressed at the funeral and all that was necessary had been done; we were now gathering to give thanks to God for her life. For my own part, I found this unhelpful as I was still feeling shocked; it might have been appropriate six months later to place such clear emphasis on thanksgiving over grief, but not, in my opinion, so soon after the death. The majority of the congregation at that service had not been present at the funeral and I would not have been surprised if their responses had been similar to my own.

Most of the memorial services I have conducted have been

attended mainly by a congregation other than those present at the funeral. Mourners who were unable to travel to the funeral have sometimes commented appreciatively on this. It has been my experience that, the more time has elapsed since the death, the easier it is to talk about the meaning of death and its effect and to utter words of faith in defiance of death, as well as to give a more rounded appreciation of the deceased by way of tribute. I have often tried to create a link between funeral and memorial service, perhaps using the same readings or some of the same hymns. Most funeral liturgies can be adapted for use at a memorial service, usually by omitting the prayers of commendation and committal. There are, however, occasions when there is no body to commit for burial or cremation, for instance, when the deceased has donated it for medical research or when a person has been lost at sea. In such situations, if the memorial service is to take the place of a funeral, it seems appropriate to me to use words of commendation and committal. The whole person would be commended to God's care and protection as in a funeral but, depending on the circumstances, the committal might need to be rephrased in such a way as to commit the person's mortal remains, say, to medical research. Alternatively there are a number of liturgies specifically written for memorial services[4] and it is likely that from time to time such a liturgy would serve the purpose more successfully than an adapted funeral service.

Contemporary Forms of Memorial

Little research has been conducted into contemporary forms of memorial, although there has been some study of the ways in which notices in local newspapers are used.[5] These will often include a photograph of the deceased and some message which is possibly addressed to the deceased by the person placing the notice in the paper. Mention has already been made of memorial gardens which, although not a new idea, have gained in popularity alongside the growth in cremation.

Other memorials might take the form of action, perhaps bringing together people who have never met, for instance, in the creation of the AIDS Memorial Quilt which is claimed to be the largest ongoing community arts project in the world. The quilt is composed of more than 44,000 colourful panels each of which commemorates the life of a person lost to AIDS. One feature that many memorials have in common is the desire that death should not have been in vain and that some good should come of it. The goals of the AIDS Memorial Quilt, for example, are: to provide a creative means of remembrance and healing; effectively to illustrate the enormity of the AIDS epidemic; to increase the general public's awareness of HIV and AIDS; to assist others with HIV prevention education; and to raise funds for community-based AIDS service organizations.[6] Other examples of memorial action have included a scholarship established from donations in memory of the deceased, a village hall built to commemorate those who died in the Second World War and gifts of books to schoolchildren presented at the end of each academic year. On occasions the memorial might be in the form of a special day such as Holocaust Memorial Day, established to remember the victims of the Holocaust and to promote awareness of other atrocities in the hope that such events will not occur in the future.

In 1989, following the Hillsborough disaster when ninety-five Liverpool football supporters were crushed, local musicians recorded a special version of *Ferry Cross the Mersey* as a memorial to those killed. This went straight to the top of the pop charts. Its production and sales were typical of the way in which people were beginning to remember the dead in new and sometimes unexpected ways.

New ideas are now constantly on offer. We have already seen how cremated remains can be turned into diamonds or works of art and an internet search would reveal even more bizarre procedures. There are a number of websites on which a wide variety of memorial notices can be placed, one example being The Virtual Memorial Garden,[7] maintained by a senior lecturer in the School of Computing Science at the University of Newcastle upon Tyne. Memorial messages can be placed by any person although neither the university not the 'maintainer' are responsible for their content. The site describes itself as 'somewhere people can celebrate their family, friends and pets'. At present only simple text is used 'but in the future there will be more complex memorials, with sound and images combining to tell you about someone you never knew and how they touched those around them. Perhaps you will see cyber-pyramids and data-sphinxes appearing. Certainly there will be electronic crypts as pages devoted to whole families are assembled.' This site has received considerable attention from newspapers and has been featured on several television programmes including the BBC's *Tomorrow's World*. The effects of sites such as these remains to be seen.

NOTES

[1] Davies, Douglas, and Shaw, A., *Reusing Old Graves: A Report on Popular British Attitudes*, Crayford, Shaw and Sons, 1995.

[2] See Chapters 3 and 7.

[3] For those who wish to see a detailed discussion of this question I would recommend reading the following publications: Church of England Liturgical Commission, Burial, in *Alternative Services: First Series*, pp. 85–91, London, SPCK, 1966, and Church of England Liturgical Commission, 'The Burial of the Dead', in *Alternative Services: Second Series*, pp. 101–41, London, SPCK, 1965. A more contemporary account will be found in Michael Perham's essay, 'Anglican Funeral Rites Today and Tomorrow', in Peter Jupp and Tony Rogers (eds), *Interpreting Death: Christian Theology and Pastoral Practice*, pp. 157–70, London, Cassell, 1997.

[4] See for example, Paul Sheppy's book, *In Sure and Certain Hope*, Norwich, Canterbury Press, 2003.

[5] See for example, Davies, Jon (ed.) *Ritual and Remembrance: Responses to Death in Human Societies*, Sheffield, Sheffield Academic Press, 1994.

[6] The NAMES Project Foundation AIDS Memorial Quilt, 101 Krog Street, Atlanta, GA 30307, USA, www.aidsquilt.org/

[7] http://catless.ncl.ac.uk/vmg/

Tying Together Loose Ends

God be in my head, and in my understanding;
God be in my eyes, and in my looking;
God be in my mouth, and in my speaking;
God be in my heart, and in my thinking;
God be at my end, and at my departing.

Sarum Missal (11th Century)[1]

Throughout this book many questions have been raised and left unanswered, and probably different clerics will answer them in differing ways. The purpose of this chapter is not to answer those questions; rather it is an attempt to address issues that have been merely touched upon but not considered in depth. In addition there are issues that have not fitted conveniently into the chapter structure but do merit some attention.

Several people have asked me why I have not included a chapter on ministering to those who are dying or who face death in the near future. The answer is that there are many such books available. Several of them include a chapter or two on funerals, but it has been my belief that funerals merit a book to themselves. A funeral will sometimes follow a cleric's ministrations to a dying person but in the majority of cases, he or she will not have been directly involved until after the death has occurred. That in itself makes a significant difference. There is an intimacy which develops between a priest and a dying person when the priest has been a regular visitor at the sick-bed. Confidences might have been shared, perhaps regrets and hopes for the future, and concern for loved ones. The impending death and what follows may also have been discussed. On one level the intimacy of that relationship is very deep, but at the same time it has an element of disinterest. Almost every cleric must at some stage in his or her ministry have heard words similar to these: 'I knew I could tell you, but my family are too close. They wouldn't have coped.' All of this will affect the funeral, not because the priest will disclose any details of the discussions, but because he or she knew the dying person at that time. There is a growing demand for funerals that are personal and the simple fact that the person leading the service was known by the deceased can be of great importance for the bereaved.

A hospital chaplain will be accustomed to the relationship that can develop in ministering to dying persons and their families and may well be the only cleric known to a particular family. In such circumstances it is quite common for the chaplain to be asked to conduct the funeral, although this will not always be possible, due to the pressure on the chaplain's time. There will be occasions, however, when the request will be granted and this will sometimes create a tension between chaplain and parish priest. The pastoral care of parishioners is strictly speaking the parish priest's responsibility and some will resent the chaplain's assuming some of it. Yet this is not how it is likely to be perceived by the family, especially if the parochial clergy are strangers to them. Nevertheless, with tactful handling the family could be introduced to their vicar; the funeral might even be jointly conducted and a pastoral contact established by the local church.

Chaplains serve a multitude of purposes in the Armed Forces apart from being priests and carrying out duties similar to those of a vicar. They also help to encourage soldiers in what is known as 'character training' – courage, discipline, selfless commitment, integrity, loyalty and respect for others. Army chaplains take care of the spiritual and moral well-being of soldiers and, with them, often have to enter into dangerous situations. In a conflict situation this could well involve ministering to dying soldiers and, if the bodies are not taken home for burial or cremation, conducting their funerals. The particular situation will affect how that funeral is conducted, but a congregation composed mainly of young men who face the possibility of their own death in combat is likely to create its own particular dynamic. A military chaplain will also face some element of personal risk. During the First and Second World Wars, over 300 chaplains were killed in action.

The cost of funerals is sometimes a concern and from time to time the issue is raised by journalists. It is difficult to say how much a funeral should cost as what is provided differs greatly from one funeral to another. The cost of a coffin or casket, for example, ranges from a few hundred to several thousand pounds. Professional associations of funeral directors[2] do provide a code of conduct to which their members must conform and this normally requires the provision of full and fair information regarding their services, together with price lists. These should include the price of a simple funeral and itemized charges for all the constituent parts of the funeral director's services and all types of coffins and caskets available. It is becoming increasingly common to ask the funeral director for an estimate beforehand. Most will also be able to offer advice regarding eligibility for payments towards the cost of a funeral from the Social Fund administered by the Department of Social Services.

Anglicans use the phrase 'occasional offices' when referring to the services of baptism, weddings and funerals, and some friends have asked me why I am not writing a book on all three as they have much in common. They do possess shared features but there are also significant differences. In all three the Church is approached by those who do not normally attend but those who request funerals form a much higher percentage of the population. Funerals normally occur with only a few days' notice, and they are emotionally different. When one makes a mistake in a baptism or a wedding one can normally make a joke of it. One cannot do that during a funeral.

In his book *Brief Encounters*, Wesley Carr describes how a minister could not find a second curate for a church in the evangelical tradition. All those who might have applied saw their ministry as teaching the faith and could see no specific value in the large number of occasional offices they would have to perform. These may sometimes be perceived as taking the minister away from his or her real work: the proclamation of the Christian gospel. In my view, that shows a misunderstanding of the nature of the occasional offices. They are not opportunities for an all-out attempt to evangelize but, rather, occasions on which people's lives are touched by the life of the Church. We establish our presence and make ourselves known. We allow our busy schedules to be interrupted for the sake of others. We create the opportunity for people to come close to the Church, to taste the living waters of our faith and, if they so wish, to drink from that fountain. It is easy to fall into the trap of seeing a funeral (or a baptism, or a wedding) as a one-off event. From the minister's point of view, it might well be simply that and he or she will have no further contact with that particular family. From the family's point of view, however, it could be one moment in a whole series of turning points in the family's life. The family Bible which chronicled them may have been replaced by the photograph album and digital camera, but the family's experience of the clergy, and through them the Church, will be part of the experience which is passed on through the generations. A failure to appreciate the importance of such encounters will, I believe, gradually damage the way in which the Church is embraced by society as a whole.

It is my view that it could be unwise to lay down too many rules about how the occasional offices should be conducted. Different parishes and churches have different traditions, and the expectations of those who approach the clergy might not match our own, especially if they have been moulded over a long period. A couple, one of whom had been previously divorced, rather hesitantly asked for their registry-office marriage to be blessed. I have never forgotten the look of surprise on their faces when, after some conversation, I asked why they had not asked for a church wedding since the blessing clearly meant so much to them. They had expected rejection and were taken aback by acceptance. We are likely to be unaware of how strangers have experienced the Church's ministry in the past, and when they approach us to request a funeral service we do not know what kind of welcome they will be expecting. Equally we might be taken by surprise, as was I when answering the vicarage door one day. A Roman Catholic couple, whom I knew slightly, explained that an Anglican relative had come to stay and had been unexpectedly taken ill. They asked if I would conduct the funeral and I agreed after ascertaining that they were the next of kin. They then left, saying that they would contact me when he died. It had never occurred to me that their relative was still alive.

I began this book by reflecting on the training I received for conducting funerals, and my own inadequacy for the task. Over the years I hope that I have learned some lessons that will be of use to others, and it is in that spirit that I would present this book to those who might read it. It is my prayer that it may help prevent others from making some of the mistakes that I have made, so that the lives of those for whose funerals we are responsible may be marked by a fitting end.

NOTES

[1] Knowles, Elizabeth (ed.), *The Oxford Dictionary of Quotations*, Oxford University Press, Oxford, 1999, p. 592.
[2] For example the National Society of Allied and Independent Funeral Directors and the National Association of Funeral Directors.

Appendix 1

Further Reading

Abrams, Rebecca, *When Parents Die: Learning to Live with the Loss of a Parent*, London, Harper Collins, 1995.

Ainsworth-Smith, Ian and Speck, Peter, *Letting Go: Caring for the Dying and Bereaved*, London, SPCK, 1982.

Ariès, Philippe, *The Hour of Our Death*, London, Allen Lane, 1981, first published in France as *L'Homme Devant la Mort* (1977).

Autton, Norman, *Peace at the Last: Talks with the Dying*, London, SPCK, 1978.

Badham, Paul, *Christian Beliefs about Life after Death*, London, Macmillan, 1976.

Badham, Paul and Ballard, Paul H. (eds), *Facing Death: An Interdisciplinary Approach*, Cardiff, University of Wales Press, 1996.

Barker, Elspeth (ed.), *Loss*, London, J. M. Dent, 1997.

Bentley, James, Best, Andrew and Hunt, Jackie (eds), *Funerals: A Guide; Prayers, Hymns and Readings*, London, Hodder and Stoughton, 1994.

Billings, Alan, *Dying and Grieving: A Guide to Personal Ministry*, London, SPCK, 2002.

Boadt, L., 'The Scriptures on Death and Dying and the New Funeral Rite', in A. F. Sherman (ed.) *Rites of Death and Dying*, Collegeville, Minnesota, The Liturgical Press, 1988, pp. 7–29.

Bowker, John, *The Meanings of Death*, Cambridge, Cambridge University Press, 1991.

Bradshaw, P. B. and Hoffman, L. A. (eds), *Life Cycles in Jewish and Christian Worship*, London, University of Notre Dame Press, 1996.

Brown, Adele, *What a Way to Go: Fabulous Funerals of the Famous and Infamous*, San Francisco, California, Chronicle Books, 2001.

Bunting, Ian, *Preaching at Funerals*, Nottingham, Grove Books, 1981.

Carr, Wesley, *Brief Encounters: Pastoral Ministry through Baptisms, Weddings and Funerals*, London, SPCK, 1994.

Charmaz, Kathy, Howarth, Glenys, and Kellehear, Allan (eds), *The Unknown Country: Death in Australia, Britain and the USA*, London, Macmillan, 1997.

Clark, David (ed.), *The Sociology of Death*, Oxford, Blackwell, 1993.

Curl, James Stevens, *Death and Architecture: An Introduction to Funerary and Commemorative Buildings in the Western European Tradition with Some Consideration of their Settings*, Stroud, Alan Sutton Publishing, 2002.

Davies, Douglas James, *British Crematoria in Public Profile*, Maidstone, Cremation Society of Great Britain, 1995.

Davies, Douglas James, *Death, Ritual and Belief*, London, Cassell, 1997.

Davies, Douglas James and Shaw, Alistair A., *Reusing Old Graves: A Report on Popular British Attitudes*, Crayford, Shaw and Sons, 1995.

Davies, Jon (ed.), *Ritual and Remembrance: Responses to Death in Human Societies*, Sheffield, Sheffield Academic Press, 1994.

Dean, Stephen (ed.), *The Parish Funeral*, Great Wakering, McCrimmons, 1991.

Despelder, L. A. and Strickland, A. L., *The Last Dance: Encountering Death and Dying*, McGraw-Hill Higher Education, 2001.

Dombeck, M., 'Death Rituals and Life Values: The American Way', in A. F. Sherman (ed.), *Rites of Death and Dying*, Collegeville, Minnesota, The Liturgical Press, 1998, pp. 30–66.

Enright, D. J. (ed.) *The Oxford Book of Death*, Oxford, Oxford University Press, 2002.

Episcopal Church of the United States of America, *The Book of Common Prayer and Administration of the Sacraments and Other Rites and Ceremonies of the Church*, New York, The Church Hymnal Corporation and the Seabury Press, 1979.

Freeman, Penny, *A Straightforward Guide to Handling Bereavement: What to Do on the Death of Another*, London, Straightforward Publishing, 2000.

Gill, Sue and Fox, John, *The Dead Good Funerals Book*, Ulverstone, Cumbria, Welfare State International, 2004.

Gittings, Clare, *Death, Burial and the Individual in Early Modern England*, London, Croom Helm, 1984.

Gorer, Geoffrey, *Death, Grief and Mourning in Contemporary Britain*, London, Cresset Press, 1965.

Grainger, Roger, *The Unburied*, Worthing, Churchman Publishing, 1988.

Grant, Len, *A Way of Life: Portraits from the Funeral Trade*, Manchester, Len Grant Photography, 1999.

Green, Jennifer, and Green, Michael, *Dealing with Death: Practices and Procedures*, London, Chapman and Hall, 1992.

Hockey, Jennifer Lorna, *Making the Most of a Funeral*, Richmond upon Thames, London, Cruse-Bereavement Care, 1992.

Hockey, Jennifer Lorna, 'The Acceptable Face of Human Grieving? The Clergy's Role in Managing Emotional Expression during Funerals', in D. Clark (ed.), *The Sociology of Death*, Oxford, Blackwell, 1993, pp. 129–48.

Hockey, Jennifer Lorna, Katz, Jeanne, and Small, Neil (eds), *Grief, Mourning and Death Ritual*, Buckingham, Open University Press, 2000.

Horton, Anne, *Using Common Worship: Funerals*, London, Church House Publishing, 2000.

Houlbrooke, Ralph (ed.), *Death, Ritual and Bereavement*, London, Routledge, 1989.

Howarth, Glennys, and Jupp, Peter (eds), *Contemporary Issues in the Sociology of Death, Dying and Disposal*, London, Macmillan, 1996.

Howarth, Glennys, and Jupp, Peter (eds), *The Changing Face Of Death: Historical Accounts of Death and Disposal*, London, Macmillan, 1997.

International Commission on English in the Liturgy, *Order of Christian Funerals No. 22*, Washington, Washington DC, International Commission on English in the Liturgy, 1985.

Jupp, Peter, *From Dust to Ashes: The Replacement of Burial by Cremation in England 1840–1967*, London, The Congregational Memorial Hall Trust, 1990.

Jupp, Peter, and Rogers, Tony (eds), *Interpreting Death: Christian Theology and Pastoral Practice*, London, Cassell, 1997.

Kastenbaum, R. J., *Death, Society and Human Experience*, Allyn and Bacon, Upper Saddle River, New Jersey, 2003.

Kearl, M. C, *Endings: A Sociology of Death and Dying*, Oxford, Oxford University Press, 1989.

Klein, D. and Hughes, T. E., *Family Guide to Wills, Funerals, and Probate: How to Protect Yourself and Your Survivors*, Facts on File, New York, 2001.

Kohner, N., and Henley, A., *When a Baby Dies*, London, Pandora Press, 1991.

Krieger, W. M., *A Complete Guide to Funeral Service Management*, Englewood Cliffs, New Jersey, Prentice-Hall, 1962.

Kubler-Ross, Elisabeth, *On Death and Dying*, London, Routledge, 1989.

Lapwood, Robin, *When Babies Die: Some Guidelines for Helpers of Bereaved Parents*, Nottingham, Grove Books, 1988.

Leming, M. R. and Dickinson, G. E., 'The American Ways of Death', in K. Charmaz, G. Howarth, and A. Kellehear (eds), *The Unknown Country: Death in Australia, Britain and the USA*, London, Macmillan, 1997, pp. 169–83.

Lewis, C. S., *A Grief Observed*, London, Faber & Faber, 1961.

Liturgy Office of the Bishops' Conference of England and Wales and the International Commission on English in the Liturgy, *Order of Christian Funerals Approved for Use in the Dioceses of England and Wales, and Scotland: Study Edition*, London, Geoffrey Chapman, 1991.

Litton, J., *The English Way of Death: The Common Funeral since 1450*, London, Hale Books, 1991.

Lloyd, Trevor, *Dying and Death: Step by Step: A Funerals Flowchart*,

Cambridge, Grove Books, 2000.

Lysons, K., 'More on Hymns for the Funeral', in *Funeral Services Journal*, July 1996.

Matlins, S. M., *The Perfect Stranger's Guide to Funerals and Grieving Practices: A Guide to Etiquette in Other People's Religious Ceremonies*, Skylight and Paths Publishing, 2000.

McCarthy, Flor, *Funeral Liturgies*, Dublin, Dominican Publications, 1994.

Metcalf, Peter and Huntingdon, Richard, *Celebrations of Death; The Anthropology of Mortuary Ritual*, Cambridge, Cambridge University Press, 1991 (In the earlier 1979 edition Huntingdon's name appears first.).

Miller, Albert Jay and Acri, Michael James (eds) *Death: A Bibliographical guide*, London, The Scarecrow Press, 1977.

Mitford, Jessica, *The American Way Of Death Revisited*, London, Virago Press, 1998.

Neuberger, Julia, *Caring for Dying People of Different Faiths*, London, Austin Cornish, 1991.

Richardson, Ruth, *Death, Dissection and the Destitute*, London, Routledge and Kegan Paul, 1987.

Robinson, John, 'Learning from Cancer', in *Where Three Ways Meet: Last Essays and Sermons*, pp. 189–94, London, SCM Press, 1987.

Rowell, Geoffrey, *The Liturgy of Christian Burial: An Introductory Survey of the Historical Development of Christian Burial Rites*, London, SPCK/Alcuin Club, 1977.

Rudinger, E. (ed.), *What To Do When Someone Dies*, London, Consumers' Association, 1967.

Rutherford, R., 'Funeral Liturgy – Why Bother: A Practical Theology of Death and Bereavement', in A. F. Sherman (ed.) *Rites of Death and Dying*, Collegeville, Minnesota, The Liturgical Press, 1998, pp. 67–102.

Seale, Clive, *Constructing Death: The Sociology of Dying and Bereavement*, Cambridge, Cambridge University Press, 1998.

Sheppy, Paul, *Death, Liturgy and Ritual: A Pastoral and Liturgical Theology*, (Volume One and Volume Two), Aldershot, Ashgate Publishing, 2003.

Sheppy, Paul, *In Sure and Certain Hope: Liturgies, Prayers and Readings for Funerals and Memorials*, Norwich, Canterbury Press, 2003.

Sherman, A. F. (ed.) *Rites of Death and Dying*, Collegeville, Minnesota, The Liturgical Press, 1998.

Sherrin, Ned, *Remembrance: An Anthology of Readings, Prayers, and Music Chosen for Memorial Services*, London, Michael Joseph, 1996.

Singer, Peter, *Rethinking Life and Death: The Collapse of Our Traditional Ethics*, Oxford, Oxford University Press, 1995.

Smith, M., *Facing Death Together: Parish Funerals*, Liturgy Training Publications, Chicago, Illinois, 1998.

Snell, Beatrice Saxon, *Horizon: An Anthology of Prose and Poetry Suitable to be Read at Quaker Funerals and for Private Devotion*, London, Friends Home Service Committee, 1972.

Speyer, Josefine and Wienrich, Stephanie (eds), *The Natural Death Handbook*, London, The Natural Death Centre, 2003.

Walter, Tony, *Funerals And How To Improve Them*, London, Hodder and Stoughton, 1990.

Walter, Tony, *The Revival of Death*, London, Routledge, 1994.

Watson, Julia (ed.), *Poems and Readings for Funerals*, London, Penguin Books, 2004.

Watson, Nick, *Sorrow and Hope: Preaching at Funerals*, Cambridge, Grove Books, 2001.

Weller, Sam, *The Daily Telegraph Lifeplanner Guide to Funerals and Bereavement*, London, Kogan Page, 1999.

Whaley, Joachim (ed.), *Mirrors of Mortality: Studies in the Social History of Death*, London, Europa Publications Ltd, 1981.

Wilcock, P., *Spiritual Care of Dying and Bereaved People*, London, SPCK, 1996.

Wilkins, Robert, *The Fireside Book of Death: A Macabre Guide to the Ultimate Experience*, London, Warner Books, 1992.

Willson, Jane Wynne, *Funerals without God: A Practical Guide to Non-religious Funeral Ceremonies*, London, British Humanist Association, 1989.

Appendix 2

Websites

Bereavement Support

The Compassionate Friends www.tcf.org.uk/ (An organization of bereaved parents and their families offering understanding, support and encouragement to others after the death of a child or children.).

Cruse Bereavement Care www.crusebereavementcare.org.uk/ .

Epilepsy Bereaved www.dspace.dial.pipex.com/epilepsybereaved/ (For those bereaved by epilepsy and others interested in the work of Epilepsy Bereaved.).

The Foundation for the Study of Infant Deaths www.sids.org.uk/fsid/ (Information about cot death.).

The National Association of War Widows of Great Britain www.warwidowsassociation.org.uk.

The National Association of Widows www.widows.uk.net.

Papyrus www.papyrus-uk.org (For those faced with young suicide, particularly teenagers and young adults.).

Patient.co.uk www.patient.co.uk/display.asp?parent=16777249 (Lists a wide range of bereavement support and self-help groups for adults and children, and their contact details.).

The Royal College of Psychiatrists www.rcpsych.ac.uk/info/help/bereav/index.asp (Information about bereavement.).

SAGA www.saga.co.uk/health_news/pages/resource_centre.asp?Iss=final_things&bhjs=1&bhqs=1 (The SAGA Resource Centre offers a wide range of contact details under 'Final Things'.).

Stillbirth and Neonatal Death Society www.uk-sands.org/ (Support for parents and families whose baby is stillborn or dies soon after birth.).

Funeral Supplies

The Funeral Shop www.funeralshop.co.uk (A website which describes itself as 'the UK's most popular funeral website'.).

Office of Fair Trading www.oft.gov.uk/ (*A Consumer Guide to Funerals* may be obtained from this website.).

Liturgical Resources

The Church of England www.cofe.anglican.org/commonworship (A website containing all the common worship texts.).

Medical Research and Organ Donation

British Organ Donor Society www.argonet.co.uk/body (Information about organ donation.).
Royal National Institute for the Blind www.rnib.org.uk (Information about eye donations for corneal grafting.).
UK Transplant www.uktransplant.org.uk (Information about organ donation.).

Miscellaneous

British Humanist Association www.humanism.org.uk.
Rights of Women www.rightsofwomen.org.uk (A website run by women lawyers giving free advice to women.).
The Samaritans www.samaritans.org.uk.
Voluntary Euthanasia Society www.ves.org.uk.

Statistics

Government Statistics Website.
www.statistics.gov.uk/ (Provides many official statistics for the United Kingdom).
www.statistics.gov.uk/CCI/SearchRes.asp?term=deaths (National Statistics for the UK: this particular page has links to death statistics.).
Department of Trade and Industry www.dti.gov.uk/homesafetynetwork/gh_intro.htm (Information about accidents.).
www.consumer.gov.uk ('The Consumer Gateway' run by the Department for Trade and Industry.).
Department of Transport www.thinkroadsafety.gov.uk/statistics.htm (Road statistics provided by the Department for Transport.).
Royal Society for the Prevention of Accidents www.rospa.co.uk/cms/

Undertakers and Funeral Directors and Professional Organizations

Funeral Services UK www.funeralservicesuk.com/ (An Online Directory of Funeral Directors, Monumental Masons, Caterers & Florists in England, Northern Ireland, Scotland & Wales.) .

The Funeral Standards Council www.funeral-standards-council.co.uk/ .

Green Burials www.greenburials.co.uk (Woodland burial services.).

The National Association of Funeral Directors www.nafd.org.uk/ .

The National Society of Allied and Independent Funeral Directors www.saif.org.uk.

The Natural Death Centre www.naturaldeath.org.uk.

UK Funerals www.uk-funerals.co.uk/index.html (Advice on funerals and contact details for undertakers and funeral directors.).

Appendix 3

Addresses

Bereavement Support

The Compassionate Friends (Helping bereaved parents and their families), 53 North Street, Bristol, BS3 1EN. Telephone: 08451 203785. Helpline: 08451 232304 (10.00am–4.00pm and 6.30–10.30pm 365 days a year).

The Cot Death Society, 4 West Mills Yard, Kennett Road, Newbury, Berkshire RG14 5LP. Telephone: 01635 38137. Helpline: 0845 601 0234.

Cruse Bereavement (Nationwide service for bereavement counselling and information), Cruse House, 126 Sheen Road, Richmond, Surrey TW9 1UR. Telephone: 020 8939 9530 (9.30am–5.00pm Mon–Fri). Helpline: 0870 167 1677 (9.00am–5.00pm Mon–Fri).

Foundation for the Study of Infant Deaths, Artillery House, 11–19 Artillery Row, London SW1P 1RT. Telephone: 020 7222 8001. Helpline: 0870 787 0554 (9.00am–5.00pm Mon–Fri).

The National Association of Widows (Provides helping hand to all widows and their families), 54/57 Allison Street, Digbeth, Birmingham B5 5TH. Telephone: 024 7663 4848.

The Rights of Women (Group of solicitors and barristers which offers free telephone advice to women), 52–54 Featherstone Street, London, EC1Y 8RT. Telephone: 020 7251 6575/6. Helpline: 020 7251 6577 (2.00pm–4.00pm and 7.00pm–9.00pm Tues–Thurs and 12.00–2.00pm Fri).

The Samaritans, The Upper Mill, Kingston Road, Ewell, Surrey KT17 2AF. Telephone: 020 8394 8300. National Emergency Line: 08457 909090 (24 hours 365 days a year).

Stillbirth & Neonatal Death Society (SANDS) (Support to parents bereaved through pregnancy), 28 Portland Place, London W1B 1LY. Telephone: 020 7436 7940. Helpline: 020 7436 5881 (10.00am–4.00pm Mon–Fri).

The War Widows Association of Great Britain (Provides advice, help and support), 1 Coach Lane, Stanton-in-Peak DE4 2NA. Telephone: 0870 241 1305.

Medical Research and Organ Donation

British Organ Donor Society (Information about organ donation), Belsham, Cambridge, CB1 6DL. Telephone: 01223 893636.

The London Anatomy Office (Enquiries about leaving one's body for medical teaching), Imperial College London, Charing Cross Hospital, Fulham Palace Road, London W6 8RF. Telephone: 020 8846 1216.

The Royal National Institute for the Blind (Eye donations for Corneal Grafting), 105 Judd Street, London WC1H 9NE. Telephone: 020 7388 1266. Helpline 0845 766 9999.

Miscellaneous

Britannia Shipping Company Ltd (For Burial at Sea), Unit 3, The Old Sawmills, Hawkerland Road, Colaton Raleigh, Sidmouth, Devon EX10 0HP. Telephone: 01395 568652.

The British Humanist Association (Help and advice on arranging a humanist funeral service), 1 Gower Street, London WC1E 6HD. Telephone: 020 7079 3580.

Federation of British Cremation Authorities, 41 Salisbury Road, Carshalton, Surrey SM5 3HA. Telephone: 020 8669 4521.

Funeral Standards Council (FSC), 30 North Road, Cardiff CF1 3DY. Telephone: 029 2038 2046.

Green Woodland Burial Services, 256 High Street, Harwich, Essex CO12 3PA. Telephone: 0800 374759.

National Association of Funeral Directors (NAFD), 618 Warwick Road, Solihull, West Midlands B91 1AA. Telephone: 0845 230 1343.

National Funerals College, 3 Priory Road, Bristol BS8 1TX. Telephone: 0117 954 5558.

The National Society of Allied and Independent Funeral Directors (SAIF), SAIF Business Centre, 3 Bullfields, Sawbridgeworth, Hertfordshire CM21 9DB. Telephone: 0845 230 6777.

Natural Death Centre, 6 Blackstock Mews, Blackstock Road, London N4 2BT. Telephone: 0871 288 2098.

The Voluntary Euthanasia Society (Campaigns for wider choice at the end of life), 13 Prince of Wales Terrace, London W8 5PG. Telephone: 020 7937 7770.

Useful American Addresses and Websites

The Academy of Professional Funeral Service Practice, PO Box 2275, Westerville, OH 43086-2275, USA. Telephone: +1 614 899 6202.

American Association of Retired Persons, AARP Fulfillment, 601 E Street,

NW, Washington, DC 20049, USA. AARP is a nonprofit, nonpartisan organization dedicated to helping older people achieve lives of independence, dignity and purpose. AARP publishes *Funeral Goods and Services* and *Pre-Paying for Your Funeral?* These publications are available free by writing to the address listed above.

The American Society of Embalmers is established to promulgate and promote excellence in the 21st century practice of the mortuary arts of embalming and restorative art. Melissa Johnson Williams, CFSP MJohnsonCFSP@aol.com, Robert G. Mayer, CFSP RMayer@aol.com

The Compassionate Friends, Inc, PO Box 3696, Oak Brook IL, 60522-3696, USA. Telephone +1 630 990 0246. www. compassionatefriends. org/index.html.

Most states have a licensing board that regulates the funeral industry. You may contact the licensing board in your state for information or help, or The Conference of Funeral Service Examining Boards, 15 Northeast 3rd Street, PO Box 497, Washington, Indiana 47501, USA. Telephone: +1 812 254 7887.

The Conference, which represents licensing boards in 47 states, provides information on laws in various states and accepts and responds to consumer inquiries or complaints about funeral providers.

Continental Association of Funeral and Memorial Societies, 6900 Lost Lake Road, Egg Harbour, Wisconsin 54209, USA. Telephone: +1 800 458 5563

CAFMS is a consumer organization that disseminates information about alternatives for funeral or non-funeral dispositions. It encourages advance planning and cost efficiency.

Cremation Association of North America, 401 North Michigan Avenue, Chicago, Illinois 60611, USA. Telephone: +1 312 644 6610. Email: CANA@smithbucklin.com.

CANA is an association of crematories, cemeteries, and funeral homes that offer cremation. More than 750 members own and operate crematories and encourage the concept of memorialization.

Funeral Consumers Alliance, 33 Patchen Road, South Burlington, Vermont, 05403, USA. Telephone: +1 800 765 0107. www.funerals.org.

A Federation of non-profit Consumer Information Societies.

Funeral Help Program (FHP), 1236 Ginger Crescent, Virginia Beach, VA 23453, USA. Telephone: +1 757 427 0220. www.funeral-help.com.

Funeral and Memorialization Information Council (FAMIC), 70 Market St, Mt Sterling, OH 43143, USA. Telephone: +1 740 869 3113. Emails: psabel@hotmail.com; Webmaster: tmonahan@assnhdqtrs.com.

Funeral Service Consumer Assistance Program, National Research and Information Center, 2250 E. Devon Avenue, Suite 250, Des Plaines, Illinois 60018, USA. Telephone: +1 800 662 7666.

FSCAP is a programme designed to assist consumers and funeral directors in resolving disagreements about funeral service contracts. It is a service of the National Research and Information Center, an independent, non-profit organization that researches and provides consumer information on death, grief, and funeral service.

FuneralWire is a free business daily email news service dedicated to the funeral services industry. It is required reading for funeral directors, cemeterians, industry suppliers, and any other death care industry professionals. FuneralWire brings you current news www.funeralwire.net.

Growth House, Inc, located in San Francisco provides information and referral services for agencies working with death and dying issues. www.growthhouse.org

Health Cyclopedia provides links to many on-line support groups. www.healthcyclopedia.com/mental-health/grief,-loss-and-bereavement.html

Hospice Foundation of America is a not-for-profit organization that provides leadership in the development and application of hospice and its philosophy of care. Through programmes of professional development, research, public education and information, it assists those who cope either personally or professionally with terminal illness, death, and the process of grief. www.hospicefoundation.org/about.

International Order of the Golden Rule, PO Box 3586, Springfield, Illinois 62708, USA. Telephone: +1 217 793 3322.

OGR is an international association of independent funeral homes in which membership is by invitation only. Approximately 1,500 US funeral homes are members of OGR.

Jewish Funeral Directors of America, Inc, 250 West 57th Street, Suite 2329, New York, New York 10107, USA. Telephone: +1 212 582 9744.

JFDA is a national trade association of funeral directors serving the Jewish community. It has approximately 200 members.

National Funeral Directors Association, 11121 West Oklahoma Avenue, Milwaukee, Wisconsin 53227, USA. Telephone: +1 414 541 2500.

NFDA is the largest educational and professional association of funeral directors. Established in 1882, it has 14,000 members throughout the USA.

National Funeral Directors and Morticians Association, Omega World Center, 3951 Snapfinger Parkway, Decatur, Georgia 3951, USA. Telephone: +1 800 434 0958.

NFDMA is a national association primarily of black funeral providers. It has 2,000 members.

National Selected Morticians, 1616 Central Street, Evanston, Illinois 60201, USA. Telephone: +1 708 475 3414.

NSM is a national association of funeral firms in which membership is by invitation only and is conditioned upon the commitment of each firm to comply with the association's Code of Good Funeral Practice. Consumers may request a variety of publications through NSM's affiliate, the Consumer Information Bureau, Inc.

The North American Woodland Burial Society is a grass-roots volunteer network comprising individuals from all vocations and religious beliefs who have the desire to further the dignified and loving practice of natural woodland burials. www.woodlandburial.htmlplanet.

Pre-Arrangement Association of America, 6321 Bury Drive, Suite 8, Eden Prairie, Minnesota 55346, USA. Telephone: +1 612 937 5879.
PAA is a national association with more than 400 members in the cemetery and funeral home business. Its primary purpose is to provide pre-arrangement purchases of funeral and cemetery goods and services.

Samaritans USA, c/o Samaritans of New York, PO Box 1259, Madison Square Station, New York, New York 10159, USA. Telephone: +1 212 677 3009. www.Samaritansnyc.org

For information on organ donation and transplantation, call the National Women's Health Information Center (NWHIC) on +1 800 994 WOMAN or contact the following organizations:

US Department of Health and Human Services, Secretary's Organ Donation Initiative. www.organdonor.gov.

Office of Minority Health, Office of the Secretary. Telephone: +1 800 444 6472. www.omhrc.gov.

American Heart Association. Telephone: +1 800 793 2665. www.americanheart.org.

American Kidney Fund. Telephone: +1 800 638 8299. www.akfinc.org.

American Liver Foundation. Telephone: +1 800 465 4837. www.liverfoundation.org.

American Lung Foundation. Telephone: +1 800 586 4872. www.lungusa.org.

American Medical Association. Telephone: +1 312 464 5000. www.ama-assn.org.

American Organ Transplant Association. Telephone: +1 281 261 AOTA. www.a-o-t-a.org

Children's Organ Transplant Association. Telephone: +1 800 366 COTA. www.cota.org.

Coalition on Donation. www.shareyourlife.org.

National Marrow Donor Program. Telephone: +1 800 627 7692. www.marrow.org.

National Minority Organ Tissue Transplant Education Program. Telephone: +1 202 865 4888. www.nationalmottep.org.

United Network for Organ Sharing (UNOS). Telephone: +1 804 330 8500. www.unos.org; www.organdonor.gov/newdonorcard.pdf.

Index

affirmation of deceased's life 51–3
afterlife 21
AIDS 98–101
Alban-Jones, Tim 134–5
All Souls' Day 36, 153
Alternative Service Book 26
American influences 103–5
An Order for Christian Funerals
    29
Anglican Church of Canada 58
anthropology
    dualist 4
    unitary 4
Ariès, Philippe 18
Aristotle 5, 138
ashes 46
Augustine of Hippo 138

babies 101
bureaucracy 15–16
body–soul dualism 4
Book of Common Prayer
    1549 30
    1552 31
    1559 32
    1662 14, 32
    1928 32
    Church in Wales 30
brain death 3
breaking down 142–3
burial 119–23
    site 151–3
Burial Acts 47

categories of difficulty 129–30
contemporary beliefs 20–3
cemeteries 7
    public 91
    Victorian 47
certification 2
chaplain
    armed forces 160
    hospital 160
children 71
    death of 136–7
church 87–8
churchyard 47
    regulations 122
    maintenance 120
clergy 38, 74–7
close friends 142–3
closely bereaved 66–9
commendation of deceased 30–5
Common Worship 28
community 38, 77–8
conflict 78–9
Consumers' Association 84
Co-operative Movement 85
cost of funerals 161
couples 67
cremated remains 70
cremation 16, 123–6
crematoria 84
    design of 114
culture 105–7

Davies, Douglas 21

death
  perceptions of 10–12
death certificate
  rules 11
deceased 63–6
Department of the Environment
  82
Department of Trade and Industry
  83
disposal of corpse 45–8, 151–3
divorce 19
doctor 1
domestic violence 135
Donatists 138
dying
  ministry to 159–60

Easter 36
environmental effect 84
environmentally-friendly 116
eschatology 7

family 67, 92–3
family feuds 141–2
family members 69–72
First World War 12–13
forgiveness 145–6
Funeral Centre 114
funeral congregation 38–40
funeral directors 72
funeral industry 83
Funeral liturgy 26–9
Funeral Services Exhibition 25
Funeral Standards Council (FSC)
  85
funeral supermarket 114
funerals
  alternative 115–19
  do-it-yourself 112–15
  large number of 143
  life-centred 51
  private ix
  public ix
  secular 51

gender 94–8
Gorer, Geoffrey 17
government 82–4
  local 82
grave 151
Greek 5
Green Movement 116
grieving 53–5

Hamlet 139–40
Hebraic 5, 7
Hellenistic 5, 7
Hockey, Jenny 28, 36
homosexuality 98–100
Humanist Association 115
hymns 109

immediate disposition 105
immortality 5, 7

Judaism 5

laments 109
land use 84
language 105–7
layers-out 86
life after death 21
Liturgical Commission 35
liturgical revision 33

Maimonides 5
maintenance of a grave 151
managing strategies 146–7
marking a death 49–50
media 78, 101–3
mediaeval England 55
mediaeval man 10
medical research 50
memorial
  contemporary forms 156–8
memorial services 49, 155–6
Middle Ages 10, 18
military cemeteries 14
missing persons 50

Mitford, Jessica 103–4
murder 135
music 109–12
Mystery of Salvation 8

National Association of Funeral
  Directors (NAFD) 85
National Funerals College 84
Natural Death Centre 114
New Age 23
New Testament 5
no body 49

occasional offices 161
Order for Christian Funerals 27,
  29
Order of the Burial of the Dead 29
ordination of women 95–7

paperwork 144
partner 67
Pastoral Services 28
Plato 5, 138
popular modern songs 111
preacher 37
preaching 37
pre-paid plans 83
proclaiming faith 35–8

Reformation 7, 28, 51
register 15
relatives 142–3
requiem Masses 153
resurrection 5, 7, 9, 37
re-use of graves 92
Robinson, John 9

scripture 40–3
Second World War 13–14
Series One 33
Series Three 34

Series Two 26
Service Corporation International
  (SCI) 103
Sheffield 36
Sheppy, Paul 40
social phenomenon 55–9
society 89–91
Society of Allied and Independent
  Funeral Directors (SAIFD) 85
sociologists 16–20
Soham 134–5
South Africa 56
spiritual growth and development
  146
sociology of death 16–20
stillborn children 18
sudden death 130–2
suicide 137–40
Sunday service 36
support 147
survival 37

terrorism 12, 101
theological language 4–6
theology of death 7–10
Thomas Aquinas 138
training x

undertaker 72–4
undertaking profession 85–7

violent death 133–5

Welsh language 106
Welsh-speaking 57
West Wales 36
women 86–7
women priests 95
women rabbis 96
woodland burial 116–17
war 12–14